What readers say about *Femme Tales*

. . . these seven classic fairy tales weave together the magical and the political. . . . unique humor and wordplay. Parry may be serious about her politics, but she allows her heroines to have fun. . . . timely and fun.

Kirkus

Each story . . . with (its) interplay of intelligence and fantasy brings understanding and wisdom. *Femme Tales* leaves you wanting more regardless of your gender. In this case, the pen is indeed mightier than the sword and much more fun.

Linda Carfagno,
Photographer/Film Maker

Like any good folk talk, these stories seem to be set in an alternate-reality version of the recent past. . . . Highly recommended.

Sondra Spatt Olsen,
Writer

I loved this book! As a teacher and mother of two girls I think the idea of allowing girls to dream, but still create their own destinies is amazing. This book was a quick read and so worth the time and money!!!

Andrea Day,
Educator

. . . what she's done with some of *Grimms' Fairy Tales* . . . is both funny and intriguing. The book is short but piquant . . . a funny, herstoric book I highly recommend . . .

Vicki P. McConnell,
Writer

The book is just fabulous and so witty! . . . giggled nervously at the ridiculousness of our society and the continued stereotypes of women.

Alexis Drabek,
Ballet Dance Mistress

Sharp and provocative and filled with wry humor . . .

This book is hilariously funny and clever. Dry deadpan humor that will have you smiling and laughing out loud. And it is full of current, up to date, witty, wry commentary on our present day state of affairs. . . . Men: do not be scared off by the title or back cover, I did not find it at all anti-man bashing.

Killing Time

Happy reading!
Roberta Parry

ALSO BY ROBERTA PARRY

Femme Tales

Killing Time

A Novel in Two Acts by

ROBERTA PARRY

mill city press • minneapolis, mn

Mill City Press, Inc.
322 First Avenue N, 5th floor
Minneapolis, MN 55401
612.455.2293
www.millcitypublishing.com

The town of Harden and all characters in this novel are fictional. Any resemblence to persons living or dead is coincidental. The Hopi content is based on personal experience and research.

Excerpt "The Hopi Clowns" previously appeared in New Frontiers, Tijeras, NM, Fall 1996.

Excerpt "Billy of the Hopi Way" previously appeared in Writers' Forum, Volume 24. University of Colorado, Colorado Springs, CO, Summer 1996.

ISBN-13: 978-1-63413-923-6
LCCN: 2015920176

Cover illustration by Roberta Parry.
Cover Design by Alan Pranke
Typeset by B. Cook

Printed in the United States of America

To the memory of Nicholas Anastasiow,
who introduced me to the Hopi mesas

For everything there is a season, and a time for every matter under Heaven:

> *a time to be born, and a time to die;*
>
> *a time to pluck, and a time to pluck up what is planted;*
>
> *a time to kill, and a time to heal;*
>
> *a time to break down, and a time to build up;*
>
> *a time to weep, and a time to laugh;*
>
> *a time to mourn, and a time to dance;*
>
> *a time to cast away stones, and a time to gather stones together;*
>
> *a time to embrace, and a time to refrain from embracing;*
>
> *a time to seek, and a time to lose;*
>
> *a time to keep, and a time to cast away;*
>
> *a time to rend, and a time to sew;*
>
> *a time to keep silence, and a time to speak;*
>
> *a time to love, and a time to hate;*
>
> *a time for war, and a time for peace.*

Ecclesiastes 5:3:1–9

Killing Time

ACT I

SCENE 1

Day sinks. She watches.

Twilight rises, seeps from behind trees, spreads across street and lawn, spills over sill, floods across floor, splashes onto lamp shade and chair cushion, drifts across the toe of her shoe, and comes to rest in dark corners. She listens. Only the swing of the pendulum in the Seth Thomas on the mantle.

The gray tide withdraws, dragging with failing fingers at table legs, fringes of throw rugs, leaving behind darkness. Street lights come on and gradually drown in waves of fog. The silence mounts, like wind at sea, like gathering clouds.

Headlights sweep across the window and onto the drive. She stiffens. A car door slams, footsteps scrape across asphalt, strike solidly up the walk. A key fumbles at the lock. She smiles. No porch light. The door pushes in and for a moment while his hand searches the wall she can see him silhouetted against the pallid night. Howie in regulation dark suit, with briefcase and overcoat.

The overhead flashes on. He blinks in the sudden bright, then blinks again at his wife huddled in the wing chair, purse on her lap, scowling against the light.

—Reggie? What're you doing . . . ?

—Contemplating the dark.

He stares.

—Why the coat? Is the furnace out?

—Dead out.

—Are you sure? It doesn't feel like it.

He drops his briefcase and coat, starts for the kitchen.

—It's Tuesday night, Howie.

He stops. It takes him a second. —Oh my god— His hand slaps his forehead. —I'm sorry, Reggie. I got so involved . . .

—You're always involved. With someone else.

—There was this important meeting, the Barrettes . . .

—The Barrettes, the Babbitts, the Whozits and Whatums, the Dowhats and Dwadiddleys, I don't give a damn. You promised this time you wouldn't forget.

—Why didn't you call? I asked you if you'd just call . . .

—No! It's bad enough I have to ask you, *beg* you, please, Howie, take me to dinner and a movie. I have to call and remind you? If you don't care enough to even remember . . .

1

—I *do* care. It's just— His hand flutters. —You don't know what it's like these days, the pressures I'm under, the things I have to keep in mind.

—How could I know? You never have time to talk to me anymore, you're always too tired or have too much work. How could I know, anymore than you know what *my* days are like.

He looks at his watch. —It's not too late, only a little past eight. We could still . . .

—No!— She stands, purse tumbling to her feet —It is too late, *months* too late— and flees, tripping over strap, dragging purse, strewing contents in her wake.

His voice follows her. —Reggie, wait. Give me a chance . . .

She leaves him listening to the hard beat of her heels receding up the hall.

—Reggie? . . .

She slams into the bedroom, heart pounding, leans her head against the door.

She hears him moving about, imagines him: stooping, retrieving lipstick, brush, compact, handkerchief, breath mints, wallet; stuffing and clutching her purse, looking around; turning off the overhead, switching on table lamps.

His footsteps start up the hall. She dashes for the bed, hunkers on its edge. He stops outside the door.

—Reggie? Can I fix you something to eat?

—No. You've killed my appetite— Her stomach's a clenching fist.

She listens to his retreating steps, hears the kitchen door's swing, the refrigerator's opening suck, sees him staring into the white glare, hears the refrigerator thunk shut.

Hears him shuffle into the living room, wander about. After a few minutes he wanders back up the hall.

She tugs her coat tightly around her. She's shivering.

—Reggie? Am I supposed to pick up the girls?

—If you want them home tonight— Muffled into her pulled-up collar.

—Should I get them now?

—I don't care what you do when.

—I'd rather stay here and talk.

She lifts her head, stops rocking.

—Leave me alone, Howie, will you? I've gotten used to it and now I find it's what I want. Just leave me alone!

Outside the door, he holds his breath and waits. Inside the door, she holds her breath and hopes. His shadow shifts, a soft plop.

—I've left your purse by the door.

She sits rigid as his footsteps withdraw.

Oh, god. He didn't even try the knob. She stumbles up, turns the lock.

The front door opens and closes. The car engine rasps to life, hums out the drive, fades down the road.

She listens.

Oh, god. The silence tears her apart. And out of the riven hollow comes a wail. She flings herself across the bed. The storm arrives.

A mistake, a terrible mistake, I wish I'd never done it, I knew I shouldn't do it, I didn't want to. I warned you, Maggie, I told you . . .

—I don't think I can go through with this.

—What're you talking about? Of course you can go through with it.

—I'm not joking. This whole thing's a terrible mistake.

—The invitations are out.

—Send regrets. Issue rain checks.

—We've ordered the food and flowers.

—Cancel them. Send back the presents. With the money you and Daddy'll save, you can hide me out in Europe until the stink blows over.

—You know your father and I don't worry about putting a few noses in the air. It's your future we care about.

—And I'm telling you. This isn't going to work.

—What do you mean? Howie adores you. He'll make a wonderful husband and father.

—It's not Howie, Maggie, it's *me.* I don't think I'm right for Howie.

—You'll break his heart.

—Better now than in ten years.

—You're being silly, I don't know what's gotten into you.

—I don't feel the way I should.

—You're having bridal jitters, that's all.

—I don't think I understand love.

—That's not what you said four years ago.

Oh, Casey.

—That's just it. I don't feel the way I did then.

—And thank god for that. What an adolescent fiasco that was! We thought you'd never outgrow it. You had us scared to death you were going to marry him.

Oh, Casey . . .

—You talk about mistakes, what a mistake that would have been.

Oh, Casey . . .

—Can you imagine? Where would you be now?
. . . *Where would we be now?*

—We'll buy a nice little house in a nice little town, and I'll paint it white, and build you a white picket fence with red roses on it, and you'll put up pictures and ruffled curtains. And I'll open that door at night and call out, Hi, Honey, I'm home, and you'll come popping out of the kitchen in a cute little apron and great big smile, and you'll sing back, Hi, Honey, how'd your day go? And I'll give you a hug and kiss, and take you on my lap, and tell you all the great things I did, and the funny things I said, and what a horse's ass the boss is, and how I told off some old fart.

—Then you'll call the kids in to wash their hands and face and comb their hair. And after we've said grace, you'll serve us fried chicken with mashed potatoes and gravy, corn on the cob, sliced tomatoes with mayonnaise, iced tea with sugar and lemon, and strawberry Jell-O with fruit cocktail and whipped cream. And while you clean up the dishes, I'll put the kids to bed.

—Then we'll sit on the couch, just the two of us, my arm around you with your head on my shoulder, and we'll watch TV together . . .

Just the two of us. Together. Oh, Casey . . . Where are you now?

The bedroom walls recede, space becomes nebulous, time closes in. She's seeing him, eyes crinkled, smile teasing, as he wrapped them in this homespun fancy they grinned at, and bought whole fabric.

Katelyn's shrill giggle pierces the darkening nimbus and pricks Reggie back to the present. She struggles to sitting position, reaches for a tissue, knocks the box to the floor, gropes down on her hands and knees, bumps the box under the bed, slides to her belly, arm outstretched, and hits her head on the iron railing. She's still dizzily sprawled in dust and tears when Howie tries the door.

—Reggie. I'd like to come to bed.

She struggles to her knees.

—Then go. The guest room's down the hall.

—What about the girls?

—They live here. They have their own rooms.

—They're confused. They don't know what to think.

—Tell them I'm sick, having a nervous breakdown. Like poor Mrs. Rochester I've gone mad and locked myself in the attic.

She holds her breath through his heavy silence, then sags relief as he turns and heads down the hall. She pulls onto the bed, buries her head under the pillow, and cries herself to sleep, clutching the tissue box.

A sharp screech screech slowly cuts through her suffocating stupor. She lifts her head, it aches, her nostrils are dry and stuffy, her eyes hot and tight. Gray light filters through the frosted panes. It's morning, she forgot to close the drapes. She pushes the covers aside and is surprised to find herself fully dressed, in coat and one shoe on. She stumbles to the window, crumpled, dull, disoriented, like a drunk after a binge. A glitter of thin ice. A black branch bent low by the burden grates across the glass.

She undresses, washes and creams her face, brushes her teeth and hair, ties on her robe. She's a wreck, eyes swollen and shadowed, skin sallow and blotched. The clock radio sings on. The girls will be up, Howie has work. She spreads a towel in the middle of the floor and assembles his toiletries—toothbrush, toothpaste, deodorant, brush and comb, electric shaver, talcum powder, aftershave—then unlocks the bedroom door and locks herself in the bathroom. From her listening post on the toilet seat she can track her family's progress: doors opening and closing, toilets flushing, faucets squealing, pipes crackling. She imagines hushed voices.

The bedroom doorknob jiggles. Howie. She smiles at the thought of his surprise when he finds the door unlocked. The pattern of his feet betrays the pattern of his mind. Pad, pad, into the room, uncertain, pad, pad, pause, as he spots the towel, folds and picks it up. *Well, all right, I'm out here, she's in there.* Pad, pad, pad to the closet, businesslike now, certain. His assurance gives her courage. Scrape, scrape, squeak, pushing hangers, selecting suit and tie. Slide of drawers, collecting shirt, socks, underwear. Another smile. He must be overloaded. Pad, pad, pad. She listens for the door, he closes it firmly.

What now?

Breakfast.

A qualm of guilt. I should be fixing the girls breakfast. Howie'll give them toast and dry cereal. I never let them go to school on a cold stomach, especially in cold weather. Eggs, bacon, ham, sausage, hot cakes, waffles. Cream of Wheat with butter and syrup, oatmeal with raisins and brown sugar. He'll leave a mess. The guilt passes.

The toilet seat grows hard. Reggie abandons her perch, slips into the bedroom, listens at the door, quickly turns the lock, and looks around. Seven forty, they should be leaving. Another qualm. They'll be late, I should be driving them. For all his long hours and conjugal sacrifices, no chauffeured limousine for Howie's family. *I'm* the chauffeur. Abby had the last hired driver. *My* family. The qualm passes. Let him take *his* turn.

The doorknob rattles, she starts.

—Reggie? We're leaving—   Pause. —We missed you this morning, we're sorry you're not feeling well—   Another pause. —I know I've been distracted lately. I guess I haven't been much of a husband. But you know what these past months have been like, what the partnership means to me. To *all* of us. I thought you understood— He waits again, giving her a last chance. But she's taken her stand and can't go back. —The girls are upset, so am I. We hope you're better when we come home tonight.

His steps recede down the hall. That's it? Her conscience pinches with second thought. She unlocks the door, patters on bare feet down the hall after him. Too late. She watches from the kitchen window as he loads the girls into the car, laughing and bantering, their breaths swirling in the air like the exhaust from the warming car. It's the laughter that chills her. The BMW backs down the drive.

That's it.

She turns and surveys the kitchen and for a moment panics. Perfect order, they didn't eat, they'll get sick. Then she spots the pot and spoon soaking in the sink. She fingers the residue. Oatmeal. With brown sugar? She opens the dishwasher. Bowls, juice glasses, spoons, rinsed spotless. Her stomach lurches and burns. She forces down toast and milk, leaves the plate, knife, glass in the sink, wanders into the living room.

What now?

The world outside the bay window lies cheerless, the neighboring houses dark and distant, the sky low and dreary. No color, no warmth, no life. A cold day in hell. She wishes something would break the numbing silence.

She wishes for snow . . .

. . . Snow as soft and fluffy as goose down, flakes the size of a quarter, fragile jewel designs, no two alike. Casey laughed as she stood spellbound, catching them on the outstretched sleeves of her coat and back of her mittens. —What's the matter, stupid, don't they have snow in Boston?

—I've never seen snow stars before. We just cut them out of tissue.

—Sure, every kid makes those, even here in Hicktown, Arizona.

—But they aren't as beautiful as these.

—Of course not. They're not real.

As Reggie watched, the first scattering of stars dissolved into the heated wool of her sleeve, beneath the second scattering to be dissolved beneath the third. She dropped to her knees and scooped up flakes. Melded to one another the stars lost their distinction. She was holding a handful of snow.

Casey grabbed her. —Come on, we're going to be late.

He knocked the snow from her hands and pulled her to her feet, pounding snow off her coat, dusting her nose and cheeks, fingers gentle, flakes on his lashes, in his cropped hair. No cap, no gloves, no muffler, only a leather flight jacket and Levis. Two degrees below zero, air crisp and dry, sky high and light, he tugged her along, snow scrunching and squeaking beneath their feet, swirling with his laugher . . .

Oh, Casey, where would I be now?

Reggie turns from the window, drifts past the cold fireplace *sun on snow* into the family room, to a chest in the back corner, Maggie's castoff, age-mellowed oak. She digs, past photos of Katelyn and Lindsay yet unmounted, past baby albums, past wedding pictures, past college. Past gold-embossed leather and plastic inserts to dime-store cardboard and coarse black sheets, to the bottom and in the back. She lifts. Dusty fibers of decomposing cheap paper sting her nostrils. She sneezes, stumbles in search of the tissue box, blows her nose, settles on the couch with the box, and opens the album.

Sun on snow. She slowly turns the pages, each page a collage of painful memories she wills herself past, until she finds it: San Francisco Peaks rising into the sky, sky opening to receive them, sun turning snow to a blaze of white, depressions to bowls of blue pooling the sky, pure blue sky. San Francisco Peaks, home of the Hopi kachinas, emissaries to the gods. Casey in the foreground laughing, eyes squinted against the light, arm around her laughing up at him, eyes squinted against *his* light.

—What did you tell Mack?

—When?

—In the car, when you went to town with him.

—I don't know. We just talked.

—About what?

—I don't know. Just stuff.

—What kind of stuff? You must have said something.

—He made me uncomfortable. I didn't know what he was getting at. Why did you want me to go with him, anyway?

—Mack's a good old boy, a good mechanic and a good talker. I thought you'd have fun getting to know him. Better than hanging around the airport while I cleaned up. So why'd he make you uncomfortable?

—He kept asking me all these questions.

—What kind of questions?

—Like where I come from, what kind of house I live in, where I go to school.

—Anything else?

—Yeah. A lot of things I didn't think were any of his business. Like how much money my father makes, and what kinds of cars we drive, and where we go on vacations. I just met him, I don't see where he gets off thinking he can ask me those kinds of questions.

—He's my buddy.

—He didn't sound much like one.

—Why? What'd he say?

—I don't want to make trouble between you and your good old buddy.

—Come on, I can take it. What'd he say?

—He asked me out. How can you laugh? I don't think it's a bit funny.

—He was testing.

—What? To see if I'd go? He's got to be at least forty, looks like a dried-up lizard, and he's married. That's no test, it's an insult.

—He wanted to see if you're really my girl. I told you, he's my buddy.

—Some buddy. You know what he said? He said he doesn't know what I see in you, why I go with you, he knows a lot of guys, smarter, better looking, with more money. He'd introduce me. Stop laughing, it isn't funny. He made me feel like some piece of goods.

—And you got red hot mad and told him off.

—How'd you know?

—And told him exactly why you like me and why you stick with me.

—You knew all about it, he told you? You . . . Did you know he was going to do this?

—He said, Case, you're one hell of a lucky man, that woman's crazy about you. To her, you're some kind of god.

Mack thought it was a joke but Mack was wrong, Casey *was* a god, a young Greek god. But Mack didn't know Grecian from Italian from Egyptian, he'd never seen a statue or an urn. Hellenic, that was how she thought of Casey. The way she visualized the Spartans. Tall and blond, strong-armed and strong-legged . . .

. . . long strong legs, dripping water, glistening sun beating off lapping water, splashing children's voices shouts laughter . . .

She was pinning up her hair, head bent, fingers twisting at the nape of her neck, when shadows fell across her. She raised her head, bobby pins in her mouth, and found herself trapped between two pairs of legs, water beading off short hairs, blazing shiny trails over rounded muscles into curved crevices. Hairs to the left coarse and swarthy, hairs to the right fine and golden.

—What do you say, shall we throw her in?

Her eyes follow the golden legs up, over tight boxer trunks, over taut belly, over hard smooth chest, to the voice. Head silhouetted against the overhead sun, face in shadow, all she can tell is the smile.

—She looks to me like she needs a good dunking.

Hands reach for her feet.

—No! Wait. I'll ruin my hair.

She quickly tugs on her bathing cap.

Swarthy grabs her legs, Golden lifts beneath her arms. She's swinging, swinging into air, over concrete, over tile, free-falling. They jump in on top of her, pushing, pulling, tumbling, otters at play under water. She splutters to the surface, gets a faceful of spray, turns in the opposite direction, gets a second faceful. She fights back, frantically slapping and batting water. Two against one. She flops onto her back and kicks furiously, out-splashing free of their line of fire. She rolls over onto her stomach and strokes to the opposite side. She's climbed out and is sitting on the pool edge by the time they catch up.

—You're a good swimmer.

She dangles her feet in the water and allows them to admire her.

Golden cocks his head, gives her a crooked grin. —I'm Casey, this is Les.

They cling to the edge, on each side of her, smiling up, teeth white in tanned faces, inviting her to admire *them*.

—Hi. I'm Reggie.

—Reggie? Like a British officer?

—She doesn't look like a British officer to me.

—I say, Reggie, old boy . . .

—She doesn't look like a boy either.

She draws her knees up, stands, looks down on them —It's short for Regina— and walks away, stiffly aware of each step, the swing of her legs, the sway of her hips, as their eyes follow.

She stretches out on her towel and removes the cap. Casey plops down beside her.

—You're new in town, aren't you?

—You haven't seen me before, have you?

—Are you visiting?

—In a way.

—Who're you staying with.

—My mother and father.

—Are you going to live here?

—For a while— She fingers her hair. —It's wet. I knew it would be. It's going to be a mess.

—Why don't you take the curls out, it'll dry faster.

He reaches and starts taking out pins.

—No— She grabs her head. —It'll look awful.

He keeps removing pins.

She lowers her hands. —It's straight as a string.

—There— His fingers pluck and fluff the strings. —Where's your comb?

She digs in her bag and hands him the comb. He pulls through the tangles, in short easy tugs, working down the strands, holding the roots against her crown with the palm of his other hand. From the corners of her lowered eyes she watches him, intent on his job, frowning slightly.

He gives a final pat, leans back. —That's not so bad— He studies the effect. —You need bangs, your forehead's too high.

She wants to bury her head, wrap up in her towel and roll out of sight, like a potato bug, an armadillo. He looks her full in the face, fixes her with his eyes, brown, dancing with green and gold flecks, and smiles, twinkling, dazzling.

—You want to go for a ride?

SCENE 2

The telephone shrills, Reggie starts, throws a pillow over the album. Heart pounding, she waits it out, it rings a long time. Her eyes sting, her nostrils burn. She smells chlorine.

She lifts the pillow off the album, stands and looks around, getting her bearings. Ships. Walls of ships, in dark frames, sails unfurled, billowing with wind, straining toward sea, set to go somewhere. Howie's sailing trophies on the mantel. Ship models, ships in bottles on shelves and tables. She shivers, her feet are freezing. Beached, dry docked, going nowhere. She grabs the album . . .

Oh, Casey, where am I now?

Her teeth chatter as she scuffles up the hall. She checks the thermostat, sixty-eight, Howie's setting. She moves it to seventy-two. She forages on the closet floor for her slippers, furry foot-muffs with puppy-dog heads, a Christmas gift from Katelyn. She thought them funny at the time. She sits on the bed, slips them on, and stares at the floppy ears, droopy eyes, little plastic noses. Suddenly she's weighted down by cold and gray, exhausted, her brain closed in on itself. She shoves the album under the pillow and falls into bed, puppy-dog slippers and robe, and pulls the covers over her head. Sometime in the afternoon the phone rings again, she hears it dimly. But her cave is dark and warm and comforting. She burrows deeper.

It's Lindsay who digs her out. —Mummy? Mummy? She's in here, Aunt Buffie, in the bedroom.

Small hands tentatively peel the covers from her head. She opens blurry eyes into Lindsay's worried face, inches away.

Buffie strides in, measuring the situation, taking stock, preparing to take charge. —My god, are you sick?

Katelyn hangs by the door, in abeyance, not risking an entrance until she's sure of her line.

Reggie smiles, tries to look reassuring. —Hi— But under the pillow her hand searches for the album. —What time is it?

—Howie couldn't get you on the phone, he was worried. He asked me to pick up the girls.

—Thank you, I'm sorry . . .

—Do you think it's the flu? Get back, Lindsay, in case she has the flu.

Lindsay holds her ground, Katelyn backs to the hall.

—Do you have a temperature?— Buffie's cold hand coolly assesses Reggie's brow.

Reggie's hand grasps the album. —I'm just so out of it . . .

—Have you eaten?

—A little milk and toast.

—Katie, put the kettle on, we'll fix tea. You're probably dehydrated. You feel hot and dry.

—I've been under the covers . . .

—Lindsay, go help Katie. Tea for the four of us. And some cookies or whatever you and Katie want for a snack. No candy.

—Mummy doesn't buy candy— Lindsay, letting Aunt Buffie know Mummy knows how to care for us, and Mummy is still in charge.

Reggie musters the energy to smile Lindsay a thank you, but she's already out the door. Buffie intercepts the effort and returns it with a smile of her own, benevolent, understanding, her have-no-fear-Buffie-is-here Red Cross smile.

—Do you think you should see a doctor?

—No, no, I just need a little rest. I'll be fine by tomorrow.

—I'll call Howie.

—No! I don't want to bother him. He has so much on his mind.

—Well— Buffie looks disapproving —it's up to you. I'll get the tea.

Buffie bustles out, efficient, confident, in command, like her brother, never at a loss, never lost, never a loser. Buffie in her plaid wool slacks, navy blazer, and cashmere turtleneck. Always correct, always in good form, even when puffing cigarettes, tossing out cuss words, and swigging down scotch . . . scotch on the rocks, no water . . .

straight . . .

. . . straight bourbon, in a shot glass *Betts* What would Betts think of Buffie, and vice versa? The sudden thought of Betts makes Reggie smile, her spirits lift enough to rouse her. She grabs the album from under her pillow and shoves it to the foot of the bed beneath the sheets, plumps Howie's pillow behind her, and braces for Buffie's return.

—You need a table in here, something round, with a fringed chintz cover, to match your spread and drapes. Over here by the slipper chair— Buffie sets the tray on the bed, drags over the bench from the makeup table —This will do for now— moves the tray to the bench, pulls up the slipper chair.

Reggie eyes the tray: china cups and saucers, silver teaspoons, linen napkins. Buffie's hunted it all up. Even in illness propriety must prevail. —Where's the rose in the bud vase?

—What?

—I said this is nice of you.

—Oh. Well.

Buffie parks her behind on the slipper chair and primly pours.

—Cream or lemon?

—Lemon.

—Sugar?

Buffie holds trapped cube in poised tongs.

—Yes. Thank you. Two.

Plop. Plop. Reggie smiles . . . like little horse pucky *Betts* She accepts her cup and delicately sips with raised pinky in tandem with Buffie's fastidious tipplings.

—Cookie?

—No thank you.

—Come on, you have to keep your strength up.

Reggie gingerly selects a ginger snap and gingerly nibbles. Buffie smiles, magnanimously, expansively, closed lips curled like a smug cat. She uncrosses her legs and leans back, her shoe body slackening, spreading in the slipper chair. Reggie enjoys noting how in unguarded relaxation Buffie's body becomes larger, coarser, her thighs fleshy, not solidly thick like Betts's . . .

. . . Betts leaning forward, hands clasped between thighs straining in brother's Levis over sides of kitchen chair too stingy for her generous butt. Betts sprawled in school desk, skirt stretched high over cones of flesh, peeking triangle of white cotton, Janie going *Psst, psst*, Trixie sniggering behind hand, pointing, "I see London, I see France . . ." Betts opening legs in defiance. So many of the girls in Harden defied with open legs. . . .

—What? Oh, I'm sorry, Buffie, I must have been drifting.

—Never mind, I wasn't saying anything important.

Of that, I can be certain.

—I can't seem to keep my head up.

—No need. Here, let me take your cup, I'll clean up.

—I really appreciate . . .

—Don't give it a thought. I'll stay with the girls until Howie gets home.

—There's food . . .

—We'll manage.

—And please close the door behind you.

Reggie snuggles into the blankets, grabs the album between her feet, pulls it within reach, and falls asleep with the album clutched against her chest.

Black, very black. A swirl of lights, swiveling beams spiraling, searching the night Becoming balls, closing in, getting brighter and brighter Focusing, forming a circle, a circle of light On asphalt, black asphalt, dried weeds in the cracks Crackling music . . . *I told you, baby, from time to time, but you just wouldn't listen or pay me no mind. Now I'm movin' on, I'm rollin' on . . .*

Hank Snow calling them in, rounding them up . . .

They're all there in the circle of headlights—Betts, Billie, Trixie; Faye, Ruthie, Lester; Tex, Freddy, Walt; Janie and Glenn—dancing, doing the two step, dipping and swinging *You switched your main engine now I ain't got time* She can hear the scrape, feel the cut and drag of grit under her leather soles *for a triflin' woman on my main line . . .*

She's dancing, dancing with Casey, up down, in out He's twirling her, twirling and twirling *You done your daddy wrong* spinning her like a top He drops her hand She keeps spinning, faster and faster, away from him The circle of light pulls back, farther and farther Casey gets smaller and smaller She can't stop spinning, she reaches out Casey! He waves back *You were flyin' too high for my little old sky* raises his arms *So I'm movin' on* rises into the air *You had the laugh on me* lifts higher and higher *So I've set you free* a ball of light on the end of each wing *I'm movin' on.*

The headlights have become pinpoints on the runway She starts whirling her arms, like propellers, trying to lift after him Casey! Grab her, she's trying to take off *But someday, baby, when you've had your play* Hands grip her arms, drag her back *You're gonna want your daddy* She struggles I want you now! Her cry comes out soundless *But your daddy will say, Keep movin' on* She fights Come back! flailing out, trying to make him hear her Hold her down! Keep her grounded! *You stayed away too long* Kicking Chock her wheels! Arms tackle her legs Anchor her! Hands pin her feet to the asphalt Don't leave me! He's fading *I'm through with you* He smiles down *Too bad you're blue* and disappears into the black night *Keep movin' on.*

Her cry finally breaks free.

—*Casey!*

—Reggie . . . ?

He's leaning over her, swarthy, his face in shadow, dark. Lester?

—Reggie.

No! Mack! She screams and strikes out.

—Reggie, it's me. Howie.

She stares at the pale face and dark eyes. She registers the concern before she recognizes the man.

—Howie?

He releases her wrists. —It's all right.

Her eyes search his face. —The airstrip, Howie, the abandoned airstrip . . . Where we used to dance . . .

—In Harden— His tone, like his face, is flat.

She nods. She's trembling.

He sighs —You were having a fever dream— and stands. —I'll get a cold cloth.

She closes her eyes. The lights start swirling again, her head spins. She opens her eyes and stares at the ceiling. Howie lays the wet cloth across her forehead, water drips from its folded ends into the hair at her temples. Her skin gulps the soothing coldness, she moves the cloth to her neck.

She tries to smile. —I feel like the old miner who's just had his first drink of water after days lost in the desert.

Howie doesn't smile back. —Do you think you can eat some soup?

—I could try.

—I'll have the girls bring you some.

—No! Howie— He stops and turns. —I don't think I'm up to them.

—They need to be reassured.

—I don't want them to catch whatever I have.

He studies her, expressionless. —I don't think they will— She stares back.

—For just a few minutes, okay? Just talk to them. I'll tell them not to get too near.

He closes the door.

She raises and bumps against the album. She can feel the dents in her flesh where she squeezed its edges into her upper arms. She looks quickly to where Howie stood, trying to gauge whether he might have seen it. She shoves the album under the bed, props up the pillows, arranges the blankets around her, leans back, and closes her eyes.

The pain is sharper, deeper, more defined, lodged in her chest, cutting up into her throat. She was ready to talk to him, could have, would have, wanted to, if only he had stayed. If only he'd given her the chance, made some opening. The tears well and slide slowly, quietly. Not a muscle of her face betrays her emotion.

SCENE 3

—What do you mean a ride, what kind of ride?

Mummy is in rumpled khaki pants and stretched-out white T-shirt, roller in hand, arrested in midstroke, paint pan on the stool beside her.

—Just a ride. In his car.

—Doing what?

—I don't know. Riding around, talking, looking at things.

—There's nothing in this town to look at. One main street four blocks long, two side streets, a Safeway, a post office . . .

—Your roller is dripping.

Mummy sets roller on pan, looks over at Daddy, cross-kneed in the only upholstered chair in the house, a dusty frazzled thing I know won't be around long. But he's studiously engrossed in his book. So she glares back at me.

—I don't know a thing about this boy, I don't know his family . . .

—You don't know anyone's family here, Mummy, we're strangers, remember?

—I can't even call the minister. Do you realize there's no Unitarian church in this town, not even a Congregational?

—So we'll go Catholic.

—God forbid.

—All right, Episcopalian.

Daddy's eyes flicker up. —Personally I prefer the Church of Christ, the hymns are more rousing.

Mummy shoots him a frown of disgust, but he's intent again on his book. I stay intent on Mummy.

—His name's Casey.

—Casey what?

—How do I know? When you're at a swimming pool, trying to make friends as the new girl in town, you don't go around saying, Pardon me but I didn't catch your last name.

Mummy picks up the roller and returns to her wall. I'm right behind her.

—He's very nice.

—How do you know?

—He looks nice.

—You can't judge by appearances.

—When did you change your mind about that?

Daddy snorts. Mummy looks over sharply but he's innocently entrenched behind his book.

—I told him to come by at seven thirty.

—Oh, I don't know— Mummy turns to the upholstered chair, exasperated. —What do you think, Artie?

Daddy looks up as if surprised to find himself invited into this conversation. He tilts his head and assesses me.

—Well I'd say the boy's taking somewhat of a chance himself.

Mummy scowls then turns her back and vigorously swipes the wall with her roller, making it clear she's through with the both of us.

I dress carefully. Full circle blue-and-white striped skirt, sash tied in back with a wide bow. White gathered blouse with puffed sleeves and scooped elastic neck that can be slipped off the shoulders. White thong sandals. I paint my toenails Fire Engine Red, then wipe it off and repaint them Petal Pink, to match my lipstick. No fingernail polish, cheap for a girl my age, Mummy's decreed.

Daddy's in the armchair, Mummy's in the rocker, there's no more seating space. For once no one can say, For heaven's sake, Reggie, sit down. I wander around the living room trying to look indifferent. Mummy has banished the yellowed window shades to the garbage pile, so I stick close along the front wall.

Casey arrives promptly at seven thirty and sits in his car. Mummy and Daddy pretend he's not there. It's a tense wait. Finally he turns out his headlights and swaggers to the front door. Daddy stands, I make introductions.

—Casey, I'd like you to meet my mother and father, Mr. and Mrs. Patterson. Mummy and Daddy, this is Casey.

Casey shakes Daddy's hand. —Mr. Patterson.

Mummy leans forward. —I'm sorry, Casey, I didn't catch your last name.

—Colter, ma'am.

Mummy extends her hand. —We're pleased to meet you, Casey Colter.

Casey looks around. In the glare from the white walls he looks younger and smaller.

Daddy smiles, Mummy assesses. It's up to me.

—I'm sorry I can't ask you to sit down, all the chairs are wet.

He can see them lined against the back wall, five wooden chairs in three different styles, behind a rectangular table, all freshly painted white.

—That's okay— Casey decides to take the bull by the horns. —If it's all right, Mr. and Mrs. Patterson, I'd like to take Reggie for a ride.

—Anywhere in particular?

Mummy and Casey take each other's measure.

—Just around town. To show her where things are. Then maybe to Dairy Queen.

Daddy wraps his arm around my shoulders. —That seems all right.

I cast him a grateful smile and head for the door. Mummy's right there beside me.

—What time will you be back?

Casey doesn't hesitate. —Ten thirty, ma'am.

She looks at her watch. —No later.

The car is tan, a four-door Chevrolet, old but spotlessly clean inside and out. The plush in the window frames is still wet. But the upholstery gives up a poof of dust when I slide in.

—What'd you call your mother?— I look at him. —When you introduced us.

—Mrs. Patterson.

—You called her Mummy.

—What do you call your mother?

—Catherine.

—It's disrespectful to call your mother by her first name.

—And calling her a mummy isn't?— He snickers. —She must be some kind of nut for white.

—She likes it clean and light. It's a small house, the rooms are dark.

—Well wait until the first dust storm, she's going to wish she'd left it dark. But your dad seems nice.

He's driving randomly up and down the streets, turning corners on apparent impulse, casting frequent glances my way. I look out the window.

The early evening has brought everyone out. Children are playing street games, fathers are watering grass, mothers are gossiping with neighbors. Grandmothers and grandfathers relax in porch swings or on lawn chairs, sipping cool drinks, waiting for the sunset, the highlight of any summer day in Arizona.

The houses are low and for the most part small, here and there a would-be pueblo or Spanish villa, but mostly bungalows. Cinder brick bungalows with townhouse fronts that remind me of the East. Wood shingle bungalows with points of stained or beveled glass that remind me of the Midwest. Spare frame bungalows with tall narrow windows that remind me of the Prairies. No colonial or ranch types. I can't tell neighborhoods. The styles are mixed haphazardly, Indian adobe next to Eastern brick next to Spanish stucco. Dirt and rain have splashed red stains up lower walls, sun and wind have burned bleached streaks down upper walls. Paint and wood don't fare so well as adobe and brick.

We drive in and out of blocks where the lawns are drier and sparser, the houses shabbier, but even here I can't find a pattern. I feel only the town. Except for a single hill, there are no lowlands or highlands to explain the poorer from the more substantial.

There are trellises of trumpet vine, sweet pea, and bougainvillea, pots of geranium, marigold, and petunia, beds of stock, snapdragon, and hollyhock. The air is warm, moist, and fragrant. I keep the window down and don't mind about my hair.

—So how long have you been in Harden?

—Five days.

—How much have you seen of the town?

—Not much. Main Street . . .

—We call it First Street.

—The Safeway, the post office. And my walk today to the swimming pool.

—That's it? What've you been doing all that time?

—Unpacking. Moving in.

—And painting everything in sight white— He considers, drops the snideness. —I guess there's not that much more to see.

—That's what Mummy said.

—What's your mother's name anyway?

—Margaret.

—So call her that.

—The family calls her Maggie.

—So call her Maggie.

His driving becomes purposeful. He whips around corners, down-gearing with the intent split-second revving of a Grand Prix racer. He heads east, to the edge of town where the houses end, and stops in front of a large square brick building.

In the last red rays of sun I make out a flight of concrete steps leading to double glass-and-steel-frame doors, and three stories of steel-framed sash windows. Behind, baseball field with backstop, football field with bleachers. No tennis courts. To the side, a small parking lot. No trees. The efforts at grass—in front, on the playing field—are scruffy, tired-looking, pocked with patches of packed dirt. Beyond, desert takes over.

—This is the high school, our new one.

He waits for comment but all I can see is Wexler, my private girls' school back home, its dignified gray-and-white Georgian buildings and twenty-five acres of green playing fields surrounded by hilly forest. Not for the first time, I'm having serious misgivings about this adventure my father has brought us on. I say the only thing that strikes my mind.

—My god, what was the old high school like?

He puts the car in gear. —Where're you from, anyway?

—Boston.

—I figured it was some place East. From the funny way you talk.

—What's wrong with the way I talk?

—It's high and in the back of your nose, kind of tight and prissy-like. Like you have to say everything just right.

He's heading back toward the center of town, taking his time, steering by his wrist draped over the steering wheel.

—What year are you?

—Sophomore.

He whistles, with raised eyebrows. —I thought you were older.

I assess him. —What year are you?

—Senior— Proudly.

—Really?— Archly. I widen my eyes. —I thought you were younger.

He looks over, eyes me speculatively, then grins.

The street lights are furry against the blue night. Front doors are open. Figures move across bright living rooms, children play tag and wrestle on dark lawns, dogs bark. Casey slows down as we pass a dark hulking building set in a block of hard dirt enclosed by cyclone fence. Backstop, bicycle racks, a rectangle of blacktop with a basketball hoop at each end.

—The old high school. Washington. Once the only school in town. Then they built Jefferson Elementary.

He's slowly moved into the next block, another square of hard dirt enclosed by another cyclone fence, in the middle of which squats another dark building with another backstop and basketball court, but in addition, swings, monkey bars, jungle-gym, and merry-go-round. —This is where Denny goes.

—Who's Denny?

—My little sister. She's starting first grade. They moved the sixth, seventh, and eighth grades over to Washington when they built Lincoln.

I giggle.

—What's so funny?

—It just strikes me that way.

—What?

—The names of everything. Washington, Jefferson, Lincoln. The avenues are states. Dakota, Wyoming, Ohio, Montana. The streets are trees. Elm, Maple, Cherry, Oak.

—So what?

—It just sounds so, I don't know, like something out of Sinclair Lewis.

—What do they call the streets where you come from?

—Brookline. Commonwealth. Beacon.

—What's so great about that?

I shrug and look out the window. —Forget it, you wouldn't understand— He gives me a narrow look, I return it. —What time is it?

He tilts his watch to the dashboard light. —Nine thirty. Am I keeping you up?

—It's too dark, I can't see anything.

He jams the car into gear, slams his foot to the accelerator, and doesn't slow until we're half a block from my house. He glides to the curb and stops, looking straight ahead, car motor still running. Behind the shadeless windows, our white living room glares like a klieg-lit Hollywood set. Mummy and Daddy sit poised, reading in their chairs, ready for the cameras to start rolling. Casey makes no move, so I open my door myself and slide out.

He shifts in his seat, glances toward me. —What's Sinclair Lewis anyway?

—A man who writes books about provincial minds in provincial towns.

I slam the door and sashay up the walk without a backward look. Casey peels out, leaving behind rubber and smoke.

SCENE 4

She lies in the darkened room, listening to her family stir, start their morning rituals, hoping someone will make a move toward her that will give her motivation and direction, get her out of bed. Minutes pass. Resigned, frustrated, curious, she swings her feet to the floor, peeks down the hall, and tiptoes past the closed doors to the guest bedroom. Howie is in the guest bath, preparing to wet his toothbrush. He spots her in the mirror and registers surprise, then, she thinks, a little irritation.

—It's all right, Howie, you can use our bedroom and bath.

He vacillates, then collects his toiletries in the towel, assessing her uneasily.

—How're you feeling?

—Wobbly.

—Do you think you should be up?

—I can't give in to it.

He hesitates, tries to read her face, looks as if about to speak, then turns and starts toward their bedroom. She wonders what he might have been going to say.

After a moment she follows, watches from the edge of the bed as he brushes his teeth and shaves. She's seen him shave a hundred times, in T-shirt and plaid boxer-shorts, with electric shaver and talc. Casey wore white cotton briefs that hugged his fanny and pouched in front. She saw him shave once, with lather and safety razor. She studies Howie's movements intently, as if the way the two men deal with face hair might reveal their significant difference. Howie pats on after-shave cologne and closes the bathroom door. In fifteen years of marriage, she's never seen him urinate. Casey thought cologne was for gigolos or sissies.

She tries to make small talk while Howie dresses.

—What's your day going to be like?

—Busy. We're finalizing the briefs for the Levitt suit against Tryon. We take it to court next week.

—Do you think you have a good chance to win?

—We better. If we don't, we lose an important client— He jabs his arms into his shirt sleeves, yanks at the buttons. —And the loss will be counted as mine.

She could say, Don't worry, you're such a good lawyer, of course you'll win. Or, Levitt's been with you for years, they won't leave you over one loss. Or, So you lose one big client, you'll get another even bigger. There are a dozen encouraging, supportive things she could say, but she has no heart for it. She knows they'll be trivial, have no consequence in the hard facts of Howie's reality. She wonders what she might say that *would* make a difference. About anything.

Howie knots his club tie loosely around his open collar and turns to her.

—What is it, Reggie? You've been moping around, hiding out now for two days. I know I let you down, and I admit not for the first time. But I don't think it was that big a catastrophe, not big enough for all this. I tried to explain and apologize. Isn't there some way we can smooth this over and get on with our life— He pauses, his voice darkens. —Unless you're tired of our life— His eyes search hers. —Or maybe it's just me you're tired of.

She suddenly sees how drawn his face is, how hollowed with shadow. Her hand flutters toward him. —No, it's me, Howie. Me I'm tired of.

—I don't understand, Reggie.

—I know. Neither do I.

—I do the best for you I can, give you the best kind of life I know how, and I don't think I've done all that badly. By most standards, we live pretty well. But lately I've felt I'm not enough. You're dissatisfied. Unhappy.

She shakes her head. —It's not you, Howie. Something's wrong in me, something is missing— Her eyes fasten on his, willing him to understand. —I feel like a jumbled puzzle inside, all tossed around. I have to sort out the pieces, find the missing parts, put them together again in a pattern that makes sense. Has some meaning.

He sighs heavily, she looks away with irritation. —I'm sorry, Howie. I'm like you, doing the best I can. I know right now that doesn't seem like much.

He shifts uneasily. —Would it help if we sat down and talked, tried to work it out together?

Something inside her twists, something cold and angry and sorry. Where was he all the other times they needed to talk? All the other nights of loneliness and confusion. She looks down at her folded hands.

—I need time, Howie, time to be alone and think.

He shrugs, exasperated, impatient.

—And what are the girls and I supposed to do during all that time, pretend you don't exist?

—Can't you just be understanding and supportive?

—While you've locked yourself away from us in the bedroom?

—What if I were recovering from a long illness?

—I don't know, I'd have to think about it— He grabs his jacket off the hanger —I guess I don't have much choice— and throws the hanger on the bed. —I'm fixing scrambled eggs. You want any?

It isn't that she's still angry, she doesn't want to hurt him, isn't trying to get back. It's just that she feels so distant, so detached. She wants to get up and follow him into the kitchen, join her family in their morning busyness and chatter, but it's an empty wanting. There's nothing inside her pulling her up, leading her on, nothing to reach out to and grip. She's drifting. Purposeless. Everyone and everything can get along quite well without her. And so she sits and waits, staring at her hands, until the BMW whirrs out the drive.

She listens to the silence for several minutes, then laboriously, begrudgingly, as if old and weary, lifts herself from the bed and forces herself down the hall.

She has to eat. But once in the kitchen, she can't stand the thought of food. Perhaps a cup of coffee. Howie hasn't fixed any, he's gone without, she usually sets the coffeemaker on the timer the night before. He won't drink instant, only brewed decaf. She doesn't keep instant in the house. She wants a cup of real coffee, something to fill the room with strong dark aroma.

She rummages for the Colombian, mixes in a little French Roast kept for company, which they haven't had much of lately, and hunches at the table while the water boils up and drips down through its cycle. The hot, acrid liquid scalds her tongue and gullet and braces her like deserved punishment. She cups her hands around the mug, takes the heat into her palms and fingers, and stares into the dark contents, reading her past.

Catherine always had a mug and a cigarette burning in an ashtray, she carried them around with her. She kept the pot on all day, a Pyrex percolator. The women would drop by, bearing cookies or donuts, sometimes a freshly baked pie or cake, they'd come in the morning after the men left, or in the afternoon before the older kids came home. Catherine would give someone a haircut, a set, a home perm, they'd sit around the table sipping coffee, smoking Pall Malls, and swapping news, histories, and confidences.

They'd report on their children: Sally got a perfect report card, Jimmy got in a fight at school, Bobby was learning the clarinet, Jeannie got invited to Mary's party. They'd report on their husbands: Al got a promotion, Jack got drunk again, Lew was taking the boys fishing, Hank was starting an auto shop in the garage. They'd report on themselves: Liz bought a new dress, Joan was thinking of getting a job, Jo Ellen was going to visit her parents, Gail had joined the church choir.

Accountings of the present wove into recountings of the past. Their children's deeds and misdeeds recalled memories of their own childhoods. Their husbands' adventures and misadventures provoked comparisons with fathers, uncles, and brothers. Their efforts and failings as mothers and wives prompted reassessments and new understandings of their own mothers.

These recountings were cast as stories, human tragedies or comedies, that built through beginning and middle to a fitting climax and denouement that provided some insight, lesson, or message relevant to the issue at hand. Once worked through and survived, the raw events of the present would in their turn be refined as stories, and in their telling and retelling, around tables, through generations, eventually become embellished and polished as histories.

The women shared unabashed tears, raucous laughter, and bawdy language. Liz confessed she'd had to sneak the money from Ray's pants and wallet over months to buy the dress. Dottie admitted Al's promotion was in name only, there was no raise, and she was afraid it was a way of pushing him aside and easing him out. Kaye was worried about Jimmy's temper, she couldn't handle him anymore, he was getting in more and more trouble. Annie didn't think she could take Jack's drinking and ugly mouth any longer and was considering divorce. Vera resented Lew's relationship with their boys and the way they excluded her from their activities. Norma had missed a period and didn't know how to tell Hank because they'd been saving their money for the auto shop. The women offered empathy, advice, support, and acceptance.

The younger children played among themselves and listened and learned with half an ear. When Casey and the older boys arrived, the talk turned to joking. When the men came around, the talk turned to the men.

Reggie's presence among the women was accepted unquestioningly; she was one of them, preparing. She quickly understood they were not gossiping. They were comparing notes, gathering information on how to live, benefitting from their collective experience and wisdom, and in the process expanding themselves as story tellers and having a hell of a good time at it. She saw these sessions as combined problem solving, therapy, and entertainment. There were no psychiatrists or counselors in Harden, only friends, neighbors, and relatives. If the talk turned to women not present, it was not to belittle them but to consider their circumstances and choices, the alternatives, the merits, the consequences. Right and wrong were judged on how to hold things together and get on; getting on had to do with taking the responsibilities of a role and doing the job well; "well" had to do with the fostering of all concerned. Those concerned were primarily children, husbands, and parents, secondarily friends and other relatives, lastly the community. The women considered themselves involved with the world but they did not see the world as involved with them. They listened to the news and discussed it, but did not see themselves as capable of affecting it.

Reggie realizes, as she swirls the grounds in the bottom of her mug, that she has never participated as an adult in such a cow session, as Casey's father Scotty called them, only listened and observed as a teenager. Coffee klatching doesn't occur in Boston, at least not in her circle. She only listened and observed as a teenager. And Katelyn and Lindsay have been denied even that.

She misses Catherine. She suddenly wants a cigarette.

She goes hunting in the dining room sideboard for the silver humidor and ashtray she keeps for guests, fills her mug, and returns to the table. The cigarettes are stale, most of their friends have stopped smoking, those who still do sneak them out of pockets or purses away from the group. She pulls smoke into her throat, gags, blows it out in a cloud that stings her eyes and nostrils. The second drag is easier. She leans back, knees crossed, cigarette held high between fingers, and closes her eyes as the nicotine rush tingles her cheeks. Casey didn't like her to smoke, he yanked the cigarette from her mouth when Billie tried to teach her.

—What're you doing? Where'd you get that?

Billie has sauntered off to the group around Tex and his guitar. Casey yells across the camp fire at her. —Billie, what the hell do you think you're doing?— Billie thrusts out a hip, crosses her arms, inhales and seductively French exhales at him. He grabs my arm. —You wanna look like that? Look at her. You ever smell her? She reeks of stale smoke. Her clothes, her hair, even her skin. It seeps out of her, that's why her complexion's so dingy. You ever kiss anyone who smokes?

I don't dare answer yes.

—Your mother smokes.

—You leave my mother out of this. No girl of mine is going to smoke.

Reggie thoughtfully traces the monogram engraved in the top of the silver humidor. A car pulls into the drive. She stubs out the cigarette, dumps the ashes in the trash, stuffs the ashtray and humidor in her robe pockets, and hurries to the living room, then hovers in the middle of the floor facing the door. The doorbell chimes. She doesn't move. No steps retreat, no car withdraws. She tiptoes to the dining-room window and checks the driveway. My god, Pat's Cherokee, it must be Friday. The chimes sound again. She reluctantly opens the door.

—Oh! Mrs. Kendall. I was beginning to think no one was home.

—I was in the bedroom. I haven't been feeling well . . .

—You want me to skip today?

—No. . . . Come on in . . .

Reggie idly follows into the laundry room and watches while Pat takes off and hangs her coat, puts on an apron.

—Sorry you're not well, what is it, the flu, you think?

—Just a little cold.

—Probably this weather we're having, awful isn't it, chill you to the bone.

Pat loads the caddy with glass cleaner, tile cleaner, scouring powder, ammonia with lemon, woodwork cleaner, furniture polish. —No one else sick, I take it.

—No, everyone else is fine.

—That's good. We can't have Katie getting sick on us, can we, so close to her recital, she's so excited. Can't say I blame her. She showed me her tutu and toe shoes. She's going to be beautiful, all that pink fluff with that dark hair and those blue eyes, I can hardly wait to see her.

Pat pulls out Rubbermaid pail and stuffs it with toilet brush, paper towels, and cleaning rags. —It was really nice of you to invite me.

—We wouldn't think of not having you, you're family, besides being Katelyn's favorite audience.

—She was wonderful in the Nutcracker.

—Well, this is going to be a bit different. No big stage, fancy sets, or fifty-piece orchestra. Just a bare floor and piano. So prepare yourself, you might find it a little boring.

—Not on your life. I can't imagine doing such a thing, getting up there in front of a roomful of people and dancing all by myself. I'd die of fright.

—Not Katelyn. She thrives on it.

Pat laughs, her round face crinkled, eyes shining, teeth almost perfect in her wide smile. And for a moment Reggie sees her as beautiful.

—No. That one lives for the limelight— Pat grins —I guess she takes after her mother— looks wise —Lindsay told me about you and your acting career— sees Reggie's face and goes anxious. —I hope that wasn't meant to be private, she's so proud of you.

Reggie shrugs. —It wasn't much of a career. I studied drama in college, did a few plays, that's all.

Pat appraises Reggie appreciatively —I can picture you as an actress— then loops the pail handle over her arm, lifts the caddy in one hand, and grabs the broom and dustmop in the other. —Where you want me to start? The bedroom so you can lie down?

Reggie doesn't answer, she's seeing Pat's face, Betts's face, Catherine's face, women's faces around a table, weathered, prematurely aged, full of laughter, full of light, full of wisdom. Beautiful. Women telling stories, making histories, creating their own theatre.

Pat's waiting turns to concern. —You sure you're all right? Maybe you should lie down right now.

—No, no, I'm fine, just a little weak. I probably need to eat.

—You haven't eaten yet? You want me to cook . . . ?

—No, no, I can do it. I've got to get myself moving, I have so much to do.

—That's the worst of being sick, isn't it, you get so far behind. Well, just call if you need something— Pat hefts the pail, caddy, mop, and broom as if they were empty shopping bags and takes the shortcut through the family room.

Reggie watches her broad back and butt, a big woman, not as big as Betts, but conveying the same sense of solid strength, a steady force, moving ahead, taking whatever in stride, head out of the clouds, feet firm on the ground, not to be tripped or toppled.

Reggie takes a pan, bowl, fork, and spatula out of the dishwasher, eggs and butter out of the refrigerator. In Harden, Pat wouldn't be a cleaning woman, she'd be around the kitchen table with Betts or Catherine. Who in Harden had a cleaning woman, who could afford one, who would think of such a thing? She puts the pan on to heat, breaks two eggs into the bowl, adds a splash of water, and beats with the fork. Maybe Mrs. Gergherty, who came from the East and whose husband was a Santa Fe official. Maybe Mrs. Thompson who was too old to clean for herself and received monthly checks in the mail from her daughters. But who would have cleaned for them? The women in Mexican Town? The women in Indian town? Certainly not Betts or Catherine.

She melts butter in the pan, pours in the eggs, pushes them around with the spatula. The women of Harden were tough, independent, took pride in doing for themselves, anything and everything that had to be done. They canned, built pantries, sewed, dug gardens out of hard dirt. They were two generations off the prairie, three generations out of covered wagons. It was a disgrace to ask others to do what you could and should do for yourself, an admittance of weakness of moral fiber, which was synonymous with weakness of physical constitution, like the public exposure of an appendix scar. Eyes were averted, lips pursed.

Reggie pushes the eggs onto a clean plate, puts the pan, bowl, and spatula in the sink to soak, and sits down at the table with the plate and fork. She listens to Pat industriously bumping around in the bedroom. She could never tell Betts she had a cleaning woman, a lawn man, a gardener, a man to prune and spray the trees, a boy to shovel snow off the walks. She could never exchange names of dressmakers, manicurists, hair stylists. Catherine had never had a facial or body massage, anymore than Pat. Pat has never seen the inside of a college, has never bought a tulle tutu and slippers with satin ribbons for her daughter.

The eggs are paper wads in Reggie's mouth, she hates herself for telling Pat she's family. She swallows, carries the plate and fork to the sink, puts the cigarettes and ashtray on the table, and calls up the hall.

—Pat, would you like a cup of coffee?

SCENE 5

It's hot the next day, of course, so of course I go to the swimming pool. He's there with his little sister. I know her only by name but there's no mistaking the girl splashing around him as some neighbor kid. She's a carbon of her big brother:

same stubborn jaw and determined chin, same dimples, same crinkly eyes, even the same honey-blonde hair. But her nose is perter. I can't tell all this at first glance, of course, it takes some covert watching. Casey's doing his own covert watching. He's facing the bathhouse back when I come out and I have the distinct feeling he's been waiting for me.

I use the term bathhouse loosely. A square of concrete block coated with glossy gray paint, men's wing to the left, women's to the right, check-in counter recessed in the center. Six dressing stalls, about thirty-six inches by thirty-six, narrow wood board to serve as bench, dingy canvas sheet as door, attached here and there by metal clips over a metal pole. Two shower stalls with no curtain, one toilet stall mercifully with door. No lockers. When you pay, you pick up a denim bag over a wooden hanger with a numbered metal tag and matching numbered safety pin. You put your belongings in the bag, pin the safety pin to your bathing suit, and return the bag to the counter. Primitive, but it saves the cost of lockers. The coach's wife could have made the bags.

To get from bathhouse to pool, you have to walk through a five-inch-deep sickly solution the color and consistency of watered milk and smelling to high heaven of warm disinfectant you're sure is going to corrode the skin off your feet. I hold my nose and tiptoe through quickly.

Casey turns away the minute he sees me and makes a big deal out of playing with Denny. I walk to my removed corner of yesterday, spread my towel, adjust my suit, and stretch out. I've hardly had time to settle before someone plops down beside me. I take my time opening my eyes. But it isn't Casey.

—Hi, I'm Fred.

I pull to sitting position, tuck my legs to the side, suck my stomach in, arch my back, and straighten my scarf. I pinned my hair at home.

—Hi.

I see Casey watching sidewise as he tosses Denny in the air and twirls her through the water.

—You're Reggie, aren't you?

—How'd you know that?

The stranger grins and shrugs, a medium-sized boy, a little on the thick side, with brown crew-cut and brown eyes. Not bad but nothing to get excited about.

—I saw you here yesterday. You're from the East and you're staying in the Ferguson house.

—Word travels fast in this town.

—It's a small town. Would you like a ride home?

—I just got here.

—I mean when you're ready to leave.

—Well that's really nice of you, but my parents don't like me driving with anyone they haven't met.

I stand and pull my cap on.

—How about if I come by this evening and meet them.

—If you want.

I'm on my way to the pool.

—What time?

I knife a neat dive into the water.

Casey stays away from me all afternoon. Fred does too. I guess he got the message. I walk home.

I'm sitting on the porch in the green wicker settee Maggie hasn't painted her way to yet when Fred drives up in a shiny new Buick. He's barely made his way to the top of the steps when Casey's dated Chevy comes skidding up. Fred looks at me uncertainly.

—I thought you said it was okay for me to come by.

—I did.

—Am I here at the wrong time?

—We didn't set a time.

—Were you expecting Colter?

—I wasn't.

Casey bounds up the steps, he doesn't bother to glance at me.

—What're you doing here, Herren?

—Same thing you're doing.

—Was Reggie expecting you?

—She was. Which is more than you can say.

—She was expecting me.

—That's not what she says.

—Reggie and I have unfinished business.

—Yeah, well, I got here first.

—No you didn't, Herren. But you're leaving first.

Casey's taken a braced-leg, arms-out-at-sides stance, shoulders and head hunched. I think, *Oh god, he's going to start a fight, Mummy'll have a fit, Daddy'll have to break it up,* but Fred doesn't accept the challenge. Instead he turns on me.

—You should have told me Colter's got this territory staked out— and with a dirty look, he departs.

I spin on Casey.

—You had no right to do that. You don't own me.

—Fred Herren's an asshole.

Mummy immediately appears at the screen door.

—Oh, hi, Mrs. Patterson, sorry for the little disturbance, but Reggie doesn't want a thing to do with Freddy Herren, believe me, he's an . . .

—I heard.

—He thinks because his dad owns the trading post that makes him big, but no one around here likes him. If Reggie's seen hanging out with him, it'll hurt her with the other kids.

Mummy's smile is acid. —It's so thoughtful of you, Casey, to be so concerned about Reggie's welfare.

Casey sweetens Mummy with one of his smiles. —No trouble at all, ma'am. I'm just trying to look out for her interests, her being new in town and all. I want her to get off on the right foot.

Daddy joins Mummy at the screen.

—Evening, Mr. Patterson. I thought I'd drop by and take Reggie for a Softy at Dairy Queen.

Mummy frowns. —You went there last night.

—Well, not exactly, ma'am, the evening ended a little abruptly. I think Reggie got put off by the new high school.

Daddy snuffles a laugh, he's heard my description, and returns to his chair and book. Mummy glares at his back, then sighs with resignation.

—Well, all right. But home by nine thirty.

—How about ten thirty?— Another dazzling smile. —The whole crowd'll be there, I want Reggie to meet them.

—Ten.

Casey drives with one hand, elbow out the window, cocky, smiling to himself.

—You look very pretty tonight. I like you in pink.

—Thanks— Mummy says it's my best color. —Who's the 'whole crowd'?

—Just the kids I pal around with. What're you nervous about?

—I'm not.

Casey puts his hand on my knee. —You just smile and be your sweet self and you'll do fine— I brush his hand off.

The Dairy Queen is almost as big a letdown as the high school. A long, low wooden shack with peeling white paint, windowed counter across the front, to the side and back a concrete-block appendage with linoleum floor and red vinyl booths. White neon tubing rims the roof. From the jukebox chained against the outside wall, Hank Williams wails into the glare. *Hey, hey, good-lookin', What'cha got cookin'? How's about cookin' somethin' up with me?*

And Casey thinks *my* voice is tight and nasal.

Sedans and pickups clutter the surrounding dirt in haphazard angles. Teenagers mill along the wide sidewalk around the take-out counter, spill over into the parking lot, sit on fenders, stand on running boards. They're dressed in Levis and shirts, a few girls in shorts. I feel stupid in my dress but I know it's no use going home, I don't own Levis and, except for the beach, Mummy won't let me wear shorts in public.

Hey, sweet baby, Don't cha think maybe, We could find us a brand new recipe?

Casey brakes to a sharp stop, spraying dust, and climbs out. Behind their smiles and tossed greetings, I see their curiosity, they're waiting for me to emerge. Casey's obviously expecting me to get out on my own and follow in his wake. I sit transfixed between indignation and agonizing self-consciousness.

I got a hotrod Ford and a two-dollar bill, I know a spot right over the hill.

A large figure detaches itself from the group, ambles toward me, and leans a large, round face with Dutch-bobbed hair into the window. I can't tell if it's male or female.

—Look at the son-of-a-bitch. He's so proud of himself for having picked you off he's forgotten all about you— The voice is strong and rough, but definitely female. —Hey, Colter, get your sorry ass over here and take care of this girl.

Casey does a comic double-take like, Oops, forgot something, and saunters back, singing and twisting with the music. *There's soda pop and the dancin' is free, So come along, take a chance with me.*

The car door opens. —Come on, who needs him, I'll take you around— She pulls me out.

She towers over me, taller than Daddy, and Daddy's five-foot-ten. She's not fat, just big, big-boned. Wide and solid. The tails of her extra-large man's shirt hang out over her extra-broad Levis. Her feet in stretched-out loafers seem small in comparison. —I'm Betts— She puts a hefty arm around me. —Hey, everybody— She turns me toward the crowd. —I want you to meet Reggie.

A small chorus, Hi, Reggie.

Casey does a fancy two-step in front of me, singing with Hank, *I'm free and I'm ready, So we can go steady, How's about keepin' steady company?* then a neat little spin and bow.

—You want a root beer float?

—Course not, you cheap son-of-a-bitch, she wants a banana split, so do I— Betts laughs at the look on his face.

"The Crowd" wanders up two and three at a time, friendly, casual. I look them in the eye, repeat their names —Hi, Trixie, Nice to meet you, Billie— try to memorize names with faces, the way they taught us at Wexler.

Trixie: Dark hair and eyes, pale skin, coy, pert. She assesses me with female wariness, what kind of competition am I?

Billie: Blonde, blue-eyed, short, bouncy. She meets me full on, open and direct. I expect her to slap me on the shoulder or shake my hand.

Faye: Tall, freckled, tough, with auburn hair and dark-framed glasses. She posts a distance, eyeing me skeptically, not to be taken in easily.

Ruthie: Pretty, sweet, demure, vacant. She smiles through me, a meaningless momentary distraction forgotten the moment she turns her back.

Janie: Plain, plump, reserved. She studies me with unabashed frankness, trying to read me.

The boys pretend not to listen, a few sidle up behind the girls, but for the most part they hold their ground, waiting for Casey to squire me.

Les is there, watching from a distance, grinning like a well-fed panther. Tex—small, handsome in a pretty, fine-boned sort of way, and older than the rest of the crowd—sits on a fender picking the strings of a guitar. Walt, Faye's twin brother, has her hair and freckles but not her glasses or toughness. Curt regards me as he does everyone, with folded arms and flat expression, saving his words for sharp insight and biting wit. Glenn has soft rolls of fat around his middle, wire-rimmed glasses, and thin lank hair. But he surmounts all with his unsquelchable good-nature. Freddy Herren leans against his shiny black sedan looking withdrawn and sulky.

The crowd's interest in me is soon satisfied and they return to each other, grouping and regrouping in familiarized patterns. I begin to relax. I tag along behind Casey, observing. He does all the talking.

My first days in Harden, I'd found the way of speech funny, almost comic. Like Mummy, I guess, I thought the local inhabitants simple, not deep, not educated, maybe not too bright. As I listen now to the kids swapping stories and inside information on persons, places, and events I know nothing of, I find my interest drifting to their faces and voices. Their expressions are animated, intent. They're enthusiastic listeners, they use their hands a lot in description. Their speech is easy, relaxed, the vowels broad, the consonants soft, sometimes so slack the words slur together, slowed down by the heat like the way of life. No place much to go so might as well take your time and enjoy yourself getting there. I've never heard so much laughter, or so much cussing. The casual use of four-letter words astonishes and embarrasses then fascinates me. It's "sonnabitch," "*shee*-it," "friggin'," "humpin'," "screwin'," but I don't hear anybody use the *f* word. Walt calls out —Hey, let's go get dronk.

This makes me nervous. I tap Casey's arm. He acts surprised to see me.

—Hey. How's my girl?

—I finished my banana split— Actually I've been wondering what to do with my plastic dish for over half an hour.

—You want something else?— I shake my head. —A hamburger?

—No thank you.

—A root beer float?

—I think I should go home.

—Okay. Whatever you say— He puts his arm around my shoulders. —Well, gang— with unnecessary loudness —I guess it's time I took the little lady home— He grins down at me. The boys return knowing smiles and size me up lasciviously. The girls' eyes go cold with speculation. I duck from under his arm and head for the car.

Casey peels out in a spray of dust. He's pleased as a peacock in a parade, playing around with the steering, swerving the car back and forth.

—I'm not your girl. And I'm not a little lady.

Casey raises his eyebrows as if surprised by the very thought.

—Who said you were?

—You did.

—I did?— He looks dumbfounded. I sit unforgiving. —Ahh— His eyes and tone cajole. —You're not gonna get mad at me again, are you? That's just a way of talking.

I consider him and relent. At least he's stopped jerking us around the road.

There's something about him that's had me thinking ever since Dairy Queen.

—You're not the same as the other kids.

He looks over. —I'm not?— The idea pleases him. —How?— He smiles engagingly, inviting confidence and flattery.

—I don't know. For one thing you don't talk quite the same, not so slurred. And you use words differently, as if you knew more and how to put them together better.

He gives a smart little jiggle in his seat. —That's probably because I went away to school.

—You did?— I perk up, thinking of Mummy. —Where? Prep school?

—Military academy— My perk droops.

—Why? Were you a behavior problem?

He laughs. —Sure. Still am— He looks over at me. —But that's not why I went away to school— The lights from an oncoming car flash across his face. His features are soft and proud, like his voice. He turns back to the road, suddenly serious. —My dad's a smart man who never finished high school. He wanted something better for me than getting stuck in Harden. He figured education was my ticket out.

—But why military academy?— I'm still having trouble with it.

—Why not? Besides, I got a scholarship— Another plus for Casey, I can't wait to get to Mummy. He grins. —Catherine wanted me to go to seminary, but Scotty said he wasn't about to have his only son become a eunuch priest.

My heart pitches to my stomach. I can hear Mummy, *God forbid.*

—Your family's Catholic?

—Just my mom, Denny, and me.

I just won't mention it.

—What's your dad?

—An engineer.

I perk up again. I feel like I'm riding a high-speed elevator, up down, up down, crashing from floor to ceiling. —So's my Uncle Jack, he's a graduate of M.I.T— Even to my own ears, my voice sounds overly bright.

—What's M.I.T.? Some university?

I try to be matter-of-fact. —The Massachusetts Institute of Technology. It's very famous. Jack's my father's younger brother, he's an electrical engineer. What kind's your father?

I realize Casey's no longer smiling.

—Railroad. Graduate of Santa Fe.

It takes me a moment. Then I get it. Of course he'd told me his father hadn't graduated from high school. I see his father in billed cap and greasy overalls, red kerchief around his neck. My reaction is not matter-of-fact. —You mean he drives the engines?

Casey looks hard at the road. —He gets them to Gallup and back— I know I deserve the cold edge.

We watch the shadowed houses drift by as we slip from pool to pool of street light in silence. Casey slides to the curb and turns the engine off. He studies my parents in their frame of curtainless window, encased in white.

—So what's your dad do?— His tone is flat. —Beside read books and buy your mother white paint— I ignore the snipe.

—He's an anthropologist.

Casey raises his eyebrows. —And that's what he's doing in Harden? Studying us provincial natives?— I decide to let this pass, too.

—The Hopis. He specializes in primitive ritualistic music and dance.

But Casey isn't about to let me off so easy, he's been saving up. —You didn't think I knew that word, did you, Miss Priss?— He smiles, cocky.

—Please don't call me that.

His chin lifts. —Why not?— But I'm relieved to see he has his good humor back. I change tack.

—So when do you go back to school?

He looks surprised. —September, just like you.

—Will you be coming home for any of the holidays?

He turns, leans against the car door to face me full on. —Why?— A little smile.

—I just wondered.

—Why?— A playful taunt.

I lift my own chin and regard him back through slanted eyes. —I was just making conversation, to be polite.

—So you can report on me to your mother?

—My mother knows all she needs to know about you.

He snorts. —I'll bet she does.

—What makes you think I talk about you to my mother?

—What makes you think I'm not going to stay in Harden?

Something inside me lifts, I feel suddenly gay and light.

—Why? Did the academy give up on you?

—They finished their job. You see before you the model cadet— I visualize him in the red, white, and blue of marine dress, the arrogance and gold trim suit him. He's eyeing me with interest.

—What does your mother know about me?

—Nothing— I give him a smart smile. —And that's all she needs to know.

—She doesn't think much of me, does she?

—She doesn't think much of anyone in Harden.

—She should have stayed in Boston.

—She and my father have never been apart. She even went with him to Kenya.

—How old were you?

—Eight. But I didn't go. I stayed with Abby.

—Who's Abby?

—My father's mother.

—You call your grandmother Abby?

—Why not? That's her name. You call your mother by hers. Where's the difference?

He shrugs. —I thought you'd call her Grummy.

I have to laugh. —I was supposed to say Grandma Abby, but it came out Grabby, so she settled for Abby.

—I can understand why— He turns and stares out the window. —I never met my grandmothers. And I remember only one grandfather, my dad's dad. He's dead now, too.

His thoughts are focused beyond the windshield, somewhere out there in the night. I can't believe the change that's come over him, his voice and face have lost years, he's suddenly young and vulnerable. I'm embarrassed, I don't know what to say. I fumble . . .

—Well, sometimes a large family isn't all that great, they always know your business.

—Yeah. Like a small town— He turns back toward me. —That's why I decided to stay in Harden for my last year of high school. I was losing touch with my friends and family. I'd come home for summer or Christmas and it'd be like getting to know them all over again, I'd be an outsider, they'd have gone on without me. Little Denny was growing up so fast, she'd be a different person every time I saw her. And I hadn't been there to enjoy the changes or help her make them.

His mood's infected me. I'm feeling deprivation. —I've always wished I had a brother or sister. It's lonely being an only child.

—And not good for you. It makes you selfish and self-centered. Spoiled. You don't learn how to share or think of other people.

I twinge with guilt and shame, recognizing how this applies to me, then bridle with defensive indignation.

—I don't think that's necessarily true, the only child doesn't have to be spoiled. Sometimes it makes you overly sensitive and gives you feelings of inferiority. You have to be perfect, everything your parents wanted. They're always watching you, expecting you to measure up. There's no one else to compare to or worry about.

—That's why I'm going to have five kids.

—*Five!*

In my parents' circle, two is the acceptable number, permissibly three, anything beyond is low-class tacky and financially irresponsible.

—Two boys and three girls, all two years apart.

I quickly calculate. —That means your wife's going to be pregnant, giving birth, and changing diapers for twelve years solid.

Casey seems cheerfully unperturbed about this. —We'll start when she's young and strong, in her early twenties. We'll have two years of honeymooning then begin our family.

I'm figuring. —So she'll be in her thirties when the last one's born— This doesn't seem so bad.

—Right.

—And fifty when the last one leaves— This seems less enticing.

—By that time, the older ones will have started their own families. And by seventy I'll be a great-grandfather— He's delighted by the prospect, he laces his fingers behind his head and grins. —Can't you just see it? We'll have kids all over the place, all shapes and sizes, running around, laughing and fighting. For family gatherings, we'll have to rent a hall.

Who's this "we"? But as I ponder it, the picture seems increasingly attractive. A pyramid of people, all ages, all related, bound together by responsibility and love, looking out for one another, perpetuating a lineage of genes, values, and traditions, starting with one man and one woman. And five kids . . .

. . . *Five.*

I remember Casey's Catholic, another wave of shame and guilt, I feel a traitor—to *my* lineage. I call upon Daddy's and Mummy's concerns about over-population, the propagation of large families among the poor, their belief in planned parenthood. —Raising five kids can be pretty expensive.

Casey's undaunted. —It's done all the time.

—The cost of food alone . . .

—So we eat steak only on birthdays. That way we appreciate it more.

—And the clothes . . .

—You buy for the first kid, after that you pass them down.

—I want my children to have better than hand-me-downs.

—What's wrong with hand-me-downs? Kids outgrow things so fast, they hardly wrinkle them. You have to buy new shoes and socks and underwear, of course, and now and then a pair of Levis, but . . .

I've arrived at the crowning consideration. —What about college? I want my children to go to college.

—So do I. So they work their way through, or get a scholarship, like I plan to do. If you have to work for it, you make more of the opportunity.

I register this for Mummy: Casey plans to go to college.

I can't come up with any other reservations, Mummy's and Daddy's arguments have all been exhausted. I look at Casey, still with laced fingers behind his head. The street lamp casts soft light along his profile. His cheekbone is high and strong, his nose narrow and straight, his mouth full and pouty. He looks sculpted in white marble. I smile.

—You have it all worked out.

He smiles back. —Sure. A man has to know what he wants and how he's going to get it— He holds my eyes for a long moment, until I get uncomfortable.

I look at my watch, I can't believe the time. —I guess I better get in.

Casey takes his hands from behind his head, reluctantly opens his door, walks around to open mine.

He escorts me to the door, calls through the screen —Thanks, Mr. and Mrs. Patterson— holds my gaze another long moment, then with a sudden brilliant smile, turns and bounds down the steps.

I stand where he left me. As he gets into the car, he looks up. —See you tomorrow.

I lie awake a long time thinking about him. I think of the shifts in him, from man to boy, from confidence to uncertainty, from hope to hankering, and back again. I've been hanging out with boys since I was at least twelve, mostly in groups— at dance classes, house parties, school socials, beach outings—and last year I went steady for eight months with Andrew Dickerman, who was almost seventeen, had gone steady three times before, and was known for his winsome way with girls. I've been with Casey only twice but I've never talked with a boy so seriously, or so long. I think maybe it's because Casey's life's been harder, he's had to grow up faster, it's made him older. Maybe because things haven't come so easily it's made him thoughtful. Those other boys had life easy, had no need to think, no reason to grow up. I feel sadness for him and respect. I wonder what kind of wife he wants.

I want to call him up and talk another hour.

SCENE 6

Reggie peers through the windshield, eyes flickering with the flick of the wipers. The hard cold has finally broken, the snow has come, clearing skies and softening landscapes. She imagines her family's surprise and pleasure when she pulls into the drive with a wagon-bed of groceries and they realize she's maneuvered the ice and snow all the way to and back from the shopping center. She's surprised and pleased herself, she's glad she forced herself up and out. The routine of planning meals, going through cupboards, making a shopping list cleared and focused her mind. The challenge of making her way up and down aisles around parked or hell-bent shopping carts gave her a sense of control. The calculation of evaluating shelves and cases of brightly labeled choices made her feel competent. Contadina tomato sauce or Hunts? Six ounces for seventy-six cents or eight ounces for ninety-eight? In Harden Safeway there were few such choices.

As she pulls into the drive, she notes no tire tracks in the fresh snow. She reaches to her visor, pushes the electric door-opener, and is disappointed to find the garage empty. She considers leaving the groceries until help arrives, reconsiders, and resolutely hefts the eight bags from the wagon into the house, one at a time, slipping but not falling. They really should get a carport over the backdoor, she'll have to talk to Howie.

She's tempted to leave the bags on the table as testimony, resists temptation, and begins to unpack. The sacks are empty, folded, and stashed by the time her family arrives. She has apron on, pots and pans out, and is ready for their entrance.

Katelyn dances in. —Hi, Mummy, did you see the snow, Daddy says if it's heavy enough, we can go sledding tomorrow.

Reggie would like to kiss her but she doesn't stand still long enough.

Lindsay follows. Her eyes light at the sight of her mother, she smiles shyly. —Hi, mummy.

Reggie would like to kiss her but she doesn't want to miss Howie's face.

He's pleased, she sees it in the soft lift of his mouth, but he's still hurt, she can tell by the pinch around his eyes. She thinks now would be a good time to talk but there isn't the chance, she can't say, Excuse me, girls, I'd like to be alone with your father, not under ordinary circumstances but especially not after her disturbing absence. She must appear casual, nonchalant, everything back to normal. For once she's happy for Katelyn's self-absorbed unconsciousness, she doesn't allow an awkward silence.

—Did anyone call me?

—I don't know, I wasn't here, I was . . .

—Wasn't Pat here, it's Friday, didn't she write down any messages?

—I don't see any.

Katelyn looks with irritation at the clean chalkboard above the telephone. —Debbie was supposed to call, she's going to ask me to spend the night, can I spend the night with her?

Reggie smiles indulgently. —Wait until she asks you— It feels good to be a mother again.

Lindsay looks at her sister with dismay. —But we're going sledding tomorrow.

—So what.

—So how can you go if you're at Debbie's?

Katelyn regards her younger sister with disgust. —So you can pick me up at Debbie's.

—But that will be rude to leave so early.

—Okay, so we'll take Debbie with us.

—Daddy, is Debbie going to go with us?— Lindsay's face begs her father to say No. With friends, Katelyn excludes her sister.

Howie's eyes meet Reggie's. —Wait until she calls— Reggie smiles gratefully. In dealing with the girls, they're in perfect accord.

Lindsay takes her mother's hand uncertainly. —Are you going, Mummy?

Reggie touches her cheek —Yes— while she holds Howie's gaze. —I went to the grocery store— She hopes it tells him what she can't say.

Casey starts coming by three, four evenings a week, promptly at seven thirty. He never says, See you Tuesday, he never calls, he just shows up. I'll be waiting for him, in the living room pretending to be visiting with Mummy and Daddy, or on the porch pretending to be reading, trying to look surprised when he arrives. But he takes in my fresh clothes and combed hair and grins. The evenings he doesn't come, I give up at eight and retire to my room to read or write in my diary. I'm upset, but I tell myself I don't care and try not to show it. Mummy accepts the whole thing grimly. Daddy seems mildly interested, and amused by Mummy.

Sometimes Casey and I go for a drive. He takes me to Indian Town, a clutter of pueblos on the outskirts of town that seem to be tumbling and eroding back into the red clay from which they were made. Children scramble up and down the hill, play ball in the courtyard or Kick the Can in the unpaved street. Adults in groups of two or three sit quietly in metal chairs in front of dark screen doors. Dogs watch.

He drives me out past the Indian sanitarium for tuberculosis, a major problem among Indians, especially the Navajo. We cross the tracks into Mexican Town, shacks put together out of adobe brick, plywood, scrap lumber, tar paper, rocks, corrugated tin. Young children squabble in the dust in shirts and underpants, shoes with no socks. Older boys in jeans fight among themselves or tease girls in puffy dresses. Mothers struggle with babies. Men lounge around cars with raised hoods, drinking beer in brown bottles. It's my first exposure to such poverty and I don't know what to think or say. I'm appalled, and fascinated. If Casey has thoughts, he keeps them to himself.

We go to Dairy Queen for a root beer float, or cruise First Street, the roller-skating rink, the bowling alley, the Texaco, looking to see who's out doing what where. If he spots someone interesting enough, Casey'll stop and exchange a few words. But most of the time, we just sit on the porch and talk.

We talk about his sister and parents, his experiences at the academy, his exploits in football. We talk about my mother and father and friends and family in Boston and the kinds of things we do there. We exchange opinions about issues large and small, any topic that comes up, what we like and don't like, what we believe is important and want out of life. Often we disagree, sometimes we argue, but the arguments are always friendly, explorations of differences that open new lines of thought to be pondered the next day and pursued the next night or the next. These talks draw us closer and closer.

Sometimes I ask Mummy's and Daddy's opinions, then weigh them against Casey's, to come up with my own position. It's like being on a debating team. I organize my ideas logically, I select and rehearse my words, to present the winning case, to win Casey. To be a worthy adversary.

Wexler Valley under snow is like a Chinese porcelain bowl, translucent white with tiny black trees brush-stoked around the inner rim.

—There's nobody here— a wail from Katelyn; it's the final blow. She's been sulking in her corner of the backseat, punishing her family with silence, she imagines, for refusing to let her spend the night with Debbie and bring her sledding. A family day, her parents agreed.

Lindsay is ecstatic. —We have it all to ourselves— Katelyn's moods don't bother her so long as she's guaranteed her sister's unshared company.

Howie brings the wagon to a stop and turns off the ignition.

—Are you going to park here?— Reggie's measuring the distance to the highest hill in the far left corner.

—Why not?

—It's too far. And we'll be pulling sleds.

—This is where we usually park.

—I know. But I just don't feel up to it today. I'm still not quite myself.

—What would you suggest? This is as close as I can get.

—Why don't you drive out onto the field a ways?

Lindsay slides up onto the edge of her seat. —We're not supposed to drive on the field, Mummy, it tears up the grass.

—What grass, stupid?— Katelyn's against unnecessary exertion on any day.

Howie's gauging the depth of the snow. —I don't think it's safe, we might get stuck.

—The snow's not that deep and there's a hard crust underneath. I did fine yesterday. The radials should give enough traction if you go slow and steady.

—All right, if that's what you want— Howie starts up the wagon and inches out of the cleared parking lot onto the covered field.

Reggie sits erect, judging conditions. She knows if there's trouble, it'll be on her head.

She touches Howie's arm. —This should be far enough— He obediently brakes to a stop.

The girls clamber out, pulling on mittens and caps, arguing over who's going to pull their sled first.

—First person pulling the sled gets the first ride.

—Pulling last is hardest. Whoever takes it up the hill gets the first ride down— They're still negotiating as Lindsay starts across the field with the sled.

Reggie follows with the larger sled. Howie locks the wagon, catches up, and takes the tow rope from her, smiling. —I'll pull all the way and you can still have the first ride.

—Gee, thanks, sport.

—I guess we need to buy another sled.

—We don't use them all that often.

—It's not that big an investment and they last forever.

—We should have brought the lid to the garbage can.

Howie's thinking of the generation to come, Reggie's thinking of a generation past. The kids in Harden came down Ohio Hill on everything: garbage can lids, squares of plywood, pieces of stiff plastic or hard rubber gleaned from garages or scavenged from dumps and junk yards. Many pulled the sled of their mother or father or grandfather, a few handmade, large and heavy, runners dull and rusty, varnish scratched and chipped, wood dry and splintery, but beautiful in their substantial old-fashioned lines. Some had new sleds, Christmas presents from Sears, with shiny surfaces and red runners.

When it snowed heavily enough, the Harden sheriff's department barricaded off the hill. During the earlier part of the day, fathers came from all over town to teach their younger children the thrill of flying on ground. The older children took over after school, when the aerotechnics became decidedly showier and more dangerous. Residents had to park at the bottom of the hill and walk up but no one minded. They were happy to have their street turned into a winter playground. They sat bundled on porches and watched, their home brand of Ice Capades. By evening, the hill's surface had become so packed and slick, you could slide down on your belly.

Reggie sits on the crest of the hill at the edge of the trees and watches the girls go up and down, taking turns on the larger sled with Howie. The crisp air rings with their laughter. Their cheeks are pink, their noses red, their eyes shiny. In their powder blue snowsuits, Lindsay's light hair straggling wetly out under her striped stocking cap, Katelyn's dark hair tucked neatly beneath her fluffy fur bonnet, Reggie thinks how beautiful they are, and how lucky. Few children in Harden had snowsuits, none had after-ski boots. Catherine wrapped Denny in long underwear, turtle-neck T-shirt, long-sleeved sweater, padded windbreaker, and corduroy pants tucked into rubber boots pulled over school oxfords. After an hour and a half, Casey had to take Denny's boots and shoes off and massage her feet, the two pairs of socks had cut off the circulation.

Denny's nose and lips were blue but like her brother she wasn't a quitter. Casey took her down on her stomach, braced over her on his elbows and knees, his hands guiding hers in steering. He took her down sitting between his knees, arms around her, feet steering. He lay on his stomach and took her down on his back, hands guiding her feet in steering. He took her down on his shoulders, hands gripping her knees, while he steered with his feet. Reggie watched from the sidelines, it was Casey's day with Denny, watch me and my little sister. They adored each other. Denny had come late to Catherine, after several miscarriages, and with Scotty out of town on runs and home at odd hours, Casey had designated himself Denny's protector and teacher.

Katelyn and Lindsay scramble up eagerly. —Are you rested yet, Mummy— Howie trudges behind panting. Reggie takes the sled from him and pulls it to level ground.

—Okay, who wants to go down with me?

—Me!

—Me!

—Okay— Reggie points the sled downhill. —Katelyn first, Lindsay second— Katelyn flops down, Reggie grabs her by the collar. —No, sitting up— Reggie seats herself behind Katelyn, legs extended, arms around her. —You hold the line, I'll steer with my feet. When we're ready, Howie, give us a shove. Okay, ready!

They fly down the hill, Reggie's cheek pressed into Katelyn's furry cap, wind squinting their eyes. It's an easy line, not much fancy footwork, just a few quick curves, but Katelyn squeals with delight.

Lindsay meets them halfway up —My turn next!— helps pull the sled to the top, and plops down in Katelyn's place, sitting up.

—Oh no you don't— Reggie pulls her off —I have another trick— and stretches flat on her stomach, hands on the steering bar. —Now sit on me, that's it, knees bent, feet back. Grab my shoulders. Are you ready? Okay, Howie, push!

Halfway down, Lindsay frees her hands, grips Reggie's sides with her knees, and leans back, arms in the air. Like riding bareback. She's twice the age of Denny, and probably twice the size, but Reggie hardly feels her. They're birds, plunging into the downdraft.

—Daddy, did you see us?

Howie's on his back in the snow, staring at the sky. —Yeah, you were great.

Katelyn's jumping around. —Do me that way, Mummy, do me.

Reggie straddles a leg over Howie and looks down into his face. —Take me down on your shoulders.

—What?

She squats and lifts him by the front of his parka. —Take me down on your shoulders.

—You're too big.

—No I'm not. You're bigger.

He frees her hands from his parka. —I'm too tired.

Reggie steps off him. —Take the girls down on your shoulders.

—I've had enough.

—Take us down on your shoulders, take us down on your shoulders!

Howie rises, brushes snow off, looks at his watch. —I think we've all had enough— He collects the sleds, and slowly rides one down, towing the other.

Reggie watches until he reaches the bottom of the hill, the girls beside her, then suddenly takes several steps back, gets a running start, and throws herself over the crest, onto her stomach. She can hear the girls' shrieks behind her. Halfway down, she gets stuck, turns sideways, and rolls over and over to the bottom. She raises her head and sees the girls rolling down after her. They tumble into a snowy mass of arms, legs, and laughter. Howie is halfway to the wagon.

He sits glowering behind the steering wheel as they scrabble in, still giggling. —I don't like the looks of this— The girls perch red, wet, and bright on the edge of the backseat, ready for more adventure. —The snow's a lot icier.

Reggie smiles complacently. —Just go slow and steady.

Howie's head jerks toward her. —You said that— He puts the gear in reverse, starts the wagon backwards.

Reggie twists to watch out the back window. —Try to stay in the same tracks— The tires slip, slide, spin. —Take your foot off the gas.

—I know that— They come to a standstill.

—Now try going forward. If you get traction, turn slowly.

—I know how to drive in snow, Reggie, I wasn't born in the desert.

He puts the gear in second, eases forward, spins, throws it into reverse, rocks backward, spins, throws it into second, rocks forward, spins. Reggie stares clamp-jawed out the window. He turns his frustration on her.

—Now what's your big idea, you got us into this.

She opens the car door. —All right, all girls out to push.

They brace themselves against the back of the wagon, Reggie in the middle. —Okay, Howie, on the count of three. One, two, *heave*— The wagon lurches forward, drops back, spins. —One, two, *heave*.

—Daddy's swearing.

—That's why we're out *here*. One, two— the tires whirr madly, Reggie and the girls drop their arms and jump back. Reggie charges around to Howie's window. —What're you doing, Howie?

—I'm cutting through the snow and ice to solid ground.

—Very good. There is no solid ground. Now you're stuck in mud.

Howie gets out and surveys his brainstorm. Reggie reaches into the backseat, pulls out the Hudson's Bay blanket she'd put there for the girls, heads for the nearest hill.

—Where're you going?

—To collect brush— Katelyn and Lindsay race after her. —Do you have your mittens? Pick up anything you can find, twigs, branches. No leaves or grass, nothing slippery. Katelyn, go over to the garbage bins, see if you can find any scrap wood or cardboard.

They pile their gleanings onto the blanket and pull it back to the wagon. Wordlessly, Howie helps Reggie lay wood in front of the front wheels and pull the brush-covered blanket in front of the back wheels.

Pushing past Howie, Reggie climbs into the driver's seat. —You're stronger than I am.

Howie takes his position between the girls at the back of the wagon.

—One, two, *heave*— The wagon moves. —One, two, *heave.*

The twigs and branches crack beneath the tires, the girls stumble and fall back. Howie runs with the wagon, pushing, until its momentum exceeds his.

Reggie leans out the window. —I'll meet you in the parking lot.

Howie sits stonily in the passenger seat. Katelyn and Lindsay huddle together in the backseat, torn, wet, stained blanket under their feet.

—Where'd you learn to do that, Mummy?

Reggie smiles smugly as she steers them onto the main road. —In the desert.

SCENE 7

For our first excursion out from Harden, Daddy drives us to Flagstaff for the All-Indian Pow Wow. We climb steadily out of high desert into fir and pine. The sun cools, the air thins and becomes tangy with resin. Mummy rolls down her window and hangs her head out, her hair blown back like the ears of a cocker spaniel. You can actually hear her sucking it in.

I get my first glimpse of the San Francisco Peaks. Suddenly the highway turns red, I can hardly believe it, a bright brick red. I think of *The Wizard of Oz.* From volcanic ash, Daddy explains. Like all communities, they use the materials at hand. Daddy can be counted on as a font of information.

He's also filled us in on the Pow Wow. It's held once a year for four to six days, usually over the Fourth of July. Indians come from hundreds of miles. Over a dozen groups are represented: Hopi, Navajo, Cherokee, Apache, Coconino, Pima, Papago, Arapaho, Havasupai, Cheyenne, Zuni, Acoma, and other pueblos from the Rio Grande and Jemez River valleys. We see them on the way in, in horse-drawn wagons and pickups, or on burros and horseback. A few walk, backs loaded, or pulling carts.

On the outskirts, we pass a lumber yard, stacks of raw new boards gleaming golden in the soft morning light, a tall conical furnace belching black smoke and orange sparks against the blue sky. Daddy points out a sign to the college. Mummy can't believe it, a real live college right here in Nowhere-dom. It gives her courage. The substantial stone and brick buildings and clean wide streets make Flagstaff feel like a metropolis after the adobe and dust of Harden. Neat bungalows with steep-pitched roofs and chimneys climb hills. Trees are the rule rather than the exception, but gardens seem to have a hard time of it. Lawns are scrubby. It fits my idea of the East more than the West.

The streets are jammed with cars and pickups, we drive around for half an hour before we find a parking spot in the dirt-and-cinder strip along the railroad track. We have to walk back half a mile to the main street. People line both sides for blocks, in Levis, boots, and western shirts, some women in squaw boots or moccasins and Indian-style skirts or dresses. I make up my mind to ask Mummy for a squaw dress; I know it's too much to hope for Levis. Everyone has a Stetson or farmer's straw hat.

The parade begins around ten, up at the high school, winds down through the business district, and ends at the fairground. It's led by important Indian leaders: governmental figures, organizers and spokesmen, and other dignitaries influential in Indian affairs. Chiefs or tribal heads walk in front of their tribes. Bands march at spaced intervals—some from Indian schools as far away as Phoenix—wearing standard uniforms of red and black, blue and white, green and yellow, and playing standard marches on standard instruments. I'm disappointed, I expected something Indian.

This is my first awareness of Indian boarding schools and I try to pursue it with Daddy. We'll talk about it later, he whispers curtly, eyeing the crowd, and I understand there's controversy. One of the adult bands, carrying a VFW banner, is led by a man in Marine dress in a wheelchair, his chest covered with medals, including the Purple Heart. There's even a corps of strutting baton twirlers, long black hair streaming down their white-satined backs, and a contingent of Indian sheriff's deputies, on horseback and in sheepskin chaps.

I love parades, and this is the most exotic I've seen, more colorful even than Macy's New York City Thanksgiving Day parade. The people are striking. Rich skin in shades from honey to brown. Black hair, thick and lustrous. Dark eyes, proud and private. High cheekbones, square jaws, strong chins. They walk with quiet dignity, backs straight, faces impassive.

With the exception of the dignitaries, who for the most part wear western clothing, the paraders are in traditional ceremonial finery. The Hopi women wear woven black tunics and, even in this heat, white mantas with red, black, and green borders, or colorful Mexican shawls. The men are bare-chested above woven white kilts with red, black, and green belts tied at the sides, fox pelts hanging from the back. The Cheyenne, Cherokee, and other Indians from Oklahoma and the Plains seem to favor fringed leather with feathers and fancy beadwork. One quintet of vigorous dancers sports large, colorful feather headdresses and a large circle of feathers on their breech-clouted backsides.

The Cherokee chief is the most perfect physical specimen of a male I've ever seen, a giant, close to seven feet, the color of ripe wheat, with startling light eyes. The muscles of his chest fairly burst out of his skimpy bolero, his arms bulge like rock, his thighs and buttocks ripple and strain against his supple leggings.

Mummy's as affected as I am. —My god— she sounds breathless —the man's gorgeous.

Daddy considers, head cocked. —Would you like to follow him home?

—It's an idea.

—You'd have to get used to walking ten paces behind.

—With that view, who'd mind?

—Remind you of a good horse?— Mummy grins, starts to say something, thinks better of it, closes her mouth. Daddy's laughing. —I'm sure he'd give you a good ride.

—Never mind.

I can't believe this, I've never heard them joke this way. Has the sun got to them or do they actually think I don't understand? I concentrate on the parade, embarrassed, but I'm not sure exactly for whom.

The chief's wife is a match for him, a soft rounded beauty half his height, her hair, like her husband's, in a thick plait down her back with beaded browband. And she does indeed walk paces behind. Indian women are humble and modest, Daddy has told me, as an example, I suspect. But you can see from the lift of this woman's chin and her sidelong glances that she's taking in the crowd's admiration of her husband and their recognition that it is she who has won him.

The Navajos don't seem to have special dress, they look the same as I've seen them on the streets of Harden, the women in layers of full, tightly pleated long skirts and long-sleeved velvet overblouses, the men in faded Levis and colorful satin or velvet shirts. But today they're led by a remarkable pair. The man is tall, not up to the Cherokee chief's standard but well over six feet, lanky, long-waisted, raw-boned, and wiry. It's hard to tell his age, but the expression lines around his mouth and nose are carved into deep crevices, his cheeks are eroded with wrinkles. You can feel his strength, not only of body but of character. Like the woman behind him, his hair is steel gray and has been folded into a thick bun wrapped in the center with string at the nape of his neck.

But what's so riveting is their ornamentation. The fronts, backs, and sleeves of their black velvet overblouses are covered with vertical rows of nickels, dimes, and quarters. Strands of silver and turquoise drape their necks. Curves of turquoise and silver bracelets climb their arms. Silver and turquoise rings weight every finger. Looped strings of turquoise dangle from their stretched earlobes. Belts of oversized silver and turquoise conchas encircle their waists. And the band of the man's wide-brimmed, high-crowned felt hat is encrusted with turquoise and silver pins.

Mummy grabs Daddy's arm.

He nods. —He must be very important.

—It's a wonder they can move under all that.

—The Navajos display their wealth to show their status. They used to solder pins on coins and literally wear their money. But the government put a stop to that. So now they invest in silver and turquoise. That's what they use at the trading posts for pawn.

Mummy's staring in awe. —Given the age of those two, most of those coins have to be worth more than face value.

Daddy nods. —He's probably walking around with a backful of buffalo heads.

I have a dozen questions, things I want to know and think about. I make a mental list to discuss with Daddy: boarding schools, trading posts and pawn, status and hierarchy, war veterans, even little Indian baton twirlers. That confuses me, too.

Group after group passes, each with its distinct look, culture, and language, separate pieces in the puzzle "Indian," but fitting themselves together for this occasion to present a unified pageant of Amerind history. Like Mummy with the clear, green air, I can't get enough of it. I drink it in, in deep, greedy gulps. My heart is pounding, I feel light-headed and short of breath, I close my eyes.

The air throbs with the low dull beat of drums, the steady shuffle of feet, the rhythmic jingle of bells, the clatter of turtle-shell and gourd rattles, and, high above, weaving in and out, the floating drift of trombones and chimes. But for all the sound, it seems strangely quiet. My throat aches, and for a crazy moment I think I'm going to cry.

The pine-shaded grounds around the fairground arena are crowded with tents, pickups, and wagons, the Indians' lodgings for the duration of the celebration. Some wagons and truck beds are covered, to give close but private quarters; otherwise families spread bedrolls on the open dirt at night. Horses and burros nap and flick flies in corrals off to one side. The strip in front of the wagons and pickups has been set up as an informal shopping district, for this—the selling and exchanging of crafts—it immediately becomes apparent to me, even before Daddy's edification, is a major activity of the Pow Wow.

Makeshift stalls of canvas and plank shelving display carved kachina dolls, sand paintings, woven baskets and plaques, beadwork of all types. Men carry trays of rings, bracelets, and pins. Women sit on chairs outside tents, painted pottery spread at their feet on blankets. Handloomed rugs and blankets drag from cords strung between stout pines. There is no hawking, no gesturing, little direct eye contact, even when purchasing. I get a feeling of stoic remoteness, as if trading is a distasteful and perhaps demeaning necessity, done outside of, and not touching, the craftsman or artisan.

Mummy, not usually a shopper, goes crazy. She buys a Navajo rainbow-god wall hanging, a polished black-on-black plate, a pottery Zuni owl, a Hopi bowl, a Pima basket, and a tooled leather belt and bolo tie for Daddy. I buy beaded moccasins and purse, tiny carved-stone bear fetish, and point out my request of turquoise ring and bracelet for Christmas. Even Daddy succumbs and picks up a painting of Navajo boys on horseback herding sheep in Monument Valley.

Mummy and Daddy return to the station wagon with our load of treasures. I wander among the crowd, absorbing faces, voices, interactions, when up ahead I recognize a tall gray-bunned head and straight back. I push through sightseers and idling shoppers as politely but as quickly as I can. He's standing to the side, alone, completely immobile, and for a minute I'm afraid there's something wrong. He's taken off his pin-studded hat and tied a red bandana around his brow, and exchanged his coin-laden shirt for a denim one. Other than that, he's the same as in the parade. I don't see the woman.

I work my way slowly around to his side. He's like a totem. His left arm is hung from wrist to elbow with necklaces. It hurts me to see him standing in the middle of the indifferent, jostling crowd holding out his wares like any common peddler. He shouldn't have to, and I wonder why, with all his coins and turquoise, he does.

I step up, his eyes flicker toward me then over my shoulder. He offers his arm, I gingerly examine the necklaces. They're all the same, strands of crude cylindrical white beads strung on coarse dirty string, interspersed with triangles of red, white, and turquoise chips glued on black backings, with a wing-spread red, white, and turquoise eagle suspended in the center.

I want to say, Did you make these? but I'm afraid I'll show my dismay. Of course he didn't make these. Instead I ask How much? He doesn't so much as blink. Three dollars. His voice is surprisingly youthful. I dig in my purse, go through my wallet, shake my head. I have only a dollar and a half. I hold my hand out to show him. He nods. —Okay— Again I'm surprised, at the offhand colloquialism. Was I expecting something in Navajo? I lay the money in his creased roughened palm, lighter in color than the back of his hand, almost as light as mine. It's our closest contact. He extends his arm and waits, his faded eyes again above my head, contemplating the distance. I want to paw through the crude strands, pick out the least objectionable, but I feel crass. I take the first, hold it toward him, he nods. I hesitate. But there's nothing more to say. For him, I've already left. I have no choice, I turn and walk away.

Mummy and Daddy meet me at the entrance to the stands just in time to find seats. The rodeo begins with a grand march on horseback led by flag bearers, just like any other horse show. From there, similarities end. It's the first live rodeo for all three of us, but Daddy's boned up of course, so he explains as events progress the practical purposes of each activity: steer wrestling, calf roping, bronc riding. I can understand the reasons behind the women's barrel race, but I fail to see any sense at all in risking life and limb on the back of an outraged bull. How many cowboys eat or ride Brahmas? Daddy decides it's for show of skill and courage, I decide the clowns take the purse on both counts. They're hysterically funny and death-defying in their antics to distract the antagonized livestock from stomping or goring their cowboy tormentors. Daddy enlightens me that this is a traditional role of clowns, the dispelling of negative forces. I'll see many clowns, he assures me, when we get to the mesa dances. And then it hits me, the awareness that's been nagging at the back of my mind. I start to giggle, Daddy eyebrows raise in question.

—The cowboys are all Indians. Don't you get it?— Daddy smiles. —What'll Hollywood do when it hears about this?

Mummy leans toward Daddy. —What?— Daddy repeats the joke. Mummy makes a "That's dumb" face and leans back, but I don't take it personally. The sun beating down on her bare head and pulsing back off the parched boards has given her a headache, she's not in a mood for irony.

She's so sick, in fact, by the end of the rodeo, we decide to take her home. Daddy says maybe we'll return another night. The evening dances were to be the highlight for him. I was looking forward to the fireworks. But I don't feel cheated. We give Mummy two aspirin and stretch her out in back. I climb in front with Daddy.

My shirt smells of sun and dust, my hair's stringy, my nose dry, my teeth gritty. My hands and face need a good soaping. And I'm blissfully happy. All the way home, Daddy and I talk Indians.

Howie finds Reggie sitting on the bed, her lap covered with a cloth holding an assortment of unfamiliar objects. He bends closer.

—What's that? Indian jewelry?

—I'd forgotten I had it.

—Your treasures from Harden?— His voice is edged. She doesn't answer. He reaches and fingers the pieces: two rings, a pin, bracelets, earrings. —They're pretty. How come I've never seen you wear them?

She hesitates. —They weren't in style here.

He notices the strand of beads dangling from her clasped hand. —What's that?

She opens her palm. —A Navajo thunderbird. It brings thunder and lightning.

—And rain?— He looks at her sidewise. She doesn't meet his eye. He lifts and examines it. —It looks like some school kid made it.

Reggie's chin goes up, there's tightness in her eyes and mouth, and in her voice. —They don't make them like this anymore. The backing is carved battery casing. Sometimes they used old phonograph records. The chips are turquoise, shell, and plastic, probably from some old store container. They used whatever they could find.

Howie rolls a bead between his fingers. —And what's this?

—Bone. Animal bone. Rounded, cut in short sections, then hollowed. All by hand, with handmade tools.

Reggie's composure slips. The bone was white when she bought it. Now it's shades of yellow, some pieces porous and opaque, others shiny hard, slightly translucent.

Howie hands back the necklace. —I still say it looks like a piece of junk.

Reggie's face contorts. She clutches the necklace, her chin trembles.

—It's a collector's item. Last time I had it appraised it was worth several hundred dollars— Her tone is shrill, accusatory.

Howie throws out his arms. —Now what did I do?

Reggie's face crumbles. —I loved that old Indian— She's openly crying.

Howie stares at her, then with a shrug gives up and exits.

I get my fireworks anyway.

I end up spending the Fourth of July with Casey. He hasn't bothered to arrange ahead, he just calls at nine in the morning, How'd you like to go to the parade with me and Denny? I'm insulted enough to want to say, I'm sorry, I have another date. But Mummy still isn't feeling well, Daddy isn't interested, and I see no sense in sitting it out or going alone. Beside, I'm curious to get to know Denny.

Harden's offering isn't much in the way of parades, especially after the Pow Wow. The usual fraternal organizations, community services, politicians, and school bands. Except for a few musicians, one Tribal Council representative, and the sheriff's special mounted deputies brought over from the Pow Wow, there are no Indians. I'm tempted to think of this as Harden's All-White-Man's Display of Independence. Especially after Daddy told me yesterday that Native Americans were considered good enough to be drafted into World War II but not good enough to vote until 1948. Even with their Purple Hearts and after a group of Navajo men created an unbreakable code that helped save countless lives and hastened the end of the war.

The best part of the parade is watching Casey and Denny. She sits on his shoulders pounding his head, kicking her feet, and tugging his ears in excitement. He holds tight to her straddled legs, ducks now and then, and keeps laughing.

Harden evidently intends to make a day of it, and from the looks of the cars and crowds, the whole town is turning out. In the afternoon there's to be a baseball game, followed by the Firemen's Pig Out, all you can eat for three fifty. And in the evening, there's a band concert and fireworks. Casey drops me off to check in with Mummy and Daddy and get permission to spend the rest of the day with him, while he takes Denny home to nap in preparation for her late evening. Then he picks me up and we join the sweating spectators in the sweltering uncovered stands of the ball park.

I'm not much of a baseball fan, in fact I find the game downright boring. But Betts and Billie are there, along with Faye, Trixie, Walt, and Glenn, and I'm happy to be seen with Casey. I entertain myself watching the bleacher boisterism—beer's being passed around everywhere—and staying in touch enough to yell the right things at the right times with Casey.

When the game finally fizzles out, Casey and I file with the rest of the crowd over to the football field; there is no park. Behind long portable tables draped with red, white, and blue bunting, men in white shirts, black trousers, wide red suspenders, and red plastic firemen's hats dish out whopping portions of food onto floppy paper plates. Hotdogs, Boston baked beans, corn bread, cole slaw, potato salad, corn on the cob, watermelon, and waxy cups of sugary iced tea. Soda and ice cream can be bought extra at a little stand. It's the first time I've seen dry ice, small blocks of steaming glacier that'll burn your hand and tear off your skin if you touch it, Casey warns me. Casey goes back for seconds of everything, then drives us to his house to rest his stomach.

I'm a nervous wreck. I'm going to meet his mother. I fuss in my mirror.

—What's the matter with you?

—Look at me. I'm a sweaty mess, my hair's limp and stringy, my shirt's sticking to my back, my hands and face are filthy.

—You can wash up when we get to the house.

—I don't want your mother to meet me like this.

—My mom's not like that, she doesn't judge by appearances.

I know somehow this should make me feel better, but it doesn't. What *does* she judge by?

The house is a small brick with no porch, two low front steps, asphalt-tile roofing. No shrubs, no flower beds, a thirsty lawn ending abruptly at the brick.

Casey opens the screen door, I hesitate behind him. Inside, it's dark, the shades pulled. It takes my eyes a minute to adjust.

A living room—couch, coffee table, floor lamp, two upholstered chairs, an end table with lamp, all facing the small-screen television. One picture, of Mary praying at the foot of the Crucifixion. A hanging knickknack shelf holding what I realize on closer inspection are salt-and-pepper shakers: barrel cactus, dogs and cats, gasoline pumps, outhouses, flowers. The carpet feels thin and hard, unpadded. I get an impression of no color, a bland blend of beige and brown. The plaid sofa looks like a hide-a-bed, with pleated dust-ruffle, two large floral pillows crushed into the corners. Nylon curtains, no drapes.

—Hey, Mom. We're home— We wait. —She must be taking a nap— Casey turns, I follow him into the kitchen. —You want something to drink?

I can't answer, I'm in a state of shock. No dining room. A Formica table with four chairs, two more against the wall. The yellow paint of the cupboards is chipped, the stove and refrigerator are vintage. No dishwasher. Plates and cups drain in a rack on the counter.

Casey takes a jug of iced tea from the refrigerator and goes to the cupboard.

—I thought I heard you come in.

I jump. A woman has entered behind us.

Casey grins. —This is my mother Catherine.

I don't know what to do. My arms waver at my sides. She reaches a hand to me.

—I'm glad to meet you, Reggie— Her smile is warm. —I've heard a lot about you.

Again I don't know what to do. How do I answer? I've heard a lot about you, too? I feel foolish and awkward, I ineffectually take her hand.

Casey's setting out three glasses, pouring the tea —Yeah, and all bad— He exchanges a grin with Catherine.

—Why don't you sit down, Reggie? I have to start dinner, you can keep me company.

Catherine initiates conversation, we talk—about the parade and Denny, the ball game, the Pig Out, the upcoming fireworks. I start to relax.

I can think of only two words to describe her: medium—medium hair, medium build, medium height, medium voice—and comfortable. There's humor to her, and spark. She takes in everything and I see it register: a soft smile, a twinkle, a flashed look, a frown. She feels easy, no fast abrupt movements, and it feels easy to be around her. She comments freely, making no bones, but she doesn't impose her opinions. Instead she makes me feel encouraged to be equally free and direct.

It's her face that draws me. She was pretty once, probably very pretty, she's still not unattractive. But her skin looks tired, not properly cared for. I wonder if she uses face creams. I wonder about her age. She can't be much older than Mummy, at the most in her early forties. She chain-smokes.

We're discussing the Pow Wow—Catherine's careful not to ask about my mother and father or my life in Boston and I'm careful not to volunteer—when suddenly a man appears: Casey's father. I hadn't counted on this, hadn't even considered it.

—Well— He smiles at me. —We have company.

Casey beams.

—Meet Reggie. Meet my dad, Reggie.

I don't know whether to sit or stand, offer my hand or curtsy.

—I'm pleased to meet you, Mr. Colter.

—Scotty.

He pulls up the chair next to me, looks me over. —You were right, Case. She *is* pretty.

I feel completely stupid. I try to make a joke of it. —My forehead's too high. Casey says I need bangs— Casey bursts out laughing.

Catherine glares at him. —She looks nice the way she is.

He grins sheepishly.

Scotty's wearing Levis and western denim shirt. He pulls out a pack of Camels and lights up.

Catherine shoves over the ashtray. —Like some iced tea, Scotty?

—Think I'll have a beer. How about a beer, punk?

Catherine gives him a stern look. —Casey's having iced tea.

Scotty pulls back, smiles around. —On second thought, think I'll have iced tea, too.

Scotty's a handsome man—tall, lean, hard-muscled—but like Catherine, tired looking. Casey's not like either of them, rather a blend. His father's intense eyes and aggressive jaw, his mother's sensuous mouth and classic nose.

Scotty places his hands on the sides of his glass, burning cigarette between his fingers, and fixes me with interest.

—So, Reggie, how're you finding life in Harden?

—Fine, sir, I like it.

—Casey treating you all right?

—Yes, sir— I blush.

—Taking good care of you, showing you around?

Casey puts his hands on the back of my chair. —You bet I am. Took her to Dairy Queen and the high school.

Scotty laughs. —The hottest spots in town.

Catherine hands Casey plates, he sets the table while we discuss my first reactions to Harden.

Catherine places a stack of paper napkins in the middle of the table.

—We're almost ready, Scotty. You can go get Denny.

—Where is she?

—At Ralston's.

Dinner is meatloaf, scalloped potatoes, and sliced tomatoes. Ice cream with frozen strawberries for dessert, a special treat, I gather. Casey eats a full serving of everything. I say I'm still too full from the Pig Out but get a small plate anyway. The food is good but plain, basic, no wine or herb cookery here. I end up forcing down bites and apologizing when I can't finish. I feel terrible. In our family, an empty plate is requisite.

I help Catherine clear up while the men retire to the television. Catherine looks over casually.

—You have beautiful hair, shiny and healthy.

I smile shyly. —Thank you.

—Is it getting blonder since you've been here?

—I think so. From being at the pool.

—It looks a little sun-bleached— She reaches out, crumples my hair. —I was a beautician, you know, before I met Scotty. Did hair, nails, makeup, the whole works. I still do for my friends. I give a lot of home perms.

I'm stunned by the news, I search for a covering answer.

—My hair can't take a permanent.

It's not true, I've never even attempted one. Mummy doesn't believe in them, says they're damaging. But it's the best I can come up with.

Catherine fingers a few strands, nods. —Too fine. You don't need one anyway, you have a natural wave— She's fussing, pushing my hair this way and that. —You'd look cute with bangs, parted on the side, swept over— She lets her hand drop. —If you ever decide you want them, just let me know. I'll be happy to cut them for you.

I think of Mummy, she'd have a fit.

—Thank you.

—And be careful, too much sun and chlorine will dry it out.

She calls Casey in to wash the dishes, I dry, while she gets Denny ready.

The fireworks are held on the flats north of town. The last miles of road out are dirt. There's already a large gathering of cars and pickups lined across the desert. We find a slot and climb out. Following Casey's instructions, I take off my sandals, crawl up on the blanket he's spread over the hood so as not to scratch it, then pull myself onto the roof. He helps Denny up and settles her between us. Up and down the line, to left and right, families sit on hoods and roofs, sipping soda pop and beer, laughing and talking in the deepening twilight, savoring the cooling air, waiting for dark.

The fireworks are better than I expected, a few, in fact, are spectacular. Against the vast clear night, they seem almost touchable. Denny squeals, oohs and aahs with the rest of us, her head leaning against Casey, his arm around her. The finale's rapid succession of multi-colored bursts lights up the sky and casts our uplifted faces in brilliance. We yell, whistle, and clap, a sound of happy fulfilled community that becomes lonely as it echoes and floats across the desert and fades with the last sparkles.

We pile into the car, roll up our windows against the dust, and join the long stream of headlights slowly weaving its way back to the deserted town.

Denny lolls against me, her eyelids droop. I take her on my lap, cradling her, and she falls asleep, legs dangling over mine, head nestled into my shoulder. I've never been this close to a child. She smells warm and dusty, sweet and sweaty. Casey smiles over at me, his eyes softly slitted. We don't talk, there's no need to, we feel each other's contentment.

At my house, Casey gently takes Denny off my lap and lays her across the backseat. She doesn't so much as whimper. He walks me to the front door. Thankfully Mummy and Daddy have gone to bed. He puts his hands on my shoulders, leans closer, his eyes holding mine. My heart thumps, my stomach flip flops. I close my eyes, body straining toward his, lips ready.

Then I feel him lean back.

I open my eyes, he's smiling down at me, teasingly, mockingly. He gives my shoulders a quick squeeze, grins —See ya— and skips down the steps. I think I hate him.

I lie in the dark and watch the day replay across the ceiling: the parade, the baseball game, the Pig Out; Denny, Catherine, Scotty. I feel myself smiling. What a day. A perfect day.

I got my fireworks all right.

SCENE 8

—Harden, please.

Click, buzz.

—Yes?

—Bailey. On McKinley Street.

—The number is 436-5752.

Heart pounding, she dials.

—Hello?

—Mrs. Bailey?— Deep breath. —This is Regina Patterson. You probably don't remember me but I was a friend of Betts. I lived in Harden one year when we were in high school. I—

—Of course I remember you, Reggie. How are you?

—Fine, thank you. Just fine— She gulps. —I've been trying to get in touch with Betts but I don't have her number. Could you by any chance give it to me?

—Of course. It's 434-2271.

—What area code?

—Why, right here in Harden, Reggie.

—Thank you. Thank you, Mrs. Bailey. I really appreciate it— She remembers her manners. —How have you been, Mrs. Bailey?

—Well, I can't complain. I still have my wits. Mr. Bailey died twelve years ago. I guess you wouldn't have heard about that. But Betts and the boys and my nine grandchildren live in town, so I have plenty to keep me busy.

—That's wonderful. Maybe I'll see you one of these days.

—That would be nice. Betts'll be glad to hear from you, Reggie.

—I'll call her right now.

Mrs. Bailey's voice hasn't changed a bit, still deep, husky from a cigarette cough. She was the smallest in the family, a medium five-six. Mr. Bailey stood well over six feet, Betts's older brothers David and Robby were closer to six-five. Handsome men, big-boned and muscular, they treated Betts like another brother. Reggie can't believe Betts is in Harden, why did she come back, she was determined to get away.

Reggie lets the phone ring four times, loses courage, starts to hang up.

—Hello.

—Betts?

Of course it is, she'd know that voice anywhere. Betts was a powerful singer, another Kate Smith, but with the sweetness of Mama Cass. She sang for every event.

—Yes.

—This is Reggie Patterson. You'll have to reach back about twenty years.

—Reggie? Reggie Patterson? My god! Reggie Patterson, how the hell are you?

—I'm fine, Betts, how the hell are *you*?

—Good, really good. Where are you?

—Here. Here in Boston. I'm sorry I haven't written, or gotten in touch with you sooner. I've been meaning to, but life's been pretty hectic. I keep getting caught up . . .

—I know how it is. I could have lifted a phone, too.

—Are you still teaching?

—Not really, just a little substituting now and then, when the kids aren't sick.

—You have kids?

—You mean you hadn't heard? I thought I'd blasted it to the ends of the earth. Four. Five including my husband— She laughs. —How about you?

—Two girls, thirteen and eleven.

—You still in theatre?

—Nah, that was a pipe dream. I had to give it up when reality set in. Not enough talent.

—I don't know about that. I thought you were pretty good. Everyone did. At least the best we'd had in Harden.

—Gee. Thanks.

Betts chuckles. —Remember "Our Town"?

—How could I forget.

—And "Seven Brides for Seven Brothers"? You did everything, sing, dance—

—Tell me about everyone else. Trixie, Janie, Ruthie . . .

—Well, Janie's in Phoenix, she married a doctor she met in nurses' training. Trixie's here in Harden, still married to Curtis Wheelock, two kids. And Ruthie's in town, too, married to Glenn Garvey, he's selling insurance. They have one daughter and one grandchild.

—What about Lester Jennings?

—Les's in the sheriff's department, a deputy. Married and divorced two times.

Reggie takes a deep breath —And Casey?— Her heart's pounding so hard in her throat, she doesn't think she can choke out the words. —Casey Colter?

—Oh, Casey's an agent for the FBI somewhere in Texas, Galveston, I think— Betts laughs —Can you beat that? Him and Jennings are still playing cowboys.

—Did he marry?

—Hell, yes, some rich gal from the South. They were up here visiting Catherine and Scotty once a long time ago. He was driving around in a fancy red sports car, making sure everyone saw him.

—Did you meet his wife?

—Nobody did. Guess Case thought she was too good for us. But Trixie saw her, said she had big boobs and long black hair— Betts chuckles. —Just like old Colter.

Reggie's stomach's pitching so violently she's afraid she's going to be sick. —Well, tell everyone Hi for me, will you? It's been great talking to you, Betts, great hearing your voice.

—You too. You really surprised me.

—I'll call again.

—Better yet, why don't you come out and visit. You can stay here. I'll put Will on the sofa.

—I just might. Meanwhile, I'll be sure to stay in touch.

—You do that, Reggie, stay in touch.

She can't get her bearings, everything's whirling, her head, her heart, her stomach. What did she expect, what was she thinking? It's been fifteen years, of course he's married, of course he has a wife. She sits down, puts her head between her knees. Big boobs and long black hair. What did Betts mean, Just like Colter? Casey didn't like brunettes, he always preferred blondes. Made her rinse her hair in lemon juice and dry it in the sun. But he did like it long. She let it grow for him, by Prom time it was past her shoulders. She wore it in a pony tail all summer, but Mummy made her cut it for Wexler. Back to the same old boring bob just below her ears that she couldn't do anything with except wash and comb. That's the point, said Mummy, so you can relax and act natural, forget about yourself.

Reggie stands and goes to the mirror. She stares at her face, runs her hands through her hair, lifting and pushing. —I'm tired of forgetting about myself.

She goes to the bedroom, strips to her Calvin Klein bikini briefs and studies her body in the full-length mirror. She turns sideways, sucks in her tummy, pushes out her chest. She turns backwards, head over shoulder, and surveys the condition of her fanny. She runs her hands over her high breasts, slim waist, taut abdomen. Well I may not have big boobs, but all things considered, I don't look so bad.

She won't say it to herself but in fact she thinks she looks terrific. Sexy. She wonders if Howie notices her body, he never comments, doesn't approach her sometimes for weeks. She wonders if it's the sex she misses or just the feeling sexy. Casey made her feel pretty. At fifteen, was that the same as sexy?

She has to laugh, an FBI agent, can you believe it? As usual pitting himself against worthy adversaries and proving himself top man. Well good for you, Casey, you're living your fantasy. Glamour, adventure, honor and glory. Hero billing. Last time she heard, he was playing football at Rice University. He got his scholarship. She received a clipping in the mail. *Rice Victory, Led by Star Quarterback Casey Colter.* No note, no return address, just a postmark from Houston, Texas. She knew it had to be from him, just to let her know: I'm in college, I made it, Reggie. Eat your heart out.

And that's exactly what she's doing.

But she knows now how to find him, she's blown his cover, *she* can be a worthy adversary.

Would he find her sexy now? She pulls on her gray slacks and fisherman's knit sweater and assesses the effect in the mirror. Not like this. She takes off the obliterating bulkiness, goes rummaging through closet and drawers. Cashmere sweaters, plaid skirts, flannel slacks, blouses with Peter Pan collars. Where did she get all this shit? She hears the word in her mind and laughs out loud. —*Shit.*

She pulls sweaters out of drawers and strews them around the room. —Sexless shit— She settles on black slacks, scooped-neck black sweater, wide black belt, and tiny black and red scarf tied around her neck.

Mummy's discovered the library.

—It's a house, Artie. A little, two-story, wooden house, stuck in the middle of a bunch of other small houses, not even in a decent section of town. The lawn's brown, the paint's peeling, you'd think they could at least paint it.

—They probably can't afford to— Daddy always takes the practical reasonable approach, and it maddens Mummy.

—Of course they can't. Who in this place is going to support a library?— She's disgusted and disturbed. —And inside, I can't tell you how depressing. The rooms are small and dark, with the original overhead fixtures, probably dated eighteen-ninety. In one room there's a bare bulb hanging from a wire. You need a flashlight to read the book spines.

Daddy's laid *The Kachina and the White Man* across his knees, face down, and is attentively listening to Mummy. He knows when she gets wound up like this, there's nothing to do but let her talk it out.

—The walls are lined with dusty wooden shelves, half of them half empty. Some of the books are so old they look like they came across in a covered wagon.

—Maybe you could find a few first editions to finance new acquisitions.

—And the children's section, Artie. You ought to see it. Two walls. The picture books take up a space no larger than the *Encyclopedia Britannica*.

This is serious business. Mummy has a degree in library science, with a specialty in children' literature.

—What do they do with their children in the evenings? Play Tiddley Winks?

We are not talking now about an impoverished small-town library. We're talking about starving children, little minds and souls wasting away, withering into empty-eyed hulks and heartless monsters.

—How can they expect their children to develop any imagination, have any understanding of the achievements of the past and the possibilities of the future, if they don't read? How can they expect their children to become readers if the parents don't read to them first?

Daddy shifts his leg, *The Kachina and the White Man* slips to the floor. —Maybe the children's books were just checked out.

Mummy gives him a withering look but he's reaching to the floor. —I checked the card catalog. And don't tell me they buy them. Have you seen what passes for a book store in this town?— Daddy waits. —One skimpy little department in Babbitt's. *Golden Books*. No Bemelmans, no Sendak. And in the Current section, not one book I haven't read— She sniffs. —But I'll tell you what they do have. Mysteries. Gothics. Westerns. Walls of them in the library, shelves of them at Babbitt's, racks of them at the Walgreen's. I always said you could tell a person by his library. Well, the same applies to a town.

She's in a state of high agitation. Daddy tries to mollify her. —That doesn't seem so unreasonable. The westerns are part of their background. And I always enjoy a good detective novel myself. It's just a matter of exposure. At least they're aware of books, and at least they read. Aren't you the one who told me once if you could get a kid to read a comic book you could get him to read anything?

Mummy's head jerks up, she fixes him with a long, intensely thoughtful look.

Later that night we see her in the glare of the white kitchen, writing away on sheets of white paper I don't see how she can distinguish from the white table.

Daddy has a new chair, brown leatherette with brass studs, not bad for fake, and a matching ottoman. I have a chair of my own now too, tan tweed not too scratchy for the price. These are not things Mummy plans to ship back, she'll leave them for future occupants.

She's ripped up the stiff dusty carpet and discovered hardwood boards, which she's washed and waxed to a dark luster. I can't believe this is my mother. But Daddy assures me she showed the same ferocious nest-building behaviors with their hut in Kenya. Something about carving a home out of the wilderness.

—Reggie— I look up from my book, *Franny and Zooey*. Mummy's wandered into the living room, a frown worrying her brow, pen and writing pad in hand. She settles in her companion tweed chair, pad supported on her knees, pen poised to write, and regards me intently. —List for me all the books you remember ever reading or having read to you.

Reggie chops vegetables and amuses herself by imagining an entrance. She wouldn't go to his house. His wife would be there. Besides she doesn't know where he lives. She'd have to go to his office. She doesn't know where that is either but it would be easy enough to find out. All she'd have to do is call Information and ask for the FBI. She'd have to telephone ahead, make sure he'd be there. But then he might refuse to see her, or worse yet, hang up. No, she'd have to take him by surprise.

Howie comes in.

Reggie lays down her knife, smiles.

—You're home early, how nice.

Howie gives her cheek a peck. —Do you think you have enough?

She looks down at the pile of yellow and red peppers, carrots, scallions, celery, enough for three salads.

—I'm planning ahead.

—The girls home?

—In their rooms studying.

She watches his back as he dumps his coat and briefcase on the family-room sofa, heads for the hall. She picks up the knife, calls after him —The mail's on the table.

He knows it is, she always leaves it there. Just like he knows the girls will be in their rooms studying. It's ritual talk, a way of making limited contact, easing the transition from office to home. Perfunctory. Just like the peck.

How long, she wonders, since they've really talked? *Communicated.* She can't remember. Did they ever? She doubts it, she would have remembered. She remembers talking about boats and boating, about shipbuilding and his shipbuilder grandfather. She cheered Howie through many a regatta.

They talked about the legal system, and corporate structure, and government regulation. She learned a lot about the politics of law.

And they talked about the future. Howie's future, their future as a couple. But it was like laying out a blueprint and making sure all the lines were straight and all the rooms in proper sequence. A pre-drawn blueprint by some master draftsman who passed on the same plan to everyone they knew with slight variation. No provision for digging out your own foundation, no allowance for hammering up your own framing, no lenience for improvising your own room arrangement.

She scrapes a third of the vegetables into the bowl on top of the lettuce, stores the rest in the cooler, lays the chicken out on the broiler pan.

If she were a case, a damsel in distress or a fugitive from justice, Casey would have to see her. The idea pleases her. An outlaw. Yes, a deviate from society. A worthy adversary.

—Are you planning a trip somewhere?

She looks up. Howie's tone is light, but there's something disturbed in his eyes. Anxiety? Alarm?

—No— Then she realizes. —Oh. The clothes— She'd left them piled on the bed. —I've just been cleaning out my drawers and closets.

The pinched look relaxes. They've been putting a good face on it, going through the motions, but Howie knows things aren't right between them. She's sorry about the look, and grateful for it. It means he still cares. It surprises her that it matters to her, that he should care. She wishes she could say, don't worry, Howie, I won't leave you. But right now she's not sure. Instead, all she can do is keep up the pretense.

She gestures with the knife. —They're discards, old clothes I'm taking over to the League. I need a big box.

—From the looks of it, you need ten boxes. You must be getting rid of half your wardrobe.

Reggie frowns. —Maggie's wardrobe.

It's been a bone of contention for years, one that until now she's gnawed at in silence. Maggie started it for her in high school. Separates with accessories carefully coordinated to be mixed and matched so as to look as if she had more outfits than the actual investment. A few basic dresses, one black, one navy; two suits, one tailored, one dressy; four skirts, gray, navy, black, camel; four slacks, gray, black, tweed, plaid; sweaters and blouses. Scarves, belts, and jewelry. Shoes and matching bags, of course. All she had to do was fill in holes and keep things updated.

She feels quarrelsome. —Do you realize some of those things are more than twenty years old?

Howie looks nonplused. —But they're still good, aren't they?

—Of course— That was Maggie's master plan. Classic lines, good fabric. She's hearing, Quality never goes out of style; she's thinking, You can't kill it with a stick.

—So what's wrong with all those things?— He's counting up the dollars.

—I'm sick of them, Howie, that's what. They're not the way I want to look.

—I always thought you looked nice.

—You did? You didn't tell me— She pulls straight, in semi-profile, hands on hips, blatantly fishing. —Tell me now.

He looks at her, confused. —You look good.

—What's "good" mean?

—I don't know— He shrugs. —Just good. How you're supposed to dress. In good taste.

Reggie drops her hands, slumps. She feels like a reject worm. Even in her apache-effected outfit she can't hook him. She wonders what kind of bait it would take.

She picks up the knife, stabs it into the chopping block. —Exactly. Like everyone else.

With Howie, that's the standard. He's fond of the Chinese saying, It's the nail that sticks up that gets hammered down. Casey was attracted to her because she was different from the girls he knew, a conspicuous nail, a challenge, a commending conquest.

A worthy adversary.

She'd like to say, Howie, have you noticed my body lately? but she's afraid to start something she doesn't want to finish. She slams the chicken under the broiler, glares at Howie.

—So maybe it's time I try a little bad taste.

SCENE 9

—Just a minute, I'll ask— I turn from the phone. —Mummy, Casey wants to know if I can go to the movie.

—Which movie?

I know what she's getting at. She's discovered there's a drive-in. —The Rialto. The one downtown.

—What's showing?

—How do I know?— I turn to the phone. —Maggie'd like to know what's showing— I turn back to Mummy. —He doesn't know either. He just thought it'd be something to do on Saturday night.

—Ohhhh— she can't think of a good objection —all right— But she's not happy about it.

Back to the phone. —Maggie says it's all right. What time?

She's regarding me with hands on hips as I hang up. —Since when did I become Maggie?

I shrug. —The kids think it's stupid when I call you Mummy.

She starts to say something, snaps her mouth shut, lips tight, and swipes at the counter with her wash cloth. —I thought Casey wasn't in the picture anymore.

—What made you think that?

—I haven't seen him around much lately.

—That's because he got a job.

—A job? What kind of a job?

I never volunteer about Casey. Anything I say might be used against him. If she wants information, she's going to have to work for it. —Out at the airport.

—The airport? Doing what?

—Driving the truck.

—Driving a truck? That's it? He's a truck driver?

—No, he cleans up, too.

—Like a janitor?

—He does all kinds of things— I try not to sound defensive, if she senses I'm on shakey ground, she'll move in to seize her advantage. —Answers the phone, hauls supplies, loads the planes. He's training to be on the ground crew.

—God forbid.

—What's so god forbid about that?

—It's not much in the way of a career, is it?— The counter's done for, now she's taking it out on the sink.

—He's not doing it for life, Mummy, it's just a summer job. Better than sitting around gathering moss. Isn't that what you always say?— She's giving me a silent back, engrossed in the sink. —Besides, it gives him money for college.

That grabs her attention. I've been saving up, waiting to spring my little surprises.

—Casey's going to college?

—Sure. Why not? He's smart enough.

—Who determined that?

—He went to private school.

—Private school?— It's the last thing she expected.

—Three years, he just returned to Harden. And he did very well— I pause for effect. When you have 'em off balance, keep your volleys coming. —He got a scholarship.

She doesn't know how to deal with this, she throws the cloth into the sink. I quietly exit before she has a chance to think Which school? Where? try to pin him down like a bug and squash him.

Casey's dressed up, baby-blue polo shirt, pressed tan slacks, polished brown loafers. Even Maggie's impressed at how nice he looks, though she's quick to cover it. I'm in yellow dotted-swiss, white Mary Jane's, a pearl pendant at my throat.

—I'll have her home by twelve, Mrs. Patterson.

Maggie pulls up short, looks around for assistance. But Daddy's in Flagstaff, doing research at the Museum of Northern Arizona. —Isn't twelve a little late? I think ten thirty should be more like it.

—It's a double feature. And I'd like to take her to Dairy Queen afterwards— He takes my arm, holds me out, dazzles Maggie with one of his smiles. —Show 'em how pretty she looks.

It's too much, Maggie resigns herself. —All right. Twelve— She fixes him with a firm look. —No later.

Casey opens the screen door, steps aside while I precede him down the steps, opens the car door, helps me in, lifts my skirt out of the door jamb. I'm suspicious of his sudden courtliness.

We start west. —Where're you going?

—To pick up Les.

—You didn't say Les was coming— I'm a little put out, I thought we'd be alone.

—Didn't I?— He grins, tries to sound casual. —I guess I forgot. He's bringing Diane.

I search my memory. —Who's Diane. I didn't meet her at Dairy Queen.

He tosses an explanation. —She's older.

Older is the exaggeration of the century. She looks at least twenty, smokes, has peroxided hair, and bosoms so large her low-necked blouse can barely cage them. She doesn't wait for Les to go to the door and escort her. She comes bounding down the steps into the backseat the moment Casey honks the horn. Les has his arm around her before Casey can get the car in gear. I hear them whispering and giggling all the way to the Rialto. I see Casey out of the corner of my eye keep smiling over at me, but I refuse to acknowledge him. I stay far to my side, pressed against the door, staring out the window.

The theater's dark when we come in, the previews are on. Diane wants to sit in the balcony where she can smoke. Les leads the way up the side aisle then steps aside. I don't like the side but nobody's bothered to ask me. We file in, Diane, Les, Casey, then me. And I don't like the order of entry. I feel like the tail tagging along behind the dog. Casey's loaded us down with coke, candy, ice cream, and popcorn with extra butter. We put the cokes under our seats, Casey holds the popcorn between his knees, I take the candy in my lap, and we start on our Eskimo Pies. Then Casey holds the popcorn between us and we sip our cokes.

As my eyes adjust to the dark, I take in my surroundings. I haven't been in many movie houses, in Boston we prefer live theatre, but immediately I can tell this one is beyond the ordinary. The side walls have gilded boxes that meet the balcony in a graceful curve topped by a gilded molding carved like a twisted cord. Above the boxes giant bas-relief gods and goddesses dance and frolic—singing, playing flutes and lyres, strewing garlands—their satiny pastel plastic surfaces glowing as if suffused with inner light. The stage is as large as the theatre stage at Wexler, but with an orchestra pit and grand piano.

To the left of the pit, gleaming organ pipes rise the height of the ceiling, at least thirty feet, and from the center of the coffered-and-gilt dome, a Herculean chain drops a huge brass-and-crystal chandelier, sadly in need of scrubbing. The heavy red-velvet drapes seem still in decent condition, but the red cushions of the seats are almost completely worn of plush. The hard black enamel on the seat arms is chipped, the seat backs are carved with initials. Cigarette butts, discarded wrappers and cups, and spilled popcorn litter the scraped gray paint of the concrete floor. My shoes stick to dried puddles of days-old ice cream and soda. The air is close and smells stale and strong, like a dirty T-shirt. I fear I'm going to wake in the night scratching flea bites.

I twist in my seat and scan the balcony. Its patrons obviously aren't there to see the movie. A few preadolescent boys whoop and hoot, happy to have a high dark place where they can make rude noises and puff illicit cigarettes. The rest neck. I quickly twist back, embarrassed and ashamed, as if I'd been caught peeping through someone's bedroom window. And indignant at having my sense of propriety unwillingly imposed upon in a place of public gathering.

The movie is a science fiction, "The Slug," about gastropods from outer space that've devoured their own planet and invade Earth in search of new vegetation. They're moving across the United States, eating everything in sight, leaving behind a shiny slick path of stem stubs and barkless tree snags. They've been spotted at night by flashlight and search beams, giant snail-like creatures with antenna-like extensions for arms and legs, but no one can capture or kill them. They're too big to step on, bullets go through their spongy bodies, and they have no blood so they can't bleed to death. A farmer tries throwing salt on one, its flesh foams and shrivels. But the farmer has only one bag of salt so the wounded slug throws its slimy body over the farmer and disintegrates him with its acidic digestive juices.

In the middle of the movie, the snails are attracted to a cabin in the woods where a group of sorority and frat kids are having a beer bust. The snails take over the cabin, frizzle up all the students, and drain the beer kegs. It's a pretty gruesome episode, but it gives the sheriffs an idea. They know which way the slugs are headed by their shiny trails, so they fill a huge sunken water tank with beer and surround it with mounds of poisoned snail bait. The last scene shows the over-sized slugs frothing and writhing on the mounds and floating bellies-up in the beer tank.

I'm not a science fiction fan, but this one is gory and scary enough to keep me interested. In the woods scene, when the slugs are creeping up on the students, I scream and grab Casey. He laughs and puts his arm around me. As things get more horrific, I move closer. I've never done this before, sat in a movie with a boy's arm around me. I've kissed of course. I had my first kiss in sixth grade playing "Spin the Bottle." And I pulled down pants and exchanged looks with the son of my mother's best friend when I was seven. I've even necked a little, at house parties. But that was in the dark, alone, just to experiment, with nobody I cared about. I didn't even care about Andrew Dickerman, he was just a feather in my cap. With Casey it's different.

At first I feel self-conscious, exposed, a little shameful. What if Mummy were to catch me? But bit by bit I relax and let myself sink into it. Casey's arm feels strong and protective. He smells warm and soapy. I can feel the heat of his body. I snuggle in, he pulls me closer. I lay my head on his shoulder, he turns his face toward mine—and from under his chin I see what's going on next to him. Les is twisted half out of his seat, on top of Diane, kissing her in a frenzy, his hands all over her body. I bolt upright, as far as I can get away from Casey.

—What's the matter?

I shake my head. I feel cheap, like another Diane. After a few minutes, Casey reaches for my hand, I let him take it. But when he tries to pull me to him, I pull back.

"The Slug" ends and the lights come on. Casey exchanges a few words with Les while Diane combs her hair and repaints her mouth, then he stands and lifts me by the arm.

—Where're we going?

—We're leaving.

—But we haven't seen the second feature.

—It's dumb.

As if the first one wasn't?

As we near the car, Casey hands Les his keys. —Do a buddy a favor.

Les and Diane scramble in front, Casey and I slide in back. Les doesn't turn toward Dairy Queen. I think that's just as well, my stomach's a little queasy. Halfway through the movie, I peeled the wrapper off my Butter Finger, Casey shared his Milk Duds, and Les passed over JuJuBes. Instead Les takes a narrow road west. I don't ask where we're going. I'm uneasy but I feel stupid showing it.

Les is driving slowly, his arm around Diane, her head on his shoulder. The windows are down, the cooling night air gently floats in, full of the perfumes of the desert, smells I'm just learning. Sage, mesquite, greasewood, creosote. Warm sand. Soft wind. Casey puts his arm around me, I cuddle in. I forget my unease.

We're out of town. The road has reduced to one lane. Les pulls over onto the sandy shoulder and turns off the ignition. It's a dark night, half moon, but still I can see Les's and Diane's silhouettes against the windshield. They go into a clinch, in minutes their heads disappear below the seatback. I try not to listen to their sounds.

Casey stretches out across the seat, ankles crossed, hands behind head, leaving just enough edge for my fanny to cling to. He reaches and pulls me toward him. This is not the way I envisioned our first kiss. I thought we'd be alone, I thought it would be more romantic. Still . . .

I remember him on the front porch, his body leaning close, his eyes holding mine, his smile teasing. I let him pull me down.

—Why don't you give me a little kiss— I give him a little kiss, he gives me a little grin. —That wasn't bad for starters, but maybe we should try it again.

The second kiss is smoother, easier, better placed, I'm not so nervous. I'm thinking now about proving myself a good kisser.

Casey suddenly pushes me back. —Jesus christ, woman, where'd you learn to kiss like that? Close your mouth before I fall in— I hear a muffled laugh from the front seat, I jerk upright. But Casey's not through with his fun. —Is that the way they do it in the East, don't you ever come up for air?

I perch on the edge of the seat, chin up, struggling to keep my voice light and steady. —I never had any complaints— but my cheeks are hot and my eyes are stinging.

—I'll bet you didn't. The poor guys probably drowned— Another giggle. —Come over here and let me show you how we do it in the West.

—No.

—Come on now, don't be like that. What's the matter, you're not mad at me, are you? Aahh, she's mad at me— His tone turns soft, sweet, cajoling. —Don't be mad at me, Honey, I was only kidding— He keeps trying to pull me toward him, I keep pulling back. —I like the way you kiss. It's just a little different from the way we do it here. Come on, let me give you a few lessons.

—No.

—Aahh, come on— He gently tugs on my arm. —Would it help if I said I'm sorry— I stop resisting. He takes my face in his hands. —All right, close your lips, not that much, a little more open, that's it, just like that. Now let me do the work. And keep your damn tongue in your mouth.

A sharp laugh from the front seat. I shove away to the other side of the car.

—Now what's wrong?

—I'd like to go home— Dead silence in the front seat.

—Now what'd I do?

—I want to go home, Les. Right now.

Les slowly rises, looks at Casey.

—I don't know, I guess I did something I shouldn't of— He shrugs. —Take her home then if that's what she wants.

Diane rises and glares at me. I give her a cold look, head high, then stare out my side window. Les starts the car, shoves it into gear, touches his foot to the accelerator. The tires spin.

—Damn— He puts it in reverse, tries to back up, the tires spin. —I don't know, Case, I think we might be stuck.

—Try rocking it.

Les rocks back and forth, from reverse to second, the tires spinning deeper and deeper. He climbs out, Casey joins him, they survey the situation, kick sand, kick the tires.

Les grins at Casey. —You still have that blanket in the trunk?

Casey opens the trunk, hands Les an old army blanket. Les comes around for Diane, they take off across the desert. Casey climbs into the backseat. I watch the receding figures.

—Where're they going?

—To collect brush for under the tires— We sit in silence.

Finally Casey looks over. —I guess I hurt your feelings.

—You made me feel like a fool.

He considers. —I guess I did kinda act like a jerk— He sounds sincerely contrite. He gets no argument.

I look out the window, letting him think about it.

—I didn't mean to make you feel bad, I was only horsing around, trying to be funny— I look at him. He looks down. —I guess I was showing off— He takes my hand, plays with the fingers. —You probably don't think much of me anymore.

I feel the strokes of his fingers along mine, their soft exploration onto my palm. I waver.

—I don't know. I guess you're all right.

He looks up hopefully, leans toward me. —Forgive me?— I can feel his breath on my cheek. I nod. After a moment, he moves next to me. —Would it make you mad again if I put my arm around you?

—No.

We sit quietly, listening to the night sounds: crickets, an owl, the whispering wind. I can feel him studying my profile. He lifts a finger and gently loops my hair behind my ear. He kisses my ear. I shiver. —Your hair's so soft— He runs his fingers through it. I'm paralyzed, like a snake stroked by a feather. He touches my chin, lifts my face to his, kisses me softly, my lips, my nose, my cheek, my lips again. Our kisses get longer and deeper, our mouths wetter, our breathing quicker. I feel myself sinking, I feel . . . a hand on my breast. I break away.

—Don't.

—What?— His mouth searches for mine, trying to reestablish contact. The hand remains.

—Don't touch me there— I push his hand away and sit upright.

—Now what?

—You know good and well.

—You mean touching your breast? There's nothing wrong with that.

—It's not nice.

—I think it's very nice.

—Nice girls don't do it.

—What're you afraid of?

—I'm not.

—Sure you are. You're afraid you'll like it so much you won't want to stop.

I study him, disgusted. —Next you're going to ask me if I plan to save it all my life.

—Well do you?

—Yes. Until I'm married.

—Well I'm saving myself, too. For the girl I marry. That doesn't mean I can't do a little petting.

—You've done this sort of thing a lot before?

—Not a lot. But some.

—Then why aren't you out with those girls?

—There's more to liking somebody than petting.

—So you can pet somebody without liking them?

—Sure. But it means a lot more if you do. It means even more if you love them. And when you love somebody enough to go all the way, it means everything. It joins you as one. It means you're married forever in the eyes of God and can't be separated.

—What about divorce?

—The Church doesn't recognize it. Divorce is man's law, for man's convenience, not God's law.

—How much have you done with other girls?

—I don't know, about everything I guess, except the final thing. A guy has to learn.

—Well you're not going to learn on me.

—Why not? We can learn with each other. We're friends, we can talk and laugh, we have a good time together. We even like each other a little.

—I've liked a lot of boys before and I'm going to like a lot more. Does that mean I should let every one of them paw around on me short of Doing It?

Casey stops short. His face goes dark, his jaw juts, his eyes narrow. He looks at me a moment. Then he drops my hand, opens the car door, and climbs out. —Les! Where the hell are you?— His yell sounds hollow in the empty night.

I climb out, too. —What's taking them so long?

In a few minutes, we see Les and Diane trudging toward us across the desert, dragging the blanket between them. It's loaded with rocks, dead wood, dried twigs, and crushed tumble weed.

Casey and Les scoop the sand away from the tires, lay a bed of rocks and wood under the rear tires, spread the blanket with twigs and tumble weed under the front. Diane takes the wheel, Casey and Les get behind and push, and on one try the car's back on the road. I guess the tires weren't all that deeply embedded. Diane leaves the motor running while she climbs into the back, I climb in front. Casey and Les walk up laughing.

—You son-of-a-bitch— Casey gives Les a playful punch.

—How'd you do?

—How about you?

Les laughs, his eyes shifting suggestively. —Bagged one good snipe.

Diane has a twig in the back of her hair, and her blouse is out over her skirt. She hasn't even cared to have the decency to stuff it back in.

It's after twelve by the time we get home. We'd dropped Diane and Les off first so we wouldn't have to explain them. Mummy's waiting.

—Sorry, Mrs. Patterson. We got stuck in the sand— My heart jumps.

—What sand— Mummy's stiffened like a bird dog, sniffing out snipe hunters.

—The Dairy Queen parking lot. This time of year it gets pretty torn up and soft. Luckily we found some able bodies to push us out.

Mummy opens the screen, Casey gives me a quick salute, bounces down the steps, hops into his car, and revs out of sight.

I know I won't see him again. And I tell myself, Who cares?

SCENE 10

Reggie sits in the wing chair, watching the last embers of the fire. It's become her favorite time. Everyone in bed, lights out, the house a dark silent conspirator in the unraveling of her thoughts. And she's had a lot of unraveling to do these past weeks. But tonight her thoughts are not heavy and thickly gnarled requiring tight-fingered unknotting. Tonight she's excited, in anticipation. Tonight she's raveling. She's thought up a story—a fiction, a fantasy out of the fragmented threads of her life—that for the past few days has increasingly preoccupied her.

It took hold slowly then gradually progressed. She'd be going through the routines of her day when suddenly it would take over. She'd find herself walking around with half a mind—doing her work, listening and talking, dealing with Howie and the girls—while the other half had visions, saw scenes, heard voices, concocted situations and problems. Situations that were more enticing than the ones she was in because their possibilities were limited only by her powers of invention. Problems that were more rewarding than her own because their solutions were within her control.

She had wandered into a world of would-be, could-be, should-be that made it easier for her to get through the immediate.

She knows exactly when it began—in the kitchen, chopping vegetables, pretending her re-entry into Casey's life. A fugitive damsel in distress intriguing the FBI agent into pursuing her. That's how the creative process works, she informs herself, thinking of Einstein on his trolley watching the whizzing-by buildings. That's where connections are made, in the suspension of time and space. Not on the edge of one's seat, straining at a blank wall, struggling to fill it with original insight and meaning. No. The imagination flows most freely in mundane surroundings, at menial tasks, leaving the mind unencumbered to commune with the lonely heart and longing soul. To make beauty and order out of chaos.

She smiles at herself. Ah yes, Reggie, that's all very fine, very grand, very inspirational. But what you're preparing to ravel here hasn't much chance at beauty. You haven't written so much as a classified ad since college, and your last piece of fiction was in high school. She sighs. At any rate, it won't be chaos.

She picks up her pine lap desk.

She even has her title. She writes it in capitals, at the top of the page, and underlines it, adds her pen name below. She's decided on that, too. She will not go as Regina Kendall, her married self, she will go as her *own* self, as she came into this world. A kind of rebirth.

And she has her protagonist. She sees her clearly. Tall, willowy. Long platinum hair, not cheap or brassy. Smokey. Long limbs golden tan. Glamorous, seductive, expensive. Early thirties with lots of money. Class—and dangerous. A damsel in distress, he has to protect her. A fugitive from the law, he has to track her down. Only she's out to get *him*. A gangster's moll. Drug trafficking. Off the Gulf of Mexico. She's made her big move, now she's on the run.

A WORTHY ADVERSARY

by Regina Irene Patterson

CHAPTER ONE

Smokey stacked the money in the suitcase, one hundred dollar bills, a hundred bills to a packet, two hundred packets. Not a lot, but as much as she dared take without arousing suspicion, though that suspicion could only come on the part of Vinnie. There was still plenty left in the wall safe. None of the boys knew she had the combination, because none of them had it except Vinnie. That's how much Artie trusted her, poor sap. And none of the boys knew exactly how much he kept in there, not even Vinnie, only that it was a few million. So five minus two. Three million could be considered a few, enough to satisfy Vinnie.

It was Artie's fast-getaway stash, and that was exactly how she was using it, along with his forty-five automatic. She checked to be sure the pistol was still in her purse; she knew how to use it and wouldn't hesitate if she had to. She slipped the purse strap over her left shoulder, lifted her overnight bag in her left hand, and gave one last look at the closet wall of beaded, sequined, satin, and lamé dresses; the rack of sable, chinchilla, and mink coats and jackets; the shelves of hats, purses, and shoes. She couldn't take any of it. Only what she would have had with her on the boat. Anyway, she wouldn't be needing sequins and sable where she was going. And what she did need she could buy.

She grabbed the suitcase in her right hand, checked the hall, and headed for the fire exit. Rubber-soled sneakers so her heels wouldn't clack on the concrete stairs, white slacks, white T-shirt, white jacket, hair wrapped in a scarf, dark glasses, just the way she'd looked on the boat. They'd all seen her, waved good-bye, a little holiday with Artie, plus tomorrow a contact in international waters. Artie was going to make contact a little sooner and a little closer-in than he'd expected, and a little deeper. She checked her watch. Three twenty. Only forty more minutes until four. The darkest hour before dawn—and her finest.

She checked the street and hurried across to the supermarket lot where she'd parked the car, rented with a phony driver's license and charge card, all in the name of her new identity. Artie had a cache of supplies for every contingency. She even had a phony birth certificate and passport. She stowed the overnight bag and suitcase in the trunk, started the engine, and didn't turn on the headlights until she was halfway up the block.

Tomorrow she'd be in Galveston.

The librarian's name is Dorothy, and she and Maggie have become friends. Now that the house is purged to her satisfaction, Maggie has started on the library. With Dorothy's almost tearful gratitude and re-inspired industry, she has dusted shelves, cleaned windows, and mended book covers. Even the bare bulb has been hoisted into proper position and decorously covered.

Maggie has a dedicated project. She and Dorothy have rearranged books so that the children's literature is in a room by itself, a corner room. On the newly polished floor, Maggie's laid a circular braided rag rug, gratis Mr. Babbitt, and on the rug she's placed a rocking chair, gratis Dorothy's mother. Large broadcloth-covered pillows are plopped here and there, in casual clumps of red, yellow, green, and blue, and blue broadcloth drapes frame the windows. The rocking chair has been painted red. Maggie is proving to be a demon with a paint brush. And Dorothy, evidently, is a whiz at the sewing machine. The room smells of wax, new fabric, and sun.

Reggie smiles around the room, complacently, even a little smugly. The whole family's there. Arthur and Maggie. Buffie and Mark, Brianna, and Matthew, the BMs, as Reggie likes to think of them. Jack and Miriam, lanky Lawrence slouching in the corner, home from Cornell for the occasion. And of course, along with her, Howie, Katelyn, and Lindsay. Caroline and Paul are not conspicuous by their absence, as usual they're traveling. Bad form to miss Abby's birthday.

They've all noticed the change in Reggie. They can't avoid it. But no one's said a word. Appetizers have been served and they're into their second round of drinks when Reggie looks up and finds Abby studying her.

At eighty-four, Abby's still a beauty, silver-white hair, figure trim in silver-blue silk and white lace, blue eyes penetrating. She still paints. Flowers from her garden. They're good but she refuses to sell them. Instead they cover her walls. A few have found their way onto walls of friends and family. Reggie has one over her bed, two others in the dining room. But they dominate. She's had to adjust the decor to soften and absorb their impact.

—You look very nice tonight, Reggie.

Reggie smiles primly. —Thank you, Abby.

Buffie stares, but she'd die before she'd say a word. Maggie doesn't need to, she's already curtly expressed her opinion.

—Is that a new haircut?

Reggie wants to burst out laughing. Is Uncle Jack really that obtuse or is this just more of their matter-of-fact down-playing? Her head is a mass of short, fluffy curls, peaks pulled into the hollows of her cheeks to emphasize her high cheekbones. Very French, perhaps Italian, but definitely European and definitely sexy. She's wearing eye shadow and large earrings.

—Yes, it is, Uncle Jack. Thank you very much for noticing.

She smiles sweetly at Buffie exiled to the corner because of her cigarettes. Buffie exhales a cloud of smoke without changing expression.

Reggie's dress is silk, a dark impressionistic print of navy, green, brown, and red, chaste long sleeves and high neck but unchaste skirt. When she stands to go to table, she's aware how closely the silk slips and slides with her. Her hose are navy, to match her kid pumps. She has gold bangles on her wrist and gold chains around her neck.

There's no confusion as to who is to sit where, no need of place cards. Everyone knows their station. Abby at the head of the table. Arthur as older son at the foot, Maggie and their family to his right. Jack and his family to Abby's right. The BMs next, on Arthur's left. Reggie's on Abby's left, across from Jack.

Casey sat at this table once, where Reggie's sitting now. He didn't know how to deal with a table that could seat twenty. He didn't know how to deal with all the shiny surfaces: the polished mahogany, the silver and crystal, the gilded frames and beveled mirrors. He didn't know how to handle eight courses. What did they teach him in that academy? Maggie fumed afterwards. How to obey orders, was Arthur's response. How to give them, had been Reggie's. Things hadn't been going well.

The food is excellent, the service exemplary. Randy serves, with long wiry hair and beard. Marta cooks, with long lank hair and granny glasses. An exhippy couple of Reggie's generation but marked by a decade she somehow missed. She marvels at how Abby finds these people. Alone, Abby eats simply, with guests, she goes the full nine yards. She lived in Paris a year, studying painting, and returned a connoisseur of good food and fine wines. Tonight is special. She's serving a different wine with each course. She'll tipple all evening: a martini or two with hors d'oeuvres, wine throughout dinner, port with fruit and cheeses, Courvoisier with coffee. But Reggie's never seen her tipsy.

Maggie tends to get frowsy. Arthur grows quieter and remoter, with a soft secretive smile. Jack winds into a talker, Miriam a giggler. Buffie gets looser and coarser, sometimes contentious. Howie becomes expansive, smiles and laughs a lot. By the end of the evening they'll be one big happy family, immensely admiring of one another.

The conversation is genial, polite. Jack has developed an ulcer, no one mentions it. Miriam and daughter Caroline aren't speaking again because of Caroline's continued refusal to have children. Nobody mentions it. There is also tension with Buffie, who as an avid volunteer for Planned Parenthood is suspected by Miriam as partly responsible for Caroline's unmotherhood. But it isn't mentioned. The favorite topic is service.

Maggie and Arthur are patrons of the symphony, Reggie and Howie benefactors, and the black-tie benefit is coming up. They'd like to recruit Jack and Miriam. Abby has maintained her involvement with the art museum. She long ago dropped volunteer activities. But she can still be counted on to help out with new acquisitions, even ones she doesn't care for, so long as the curator can convince her of their merit. Buffie's and Mark's house is on the Junior League house tour, and Buffie is trying to talk Abby into opening hers.

—I don't like the idea of a bunch of strangers trampling over my good rugs, goggling at my possessions.

—We'll cordon if off and put down plastic runners.

—It's an invasion of my privacy.

—But your house is beautiful, Grammy, so tastefully, *artfully* done. You have so many beautiful things: your Persian rugs, your impressionistic paintings, your European antiques. The gardens will be in bloom. You've put so much time and thought and energy into it, it seems a shame not to share it.

Reggie is fascinated. This is Buffie at her most persuasive, her voice low, melodious, almost sing-songy. Buffie is sitting to Arthur's left so she's speaking the length of the table. Everyone is mesmerized, except Abby.

—I'm sorry, Buffie, but this is not a museum, it's my home. But you're right about one thing: this is for me very much a matter of good taste. There are any number of beautiful homes in the Greater Boston area, small but tastefully, *artfully*, decorated, whose owners have put in as much time, energy, and thought as I have. But those houses are not considered for the League's tour because there is one thing they do not exhibit— She pauses. —They do not make a show of money. And *that*, Buffie, is what your house tour is really all about. The display of money. Which I consider to be in very *poor* taste.

Abby returns her attention to her meal, discussion finished. It's as close as the family will come to discord during dinner. Buffie's been reproved and she knows it. She knows she's not a favorite with Abby. And, although it's never been officially declared, she knows Reggie is.

This is perhaps why Buffie now turns to Maggie sitting opposite.

—Speaking of Junior League, Maggie, I hear Reggie gave them all her clothes. Her wild shot is a direct hit.

—Reggie— Reggie leans forward to meet her mother eye-to-eye down the long table. Maggie's look is worse than Reggie'd prepared for; she's appalled, on the verge of injured outrage. —Is this true? You didn't give away all those good clothes I bought you?

Reggie sits erect, smiling pleasantly. —No. I donated them, Maggie. To a worthy cause. And I didn't donate all. I saved a few things.

Buffie's delighted, she chimes a little laugh. —I couldn't believe it myself when I heard it. I had to go down and see. I don't know what they're going to do about all those monograms— Buffie looks over at Reggie with helpless humor, as if at a small hopeless child. —Whatever possessed you, Reggie?

—I'm thirty-five, Buffie, I'm tired of being a preppy.

Abby can't help herself, she laughs, a sharp, short bark.

—Once a preppy, always a preppy— Mark leans back in his chair and grins around the table, proud of his witticism. Reggie would like to rejoin, And nobody should know better than you, Mark. Instead she smiles sweetly.

But Buffie's not finished. —They're going to nominate you as Chair.

—Of what?

—From Rags to Riches— Obviously, Buffie thinks this a great joke. —So be prepared.

—Oh believe me, I am.

—You're not going to accept it— Howie's right to be surprised.

—Of course not.

—But why not?— Even Aunt Miriam's drawn in. She'd give anything to be nominated Chair of something.

—I'm over-committed.

—To what?— Buffie's disdain is barely concealed. She prides herself on her volunteerism.

—The dance classes. The mothers' auxiliary. The Vassar alumnae association. The League— Even to her the list sounds paltry. —And I'm considering starting a children's theatre.

The children, drowsy from the adult talk, immediately pop to attention.

—Oh, Mummy, can I be in it?

—May I, Mummy?

—Me, too, Aunt Reggie.

It's a stroke of genius. Necessity, the mother of invention.

—Reggie, what a good idea!— Abby never did agree with Maggie's disapproval of Reggie's interest in theatre.

Maggie leans forward. —I think I might get you some space at the library.

Reggie stares at her mother in disbelief. —Why, thank you, Maggie— Her smile is soft with gratitude.

Maggie smiles back, they glow. It's beautiful. Reggie's won the moment. She nurses her triumph the rest of the evening, like a chocolate in her cheek.

Buffie, on the other hand, seems to be sucking a lemon ball she tries to wash down with brandy. As she waits by the drive with Brianna and Matthew for Mark to bring the car, her laugh is too loud and her gestures exaggerated. Reggie, just starting down the walk with Howie, Katelyn and Lindsay skipping ahead, pauses to observe her.

—Do I act differently when I drink?

—Sure.

—How?

Howie considers. —Two drinks, you get sentimental. Four, you get philosophical. Six, you turn maudlin. I've even known you to sit down and have a good cry.

Mark has loaded Buffie into the front seat. As he whisks her away, she wrinkles her nose and wriggles her fingers at them with a smile that borders on malevolence.

Reggie toodle-oohs back. —I don't think Buffie approves of my new look.

—Buffie can be a real bitch.

Reggie stops in her tracks. —Howie, that's the nicest thing you've said to me in years.

He grins. —*I think you look terrific.*

—I take it back— She touches his arm. —*That's* the nicest thing.

Howie tucks her hand in the crook of his elbow and walks her to the car.

Reggie pokes the fire, picks up her lap desk, and poises her pen. All right, Smokey's in Galveston. She's rented a furnished room, picked up a few groceries. All uninteresting transition stuff that can be filled in later. The important thing is Smokey's meeting with Casey. She can't just walk in and say, Hello, Casey. After all these years to suddenly turn up, he'd suspect her motives. He'd know she was trouble. Besides, it isn't convoluted enough, not strong enough plotting. No, she has to get to him obliquely, so he thinks it's coincidence. Another FBI agent, a buddy, in the office down the hall. Single, susceptible to women, not too smooth, not too experienced. She gives a mischievous giggle. She has just the man in mind. She starts to write.

CHAPTER TWO

Fred Herron stood as the hall guard opened the door and ushered the woman in, a tall brunette in a wide-brimmed black hat with patent purse tucked under her arm.

"Miss Carter?"

She extended a white-gloved hand. "Thank you for seeing me."

"Would you like to sit down?"

The brunette arranged herself neatly on the chair, knees together, gloved hands folded in her lap on top of her purse. A lady, Fred assessed. A nervous lady.

"There seemed to be some urgency in your phone call. You said you were in trouble and needed someone you could trust."

"Yes." The brunette looked around, her fine-boned features tense. "Are we safe?"

"Completely. You're in good hands."

She studied his face, trying to read his eyes, her small hands twisting the strap of her purse, then made her decision. "Mr. Herron, you are looking at a dead woman." Her right hand plucked off the dark glasses, her left hand removed the hat then brunette wig, and a cascade of platinum hair tumbled to her shoulders.

Fred stared, grabbed a folder on his desk, and fumbled through to a picture. "My god," he said, looking up, "you're Smokey Lorraine." She gave him a moment to absorb the realization. "You're supposed to be in a thousand pieces at the bottom of the Atlantic Ocean."

"And I'd like to keep it that way."

Fred got up from his desk and hurriedly locked the door. "Why don't you start from the beginning."

"This is the beginning, Mr. Herron. The first day of my life." She took a deep breath. "I've been trying to get away from the rackets for years. But as long as Artie was alive, I didn't stand a chance. I knew too much. He would have hunted me down to the ends of the earth."

"Why did you come to the Bureau? You could have stayed at the bottom of the ocean."

"And been hiding out the rest of my life? It isn't often you get a second chance, Mr. Herron. This time I want to do it right."

Fred tapped the desk, flipped the folder from side to side. "And what exactly is it you want from us?"

"Protection. I want to stay alive."

"In exchange for what?"

"I can give you everything you need to put the lot of them away. Names, dates, times, places." A small, smug smile. "I have a little black book."

"You kept a record?" Fred's eyes narrowed. "Isn't that rather unusual for a woman in love?"

"Ours was a business arrangement, Mr. Herron. I was young when I met Artie Palmerini. Young and poor. But I wasn't stupid. I knew someday I might need an insurance policy."

The agent assessed her as she replaced the wig and tucked the platinum tresses safely out of sight. "And this is the day?" She nodded. "You understand what's involved if you turn state's evidence? You'll be the government's star witness." She nodded again, replacing the hat and dark glasses. "It won't be pleasant."

"I've lived through worse. All I ask is protection. And complete anonymity until the trial."

"Seems fair enough. But I have to clear it higher up. Where can I reach you?" She handed him a slip of cheap paper on which were neatly written in a slanted, full-looped script a name, address, and phone number. "Ann Carter." He'd have to pass this on to the boys in handwriting analysis. He'd need to do a little deeper checking on this beauty he was bargaining with. "Does anyone else know you're alive?"

"Only you, Mr. Herron. My life is in your hands."

"How'd you get off that yacht, anyway?"

She smiled and stood. "An unexpected little act of nature, for which I'll be eternally grateful." She started for the door.

All right, he could wait for her story. They'd have plenty of time. "This may take a few years, you realize."

"I've already waited several." Her hand reached for the door lock.

Fred looked at the address in his hand. "How'd you get here?"

"Bus."

"I'd like you to go home in a taxi."

"I'm on limited funds."

He reached into his pocket. "I think we can arrange a little financial assistance. This will be for starters."

She shook her head at the bills he held out. "I can take care of myself."

"I'm sure you can."

"I'm planning to get a job."

"I don't think that would be wise. I'd rather you stay close to your rooms."

"And be so stir crazy by the time of the trial I couldn't testify?"

"The more you expose yourself, the more you risk being spotted."

"I'm good at disguises." She smiled. "Or hadn't you noticed?" Fred returned the smile. "Besides, what could be more conspicuous than a young, single woman never leaving her room? No, I think it's better to keep up the appearance of a normal life. A job from nine to five, a movie or two on the weekends."

"You like movies?"

"I'm ashamed to admit I'm an incurable buff."

Fred's smile was quick. "Me, too."

"Really? What a coincidence." Her smile was wide and innocent, her eyes self-satisfied. Did the FBI think they were the only ones who did their background research? "It'll give us something to talk about."

She turned the knob.

"Okay, Ann Carter," Fred rose from his desk, moved toward her, offered his hand, "I'll be seeing you."

She returned his grip, eyes meeting his, holding. "With you, Mr. Herron, I think I'd like to be Smokey Lorraine."

SCENE 11

I've never seen anything like Jack's Canyon. The road out is a thin black trail seemingly blazed across the flat desert by the high beams of Betts's pickup. It's a dark night, and what piece of moon there is seems high and distant, like the sky and pinprick stars. A jackrabbit bolts out of the low brush, tall ears stiff, eyes bright in the headlights. Veers toward the road in panic, then jerks into reverse, and with powerful pushes of his long hind legs bounds over the scrub out of sight. Other than that, Betts and I seem to be the only living beings in the night.

We don't talk much. —Jackrabbit— she says when he makes his appearance, followed by —Sonofabitch— when he starts across our path. After that we sink back into the forward pull of the headlights and the hypnotic drone of the engine, surrounded by outside silence. I feel like we're driving toward the end of the world.

Suddenly the black framework of a bridge looms in front of us, sinister in its imposing unexpectedness. The roadbed is barely wide enough for two cars. We're skimming so close to the side railing I grab the dashboard. I catch a glimpse below of a sinuous black gulf.

The other side of the bridge is another land. The road rises into clusters of huge sandstone boulders piled atop one another like toppling pagodas. I think of the dollops of sand I used to dribble on top of one another at the shore to build towers and spires.

Betts turns left onto a dirt track that bumps and cuts over and around rocks, down to a wide flat area, and I see that after all we are not the only living beings in the night. Betts was right, all the gang's here—or almost all. Among the Fords, Plymouths, and Dodges lodged at tilted angles among the rocks, I do not see a tan Chevy.

We're on a beach. A wide creek ripples in front of us to disappear at a rapid descent beneath the bridge to our left. Fragments of moon glint off its surface. Levi-clad figures lounge on rocks or stand at water's edge. The murmur of their voices floats on the air above the water's soft rush. They turn at our approach but their greetings are subdued, not the hail-fellow-well-met gregariousness I've heard before. Their calls to Betts are warm, me they accept matter-of-factly. I'm not one of the crowd but I'm not made to feel an outsider. A few of the kids I've seen at the swimming pool, or run into at Walgreen's when I've gone with Betts for a cherry coke. We've waved and said Hi. And of course there was the July Fourth baseball game. But it's not like we've talked, it's more like I've hung out with them while *they* joked around and talked. Which has been just fine with me. It's given me time to catch on to their style and lingo. So I feel a little self-conscious but not really uncomfortable as I tag along with Betts.

Faye, Walt, and Glenn have climbed up onto a large, flat rock. They make me think of Alice on her toadstool. As Betts stands talking up to them, I hear a hissing sound and jump, wary of snakes, but no one else seems alarmed. I see Walt pass a can to Glenn and realize that what I'm hearing is the escaping gas of a punctured beer can. Walt bends again to his work and I count three six-packs lodged between him and Faye. Several cans look already emptied. I turn to Betts and find she's taken off toward the pickup. But as I start to follow, Billie pulls away from a group by the water and calls out to me.

She saunters over, beer can in hand, and confronts me, head tilted, face friendly. —So, how're you taking to life in Harden?

—Good— I try to sound as casual. —I like it.

—Not much like what you're used to, huh?

—That's why I like it.

She grins, takes a swig from her can, studies me frankly, then notes my empty hands.

—Want a beer?— nodding toward the stash of six-packs cooling in the water.

—No thanks.

—You don't drink?

I try to make it humorous. —My mother waits up for me.

—Yeah, my mom does, too. If she can stay awake that long. I've got three younger sisters, the youngest is four, and she's usually so pooped from chasing after them, she craps out by ten.

—Doesn't she worry about what time you come home?

—Sure. So I just come in when I'm supposed to, bang around, flush the toilet, then sneak out again.

—Doesn't she hear you?

Another grin. —I give it fifteen minutes, then climb out my bedroom window. Faye waits for me at the corner.

I don't know what to think of this, so I fall back on the truth. —I'd get caught.

Billie shrugs. —If I get really soused, I go home with Betts and have Mrs. Bailey call my mom and tell her I'm sleeping over.

—Betts's mother doesn't care if you get drunk?— I try to fit this information to the salt-and-pepper-haired matron in shirtwaist dresses and Naturalizer shoes.

—She's not crazy about it but she takes it in stride. She's had Betts's two older brothers to get through, great big bruisers, and, believe me, real hell-raisers. Out drinking and fighting every night. I guess in comparison, we seem pretty tame. She says she'd rather have us making fools of ourselves on her living room floor than driving around 'til we sober up. There was a bad accident out on 66 a couple of years back, a head-on between a family of tourists driving the desert at night and a carload of high school kids who'd been drinking. Eight people got killed.

I see Betts returning from the pickup, lugging a six-pack in each hand.

—Does Betts get drunk much?— I'm thinking of the long drive home.

—Are you kidding?— Billie turns and gestures toward the bulk of the approaching Betts. —Look at her. It'd take a keg to knock that out.

—Two— Betts grins and holds out her six-packs. —One for you and one for me.

—Reggie doesn't drink.

—None for you and two for me.

Betts sets her six-packs against a rock and takes out a can.

—Who's got the church key?

—Trixie. On a chain around her neck.

They laugh. Like a skate key, I think. We head for the group on the beach. I recognize Trixie, Ruthie, and Curt. The fourth figure, I'm sorry to see, is Freddy Herren. He stands back a little, watching my approach. Fine, I think, let him keep his distance. But after a few minutes, he saunters over, hands in hip pockets.

—Where's your bodyguard?

My heart lurches, I was hoping to avoid this. I lift my chin and match his tone of belligerence. —I don't need one.

—She has me— Betts fixes Freddy with a look that clearly says, And don't mess with me. I resist a desire to move behind her.

—How come Colter isn't with you this evening?

—He wasn't invited— Billie steps up and puts herself in Freddy's path, and I think I'm safe, they're going to fight my fight for me. But Freddy steps right around her and plunks himself directly in front of me.

—Oh yeah? You two break up?

—We weren't ever going together.

—That's not the story Colter's putting out.

—Then you ought to be more careful where you get your information— and I turn my back on him and remove myself to the other side of the group.

Jagged laughter suddenly cuts across the warm quiet, like a diving flock of raucous crows. We all turn.

—Walt and Glenn are telling jokes.

—Com'on.

Everyone grabs up six-packs and hurries to the foot of Faye's, Walt's, and Glenn's rock.

—You hear about the new laxative?— Glenn waits for us newcomers to settle in, fixes on Freddy. —You're always constipated, Herren, this oughta interest you. It's called Feather Lax. It'll tickle the shit out of you.

Laughter.

—Well, if Herren can't use it, I know a critter that sure can— Walt picks up the cue —There were these three colored guys, see? arguing about the meanest animal in the world. The first guy says, I tell you, man, the meanest animal in the world is the tiger. Why, the tiger's so mean that with one pounce he can knock you to the ground and rip you to shreds with his sharp teeth and claws until you're nothin' but bone and gristle.

—The second guy says, Well, the tiger's mean all right, but he ain't the meanest animal. No sir. The meanest animal in the world is the elephant. Why, the elephant's so mean that with one lift of his huge foot he can squash you flatter'n a pancake, and with one swing of his mighty trunk he can bash you against a tree 'til you're nothin' but bloody pulp.

—The third guy says, No, no, you're both wrong. The tiger's mean, and the elephant's mean, but they're not the meanest animals. No sirree, man, the meanest animal in the world is the hippogator.

—The hippogator, man? What's a hippogator?

—Why, a hippogator's a critter with the head of a hippopotamus at one end and the head of an alligator at the other.

—But, man, if he got the head of a hippopotamus at one end and the head of an alligator at the other, how the hell do he shit?

—He don't, man. And that's what makes him so goddamn mean.

Raucous laughter.

—Give him Feather Lax.

—Maybe that's what makes Herren so goddamn mean.

—He's always full of shit.

—You got two heads, Herren?

—You got a head where your ass oughta be?

—Hell no, Herren's got an ass where his head oughta be.

—You mean he's got his head up his ass.

—You're all wrong. The reason Herren's so goddamn mean is 'cause he don't get no head.

Loud, hooting laughter. Freddy looks disgusted, but he stands there and takes it. I don't understand this. And I don't understand the jokes. What, I want to know, is so funny about shit and not shitting? It seems in bad taste to me. And it seems insulting to use the word colored or to tell a joke using a phony Negro accent.

I stop listening and drift down to the beach, I want to be alone. All of a sudden I don't feel like being one of the crowd. I'm irritated when Freddy comes up beside me. I feel sorry for him but I don't respect him.

—I was watching you at the swimming pool. You're a good swimmer.

I stare at the water. —Thanks.

—You ought to join the swimming team.

—What swimming team?

—The one at the high school.

—The high school has a swimming team?

—Sure. A good one. They've won a few championships.

This interests me. Swimming and diving are my specialties. I've won a few awards myself. But I'm not about to mention this to Freddy.

—How do you get on it?

—You have to try out— He watches while I consider this. —You think you're good enough?— Again the mocking.

—I might be.

—You think so, huh? How good are you?— I don't bother to answer. —Maybe we should find out— I'm not looking at Freddy, so I'm not prepared when he swoops me up and heads with me toward the creek. I holler and kick. —So you think you're pretty good, do you?— he jeers in my face. —Let's see how good— and he tosses me out into the water.

It's cold as ice, the current is strong and swift. It takes me a minute or two of splashing and scrabbling around before I can find footing on the slippery rocks and loose sand and struggle to shore. The whole crowd has run down. Herren stands with his hands on his hips. Arms grab and pull.

—Herren, you stupid sonofabitch.

—Why'd you do a thing like that?

—She could've cracked her head.

—You all right, Reggie?

—Look at her, she's sopping.

—Anyone got a blanket?

They lead me up the beach and settle me on a rock.

—Give her a beer somebody.

—She doesn't drink.

—You asshole, Herren.

—You're just lucky she didn't get caught in the current.

Curt puts his Levi jacket around me. I sit shivering and trying to laugh above the chattering of my teeth. The group stands around me, opening fresh beers, grumbling about Freddy, who leans against the base of Faye's and Walt's abandoned boulder, glaring back defiantly.

Headlights bounce down the dirt track, come to a halt, and go out. A figure emerges from the dark and heads toward us. My heart leaps. I recognize the walk.

—Colter.

—Shit.

The group scatters, ambling around, nonchalant.

—Hey, Case.

—How goes it?

—Just get off work?

I don't know which way to go. So I sit on my rock. He moseys around, sipping on his can, exchanging quips, checking out who's there. No one mentions me. It takes a while before he becomes aware of the lone figure hunkered on a rock.

—Who's that?— mildly curious. No one says a word.

I think how stupid I must look, so I stand as he nears. He's almost on top of me before he recognizes me. I'm a shock.

—What the hell're you doing here?

—Betts brought me.

—Betts?— then he notices my condition. —What the hell happened to you?

—I fell in the water.

—You been drinking?— He looks ready to shake me.

—No.

—Herren threw her in.

—Herren did *what*?

The gang has collected in a loose circle around us. Casey turns and pushes his way back to Freddy, still stationed against his rock, though now not so confidently.

—Herren— Casey pokes a finger into his chest —you sonofabitch. Don't you ever touch Reggie again— The finger pokes. —You hear me?— Poke. —I don't ever want to see or hear of you near her— One final pointed jab —You got that, you bastard?— and he pushes back through the crowd. —Come on.

—Where're we going?

He grabs me by the arm and starts dragging me toward his car.

I pull back. —Wait! Curt's jacket— He yanks it off and throws it back toward the crowd. I call back over my shoulder —Thank you, Curt— as I stumble to keep up.

Casey shoves me in the front seat and storms around to jerk open and slam shut the trunk. —Here. Put this around you— He throws the beat-up army blanket at me. It's been shaken free of grit, but the smell of dust and tumble weed lingers. I sneeze. —Goddamn that Herren. If you catch cold . . .

He drives like a maniac, hunched over the wheel, both hands wrestling the steering. He glares straight ahead, the miles pass in silence. I stare out the window, watching the brush flare up at the side of the headlights then dim past like small desert spooks, feeling strangely self-possessed and detached.

Casey slams his fist on the steering wheel. —All right. You win— He sounds furious. I turn slowly to look at him. I wasn't aware there was a contest. —Have it your way, I won't lay a hand on you.

I have no answer for this, since it was never in question. I turn back to my window. But in my detachment I feel elation, I might even say triumph. If there had been any contest.

Another silent mile.

—So does that mean you'll be my girl?

For the second time tonight, I feel the shock of cold water. I catch my breath—I don't know where I thought this thing between us was going, what I thought I wanted out of it—and flounder around, stalling for time.

—What does that mean?

—What the hell do you think it means? Are you stupid, haven't you ever gone steady?

I decide to add lying to my growing list of crimes. —No.

He exhales heavily, but I think it sounds more out of relief than irritation. He instructs me with exaggerated patience, as if I'm an exasperating three-year-old.

—It means you won't go out with anybody but me. And you'll wear my class ring and letter sweater.

I think about Mummy. I think about all the boys in Harden I haven't met yet. I'm surprised by my sudden panic.

—I don't know— My voice sounds small and apologetic. —I'll have to think about it.

I strain toward the lights of town as if they're buoys.

SCENE 12

Maggie's newest dog is driving her crazy. Reggie can hear him the minute she steps out of the car. Maggie says he runs and barks twenty-four hours a day. Reggie rings the chimes, she hears the dog scrabbling on the polished oak floor. Maggie says his nails are scratching the tar out of it.

—Stay! Stay!— Maggie's most authoritative voice. The door swings open

—Oh!— Reggie braces herself. The setter pokes his head between Maggie's legs, panting and drooling, his tail wagging frantically behind her. —I was expecting him to come charging at me.

Maggie grabs the dog's choke chain. —No, we're making some progress.

Maggie leads the way up the hall. Jake stumbles over himself twisting to walk backwards, trying to get to Reggie.

Reggie shoves at him. —Down! Down!

—Down, Jake!— Maggie flourishes a horse's crop. —It's the only thing he understands. He thinks the rolled-up newspaper's a hilarious joke. He chews it up the minute I set it down— She's in jodhpurs, riding season's begun. —Sorry we have to use the family room. It's the only room I don't care that much about and can close off— She's put a child's barricade across the top of the short flight of stairs down to the sunken room.

Maggie's never been known for her housekeeping but the room's a particular mess: shreds of paper littered across the carpet, a strip of burlap wallpaper torn loose from the wall, teeth marks in table legs and chair arms.

—Why don't you keep him outdoors?

Maggie gives her daughter a tired look. —Come on, I'll show you— She grabs the setter by his choke chain —Heel, Jake!— and marches him out the sliding glass doors across the patio and across the lawn.

At the back of the lot Maggie's installed two metal posts between which is suspended a thick metal cable, from which hangs a horse's lunge line. A trough has been worn deep between the posts. Maggie snaps the lunge line to the dog's choke chain, takes Reggie's arm and starts her back toward the house. —Watch this.

Immediately the dog sets up a wild yelping and barking, racing back and forth on his line between the posts, digging his trench deeper.

—He'll keep it up for hours. The neighbors have complained, the police have been here twice— She goes back for the setter, who licks and gnaws her hand and arm as she unhooks him. —What am I to do?

—Give him back.

—They won't have him.

—Sell him.

—Who'd buy him?

—He has papers, hasn't he?

—Excellent ones. Serves me right. I got exactly what I asked for. The largest male in a litter of nine, sired by a field hunter, birthed by a farm bitch who'd been given fertility shots, or fed hormones, or whatever. Every time he sees a bird or squirrel, he quivers and freezes into a perfect point. It's in the genes, he's a natural.

—So sell him to a hunter.

—You know I don't believe in hunting.

—But he does.

Maggie shakes her head. —It'd be like selling my own child. I took him on in good faith, he accepted me with equal trust. I can't admit myself an inadequate mother.

They've settled on the couch, the setter happily at Maggie's feet, chewing a huge leather bone she's unearthed from beneath a pile of newspapers. She pats his pointed head and scratches a floppy ear. —I'm committed to him.

Reggie thinks of Maggie's prime reason for having Jake. —Is he ever going to settle down enough to breed?

Maggie shrugs. —Who knows. If he ever gets out of adolescence. Look at him. Six months, eighty-five pounds, a head the size and shape of a football. And he won't mature until he's a year and a half, maybe two. Can you imagine what he's going to end up like?

—Poor Erin— Reggie looks around, suddenly aware of the high-strung bitch's absence. —Where is she, anyway?

—Hiding out, shaking herself to death in contemplation of her future.

Reggie smiles grimly. —I empathize.

Maggie casts her daughter a sidelong look. —I'll fix tea.

The setter picks up his bone, plops it on Reggie's foot, and resumes scratching his teeth. Reggie watches the saliva spatter her shoe.

Maggie and her animals. Reggie's been raised with everything: parakeets, white rats, hamsters, rabbits, guinea pigs. For a while, Maggie bred and sold pedigreed cats. Then she went to a dog show. She's had a French poodle, a golden retriever, and a Norwegian elkhound. Her mission now is to produce from the union of the aristocratic over-bred Erin and the rusticated happy-go-lucky Jake the perfect Irish setter.

Maggie sets the tray on the coffee table. She's made cinnamon toast, Reggie's childhood favorite. She pours, hands Reggie her cup, then purposefully sets her own cup down. —All right. Now just what's going on?

With equal purposefulness, Reggie languorously sips her tea.

—Well, let's see. Katelyn's so thrilled with her recital triumph, she's decided to dedicate herself to becoming a professional ballerina.

Maggie gives a short laugh. —She'll soon enough change her mind about that. It's hard work.

—Like I did about acting?

Maggie lets it pass. —I'm concerned about Lindsay though. Katelyn's such star material, I don't want her overshadowed.

—Don't worry. Lindsay knows how to look out for herself. She has big plans, too. She's determined her heart's desire— Reggie fixes her mother with a pointed look. —She wants a horse.

Maggie raises her eyebrows. —Are you going to get her one?

—No. I'm leaving that honor to you. It's your fault.

Maggie lets this pass, too. For the time being. But Reggie knows she'll mull it over. Maggie knows she's the one with the stable facilities, the riding-club connections. Reggie's lost contact. She rides with her mother now no more than four times a year.

Maggie lifts her cup, sips. —And how's Howie?

—Good.

—He looked good at Abby's.

They're fencing. Thrusting, parrying, dodging.

Reggie's face goes hard. —Good and busy, doing good work, getting good evaluations. And worrying a good deal. But he's a shoo-in for the partnership.

—So what's the problem?

Reggie looks surprised. —Problem? What problem? Katelyn's happy, Lindsay's happy, Howie's happy. So what problem could there possibly be?

—You're talking to your mother, remember? I haven't seen you so tightly wound in years.

Reggie's face is proof of the words. —You're just like everyone. My kids are fine, my husband's fine, so I must be fine, too. Like there's nothing else to me.

Maggie hears the contained shrillness. —That's why I invited you.

—And you're right. There isn't. Not anymore— Reggie's mouth twists with bitterness.

—You know what I am, Maggie? What I've become? A Boston Proper manequin playing out a shop-worn role.

—We're all caught up in roles, Reggie. You think Howie isn't? Husband, father . . .

—But at least Howie has some larger purpose in life, some accomplishment he can show the world. He's a major player, a man of power, manipulating monies, corporations, and people, grappling with the law and government. And often winning. I'm strictly minor, a supporting role that's coming to look more and more like a bit part. And I feel like a loser.

—From my perspective, you have a privileged life.

—Sure. Smug, superficial, and superfluous, with little freedom and even less excitement. I look at my future and all I can see are days ahead just like the days past, a cycle of pleasant and inconsequential repeat performances. Days of insignificance— Her voice catches. —Even Katelyn and Lindsay don't need me anymore.

—Of course they do.

—No, not *me*— She's trying hard not to cry. —I'm a face and name in a long history of faces and names, most of them forgotten. If I weren't performing these roles, some other woman would serve. It's not *myself* that matters.

Maggie puts her hand on her daughter's knee. —That's not true at all, Reggie. Katie and Lindsay love you.

—And take me for granted. And why shouldn't they? They're caught up in their own busy lives. Classes, parties, dances. I'm the good mother. Just like Howie takes me for granted, as the good wife. But there's not one thing in my life *I* can take for granted— She sobs. —Not even my husband's showing up for a simple movie and dinner out— She tries to choke it back, gives up, and lets it pour out.

—Is that what started all this? Howie forgot a date?

—Not one date, Maggie. Three. Three times in six weeks— Reggie's sobs choke her throat, shake her shoulders. Maggie looks around for a kleenex, hands Reggie a linen napkin. —I've disappeared, gone up in smoke. I'm not real anymore. All I am is an image left in someone else's mind. A photo in a gold frame on Howie's desk, to be looked at, smiled at, and forgotten— Maggie pats her daughter's knee. Reggie's eyes fasten on hers, beseeching. —I'm a phony, Maggie, a two-dimensional paper doll with a two-dimensional wardrobe and two-dimensional cardboard set to parade around in— She sobs. —*I'm a goddamn Barbie doll.*

Maggie nods. —So that explains the clothes.

—I have to make a clean sweep, get rid of the tinsel and tissue.

—Not too clean, I hope. Be careful you don't throw the baby out with the bathwater.

—I'm not like you, Maggie— Reggie sniffles into her napkin.

—I never wanted you to be— She smiles. —I'd like to think of myself as an original.

—That's just it. You are. Full of your own color and light— Reggie wads the soiled napkin —I'm dull and flat— takes a breath, looks at her mother. —The only time I felt full of sunsets was in Arizona.

Maggie looks hard at her daughter, puts her hands on her thighs, nods and sighs —I was afraid of this— and stands, going to the glass doors, looking out. —Taking you to Arizona was the worst decision your father and I ever made.

—No! It was the best. It opened my life, expanded my horizons.

—You were too impressionable. We should have left you with Abby.

—And closed off all those doors? How would I have ever learned how other people live? What other possibilities there were for being a person and making a life? You would have left me with only one room.

—You were too young. You didn't know how to discriminate, to be selective. Not every door you open is marked with your name, Reggie. Not every room you enter holds *your* bed.

Reggie throws the napkin to the floor. Her voice is harsh. —So that's it then, I guess. That's what I have to learn now. How to discriminate *my* door, select my *own* bed.

—Be careful, Reggie— Maggie turns from the glass, regards her daughter thoughtfully. —Those sunsets. Were they the big sky . . . Or were they Casey?

Reggie's eyes are full of pleading. —I don't know— Her voice becomes a whisper. —That's what I have to find out.

Maggie's face is tight with grim irritation as she moves back into the room. —That boy's like a bad penny, he keeps popping up— She picks up the crumpled napkin and tosses it onto the tray with finality. —This thing has got to be put to rest.

Reggie looks up at her mother, feeling young and frightened. —I couldn't agree more.

Maggie shakes her head. —You're like this pup here. A late maturer.

Reggie smiles through her tears. —I thought you said I was an early bloomer.

—When did I say that?

—When I started menstruating at ten.

—Well maybe physically, and *maybe* intellectually. But certainly not emotionally— Maggie starts collecting the cups and saucers. —You may be intelligent, Reggie, but sometimes you're not too smart.

—Meaning what?

Maggie sets the last cup on the tray —I leave that for you to work out— picks up the tray —You're the one searching for meanings— and disappears into the kitchen.

The new books arrive, boxes and boxes. Maggie is in a frenzy to unpack them. We make a party of it, Maggie, Dorothy, and I. Maggie makes chicken salad sandwiches. Dorothy supplies sweetened iced tea, which Maggie can't abide. I bake Toll House cookies.

There are several hundred books ranging from de Angeli's *Mother Goose* to Hawthorne's *Scarlet Letter*. No reference is made as to how they've been paid for, but the shipment's been sent to our house, with the invoice in Maggie's name, and I'm wondering what fiction Dorothy's laboring under. Maggie considers it tacky to mention trust funds.

My job is to lift the books out of the boxes and carry them to the designated shelves. Their actual arranging isn't all that involved, cut-and-dried work for librarians. It's the ceremony that takes so long. Maggie knows the boxes' occupants, but for Dorothy it's like a surprise birthday, with each guest making a special announced entrance, something like Ralph Edwards's "This Is Your Life." She greets each new arrival with an exclamation of delight and a few words about the book's special merits. Maggie follows with her own reasons for including it. This digresses into discussions of illustrations and illustrators, stories and characters, authors and style. Dorothy recalls the effects of certain books on her, their impact on her life. Maggie shares kindred experiences. They reminisce. This is fascinating to me, I see them as girls. Dorothy in pinafore and ribbons weeping over the loneliness and goodness of *The Secret Garden*. Maggie in jodhpurs and hard hat ravaged by the brutality of man over gentle beast in *Black Beauty*. The girls resolved to be humane and courageous women.

—And this!— Dorothy has peeked into the box meant for the lower shelves, for the littler people, and pulled out a picture book. —I adore this book!

Maggie smiles. —That was Reggie's favorite when she was three. She could recite it cover to cover.

—Oh, read it for us, Reggie— Dorothy thrusts the book at me.

I look at the cover and feel the warmth of familiarity. I haven't thought of this book in years, but as with Maggie and Dorothy, it has associations, it brings back memories. I hear Maggie's voice, reading to me. I hear my own voice, reading to Katelyn and Lindsay. I sit down in the rocker and open the book across my knees.

—*The Biggest Bear*. By Lynd Ward.

This is easy for me. I like to read, and I like to hear my voice. I like to play with it, make the sound give added interest and feeling and heighten the words. I've been in several skits and short plays at Wexler, mostly ones we've had to write ourselves. And in English we've had to memorize and recite poems.

When I'm finished, Dorothy claps. —Bravo! Bravissimo!

I flush. Maggie is smiling bemusedly, a peculiar glint in her eye.

SCENE 13

Reggie lifts the glass, gazes through it into the fire, sips, sets it down again. It's become part of her late-night ritual, the glass or two of wine. Low flames within to fuse with low flames without. It helps her think, relaxes her, frees the images. She picks up her pen.

CHAPTER THREE

Fred Herron held open the heavy plate-glass door, then hurried to catch up beside Smokey.

"I could see that movie a hundred times." He self-consciously missed a step as she smiled up at him.

"I think I have."

Casablanca had been her idea. She thought it might stimulate him, give him ideas. They'd been to several movies together now, part of his surveillance over her, her own private body guard, though his official on-duty hours were increasingly extending into unofficial off-duty hours.

He steered her toward the curb and started to signal. "I'll get a cab."

"No. It's a beautiful evening, I'd rather walk." Fred looked uneasy, then gave over his better judgment to his desire to please her.

He offered his arm, and flushed as she took it.

"So, how's the job going?"

"Same old thing."

"You're probably the best saleslady that store's ever had."

"I wouldn't know about that. But it's good experience. I'm learning a lot."

"Still thinking about opening your own dress shop?"

Smokey looked up at him, gave his arm a little squeeze. "I'm bored with me. Let's talk about you for a change."

Fred looked flustered, and pleased. "There's really not that much to talk about."

"You mean, not much you *can* talk about."

"No, there's just not much to tell. I'm a pretty uninteresting guy."

"Oh, I wouldn't say that. Why don't you start with your childhood?" Fred grinned and flushed. "For starters, where were you born?"

Fred started talking. They walked past the bright, peopled, store-fronted streets, out of the business district, into the soft, peaceful, lawn-fronted sidewalks of the residential district. Fred kept talking. When he showed signs of running down, Smokey spurred him on with questions. By the time they reached her apartment in a modest middle-class neighborhood, Fred had told her most of his life. As they stood outside her door, he was still talking and didn't seem inclined to stop.

"Would you like to come in?"

Fred looked startled, as if suddenly recalled to who and where, and what, he was. "Oh—no—I really don't think I should." He started backing away, as if from a mortal temptation he'd barely been saved from. Smokey chuckled to herself.

"All right. I guess I'll see you Monday then. Thanks again for the movie." She took the key from her purse and fitted it to the lock. But Fred remained a few feet away, hands in pockets. "You want to check the apartment out?"

Fred looked uncomfortable. "No, no. I'm sure the boys in the van have everything under control." But he still didn't go.

Smokey considered him with a small smile. "Is there something else on your mind?"

He made his decision. "I was just wondering what you were doing Sunday."

"Sunday?" Smokey turned the lock and put the key back in her purse. "A load or two of washing, some dusting and vacuuming, a little grocery shopping."

"Would you like to go to the beach?"

Smokey's smile was wide, and tinged with humor. "Was that question serious?"

Fred grinned back. He knew how much she loved the beach, she went every chance she could. In spite of five days' work a week, she maintained her golden tan, aided by self-tanning lotion Fred couldn't know about, which she smoothed on in long, even strokes out of a tube.

"A buddy of mine in the Bureau asked me to join him and his family, and he said I could bring along a friend."

"Thank you, Fred," Smokey's voice was soft, her smile bedazzling, "for considering me more than a job." Fred's confusion was so great, Smokey almost laughed. "I'd love to go to the beach with you."

Dorothy has invited us to dinner. It's our first social engagement in Harden. Maggie has mixed feelings. She likes Dorothy and is pleased to be fixing up and going out. On the other hand, she's not sure how it's going to go as a family. Daddy isn't easily gregarious, and Mr. McElvrey is an unknown entity. I have no feelings one way or the other. As an only child, I'm used to occupying myself in a group of adults. It's only after we're in the car, on our way there, that Maggie happens to mention Dorothy's son.

—Oh, yes. Didn't I tell you about him? Dean. He's going to be a freshman at the University of Arizona. In premed.

—And he's going to be there?

—Of course.

I am now dreading this outing.

To Maggie's relief, we're the only other couple. Mr. McElvrey's the enthusiastic type, full of loud laughs, hearty handshakes, and too many grins, the type that drives Daddy into a corner. I see Maggie starting to get nervous. But Dorothy knows how to move in on her husband and settle him down, keep things calm and directed.

Dean is tall and slender, not bad looking, with wavy blond hair, vivid blue eyes, and light freckles across his nose and cheeks. He's a nice combination of his mother and father, twinkly and reserved. I see him watching the proceedings with humor and awareness. I decide I like him.

I'm surprised to find dinner parties here much like dinner parties in Boston. I don't know what I was expecting. We talk about the contrasts of life between the East and the West. Daddy's work. Mr. McElvrey's work, he's some kind of administrator with Santa Fe. Books and the library. A little time is spent on my upcoming adjustment to Harden High School, more time is spent on Dean's upcoming adjustment to college.

We adjourn to the living room. Dorothy is passing around tea and coffee, sees Dean and me just sitting there, hands in laps.

—Dean. Perhaps Reggie would like to play a game of Parcheesi.

He raises his eyebrows at me, I nod. I follow him into the study, a small, dark room lined with books. Dean unfolds a card table.

—So what would you like to play? Parcheesi or something else?

I shrug. —I don't know. What have you got?

—Name it. Checkers, Chess, Monopoly.

—How about Scrabble?

—Scrabble it is.

He's a good player, we have a good time, I learn some new words. I'm disappointed when Maggie comes to say it's time to go home.

We're standing at the door, making our good-byes. Dean makes his niceties to Maggie and Daddy, then turns to me.

—Friday's my birthday. Would you like to help me celebrate?

All the adults look at me with a smile, even Daddy. I think What is this? I think of Casey. I'm stricken. Maggie leaps in.

—Of course she would.

I manage a smile. Dean takes it as acceptance.

—Great. I'll pick you up at seven.

Reggie sips her wine. She is not writing, just staring at the fire. Sips again, sets the empty glass down, fills it from the bottle beside her. Sips.

She stands, takes the glass with her into the family room, sets the phone on her lap, dials.

—What city, please?

—Galveston.

—Yes?

—Colter. With a C. Casey.

—What street?

—I'm sorry, I don't know.

Long pause.

—I'm sorry, that number is unlisted at the party's request.

—This is an emergency.

—I'm sorry.

—Could you just give me the street?

—I'm sorry. That information is restricted.

Click.

Buzz.

CHAPTER FOUR

Sunday was a perfect day, the sky high, clear, and blue. It wasn't yet eleven but everyone was out. Like Smokey and Fred, going to the beach. Smokey glanced over at Fred as he cut his way through the heavy traffic. However mild he might be otherwise, he was an aggressive driver. She liked that.

"You look nice in your madras shirt and suntans." This was the first time she'd seen him out of a suit.

Fred flushed. It was so easy to disarm him, like spreading toast with soft butter. There wasn't much fun in it, and wouldn't have been worth the effort if the stakes weren't so high. She'd taken care to cover herself decorously in a full-skirted cotton wrap-around, to ensure the full impact of contrast when she eventually unwrapped it.

"So, who are these friends I'm going to meet?"

"A guy I went through training with and his wife and kids."

"Are they prepared for me?"

"I just told them I was bringing a friend. Casey knows about you, of course, but he just got back, he's been out of town on a case."

After years of disciplined self-control, Smokey didn't think it possible for her to react this way anymore. Her heart leapt to her throat, the air squeezed from her lungs. She turned so Fred wouldn't see the rush of blood to her face.

"Casey who?" Her voice sounded breathy. It was hard to keep it steady with the pounding in her chest.

"Colter. His wife's Glory. The kids are Denise and Lester. I thought I'd have a little fun with Case and spring you as a surprise."

"I'm not sure I like being sprung. Surprises like that can have a way of backfiring."

Smokey was thinking rapidly. She hadn't had time to prepare. Before important encounters she always planned out the scenario, scripted her lines to prompt the desired responses. She'd have to ad lib, improvise. Thank god for her background in *commedia dell'arte*.

"They might not be so happy to have me at their little party. In fact, they could be quite upset."

Fred looked concerned. "Oh, no, you don't have to worry about that. Case has a great sense of humor, and Glory'll go along with anything."

"Am I to take it then, I'm some kind of joke?"

He pulled back in hurt confusion. "That isn't what I meant at all."

"After all, if you remember correctly, I'm something of a fugitive. Do you think they'll want me around their children?"

Fred stared out the window, truly agitated now. Good, Smokey mentally nodded. Keep him off balance. He'd be easier to handle. She let him stew in his muddle for a minute, gauging out the corner of her eye his creeping self-doubt, the feeling he'd let her down; playing him like a yo-yo.

Now to pull him back in, swing him around, bolster him up again. Get him working on her side.

"I'm sorry, Fred." She leaned toward him, gently touched his arm. "I'm just nervous." He ventured a look in her direction. She let him see how remorseful she was. "No need to take it out on you."

His face was hangdog with apology. "I should have seen how hard this would be for you. I guess I didn't think it through."

"It's not your fault. I'm the one put myself in this miserable position. I want so badly to make up for my past. I want so much for your friends to accept me. I'm just afraid they won't."

Fred's smile beamed buoyant reassurance. "Sure they will. Glory won't know who you are, she'll meet you as Ann Carter. And Case'll think you're great for your courage. Just the way I do."

"Thank you." Smokey's smile was warm and brave. "I needed that." Her eyes reached to him. "I'll be all right. As long as I have you there looking out for me."

She choked on her suppressed laughter.

Fred understood the sound as emotion. His face went hard and strong, his eyes soft and protective.

For a moment, Smokey found him almost attractive. But she couldn't get fond of him. He might have to be sacrificed.

Fred stayed right beside her as they picked their way through the sand, around the sunbathing bodies. Smokey spotted Casey before Fred did. He looked just the same, only maturer, handsomer, if that was possible. Casey had been keeping a lookout, and stood to wave when he saw Fred. Fred waved back. Casey glanced at the woman by Fred's side, but in her dark wig and sun glasses, he didn't recognize Smokey at first—and then she saw that he did. Something in her walk? the way she carried her body? His face went hard, his body stiffened. Good, she thought, there's still feeling. It's only indifference I can't work with. By the time she and Fred reached him, Casey was in complete command of himself.

His wife had risen behind him. Fred introduced them.

"Glory, I'd like you to meet Ann Carter."

"Ann." Glory extended her hand, Smokey took it—but she could tell they were having the same stunned reaction. It was like looking in a full-length mirror, seeing your double, only Smokey was taller, Glory thinner with fuller breasts.

"We're so pleased to have you join us." Glory's voice dripped with thick Louisiana sugar, a true Mardi Gras queen.

Smokey smiled with equal sweetness and did her own dripping. "It's so nice of you to have me. I can't tell you how much I appreciate it." You'll never know how much, she thought with sardonic humor.

And now it was Casey's turn for introductions. Fred's smile was full of pride, and a hint of mischievousness.

"Casey, this is Ann." Smokey offered her hand, but Casey pretended not to see it.

"Ann Carter, is it?" The look he gave her was pleasant but indifferent. Then he turned his back.

Fred spread their blanket and he and Smokey spent meticulous minutes straightening and smoothing it. Smokey laid out her towel and tanning lotion, her hat and scarf, took off her sandals.

Casey kept his back to her.

"How about a beer, Fred?"

"Don't mind if I do."

"Or are you still on duty?" A nod toward Smokey.

"Nope. Today is strictly pleasure." He grinned.

Fred had removed his suntans and shirt and settled on the blanket in his bathing trunks. His skin was sickly pale, as if it had never seen the light of day. And for an FBI man he looked surprisingly out of condition, with loose little rolls of flab around his middle. Casey was deep bronze, his body even tighter and more developed than Smokey remembered, as if he worked out with weights. Glory was tanned so dark she was almost black, which Smokey found unattractive. Her pelvic bones jutted sharply against her skin above her purple bikini. And across her lower abdomen pooched a fleshy little pad, which on furtive inspection revealed shiny stretch marks, as did her over-blown breasts.

Smokey decided it was time for the unveiling. She stood and demurely turned away, undid the two buttons, and let the wrap-around drop. She pulled the dress to her front and neatly folded it, giving Casey the full benefit of her strong back and slim legs. Then turning, she knelt to put the dress in her beach bag and pick up her scarf and hat, giving him an exposure of the firm, unmarred drop of her breasts. She stood and took her time tying on scarf and arranging hat, arms raised, presenting to best advantage her high ribcage, narrow waist, and concave abdomen. Her skin was golden brown. Her bikini was silky blue, the color of her eyes. She shimmered sand and sky. She languidly stretched out on the blanket, as if unaware of the silence.

"Where are the kids?" Fred suddenly asked, looking around.

"Down by the water." Casey was scowling. "Where else?"

Glory sat up and worriedly scanned the beach. "I don't see them." She leapt to her feet. "I better check."

Fred jumped up after her. "I'll go with you."

Smokey sifted sand through her fingers and waited.

Casey finally spoke. "Well. You were a nice little bomb shell dropped down on my Sunday."

"If you were surprised, think how I must have felt. At least you knew I was in town, that you'd have to run into me sooner or later. I thought I'd never see you again."

"Too bad we couldn't have kept it that way."

"Don't worry, Casey, I have no intention of interfering with your business. I have troubles of my own."

"So I've heard. A neat little mess you've made of your life."

"I had a lot of help. But I'm trying to set it straight. It's been hard enough, please—don't make it any harder." For the first time, she looked at him. "Give me a chance."

"Unfortunately, I guess I'm going to have to." His profile was grim. "I've been assigned to your case as Fred's back up."

Again that wild racing of the heart. Smokey turned to the ocean, her face and voice impassive.

"I'm sorry, Casey."

"Not half as sorry as I am."

"Given the way you feel, what good are you going to be in helping me?"

"A question I've asked myself."

"Maybe you should have yourself removed. I assume they don't know about our history."

"I thought about it. I decided you deserve a break. The Bureau needs someone who can fathom your psychology, hold you steady, get you through the trials." For the first time, he looked at her. "And no one knows you better than I do."

She met his look, *Oh, don't be too sure, Casey.* And looked away.

Glory and Fred were returning up the sand, accompanied by a boy and girl. Now it was time to deal with the children.

SCENE 14

—What city, please?

  —Harden.

Click.

  —Harden.

  —Information, please.

  —Yes?

  —Colter. C-O-L-T-E-R. Scott.

  —One moment, please.

Reggie takes a quick sip of wine.

  —That number is 436-2417.

She tries to write it on the paper.

  —I'm sorry, operator, my pen slipped. Could you give me that number again?

  —Certainly. 436-2417.

She concentrates intently on the formation of each digit.

  —Thank you.

Harden keeps popping surprises at me. I've been to a lot of fancy places in Boston and New York, but for beauty this place has to beat them all. And it's stuck right here in the middle of town, right on First Street. I must have passed it dozens of times and never given it a second glance. I guess that's because it's attached to the railroad station and surrounded by a high wall. *La Descansada.* The Rest.

On the outside, it's a huge adobe Spanish villa, with heavy arched wooden doors, and spiraled wooden bars over the arched windows. Flower boxes of geranium grace the windows, and trellises of bougainvillea climb the walls— salmon, pink, white, yellow, ruby, purple. The roof is red Spanish tile.

Inside, it's a grand Mexican palace. Terra-cotta tiles pave the wide long halls, hand-hewn rafters support the high ceilings, from which hang huge circular iron chandeliers with real candles. The lower halves of the walls are covered with glazed ceramic tiles, in a variety of designs and colors. The rose-adobe upper walls are ornamented with copper bowls, tin masks, brass plates, peasant stitchery, woven baskets.

The furniture is oversized, of elaborately carved wood and hand-tooled cow hide, or upholstery of tapestry with tassels. Glass cases display matador outfits in silver and gold, full-skirted fiesta costumes painted with flowers outlined in sequins, multi-tiered white lace dresses and black lace mantillas. Diminutive coats of arms stand at attention beside main entrances.

There are Spanish-tile fireplaces in every room, sometimes two, small and curved in corners, or high and rectangular on long walls, with heavy iron andirons, carved wood mantles, and tall brass candlesticks. Even in summer with the temperature outside over a hundred, the rooms are cool, almost chilly, and here and there logs burn.

Dean lets me take my time. At first I exclaim over everything, then fall silent, there seems nothing left to say. I wander through smoking rooms, card rooms, music rooms, sitting rooms, reading rooms, rooms that had real functions in earlier eras. Now for the most part, they're empty. The upper two floors are the hotel, also for the most part empty. I think of the waste. The top floor is used as offices by the railroad.

When I'm finally satisfied, Dean leads me to the dining room, and again I'm left breathless. Vertical turquoise beams break the walls at regular intervals. The white stucco spaces between are painted in vibrant floral and bird designs. There are brass chandeliers, wall sconces, and candelabra. One whole wall is fireplace, the wall opposite is a bank of lace-curtained glass doors leading out to the gardens, which Dean promises to show me later. Our tablecloth and napkins are white linen with Greek key border, which here I think of as Aztec. In the center is a crystal vase of pink roses. The silverware is heavy and ornate, the china turquoise blue and gold-rimmed.

—I love this place.

—I thought you would. It used to be a Harvey House.

—You mean like the Harvey Girls?

—Fred Harvey built them a day's ride apart all along the Santa Fe line and staffed them with attractive young girls. That's how my dad's family got out here. His mother was a Harvey Girl. She came West looking for a husband.

I'm nonplussed. I've heard stories about the Harvey Girls, and this is his grandmother he's talking about? —Well evidently her trip was a success.

I know it's stupid but it's all I can think of. Women who did that sort of thing in that time of history had to be, to say the least, *adventurous*. Dean smiles as if I've been delightfully clever.

—So— he leans forward, regarding me with courtly attentiveness. —What're you going to have?— I consider the menu. I'd been expecting Mexican food, I'm disappointed, instead it's steak, chops, chicken, and fish. —I highly recommend the steak.

—I'm not much of a beef eater. I was thinking maybe the lamb chops.

—They're pretty skimpy. Unless you're not that hungry.

—That leaves chicken— I shake my head. —Maggie cooks chicken all the time.

—How about fish? The trout's good.

—It's frozen.

—The heck it is, it's fresh out of Oak Creek. The perch is from Pine Lake, the catfish from the Colorado River.

—What's catfish taste like?

Dean grimaces. —Muddy fat. Or fatty mud— I grimace back. —My dad says it can be good if you know the right way to cook it.

—I think I'll try the quail.

Maggie and Daddy are always encouraging me to try new foods. Quail's a bird, like chicken and turkey, so how can I go too far wrong?

The menu is *a la carte* or dinner. *A la carte* you order the side courses you want, on the dinner they choose them for you but it's less expensive. Maggie always orders *a la carte*, Dean orders on the dinner.

I can't eat my quail. It looks like a tiny sparrow laid out on a bier of toast. It's leg bones are the size of toothpicks. All I can think is, thank god they didn't serve the head. I try to get down my rice and peas. But every time I see the poor little fellow just lying there, his Q-Tip drumsticks sticking up, I start to cry.

Dean feels terrible, he encourages me to order something else, but I've lost my appetite. I finish my salad, and for dessert decide on vanilla ice cream with *creme de menthe*, to sooth my distressed stomach. Dean passes over half of his chocolate cake. I manage it, in honor of his birthday, and pass back half my ice cream. We don't have tea or coffee.

Dean's very solicitous. He worries about me. He helps me in and out of my chair. He orders another knife and fork when I knock mine to the floor in dismay over my quail. He escorts me to the restroom and retrieves my napkin from the floor on our return. He looks nice in his sports jacket and tie, shades of tan and blue, that match and make manly his Huck Finn freckles and eyes. He's good company, I'm comfortable with him, the conversation doesn't lag.

He takes me out to the gardens. The air hits me, warm and moist from recent sun and watering, heavy with flower fragrance and cut grass. I close my eyes, lift my nose, and breathe deeply. My eyes adjust to the moonlight and I get an idea of how extensive the gardens are, almost a full town block. There are gracefully spaced shrubs and trees—one of each kind of those indigenous, Dean tells me, like in a small arboretum—expanses of lawn, and bed after bed of flowers. Stock, marigold, snapdragon; petunia, nasturtium, verbena; zinnia, hollyhock, delphinium. And roses. Roses and roses and roses, every kind imaginable. I'm in ecstasy, light-headed from the perfume, I plan to bring Maggie and Daddy. I tell Dean about Abby and her prize-winning irises. Dean tells me about his grandfather's enormous melons. We laugh. In spite of the quail, the evening's a success. On the way to the car, Dean puts his arm around me and I let him.

At the door, we start to say good night. Maggie and Daddy aren't in the living room but they've left the porch light on. Dean puts his hands on my waist and pulls me to the side of the screen door. He bends toward me. I think, all right. He kisses me. It isn't bad. I don't stop him when he moves in for the second kiss. But this time, he really gets into it. He goes for the long count, his breathing heightens, he pulls me into him. The next thing I know, there's a tongue in my mouth. I don't push away, I'm too surprised, in a kind of abeyance. I'm thinking of Casey. Is this what he felt, this sudden intrusion, this unanticipated thrust of passion and possession without permission? I don't think I used that much tongue, just more insinuated, but it's hard to gauge.

Then I realize Dean is grinding his pelvis against mine with small moans. I shove him back. The break of our kiss is so abrupt there's a small sucking sound, like a wine cork leaving the bottle. I slam through the screen, without even bothering to say Happy Birthday, much less Thank you for the dinner.

What is this? I ask myself as I tear off my clothes and sling them around the room. Why does kissing have to be so damn complicated in Harden?

Reggie puts the bottle and glass on the desk and pulls the telephone to her. The study is dark, lit only by the streetlight falling across the desk. She puts a piece of paper on the blotter and smoothes it out. Then she dials.

—Hello.

—Mr. Colter?

—Yes.

—Oh. Mr. Colter, this is Regina Patterson, you may not remember me, I . . .

—I know who you are, Reggie.

—Oh. How are you, Mr. Colter?

—I'm all right.

—Well, Mr. Colter, I need to talk to Casey and . . .

—He isn't here.

—I can't seem to find his number and . . .

—What do you want with Casey?

—I really need to talk with him and I'd be grateful if you could give me his number.

—I can't give it to you.

—This is really important, Mr. Colter.

—Then give me your number. I'll tell Casey you called and he can get back to you if he wants.

—Is Catherine there? I'd like to say hello to Catherine.

—So would I.

—May I speak with Catherine, please?

—She's dead.

—Oh. My god. I'm sorry.

—So am I.

—How long . . . ?

—Eight years.

—My god . . . I'm so sorry, I didn't know, I would have sent flowers. Eight years? She was still young, not much older than my mother. How could that happen?

—Lung cancer.

—You must be lonely, are you there all alone?

—Have you been drinking, Reggie?

—Just a little.

—Sounds to me like a lot.

—I get lonely, Mr. Colter, I'm going through a bad time.

—I'm sorry to hear that but I can't help you.

—I need to speak to Casey.

—Casey can't help you either. He's married and has a family.

—I know that. I just want to talk to him.

—Leave Casey alone.

Click.

CHAPTER FIVE (?)

Smokey had made great headway in a short time. Little Denny and Les loved her. She'd won them over completely. They'd read books together, written stories, presented puppet shows. They called her Aunt Ann, according to southern custom. Not bad for a woman who didn't even like children.

Glory had come to accept her as almost one of the family. Smokey babysat, helped with weekend errands. She went with them to the beach or fishing, but always with Fred; Casey wasn't so threatened when Fred was around. Because Casey *was* threatened—by what he was fighting inside.

He watched Smokey with Glory and the children, he watched her with Fred, fascinated and distrusting. And she played him. She drew near, letting him feel the heat of her presence. She pulled away, letting him know the cold of her absence. He was becoming increasingly roped in. But Smokey kept him on a loose tether. It was not her sexiness *per se*; she was keeping that on a low burner—for the time being. It was the challenge. I am a worthy adversary, she whispered through her body at each encounter. This was the sex of it, the seductiveness. Casey was coming to crave her, hungering to conquer her. She fed his hunger in nips and nibbles. She whetted his appetite.

Reggie sets down her pen. That's good, I like it. She smiles, picks up her glass, sips, stares into the fire. Ponders, considers. But maybe I'm moving a little too fast, need to do a little more development between chapters four and five. Show Casey and Fred working with Smokey in their professional capacity. Get in a little more of the FBI and mob stuff.

She sips, stares into the fire. The images start to flow again. She hears them, Fred, Casey, she sees them, Smokey, Glory. Ah yes, that's it, what a good idea. She writes, pausing only for a sip from the glass, a pour from the bottle, the thoughts springing easily, the words coming freely. When she finally stops, she is spent in a euphoria of creative satisfaction. A whole new scene, a new chapter five, full of tension and revealing interaction. She's amazed. Where does it come from? She tries to read the pages, the words blur, become unintelligible squiggles, run downhill. Never mind, it's late, she's tired. Tomorrow she'll make sense of it.

Maggie's roped me in on her project. I'm story teller for her newly initiated Story Time. Saturday mornings at ten thirty, I take my place in the rocker and read to a circle of shiny-faced urchins perched cross-legged around me on Maggie's bright pillows. I love sharing with them, their eager eyes, their adoring smiles, their appreciative little noises.

—You're good!— Dorothy beams at me. —You ought to be an actress.

—God forbid— But in spite of her deprecation, Maggie's pleased with me, too.

SCENE 15

Maggie has found the horse for Lindsay. She wants Reggie to check him out.

—I don't need to check him out, Maggie. You know I trust you completely.

—Just the same, I want you to see him. I'll feel better with your approval.

So Reggie stands in front of the mirror in jodhpurs, English boots, and tweed jacket. She wants to laugh out loud. What a farce. I'm no equestrian. I'm strictly pedestrian. And not even good at that. I can't even walk my way through life.

But she shows up at the stable for Lindsay and Maggie.

—He's gorgeous, Maggie— A bay, with dark mane and tail. —A real beauty.

—Well, he's a little younger than I wanted. But this way she'll have him for years. He's quality, good blood lines, fifteen hands. He'll make a rider of her.

—She's going to go out of her mind. I can hardly wait to see her face— Reggie imagines it'll look something like Maggie's does now, full of love and light and pride. —For her birthday?

—I thought. If it's all right with you.

—I'll get her the saddle.

—And tack?

Reggie smiles. —And tack. If you'll help me fit him.

—Deal.

Maggie holds out a brush.

Reggie starts brushing automatically, admiring the ripple and sheen under her hand. The horse's coat is warm in the sun, smells of hay and dust and stale sweat. She puts her nose to him.

Maggie looks over from her brushing on the other side. —There's nothing like a horse.

—I'd forgotten how good they smell.

—Gamey.

—Sexy.

Maggie returns to her brushing. —So, how're things going?

—Okay.

—You look tired— No response. —Howie says you've been keeping late hours.

Reggie flares. —What the hell've you got going around here, some kind of spy system?— She's been swearing more lately, it feels good.

—What're you so prickly about? I just called to ask him about some stock I was considering, and in the course of politenesses I said, How's Reggie? and he said, Tired, she's been staying up late a lot. That's it. Does that make us spies?

Reggie brushes in hard short strokes, her face dark and closed off. Maggie works on the horse's mane.

—I'd rather hear about you from you, of course, but you don't seem inclined to talk to me these days. You don't answer the phone and if you do, you tell me you're too busy to talk and promptly hang up. I get the impression you're avoiding me— Again no response. —I'm not planning to spring a lecture, Reggie.

—Good.

—I just want to know how you are. You may not realize this, but I care about you.

Reggie relents. —I have a new project.

—Oh?

Reggie concentrates on her brushing. —I'm writing a book.

Maggie raises her eyebrows. —A book? What kind?

Reggie grimaces wryly. —A mystery.

Maggie grins. —A murder mystery? Where the wife bumps off the husband?

Reggie smiles in spite of herself, gives Maggie a quick look. —I guess you'd call it a romantic mystery— She's sheepish.

—God forbid.

Another smile. —Not a gothic.

—Well thank heaven for that— Maggie fusses with the horse's forelock. —I gather Howie doesn't know about this.

Reggie looks up sharply. —Why? Because otherwise he would have squealed that, too?

Maggie shrugs. —To give you credit.

—And excuse my late hours?

—You may not want to realize this either, but Howie cares about you, too— Reggie flashes a black look, resumes brushing with a vengeance. Maggie studies her earnestly. —Don't shut yourself off, Reggie. You've got to keep contact.

Reggie's control shatters with a crash. She squares off across the horse's back. —Contact, for god's sake, let me tell you about my contact. I get up in the morning, fix breakfast for Howie and the girls, throw on some clothes while they eat, drive the girls to school, rush home, clean up the dishes, check my day's schedule, dress decently, for whatever role I'm to play that day, which usually involves the momentous business of making phone calls, asking for this, setting up that. I dash to meetings, listen to silly women talk silly nonsense about silly projects. Dash back to school, pick up Lindsay and Katelyn, dash them to music, dance, swimming, riding, skating, tennis. Then dash to the store for groceries, dash back for Katelyn and Lindsay, dash home to fix dinner, dash . . .

—And then stay up half the night writing about romance and mystery.

Reggie throws her brush to the ground. —Goddamnit!

—Tell me, Reggie. How's your sex life?

Reggie glares at her mother, eyes red and hot. —I'll send you the book when it's finished.

—So— Maggie sets her brush down, picks up Reggie's. —I think we've spent enough time making friends with him. Are you ready to take him out?

Reggie's head snaps, her anger abruptly displaced by anxiety. —Me? I thought you were going to take him.

Maggie smiles with satisfaction. —I've already ridden him. I thought you'd like to see how he sits.

—I'm not that much of a judge.

—Just around the ring a few times.

—I'll take your word.

—Get me that pad over there, will you?

Reggie gets the pad, settles it on the horse's back. Maggie throws the saddle over, tightens and buckles the girth. Reggie awkwardly attempts to help.

—I haven't been on a horse in months.

—Don't let him know that— Reggie mounts, starts the horse toward the ring. —He's proud and spirited. He's got to respect you, know you're worthy.

—I know that!

—Don't let him get the upper hand.

While Maggie watches at the railing, Reggie walks the horse around the ring a few times, getting the feel of him, getting the feel of herself on him, feeling them as a unit. The horse is tense with pent-up energy; this is one of his first Spring rides after months wintering in the stable. He wants to pull out, stretch his legs, release power. She can feel him straining, testing and gauging. He arches his neck, jerks his head, trying to take the bit. She pulls his head down, a rein in each hand, and holds him back until he accepts her authority. Gradually she picks up pace, keeping control, then cues him into a slow trot. He makes the transition smoothly, obediently. Gently posting, knees gripping, she slackens rein, bit by bit giving him his head, allowing him freedom within her constraints.

They've moved into a fast trot, when she slips her right stirrup. —Shit!— The horse knows immediately; his rider has become unsettled, lost command. She hears Maggie yelling but she can't make out the words. Already the horse is picking up speed, in a moment he'll break into a canter. Then she'll really be in trouble. In automatic reflex, mind racing too fast to monitor, she shifts her weight to her left stirrup, throws her right leg behind her, grasps the horse's mane, slips her left stirrup, and drops to the ground. Unbelievably, she's upright. She takes a hard tug to the body, braces against it, looks at her hand. Even more unbelievably, she's still holding the reins, the horse jittering at the other end.

Maggie's at her side.

—Did you see me, Maggie? A moving dismount, I made a perfect moving dismount.

—An unnecessary moving dismount. How many times have I told you, keep your heels down.

—I never made a moving dismount in my life— Reggie smiles archly. —I guess for some of us, some things just come naturally.

Maggie's eyeing her daughter knowingly: Reggie's face is white but there's life back in it. —Like falling off horses? Next time, you'll land on your butt, your head if you're less lucky.

Reggie starts forward, leading the horse.

—Where do you think you're going?

—Back to the stables.

—Oh no you don't— Maggie puts her hand on the horse's chest, stops him. —Get back on this horse.

—I've had enough riding for one day.

—Get back on this horse— Reggie's face has gone white again. —You've got to show him his rider has enough guts to get back on and ride him in. I'm not going to have you disgrace a good horse.

Reggie takes a deep breath, she hadn't realized how shaky her legs were, and mounts.

Maggie walks on ahead. —I'll tell Murphy you're coming in.

It's a slow, calm return. The horse, as well as Reggie, seems pleased. Reggie's smiling as she hands over the reins. —He's a beautiful horse, Murphy. We'll take him.

Maggie puts her hands on her hips —Who's this We?

Reggie circles an arm around her mother's shoulders —Maggie'll take him— and kisses her cheek.

—What was that for?

Reggie looks into her mother's eyes with her own knowing smile. —Satisfied?

The station wagons are side by side. Maggie stops by her door, calls across —Wanna come by for a cup of tea?

Reggie looks at her watch. —I don't think so.

—All right then, how about a drink?

—Now you're talking.

CHAPTER SIX (?)

Smokey watched Glory lock the car, cross the parking lot, and disappear with a shopping cart into the A&P. Then she picked up a spiral-bound notebook and recorded: Tuesday, March 19, 9:30 A.M. Grocery shopping, A&P.

When Glory reappeared, Smokey studied the cart a moment, picked up the book again, and made an addition to her entry: 45 minutes, 5 bags.

It was her newest game, she'd come up with it New Year's Eve, and she was delighting in it—no, glorying. She laughed at her little pun.

She'd spent a lot of time with Glory these past several months; she understood the strategy of joining the enemy's camp. But she hadn't really paid her that much attention or given her that much thought. She'd had to learn her as a personality, of course, to win her friendship and trust. But that hadn't been any great challenge requiring any keen cleverness. Glory was basically a pleasant, not-overly-bright, unquestioning type who was more or less happy to just go along—making Casey's job as male authority and Smokey's as female infiltrator that much easier. Smokey hadn't explored Glory beyond surfaces, hadn't felt the need or interest, and hadn't cared—until New Year's Eve.

They'd gone to a large party with a bunch of boys from the Bureau, Smokey as Ann Carter, Fred's steady date; her identity was still carefully guarded. She'd dressed as a twenties' flapper in beaded-and-fringed red satin, red-bowed headache band, and red satin pumps. She'd been a knockout, and she knew it. She'd seen it in every man's face, including Casey's, the moment she'd entered the room.

But Casey had refused to dance with her. She'd tried to coax, then kid, then shame him into it, playfully acting the rejected female. But he'd consistently dodged her until finally Glory had stepped in. "Honestly, Casey, I don't know what's the matter with you, you're acting like a bashful schoolboy," and she'd pushed him out onto the dance floor. But Casey still wouldn't look at Smokey or talk to her, and halfway through the number he'd dropped her hand and stalked off in the other direction.

He'd spent the rest of the evening showing off Glory, laughing and dancing with her, holding her close, parading her around to other tables, bragging about what a beauty she was, what a great wife and mother—rather too loudly, Smokey thought. She'd felt pure hatred. She remembered when she'd been the woman in tow.

Suddenly Smokey had focused on Glory. Who was this woman Casey had married? What made him love her, choose her over other women? What was the secret quality that made her special? Know thine enemy: the thought had come unbidden. And she'd hit on it. She'd study Glory like a bug under glass. She knew all about surveillance thanks to Artie—and to her stint with the FBI.

By the time the party was over, Smokey had the outlines of her game plan. She'd need lots of time, free time, unobserved. She'd have to get rid of Fred.

It took her two weeks to set things up. She went through phone books, wrote down names, addresses, numbers. She collected and memorized maps. She bought a voice-activated tape recorder and a supply of tapes, notebooks, and pens. She recovered from secret storage two suitcases that had been shipped ahead of her to Galveston from Miami. She scripted every beat and comma of her plot. Then she made an appointment with Casey.

"What do you want?" He regarded her from behind the desk with cold arrogance. He didn't ask her to sit down. "You said it was important. It better be."

"I want a vacation, Casey."

"I can't let you leave town."

"I'm not asking to. I just need time off. I've quit work."

Casey lowered his chin in surprise. "How do you propose to get by? Go on dole with the Bureau?"

"I've set some money aside. Enough to last a few months."

"Okay. So take a vacation."

"How can I, with your hounds constantly breathing down my neck. I can't take anymore of this, Casey. I've had it. I feel eyes on me and hear footsteps behind me everywhere I go. I see figures in every shadow. I'm afraid to turn the corner. You've made me a hunted woman."

"You did that to yourself. You knew the terms when we made our contract."

"Okay. Then I want out."

"Not quite that fast. And not that easy."

"I don't see why not. I'll just refuse to cooperate."

"Consider the alternative."

"Look, Casey, what's the reason for all this? I can't take a pee without your van recording it. Is my urinary tract some sort of threat to the country? It's ridiculous. And a crashing bore. And totally unnecessary. The heat's off. You said so yourself.

That's why you've been making such great progress in gathering evidence and building your cases. They think I'm dead, blown to bits with Artie. They've relaxed back to form, business as usual. So why not the same for me?"

"What do you want?"

"I want to feel free space, I want to breathe free air, I want to come and go without tipping my hat to your van or asking Fred's permission. I want to live like a normal person."

"You'll never be normal, Smokey."

"All right, then ordinary."

"You'll never be that either."

"Leave your bugs in place, I don't care about them. Leave the taps on the phone. Just call your dogs off. Or at least keep them at bay."

Casey tapped the desk with his pencil, doodled lines on a paper. "Would you check in every hour?"

"Every three."

"I'd have to know where you are every minute."

"I'll call if I have the least suspicion. If you don't trust me by now, forget it."

"You could wind up dead."

"I'm dying as it is. Jail couldn't be worse."

Casey laid down the pencil. "I'll check with the higher ups."

"Fuck the higher ups. You can do this for me and you know it, Casey."

"What about Fred?"

"Fuck Fred, too. Better yet, you fuck him." Smokey saw the suppressed smile, the hooded twinkle. "Let word get around he's become too involved with me. He's lost his objectivity. He's become a security risk, a risk to my security. As backup, you'll automatically be moved into his place."

Casey jabbed thoughtfully at the paper with his pencil tip. Smokey stood. She knew her man—and her timing.

She stopped at the door, turned, smiled, "Best yet, fuck you," and made her exit.

She had her way.

And now she had Glory.

She put the car in gear and pulled out behind Glory's white Olds, keeping a discreet distance. Today Smokey was a stringy brunette in a Rent-a-Wreck. Yesterday she'd been a bouffant blonde in a Lincoln Continental. Tomorrow she could be a frizzy redhead in a Cheap Heap, or a dishwater drab in a Nissan compact. She knew two dozen car rentals, had a dozen wigs, and a dozen driver's licenses, part of her legacy from Artie. She was having the time of her life, every day a new disguise, a new role, a new person.

Not like her quarry. Glory, she'd learned, was a creature of habit. No spontaneity, no imagination, no surprises. Every day the same routine. Monday, washing and errands. Tuesday, groceries and ironing. Wednesday, bowling and yard work. Thursday, house cleaning. Friday, hairdresser, manicure, and shopping. Always the same places at the same times, making Smokey's list of addresses short, making Glory easy to keep track of.

She was home week days by three for the children. Weekends she left free for Casey. No close girlfriends—unless you could count the bowling team. All the better for Smokey. It left a vacuum primed for her to rush into, although as yet she hadn't taken advantage of it. She hadn't felt ready to share girlish confidences, too dangerous. The less information Glory had about her the better, too easy to get caught in lies. And she hadn't been sure she wanted to be privy to Glory's intimacies. She didn't want to hear about her frolics in bed. Safer to learn about her objectively from observation: these were the patterns of Glory's life, this was how her mind worked, this was how she functioned for Casey.

Now Smokey could anticipate and imitate Glory's rhythms and beats like a metronome. This was the way Glory moved her body, this was the way she turned her head, this was the way she laughed. This was what made her laugh. Smokey could walk down the street as Glory.

Smokey found this more than satisfying or entertaining. She sensed it was necessary. Somehow it would pay off.

SCENE 16

Reggie looks in the mirror. Another costume. White pleated tennis skirt with sleeveless top, white tennis shoes, white socks. She picks up the white tennis hat with visor, slaps it on, and laughs.

She should feel guilty. She hasn't seen Cissy for months, hasn't talked with her for weeks. She hasn't felt like it, hasn't had the energy, hasn't had the interest. But Cissy's her best friend, since twelve. Reggie knows Cissy's missed their get-togethers, she's feeling slighted, confused, hurt. She knows something's wrong and there's nothing Reggie can explain to help her understand. So she's agreed to a game of tennis. All right. Reggie picks up the racket, does a little dance. I'm practiced in gamesmanship. Swing, lob, slam. Let's get on with the game.

Cissy's almost pathetically happy to see Reggie, like being reunited with a feared-lost, barely-returned-from-the-jaws-of-death friend. Her guileless face, full of smiles and concern, scans Reggie's throughout her opening barrage of over-bright chatter. Reggie knows she should be touched by this display of anxious affection but instead it embarrasses her. She can't meet it. The thought of having to respond for two hours, smiling, without hurting her friend, exhausts her. Out of reluctance to keep this engagement in the first place, she's arrived late, fortunately making it necessary to abbreviate greetings.

Cissy's a tennis buff, plays year round, takes in all the tournaments, follows the stars. She won't waste a minute of court time. She looks great—young, happy, athletic—in her white cotton shorts, white Lacoste shirt with crocodile on the pocket, white canvas Top-Sider sneakers, and white sweat band. Her thin arms and legs and fine-boned face are deeply tanned, her straight straw-blonde hair sunstreaked, from her recent stay at the family place in St. Barth's. She bounds agilely back and forth, Reggie feels pale and lumbering as she struggles to keep up.

Cissy wins the first two sets easily and takes position for the third. Reggie lowers her racket and stumbles to the net.

—I give up.

—What? You can't. We haven't finished the match yet.

—I'm not much of an adversary.

Cissy looks puzzled. —Don't you mean opponent?

—What'd I say?

—Adversary.

Reggie grins. That damn Smokey. —Whatever, I'm just not up to it.

—All you need is a little practice. Come on, we still have court time. We'll volley.

Reggie takes her place in backcourt. It's easier than arguing. But as she raises her racket, she's distracted by a flash of white to the corner of her eye. She glances over to see Smokey reclining at courtside, one foot up on the bench, dressed, Reggie is amused to note, in an identical tennis outfit, complete to visored cap. Smokey casts her a sly grin and cool pass of the hand. Cissy's serve goes whizzing by. Reggie scowls at Smokey, grabs her racket with both hands, and faces Cissy with determination. Cissy's delighted.

—There. You see? All you needed was practice. You got much better there toward the end. Now, how about some lunch?

Reggie feigns distress. —Oh, I can't possibly, Cissy. I have a list a mile long.

Cissy's crestfallen. —But we haven't even talked. Can't you spare at least a half hour, time for one cool drink?

Reggie feels a wrench of shame, looks at her watch. —Well . . . okay. But just a half hour.

Cissy smiles gratefully, gives Reggie's waist a quick squeeze.

Up close, Reggie can see the fine dry lines prematurely crinkling Cissy's face, and thinks she ought to warn her about the dangers of sun but decides this isn't the time. Cissy's two inches shorter than Reggie and almost a year younger, of an easy-going, uncomplicated nature. Reggie has always been the leader. But today Cissy's assumed a maternal protectiveness Reggie doesn't want to upstage. She has to admit her game has improved and also her spirits. But she doesn't think she can credit Cissy for the latter. As they head for the clubhouse, she senses behind her a bobby-socked, white-pleated presence.

Cissy chooses a table for four on the terrace, white wrought iron with glass top, overlooking the golf course. They set their bags on the extra chairs. Cissy smooths her napkin across her lap and smiles expectantly at Reggie, but like a well-brought-up child bides her time until they've placed their orders.

—Iced tea. With powdered sugar and mint, lemon on the side— Cissy's special concoction.

The waiter stands with poised pad and pained look while Reggie ponders. She suddenly looks over and sees Smokey in the chair next to her, sipping limey liquid from a beaded cocktail glass. She smiles. Why not?

—I'll have a vodka gimlet— and is mischievously pleased to see Cissy hurriedly hide her surprise.

—Now— The waiter moves out of earshot, Cissy leans forward, eyes intent on Reggie, trying to read her friend. Reggie braces herself. —What in the world's been going on with you?

Reggie takes a deep breath and considers. She'd like to confide, she trusts Cissy's sincerity. She thinks how good it would be to unburden. But to raise questions about her life would be to question Cissy's. To express doubts about herself would be to cast doubt on Cissy. They and their lives are so much alike. How can she tell Cissy about Casey? Cissy knows about him, of course, though there were things Reggie never confided even to Cissy. But to confess that the past has caught up with her, that she thinks she still loves him? Cissy adores Howie, sees Reggie as a model wife and mother. She'd nod sympathetically, she'd make the appropriate noises, she'd try to understand. But she wouldn't. Inside, she'd be confused and disappointed, perhaps disapproving. And Reggie can't afford to add the weight of Cissy's judgments to her own.

—I don't know, Cissy. It's hard to explain— Reggie looks away, struggling to find a way to gently evade, to lightly dismiss her reclusive behavior and reticence, and finds herself saved. —Oh oh—

—What?

—Don't look now but I think we're about to be invaded.

Cissy checks her impulse to look over her shoulder. —Who?

—Corkie and Muffy. Coming up from the ninth hole.

—Have they seen us?— The stocky redhead and diminutive brunette wave vigorously and quicken their pace. Reggie waves back and nods. Cissy frowns. —Damn.

Corkie and Muffy are delighted at the chance encounter.

—My god. Will you look who's here.

—We were just talking about you.

—Where've you been hiding yourself?

—We haven't seen you at League for months.

—How's Howie? Still talking about the boat he's going to build?

—How's Katelyn?

—How's Lindsay?

—We saw Lindsay in the horse show last week.

—She was terrific.

—She must have a wall of ribbons by now.

—We looked for you . . .

—We thought maybe you'd been sick . . .

—But Tammy said she saw you at Katelyn's recital and you looked fine.

—She said Katelyn was a sensation.

—Like her Mummy— Muffy smiles coyly. —A born performer.

Reggie looks them directly in the eye, smiles back and answers with as few words as possible. It becomes awkward. They switch to Cissy.

—As always, you're looking great, Cissy.

—How was St. Barth's?

—I hear the weather was terrific.

—It rained in Bermuda the whole time.

—You must have got in scads of tennis.

—I hope you're being careful about too much sun.

—Chip says Buddy's a cinch to take the men's singles.

—Prissy had a skin cancer removed.

—You two going out for mixed doubles again?

Cissy is still miffed over the intrusion on her privacy with Reggie, but her gentle nature is sensitive to social disharmonies and she feels the need to ease the tension and take the heat off Reggie. Good breeding wins out and she gamely holds up her end. How's Win? How's Big Chip? How's Chipper doing at St. Lawrence?

Little Chip, it turns out, has recently sustained an injury in soccer.

—But— Corkie is proud to announce —he's still playing with his knee tightly bound.

Muffy's disgusted. —As far as I'm concerned, this whole physical competition thing is macho, and dangerous not only to the soma but to the psyche— Muffy's only child Tyler is a delicate blue-eyed blond of six.

Corkie shrugs. —Competitive sports build sound minds in sound bodies and prepare young men for real life.

Muffy laughs, head back, with no mirth. —You sound just like a slogan. Personally, I deplore this dog-eat-dog world that makes such preparation necessary.

Cissy collects her courage. —I don't see it as so dog-eat-dog—The very idea hurts. —Jamie and Bif have developed real character playing soccer. It's taught them sportsmanship, what it means to work as a member of a team.

—Right!— Corkie smacks fist to palm. —It makes gentlemen out of 'em.

Reggie follows the exchanges as she'd watch a ping-pong match, head switching back and forth from speaker to speaker. Smokey lounges in her wrought-iron chair, legs crossed, the picture of boredom, raised foot impatiently jiggling.

Reggie finds herself suddenly intrigued by Muffy. She wouldn't have suspected Muffy knew such words as soma and psyche and deplore. All through school, she'd been the ultimate helpless female, too petite and fragile to lift a finger. A Dresden Guinevere who clung and leaned without actually doing so and made a protective Lancelot out of every fumbling lad she turned her pitiable gaze upon. Yet she'd managed to make it into Sweet Briar and managed to become fluent enough in French to spend her junior year in Paris, polishing, she'd demurely made a point of, her Gallic heredity. And on her return, she'd managed to snare Winthrop Rogers, III, tall blond scion of a long line of embarrassingly wealthy bankers.

Leaning against Cissy's chair in her patchwork madras pants and child-size kiltie golf shoes, Muffy still looks the ingenue. But now she commands a full-time staff of eight plus part-time help in running a twenty-room Tudor mansion and hostessing elegant parties, famous for their fine wines and gourmet food, planned and prepared under Muffy's personal direction by her French chef in a kitchen modeled after some fancy Parisian restaurant. Invitations to her affairs are highly sought and, Reggie suddenly realizes, she and Howie haven't been included recently. She'll have to start entertaining again, she grudgingly acknowledges, or they'll be completely dropped.

Muffy is heatedly expounding her argument that cooperation can be fostered through sensitivity to others and awareness of mutual needs and benefits, when she is interrupted by the noisy entrance of three other women—Sally, Barbara, and Junie—who have arrived for luncheon before bridge club and spotted the foursome on the terrace.

Reggie seizes the opportunity to make her getaway, but before she can fully gain flight, she's netted and pinned. The litany of exclamations, questions, and explanations starts over again. How's Win? How's Howie? How's Buddy? How's Chip? Reggie slowly sinks back into her chair.

Betts ambles up, in blue dirndl skirt and white gym shirt, not the Betts of high school, an older Betts. She looks the group over, benignly assessing, then with a soft grunt spreads herself into the chair on the other side of Reggie, opposite Smokey.

—Muffy, I ran into your mother at J. Press the other day. She looked absolutely tremendous.

—I swear I don't know how you find time to shop, Junie. If it weren't for my L. L. Bean and Tog Shop catalogs, my whole family'd go naked.

Reggie assesses Sally, tries to visualize the five-foot-ten of her naked. Ponderous breasts, swollen belly, beefy thighs, broad buttocks. Dimpled cellulite and striations of stretch marks.

—Oh, I know what you mean.

—And how about Eddie Bauer?

—Have you tried Lands' End?

—I get it over with two weeks a year in New York, one trip in spring, one in fall.

—Plus you get in all those Broadway shows and French restaurants.

—Smart planning.

—In between I don't buy so much as a pair of socks.

—But how do you manage all the special things that come up?

—And all the things that get torn or lost?

Reggie eyes the women warily. They look like they're readying to move in and usurp Smokey and Betts. But they're too well-mannered to displace the tennis gear without being invited. Besides, there aren't enough chairs. Reggie slumps sideways, elbow on chair arm, chin on hand, knees crossed, foot jiggling. When the waiter passes, she signals for another gimlet.

—I hate to shop. Such a waste of good time.

—Not to mention boring.

—You ought to try catalogs.

—Are you kidding? With this figure, I have to try on everything.

—So you just order several styles in several sizes then send back what you don't want.

—And spend a fortune in shipping and handling?

—What about gas and parking?

—Not to mention the cost of your time.

—You know that dress I had on Saturday night at the symphony? I got that out of Talbots.

Reggie stops mid-sip, raises her brows above the glass rim. Smokey catches her eye and smirks. Obviously she caught the dress, too.

Reggie'd spotted Barbara and Sally at the symphony, they'd tried to wave her down, but she'd ducked behind Howie and Maggie. She's known these women more or less on and off all her life. Their paths have crisscrossed through schools, extracurricular activities, recreational interests, social and cultural functions, family and friends, clubs, charities, causes. But these last few months she's dreaded the thought of talking with any of them.

—What'd you think of Leonard Bernstein?

—I've seen him before.

—So what?

—So he's all right. With something modern like Copeland or his own compositions.

—His Mahler is good.

—I thought he was fantastic, he really pulled the music out of that orchestra. I've never heard them give so much.

—I know. It felt like they really loved playing for him.

—He's so dynamic and expressive.

—Too much bouncing around and emoting.

—I think of him as just vigorous.

—But he's also a sensitive and exacting musician.

—I think he's just plain sexy.

—That's what I mean. It distracts from the music.

—When isn't music meant to be sensuous?

—When it's Bach.

—You have to give the guy credit. He's done a lot to educate children and the public.

—So's Arthur Fiedler and the Boston Pops.

—But not the same . . .

—Speaking of educating children and the public, Reggie, I heard your mother last week at the censorship meeting.

Reggie tries to look alert and fix Barbara with interest, but the gimlets have wooed her into devil-may-care insouciance.

—Oh? How was she?

Barbara hesitates, but Junie has no reluctance.

—She was great! She stood right up there and gave them a piece of her mind. And I agree with her completely. I can't believe the people of this country much less the parents of this community are actually considering banning books.

—I think it's a little more complicated than that— Barbara's nostrils pinch and rise.

Sally's lips tighten. —It's the information, the ideas.

Barbara nods. —The *language*— Sally and Barbara always stand on the same side.

—So you want to keep your children from thinking and speaking?

—Why must you always take the simplistic view, Junie?

Junie flushes.

So does Cissy, at the slight to her friend. Timidity vaporizes, indignation overrides. —Those books they're talking about aren't trash, Muffy, they're *literature*.

—Yeah— Corkie jumps in. —We're not speaking here of *Penthouse* and *Hustler*.

It's a hot issue. Even Smokey perks up, at the prospect of a good fight.

Betts pulls a pack of Marlboros out of her shirt pocket, shakes one loose, pokes it in her mouth, offers the pack to Smokey. They light up, Smokey practices French inhaling, Betts grins and blows a smoke ring.

—It's the *quality* of the language and ideas.

—Look, Barb, it's all part of the human experience.

—Not *my* experience.

—Come on now, Sally. I seem to remember you going through *Lady Chatterley's Lover* with a fine-toothed comb, reading aloud all the dirty parts.

Reggie and Cissy, and Betts and Smokey, are happy to see Sally have the good grace to take *her* turn at a blush.

—Those weren't dirty, Corkie, they were *beautiful*.

—Pardon. I stand corrected, Junie.

Sally's not giving up, blush withstanding. —I'm not saying I'm in favor of censorship. I'm just saying there need to be controls.

Barbara hangs in there with her. —It's not the books children read that concern us. It's the age at which they read them.

—Exactly. *Portnoy's Complaint* is not appropriate reading for a six-year-old.

Cissy joins the match. —*Portnoy's Complaint* isn't in the elementary libraries, Muffy, or even the high schools'.

—But it's in the public libraries.

—So what are you suggesting, Barb? That we march on them, too?

—Come on, Corkie.

Betts loses interest, becomes captivated by the golfers, heaves up out of her chair, and wanders off toward the green. Reggie realizes this might well be Betts's first exposure to live golf, golf in the *rough*, so to speak . . . she grins . . . as opposed to golf televised. She looks over at Smokey, wishing she could share her little pun. Harden had no country club, no golf course, no pudgy businessmen in polyester pants chasing their tiny balls around with their dried up sticks, as Casey phrased it.

—Listen, if Little Chip could have been capable of reading *Portnoy's Complaint* at age six, I would have been proud as hell.

—But he wouldn't have understood a word.

—So what's the harm in his reading?

—Yeah, what're you guys so afraid of?

—It would have been emotionally and psychologically too advanced.

—It would have put disturbing thoughts in his mind.

—Unhealthy.

—Certain things shouldn't be made available to a child until he's ready.

—If a kid's curious enough to take a book off the shelf and read it, he's ready.

—I completely disagree.

—Look, it's out there, Barb. Sooner or later your kids are gonna run into it. So you might as well teach them to deal with it before somebody else does.

Something about Barbara standing there in her prim navy-blue shirt-dress and cable-knit cardigan looking so self-righteous triggers Reggie.

—Right. If you want to keep your kids from the world, don't lock up the books, lock up the kids.

The women are as startled at Reggie's sudden interjection as Reggie, who immediately rues the renewed attention her impetuousness has cost her. Muffy's mouth purses slyly.

—Considering your strong feelings, Reggie, I'm surprised you weren't at the meeting.

Reggie reassumes her air of nonchalance.

—Why? I know my mother's feelings about banning Judy Blume from high school bookshelves and jailing Huckleberry Finn and Holden Caldwell behind locked cupboards.

—I'd have thought you'd want to be there to give her support.

The shot finds its mark. The idea that her mother might have needed support had never occurred to Reggie. Ever. Not in all the years Maggie has pushed and pulled, primed and preened Reggie into fitting the mold of these women. She smiles superiorly, grasping at straws, hoping to flail Muffy with them.

—Why should Maggie need my support? She has the American Constitution.

—Bravo!— Corkie punches her fist in the air.

Cissy smiles triumphantly.

Junie claps vigorously.

Barbara's face sours with disgust.

Sally casts Barbara a look of shared scorn, turns away.

Smokey stares at Reggie, then splutters out in silent hilarity.

Reggie pushes to her feet, resisting a sheepish, vindictive grin —And on that note— steps on her own toes, steadies herself on the chair —I shall take my leave— She collects her gear, kisses Cissy's cheek —I'll call— faces the group —It's been great seeing you all— lifts her encased racket in a parting salute, and strolls across the terrace toward the parking lot, concentrating on presenting a composed, indifferent back, and walking a straight line.

SCENE 17

Reggie doesn't feel good. The gimlets have worn off and so has the false bravado. She feels young, alone, more than a little inadequate. She feels foolish. What's wrong with her? Maybe a nap would help. She glances at the dashboard clock, but there isn't time, she stayed too long. She has to pick up the girls, take Lindsay to riding, Katelyn to piano, pick up Lindsay, home for a quick dinner, then ballet tonight. Her head's closing in on itself, shrinking, squeezing her brain, she's straining to see the road through a tunnel . . .

—My god, I don't believe those women— Reggie starts, looks in the rear-view mirror. Smokey is slouched in the right corner of the backseat, staring out the window. —That Muffy is a real bitch.

Reggie smiles. It takes one to know one.

—I thought Corkie was nice— Reggie starts again, shifts her eyes. Betts is holding down the other half of the backseat.

Smokey scoffs. —That dyke?

Betts looks confused. Reggie isn't sure if Betts even knows the word. In Harden, there was no such thing as homosexuality, at least not that anyone acknowledged. No gay jokes, no swishing parodies of queens, no guys calling other guys faggots. The first Reggie had heard of such a thing was at Wexler, when an attachable dildo had reputedly been found under the front seat of Miss Lewis's car at the auto body shop. Who at Wexler had a contact in the auto body business intimate enough to confide such information had never been questioned. But thereafter everyone wanted Miss Lewis for English.

Betts is looking protective. —She's married. She even has a kid.

Smokey sniffs. —That doesn't prove a thing. All you have to do is look at her to know she's a first-class female jock.

—That's not the same thing at all. Maybe her husband's a male jock.

Reggie decides to step in, in defense of Betts *and* Corkie. —He is.

Smokey's derisive. —What kind? A crotch-grabbing football fairy?

—A golfer. Complete with beer belly and baggy khakis. He competes in the pro circuit.

—Must be a real prince. I'm surprised she snagged even him.

Reggie grins. —So was everyone else. Except Corkie.

—Did you see that skirt she had on?

Betts looks over, smiling innocently. —I thought it was cute.

—Baby blue and pink roses? With scallops around the hem? On *her*?

—Pink's a good color for redheads.

—Electric pink? in a knit shirt? with an alligator on the breast? Pardon, on her *chest*? Come on, Betts, you know you wouldn't be caught dead . . .

—I'm not a redhead.

—*I* wouldn't be caught dead.

—Why not? Pink's a good color for bleached blondes, too.

Smokey gives Betts a withering look. Betts chuckles.

So does Reggie. —Well, I'll grant you, Corkie may be no flashy showgirl— Reggie's eyes meet Smokey's in the mirror, Smokey withers *her* —but I'll tell you one thing for sure. Of all the married couples I know, she and Chip are the closest and happiest. You always see them standing together, side-by-side, his arm over her shoulder . . .

—Sure. Like locker-room buddies. And when she hops in bed, he probably slaps her on the butt and says, Hunker down, baby, get over that ball, let's get this pigskin in play.

Betts's smile is satisfied. —So, you see? They probably have a great sex life.

Smokey flicks her a look of disdain. —Preppies don't have sex lives. Right, Reggie?

Betts lifts her chin. —Oh yeah? Then how'd Sally get so pregnant?

Reggie giggles. —She isn't. At least not currently. That's her Laura Ashley smocked look.

Smokey's aghast. —You mean she actually dresses on purpose to look like an overstuffed chintz chair?

Betts guffaws, the description's too apt.

Reggie's feeling world's better, her headache's gone, her vision's cleared. She's enjoying Smokey's trashing. She wouldn't dream of venting like this with anyone. She wonders did they do it at Wexler. Gossiping certainly, plenty of that, but not bare-clawed cat slapping. Did they do it in Harden? Not Betts probably, Betts always found the good word. Billie would have said it to your face. Ruthie was too bland. Janie too proper. But maybe Faye and Trixie. She can't remember. She'd like to ask Betts, but Smokey's off again on her tirade.

—But of the whole lot that Barbara's the absolute worst. She's such a tight-assed prig, you'd think she came straight off the Mayflower.

Reggie snickers. —She did. And she has a sampler on her wall to prove it. Of her family tree growing out of Plymouth Rock.

Betts snuffs. —She's the type wouldn't say the word if she was shoved in it— Evidently even Betts can't spare Barbara a good word.

—But she sure as hell smells it— Smokey grabs her nostrils, talks nasally. —You can tell by the high white pinch of her nose. She's standing in a pile of it, no doubt *hers*.

Betts corrects. —Has to be Sally's. Dogs don't smell their own.

Reggie's laughing so hard she has to take her foot off the accelerator. —No. Barbara gets that look from sitting too long in a lab, seeing life as a cell under a microscope.

Smokey frowns. —I don't get it.

—She's a biochemist. Out of Mt. Holyoke. She wanted to be a doctor. Instead she married one.

—She would have made a great doctor. *Witch* doctor.

—Better yet, witch.

—How about witch hunter?

—Can't you just see her, standing on Plymouth Rock in a black dress and hat, clutching the holy book, skirts whipping around her, glaring down the wind?

—Like some Puritan minister's daughter.

—No, that's Junie.

Betts looks surprised. —Junie? Junie's a preacher's kid?

Reggie nods. —She directs the choir. Of one of the area's largest Congregationals. She lives to sing. She's a member of the Boston Choral Society. The highlight of her year is the Radcliffe alumnae choir's annual benefit recital.

Smokey's look is meanly calculated. —But she isn't married, is she? She wasn't wearing a ring.

—No. As a matter of fact, she isn't— Reggie's sorry to admit it.

Smokey smiles, vindictively vindicated. —You see? That's what religion'll do to you. Scar you for life.

Betts has become subdued. Pensive and withdrawn. —You don't have to be hooked on religion, Smokey, to be single and enjoy singing in a choir.

Reggie looks up, catches the look on Betts's face—and suddenly sees her, blue-robed, in the front row of the Harden Methodist choir singing her heart out, her face the reflection of heaven.

—You would've made a great choir director, Betts.

Betts shakes her head. —I'd rather have done something in medicine.

—You would've made a great nurse.

—Why not doctor?

But Smokey isn't the least interested in Betts's lost ambitions. She still has venom to spit.

—And that's exactly what's wrong with your prissy country-club pals back there, Reggie. They don't know how to let their hair down much less their pants and have a good time.

Reggie bristles, she feels included. —That's not quite true. Sally was a real party girl at Smith, one of the wildest.

Smokey hoots. —That cow?

—She wasn't such a cow then. In fact, she was quite pretty.

—My god. What happened?

Reggie grows silent, concentrates on the traffic. When she speaks her voice is subdued, pensive and withdrawn, like Betts's. —The same thing that happened to all of us. She married. And started a family. Four kids in eleven years.

A louder whoop. —And from the size of those udders, she's still got the last one to tit.

Reggie isn't enjoying Smokey anymore. She's finding her crude and offensive.

—He's almost two.

—That's what I mean. She's probably a La Leche nut or some other mother's-milk cult.

Betts has also had her fill.

—Come off it, will you, Smokey? You haven't had a decent word to say the last twenty minutes.

—What's decent to say?

Betts turns, penetrates Smokey with a look. —How come those women got to you so much?

Smokey stares back, then wrenches away with a flounce, over into her corner, looking for all the world—with her visor knocked cockeyed—like a rebuked, petulant child.

Reggie imagines young Smokey—skinny, long-legged, knob-kneed, dark-haired and tan-skinned, possibly naturally so—scuffing through the dusty outskirts of Harden. Her grandmother was rumored to have come from Mexican Town. Her father was a known drunk. No one remembered her mother. Their house was one of the shanties near Indian Town. Where did she learn to sing and dance? It must have been a natural talent, developed by desperation. Dreams and desperation. Reggie feels compassion for her, and a certain admiration.

—It's all right, they get to me, too, Smokey. I know they can seem like complete pains in the ass sometimes. I'd be the first to admit it. But they're not so bad really. Not once you get to know them— Smokey continues to stare sullenly out the window. —Really. In fact, at times they can be pretty good fun. You just have to get a few drinks in them.

But Smokey refuses to be mollified. Betts decides to lend a hand. She forces a laugh. —Come on. You don't mean to tell me those women actually drink?

Reggie sends her a grateful look. —Sure. Preppies love to party.

—Even old Barb?

—As long as you offer her good sherry— Betts snorts. —You won't believe this but underneath that severe facade Miss Puritan has the perfect body. You ought to see her in a bathing suit— Reggie considers. —In fact, maybe that's why she works so hard to disguise it. Everyone's afraid to handle dynamite.

—Ha!— Finally a rise out of Smokey. —Including the poor sap who married her. I never saw a woman so in need of a good fuck.

Betts looks heavenward, shakes her head.

Reggie's eyes twinkle. —He's a gynecologist.

—Proving what?

Betts sees it coming, starts a slow smile.

—He knows his ins and outs and its equipment.

The joke passes right over Smokey's head. —Big deal. So they drink. A glass or two of wine. I still say there's not a one of 'em could ever loosen up enough to actually let herself get drunk.

—Well, maybe not like they used to. But there was a time . . .

Reggie's getting images: Chip bellowing his Tarzan yell, diving headfirst off the ski-lodge roof into the surrounding snow drift, buried up to his boots. Tip and Wally hauling him up with ropes. Cissy and Buddy in chiffon and black tie, jumping into the Harvard fountain, splashing passers-by, dragging in shrieking silk-beruffled Muffy. Sally in doused shredded T-shirt clinging to her braless buxom body, holding up a flimsy minuscule Frederick's of Hollywood teddy, her Best Decorated T-Shirt prize. Dicky and Skip mooning out Skip's Volvo windows, one on each side, Bunny at the wheel careening them through the night, their bare white backsides shocking light into dour by-standing matron faces . . .

Reggie's smile grows distant, her look softens. —We used to party all the time, every weekend, all kinds of crazy parties. Beach parties where we roasted hotdogs and marshmallows, and sucked straws stuck in watermelons filled with rum, and went skinny dipping at midnight to try to sober up. Ski parties, where we drank hot toddies and buttered rums around a Swedish fireplace and sang bawdy songs with a guitar until the management kicked us out. Or tropical-night parties, where the men dressed in Hawaiian shirts and white pants, and the women in brilliant halter dresses with flowers behind their ears, and we drank mai-tais and piña coladas and danced and sang to ukuleles.

Reggie pauses. —We even had costumed Halloween parties where we bobbed for apples in tubs of beer and played musical chairs, spin the bottle, and pin the tail on the donkey.

She's sinking deeper.

—Then there were all the sorority and fraternity bashes, and football weekends. Homecoming was the biggest. Parents would arrive in droves, in plaid wool, with woodies crammed with food and booze. We'd form a circle in some field near the stadium, like a wagon train, and hold these great pregame tailgate picnics . . .

She's seeing Maggie and Arthur, pouring out glasses of thermosed whiskey sours and Bloody Marys, passing around plates of ham and cheese sandwiches and stuffed eggs, laughing, toasting, joking. She'd forgotten how young they were, how happy together, how much in love. Her eyes mist.

—But my favorites were the garden parties. They were held under a huge tent, southern style. The men came in seersucker suits, the women in yards of voile, long gloves, and wide hats dripping with ribbons and fake flowers. We'd sip planter's punch and mint juleps and play croquet on the lawn, then in the evening dance to a corny band . . . she drifts. She's seeing another couple. —That's how I met Howie . . .

She sinks into reverie, so deep she's not aware of her thoughts or even that she's thinking. She's brought back by a sudden realization of absolute silence.

She glances quickly in the mirror and is relieved to see Smokey and Betts still there, but not necessarily with her. They're lost in their own thoughts, staring at the passing affluent residences.

—I'm sorry, I got rambling.

—Not at all— Smokey has removed her cap and is once again the haughty showgirl. —Hearing about rich kids' partying habits was fascinating— Reggie doesn't blame her for the sarcasm.

Smokey turns back to the window, her face carved in ice, her voice hard against the glass. —That's why I left that lousy town. No place to go, nothing to do, and no imagination.

Reggie's filled with remorse. She struggles to undo her thoughtlessness, smiles brightly. —What do you mean? We had all kinds of fun things to do in Harden, all kinds of great places to go— She knows she's being falsely cheerful but she can't stop it.

Smokey casts her a resentful glare. —Name one.

Betts suddenly stirs. —The bowling alley.

Reggie grins and raises her eyes to Betts in the mirror. It's a private joke. Reggie'd been grounded for a week when Maggie found out she'd been bowling.

Smokey's face twists. —Yeah, and the pool hall.

—And I wouldn't say we were all that short on imagination and daring. Would you, Betts? What about that time we loaded the punch with vodka?

Betts grunts with amused remembrance. —And all the goody-goodies got high?

—And old maid Beamish dragged Coach Wilson out onto the dance floor?

—What?— Smokey's pulled away from the window. —In Harden?

—The Junior Prom.

—You spiked the punch?

—Reggie did. Two bowlfuls. Before the faculty got wise.

Reggie demures. —It was Billie's idea really.

—Who? Billie Franks?— Even Smokey knows Billie.

—And Billie and Trixie poured it in.

—Yeah. But Reggie engineered it. She snuck the bottles in and hid them, then gave the sign when the coast was clear.

—And you didn't get caught?

—They suspected Billie and Trixie, they were always up to something, but never our Miss Preppy.

Reggie's chin goes up. —I wasn't a preppy then.

—Like hell you weren't— Reggie stiffens. —And you wanna talk about wild parties, I'll bet you never had one in Boston that brought the sheriff out.

Reggie smiles in spite of her offended self-image. —My god— She shakes her head.

—What a night.

—We even made the *Harden Times.*

—But no names. We were all juveniles.

—Yeah but the whole town knew anyway.

—What? What did you do?— Smokey's bouncing in her seat, the child again, avid with curiosity.

—It was football season— Reggie blinks. —The second or third game.

—The third.

She's squinting it's so bright. She thinks it's headlights. But it's still afternoon

She looks up, the stadium lights are blazing, she can't see the sky for the glare. The bleachers are crammed, kids running up and down, spilling cokes, screaming; hometowners pushing in, crawling over legs, standing up waving, bawling out bets. Cars stream in, headlights competing, overflowing the parking lot into side streets. Residents flag them with cardboard signs marked fifty cents, one dollar nearer the high school, direct them into driveways, onto lawns. The visitors' side swells with the opposition's bussed-in band and cheering section, raucous students, other out-of-towners, and late-arriving locals.

The Harden band marches on, blue and maroon and shiny brass, Trixie leading them in short pleated skirt and tall feathered hat, white boots prancing, tasseled baton marking time. They boom, toot, tinkle, and blare across the field into their seats in the stands. All eyes fix on the large white circle held upright by two male cheerleaders between the northern goal posts. The pom-pom girls wait on tiptoe in short twirly waist-nipped gores of maroon and blue, pom-poms raised. Suddenly trumpet fanfare, the boosters rise, the bass drum pounds, the snares beat a tattoo. Billie crashes through the paper circle, executes a triple cartwheel, comes up arms high. The crowd goes wild, yells, screams, whistles, claps, stomps the wooden boards. The Harden Mustangs follow through the hoop one at a time, announced over the loud speaker. The air reverberates, the bleachers quake. From the opposite side, boos, jeers, and hisses, bringing forth from the poorly placed supporters name calling, shoving, and cup throwing. The beginnings of a promising night.

Reggie cranes to see around the jumping girls and waving color cards. Casey is third out, right behind Les. She catches her breath, her heart races, she can feel the heat prickling her face. He looks so beautiful, so young and strong, so masculine in his white home uniform, maroon and blue stripes up the sides of his tights, blue H and bucking maroon mustang across his chest. He's carrying his helmet. His number is eleven.

SCENE 18

Reggie smiles through the windshield, sighs. —I'll never forget those games. Football's never seemed so exciting, not even in college.

Betts looks knowing. —That's because you had a boyfriend on the team.

Smokey pulls alert. —You went with a football player?

Reggie's cheeks grow warm, she smiles. —In college he became a star quarterback. That night was his breakthrough, his first important game. He scored three touchdowns. Ran in two and caught the third. That's why I was so late getting to the party.

Betts snorts. —Oh sure.

Smokey sniggers.

Reggie prickles righteously. —We were just talking. He was excited and happy, he wanted to explain the game.

—So you were necking. Who gives a damn. I want to hear about the sheriff.

Betts waits for Reggie.

—You tell it, Betts, you're the better storyteller.

Betts settles back, expands into memory.

—We'd decided to have a slumber party. The Franks were out of town visiting Billie's grandmother, so we had the perfect opportunity.

—No chaperones? Did your folks know?

—We somehow forgot to tell them.

—Hoo hoo . . .

—The game was over around ten. Billie was cheerleader, Janie and Ruthie were pom-pom girls, Trixie was majorette, so they had to stay 'til the end. But Faye and I had the beer and sleeping bags in the pickup so we left early to set things up. Anyway, we'd already started partying.

Reggie makes a sound in her throat. —And believe me, when the rest of them got there, they worked fast to catch up.

Betts nods, chuckling. —Faye had brought a bottle and we were doing boilermakers. We got stomping drunk.

—I arrived around midnight, and you can't imagine the mess I walked in on. There were bodies all over the place. The floor was covered with sleeping bags, twisted bedrolls, discarded clothing, spilled ash trays, crushed tortilla chip bags, empty cans in every corner. The air reeked of beer, cigarette smoke, and sour sweetness.

—Yuck.

—Trixie was sitting in the middle of her bedroll crying.

—Why?

—Who knows.

—Who cared.

—Ruthie was passed out on her sleeping bag, her hair and pillow filled with vomit.

—Double yuck.

—Janie was standing over her going, Uck, uck, she makes me sick, sticking her finger up her throat.

—Trying to make herself vomit?

Betts looks disgusted. —Sometimes Janie could be a real horse's ass.

Reggie twitches her shoulders. —I guess she wanted attention.

—But no one was giving a damn.

—About anyone, including Ruthie.

—My god. What'd you do?

—I'd never been in a situation like that. I didn't know what to do.

Betts sits up with a sharp bark. —Like hell you didn't. I'll tell you what she did. She started hollering.

Betts is laughing, her cheeks round, her eyes squinted. —Faye was sitting cross-legged in a chair, smoking and drinking, watching the goings-on like it's a movie, singing dirty songs to herself. Reggie started hollering, at the top of her lungs. I thought Faye was going to jump out of her skin— Betts stops to chuckle. —I was putting cans in a sack, trying to pick up a little . . .

—But not going near poor Ruthie, if I remember.

—No. She was a little more than I wanted to take on at the time— She grins. —Reggie roared up on me, grabbed the sack out of my hand, gave me a shove toward the kitchen, and yelled, Get a bucket of water! Then she turned on Janie, Stop that this very minute! Next on her list was Trixie. She strode over, jerked her up by one arm, gave her a shake, and yelled, Get a hold of yourself. You're not helping one bit! We've got to clean this place up! Scared hell out of Trixie, I can tell you, sobered her right up.

Reggie's mouth pinches with disdain. —She was only play acting, trying to work herself up.

—Meanwhile Janie's back to retching. Faye sees this as her big chance. She leaps out of her chair, over a few sleeping bags, over Ruthie, grabs Janie's hair, and gives her a smart slap. Reggie told you to stop that! Then for good measure gives her a second slap.

Reggie's shaking her head. —Faye always hated Janie.

—Now Janie's crying . . .

—Trixie starts wawling again . . .

—Ruthie's moaning . . .

—This is the moment Billie chooses to return from the bathroom.

—I see her coming and try to head her off, but Reggie gets to her first. What's the matter with you? she yells, marching right up. This is your house. Don't you care about it? Don't you care about your parents? Don't you care about your friends? Billie just looks at her. Sure. Then do something. What? Get towels, get washcloths. Okay. Billie shrugs, heads for the linen closet. I decide it's time to go for the bucket of water.

Betts's chest is jiggling in silent mirth. —And she was the youngest in the whole damn crowd.

Smokey regards Reggie with reserved admiration. —Also the only one sober.

—I didn't remember half of what I did. Betts had to tell me afterwards.

—Anyway, she got us all shaped up— Betts lapses into bemused amused silence.

Smokey waits. —And that's it? The end? No, it can't be. The sheriff. Where does the sheriff come in?

Reggie's grim. —After the boys arrived.

—Boys? You mean you had boys there?

Betts pulls back to the story, no longer smiling. —There weren't supposed to be any. We knew they'd bring trouble. But somebody must have let it out. Probably Walt. He helped us get the beer— She sighs, heavily. —Anyway, around two o'clock, here they come.

—It was a nightmare.

—They'd been drinking for hours, three carloads of rowdy drunks. They wanted to come in. We refused. They milled around, opening beer cans, calling out, threatening to break in. We were worried about the neighbors. So finally we agreed to come out for a minute if they'd agree to go away.

—And the girls actually did— Reggie's still disbelieving. —They went out, in pajamas and shorty nightgowns.

—No!

—We'd just about talked the boys into leaving when two sheriff's cars drive up, one at each end of the street.

—A few of the girls were in backseats drinking, one couple was in the bushes.

—Shit.

Betts nods. —That's just about what we did. We had to take some pretty tough talking to, a couple of guys spent the rest of the night in jail, a few girls got punished, and the town gossiped about us for months— She gives a little shrug —But that was the worst of it— and looks out the window.

—You were lucky.

—Yeah— Betts turns back. —If it hadn't been for Reggie, who knows what the deputies might have found.

Reggie's throat swells with a sweet lump.

—God. What'd your mother do, Reggie? She must have gone wild.

Reggie swallows, the sweet lump turned sour. —I lied— It's hard to admit even now. —I covered my fanny.

Betts is watching carefully. —You see, Reggie didn't stay to finish the night.

—You left? You got out of there? How?— Smokey looks aghast. —You weren't stupid enough to call your mother?

Reggie shakes her head. —No. I called Casey.

—Casey?— Smokey's voice has suddenly gone sharp. —Casey who?

—Casey Colter. My boyfriend.

—Casey Colter was your boyfriend?

Betts's smile is mischievous. She'd been waiting for this.

—Yeah. He was the football star.

Smokey's eyes narrow. —I see. . . .

Reggie senses something. —Why? Did you know him?

Smokey considers Reggie. —He graduated before I entered high school, but yeah. I knew him. A little.

Betts rolls her eyes, looks back out the window.

—Go on, Reggie. I'm dying to hear the rest of this— Something in Smokey's tone makes Reggie uneasy. She resumes cautiously, trying to feel out the problem.

—Well, the sheriff and boys were gone. The house was in order. Ruthie was cleaned up and sleeping. The other girls were more or less sobered and in the mood to party again . . .

—*Again?*

Betts turns away from the window. —Sure. Why not? Just part of the evening's fun.

Reggie scowls. —Maybe for you, but not for me— She returns to Smokey's eyes impatiently fixed on her in the mirror. —I knew I shouldn't stay there, but I was afraid to go home. So I called Casey, told him what had happened, and he came and got me.

—Brave cavalier. To the rescue— Smokey's smile glints like an edged blade. Reggie hesitates. Smokey prods. —So?

—He took me to his house, and in the morning Catherine, his mother . . .

—Yes. I know Catherine— Curt, sharp.

By now Reggie's acutely aware of danger. She finishes in a hurry. —She called my mother and my mother came and took me home.

Smokey's studying Reggie narrowly. —There's got to be more to it than that. Why did you stay the night? Why, in the morning, didn't *Casey* take you home?

Reggie's trying to figure how to answer with as few words and as little information as possible.

—We were afraid my mother'd get angry. Catherine wanted to talk to her.

—About what?

—I wasn't sure. I just knew she was trying to help me.

They face each other across the table, Catherine's eyes soft with concern, Maggie's tight with worry. They're both expecting the worst.

What's going on around here, had been Maggie's first words as she entered the door. Sit down, let's talk, had been Catherine's as she led the way to the kitchen. And to my surprise Maggie sat. It's the first time they've met.

—Would you like coffee?

—No. Thank you.

Catherine pours two mugs anyway, and sets out a plate of doughnuts. Maggie waits.

Catherine lights a cigarette, exhales. Maggie turns her face from the smoke.

—Reggie ran into a little trouble last night.

—She was supposed to be at a slumber party.

—She was. But things got a little out of hand. There was beer, and some of the girls had too much.

I sneak a look and see the quick hard set of Maggie's jaw. She turns to me in my wooden chair at the end of the table. I sit head down, hands in lap, trying to look as contrite as I am. I'm expecting the worst, too. She's going to tell me I can't run around with Betts and the girls anymore. I can't go out with Casey.

—You should have come home, Reggie. You should have called— Her eyes are angry.

—I wanted to.

—Then why didn't you?

I stare at my hands.

—She was afraid.

Maggie's head jerks up.

Casey's leaning against the wall behind me, arms crossed, eye-to-eye with Maggie, ready to do battle. I'm grateful, and embarrassed. I feel reduced: small and scared. I don't want him to see me like this.

—Be quiet, Casey.

Catherine's tone is mild but he hears the steel in it. He clamps his jaw but its stern set is a match for Maggie's.

Catherine's eyes issue a final warning then shift back to Maggie.

—Nothing that bad went on really, just typical high-spirited teenage foolishness. But you're going to hear about it, and it's going to sound worse than it was.

—I'd like to get the story from Reggie.

I collect my courage, try to look my most sincere and sound my most convincing. I take a breath and rush into it.

—Well, after the game, I went out for a hamburger and coke with Casey, so I got to Billie's house later than the other girls. And when I got there, they'd all been drinking.

—What about her parents? Weren't her parents there?

I can't look her in the face. —They'd been called out of town. I guess Billie's grandmother got sick.

—Did you know this beforehand?

I force myself to meet her eyes. —It was sort of spur of the moment. A kind of last minute thing.

—And you stayed there anyway? You didn't come home that very minute? You didn't call?

Catherine steps in. —One of the girls was sick. Reggie wanted to take care of her.

—Is that true?— Eyes on me, hard and penetrating.

Casey steps from the wall. —My mother doesn't lie.

Maggie blinks.

—The place was a mess, Mummy, they needed help. And I was the only one could do anything. So I stayed and cleaned up.

—And then you *still* didn't come home— I can feel Catherine and Casey containing themselves.

Maggie measures our silence, takes a sip from her mug, sets it down.

—What were you afraid of? Your father and I aren't that unreasonable.

I inhale. —I was afraid for the other girls. I didn't want you to see them like that. I was afraid if I called, you'd insist on coming in, and then you'd never let me see them again. They're my friends, Mummy, I like them, and I don't want you to think badly of them— Exhale.

Catherine sits strongly. —I don't want you to either, Mrs. Patterson. They're nice girls, every last one of them. I know them all. The Baileys are one of Harden's oldest families, they helped pioneer this town. They don't come any finer than Betts. She's into every school activity you'd care to think of and volunteers at the hospital. Billie Franks is a three-year letterman in track and softball and one of the best cheerleaders we've had. Janie Smithson's an honor student and this year's representative to Girls' State. Trixie Kelly's . . .

Maggie has her hand up, shaking her head. —No, no, it's not the girls.

—They're not wild, believe me. They were just experimenting, just . . .

—I know, I know. Teenagers will be teenagers. They party in Boston, too, Mrs. Colter. That's not what bothers me. It's Reggie's role in all this.

I lift my head. —I was afraid you'd call their mothers and get them in trouble.

Catherine squeezes my leg under the table, meets Maggie's eyes directly. —She considered her friends before herself. If she were mine, I'd be pretty proud of her.

Maggie's eyes flutter and lower. —Well, that may be taking it a bit far, but . . . She pushes back her chair, rises. —You think you're ready to go home *now*, Reggie?

I obediently stand. Casey picks up my overnight case. The sleeping bag is his. Catherine follows us out to the car. I see Denny peeking from her mom's bedroom window. She'd been told to stay out of sight. I waggle my fingers, she waves.

Casey hands me into the car, sets my bag in the backseat. Maggie hesitates by the car door, fiddles with her keys.

—Thank you— It's hard for her but she includes Casey in her glance. Catherine nods. Casey stares at the dry grass.

We drive away in silence. I finally gather my courage and risk the leap, trying to make light.

—Whew! I can hardly wait to get out of these clothes and into a hot shower.

Maggie scowls. —You smell like a cigarette factory— A harmless enough mother-type complaint. But her eyes are creased and shadowed. She catches me sneaking a look at her. —You're only fifteen, Reggie— Her voice is bereft, like I'm going out on the street.

—I don't smoke, Mummy.

—Promise me one thing. You won't drive with anyone who's been drinking. Her look is so tired and crushed, I'd promise her anything.

—And did she?

—What?

—Help you?

—Who?

—Catherine.

Reggie brings herself back to the present, rapidly sorts through her mental file to relocate her place in the conversation.

—Yes. She didn't say a lot but what she did say mattered. Maggie didn't come right out and admit it, but I think she liked Catherine.

—And why not? Catherine was a likable person.

Reggie has her receivers fine-tuned, but Smokey's comment seems innocent enough.

Betts agrees. —If it hadn't been for Catherine, Reggie's parents probably would have been a lot harder on her.

Reggie nods. —I still had more to go through when they found out about the boys and the sheriff. But by then it was anticlimactic.

Betts stares out the window, her face thoughtful.

—You know, every time I think about that night, I wonder what would have happened if you'd gotten to the party when the rest of us did.

The idea surprises Reggie. —I don't know. It probably would have turned out the same.

—Yeah, probably. Probably for the rest of us— She considers Reggie's eyes in the mirror. —But for you it might have been a different story.

The stately gray and white buildings of Wexler loom into view.

Yes . . . Reggie swings up the wide circular drive . . . *For me it might have been a different story.*

Flutterings and whisperings. Shifting shadows.

Katelyn and Lindsay wait on the curb.

The backseat is empty.

SCENE 19

Reggie stands at the window watching the rain. A spring downpour, dark, heavy, monotonous. No roiling clouds, no lashing winds, no deafening thunder or blinding lightning. No dramatics. Just a steady obliterating sheet of water. It's been building for two days, two dulling gray days of increasing oppression. People will be glad it's finally come to a head enough to do something. A relief in the barometric pressure, they'll say. Good for the crops. Good for the reservoirs. Good for dispositions. But not good for Reggie.

One whole day to herself. No kids, no errands, no appointments. No schedules to keep, no expectations to meet. Nothing to do. And no place to go.

It's not entirely the rain's fault. She has no car, it's in the shop for its checkup. Howie's doing chauffeuring, bringing home pizza, she doesn't even have to cook. The irony. She has to give up her wheels to get a few free hours. Mobility for autonomy. Space for time.

She watches the drops bead on the mullioned panes, gather, flow as rivulets, hit a transom, collect, surmount the obstacle and flow on.

She used to love the rain, in Arizona. It had so many temperaments, came in so many guises. She'd seen tender spring rain, the color of young willows, like the time they'd visited the Sonoran Desert, between Phoenix and Tucson. It had been Easter break, they'd watched from their motel balcony. The sky had gradually veiled over, a high gray light suffused with pale yellow. The shower never reached them, but they could hear and smell it. A soft hushed patter sweeping across sand, releasing stored sun in moist redolent waves. It made Reggie's mouth water, literally. She'd wanted to eat sand.

Next day they drove into it. The desert it seemed had come to life overnight. They stood on a high sand dune, gazing across miles and miles of color.

Splashes of Mexican goldpoppy. Patches of purple owl clover and lavender sand verbena. Streaks of blue lupine. Strokes of white primrose. Splotches of pink and peach globemallow. Dashes of scarlet penstemon and dabs of flaming paintbrush.

The fragrance was narcotic.

They couldn't speak. Didn't want to. Finally Maggie shook her head. —I heard about this sort of thing. I didn't believe it. I still don't.

It was like being in the middle of a Van Gogh painting.

She'd seen it rain with the sun shining. The Devil's smiling they'd say. She'd never understood the expression. Why not God or the angels? She'd seen it rain on one side of the street, shine on the other. She'd seen a single white cloud float in, sprinkle a few drops, and drift off, like a lost lamb.

She'd seen cloudbursts that would put this one to shame, day after day, the whole month of July. She'd wake, the sky would be high, clear, and blue, the sun intense, the heat overbearing, temperatures rising to well over a hundred. By noon, clouds would start rolling in, she never knew from where, they'd just miraculously arrive, from all directions it seemed, though she knew this couldn't be true. They'd pile up, great cumulonimbus cotton puffs with dark undersides getting darker by the minute as they compressed together, crowding tighter, pushing higher, the only way left to go. Until the accumulated weight of their pent-up burden became too much and they broke under it. The clouds burst. The sky split.

Great quantities of water were dumped, three to six inches in an hour, too fast for the sand to absorb. It rolled off the desert into deep arroyos in flash floods that carried before them everything caught in their path, including sheep and deer. It crossed the outskirts of town, joined with runoff from roofs and sidewalks, and rushed down streets, between curbs built high expressly for this reason. Children donned bathing suits to splash and dunk in the red rivers, coming up coated with red silt that had to be hosed off by their mothers before they were fit to reenter the house.

If there was lightning, which there usually was, families took to their automobiles and the highway, in the belief that this was the only safe place to be, a moving car somehow being grounded. Casey had instructed her: stay on high ground, out of the swimming pool, away from open fields and tall lone structures. She'd seen trees split, sheds burnt, heard of cattle struck dead.

But even with Casey's instructions, and a week or two of rains to her experience, she'd not been prepared for her first full-scale electrical storm. Neither had Maggie or Daddy.

Maggie'd been fretting around the living room, dragging her finger across surfaces, fussing over the film of fine red dust.

—Look at these venetian blinds, Artie— She pulls at the blinds. —Artie?—

Daddy looks up absently, he's studying for the next Hopi dance —I wouldn't worry about it— and returns to his book. Maggie hasn't heard him.

—Artie! Take a look at this sky.

Daddy's torn, he doesn't want to leave his book, but he recognizes Maggie's urgency. He closes the book on his finger, reluctantly pulls out of his chair. —My god—

—Have you ever seen anything like that?

By now, I'm at the front screen. The sky is black, churning with turbulence, like molten lava in a slow heavy boil. Nothing cotton puff about these clouds.

We go out on the sidewalk to get a better view and perhaps spot a neighbor, and watch with horrified fascination as the sky becomes increasingly ominous. I think of a huge snake, coiling in on itself, gathering venom, collecting momentum to strike. The wind has risen to a steady insistent force, blowing the hair straight back from our faces.

Maggie grabs at Daddy. —What is it, Artie?

—I think you're getting ready to be treated to your first real thunder storm.

—What were those we've been having?

—Pikers.

—What do we do?

—Go back in the house for starters.

Suddenly the wind hits in dead earnest, whipping trees, grabbing and banging screens, shaking blinds, propelling in more grit.

—Close the doors, Reggie! And latch the screens. Artie, get the windows!

We race around, securing the hatches. It's our custom to turn off the air conditioner and open every window when the rain clouds cool the air, to get a cross current and clear the house. Maggie's a fresh air addict.

We're standing in the middle of the dark living room listening to the wind thrashing around the house, when the lightning and thunder begin. It's a ways off still, but we can tell this is not going to be like anything we've been through before.

—Quick, get under a door frame, Reggie. The hall, no, your bedroom. Daddy and I'll take our bedroom!

—That's for earthquakes and tornadoes, Mag.

—Then what do we do? Think of something!

Daddy vacillates, so I take the initiative.

—Get in the car and drive.

—What?

—That's what Casey says we're supposed to do.

—That's the silliest thing I ever heard.

—He says the car's grounded.

Daddy considers. —I think that's only if you attach a chain.

Maggie grabs. —Do we have a chain? It doesn't matter, let's get in the car anyway. It can't hurt and it's better than staying here like sitting pigeons.

—Clay pigeons. Sitting ducks— Daddy thinks it's funny.

But the lightning's advancing, Maggie's beside herself, she's almost screaming. —Who cares. I'm not a hunter. And you're no physicist either.

Daddy hurries us into the car.

Out on the highway, we get a clear view of just how major the storm front is. It encompasses the entire sky from horizon to horizon. The clouds have been absorbed in a blanket of black. We need headlights.

—Which way do we go?

—Out of town— Maggie has no question, she clearly blames Harden. She doesn't care about direction.

I'm surprised not to see more cars. I soon understand the reason.

The wind hits gale force. Daddy struggles to steer with both hands, body hunched toward the window. —I think this was a big mistake.

Maggie's jaw clenches with determination. —Keep going.

—If it gets much worse, I'm not sure I can keep the car on the road.

—What do you propose?

—Turning back.

—We'll never make it.

The first drops slap the windshield, fat and lazy, laughing at us. At that moment, I see a familiar place, bright lights. Sanctuary.

—Pull in there.

—But that's *Dairy Queen*— Maggie clearly thinks I've lost my senses.

Daddy swings a sharp left.

Maggie grabs the door rest. —Look out for the sand!

Daddy parks on the small strip of asphalt.

The personnel of Dairy Queen are having their own troubles. Two waitresses and one cook are wrestling with the juke box, which has been wrenched from its chain and sent hurtling across the parking lot. They don't give us a glance as we scurry past into florescent shelter.

Just in the nick of time. The onslaught is torrential. We huddle in the booth, wordless, getting back from the blackened window only our wide-eyed reflections.

The lightning is directly from Zeus's hand, god-sized shafts that rip open the sky, from Olympus to earth, and slash a dark afterimage across the retina. The thunder that follows is shattering, giant crashes that smash the air, shake the building, and rattle the windows. We cover our ears, Maggie starts counting. One thousand one, one thousand two, ten miles away supposedly for every second.

The wind abates, the juke box is hauled in, in time we get coffee. The bolts of lightning splinter into a network of jagged streaks gridding the sky, or diffuse into flashes of sheet lightning. The thunder becomes a series of cracklings and rumblings that gradually move off into the distance.

By five o'clock it's over.

Blow by next time, the waitresses joke, as we make our thank-you's and good-byes.

On the drive home, we see a car drowned in the underpass, overturned lawn furniture, broken tree limbs, scattered leaves and branches. The cottonwood trees have been stripped of their cottonballs, tomorrow the kids will have cottonball fights.

By seven, it's hard to believe it happened, except for the cool clean calm and the left over scudding clouds.

The sun sets in triumph. It drops as a fiery ball of orange, setting the clouds aflame. Deepens to red as it nears the horizon, turning the scuds' undersides to ash. Disappears, leaving only the storm's fire-edged remains, like smoldering embers raked across the sky as final eulogy to the day.

Maggie and Daddy sit on the wicker settee, eyes on the sky, his arm around her. I sit on the steps. We haven't eaten.

It's strange. I think something important's happened.

Reggie absently follows with her finger the flow of a rivulet as it courses down the window, her cheeks streaked like its panes.

Yes. Many important things happened. But how to define them exactly? How to order them in importance. How to fit them together to form a coherent pattern, a lesson on life?

In the desert there are creatures that have uniquely adapted to drought. They can go into a dehydrated suspension of life, deeper than hibernation, a kind of semi-mummification, that can in some cases last for years. When the first rain comes, they burst into life, crawl from their tombs, and get on with the business of eating and breeding. Without instruction, they know how to make the most of their brief stay, which for some may be a matter of days, one cycle. Such adaptations can't occur slowly, over years and generations. They must be made quickly, within the breath of a lifetime, if the species is to survive.

The rain is meant to make you feel refreshed, cleansed, ready for renewed life. Then why is she so depressed, so at a loss? Because the rain has closed off options? Because she has no car? No, even without the rain and with a car, she would lack purpose and direction. She'd still be floundering.

A project, she needs a project, something to do and be. She needs to forget, not remember. She needs to move out, not in. She needs to act, not think.

She resolutely wipes her cheeks, pulls herself from the window, and starts going through rooms, looking for a project. But everything's done, all's clean and orderly. She's a good wife, a good mother, a good organizer. All she can find is an old sewing basket of mending—a bra with untacked straps, a shirt with missing buttons, shorts with torn pocket, worn socks—articles she'd intended to salvage, gestures to her conscience, long-forgotten. She hasn't sewn in years. Zippers and buttons get replaced at the cleaners, the dressmaker takes care of larger projects, socks with holes get thrown out. But she could still repair a loose hem if she had to. She could still stitch a straight seam.

She absently refolds the mending into the basket. She's remembering her first dress. Betts had gone with her to Babbitt's to help pick out the pattern, an Easy McCall's. Mrs. Bailey had been going through her fabric chest, that's what had started it all. She'd found a four-and-a-half-yard length of plaid gingham, too fussy for Betts, too youthful for herself. —It'd be perfect on you— she'd announced happily, holding it up to Reggie.

Reggie'd been delighted at the beauty and generosity of the gift, but her face must have revealed her consternation.

—You don't sew— Betts had astutely guessed.

Reggie'd mutely shaken her head, ashamed of her inadequacy. Janie and Ruthie had made their pom-pom dresses. Betts made Billie's short pleated cheerleading skirt and, with Trixie's mother's help, Trixie's majorette outfit. Even Faye knew what to do with a needle and thread.

On hands and knees beside her, pins in her mouth, glasses slipped to the bridge of her nose, matronly rear end broad above Naturalizer oxfords, Mrs. Bailey taught Reggie to lay out her gingham and pin and cut a pattern. Watching over her shoulder, now and then reaching out a guiding hand, she instructed Reggie in the process of feeding cloth through a sewing machine and coming out the other end with a dress.

—Why doesn't anyone in this family sew?— Reggie'd accused her mother.

—What makes you think they don't?

—I've never seen anyone.

—What do you mean you've never seen anyone? Abby knits all the time, you have the sweaters and afghan to prove it. And Grandma Harrington did all kinds of handwork. Embroidery, crewel, crochet, quilting . . .

—Then why don't you?

Maggie'd looked surprised. —Because I don't want to— as if to say, Why else?

Mrs. Bailey made all of Betts's skirts and dresses because she had to, because nothing in the stores fit her except in the men's department.

Catherine taught Reggie to cut hair. Reggie'd started by trimming her own bangs, advanced to pruning Denny's split ends. Then graduated to styling Billie's bouncy curls and Betts's dutch bob. Katelyn and Lindsay go to Reggie's beauty salon.

Reggie had never so much as turned over a meat patty. Faye taught her to broil steak and bake potatoes. Billie showed her the fine art of making fudge. Janie excelled at cakes and brownies. Many an afternoon she admired as Betts's strong arms and hands slapped out and kneaded dough for buns and bread.

The smell of coffee and cigarettes reminds her of Catherine. The smells of sewing machine oil and new cotton remind her of Mrs. Bailey. The smells of oil paint and humid greenhouses remind her of Abby. The smells of animal flesh and new books remind her of Maggie.

The yeasty smell of rising dough reminds her of the warm nurturing earthiness of Betts.

Reggie wipes the renewed salty stream from her cheek and carries the mending to the trash. She can no longer afford self-deceiving gestures. But now she holds nothing in her hand but an empty basket.

Is this the message of the day then? She's dependent on other people to give her purpose and direction? Her function for others is her hold on life?

She tries to think of things that have autonomous meaning, that give private gratification. That will get her going on her own as an independent person. She can come up with only one thing: her writing. But she's not written in the daytime, it doesn't seem right. Too cold and uninspiring. The day is for business and work, for material gains and practical accomplishments. She looks around for motivation. Perhaps if she lights the fire.

She gets a good blaze going, pulls up a chair, and settles down with her lap desk. But nothing comes. She needs something to drink. Not wine, too early in the day, she won't succumb to that. A cup of coffee. Why is writing so damn oral? But by the third cup, all she's achieved is an upset stomach and a case of nerves.

It's the room, the room is too big, too much emptiness to fill. In the evenings with only the fire, she closes off the corners, creates a space just the right size for her mind. Now, in daylight, it belongs to others, to the mundane and the immediate. She needs a room of her own. She smiles. Virginia Woolf smiles back at her.

She picks up her paper and pen and heads for the study, Howie's study, but he rarely uses it. When he brings work home, he usually chooses the family room, among his ships and trophies. Howie's memorabilia.

She plops down at the desk. Dark green wallpaper dotted with flying ducks, framed Audubon ducks above the bookcase, painted decoy bookends, a sitting duck paperweight. Even a mallard lamp base. Where the hell did they get these things? Why the hell did she use them to decorate? But the room is small, uncluttered, private, looks out on the lawn and garden. Here the rain whispers close and conspiratorially. Yes, here she thinks she can write.

SCENE 20

CHAPTER ?

Smokey checked Denise and Lester one last time, turned out all the lights except one side lamp, and stretched out on the sofa. She was tired. It was past two, and they'd said no later than midnight. She didn't mind babysitting now and then, it served its purposes. But this was too much, this was taking advantage.

She was asleep when she heard them at the door. It took her a moment to recollect herself. She sat up, started to fluff her hair, then had second thoughts. She quickly pulled at her clothes and stretched out again, face to the sofa back, blouse tail out, top button undone, skirt twisted high and tight.

They clattered in, going, Shhh, shhh, stumbling as they tried to tiptoe. They'd been drinking.

Smokey struggled to roll over, twisting her clothes more awry, and faced them, looking disoriented, shielding her eyes from the light. "Oh—."

Glory tripped toward her, hand outstretched, as if trying to find her.

"Oh, god, Smokey, I'm so sorry. We thought it would be over by twelve. But everyone was having so much fun, we just lost all track of time."

Casey was rocking on his heels, grinning at her.

"You and the kids do all right?"

"Of course." Smokey considered sitting up, then decided to stay reclined on one elbow. She was fully aware of the effect she was presenting. "We always do all right."

"I know. They love you so." Glory was jittering around on her three-inch heels like she had to go to the bathroom. "I guess that's why I didn't worry." She giggled and staggered sideways. "Oops." She was drunker than Smokey had at first assessed. "I'm sorry, hon." She placed a hand on Casey's arm. "I'm so tired. Maybe I'll just toddle off to bed." And with a wobbly little bow and another giggle, "If you'll excuse me," she teetered down the hall.

Casey was still grinning, regarding her with jauntily raised chin.

"You ready to go home?"

"Am I driving?"

"No way. I taught you to drive. I know how wild you are."

"Then I'm walking."

"Are you kidding? It's more than three miles. And after midnight."

"Two forty, to be exact."

"I'll drive."

"You're in no shape."

"What do you mean? I'm always in perfect shape." He expanded his chest, flexed a bicep.

Smokey eyed him appreciatively. "Maybe. But not for driving."

She was enjoying the change in him. He'd completely forgotten his FBI persona. She smiled slyly. It was amazing what liquor could do.

He grinned. "All right, be stubborn. You'll just have to stay here for the night."

"Fine. With no pillow, no blanket, no nightgown . . ."

Casey raised his hand. "Have no fear, Old Case is here. I'll get everything." He started toward the hall, then stopped to point a finger at her. "Stay right where you are."

Smokey waited, painted toes side by side on the carpet, knees primly together, hands braced on the edge of the sofa, skirt high, blouse gaping. Casey returned, burdened.

"Pillow." He tossed it at the head of the sofa. "Blanket." He threw it to the other end. "Robe." He held up a peachy silk wrap-around.

Smokey reached for it. "Does Glory know you have this?"

He grinned. "She couldn't care less. She's dead to the world, sprawled across the bed in her shoes and dress just the way she fell on it, purse still in her hand." He found this immensely funny.

Smokey stood, slowly started unbuttoning her blouse, her eyes on Casey. He returned the look, unflinching, still grinning, accepting the challenge.

Smokey slipped off her blouse, let it drop to the carpet. Casey's gaze wavered, lowered to her full breasts pushed high in her lacy French bra. He stopped grinning.

"I guess I better go to bed."

"Suit yourself." Smokey reached for her skirt placket, unzipped. "I can think of better things to do."

Casey turned away abruptly, head down, his retreating steps sharp up the hardwood hall.

Smokey smiled in triumph. She'd finally knocked the cockiness out of him. She turned out the side lamp, stretched out on the sofa, naked beneath the silky wrap-around, and waited.

She could hear him brushing his teeth, taking a pee, drinking water. He'd forgotten to close doors. Then silence.

It took him little more than ten minutes before she heard him stumbling back through the dark, feeling his way, fumbling toward the sofa.

"Smokey?"

She didn't answer.

He reached out, groping for her, found her shoulder, stroked his hand up her neck to her cheek.

"Smokey."

She raised to meet him, arms reaching for his neck, hands embracing his head. Their kiss was hard, violent, then slow and sweet. They'd waited a long time for this. She was only sorry it had taken booze to release it. But she knew how to handle that.

She pulled him down to her, slowly, confidently. She stroked his hair, kissed his eyes, blew into his ear. Sank her teeth gently into his neck. He moaned.

She rolled over him, pushing him onto his back lengthwise on the sofa, unloosed his robe, straddled him. Then slipped down, kissing his chest, nipping his nipples, licking his belly. He groaned, quivered. She tongued lower, playing with his navel, flicking into his pubic hair. Her long nails joined the teasing, tickling his knees, up his inner thighs, across his scrotum. He gasped, arched. She cupped, squeezed. He spread his legs, began to thrash. He was ready, more than ready. She reached, gripped. He cried out. She mounted.

He was hers.

She had him.

It was a seemingly ordinary morning after. Glory had a hangover. The kids ran around in pajamas demanding breakfast. Smokey cooked. Bacon, scrambled eggs, and English muffins. Casey sat hunched at the end of the table, sullen, unapproachable. He couldn't look at Glory, and wouldn't look at Smokey. Glory accepted this humorously as his own hangover suffering. Smokey knew differently.

She smiled as she spread the kids' muffins with strawberry jam.

He remembered.

It had all come back to him.

He didn't want to drive Smokey home alone. He tried to talk Glory into coming with them, but Glory was in no shape to go anywhere. She felt like hell. And, Smokey noted with glee, she looked like hell. With no makeup and flattened slept-on hair, she looked plain, pale and drawn beyond her years. Smokey's high color and bright spirits presented vivid contrast, as she was more than aware. She made the most of it.

Casey gripped the wheel with white knuckles and glared through the windshield in silence. As she studied his stony profile, she could almost feel sorry for him. There was pain around his eyes, and confusion.

"Don't feel bad, Casey. It was bound to happen."

He cast her a dark look.

"But it won't happen again."

"Why not? It was wonderful."

He turned on her, hard and angry.

"What's the matter with you? I'm married. My wife's your friend."

"So what?"

If she hadn't known better, she would have thought from his look that he hated her.

"What kind of woman are you, anyway?"

"A woman in love."

"Don't give me that shit."

"I've never stopped loving you, Casey."

"That's why you pulled out on me?"

"You accused me of some pretty rough things."

"You deserved them."

"No, I didn't. And you know it."

He stared out the window. "What's past is past."

"You and I will never be past. You know that, too."

The fight seemed to sag out of him.

"I won't do anything to hurt my kids or marriage."

"I'm not asking you to."

"What do you want from me?" His demand was almost desperate. "I can't marry you." It was like a cry of loss hardened into angry denial.

She leaned close, knowing he could feel her breath. "You. Your mind, your soul, your body. You don't have to marry me for that."

"I don't love you." He almost shouted it. She let the words crumble into emptiness in the silence.

"Yes," she whispered against his cheek. "You told me that once before."

Reggie's enthralled. Where did she come up with all this? It's not like anything she's experienced, or even imagined. Or is it? She wonders. Even in the bright of day, are these longings she's felt in the dark of night? She ponders. Is her subconscious telling her something?

She dismisses it. Too troubling to think about.

—Hi. What're you up to?

—*Reggie.* How nice to hear from you.

She'd been prepared for hurt coldness but not cutting sarcasm.

—Did I catch you at a bad time?— She can hear Jake barking in the background.

—Not at all. You know I always have time for you— Reggie gets the implied accusation, *even though you don't have time for me.* She's going to get repaid with dividends.

—What's the matter with Jake?— The barking's closer and more insistent.

—Not a thing I'm aware of. He's in fine fettle. And fine voice, as you can hear. He's just exercising his prerogative. He hates it when I talk on the telephone, it distracts my attention from him. Is that why you called, to inquire after my dog?

Reggie suppresses her irritation. —I have a favor to ask.

—Oh? I might have suspected— Reggie forces down another hard swallow. —What may I do for you?

—You know all those things you brought back from Harden, the rugs and bowls and baskets?

—Yes. What about them?

—Do you still have them?

—I suppose.

Maggie isn't going to help one bit.

—May I have them?

—Why?

Reggie takes a breath. —I want to use them to decorate my writing room.

—What writing room?

—Howie's old study.

—Has Howie been consulted about this?

Reggie's control snaps. —Of course!

—I was just asking.

—You don't think I'm going to take over my husband's study without discussing it with him, do you?

—It's hard to know. I have no idea what you're capable of these days.

Reggie squeezes her eyes against the surge of anger, the choked-off ache in her throat.

—I'm so sorry to have bothered you. I won't let it happen again— and she gently replaces the receiver in the cradle.

After a moment, she removes her hand. Pain stabs behind her eyes, her temples throb. She opens her eyes, lifts her chin.

All right, true enough, Maggie. I guess now days there is no telling what I'm capable of. But there was a time you knew. . . .

—You're capable of anything you set your mind to.

Maggie was trying to impress on her the seriousness of her responsibility. She and Daddy had just returned from a conference at Harden High. The principal, dean of women, school counselor, and class advisor had reviewed Reggie's six weeks' performance and were recommending she be advanced to junior standing.

Principal Watts wasn't happy with the implication that northeastern schools produce better students than southwestern schools, of which he considered Harden, as under his leadership, exemplary. But he prided himself on his fairness and commitment to his students.

Maggie and Arthur weren't happy with the prospect of Reggie seeing herself as peer with students one year older and therefore supposedly one year maturer and more socially sophisticated. Or of thinking herself intellectually superior. But *they* prided themselves on the solidness of their liberal child-rearing practices and their ability to keep her grounded. Besides, they reasoned practically, they didn't want her to lose a year in her education. And, anyway, she was already running around with juniors and seniors.

So Reggie moved into trigonometry with Faye, Billie, and Janie; civics with Billie, Faye, Ruthie, and Betts; and English III with Betts, Billie, and Trixie. She remained in Spanish I, since Spanish II was taught only in Spring, but with the agreement that she could go ahead in the books and would join Spanish Club. And she continued with Chemistry I to fulfill her science requirement. With the exception of Janie, they were all together for gym.

Sixth period was the most coveted gym time. As the last class of the day, you could take extra time to repair hair and makeup damage. Or go right from gym into after-school sports then straight home without having to change or caring what a mess you got. Seniors usually had priority, followed by juniors prominent in sports, which included Billie and Betts. Fourth period gym was the second most sought-after—you had the whole lunch hour to fix up—and was usually reserved for juniors. But because of Billie's and Betts's close in with the gym teachers, they had managed to get the whole gang signed up for sixth period. And when Reggie's schedule was rearranged, they somehow squeezed her in, too.

Reggie sits swiveled sideways on the edge of Howie's padded desk chair, staring blindly at the empty bookcase, reliving events long passed, the present pain of Maggie's harshness forgotten.

Sixth period gym. What an experience. The education of my life.

I can't believe it. Sixth period gym! I don't know how Billie and Betts got me switched, they won't tell me, they just smile mysteriously and say Don't worry about it. But I know it has something to do with Billie's "favored" status. She's the best runner the girls' track team has had, no one's beat her yet, and she's brought the school three trophies. And Betts is everyone's favorite: vice-president of the junior class, secretary of the student body, president of the honor society, member of the drama club, manager of the girls' swimming team, soloist with the choir, Sunday School teacher, and volunteer at the hospital. I suppose all she and Billie had to do was make a small request to Mrs. Stanley and Miss Loomis, our gym teachers, and the strings were pulled. Anyway, however they did it, here I am now with the whole gang.

Before this, I had third period gym with a bunch of sophomores. Which meant by eleven my carefully coaxed curls were a limp wreck for the day. Casey started calling me Raggedy Ann, which didn't amuse me one bit. So Catherine plunked me down in a kitchen chair and, after fooling around for a few minutes, cut me a page boy with side part and bangs which, because she used my natural wave, keeps its shape and body no matter what. Everyone thinks it's a great success. Even Maggie's decided she likes it, once she got over her peeve. She'd been upset because I hadn't asked her permission. Which surprised Catherine, who assumed a fifteen-year-old girl could do as she wanted with her hair.

I hate gym, and I hate team sports. I don't like running around and getting sweaty. I don't like getting hit and knocked down. I bruise easily.

And I hate this gym, the locker-room part of it. The ceiling is so low because the bleachers of the boys' gym are over it. The girls' gym doesn't have bleachers. The steam from six periods of showers gets condensed between concrete, acoustical tile, and sheetrock. By the end of the day it's like a sauna, only muggier and fetid with scented soap, drugstore cologne, disinfectant, mildew, and sweat. There are two rows of three-by-three curtained dressing stalls, each with a little bench and a hook to hang your clothes on, and an attached *un*curtained three-by-three shower stall. Everyone has to wear shower shoes. When you come out, you feel dirtier than when you went in. But the gym part isn't so bad. It's big, with four-story ceiling, glossy hardwood floors, and lots of light through high banks of windows. Before the new school, the girls didn't have their own gym. They had to use the boys' after school. If the boys weren't using it.

At the end of game time my first day in sixth-period gym, I automatically head back to my individual shower. I'm happily soaping away when I hear someone call out, Where's Reggie? I freeze on the spot. I'd been listening to Betts and Billie and the other girls laughing and horsing around, aware in the back of my mind that they were some place together. But now it suddenly hits me with a shock that that "some place" is the gang shower.

Before Harden High, I'd never so much as heard of a gang shower. Such a thing would never have been conceived much less concretized by the decorous minds responsible for Wexler, and most expressly not for girls. The very name holds the onus of low-class male animalism. I'd been so embarrassed by my first sight of it—it looked like my idea of a urinal—and my realization of its function, I hadn't dared breathe a word of it to Maggie and Daddy. I was afraid they'd whisk me out of gym class if not out of Harden High altogether, into some hermetically sealed cloister. But no girls used it in third period and my alarm gradually subsided.

And now, here're my friends—my two *best* friends—romping around as if they're actually enjoying their shared exposure, and calling me to join them.

I keep very quiet.

But they catch up with me on the way out. Where was I? I make excuses:

I didn't know, I didn't hear them, I was in my regular stall, the one from third period. Which they reluctantly accept because they're not sure what to make of them.

The second day at the ending buzzer, I rush as fast as I can back to my private stall, throw on my clothes without showering, and beat them out the door. Again ignoring their calls.

As I run into them next day in class, no one says a word. And I think, Good, they got the message. They're going to leave me alone, let me have my privacy. But still I'm nervous.

That afternoon I keep an eye on the gym clock, and two seconds before buzzer time I'm out the door, on my way to my anonymous stall. I listen to the rest of the class clatter and chatter in. I listen to the rush of showers. I listen for voices calling me. But the gang shower is strangely quiet.

Suddenly the curtain on my stall is yanked back.

—Hey, Reggie— Faye stands confronting me. —What's the matter, don't you like us anymore?

I'm startled out of my wits. The girls are all behind her, in towels. They've caught me in bra and panties.

I try to laugh, make a joke of it. —Of course I like you.

—Then what're you doing in here?

—Taking a shower.

—We shower over there.

I lift my chin. —I shower here.

Billie steps up. —Why?

Faye regards me coolly. —You think you're too good for us?

—No.

—Then what're you hiding?

—Nothing.

—I agree— Faye eyes me up and down. —It doesn't look like much to me. Eyes twinkle, grins pop.

Trixie's head pokes over Faye's shoulder. —You think you got something we ain't got?

—No.

—Let's see— Billie reaches out, grabs.

—No!

I yank free the top of my pants and jump back.

—Yeah— Faye nods. —Looks about the same to me.

—All right, Regina Irene— Betts's bulk shoves into the doorway. —This is your last chance. Are you coming willingly or not?

I can't believe this, even Betts is against me. I look around desperately, grab onto the shower stall frame.

—Okay— Betts turns away. —That does it, I wash my hands of her, Faye. She's all yours.

Billie and Faye move in on me. Ruthie and Trixie reach to pry loose my fingers. They pull me out of the stall and, as a mob, half-drag half-carry me toward the gang shower. I know it's silly but I'm terrified. I kick, I scream. I jerk my arms and thrash my body.

I demand to be set free and receive hoots and jeers. Someone boo-hoos loudly. No one comes to my rescue. Mrs. Stanley and Miss Loomis must be used to gang-shower violence. So evidently are the other members of this gym period, who watch my passage with mild curiosity, then move on about their own business.

By now towels have been lost in the scuffle and I'm in a swirl of legs, arms, bouncing breasts, and pubic triangles. I squeeze my eyes tight, turn my head, but there's no avoiding their intimidating proximity. Only Betts remains decorously wrapped as she supervises from the edge of the circle.

They plop me down on the narrow concrete floor and turn on all ten nozzles full blast, five to each side, pinning me in the middle. I try to scramble up, they shove me down, Billie sits on me. I feel hands fumbling, tugging, I see flashes of beaded flesh, strands of dripping hair framing intently bent faces. When they're done, I'm on my back spread-eagle, wet and naked, surrounded by a circle of jeering wet and naked females. I lie there, helpless, spent, the spray pelting relentlessly. I don't move. There's nothing left to fight for.

They're waiting.

—Okay— I grin weakly. —You win.

They yell and cheer, stomp water in my face. Betts lifts me to my feet. She seems twice as big, an Olympian monolith, in her togaed nudity.

Later in the car, Casey listens to my story without a word, his face dark as a thunderhead as I finish.

—That Billie's a goddamn tramp! And Faye's got a mouth like a truck driver and a mind to match it.

—They were just having fun. And it wasn't only them. Everyone was in on it.

—I don't like you being in gym with that bunch, they're a bad influence.

—I can take care of myself.

—Oh yeah— He gives me a sharp look. —I want you to stay a lady.

I don't know what to say to this, I'm not happy with the distinction but I like him to think I'm special.

He touches the back of my hand, strokes my fingers. —They could have hurt you.

I don't tell him about the scrapes I feel smarting on my elbows, or the tender spots on my legs I know will soon be livid.

We're waiting for my hair to dry. My damp bra and panties are wadded in my purse. My awareness that he knows I have no underwear beneath my dress is giving me sensations I'm not comfortable with. I'm overly conscious of my unbound parts. I shift to hide the stiff poke of my nipples, and catch my breath as the cloth brushes their sensitive tautness.

I suddenly realize I want to be touched. I grab my purse.

—I think my hair's dry now. You better take me home.

SCENE 21

—Howie, what's this thing we've got going with ducks?

Howie looks up from his papers. He's cross-kneed on the family-room couch, the contents of his briefcase in neat piles on both sides of him. —What thing?

—This duck mania thing— Reggie shoves the loaded carton at him.

He looks divested. —That's the stuff from my study.

—Right. You said I could have it for my writing room.

—But what's it doing in there?

—Getting ready to go to Goodwill.

—You can't get rid of that stuff, Reggie.

—And why not?

—It came from my family.

—I seem to recognize a few things from my family as well. So what? They were so crazy about them they gave them away to us. So now they're ours to do with as we please.

Howie's rummaging through the box. —We might find some use . . .

—Do you love ducks, Howie? Do you think they're noble and beautiful and intelligent and . . .

—Not really.

—Then why do we surround ourselves with them? I mean, what's the *point*. And it's not just us, it's everyone we know. Yet I bet if we were to ask any one of them, Do you think the duck is a magnificent bird? every last one of them would answer No. Still we have them all over the place. On our walls, our shelves, our clothes, our pillows and quilts. Even our doormats, mailboxes, and weathervanes. *Why?*

Howie considers his wife. —I don't know, I never thought about it.

—Well think about it now— Howie looks thoughtful. —What's the meaning?

He shrugs. —Maybe there isn't any. Does there have to be?

—You mean we drape ourselves in dumb ducks for no reason?

—I suppose it represents the great outdoors. Back to basics. That sort of thing.

—Nature and the elements? Then why not the eagle? Why not something with a little majesty or at least a little grace? Why not a swan or a cormorant? Something inspiring. Even a pelican has more personality.

—I don't know, Reg, I'm not up on ornithology. I just study the law.

Reggie regards her husband a moment, sets the carton on the floor, sighs. —Okay. Maybe you can do something with all this at work.

Howie brightens, leans toward the box. With the partnership, he'll have a bigger office.

Reggie stops at the doorway. —On second thought, Howie, maybe all of you are right. Maybe a mindless mallard *is* the appropriate motif.

Minutes later, she's bumping around in the dining-room sideboard, minutes after that, banging around in the kitchen cupboards. Her bumps and bangs have determined purpose.

Curious, Howie wanders into the kitchen. The table is crowded with serving dishes, dessert plates, silver spoons, trays, soup tureen with matching bowls. In her arms, Reggie clutches six glasses, six more wait behind her on the shelf. Every item has one thing in common: each bears in one form or another the emblem of the duck.

—What're you doing?

—I'm freeing us from the mire, Howie. I'm digging us out of duck shit.

Of all birds, the eagle is most sacred to the Hopi. It was the eagle who first welcomed The People into the Fourth World and gave them permission to occupy the land. He also gave them his feathers as *pahos* to carry their prayers aloft, in exchange for their promise to always keep the good thoughts that would protect the life of the planet and its balance.

The eagle's down is like the breath, the breath is like the clouds, the clouds are like spirits. Thus the feathers of his breast represent the soul.

The eagle is important in medicine and healing. His tail feathers are used by Hopi doctors in curing rites to stroke "sorceries" from the patient's body and dispel their evil in the six directions: north, south, east, west, nadir, and zenith.

He also possesses the power to charm the venomous snake. In the Hopi Snake

Dance, the brushing of an eagle feather along the snake's back prevents the snake from coiling and therefore striking.

And, it is said, eagles today are descendants of Hopi children. As the Hopis themselves were once "children" of the eagle.

The story is told that during the Hopis' long migrations, children were lost in a deep canyon. The Hopis searched and searched but could not find them, until at last they were forced to give up and go on. But the children were still alive, wandering from crevice to crevice, looking for roots and wild berries. The eagles in the high cliffs glided above, to watch over and keep track of them. They felt sorry for the lost and hungry children, and brought them food and sought to comfort them. Until the children began to think of the eagles as their own people. They watched the eagles fly, listened to their calls, and imitated them. Then one morning they awoke and found themselves young eagles. They flew into the air and perched on the aeries beside their parents. That is why the Hopis treat captured eaglets like babies.

The Kachina wear the eagle's feathers because he is strong and wise and kind. With his great wings he can fly out of sight above the clouds into the upper reaches, where he can speak directly to the Sky Powers and tell the Great Father all that befalls his human children.

No bird or living soul has explored so high on his own, and none is so proud or mighty. He is Qua'hu, the eagle, conqueror of air, master of height. The bird that soars to the very face of the Sun, to Tawa, the Creator.

Singing in the shower has never had such meaning as it's given in gang shower.

We sing obvious things, like "Singing in the Rain," towels umbrellaed above our heads, leaping over and jumping into puddles, kicking water at each other, a la Gene Kelly. Or "Pennies from Heaven," where we attempt a soft-shoe chorus line. Some days we're Fred and Ginger, dipping and twirling to "Dancing in the Dark," towels swirling around us and into one another. Which often as not leads to a snapping stinging towel fight that leaves red welts on thighs and buttocks that I don't tell Casey about.

And at least once a week we degenerate into the ribald and downright dirty. In Boston, my exposure to off-color songs had consisted of exactly two ditties: the first, a variation of "I'm Looking Over a Four-Leaf Clover" that goes:

> *I'm looking under a lady's undies*
> *that I underlooked before.*
> *First come the ankles, the second the knees,*
> *The third are the panties that blow in the breeze.*

> *There's no need explaining the one remaining,*
> *It's something that I adore.*
> *I'm looking under a lady's undies*
>   *that I underlooked before.*

The second, a rather monotonous tune that has the chorus: *Roll me over, lay me down, and do it again. Roll me o-o-ver in the clo-o-ver. Roll me over, lay me down, and do it again.* The verses go:

> *This is number one and we sure are having fun.* Chorus.
> *This is number two and my hand is on her shoe.* Chorus.
> *This is number three and my hand is on her knee.* Chorus.

And so on up numbers and rhyming body parts until, *This is number ten and I'm starting in again.* Not very imaginative, something like "Ninety-nine Bottles of Beer on the Wall," it's virtues being that anyone can learn it and it keeps you going for a while, but titillating enough when you're twelve and in a private New England girls' school to make you think you're being naughty.

The songs Betts and the girls introduce me to are so scandalous by comparison they make these two seem cutely innocent. And to tell the truth, I'm so appalled by the first one I hear, I want to leave the shower. But I've learned by now this is exactly the reaction that'll earn me a second, and more affronting, dose. So I stick it out, and by the time they're into the third song, I'm so numb I actually listen. I guess that's how we get through a lot of things: one foot in front of the other in spite of paralysis.

The girls seem to have the songs in a set sequence, like serial learning, one song automatically calling up the next. Their favored starter, the one I cut my teeth on, begins, like all of them, with a robust prolonged "Ohhhhh—" then launches frolicsomely into:

> *She ran out there in the midnight air*
> *with nothing on but her nightie.*
> *The moonlight hit on the nipple of her tit,*
> *and jesus christ almighty.*
> *She jumped in bed and covered up her head*
> *and said I'd never find her.*
> *But I knew damn well she lied like hell,*
> *so I jumped right in behind her.*

I screwed her once, I screwed her twice,
I screwed her once too often.
I broke a spring or some damn thing,
and now she's in her coffin.

Reggie laughs. —Ohhhh . . . The tune's still ringing in her head. It's amazing. She remembered all the words. She hasn't thought of these songs in years. But they're all there, in the back of her mind, waiting to tumble out. Already she can hear the next in the sequence. She hums, mouthing the words, gains confidence, bursts into full voice with gusto.

Walking down Canal Street, going from door to door.
Goddamn son-of-a-bitch, I couldn't find a whore.
Finally I found one, she was tall and thin.
Goddamn son-of-a-bitch, I couldn't get it in.
Finally I got it in, wiggled it all about.
Goddamn son-of-a-bitch, I couldn't get it out.
Finally I got it out, it was red and sore.
Goddamn son-of-a-bitch, I'll never fuck a whore.

She giggles guiltily, looks around. She'd forgotten how raw these songs were. She never heard the boys sing them, she always thought of them as the girls' secret property. But now that she considers it, the boys must have been the ones who passed them on. They're written from a male point of view, definitely not the kind of thing a female would think up. In fact, on further consideration, they're actually demeaning to women.

And outside of this one song, she never heard the girls use the *f* word. They never even talked about sex, or rarely, or at least not around her. And when they did, it was usually in slurring reference to some other girl's promiscuous behavior. *Slut* was one of Billie's favorite pejoratives, *bitch* was Faye's. Unmarried girls who got pregnant were meted dark unsympathetic judgment. Trixie had been going steady with Walt since her freshman year and Walt was no choirboy, but no one questioned what they did alone. Dating was mostly in groups. But it was taken for granted that after the group split up, couples parked in the dark and necked, maybe even petted.

It was taken for granted the guys hunted around for loose girls. Les was a notorious womanizer. He knew women in Mexican Town, which was considered dangerous. He could end up with a knife in his ribs. He knew married women, which was also dangerous. He was particularly successful on his prowls into small neighboring towns, where young women eager for sexual adventure rationalized they could abandon themselves to a stranger and no one would be the wiser. Which was *their* mistake and danger. The guys talked, they openly joked about who would and who wouldn't. Which Reggie found offensive, and which is possibly why the other girls kept so closed-mouthed. Nice girls were spared, nice girls being those who were going with a particular guy. But once the couple broke up, there was always the fear her privacy would not be preserved, especially if the guy was hurt or angry.

Joking was the only way sex could be dealt with openly between the two genders. They couldn't sit down and discuss this basic human relationship. They couldn't seriously exchange ideas and seek information. But they could stand around a fire drinking beer and tell dirty jokes. Girls were allowed to contribute as freely as boys, and those with the best stories and funniest delivery were accorded special popularity. Walt was undisputed king, with Casey running close second. Billie was first among the girls, but Betts didn't do so bad holding up her end.

Sex, marriage, and race were the favored topics, followed by politics and religion. Stupidity, futility, and otherness seemed to be the favorite butts. There were dumb Polack jokes, jokes about Indians and niggers, and plenty about wetbacks. She didn't remember any about Jews, a frequent target in Boston. To the best of her knowledge, there were no Jews in Harden. Catholics told stories about the Baptists, Baptists told stories about the Catholics, and everyone told stories about the Mormons.

Mormon girls were reputed to be of easy virtue, though Reggie never understood this reputation. The Mormons she knew at Harden High were quiet, plainly dressed, conscientious students, committed to the values of the Mormon family and the perpetuation of the Mormon community. They were expected to work hard and do well, in studies, sports, and home duties as well as religious training. The girls wore little to no makeup and were well-versed in the domestic arts. The boys were clean-cut, reserved, and well-mannered. They didn't curse, smoke, or drink stimulants, and rarely dated out of their faith. Many went on to missionary service before they married. It was hard to imagine someone like Clydene Orton bouncing around in a backseat with the likes of Lester Jenkins.

Clydene Orton. Reggie smiles. She hasn't thought of old Clydene in years. She can still see the shocked repugnance on her prissy face when she'd come upon them in gang shower. She'd watched as Betts and the girls had nakedly cavorted for her benefit, books tight to her chest, spine rigid, nose high and pinched, looking for all the world—Reggie suddenly realizes—just like Barbara.

—You girls are disgusting animals— Cold judgment that had spurred the girls into wild wahoos and lariat-swinging of wet towels against the concrete floor, slapping water in Clydene's direction. Clydene had stood her ground, then raised her head and disdainfully walked away.

Reggie had brazenly confronted her with the best of them, hands on hips, exultant in her newly gained freedom, proud of her stripped pretensions. Her initiation into gang shower had released her from the self-shaming need to cover and hide herself.

No. Reggie stops herself. *That isn't true.* She hides herself from Howie. She undresses away from him, back turned, towel or slip clutched across her front as she moves about the room. And he does the same. No parading before one another in immodest pleasure. No enjoying familiarity of body. No sharing casual intimacy. Why?

What are they protecting?

SCENE 22

Reggie and the girls find the boxes waiting at the back entry. Katelyn is first out of the car to be first to inspect them.

—What are they, Mummy?

Reggie takes one look at a small-printed label, and smiles wryly. *Not at all like Maggie, she never leaves a thing unguarded. No doubt she's hoping someone will steal them before I can put them to my nefarious use.*

—They're from your grandmother.

—For us?

—For me.

—But what are they?

—Help me get them into the study and I'll show you.

Katelyn stoops to get her arms around a box, struggles to lift.

Reggie laughs. —Here. I think we better do it together. But be careful, the contents are breakable. Lindsay, you can get the doors.

The girls take turns helping Reggie maneuver through the laundry room, kitchen, family room, and up the hall. It takes several minutes of cautious exertion, but finally the boxes are safely lined on the study floor. The girls stand back and wait expectantly.

Reggie opens the first box, carefully lifts out and untissues a small round object. The girls look disappointed. Reggie smiles with understanding.

—What is it, Mummy?

—A Hopi bowl. Made by one of your granddaddy's friends, a very nice lady named Nancy. You remember Granddaddy talking about the Hopis and the mesas— The girls nod uncertainly. —This is from First Mesa. You can tell by the orangy color of the clay, and the design. See— Her finger traces as she holds out the bowl. —They use birds like this and other natural forms.

She waits for the girls to respond. When they don't, she sets the bowl on the desk and reaches for the second packet. Her unwrapping reveals another piece of pottery, this one the size and general shape of a large acorn squash.

Katelyn cocks her head. —That looks like some kind of bird, too.

Reggie smiles. —A Zuni owl, to be precise. The white coating is called slip, a mixture of fine clay and water. The black and brown of the feathers, eyes, and beak are added and fired later.

But Katelyn's impatiently turned away and is prying into the box. Reggie checks herself, watches nervously as Katelyn unwraps and comes up with a black plate.

—That's the oldest piece in the collection. A black-on-black by Maria of San Ildefonso and her husband Julian Martinez. They invented the process. Maria makes and polishes the ware, then Julian paints the design— She takes the plate from Katelyn, hands it to Lindsay. —See how the design shows dull against the shiny surface?— Lindsay runs her finger across, feeling the two textures.

But Katelyn's unimpressed. She's moved on, is again foraging through the tissue. Her eyes widen. She holds up her prize, a delicate black-on-white pot in an all-over geometric design of birds and flowers.

—Oooohh, I like this one.

Reggie reaches quickly. —Good taste, Katie.

—I'm not going to drop it, Mummy.

—I just want to hold it while you feel its wall. No, both sides, between thumb and finger. Of all the pueblos, Acoma's known for the thinnest pottery. This was made by Lucy Lewis, another famous potter.

The girls are becoming captivated. They've never seen their mother like this, her face luminous with absorption in the artifacts she's presenting almost reverently for their admiration and edification. They exchange a look as Reggie gently sets the pot on the desk beside the other unearthed treasures and opens the next box.

She reaches through the tissue, pulls out a basket. —This is from Third Mesa. See how fine the weaving is?— She sorts again. —And this is a winnowing tray from Second Mesa. Look how vibrant the colors are. And all from native plants.

Reggie bends, searches. —And somewhere in here, if Grandmummy hasn't held out on me . . . Yes— She stands, unwraps. —And this is the Hopi Hemis Kachina.

Lindsay catches her breath. —Oh, Mummy, he's beautiful.

Katelyn frowns. —What's a kachina?

Reggie smiles, pleased at her interest. —The kachinas are the spirits of the invisible forces of life. Emissaries that carry the prayers of the earthbound to the gods on high.

The girls look at one another in confusion and wonder.

Lindsay reaches. —May I hold him?

—Are your hands clean and dry? The paint lifts easily.

Lindsay wipes her hands on her pants, gingerly takes the figure. —He's so light. He looked heavy.

—They're carved from the single root of a cottonwood tree. By the uncles and fathers for the children, so they can learn to identify them.

Katelyn is studying her mother with new respect. She's hearing from her information not commonly dispensed in Boston. —How do you know all this, Mummy?

—What?— Reggie looks startled, shrugs. —Oh I don't know. From your granddaddy, I guess— She grins sardonically. —It couldn't have been anyone I knew in Harden. They didn't have that much interest.

And this is the sad truth. None of her friends had visited the Mesas and didn't seem inclined to. They couldn't understand her enthusiasm. Her father's yes, it was his business. Like the trading post was Hubert Herren's business. But for most of Harden's inhabitants, Indians were simply a fact of life, and not always an agreeable one. *Native American*, as the accurate and respectful identification, had not yet come into common usage. She remembers ugly comments, unpleasant incidents . . . she doesn't want to remember . . .

—There's still one more box— Katelyn's opened it and pulled back the flaps. —It looks like a rug.

—It *is* a rug. And if I know your grandmother— Reggie carefully lays back the heavy folds. —Now I'll show you *my* favorite— She lifts a large colorful painting of Navajo boys on horseback herding sheep in Monument Valley. —It's by Harrison Begay, a Navajo. He's famous now, too.

—Are any of these things valuable, Mummy, I mean worth *money*?

—I don't know. I hadn't thought about it that way. But, yes, I suppose some are. And they're all certainly worth more than we paid for them— Reggie fixes her daughter with a stern look. —But value can't be measured by dollars alone, Katie.

Katelyn squinches her face to show her mother what she thinks of this piece of moralizing.

But Lindsay's looking concerned. —You aren't going to sell these things, are you, Mummy? If you are may I have the kachina?

—I'm not going to sell a thing. And, no, you may not have the kachina. He stays right here, where he can carry *my* prayers. But you may visit him any time you like. We'll put him on the bookcase where you can see him the moment you enter.

Reggie sets the Hemis in the center of the top shelf and stands back to assess the effect. Since she's taken over the study, she's stripped the dark paper and painted the walls white warmed with a hint of burnt umber and yellow ochre. She's proud of the job. She did it all herself, including the tinting, without once reducing herself to consult Maggie. The room looks clean, larger, lighter, a space conducive to airing the soul and opening the mind. Cool afternoon sun filters through the window and highlights the freshly waxed desk.

—I thought I'd make drapes out of some loosely woven fabric and hang them by wooden rings across a wooden rod, kind of homespun like. What do you think?

—You're going to make drapes? By yourself?

—I didn't know you could sew, Mummy.

—You see? Wonders never cease— Reggie smiles secretively. —There're a lot of things you don't know about me— The girls are just coming to see this. —Now, how about helping me get the rest of this stuff in place.

The girls scurry to collect hammer, picture hangers, dust cloth, paper towels, Windex. They wipe and polish and, under Reggie's supervision, test objects here and there until they agree they've achieved the perfect arrangement and balance. They lay the rug across the floor. The basket goes in the corner. Picture and plaque on walls, bowls, plate, and owl strategically spaced on shelves. Only the desk is left empty. Purposefully. No distractions.

Reggie sits down in the chair and lets the room sink into her. The girls wait in respectful silence. She sighs.

—You must have liked Arizona a lot, Mummy.

Reggie looks up, surprised. —Yes. I did, Lindsay.

—Then how come you never talk about it?

—Oh, I don't know. It was a long time ago. And many miles away. I guess I didn't see any purpose.

—Didn't you think we'd be interested?

—I'm interested, Mummy.

—I am, too.

—What was it like?

Reggie becomes thoughtful. —Full of sky and endless horizons. You felt your soul and mind could go on forever, exploring and expanding. There seemed no barriers except time— She smiles, looks out the window.

Katelyn shifts uneasily, but Lindsay quickly adjusts to her mother's wistful mood.

—It must have been beautiful.

—How could it be beautiful, silly? It's desert.

Reggie looks back. —No, Lindsay's right, Katie. It *was* beautiful. But in a way different from what you're used to. Stripped down, closer to the essential. And for me, I guess that means closer to the truth— She drifts, her voice softens. —Single things took on importance. The shape of a rock formation. The silhouette of a saguaro at sunset. The waxiness of a cactus bloom— She stops . . .

blossoms of white sprays of light bursts of sparkling water cascading down tumbled smooth boulders into shallow streams deep calm crystal clear to the bottom sinuous black line stretched across white rock water moccasin sunbathing . . .

Reggie turns her head, appears to look at her daughters, but her eyes are glazed and distant. They exchange an uncertain look, Katie shrugs, Lindsay tentatively reaches out, touches her mother's shoulder.

—Are you okay, Mummy?

—What? Oh. Yes— Reggie opens the desk drawer. —I just thought of something I want to write down— She takes out a pen and note book, bends to the desk.

long lonely highway black asphalt two lanes white line dividing stretching on forever telephone poles lone felled pines merging into horizon into faded round hills distant purple peaks toppled gray mountains

weathered rubble dry dirt parched earth hard packed red desert sandstone debris piled slabs with crawling insects ants centipedes scorpions lizards camouflaged against hot rocks rattlesnakes napping in cool crevices white coils rattling in breeze . . . no breeze the human breeze . . .

Reggie lifts her head, stares out the window, pen in abeyance between her fingers. Katelyn plucks Lindsay's arm, they tiptoe out.

—Well, good— Katelyn whispers with satisfaction. —I guess it's working. She wanted a place where she could write.

Reggie turns to study the book shelf, absently notes her daughters' withdrawal. Lindsay's eyes are on her, sad and troubled, as she quietly closes the door.

School's starting, and I'm still turning my Saturdays over to Maggie's library project. Story Time's proved such a success, she and Dorothy have decided to continue it as a year-round program. Older children have started to come, leaning against the bookcases around the room with the parents, the little kids squirming on the floor. Maggie's had to divide the group: threes to sixes in the morning, sevens and older in the afternoon, with some overlapping allowed for less-mature or more-precocious children. But you have to sign up and you have to clear with Maggie.

With the older group, I read a story or chapter in a book. So now I have twice as much preparation. Maggie picks the material, gives it to me to practice and play around with, then directs me through a rehearsal, usually on Wednesday evenings. She thinks she's Harold Clurman: Back straight, Reggie, knees together. Don't slump over the book. Pause, make eye contact. Smile. More suspense now. More excitement, please. Slower. Faster. Softer. Speak up, I can hardly hear you. Why are you shouting?

I complain about all the time I'm giving up and all the things I'm missing out on, just to make sure she appreciates me and feels a little beholden. But the truth is I look forward to Story Time. Casey works weekends at the airport, Betts and Billie are busy with house chores, and what homework I have can be finished Sunday. It gives me something to fill my day until Casey comes by for me. Maggie says it's my service to the community.

One Saturday off, Casey brings Denny. It's their first visit. Dean's come several times, so I've been just as glad Casey's working. I don't know how I'd deal with the two of them, though they don't know about each other. But now Dean's safely off to college in Tucson.

Denny sits smack dab in front of me, craning up with that infectious grin of her father and brother, excited at the prospect of a new experience, feeling special because she has an in with me. Casey lounges beside the door, arms akimbo, one foot crossed over the other. He's dressed up in slacks and polo shirt. I'm nervous, I want to do my best, I want to impress him. I try not to look in his direction. Once our eyes meet accidently and I almost lose my place.

Afterwards mothers and children come up, say hi, make nice comments. I hope Casey hears them. Many are regulars, we know each other by name, chat familiarly. I play this up, take my time, make sure Casey sees I have a following.

Finally I work my way back to him, Denny hanging on me. I feel proud and shy and eager.

He smiles down at me.

—You looked real sweet up there with all those little kids around you.

He has a way now of standing close though not touching, making everything feel as if it's just between the two of us, even when we're with others. —You'd make a good mother— For a moment, his eyes are soft and deep. Then he turns to Denny, who's traded my arm for his and is dragging and swinging on it. —So what'd you think, punk? Would you like to come again?

—Yeah!

Not a word about my performance.

He drops Denny off at their house and I think, now's my chance. As soon as he gets back in the car he'll take my hand and tell me how wonderful I was. He piles in, slams the door, starts the engine. Not a word. He shifts into gear, starts up the street.

I can't wait any longer.

—So, what'd you think?

—About what?

—Story Time.

—It was great. Denny loved it.

—Did you like the story?

—Sure— He looks surprised. —Why not? It was cute.

He relaxes into the seat, thighs wide, wrist over the steering wheel, elbow out the window. I try to think what next to say. I catch him watching me out the corner of his eye.

—Did you think I read it all right?

I see the slow grin, the twinkle. —What're you doing, fishing for compliments?

He's been playing, baiting me. I'm embarrassed and delighted, like a child caught in a sly trick by an indulgent parent.

—I just wanted to know if you thought I did all right.

He puts his arm around me and pulls me to him. —You know you did.

—No, I wanted to hear what *you* think.

His face is inches away, soft and teasing. He kisses me on the nose.

—Do you need words for everything?

Yes, Reggie throws the pen down. *Yes, goddamnit, I need words.* She shoves back from the desk, stumbles to her feet. *What's gone wrong here?* She can't write, can't think. Can't see or hear her characters. They've gone, left her, with a cold blank sheet. White paper. White walls. A room of her own and she can't find words to furnish it.

Scribbled across the crumpled balls littering the floor are her attempts to create the pivotal scene of the book. Casey's capitulation and his reconciliation with Smokey, the love scene of the century. She wants to capture heights of emotion: joy, passion, ecstasy, fulfillment. The exultant physical expression of kindred spirits finally reunited. But all she's managed to corral are the usual kisses, strokes, and thrusts, the *de rigueur* sighs, moans, and gasps of the drugstore bodice-buster, the dextrose of dream-starved women. She retrieves a rumpled sheet, smooths, reads:

Casey tried to fight Smokey, but his past feelings for her had become too present.

He tried to avoid her, but the functions of his custodial role kept forcing them into constant contact. He held her at bay by assuming the punitive sternness of an impersonal authoritarian. She countered his cold commands with unarmored submissiveness.

He tried to drive her back with a barrage of bitter invective that left him spent and feeling impotent. She withstood the assault unflinching.

He threatened to put Fred back in charge, but they both knew that would be admitting defeat. It didn't matter, Smokey knew she'd won already. Casey just needed time to accept it.

(Get transition, beginning of scene here: Smokey's apartment. They've been fighting. About the past.)

"I know," she said softly. "We hurt each other." She reached her hand to his cheek. "Now we have to heal each other."

She didn't push it. She let her hand drop and waited. She could feel the intensity of his internal battle.

He turned and started for the door. Smokey let him go.

"That's all right, I can afford to be patient. Without you, I have nothing but time."

He stopped, his hand on the knob. Even before he faced her, she had accepted his surrender.

Reggie throws the paper back to the floor. *Crap.* Kicks the overstuffed waste basket. *Unmitigated shit.* Stilted language, unimaginative images, undistinguished dialogue.

She stoops for another sheet.

He stood for a long moment, his back to her. She waited, watching with satisfaction (in triumph), as the life (resistance, strength) slowly seeped (drained) out of him. His head drooped (dropped, hung), his shoulders sagged (hunched). When he finally turned, he was a whipped (beaten, conquered) man.

"I can't, Smokey. I can't fight you any longer (anymore)." His face was twisted The face he raised to her was filled with (twisted in, with) misery.

She smiled. "Then don't. Give up." She moved slowly toward him. She could feel his need, the ache in his body, reaching for her. She stopped inches from him, letting the magnetism (between them ?) pull him to her, her eyes holding (commanding) him. "Give over to it. Give in."

He grabbed her with a moan. "You win." His head sank to her shoulder.

She held him, gently (comfortingly), her hand stroking the back of his hair (head). "We both win. Your loss is *our* gain." (Italics?)

His lips sought her neck, kissed, found the soft shell of her ear. "Oh, god, Smokey. How I love you." His breath was hot (sweet, hot and sweet).

Smokey closed her eyes, sank into him. He gripped her as if he'd never let go. Her mouth hard on his, she gently pulled him down (to the floor ?).

Reggie slaps the page on the desk. Clichéd. Overwritten. Florid purple prose. No poetry, no soul. She's embarrassed, humbled, apologetic. She should be capable of better.

Words, the words are inadequate. She can't even make a decision. Which word? This? This? Because she doesn't know the right words.

She needs to expand her vocabulary. But where is the vocabulary commensurate with great emotion that doesn't somehow diminish it? Surely others have accomplished the task. She should be better read. But if others have mastered it before her, why should she try, why tread the path already taken? She wants to blaze a new trail, penetrate her own forest.

Why should she find it so difficult to write about sex, the consummate human communication?

She lays her cheek down on the crinkled page. Her head aches from the strain of unaccustomed thinking, from the stretch for inspired insight. Inside, she feels great things, senses large connections. Deep intimations of the human condition. Then why are her achievements so trivial, so trite; so callow and shallow? She turns her face into her pitiable words and weeps.

No talent.

She straightens, wipes her eyes.

Well, if that's the way it is, as Vonnegut says, So be it. Either give up or get on with it.

No quarter given to cowards is a saying she remembers from her childhood, probably from Abby.

All right, so she'll just be another no-talent writer. At least they sell, get read, make money.

She fumbles for a clean sheet, lays it on the desk. *Write from your experience.* Another old saying, from tired old university writing classes. Why not write from your dreams? Why not write from the real as a point of departure into the *more* real?

All right then, what's real here? What would she like to be real? Sex is her point of departure.

She raises her pen determinedly, and finds herself as blank as the forbidding page. She tries to think of Casey. Can't think, can't remember. Why can't she remember? Her forehead is a tight band restricting her brain. She thinks of Howie. *Shouldn't* think. She feels traitorous, ashamed, an exploiter of his privacy. Sweet considerate Howie who never envisioned himself in bed as grist for her writer's mill. Nice conservative Howie who never provided grist.

She crushes the paper, throws it at the window, and sobs bitterly.

SCENE 23

Casey finds out about Dean. Not that there's that much to find out about. I've only seen Dean a few times, and never where anyone else might see us. But Casey makes a federal case out of it.

It's Labor Day weekend, the official end of summer and start of school. We've already checked in and picked up our schedules, books, and locker assignments, but classes don't begin until Tuesday. Saturday night the Lions Club has a dance.

The hall is just what you'd expect: a large square of blond hardwood floor enclosed in white walls broken by high windows and lined with folding chairs; at one end a long table with punch bowl and cookie platters, in the corner a phonograph and record stack.

Casey and I arrive late. We've been arguing. I can't figure out the exact cause of his contentiousness but I get the impression he had expectations and I don't measure up.

He doesn't like my dress.

—What's wrong with it?

—It's dumb. What's that you've got at the waist?

—Carnations.

—They're fake.

—I know they are. I put them there.

—Take them out— He grabs.

I grab back. —They brighten up the dress, it's the style.

—Not here it isn't.

—I don't notice you brought me any real ones.

—It isn't that kind of dance.

And he stalks off, leaving me standing where I am. I think, Fine, let him go, I can get along quite well without him. I look around, trying to find someone I know—and spot Dean across the room, watching me. He's the last person I'm expecting. We'd said good-bye last week, when he'd left for Tucson to register and settle into his dorm. What's he doing back?

He knows I've seen him. I don't know what to do. If I wave, I'm afraid he'll come over. If I don't, he'll know I'm intentionally snubbing him. He might say something to his mother, who for sure will say something to *my* mother. I'm saved by Casey stepping in front of me, shoving a waxed cup of Hawaiian Punch.

I find a chair, take a ladylike perch, and daintily sip. I can feel Dean watching me, it gives me a keened edge of self-awareness. I lift my chin, pose semi-profile, glance around the room, anywhere but at Casey, a soft vindictive smile playing on my lips. But Casey isn't taking it in. He isn't the least aware of my secretive amused detachment. He couldn't care less that another man across the room is admiring me. He's on the edge of the dance floor, jiggling to the music.

—Come on— He thrusts a hand back at me without looking.

I suddenly hear the music, I'm overcome with panic.

—I can't.

I've finally grabbed his attention. But I've lost my smile.

—What do you mean you can't?

—I can't dance to that.

—Well if you can't dance why the hell did you come?

—I can dance. As a matter of fact, I'm a very good dancer. But to regular music.

—This is regular music.

—Not where I come from.

—Oh yeah? What do they dance where you come from? The minuet?

—Very funny. And what do you call this? The hillbilly hoedown?

—The cowboy stomp. To the good old "Salty Dog Rag"— He's bouncing again. —Come on. It's easy, just back and forth, a simple two-step— He demonstrates.

But I'm not convinced. I watch the crowd of dancers, old as well as young, stomping up and down, twisting, turning, bumping into each other. No one seems to mind.

—It's too fast. Wait for a slower one.

Casey gives up and turns away, disgusted. And in a minute the good old "Salty Dog Rag" gives up, too. The next number comes on, something not quite so rambunctious. I pick out a couple that looks like they know what they're doing and carefully follow their feet, frantically boning up. One, two, one, two. It doesn't look too difficult.

Casey turns back to me. A new number's come on. —Okay, this slow enough for you?

I know that someday you'll want me to want you, When I'm in love with somebody else . . .

I listen, nod, contritely rise, and let him lead me onto the dance floor. *You expect me to be true, And keep on loving you.* He puts his arm around my waist, raises my hand in his, and starts slowly moving me. *Though I am feeling blue, You think I can't forget you.*

He looks in my face. —See, this isn't so hard, is it?

I smile, shy at his gentleness. *But one day you're gonna want me to want you.* I relax, settle into the easy sway. *When I am strong for somebody new.* He's a good dancer, smooth, confident. My own confidence begins to return. *And though you don't want me now, I'll get along somehow.* I'm terribly aware of him. This is the closest we've been, the whole length of our bodies, separated by inches. *And then I won't want you.* He pulls me closer. Our thighs brush.

And though you don't want me now . . .

—Who is she?

—Connie Francis— Our cheeks touch.

I know I'll get along somehow . . .

—I like her— I can feel his breath on my ear.

And then I won't, I wo-o-n't wa-a-nt you.

We finish in a dip, his arm pulling me tight, his body pressed over mine.

We stand, drop arms, pull apart. I'm trembly.

He smiles. —You did real good— Then turns, scans the crowd. —Hey, there's Les and Diane— He waves.

I don't look. I hate Les and Diane.

Thankfully the music starts again. Then not so thankfully. It's upbeat. Not as wild as the "Salty Dog Rag" but enough to worry me. Casey grabs me up, full of grins, and starts right in, as if we've been dancing as a duo for years. I do my best to keep up, but I can't get the beat. I miss a step.

—Relax— A command. —And smile— A frown.

I take a deep breath, look over his shoulder, and concentrate on his feet, trying to remember to smile. We do okay for a minute, then I over-anticipate and step on his foot.

—Will you let me lead?— He pushes my arm back and down.

Another deep breath. I will myself to go limp, follow the music, and forget about him.

I start to get the knack. Casey's scowl smooths, he starts to hum, then he gets fancy. I hang in there as best I can. He tries a quick spin, without proper cue, in my opinion. Our legs tangle, I trip him up, and we stumble. He throws my hand down, pushes me away.

—What's the matter with you?— He glares. There is no doubt now, I am definitely not measuring up. And stomps off.

I feel a fool, completely miserable, standing alone in the middle of the dance floor, people gawking. I make my way to a chair in a dark corner and fight tears. I refuse to give Casey the satisfaction of reducing me. I see him over with Les and Diane, talking and laughing to beat the band, and suddenly I see the other side. *I'm* the one given the satisfaction, *he's* the one reduced. He made a fool of *himself* in front of his friends. I sit straight, hands in lap, chin up—to hell with you, Colter—a wallflower with her pride.

All of a sudden, there's Dean in front of me. I'd completely forgotten about him. He smiles. —Would you care to dance?

I wonder if he's witnessed my little humiliation. I smile back. —I'd love to.

He escorts me through the crowd, hand on my elbow, no dragging me by the hand like some hillbilly clod. Dean's a gentleman. He dances like one, too, leads beautifully. I have no trouble following. We start with a simple two-step, nothing showy, a modified cowboy stomp with no stomping. But as we find how comfortably we fit, how well we do together, we open up, add breaks, a little bounce. We end with a spin, me safe at the end of Dean's arm, the skirt of my "dumb" dress swirling, no legs tangled. I'm giddy with success. It wasn't my fault at all. I don't bother to see if Casey's watching, I know he is.

In no time at all, I'm a veteran stomper.

Dean and I dance a polka, twirling and hopping. We do a foxtrot worthy of Astaire and Rogers. We're the best of the handful of couples who dare the samba. By this time, we've attracted attention. Dean leads me to the turntable, sorts through the records, hands one to the Lion in charge, and leads me back onto the dance floor. I'm dying of curiosity. The strains of a waltz announce. I float into his arms.

We start with a box waltz, mock-sedately, playing around, having fun with it. Then open up, get fancy. And fancier. The other dancers clear the floor. We whirl around and around, fast as the wind, spinning and twirling, circling the floor. We end with a deep dip, my leg in the air, dripping with the wide eyelet ruffle of my petticoat. The crowd claps, Dean bows, I curtsy. He escorts me to the sidelines, we're breathless and beaming.

The lights dim, the hall fills with the sad refrain of "Auld Lang Syne." I turn toward Dean—and Casey steps between us.

My stomach pitches, my lungs collapse.

—I think this dance is mine.

I'm at a complete loss. I'd seen Casey early on, over Dean's shoulder, stomping around with some other girl, grinning like he was having the time of his life, and I'd said to myself, Fine, let him, I have Dean. Later I couldn't find him. Then I'd seen Les and Diane leave.

I look helplessly at Dean. He takes my arm.

—No, I believe the dance belongs to me. Reggie's been with me all evening.

Casey takes a step forward. —But she came with me. And a lady always saves the last dance for the man who brought her— He turns on me. —And Reggie's definitely a lady. Aren't you, Reggie?— His smile's a thrown gauntlet.

What can I say? I look apologetically at Dean and let Casey drag me away.

Our dance is not friendly. Casey stares over my shoulder past my head, his face hard with cold dark thought. I have my own confusions to work out. I haven't thought of Casey for the last two hours and I can't quite figure what to make of this. I don't bother about whether I'm following or not. He could be doing the foxtrot and I could be doing the samba, we're so far apart it wouldn't matter.

The music stops, the lights glare up.

—Let's go— Casey's fingers bite into my upper arm.

I have no doubt now about his anger. It occurs to me maybe I should worry about his becoming violent. Then I think about his gentleness with his sister, his protectiveness of his mom.

The car isn't where we first left it. Casey yanks the door open, looks away while I slide in, then pulls back his arm as if to slam it. I brace myself. Instead he steps up and firmly shuts it, resolutely but within reason. With the same deliberate precision, he opens and closes his own door, inserts the key in the ignition, and maneuvers us out between parked cars. I realize he's exerting maximum control.

He drives us to the northern edge of town, where we always seem to go to work out our problems. We haven't exchanged one word or one look. Watching from the corner of my eye, I wait while he sullenly considers the line dividing black desert and midnight gray sky. The stars are too high and dim to be clear markers.

He studies the limp weights of his hands drooping over the steering wheel. The muscle in his jaw is rhythmically bunching. He scowls.

—Why didn't you tell me you knew Dean McElvrey?

—I didn't know I was supposed to. Do you tell me everyone you know?

—Maybe you had some reason to keep it hidden.

—Maybe it just didn't come up in the conversation.

—So how long have you known him?

—What makes you think I didn't just meet him?

—You were too friendly. I saw you talking. You wouldn't talk like that with someone you'd just met.

I can feel him fighting his anger. But he better watch out, I'm fighting my own.

—Where'd you meet him?

—What is this? The Inquisition?

He lifts his head and finally looks at me, a look of ice-bound rage. —I think I have a right to ask about the guy you dumped me for and spent my evening with.

I can't believe this. Who dumped who? Inside I'm going crazy.

His glare is piercing. —Just tell me one thing. Have you been out with him?

I'm incensed. Who does he think he is? —Yes! Yes, I've been out with him. He took me to dinner at La Descansada.

Casey's face goes white, his eyes narrow.

—And afterwards taught you some fancy dancing?

—He showed me the gardens.

—I'll bet he did. In the dark?

—It was his birthday. We had a wonderful time.

—And did you try to twist your tongue around his tonsils, too?

I stare at him. To think I once thought him cute. With one quick wrench, I have the door open and my leg out.

—Wait!— Casey leans across the seat and grabs my arm. —Don't go— He pulls me back. —I didn't mean it— My hand's still on the handle, the door comes with me. —I shouldn't have said that.

—Then why did you?— I'm about ready to let him have a blast of my own ice-bound rage.

—I don't know. It upset me to see you dancing with some other guy.

—You should have thought of that when you went off and left me.

—I didn't leave you— He smiles, the beguiling boy again. —I just went to get you a cup of punch.

—You went to get built up by Les and Diane.

—But I was coming back.

—When? For the last dance?

—I didn't think you were the kind who'd pick up with another guy.

—Oh? And what kind is that? Now you're calling me a pick up?

—That isn't what I meant.

—You seem to be saying a lot of things tonight you don't mean. And you did leave. The car was parked in a different place.

—I went to get some fresh air— I let him think about it. He gently pounds the steering wheel. —So what'd Dean say about me?

—Nothing. He's too much a gentleman. He saw how you treated me, he had to, the whole hall did. He didn't want to embarrass me anymore by bringing it up again.

—I would have come and got you sooner— The sarcasm slips back in. —But you seemed to be having so much fun I didn't want to break in.

—So why didn't you just let Dean take me home? He would have been more than happy to.

—I'm sure— Casey's eyes bore into me. —But my mother taught me to always take home the girl I brought. I'm a gentleman, too.

—I'm sure— My eyes do a little return boring. —You were just exerting your mistaken rights of possession.

We sit there glaring at each other. Finally Casey looks down, picks up my hand.

—None of this would have happened if we were going steady.

—You mean if we were going steady you wouldn't have left me on the dance floor?

—You wouldn't have taken off with Dean.

—Exactly— I snatch back my hand. —That's just the way you'd see it. You'd still have the right to walk off and leave me any time I didn't please you but I wouldn't have the right to find someone I *did*.

—You please me— He reaches again for my hand.

—Sure— slapping away his hand. —As long as I look and act right. You weren't happy with me from the very start of the evening, because you didn't like my "dumb" dress. Then you got good and mad because I didn't come out of the womb cowboy stomping. But that didn't have anything to do with me, it was all about you and how *you* felt. You didn't care a thing about my feelings. I wasn't a person to you, I was— I search —an *appendage*— I'm proud of the word. —An ornament you'd dragged along to show *you* off.

—I didn't make a fool out of you, Casey. You made one out of yourself. Because let's face it, you have bad manners and you just don't dance as well as Dean. And that's what really made you so crazy. You wanted to steal the show like he did. You're not mad at me, you're mad at yourself. Because you wanted to be Dean.

I'm fairly panting from the gush of words and anger. I wait, shoulders back, chin up, ready. I can take whatever he cares to dish out. Instead he surprises me.

Head down, he hangs onto the steering wheel. Then without a look or word, starts the car and drives us out of the desert. At my house, he quietly turns off the lights and ignition then reaches for his handle, but I'm already out.

I don't slam the door. I step up and close it with firm decision. I don't run to the house. I walk, calmly, decisively. He just sits in front of the house. I open, close, and lock the screen and front doors, turn off the porch light and living-room lamp. He sits. I stroll down the hall to my room, turn out the bed-side light, and peek through my venetian blinds. He's still out there. I watch in the dark until he finally drives away.

Then I turn on the light and stand in front of the mirror. I feel grand. More than that: *regal.* Regina, the Queen. I turn my head from side to side, shoulders straight, chin still high. I'm proud of the way I handled myself, my control, the way I didn't sink to his level. I'm glad I told him off, he had it coming, and I did a good job. I'm surprised by the way I suddenly saw through him so clearly, and by the words that came so freely and accurately. I step up to the mirror and study my face, expecting to look older. I feel wiser, maturer. I didn't know I had it in me.

I undress slowly, hang my dress and petticoat carefully, align my Mary Janes on the closet shoe-rack, thinking about my newly discovered insight and eloquence. And that I really couldn't care less that I probably won't see him again.

SCENE 24

Reggie sits in the winged-back chair with her lap desk. She's reverted to her late hours in front of the fire. Only there isn't a fire, it's too late in the season. Howie has cleaned out the hearth and closed the damper. So she stares at the dried floral arrangement in front of the brass fan spread across the cold dark opening and waits for thoughts and words.

She hasn't written for weeks. The girls' stepped-up spring schedules have kept her running. And the few hours she's found for time at her desk have produced worse than nothing. Her writer's block has become a wall, shutting her off from herself and making her resentful and irritable with others.

She leans back, closes her eyes, and struggles to empty herself like a receptive vessel, the way the books instruct. She'll put down anything that comes. It doesn't matter where it fits in the novel or if it fits at all, so long as it gets her writing. She releases and reaches for images—colors, lights, faces, bits of places, pieces of scenes—anything that will fire and free her into that visceral connection she's been missing. Insight and eloquence come from feeling . . .

She opens her eyes. The images focus, become fixed and vivid: Casey hanging onto the steering wheel, head down, enduring her righteous analysis and upbraiding.

Insight and eloquence.

She smiles. She hadn't known she had such capabilities. She'd never before been provoked. She'd been so smug and self-congratulatory. But it's true. He brought that out in her: insight and eloquence.

She could use a little of it now.

She picks up her wine glass but doesn't sip, arrested in sudden realization: *He brought out so much in me. I learned so much about myself from him.*

Not that he taught her. It was something about the closeness between them. They were alike in so many ways, they even looked alike. We'll have beautiful babies, he said, they'll look just like us. At the time, she'd grown all mushy and misty. Now, she wants to laugh at the conceit and arrogance. But she can't. She dreamed for years of those blond-haired, hazel-eyed babies.

Casey painted such pictures of them, full of pride, playfulness, and laughter. How they'd learn to take their first steps and say their first words, and brush their teeth and wash their ears, and not pick noses or scratch fannies. He'd talk about taking them fishing, and camping, and skiing, and when they were older, on a special vacation to Disney Land. He'd say things like, When we have kids, they're not going to be a bunch of mannerless smart alecks; they're going to know how to go anywhere and act and talk properly. Or, Our kids are going to have to work for a car if they want one; they're not going to get things handed to them on a silver platter.

The boys were going to be athletes like him; he'd humorously describe how he'd teach them to throw a ball and swing a bat and jump hurdles and make touchdowns. The girls were going to be talented belles like Reggie; he'd make up funny stories of how she'd drag them to singing and dancing and piano, and show them how to dress and style their hair and apply makeup. And, of course, they were all going to be smart and get college degrees.

He saw it all, and made Reggie see it. She knew just what kind of father he'd be, from the way he was with Denny. And she knew just what kind of mother she'd be, from the way she was with him.

Casey made her want what he wanted. And that was part of their closeness.

But it wasn't a closeness of convex curve melding into concave curve, complements. Theirs was a closeness of friction that produced sparks and heat. They kept abrading against one another, trying to find the need in the one the other might meet. Reggie adjusted herself to make the fit.

She never wore the dumb dress again. Why? To please him? Yes. But more than that: To prove herself. She accepted his judgment; it *was* a dumb dress. He had an image of her she was challenged to fulfill.

Casey was reaching for something in her she was reaching for in herself.

She had never thought of herself as a beauty. But when the beauty contest was announced, she entered. You're the prettiest girl in this school, Casey pronounced, and he picked up the entry form himself. Maggie'd looked askance at the proposal. She didn't approve of undue regard for one's looks, much less flaunting them. She'd taught Reggie to stand straight, walk with her toes forward, and present a well-groomed understated appearance.

I don't see that it's much different from parading at a coming-out ball, Daddy had ventured. You don't nominate yourself as a debutante, Maggie retorted. But in the end, Maggie ordered a "suitable" gown from Bendel's, and Reggie floated across the stage in a cloud of pink tulle, back straight, chin up, toes forward.

She had never thought of herself as particularly talented. But when the talent contest was announced, she entered. At first she balked at the idea. She wasn't about to sing or dance by herself in front of a judging audience. You can read a story, Casey suggested. You do that all the time. Something cute, like that one where you use all the different voices.

Maggie, to Reggie's surprise, was more receptive to a competition in talent. She agreed, though begrudgingly, with Casey's choice, a selection from *Alice in Wonderland*. She coached and rehearsed Reggie. And ordered another appropriate outfit.

Reggie made it into the Christmas program lisping her rendition of "All I Want for Christmas Is My Two Front Teeth." She'd taught it to Denny as an after-dinner surprise for her parents and brother that had brought the Colter household down. You ought to do that for the Christmas show, Casey had said. So did Maggie, after Reggie used it with the children at Story Time.

Reggie joined the Drama Club, performed in the junior-class play, and in April auditioned for the school play. By then, she was brave enough, and experienced enough, to sing and dance in front of a crowd. She got the lead.

But she didn't start on top. Dolores Torres came in first in the beauty contest, with her black-haired, black-eyed fire dramatically contrasted against icy-white satin. In her sweetsy pink, Reggie had been a pallid second. Janie won the talent contest, pounding out on the piano "Rustles of Spring" with a fervor that surprised even those who thought they knew her. Again, Reggie placed second. Her contribution to the Christmas show got positioned as curtain raiser. But the student body came to know her as a major contender, and by spring, when the most popular students were selected as slaves to be auctioned off on Slave Day, Reggie was among them.

The striking of the Seth Thomas startles Reggie from her reveries. She sets the empty glass on the table next to the half-empty bottle, lowers her lap desk, and stiffly rises. It's late, the room is chilly and cheerless, and she has to get up early. But she suddenly needs to see herself more clearly as she was than through insubstantial memory.

She pussyfoots into the study, softly closes the door, switches on the light, opens the bottom desk drawer, and lifts out the album. Pandora's Box. She hasn't allowed herself to succumb to it again since that overcast day she confronted her sun god and ended up buried in bed, diseased with despair and longing. But she can't blame the album. The virulent forces had already been unleashed. This time she has a safer quest; it's not Casey she's pursing but herself. And this time, she's better prepared. She's had months of inner upheaval and outer dissembling. She's disciplined. She can handle it. She's an adversary worthy of her dilemma.

She resettles in the wing-back, places the album on her lap, and contemplates its black cover. Like a coffin lid. Holding a living corpse. She assesses the pages, slips in fingers, and lifts.

"Our Town." The cast lined across the stage for curtain call. She scans the faces, all but forgotten until now except for Betts, the perfect Mrs. Gibbs, and stops at her face: Emily. She hated that play, found it slow and talky. Nothing but sitting or standing around philosophizing. But like the rest of the actors, she's blithely smiling.

She turns the page. "Seven Brides for Seven Brothers." This had been much more to her liking. In fact she'd had the time of her life, singing and dancing as if she didn't have a nerve in her body. She'd even discovered she had a flair for comedy. What, she now wryly wonders, happened to it?

She turns another page. And there it is, the memory that sent her to her desk drawer seeking verification. Slave Day. She pours wine and lets herself sink into the picture. She and Billie side-by-side in their harem outfits. Betts and Mrs. Bailey had helped make them. Trixie had contributed the beads, bangles, and dangle earrings. Ruthie had come up with the veils.

Reggie studies her image carefully. Then slowly leafs backwards, pausing to study again the backwoods coquette in puffed sleeves and laced bodice. Pausing to study the small-town priss in white satin death-robe. Pausing to study the dreamy-eyed *jeune fille* in sky-blue polished cotton with ribbons and lace that made Reggie look, and feel, just like bewildered Alice. Pausing to study the pigeon-toed moppet in white knee-socks, short skirt, oversized hair bow, and blackened front teeth. Pausing to study the would-be debutante in stiff tulle and long satin gloves.

And stopping. To study the should-be Homecoming queen, sitting to one side of Billie on the folded-down top of the white convertible lent for the occasion, and advertisement, by Decker Pontiac, again blithely smiling. Though inside she's so hurt and angry she wants to cry.

And there, to Billie's other side, is good old Clydene Orton, waving and smiling as if she's pleased as punch with the company she's keeping and doesn't mind in the least coming in third. Though she wouldn't say a word to Reggie or

Billie during the noon parade through town or the evening half-time circling of the field. As far as Clydene was concerned, they were so far beneath her, they didn't exist.

Reggie laughs. Good old Clydene. Was this the beginning of their rivalry? No, it began in gang shower that day Reggie took her naked stand with Betts and the girls and identified herself as aligned with the Devil, while Clydene, of course, was a Latter Day Saint. Their competition progressed into the classroom where the Force of Evil vied with the Force of Good for top grades and honors, and extended into extra-curricular activities, where they continued their wrestle for ascendancy. And for the most part, it was a draw.

Clydene came in third in the talent contest singing in her clear lyric soprano "Summertime," which Reggie found a strange choice considering the Mormons' attitude toward black people, who as children of Ham could not become full members of the church. But Clydene got elected to Student Council while Reggie made it only as class treasurer. But in addition Reggie was elected president of the honor society. Clydene was captain of the women's volley ball team, Reggie was captain of the swimming team. On Awards Day, Clydene was number one in scholarship, but Reggie walked off with the class activities pin. And on and on, back and forth they went.

But you got the last laugh, didn't you, Clydene? Reggie chuckles at the picture, drains her glass, refills it, *Here's to you,* and toasts the smiling heart-shaped face surrounded by a halo of back-lighted hair, the color of orange soufflé. A true strawberry blonde. Skin as delicate and white as porcelain. Eyes like blue diamonds. Untouched by the sun. Clydene the Ice Maiden. She could bestow smiles of sheer radiance that left you dazzled but somehow chilled, longing for the warmth those smiles promised but that never came. Clydene was known and respected by everyone, even admired. But on Slave Day she was not selected for the auction block. You had to have a sense of play to be popular.

Reggie's gaze shifts to the center of the photo. Her face sobers. She raises her arm, *And here's to you, Billie.* She drinks. Whenever she thinks of her, this is how she remembers Billie: laughing, chin up, head cocked, eyes squinted against the sun. Billie the Fun Maiden, who knew better than anyone how to play.

That, Reggie supposes, is why she found it so easy to forgive her. Who could stay mad at Billie? She didn't have a mean bone in her body or selfish scheme in her head. The ticket trade hadn't been her idea, she'd just gone along with it. And who could blame her? Faye was right: Billie deserved to be queen. And Reggie's glad now, the way things turned out, that Faye did what she did. But Reggie never again trusted Faye.

Reggie stares thoughtfully at the photo a minute longer then, keeping her finger in place, leafs forward to the Slave Day picture. Compares the two, nods, sips. She was right. She changed a lot in those six months. And it's not just the difference of going from fifteen to almost sixteen. There's an awareness around her eyes in the second picture that isn't there in the first. She considers the sheer pantaloons and brief halter, the way she's standing, hands behind back, hip tilted. There's a new awareness in her body, too. And of her body.

Reggie takes a heavy swig.

She never shared her harem costume with Maggie, never told her about Slave Day, never showed her this picture. She was afraid of Maggie's reaction and wouldn't risk it. Reggie changed at school, returned the jewelry to Trixie, then left the costume with Catherine to make over some Halloween for Denny.

That's what happens when you play a character scripted by some other person.

Reggie sets the glass down and page by page carefully slips pictures from their corner mounts. She has a sudden desire to show them to Katelyn and Lindsay. She wants them to know her as she was then.

And it's safe. Casey isn't in any of them.

But he was always there. On call to run errands, in the center of the fifth row, at the curb ready to chauffeur. Behind her. During curtain calls for "Seven Brides," he strode up and presented her with an armload of long-stemmed red roses, an extravagant accolade in sand-locked Harden that spurred the audience to a greater burst of applause. On Slave Day, he bid twenty-five dollars for her, the highest for anyone—except Billie, who went for thirty to three nonjocks combining wallets. Her placement on the Christmas program—first, in front of the curtain—was, Casey assured her, to be sure the show got off to a good start.

When she took second in the talent contest, Casey was derisive in his criticism of Janie's playing (he was sure he'd heard several wrong notes though Reggie was equally sure he'd never heard "Rustles of Spring" before in his life) and the judges' low level of taste and literacy. Dolores Torres's winning of the beauty contest was, Casey accused, a blatant attempt to appease the Mexican community, where rumblings had been surfacing lately against discrimination. And for engineering the Homecoming cheat, he hated Faye Quinn the rest of his life.

Casey, too, was a major contender. But he played to win. When he didn't, he turned on those who caused his loss. And—Reggie suddenly stiffens—she had been part of his game; her losses had been his.

She sits transfixed in thought for several minutes, grappling with this understanding.

What Casey was reaching for in her, he was reaching for in himself. She foggily traces the logic. Does it follow, then, that what she was reaching for in herself, she was reaching for in him?

She sighs and relaxes with satisfaction, polishes off the last drops in the bottle, tucks the loose photos in the album, unsteadily stands, leaves her lap desk on the living-room floor, deposits the glass and bottle on the kitchen counter, dumps the album on the study desk, and bumps her way down the hall to the bedroom, feeling full of insight and eloquence.

Too few hours later the clock radio clicks into song. Reggie groans and rolls toward Howie.

—Please, Howie. Would you take care of the girls?— She touches his shoulder. —I have this terrible headache— Howie shrugs away from her hand. —Do you mind? Just this once?

His face is hardened with anger as he leaves the bed.

SCENE 25

I can't believe it. I've been nominated for Homecoming Queen. And I've only been in this school two months!

I'd heard kids talking about it, and now that I look back Casey'd dropped a few sly hints. But I hadn't really paid attention. It was just something they did here that had nothing to do with me.

And then Friday morning, deep into the boredom of Spanish I, the intercom buzzes on. We all look up expectantly, relieved at the break in mastering Spanish pronunciation, and focus on the small black box high on the wall. The voice is gravelly, staticky with the stress of school-wide communication from a single central-office mike.

> Good morning, boys and girls. This is Coach Wilson speaking for the Men's Athletic Department. The boys of Harden High are pleased to announce their nominees for this year's Homecoming Queen, to be crowned November seventeenth at Homecoming. As you know, nominations are submitted anonymously by all boys regularly attending gym class, and those ten girls named the most times become our candidates.
>
> And now, without further ado, here they are. Will the following girls please report to the office:

I hear Billie's name, Trixie's name, Clydene's, a few names I don't know, a few I recognize vaguely. And then I hear my name.

I'm stunned.

Everyone turns to look at me. It's like they're seeing me for the first time, the boys surprised and happy, the girls surprised and not so sure.

I just stare back.

—Go on, Reggie.

—What do I do now?

—Go to the office.

I stand, turn to Mr. Jacobs. He gives me a big smile. —You're excused.

I make my way to the office, I don't know how, I'm in such a tizzy I hardly recognize my surroundings. The other girls have already arrived, they probably ran. They're laughing and talking a mile a minute, loud and shrill with excitement. Except for Clydene, of course, who's standing removed with her usual cool superior smile.

I grab onto Billie, she squeezes my arm back. —Get ready for the fun— But her voice has a sardonic tinge, and her grin is wryly knowing.

—Attention. Attention, girls— Miss Walfrid, the dried-up Dean of Women, enters from her inner sanctum, hands raised. —Quiet. Quiet, everyone— She slaps the counter, fixes on us sternly. —All right, settle down— She waits until all eyes are obediently attentive. —Congratulations— She smiles dryly, lips closed. —Now— The smile vanishes. —I am sure you are all familiar with the process. We will start you with ten books of ten. You may pick up additional should you need them from the secretaries here at the office. Ballots are to be in Monday, November 13, nine A.M. One second later and you will be disqualified. That gives you exactly one week and three days. Good luck.

She reaches to the row of rubber-banded packets lined along the counter. We step up in turn, accept one, and exit to the hall, where we mill around, assessing the road to queenhood and one another's prospects. We are considerably subdued from when we entered.

I stare at my packet, shrug at Billie. —Well for a Dean of Women, ol' Wall Fridge was sure one great big help. I started out knowing absolutely nothing about "the process" and I still don't.

Billie laughs, and stuffs her packet into her pocket. —She's like everyone. She figures if you're running for Homecoming Queen you must of been born in the town or at least lived here all your life.

—Well I'm sorry to disappoint her. Remind me not to take her my problems— I examine the black printing on rectangular white stock, look up at Billie in surprise. —These aren't ballots, they're *tickets*.

Billie's enjoying my consternation. —Ever hear of buying votes? Well now you're selling them.

—You mean I have to *sell* these?

—How do you think the football team gets its crotch cups?

—Then there's no voting at all. It means nothing— I'm terribly let down.

—Sure it does. The guys aren't going to nominate some dumb dog.

—No— I'm getting the picture. —They're looking for a sweet-smiling money-maker.

Billie tilts her head, grins. —So what's wrong with being a sugar mama?

I look at her. —How am I going to sell these, Billie? I know exactly five people in town.

She considers me with amusement. —You're gonna do just like the rest of us. First thing you get home tonight, you're gonna make the rounds of everyone you know: family, friends, neighbors, your dad's business acquaintances. Next, bright and early tomorrow morning, you're gonna hit downtown and every merchant, doctor, dentist, lawyer, and public official you can dig up. Then you're gonna go to the houses in the better parts of town and work your way door-to-door. After that, you go to the poorer. They're suckers for sweet smiles, too. Until you've canvassed the whole town— She grins. —And at every one of those places, you're gonna hope to get there first. Just like the rest of us do.

I grimace, not at all entranced by the prospect, and riffle my thumb across the ticket edges. —Ten times ten is a hundred people— I shake my head. —Ol' Wall Fridge was right. I should have been born in this town.

But bright and early Saturday morning I'm on First Street, flashing my smile and tickets. I run into Billie right off. We burst out laughing and agree to take opposite sides of the street then trade. I see several of the other girls, but no Clydene. Some merchants buy from every girl, some are selective for whatever reasons, and some have a single favorite they know personally. But by the end of my circuit, I'm satisfied.

The afternoon I spend in "better" parts of town. Sunday I'm out again, but not until after one, out of respect, Maggie insists, for church-goers. She and Daddy have had surprisingly little to say about my latest enterprise. They're used to fund raisers, I guess. Even those where it's a winsome smile, comely face, and pleasing body that's the commodity. So long as no goods are exchanged. And it doesn't seem to bother them that I'm soliciting door-to-door to secure my own crown and finance a macho kingdom. It isn't the first time in history. Even in Boston a woman has to offer some material advantage to be classed as a desirable bride. Think of the dowry. Only that isn't what they call it now. Now it's a trust fund.

I'm out every day after school. Casey can't drive me because of football practice, so I walk. I learn every inch of town. And by the end of the week, I have blistered feet but over a hundred dollars. Casey's sure I'm going to win. He's bought two books, at a dollar a ticket. His mother and father bought one. Maggie and Daddy bought two and will buy more should I need them. But how can I tell? One of the rules is that each girl's sales must be kept an absolute secret. To stimulate competition, I suppose. But Casey knows what last year's winner brought in and it's much less than I have. I begin to let myself hope. And Maggie gets out my lavender taffeta and sends it to the cleaner.

Monday morning we're all there, well before nine, lined at the office counter, ready to hand our dollars in. We glance furtively at each other's envelopes, trying to gauge their holdings, and though it's too late to matter now, we spread our hands to hide our own. But there's no question: mine is the thickest.

And then things start to go funny. Faye appears at the door and motions for Trixie, Trixie exits. They stand to the side of the door, Faye vigorously talking, Trixie listening and nodding. Then Trixie comes back in and pulls out Billie. Again Faye talks, Billie shaking her head, Trixie moving over to join Faye's side. Billie finally nods. Faye takes Billie's envelope. Then I can't see what happens next because Faye catches me watching and pushes Billie and Trixie over against the wall out of sight.

Billie returns, to the other end of the counter. Trixie hangs back by the door. Miss Walfrid enters and, without so much as a Good morning, gets right to business. She calls out our names alphabetically. I wait anxiously through the first until she gets to the fourth.

—Franks, Billie.

Billie steps up, hands over her envelope identified only by a number, receives a check against her numbered name in Miss Walfrid's ledger, and goes out, head down, without a look at me or Trixie.

—Kelly, Trixie.

Trixie drags up, looking all apologetic and woe-begone, as if she's going to a funeral.

—I'm sorry, Miss Walfrid, I couldn't sell my tickets. My mother got sick, and I couldn't leave the house. I had to take care of her.

Miss Walfrid regards Trixie with impatience. —You should have told me right away. I could have gotten another girl.

—I know. I wasn't thinking clearly. I was so upset, about my mother and all, and wanting to have my chance at Homecoming Queen— Trixie's eyes appeal to Miss Walfrid sorrowfully. —I guess I just kept hoping she'd get well enough so I could still go out and sell my tickets— She lets her voice dwindle, her body droops pathetically. —And then the time was gone.

—Well— Walfrid frowns with annoyance. —I guess there's nothing can be done about it now. Just let me have your tickets.

Trixie looks devastated, as if the sky's caving in. —I can't, Miss Walfrid. I lost them.

—You *what?*

—They're somewhere in the house, I know they are. But in all the confusion . . .

Walfrid pulls stiff as a rod and beats down on Trixie with a glare. —I want those tickets!

Trixie ducks. —Yes, ma'am, as soon as I find them— and whisks out the door as if the sheriff's posse's after her.

I don't know what to think. I'm in complete confusion as I wait through the other girls to hand over my money. I even forget to size up Clydene's holdings. This is the first I'd heard about Trixie's mother and I'm sorry, Trixie seemed so distraught. And I know how badly she must feel to miss out on her chance to be Homecoming Queen.

But there's a prickling on my skin and a pitching in my stomach telling me something's not right.

My feelers are out, testing like a snail, as I run into the girls in class. Trixie's still a little withdrawn, as I'd expect, considering what she's gone through. But Billie's all smiles again, and Faye's as cocky as ever.

Betts gives me a broad smile. —How're you holding up?

—I'm a nervous wreck. When will they tell us?

—As soon as they count the money. I don't care who wins as long as it's you or Billie or Trixie.

—I wish it could be all three of us.

—And why not? You're the three best girls running— Betts beams at the possibility. —What a court that would be.

The announcement comes at eleven forty-eight. The intercom crackles on and I jump. Coach Wilson doesn't bother to introduce himself, knows he doesn't need to. His joviality overrides the static.

> Okay, boys and girls, here's the news you've been waiting for. The three beautiful ladies who are going to reign over this year's Homecoming are:

Second runner-up Princess Clydene Orton.
First runner-up Princess Regina Patterson.
And *Queen*—Billie Franks.

I'm sick, sick all over. I realize this is not what I was expecting. I was sure I was going to win. I'm vaguely aware of the whistles and cheers of my classmates through the din in my head. I somehow manage to turn and smile at them.

I manage to make it through the last minutes of class, the back pats and babble of excitement. At the sound of the bell, I manage to make it out the door and down the hall, kids turning and smiling, throwing out —Hey, atta way— and —Congratulations, Reggie— as they pass. And there, at the bottom of the ramp, is Casey.

He must have run to make it so fast; I usually have to wait for him by my locker. He's smiling up at me as if I'm some kind of celestial body, full of light that's shining off his face. I know what he's doing, and I'm grateful. I smile back as brightly as I can and promise myself I absolutely will not cry.

Suddenly everyone seems to know me. They smile, nod, point me out. Casey's basking in the reflected glory. He has a hold of my arm and doesn't let go. I don't tell him what I'm feeling. I don't say a word about Faye, Trixie, and Billie. I don't betray my share of winning. And in a little while the pain begins to ease. As he lets me off at my house for lunch, Casey gives me a quick kiss.

Maggie and Daddy are waiting just beyond the screen door, all smiles and eagerness.

—Princess, Mummy— My voice is flat, a chink to seep out the truth so it won't drown me.

—Why that's wonderful, Reggie!

—Good for you, Reggie!— Daddy smacks his fist into his palm, an uncharacteristic gesture.

My chin quivers. —I wanted to be queen.

—Of course you did.

—I was so sure I had it.

—You know what they say: Never count your chickens.

—Please, Daddy. No homilies.

He laughs, heartily, again uncharacteristic. —I'm glad your mother raised you on books, it's given you a vocabulary.

—Great. But it doesn't make me queen.

Maggie sniffs. —I'm not so sure of that.

Daddy's bright with pride. —I think princess is quite an accomplishment. Especially for the new girl in town.

—And you can still wear your lavender taffeta.

At that moment, I love my parents inordinately.

By the time I return to school I'm on top of it. I've accepted my standing as second and can sincerely return the smiles and good wishes. And then I enter sixth-period gym.

Betts and Faye are in the middle of the gym floor, squared off, Betts holding her ground like a granite boulder, Faye pecking away at her like a fighting rooster, legs spread, torso thrust forward. Trixie's to Faye's side, throwing in a word now and then, hands on hips, a clucking hen. Billie wavers between Faye and Betts, a frightened chick. Ruthie's keeping watch on the rest of the class, glaring off the curious.

I understand immediately this is a scene I should not enter. I falter, wondering which way to turn. Betts spots me and with her eyes warns me off. But before I can move, Faye's followed her look.

She turns on me.

—I don't give a damn what you think, Betts, Billie deserves to be queen— Faye's shouting, making sure I don't miss a word. —She's lived in this town her whole life, she was *born* here. She's not some goddamn precious import from the snooty East thinks she can come in here and take overnight what rightfully belongs to us.

Faye takes two stiff steps toward me. Something in me refuses to let me turn and run.

—Who do you think you are, anyway?

I wish to god I could stand up to her like Betts, like a block of impregnable granite, but I can't. I lower my head, stammer. —No one.

—Right! And don't you forget it.

—You're a goddamn bitch, you know that, Faye?— Betts's voice booms, I wonder Faye's not bowled over by it.

Faye turns and fires back. —So who gives a good goddamn.

—Billie does.

We look at Billie, forgotten, shriveled into herself like a dried mushroom.

—The hell she does, she's *glad* to be queen.

—But she's not glad about the way she got it.

There's a moment of heavy silence, into which, thankfully, Miss Loomis trots, blowing her whistle and vigorously clapping.

—All right, everyone, line up for roll call.

I do my jumping jacks, arm twirls, and toe touches. I play a decent game of volleyball. But at the end of class, I grab up my clothes and rush to a private shower. No one comes to get me. No one calls my name. The gang shower seems shrouded in silence.

I wait until the locker room is quiet before I come out of hiding. But Betts is waiting outside the gym door. We look at each other, there isn't anything to say. By now I've figured out the story.

—Trixie gave Billie her money, didn't she?— Betts nods, her eyes dull and sorry. —I would have won— Again Betts nods. —But how did they know?

—Mrs. Wilkie the secretary lives next-door to Faye. She let it slip to Mrs. Quinn you were the only girl came for a second packet.

I study a chipped tile in the floor. Another lesson in small-town loyalty.

—Don't be mad at Billie— I look at Betts. —She really feels bad.

—Then she shouldn't have done it.

Betts shakes her head. —Faye always could bully Billie.

I walk away.

Casey can see it in my face immediately. —What's wrong?

—Just take me into the desert.

He looks surprised but doesn't press. —Where?

—Anywhere. As long as it's quiet and empty.

He drives me to the northern edge of town, overlooking the flat prairie and facing the far-off mesas and Hopi Land. I wait until the sound of the engine has cleared from our space and the peace of the sky's settled in. Then I let it all pour out.

Casey stares at me, turns away, hands on each side of the steering wheel. As I talk, his knuckles get whiter and whiter, his face blacker and blacker. His jaw squares, his chin juts, his brow lowers. I get the feeling he's ready to yank the steering wheel from its socket.

The silence is frightening as I finish.

—*That goddamn dirty fucking Faye Quinn.*

His voice explodes the tension into tiny sharp fragments. His face is so ugly, I have to look away. But there's something in his anger that answers a place in the center of me, and I'm soothed. I don't even mind his using the *f* word, it seems fitting, and my mind echoes *That fucking Faye Quinn.*

I can see his mind working.

—Don't do anything, please, Casey. You'll just make it worse.

He finally looks at me, his eyes soften, he touches my hair. —Don't you worry, Honey, you're gonna be the best goddamn Homecoming princess this school's ever seen. We're gonna make it a night to remember.

The question on the way home is whether or not to tell Maggie and Daddy.

We finally decide not to, but for slightly different reasons.

Casey's concerned for my parents. —They're so proud and happy. Why ruin it for them?

I'm concerned *about* them. —They won't let me hang around with the girls anymore.

Casey's anger rekindles. —Why the hell would you want to? After what that goddamn Faye did.

—But it was only Faye.

—And Trixie and Billie.

—Just Faye really. Trixie and Billie were pawns. The other girls are nice— Casey snorts. I turn to him appealing. —Betts is the best friend I've ever had.

—Then why didn't she stop them?

—She would have. She didn't know until it was too late.

Casey considers me —I want Catherine to hear this— and he takes me to his house.

We sit around the table. Catherine listens thoughtfully, sipping coffee and puffing cigarettes. Casey interrupts. —Be quiet, Casey, it's Reggie's story.

When I'm finished, Catherine looks into my face. —It doesn't mean they're not your friends, Reggie. Even Faye— Casey splutters. —Shut up, Casey— She turns back to me. —It just means they've been each other's friends longer— Her eyes hold mine. —Don't give up on them, Reggie. Don't harden your heart. This is going to be an important lesson for them, but they'll learn it. And when they do, they'll make it up to you.

She gives my hand a squeeze.

Inside I'm trembly, the backs of my eyes are stinging, it's hard to speak.

I squeeze back. —Thank you.

And Casey fulfills his promise. We make Homecoming a night to remember.

At noontime of Homecoming day, everyone who has a car or pickup loads up with students, and we make a yelling, honking cavalcade through town, led by Decker's white Pontiac convertible, male cheerleaders on the front fenders with bullhorns, me and Billie and Clydene in borrowed letterman sweaters in the back on the folded-down bonnet, smiling and waving pom-poms at our adoring subjects lined along the sidewalks.

That night, at halftime, we have the official coronation. Bleachers crammed, band bleating and beating, we're driven to the middle of the field, again in Decker's convertible, descend to the hastily erected dais—Billie on the raised center, me and Clydene to her sides—and beneath a blaze of lights receive our crowns. Billie's is larger than Clydene's and mine, and she gets a maroon velvet robe—which, I'm gratified to note, swallows her new strapless gown and is too long for her, but would be just right for me or Clydene. Then we resume our places on the convertible bonnet and circle the field, band churning, crowd cheering. In the focus of glare and noise, I forget I'm second.

As we're climbing the bleacher stairs to our special fifty-yard-center seats behind the band, I see Denny jumping up and down, waving and squealing at me. Catherine, and even Scotty, are with her. I get a sweet pang, and wave and squeal back. Casey hadn't told me they were coming.

I suddenly miss Maggie and Daddy. I'm sorry I asked them not to come. I was worried how they'd take all this Harden cornpone, and I didn't want them to ruin it for me. So I told them the whole thing meant less than nothing to me. I'd realized how shallow and crassly commercial it was, I felt exploited and ashamed to be part of it, and I'd be embarrassed to have them see me. They were confused and disappointed, but they took me at my word. I wish now that they hadn't.

I meet up with Catherine, Scotty, and Denny after the game and we wait for Casey. He's had a spectacular night, two touchdowns and a beautiful pass reception. Harden won the game by thirteen points, a karmic number, I think, counting back five days to Monday the thirteenth when I handed in my money. I'm just glad it wasn't Friday. My luck's been bad enough.

Casey's all healthy and jaunty as he comes toward us, his skin tight and shiny from his exertion, his hair wet from his shower. He's wearing gray slacks, white dress shirt open at the collar, and his letterman's sweater. And he looks just about as good as anything I've seen.

—Good game— It's all Scotty has to say. No hand shake, no back slap. But his smile of pride is more than enough. He has the same quirky grin as Casey, the same teasing eyes, the same slow-burning charm.

Denny's dancing around, hoping for Casey's attention. But she knows she's living on borrowed time, it's past her bedtime, as concession to a special occasion. So she keeps a low profile and defers to the adults.

—Where are you going now?— Catherine seems to have more than casual interest.

Casey shrugs, hands in pockets. —I hadn't thought about it.

—Well maybe you should.

—How about the backseat of my car?— Casey's eyes haven't left my face, and he hasn't stopped smiling.

Scotty laughs.

Catherine gives Scotty a sharp look then scowls at Casey. —That isn't funny,

Casey. Tonight is a special night. And Reggie looks so beautiful you ought to take her some place special.

—Where would you suggest?

Scotty's a railroad man. —How about the Harvey House?

My heart pitches. La Descansada? I smile quickly and pluck at my lavender gown. —I'm overdressed.

Catherine shakes her head reassuringly. —They're used to formals. The girls go there all the time after prom.

—But tonight I'm just one girl.

Casey steps to my side, takes my arm. —Why don't you leave this to me, Catherine? I'm sure I can think of something.

Catherine studies him. —I want her to have a lovely time— She puts her hands on my shoulders, kisses my cheek —Because she's so lovely— then shoves Scotty, grabs Denny, and bows out.

Casey drives us south of town.

—Where are we going?

—Wait and see— He grins over at me. —The night was made for dancing. As the stars are dancing in your eyes.

I groan. He laughs, leans over, tickles me under the chin. I slap his hand. He goes *tsk*, *tsk* and waggles a finger at me.

It's my first knowledge of the abandoned airstrip. We park the car in the middle of nowhere, turn on the radio full-blast, open the car doors, and dance in the beam of the headlights.

Late-night country western, and we're fine, two-stepping and stomping, even in my taffeta and tiara.

I shiver.

—You're cold.

—No. It's just the excitement.

—Here. Why don't you put this on?— He takes off his letterman's sweater and slips it over me.

—You looked good in it today.

—It was too big. I drowned in it.

—To show the size of the man who's going to protect you.

—Thank you for lending it.

—You ought to wear it all the time— I look up at him. —Would you wear it all the time?

So I accept his letterman's sweater. And his class ring. On a gold chain around my neck. I'm going steady. What will Maggie think?

I really don't care.

By Sunday, Betts has the figures. I had a hundred-and-twelve dollars. Billie had ninety-five. Trixie had eighty-two. Clydene had seventy-eight.

Betts stares into space, at the past. —It could have been the three of you.

I think about Faye and Trixie and Billie. About the road to queendom and what I really lost.

But I never cried.

SCENE 26

Reggie can't sleep. Something's bothering her. She feels jumpy, itchy, edgy. She sneaks out of bed and tiptoes down the hall. The study seems to be calling her. She opens the door, and is struck back by the strength of the light streaming at her, like a metaphysical force released from captivity. Pandora's Box.

My, isn't the moon just terrible? Her Emily voice, coming straight out of "Our Town."

She slowly moves to the window, transported by the pure illumination washing her room, bleaching it of color, leaving it an ethereal, translucent white. Full moon. She's never seen it quite like this, not here, only in the desert. Blinding. Enticing. Deranging.

Full of revelation.

She leans across the desk, seeking upward, but the moon's too high, out of sight above the window. But she visualizes it: round, immense, sucking up the sky, swallowing stars, burning with cold heat like dry ice.

She sees the desert, blanched, trembling under such brightness. Exposed, laid bare except for scrubby puff outlines of sage and low cypress, glistening as if dipped in salt.

It must have been April, no later than early May. She doesn't remember where they'd been, or even if it was a school night and they were just out driving.

They hadn't been talking. Casey'd been in a funny mood, sunk into himself over on his side of the car. So she'd stayed on her side to give him space to work it out. She knew she'd hear what was on his mind when he was ready.

Suddenly he pulled to the side of the road and came to an abrupt stop, as if he'd reached a decision. She turned to him.

He continued to stare out the window, hands tight on the steering wheel, shoulders stiff, the muscle in his jaw working. He did that only in moments of intense feeling. She began to worry.

When he spoke, his voice was thick and gruff.

—Take off your clothes.

—What?— She was so startled, she wasn't sure she'd heard him.

—I want you to take your clothes off.

She stared at him a stunned moment. Then, in a strange kind of involuntary obedience, slowly began removing her clothes. He didn't watch as she pulled off her blouse, shucked down her skirt, slipped off her shoes, then waited.

He glanced at her peripherally.

—All of them.

She hesitated. They'd been going steady six months now, but heavy petting had been the agreed-upon limit of their intimacy.

He shifted irritably. —I'm waiting.

She unsnapped her bra, wriggled out of her panties, and sat hunched against the door, arms across her body, hands between her thighs, protecting herself from her vulnerability and whatever was to come.

—Now get out of the car.

Again she stared. She didn't understand. What was wrong? Why did he seem so angry?

He leaned across, still refusing to look at her, and roughly shoved open her door. She was too dismayed to think. She stumbled barefoot into the sand, and stood facing the moonstruck desert.

Was he going to abandon her on the side of the road?

Why?

She heard his voice behind her.

—Now turn around.

She turned. He'd slid to her side of the car and was leaning toward her. She could see him clearly.

—Put your arms down.

She put her arms at her sides.

Finally he raised his eyes to hers. It seemed to hurt him.

—I want to see you.

And for a very long time, minutes and minutes it seemed, he saw her. As no one had seen her before.

Gradually he came out of himself and became aware she was trembling.

—Are you cold?

—Just a little— She had goose bumps and her teeth were chattering.

—Then get in the car— Abrupt, impatient again, as if she were a foolish child who ought to know better than to stand around in the night air with no clothes on.

She scrambled in.

He held out her bra and panties.

—Put your clothes on— Still bossy, still in charge of the naughty girl.

She put her clothes on and he drove her home, without a word, his face conflicted, his thoughts unreadable. He left her off at the curb, didn't even kiss her good-night. She still felt naked as she scurried up the walk.

For weeks she worried she'd been a disappointment, the explanation for his anger, the reason why the incident was never mentioned.

But Reggie knows better now, she understands that gruff annoyance, that self-protective anger, that struggle with strong disturbing emotion.

She studies the moon-frosted lawn, the limn-barked trees, and sees what Casey saw: a slender teenage girl, long-limbed and narrow-waisted, white-washed under the sky, the only color the rosy circles of her nipples and dusky triangle of her mons. The geometry of life.

If Casey became her sun god at the pool, she became his moon goddess that night.

It had been an indelible experience. It had initiated between them a betrothed tenderness that had eventually been consummated by the giving of their virginities to one another. Yet she hadn't thought of it for years, hadn't even remembered it. Until her submersion tonight in moon.

What other memories lurked in the shadows to overtake her in the unguarded night? What other repressions waited to unsuspectedly surge to the surface? To remind her of the past, and merge it with the present?

Who can understand the covert world of the emotions, the secret life of the mind?

Reggie turns from the window. She feels purged. She can sleep now.

The tune wafts insidiously. Reggie struggles in her sleep to recognize it. But someone is definitely singing. A girl, in a high sweet voice that wavers closer then floats farther away, as if carried in and out on the wind . . .

Oh, she stood out there in the midnight air, with nothing on but her nightie. The moonlight hit on the nipple of her tit, and jesus christ almighty.

A lady, a beautiful lady, is standing on the edge of a high cliff, under a full moon, the wind blowing about her, lifting her fair knee-length hair into plume-like tendrils around her white face. Whipping her gossamer gown of pink veils against her naked body, revealing her slender long legs, high breasts, rosy nipples, dusky mons . . .

Oh, her lips were pink, like a rooster's dink, and her hair was a hen-shit brown. Her tits hung loose like the wattles on a goose, and her ass wobbled up and down.

The lady is running across the sand, running running, arms outstretched, toward the sea, waves cresting and crashing, spraying white, moon sliding in and out of blue clouds . . .

Oh, she jumped in bed and covered up her head, and said I'd never find her. But I knew damn well she lied like hell, so I jumped right in behind her.

A horse, a powerful bay stallion, is pounding down the beach toward the lady. She turns, runs to meet him, leaps, straddling his back. They race down the beach together, hooves pounding resounding, head tossing thrashing, reins whipping lashing, waves crashing splashing, moon gliding hiding, lady riding riding, arms high, knees gripping tight, hair flying. Veils blown from her body, face to the moon, into the night . . .

Reggie wakes with a start, sits bolt upright. —*That's it!*

Howie stirs. —Wha . . . ?

—That's it, Howie! The next chapter— Howie struggles to his elbow. —I'm sorry, Honey, I didn't mean to wake you— She's crawling out of the covers —but I had this dream— climbing over him —and I know what to write— Her feet hit the floor. —I can write again, Howie!

CHAPTER (?)

"Please, Casey. No one has to know, it can't do any harm."

Smokey gave Casey her most winsome look, pouty, appealing, like a spoiled, coaxing child. "And it would mean so much to me."

Casey stretched back on the sofa, hands behind his head, knees spread, and enjoyed Smokey. He'd finally relaxed with her, let go of his self-protective hostility. But it hadn't come easily. It had taken time, much time, and, though he wasn't aware of it, much calculated effort on Smokey's part.

Casey had agonized over his drunken night of infidelity to Glory, his lapsed self-discipline, his betrayal of his children, his conflicted need for Smokey. He swore, to himself and Smokey, it would never happen again. He was a dedicated special agent, he informed her, he intended to perform his duty honorably. He was a devout Catholic and devoted father, he warned. He meant to keep his marriage vows.

But, Smokey knew, he was also a man. She'd continued to ply her charms with infinite patience, cleverness, and variety. But she had not succeeded in getting

Casey into bed again. Finally, she had wisely determined she would have to devise a different strategy.

"Okay," she'd said. "As long as we have to work together, how do we handle this?"

She'd let Casey take the initiative, so he would think the resolution was his. And in the end, she'd guided him into a kind of moratorium: Smokey would give up all sexual pressures if Casey would let them become friends.

And they had become friends, closer than Casey realized. They'd talked, caught up on the years, covering everything. Casey's work with the Bureau, his marriage with Glory, his children. Smokey's career as a chorine, her life with Artie, her connections with the mob. And if there were things Casey necessarily left out, about his wife and job, there were certainly things Smokey necessarily neglected, like her role in Artie's death and bag of hidden money.

They had even become trusting enough to go back over their broken love affair and discuss what had happened. Thoughts and feelings had been expressed, grievances explored, confusions clarified, misunderstandings resolved. The air had been cleared. Until now, after almost a year of working together, slowly evolving their new relationship, Smokey and Casey had reached a point of complete ease and honesty. Taking them back to where they'd been years before. They knew each other as they knew themselves, and this knowledge created a bond they had with no one else. With one another, they were most truly themselves.

"So what do you think?" Smokey pressed.

Casey eyed her thoughtfully. "Where did you say this place is?"

Smokey, sitting on bent leg sideways to Casey, leaned toward him hopefully. "Just across the highway from the beach, about two miles out of town. Between a bunch of tin sheds and a place that rents farm equipment."

Casey shook his head. "I don't think so, Smokey. Someone's bound to see us."

"Two miles out of town?"

"On horseback? In broad daylight?"

"So we could go at night." Casey scoffed. "No, I mean it. They rent horses at night. Oh, please, Casey, it would be so wonderful. We could pick a starry night."

"And it would rain."

"Oh, don't be such a poop." Smokey poked him in the ribs. "You used to love to ride."

"I still do. I just haven't had that much time."

"Well, neither have I," Smokey lied; she was still enjoying her loose leash. "This will be the perfect opportunity for us to brush up."

"What if I fall off?"

Smokey grinned. "You'll be on soft sand." Casey considered her a moment longer. She nodded perkily, "Is it a deal, then?"

He grinned back and pulled upright. "Okay. Deal."

Smokey bounced up and down on her leg. "Oh, Casey, thank you, thank you, thank you." She stretched toward him as if to give an impulsive hug, then checked herself, "Oops, sorry," and pulled back, hands primly clasped in her lap. But her bit of playacting had its effect.

Smokey moved fast, so as not to allow Casey time to reconsider. She studied the calendar, then went out to personally select and reserve their horses.

"Guess what I got you today."

She stood in front of Casey, hands behind back, jouncing on her toes.

"What?"

"A caramel palomino."

"You went out to the stables today?"

"Sure. You don't think I was going to let them stick us with some mangy old nags."

Casey smiled approvingly. She could see him appreciating himself on the back of a creamy-maned palomino. "And what did *you* get?"

She jounced. "A mahogany bay."

Casey nodded. "What'll you ride, English or Western?"

Smokey looked as if he'd lost his senses. "Why English, of course."

Casey grinned. "So you can play the perfect lady?"

"I *am* the perfect lady."

"Oh, yeah? You could have fooled me."

"And what're *you* going to ride?"

"Who, me? On a palomino?" Casey looked as if *Smokey* had lost *her* senses. "Western, of course."

"Ride 'em, cowboy, huh?"

Casey grinned. "Yeah, well let's just hope we can fool the horses."

Smokey loved their teasing banter, baited Casey, played for it. And it was getting easier and more natural every day. Just like old times.

She'd watched carefully, and there was no teasing banter between him and Glory. Glory was too literal, too practical for play. She talked shopping and budgets, kids and schedules, trivial news and gossip: Who was getting divorced or married, who had bought a new house or car, who was going where on their vacation. Glory was a bore. Boring, boring, boring. And Casey was a man of imagination and challenge, a man of the romantic West.

And if things went the way she planned, Smokey was about to rope her cowboy in.

She'd picked the night of the full moon, and her luck held out. The air was clear and balmy, not a cloud in sight. She dressed—with a soft, knowing smile—in tight tan breeches, high English boots, and silky yellow blouse. No need for jacket or hard hat.

Casey showed up in Levis, western shirt, and pointed western boots. Smokey hooted at his Stetson.

"Howdy, ma'am," he drawled, lifting it and dipping into a deep bow.

Then Smokey noticed his belt: hand-tooled leather with silver-and-turquoise buckle. She wondered if he remembered where he got it.

"Say—I like your belt."

"Why, thank you, ma'am." Casey bowed again. "A gift from an old girl friend."

"Oh, I don't know. Not so old."

"Pushing thirty."

"Who're you to remind? You've climbed that hill."

"And from up here, the view's right pretty." Casey's eyes crinkled at her for a brief moment, then he turned and hobbled out to the car, legs comically bowed, feet teetering to the outer edge of his boots.

But she'd caught the compliment.

At the stable Casey took charge, and Smokey let him, demurely hanging back. He checked over the horses, made sure the girths were tight, sat her up in her saddle, and adjusted the length of her stirrups. Then he led the way out across the highway, onto the Galveston beach.

The moon was halfway over the ocean, highlighting the splashing wave crests and spikey heads of sea oats, casting their horses' elongated shadows up the sand. Smokey realized she'd miscalculated. It was too bright. She should have scheduled this ride for the darkest night.

They rode away from town, behind sheltering sand dunes, at an easy walk for several minutes, side by side, getting the feel of the horses, letting the horses get the feel of them, enjoying the warm night air, the shine across water, and the quiet. The beach was empty, except for them.

Casey smiled over at her. "How're you doing?"

"Fine."

"You have a nice seat."

"Thank you, sir." Smokey grinned at Casey's trim buttocks. "I like yours, too."

"You wanna pick it up a little?"

"You set the pace."

Casey moved into a fast walk. Smokey stayed beside him. He looked over, kicked into an easy trot. She was still beside him.

"How come you're not posting?"

"Not fast enough."

Casey kicked again, Smokey started posting. He watched for a moment, smiled, then kicked again.

Good, Smokey smiled to herself. *He's met the challenge.*

The horses were gaining momentum. Smokey could feel her bay's rhythm beginning to shift. *He's getting ready to let go.* She looked over. Casey was leaning forward, intent. He too was getting ready to let go. She pulled gently on her reins, cuing her horse to drop back as Casey broke into a canter, moving ahead. *Okay, Smokey, old girl, it's now or never.*

She slipped her foot out of the right stirrup, shifted her weight to the left stirrup, rolled her right leg over, released the reins, and dropped to the ground, in a perfect moving dismount. Then let herself fall backwards, onto the sand.

She lay quietly, arms outstretched, one knee bent, and waited. It took only moments before she heard Casey's horse pounding back, vibrating the sand beneath her.

Casey brought his horse to a skidding stop, sand spraying, leapt off, and went down on his knees beside her. "Smokey! Smokey—are you all right?" His face was bent close over hers, full of fear.

"Yeah . . . yeah, I'm all right." She wavered a smile. "Just a little shaken."

"Are you sure?" He studied her anxiously. She was breathing in short, shallow gasps. He could see her breasts heaving beneath the yellow silk.

"I slipped a stirrup." She laughed unsteadily. "Stupid damn thing. You'd think I'd know better by now."

He smiled. "Always keep your heels down."

Smokey tried to sit up, "Now you remind me," and fell back.

Casey put his hands under her arms, gently lifted her to her feet. She stumbled, he grabbed, pulling her against him.

"Sorry," she said, meeting his eyes then quickly looking away. "I'm still a little disoriented. It'll just take me a minute."

Casey held her while she took in deep, calming breaths, breasts rising and falling against his chest, face lifted to the conspiring moon.

His grip tightened. He bent, kissed her neck, the hollow in her throat, the skin exposed above the deep V of her blouse. She accepted, mute and unmoving. He slowly unbuttoned her blouse, reached behind and unhooked her bra. Then stepped back and, just as slowly, his eyes never leaving hers, unsnapped his own shirt, unbuckled his belt, undid his fly. He sat quickly to pull off his boots and socks, stood again to remove his Levis. Then, in white jockey briefs tightly outlining his bulging crotch, spread shirt and Levis on the sand.

Smokey waited, like a moon-stunned statue. The horses lingered nearby, checking out the sea oats.

Casey put his hands on her shoulders, slowly lowered her blouse, and threw it next to his shirt. He slipped off her bra. He cupped her breasts in his hands, squeezed, weighing the full, giving roundness, tweaked her nipples erect. He kissed, sucked, gently pulled his teeth over the rosy hardness. He ran his fingers across her chest, over her shoulders, down her back and arms. He tickled the palms of her hands. She moaned and fell against him.

He lifted her, and laid her on the bed of clothing. He tugged off her boots and socks, worked down her breeches and underpants, and, balanced over her on his knees, removed his briefs. He moved up on her, showing her the full extent of his desire, immense, rigid, an obelisk. A rod of power and pleasure, of life and death. A king's scepter.

He pressed his palm in slow circles on her silky mons. Squeezed the plump lips, stroked their sleek inner folds. Rubbed the tiny button until it was hard and high.

He inserted a finger, she arched. He probed deeper, exploring the creased, cushiony satin, seeking the crucial spot. His hand came away hot and wet.

His scepter sought her throne. She spread her legs, bent her knees, raised her pelvis to meet him. They rolled, writhed, slowly, gently, rhythmically, the moon basking, the sea crashing, the horses snuffling and pawing, bridles chinkling.

Smokey came first. Her sharp cry and convulsed body released Casey. He reared up for his last violent thrust, pulled out to spend himself across her breasts and stomach, then fell heavily upon her, his face in her hair, his breaths harsh in her ear.

Afterwards, they stood facing one another, in the sacral moonlight, gritty and sticky with sand and semen, memorizing each other's body so they would never again forget.

They were the other half of each other. The yin and yang of it. The anima and animus.

Reggie sets down her pen. She's finished. The pale gold of dawn filters through the window. She turns out the lamp. She's exhausted. She lays her head down on the manuscript.

How strange, she thinks, that a vulgar song, a piece of coarse Americana, should have stimulated all this. She sees again the lady on the cliff, hears the song floating on the wind. She never heard the last verse, she woke too soon. Or the lady stopped singing. She reviews the song, quickly running through the verses, until she comes to it.

I screwed her once, I screwed her twice, I screwed her once too often. I broke a spring, or some damn thing, and now she's in her coffin.

She winces, sorry she's recalled it. Why does it always have to end like this? In ugliness, dirty words, the death of the woman?

A song written by a man.

She pulls wearily from the chair, looks at her watch. The clock radio will soon go off. To hell with it, it doesn't matter. Nothing matters. She'll do what she has to do. She'll take care of the girls, get Howie off.

She stumbles to the kitchen, numbly takes out the frying pan, puts on the coffee.

She wishes there was someone she could talk to. She wishes for Catherine.

SCENE 27

—I'm really glad we decided to go tonight— Reggie's fingers pluck at the soft folds gathered horizontally down the center of her gown.

—It wasn't my decision. I was willing to go all the time.

Reggie looks up from herself in the mirror to the reflection of Howie behind her. But he's busy putting on his cuff links, frowning. He's been irritable lately, not his old agreeable self. But who can blame him? Neither has she.

She adjusts her spaghetti straps, smooths the silk across her hips, and turns expectantly. But now he's fussing with his bow tie.

—Here— she moves toward him —let me help you with that— She reaches to the tie, smiles up at him. But he's staring over her head.

Daddy taught her to tie ties, out of desperation, so he'd have someone to help him. Maggie didn't have the patience.

She gives the tie a final twist —There— and steps back. —You look very nice tonight— and he does, in white dinner jacket, plaid tie, and matching cummerbund.

—Thank you— His eyes flicker toward her but he doesn't return the compliment.

She gestures at the dress. —What? Am I too much for you?— She doesn't mean to make it sound like a challenge.

He looks uncomfortable, he doesn't want to fight. —No. It just isn't what I expected.

She doesn't want to fight either. But he knows she designed the dress herself, picked out the fabric, a crepey mauve the color of one of Abby's hybrid irises. And the dressmaker has done a perfect job; the dress slips and slides on its slinky satin lining like the outer shell of her body.

—Well. I. Like. It— each word emphasized.

—That's all that counts— He still won't look at her.

Reggie puts her hand to her throat. —Recognize these?

He glances toward her hand, nods. —My mother's amethysts— Graduated teardrops of violet surrounded by tiny diamonds, dangle earrings to match.

—I made the dress expressly to go with them.

—They look nice.

—They're my favorite set, I think of your mother every time I wear them— Howie lifts his foot to the blanket bench, buffs the toe of his patent loafer. Reggie fumbles, grasping for straws. Steps closer, watching him. —I wish the girls could have known her. She was such a special person.

It's probably not the wisest thing to say in preparation for a party, but she's trying to reach him. Howie was very close to his mother.

She'd died young, at fifty-one, of cancer. His father had gone three years later. Of high blood pressure and a massive coronary, so the doctors said. But Howie and Reggie knew better; it had been of grief and loneliness. They'd been a devoted couple, in that undemonstrative, nonverbal way of New Englanders. The way Howie understands.

Reggie watches Howie finish buffing his shoes, stand, reach for his jacket. She goes to him, helps him straighten it on. Looks up at him, holding both lapels, her eyes searching his.

—I want us to have a good time tonight, Howie.

He meets her look, and she hates what she sees there: pain, distrust. She hates even more knowing she's responsible.

She feels sorrow, remorse. She wants to reestablish contact. She reaches inside his jacket, arms around his waist, cheek against his chest. After a moment he returns the hug, cheek on top of her head. They hold each other in long silence. She'd like to say, I love you, Howie. That's what she's feeling right now. But she doesn't trust it, anymore than he does.

The intimacy of the car—the hum of the engine, the whirr of the tires, the flash of the headbeams as they cut through the night—brings them closer.

It's a beautiful spring evening, full of black sky, bright stars, and new green. Reggie stirs with excitement.

—You know what we ought to get, Howie? A convertible. For just this kind of night— She suddenly feels young and giddy.

—What about your hair?

—To hell with my hair. What about romance?— But she doesn't roll down the window.

She slides over next to Howie. —We're going to have such a good time tonight. We're going to sing and dance and laugh. Just like old times.

Howie smiles, lifts his arm, Reggie snuggles under. —They don't allow sing-alongs at the country club.

—Well pooh on them. Then we'll just have to do it right now— She turns on the radio, finds a station with seventies' music, songs they know the words of. She lays her head on Howie's shoulder, listens.

. . . *Yesterday. All my troubles seemed so far away. Now it looks as if they're here to stay.* She starts to sing. *Oh, I believe in yesterday. Yesterday. I'm not half the man I used to be. There's a shadow hanging over me. Yesterday came suddenly.* She doesn't expect Howie to join in, too shy, except on their occasional appearances at church. And once in a while she and the girls can coax him into a round. *Love was such an easy game to play. Now I need a place to hide away . . .*

She snaps off the radio —Too sad— leans into Howie, starts singing softly. —Row, row, row your boat, gently down the stream— He glances down at her, grins. —Merrily, merrily, merrily, merrily, life is but a dream— She starts again, stronger —Row, row, row your boat— nods, Howie kicks in. —Row, row, row your boat— They finish in perfect time and harmony.

They've polished off "You Are My Sunshine" and "My Bonnie Lies Over the Ocean" and are into "I've Been Working on the Railroad" by the time they turn into the drive of the club.

The place is packed. The May Dinner Dance is one of the most popular events of the year and everyone has turned out: Cissy and Buddy, Muffy and Win, Corkie and Chip, Barbara and David, Sally and Ted, Buffie and Mark, and a dozen other couples Reggie's known for years but hasn't seen in months. She and Howie make the rounds, pumping hands, brush-kissing cheeks, reciting the litany:

—Hey, Teddy, how the hell are you?

—Hi, Muffy. It's so good to see you.

—Chip, old boy. How you doin'?

—Sally! How nice you look.

—How's Chipper . . . ?

—How's Tyler . . . ?

—How's your mother?

Reggie gushes in, all gregarious charm and swift vivaciousness, giving no room for upstaging. She's in charge of this show tonight, and no one's getting a line she doesn't hand them. There's been talk, she knows, and so does Howie. Problems with Reggie, trouble between the Kendalls, rumors of divorce. Reggie's out to dispel them. Their faces are a joy to behold. Surprise, speculation, consternation.

Howie sees what she's doing and is amused. What he can't do himself but enjoys in her; what he married her for. She's beginning to feel like her old self, the self she hasn't let herself be around these people for years, if ever. Her Harden self. So let 'em look!

Buffie's been expecting them of course; she keeps close track of her little brother, or tries to. And the look on her face when she sees Reggie's dress is worth the whole evening. Her eyes fairly pop out of her head and her chin almost drops to her chest, her mouth's that big and her chest that ample. Reggie lifts her skirt and makes a little curtsy, giving Buffie the full benefit of shapely leg poking from center slit, and waggles her fingers in sweet greeting. Buffie also spots the amethysts, which she thought should have gone to her. Reggie's triumph is complete.

Reggie's arranged for them to sit with Cissy and Buddy. Her reclusiveness these past months, including her avoidance of even Cissy, has put a strain on their friendship. She's hoping this evening will ease it. Their table is well situated, just off center and one row back of the dance floor; some of Buddy the club tennis pro's influence, Reggie suspects. Buffie and Mark, she's delighted to note, are near the back corner.

Dinner is heart of palm and pimiento salad, *cordon bleu* chicken with mixed rice and asparagus tips, and raspberry mousse with chocolate wafers. Not *haute cuisine* but pretty good for a country club.

Reggie'd started with Perfect Rob Roys during cocktails, shifted to champagne with *hors d'oeuvres*, and is now working on a fine white wine. Howie's not much of a wine drinker, like Buffie he prefers scotch, but he knows his wine list.

Conversation is going swimmingly. Cissy's had enough to drink to get girlish and giggly, Howie's growing expansive, and Buddy never shows his liquor. Reggie herself is a little light-headed. But given her late-night hours with her lap desk, her capacity is greater than it used to be.

The orchestra's past warming up and is beginning to get hot. During cocktail hour, they provided soft background, to help absorb the shrill laughs and abrupt guffaws. Between dinner courses, a few couples got up to initiate the dance floor. But the real dancing begins once the tables are cleared.

The crowd ranges widely in age, so the orchestra pulls out a little of everything, to give everyone a chance to shine. Members and guests who come to the dances are *dancers*, whether they're good at it or not. Buffie and Mark relish the samba, where Buffie seems to think the main object is to toss her hips, battleships on a wind-torn sea, her idea of sexy. Cissy does a mean Charleston. Corkie and Chip like all the fast numbers, where they can sling one another around and bounce. Barbara and David prefer the sedate selections, slow waltzes and dreamy foxtrots. Sally and Ted never get up, and Muffy and Win never sit down. There are even a few takers for the Twist and, later in the evening, a frolicsome line for the Bunny Hop.

Reggie talks Howie into a few foxtrots, two sambas, one tango, and one waltz, but beyond that he balks. Like everyone, he's been to the dance classes, he knows the steps, but he lacks confidence. He dies a thousand deaths when he bumps into someone or steps on Reggie's foot. Yet he can stand up in court before a judge and roomful of power brokers and argue a case involving millions of dollars.

Reggie tips her wine glass and finds it empty, signals to Howie across the table, lifting her empty glass.

He reaches for the bottle —No more— shaking it to show her.

—Order another— They have to speak loudly to hear each other above the music and conviviality.

—We've already had three.

—Cissy and Buddy are going to be thirsty when they get off the dance floor.

Howie looks uncertain. —You've had a lot to drink.

—I'm *fine*, Howie— pulling straight and smiley. —Do I look sloppy? Am I the least maudlin?— He still hesitates. —Come on, Howie. It's a *party.*

Howie motions for the waiter.

Reggie smiles, hand holding the stem, while the waiter refills her glass. Then lifts and sips, looking around the room, absorbing the lowered lights, the candles and flowers, the swaying figures in cocktail dresses and summer tuxedos, shushing shuffle of feet and seductive croon of sax. Black and white with notes of subdued color. It's one of those quiet spacings between hot licks, to allow wiping of brows, sipping of drinks, and catching of second breaths.

She's remembering how well she used to dance. How she and short Bobby Briggs became the hit of the Harden High Friday afternoon sock hops, jitterbugging like Warner Brothers' forties, jigging like the fifties, jiving straight out of Mo Town; whirling, twirling, swinging, dipping, feet flying faster than train wheels; bending backwards, down, down, knees bent, backs to the floor, closer and closer; leaping up in perfect timing, never missing a step never missing a beat.

In Harden, when there was nothing else to do, they could always dance.

She's remembering:

How they drove their cars to the abandoned airstrip, parked in a circle, radios on the same station full blast, doors wide, and in the beams of the headlights, danced on the sandy asphalt. Gritty gyration, small-town salvation.

How she chaired decorations for the Junior-Senior prom, Parisian Nights, with blue-and-white striped awnings, murals painted by the art club, of which she was a member.

Betts in her oversized midnight-blue taffeta formal, made by her mother, Betts on the arm of her father.

Oh, Betts.

No one else would bring her, she didn't have a date. So her father was her escort.

Oh, Betts . . .

—Why, *Reggie.* What's the matter— Reggie starts, finds herself staring into Cissy's concerned face leaning toward her. —You look like you're about to cry.

Howie gives Reggie a sharp look. —She's getting maudlin.

—I am not getting maudlin.

—She always gets maudlin when she's had too much to drink— Howie's voice itself is a little thick.

Reggie speaks very distinctly. —I am not maudlin. And I have not had too much to drink— Cissy looks uneasily from one to the other, Howie cynical, Reggie defiant. —I'm just bored, that's all.

Reggie pushes to her feet —I want to dance— and stares at Howie, hip out.

—Not now.

—I want to dance, Howie.

—Maybe a little later.

Reggie glowers across the table, turns on Buddy. —Dance with me, Buddy.

—I just sat down.

—All right then— she spins around, scans the crowd, hands on her hips.

—Sit down, Reggie.

—I'll find someone who *does* want to dance with me.

—And keep your voice down— Howie is no longer expansive.

—Will you stop picking on me?

Cissy darts a worried look around the room, leans forward in a hushed tone.

—She's okay, Howie. She's just having fun. She's been shut away so long, she . . .

—Stay out of this, Cissy— Buddy's scowl warns. She shuts her mouth and lowers her head obediently.

Reggie's turned belligerently on Howie. —You're acting just like my mother.

—You're making a spectacle of yourself.

—A *what*?

—People are looking.

Reggie glares at the crowd, at Howie, at Buddy and Cissy. Sits, grabs the bottle, pours wine, sets the bottle beside her glass. Drinks and glares at the dance floor.

Cissy pipes up cheerily. —Isn't the orchestra just wonderful this year? Last year they had so many complaints, the management just had to . . . She flutes on, nervously, inanely.

Reggie ignores her. Her brain is buzzing with fury, like a bunched bundle of shorted electric circuits.

The orchestra stops playing, holds a long silent beat, then abruptly breaks into a conga. Cheers from the crowd, couples scramble up. Reggie's chin lifts, her eyes narrow. She shoves again to her feet.

—Where are you going?— Howie alerts, back suddenly stiffening, voice sharp.

—It's a line dance. I don't need a partner— She starts pushing between the chairs. —You coming, Cissy?

Cissy pulls back. —Oh, I couldn't possibly. It's too fast and crazy. I'm always afraid I'll fall down.

Reggie sashays onto the dance floor, grabs the end of the line, swings into rhythm, One, two, three, la con*ga,* feels her own waist grabbed. One, two, three, la con*ga.* The line weaves around the floor, circling and snaking, stamping and kicking, laughing and singing out One, two, three, la con*ga,* getting faster and wilder, until finally, with one mighty crack of the whip, it snaps and falls apart.

Reggie staggers back, laughing, head spinning—and feels her waist still caught in the viselike grip. She twists, looks over her shoulder.

—Hey, Skipper. Was that you back there all the time?

Skip leans into her face. —Hanging on for dear life— He's swaying, loosely, unrhythmically, as if there's still music.

—Well you can let go now.

—What if I don't want to?

Reggie wrenches free, looks around. —Where's Marla?

—At the table. She won't dance with me. Says I'm too drunk.

—That's what Howie says, too.

Skip looks aghast. —He said that about *me*?

—No. About me— They laugh into each other's face.

—Well you look just *fine* to me— Skip leers, listing unsteadily.

Reggie poses. —You like my dress, huh?

—I like what's in it.

The orchestra starts up again.

Reggie tilts her head. —So how are you at the foxtrot?

—Why don't you try me?— Another leer.

He reaches for her, both hands. She grabs up one, plants the other firmly at her waist. They shuffle back and forth, in a slow two-step, wearing out the same square of polished hardwood.

Reggie slits her eyes, sinks into the music, letting it sing to her body. She feels the slippery shift of her dress as she sways from foot to foot, hears the murmuring crowd at a distance, like soughing waves. Lifts her face to the fractured mirror ball revolving above her, fragmented full moon sending secret signals into the night. She shakes her head, imagining the soft brush of long platinum hair against her back and shoulders.

Skip lurches and pulls her closer. She smiles, beguilingly, and pushes him back. His hand slips to her hip and tightens.

—You shake a mean hip there.

—I'm a dancer— She's seeing herself a chorine, in Las Vegas.

—What else do you do?

The music stops, she drops his hand, steps back and gives him a slow heavy grind and mean hard bump, topped with a jelly-jiggling shake of the bosom.

His bloodshot eyes pop. —Wow!— She laughs, a light tinkly laugh, and tosses her long platinum hair. —Stay right here— He starts away, turns back. —Don't go away— She cocks her chin, teasingly, tauntingly, throws out a hip. He points a finger. —I'll be right back.

She watches him hurriedly stagger toward the bandstand. The room spins, recedes, blurs, for a moment she's not sure where she is. She frowns in concentration as a man, somehow familiar, motions to the orchestra leader, leans forward whispering, hands him something. Then turns and weaves toward her, his ruddy face split in a wide toothy grin, eyes riveted on her.

She smiles, lifts her hand and floats into his arms. His face is coarse and sweaty. She doesn't see it. His breath is hot and acrid. She doesn't smell it.

She's listening to the music, something she knows but just can't quite recall the name of. A strong elemental beat, sensual, fun to fool around with.

She gives herself over to it.

Her partner pitches and stumbles sideways.

It doesn't matter.

She's dancing alone.

SCENE 28

Gradually, like slowly lifting the hood from a parrot's cage, Reggie's brain registers awakeness. She resists the message. She keeps her eyes shut and stays very still, somehow sensing that the slightest movement will prove a disaster.

She hears a soft whir and click, the light outside her lids brightens. Someone has opened the drapes. She squints an eye. She's home, in bed. She turns her face into the pillow.

—Reggie?— *Howie.* If she ignores him, maybe he'll go away. —It's eleven o'clock. Don't you think it's time to get up?

She burrows deeper into the pillow. —No . . . A barely audible whimper.

—All right then. I'm leaving with the girls.

Her eyes snap open. This sounds ominous. A threat? She rolls her face out of the pillow. The light cuts across her retinas, stabs into her head. She raises a hand to shield them.

—Where? Where are you going?

—I promised to take them biking.

—Oh— Now she remembers.

—You said you were going with us.

—I know— She moans. —But I can't possibly, Howie. My head's splitting.

—I'm not surprised.

She opens her fingers, peers through them at him. He's assessing her, arms crossed.

—I guess I had too much to drink.

No comment.

She struggles to sitting position, squinting against the brightness and pain, finds herself naked. —How'd I get undressed?— She looks up. —You must have put me to bed— The realization of this intimacy shocks and fascinates her. A first. Howie taking her clothes off. She pulls the sheet to her chin.

—You certainly weren't in any shape to do it.

—I'm sorry, Howie— She smiles weakly, apologetically. —I don't remember a thing— He continues to regard her impassively. —Did I pass out?

—Only from the neck up. The rest of you was quite active— A hint of amusement?

—Thank you— Another attempt at a smile. —It's not easy undressing a floppy drunk— Another weighted silence. —I don't even remember coming home.

—Lucky you— She looks up at him sharply. No amusement.

—I didn't get maudlin, did I? I hope I didn't get into a crying jag.

—I wish you had. It would have been better.

Her eyes widen with alarm. —Better than what?

—You sang.

She laughs, trying to coax him into a little humor. —Was I that bad? What'd I do? More rounds?

He doesn't smile. —Dirty songs.

—Oh. No— Her heart pitches. —Not about a lady in the moonlight in her nightie?— She's hearing the words. *The moonlight hit on the nipple of her tit.*

Howie nods. —That and Canal Street. Which I'd heard before. But not from a woman.

. . . goddamn son-of-a-bitch, I couldn't find a whore . . .

—Oh no.

—And a nice little ditty about the mountaineers.

. . . they screw their wives with butcher knives . . .

—Oh god. I *hate* that song.

—And just about the filthiest thing I've ever heard.

—No. Don't tell me— She wants to block her ears.

—With the cute catchy refrain of "Ring Dang Do."

. . . so soft and furry like a pussy cat . . .

—Oh no. Oh *god.* I'm so sorry, Howie.

—So am I. I haven't been able to get it out of my ears.

—Believe me, I wouldn't have sung those songs for the world if I hadn't been drinking.

—I must say, you have quite a repertoire. Rougher than any I heard in all my years at Yale and Harvard.

—I haven't thought about those songs for years.

—I don't need to ask where you learned them.

—I can't imagine what made me do such a thing.

—For the shock value, I suspect.

—But why? Why would I want to shock you?

—That's what I've been asking myself all night. Why would Reggie want to disgrace herself in front of the whole country club?

—The whole country club?— She stares at him, horrified. —Howie. I didn't sing at the country club?

At last he allows himself a small smile. Tight, thin-edged, and sharp, like the blade of a knife.

—No. For them, you danced.

Reggie doesn't know what to answer, can't answer. —The last thing I remember is the conga line.

—What about Skip?

—Skip?— Red face, white-toothed grin, sweaty palm. —Yes— Revolving ball, reeling room. —I danced with him.

—And then *for* him.

She stares, uncomprehending.

—You still don't remember?

She shakes her head.

—"The Stripper"?

Her face goes white, her eyes widen, her hand clumps the sheet at her chest.

—*David Rose's "Stripper"?*— Aghast, disbelieving. She remembers only too well the way she used to dance to it.

Howie nods, grimly. —Selected by Skip Wallingham, the preppy set's exemplar of "The Lost Weekend." Choreographed by Reggie Kendall, the country-club set's reincarnation of Gypsy Rose Lee.

—No— Reggie catches a remembrance of long platinum hair tossed against bare shoulders. A Vegas chorine imagined. *Smokey.*

—Why didn't you stop me?

Howie suddenly looks tired. —To tell you the truth, Reggie, I didn't know how. I felt completely defeated. If I went out on the dance floor, I was afraid you'd fight me, creating a worse scene. If I stayed at the table, I'd look like some spineless wimp, shaming us both. I was in a strictly lose-lose situation.

—So you just let me *go*?

Howie studies his wife.

—Cissy went out and got you. Led you back, still dancing, still swinging your hips, smiling and waving to your audience.

Reggie sinks her face into her hands. —Poor Cissy.

—Marla took care of Skip. He'd been literally bowled over by your performance, toppled to the floor. Where he sat ogling you.

—Please, Howie. No more.

—But it wasn't a total loss. You roped in a few whistles and cheers. I'm sure there would have been more if there hadn't been wives.

—Don't. I don't want to hear . . .

—But I think you ought to prepare yourself.

—For what?

—The talk.

—Oh, *god*. It's going to be all over town.

—You're going to get some calls. First most probably from your mother. Then your grandmother.

—No! I can't face them. What will I say?— She looks at him desperately. —Don't answer the phone, Howie. Don't talk to anyone.

—We can't hide out forever, Reggie. I have to go to work.

Work. Oh no.

—Oh god, Howie. Your *promotion*!

Howie smiles, a dark twisted smile. He nods, curtly, with finality —Exactly— and starts for the door.

—Howie— He stops. —I'm sorry. So terribly sorry . . .

He looks at her, eyes shadowed with pain. —I don't know what you're trying to prove, Reggie, or why. But I'll say one thing for you. You sure can bump and grind— And he quietly exits, closing the door behind him.

Reggie sits clutching the sheet, staring blindly at the closed door, as she gradually absorbs the damage she's done, and those she's damaged. Howie. Katelyn and Lindsay. Maggie and Daddy. Abby. Understanding, with sudden cruel insight, the selfish consequences of her defiance.

You do not fly in the face of propriety. You observe the code, obey the rules. To show you are reasonable and rational. In control, stable. A person of taste, moderation, and judgment. Dependable, conscientious, responsible. In a word, trustworthy.

Reggie slowly untangles from the bed, shuffles to the bathroom, each step a punishment, to assess the rest of the damage. Her reflection in the mirror is a reproach. Red swollen eyes, puffy dark circles, blotchy dull skin. Hair poking up in matted peaks, the result of sweat, fitful sleep, and hair spray. This is what Howie stood looking at. A harridan, a haggard harpy, who had wrought havoc.

She brushes her teeth, gagging. Splashes water on her face, wiping away mascara smears and crusted sleepers. Jerks the comb through the spiked clumps, shaking out white dust of residue lacquer. Washes down three aspirin, feeling a wave of dizziness and nausea as the water hits her raw stomach.

She drags to the closet. Howie's hung her dress neatly on the back of the closet door. The slit is torn several inches up, the crepey silk is puckered in rings from sloshed drinks. The dyed-to-match satin pumps, neatly lined on the closet floor, are scuffed and stained beyond salvage.

She puts on her robe and crawls back into bed. Her body aches, her head throbs, her eyes burn, her stomach gurgles and lurches. But these are nothing beside the distress of her conscience. She must do the right thing, try to make amends, repair the damage as best she can. She reaches for the bedside phone. And this will be her greatest agony.

She dials, takes a deep breath, waits trembling.

—Hello, Maggie?— Her voice sounds small, young, frightened. —It's me. Reggie.

—Yes, I think I recognize your voice by now— Does Reggie hear a hint of a smile, a touch of humor? —How are you?

Another breath. —Well, to tell you the truth, Maggie, not so good.

—Oh?

—I've done something terrible.

—Have you now? Would you like to talk about it?

—Yes. But not over the phone. Could I come over?

—Any time you like, Reggie, this is your home. You know I'm always happy to see you. After all, you may remember, you're my daughter— And after Reggie's been so rotten to her these past months. She feels her chest tighten, her eyes water.

—I'm not much up to going out today, but I was thinking maybe tomorrow morning. As soon as I get the girls off.

—Fine. We'll have breakfast— The thought of food sickens Reggie.

—And, Maggie?— Maggie waits. Reggie's voice quivers. —If anyone calls, please try not to pay any attention. Just wait until I get there.

—I was planning to do just that.

Reggie's heart sinks. —You've already heard . . .

—Just one person's story, Reggie. I was hoping for yours.

—Buffie.

—Via Aunt Miriam.

—How many other people must they have told?

—It doesn't matter. We'll take care of all that tomorrow. And, Reggie— Softly. —Thank you for calling.

Reggie replaces the receiver and, squeezing her eyes tight, quietly, acquiescently, lets the tears fall. Her body jerks in short sharp spasms, the sobs catch and squeak in her throat, like the whimpers of a lost puppy.

After several minutes, her shoulders still, she opens her eyes, wipes her face on the sheet, and, holding the phone on her lap, dials again. This time her voice is stronger.

—Hi, Abby, it's me, Reggie.

—Why, Reggie, how nice to hear from you.

—Well maybe, and maybe not. I need to talk to you.

—Certainly.

—Could I come over tomorrow?

—I'd be delighted. Plan on lunch.

—Do you mind if we make it a little late? I have to see Maggie first.

—Good. I'm glad you called her.

—Oh. I see Buffie got to you, too.

—Of course, dear. Bright and early. You don't suppose she was going to pass up such a juicy opportunity.

—And it's probably every bit as bad as you heard.

—Don't be silly. I've lived long enough to know nothing is ever as bad as you hear. Would one o'clock do?

—Perfect. It'll give me just enough time to bare my soul to Maggie, with an excuse to leave before I bleed to death.

—I wouldn't worry it'll come to all that. Remember what we painters say: There isn't a canvas can't be painted over.

—Yeah, well I think I need to scrape this one clean.

SCENE 29

Reggie stops the car in the shoulder just short of the drive up to the house, turns off the engine, and quietly sits, collecting courage. She's early. Howie'd offered to take the girls to school, as a show of support. Or, she suspects, in an effort to get her out the door before she changed her mind. He'd been relieved and approved, she could see, when she told him about her arranged visits with Maggie and Abby, though he'd been keeping removed from her these last miserable twenty-four hours, morose and uncommunicative. And who could blame him? She was ruining his life, and hers.

She studies the commodious white colonial congenially set on its sloping expanse of green lawn, the spaced trees and trimmed shrubs. This is your home, Maggie had said. And though Reggie lived here twenty-one years, it seems as strange to her now as her own house has seemed these past months each time she drives up to it.

She sighs, there's no putting it off any longer. She starts the car and turns up the drive.

She rings the bell and waits, tensed, for the slipping clicking onslaught of Jake's toenails. Unnerving silence. Maggie opens the door, and for a moment, Reggie just dumbly stands.

Maggie smiles. —Well, come on in. I'm not going to bite.

Reggie returns the smile, uncertainly, enters, and waits while Maggie closes the door. She needs reassurance, although she knows she doesn't deserve it. In the West, visitors are always received with a solid hug and hearty greeting. Not so in the reserved East. Even when the visitor is family, unless, that is, you're a child. Reggie feels right now she qualifies.

Maggie gives her daughter a quick once-over, then briskly heads for the kitchen. Reggie meekly follows. The table is set with place mats and napkins, second-best silver, and even a vial of flowers. On the counter are lined what look like preparations for an omelette. Maggie, not an inspired or enthusiastic cook, has gone to some effort, and Reggie is touched.

—Daddy wanted to be here but he had class. He sends his love.

Reggie nods, thinking it's just as well, one parent at a time is about as much as she can handle, and watches as her mother cracks eggs into a bowl. The silence seems disconcertingly unnatural, and she suddenly realizes why.

—Where's Jake?

Maggie's face clouds, she picks up a wire whisk. —I had to give him away— Reggie looks at her mother incredulously. —I know. You don't have to say it— Maggie whips at the eggs furiously. —But there was nothing left I could do. No matter how many times a day I worked with him, he refused to be trained. So finally, I enrolled him in obedience school— She whacks the whisk on the edge of the bowl. —He flunked sub-novice three times— Sets the whisk on the counter. —They kicked him out.

Reggie resists a grin. This is serious business to Maggie. —I never heard of such a thing. Kicking a dog out of school.

—Even dog schools have an image of respect to maintain. Like all private schools. He was wasting their time and setting a bad example. Presenting a bad influence.

—So where is he?

Maggie turns on the burner under the omelette pan. —I found him a home on a farm with five children and all kinds of livestock— She scowls. —He's having the time of his life. I've been out to see him twice. He doesn't even recognize me— Reggie can see how much this hurts. —He's too busy chasing after the horses and cows, and the kids on their dirt bikes.

Reggie tries to be reassuring. —It sounds like the perfect place for him.

—Oh it is— But Maggie doesn't sound too happy about it. —He stays outdoors all the time, refuses to come in even when lured with a bone. The boys built him this huge dog house. I wish you could see it. He's chewed around the entire doorway, absolutely shredded it. He must have a stomachful of splinters.

Reggie laughs. —Better his woodwork than yours.

—Have you seen the family room? Take a look before you leave. We're going to have to completely repaper it. He somehow discovered he could catch his teeth in the burlap. So every time he passed, whenever we weren't watching, and how could we watch him all the time, he'd snag an edge and rip.

Maggie slams English muffins into the toaster oven. —We couldn't put butter on the table. He'd casually walk by and with one flick of his huge tongue leave the plate clean, with a look of saintlike innocence.

Reggie's grinning, enjoying her mother's exasperation and the relaxation of tension between them.

Maggie slops the eggs into the omelette pan, too worked up to notice the dribbles smoking on the burner.

—Your poor father. One day he was taking a nap on the sofa. The dog knew he wasn't allowed on the sofa. But every once in a while he'd back his fanny up to it and sit on the edge, just like he was proper people. He was that big. You never saw how big he got. I guess that's what he tried with your father. And when he didn't get scolded off, he took advantage. The next thing I knew, I heard your father yelling for help. Jake had backed up until he was completely on top of him, in the middle of his back. Daddy couldn't shove him off because his arms were pinned under his chest. And he couldn't buck him off because he was hefting close to a hundred pounds. The dog just kept riding up and down, and, I swear, grinning for all the world as if this were the best fun he'd had in months.

Reggie's laughing so hard, she has tears.

Maggie throws diced ham and cheese into the omelette. —Our whole lives were taken over by that dog. We were being ruled by a good-natured imbecilic tyrant.

—So you did what you had to do. You were fighting for house and husband.

—I know. But I still feel terrible about it.

Maggie flops the omelette onto a plate, cuts, slides half onto a second plate, under-cooked center oozing.

Reggie saves the muffins from the toaster oven. —This just wasn't his environment or life style— She hears her words, thinks of her own situation. Maggie sees the darkness come over her.

They settle at the table. Reggie gingerly takes a bite, Maggie watching.

—Good— Reggie nods. She knows how much her mother hates to cook.

Maggie nods in return, curtly. She knows Reggie knows how much she hates to cook.

—So— Reggie takes a discreet pause between bites. —After all that, dare I ask? Where's Erin?

Maggie's mouth pinches, she frowns. —That's another sad story. She's at the vet's. I decided to have her spayed— Abrupt. Dealing succinctly with the painful.

—Oh, Maggie. There go all your beautiful plans for breeding the perfect setter.

—No— Maggie shakes her head. —She was too high-strung. She would have made a terrible mother. I'd have all these nervous neurotic pups. She'd either worry at them all the time or neglect them. This will be better for her. Without the stress of being procreative, maybe she'll relax and be easier to live with. She can stop looking over her shoulder for the next stud.

Reggie sets her fork down.

Maggie looks over. —Is that all you're going to eat?

Reggie lays her hand on her stomach. —I'm still a little queasy.

—The wages of sin, eh?— Maggie stands. —So I don't suppose you want coffee.

Reggie makes a face, sticks out her tongue.

Maggie pours her own cup, returns to the table. —Are you ready to talk?

—I guess. If you are.

—So. Exactly what happened?

—What was Aunt Miriam's story?

—I'm not interested in Aunt Miriam's story. Or Buffie's. I'm interested in yours.

Reggie braces. —Well, the facts are simple enough, and not too pleasant. I went to the country club dance, had too much to drink, and danced the bumps and grinds to David Rose's "Stripper."

Maggie nods. —That's pretty much Miriam's story, stripped, if you'll excuse the pun, of her embellishment.

Reggie tries to grin. —You've been living too long with Daddy.

Maggie raises her eyes, looks earnestly at her daughter. —But why, Reggie?

Reggie returns her look, distressed. —I don't know, Maggie. I honestly don't know. I've done nothing but think about it all day and all night. But I can't come up with any answer because I don't remember any of it. It's like it was some other person. All I can say is, I guess I was drunk.

Maggie shakes her head. —That's not enough. You've had too many drinks before and never come close to doing anything like this, not even in college.

Reggie lifts and drops her shoulders. —Howie says it was for the shock value.

Maggie's lips pull thin, she considers. —Yes, I can see that. An act of defiance. By a rebellious child.

—Only I'm not a child.

—No— Maggie gives Reggie a direct look. —You're a grown woman. With a husband and family.

Reggie lowers her head. —Whom I'm hurting very much.

Maggie studies her daughter, her face pained for both of them. —I'm sorry, Reggie— Reggie looks up, startled by her mother's sincerity and sorrow. —Sometimes I'm not a very good mother. I want to help, but I'm like Erin I guess. Either I worry at you all the time, or I neglect you. I try to reach out, but all I can offer is what I understand, the do's and don'ts of things. And when that doesn't work, I pull back. Not because I'm angry or don't care but because I'm frustrated. Because I just don't know what else to do.

—No. It's not your fault, Maggie. I pushed you away.

—Because I couldn't give you what you needed.

—Because I have to work this out for myself.

Maggie fiddles with her knife. —But that doesn't seem to be going too well, does it?

—No. I guess not. I'm not being a very good daughter. *I'm* the one should be sorry. And I am, Maggie. Truly sorry.

—Yes. I can see that.

—I didn't mean to disgrace you and Daddy.

—You know that isn't what matters to us. I told you a long time ago, we don't mind putting a few noses in the air. As your father says, it gives them something to smell besides their own dirty laundry. *You're* what matters.

—Don't give up on me, Maggie. I'm still trying, I know I can work this out.

—Maybe— A deep breath, like a sigh. Or a reach for courage. —And maybe it's time for outside help. Someone objective— Another deep breath. —A professional.

Reggie looks up, stunned. —Are you saying I need a psychiatrist?

—I'm saying I think you need help.

—You think I'm crazy.

—Not at all. I just think this thing has gotten beyond you. You're confused. And a psychiatrist can help you sort it out.

—I don't believe this!

—Think about it. Please, Reggie. That's all I'm asking.

—My own mother.

Maggie fumbles in her pocket, extends her hand. —And just in case . . .

—What? A card? You even have a card?

—I wanted to be prepared.

Reggie pushes back in her chair. —You're farming me out!

Maggie's hand trembles, her voice falters. —I was hoping you'd be receptive.

Reggie grabs her purse, shoves to her feet. —Next thing I know, you'll want me sterilized! Have *me* spayed.

Maggie winces, her arm falls heavily across the table.

Reggie spins on her heel, leaving Maggie with her eyes pleading, the card twitching between her thumb and finger like a white eagle's feather, a prayer feather, as Reggie stalks out the door.

SCENE 30

Reggie's driving erratically. She knows she should slow down, pull over to the side of the road. She's not processing. But she has to get out of this neighborhood, away from that house.

She feels duped, taken in, completely and utterly sold out. Her face stings with heat and sweat and humiliation, her stomach churns with betrayal. She fights dizziness and the desire to vomit as she tries to think what to do.

She can't go to Abby's, it's too early. She can't go home, it's too empty. And too far back to Abby's. The abrupt ending with Maggie has left her too much time and not enough.

Too much, and not enough . . .

She drives aimlessly, letting the car take over. She has to calm down, get control of herself. Has to be rational, reasonable . . .

What was it Maggie did that was really all that terrible? Suggest she see a psychiatrist? So what? Big deal. Half the families Reggie knows have had one if not several members in therapy at one time or another. Why should that be so threatening? It's what educated, affluent people do when they can't work out their problems for themselves. When they have no one else to talk to.

What did she expect of Maggie anyway? That she'd take her hand and tell her what a darling girl she was? That she'd offer unqualified love and support? Regardless of her actions?

No. She has to be fair to Maggie, honest with herself. She's been behaving badly. Jeopardizing her entire family, their stability, their standing. Social associations. Business connections. They're one and the same.

She's been thinking only of herself, though that isn't how she feels or how she means to be.

She has to see it from Maggie's side, the side everyone else will see. And take.

But who is there to understand and take Reggie's side?

Perhaps she doesn't have a side. Perhaps she *has* become an egocentric monster.

Perhaps after all Maggie is right. She needs a psychiatrist.

Reggie resurfaces from her quagmire, looks around. She's been driving on automatic, completely unawares. But landmarks seem familiar. With sudden recognition, she realizes that the BMW, in its fey Celtic wisdom, has carried her toward the one place that can give her the solitude and solace she's so sorely in need of.

She parks at the bottom of the hill, takes the path up through the trees, comes out behind the gardens. The azalea and rhododendron are in full bloom, a blaze of pink, ruby red, white, salmon, fuchsia. She's missed the iris. She didn't even make it to the garden show, to applaud Abby's contributions and her assured annual ribbons. She *is* a self-obsessed monster.

She circles the large lawn, set up for croquet, staying close to the trees, clear of the view from the back windows, pausing to admire jack-in-the-pulpit, shooting star, bleeding heart, trillium. But when she reaches the gazebo, her planned destination, it feels too formal and structured, too closed in. She moves on, carefully picking her way back into the woods, lifting low branches, watching where she puts her feet, mindful of nascent buddings, until she comes to the brook. She knows her spot. She crawls in and settles among the ferns, mossy hummocks, and lichen-covered rocks. The trees form a high stippled canopy, its shifting pattern repeated on the moist ground. Beds of windflower nod along the banks, clumps of wild ginger cling among exposed roots. The sway of light and leaf is calming, the shaded breeze cooling, the smell of rich humusy earth comforting, the melody of water soothing.

Reggie drinks it in with deeply thirsting gulps, swallowing it to the pit of her stomach, filling her lungs, letting it seep through her body. Her face relaxes, her taut nerves release. She doesn't think, she doesn't feel.

She lets go.

After a long while of perfect stillness, she stirs, looks at her watch, slowly rises. Extricates herself from the ferns, takes a lingering last look at the brook, and retraces her route to the house, arriving on the front porch at exactly three minutes to one.

Abby opens the door herself, erect and smiling. Reggie doesn't check her impulse; she moves not past but straight to her grandmother, kisses her soft powdery cheek. Abby stiffens with pleased surprise, awkwardly pats her granddaughter. Then, without a word, leads to the dining room.

The table is colorfully set with blue-rimmed, flower-splashed porcelain, heavy blue goblets, and blue-embroidered linen. A large bowl of gem-like fruit sits between tall blue-and-white china candlesticks. The sideboard is laid with cold soup, tossed salad, tiny triangular sandwiches, and lacy cookies.

—I told Randy and Marta we'd serve ourselves. I thought we'd prefer to be alone.

Reggie nods, grateful.

Abby spoons cracked ice into a cocktail mixer, shakes, strains frothy yellow liquid into two tapered glasses, adds carbonated water, and hands one to Reggie.

Reggie looks doubtful.

—Go ahead. It's a Golden Fizz. It'll do you good— Reggie takes a tentative sip. —See? A bit of the hair of the dog that bit you.

Abby takes an enthusiastic sip. Reggie smiles at the line of froth left on Abby's lightly downed upper lip.

Abby notes the smile, nods in approval. —That's better. You look a little more like you're going to live. I'm sorry things didn't go well with your mother— Reggie's head jerks. —No, I didn't talk to your mother. And I didn't see you go into the woods. I didn't need to. The stain on the back of your slacks told me— Reggie twists to look. —I always knew when you were a child and turned up missing where I could find you. It's a good place when you're hurt or angry. I've used it myself a few times.

Reggie twiddles her glass. —She thinks I need to see a psychiatrist, Abby.

—Why? Because you danced the seven veils of Salome for the country club?

—It's a little more than that. That was just the straw that broke the camel's back. But a big one. It's the last several months, the way I've been acting— Reggie tries a weak smile. —I guess you know, I haven't been myself.

—It's been mentioned.

—I don't know what's the matter with me, Abby. I thought I did, but— Reggie shakes her head. —I'm not happy. I keep hiding out. I don't want to see anyone or go anywhere. Look, I didn't even go to the garden show, I didn't come see your iris.

—Your absence was noted.

—The very first year I've missed. I didn't bother to call you. I don't call Maggie. I'm hurting her. I'm hurting everyone.

Abby studies her granddaughter. —Why don't we get some soup.

Abby ladles out two bowls of bisque the milky green of water jade, pours wine. Reggie's surprised to find she has an appetite. The Golden Fizz has settled her stomach. She savors the smooth minted coolness of the pea puree as it refreshes her mouth and gullet. The dry fruity sparkle of the chardonnay refreshes her mind. She feels almost human again.

—So what do you think, Abby? Am I crazy?

Abby smiles. —You're spirited, Reggie. And dramatic. It's part of your artistic temperament. You get that from your father.

Reggie stops mid-spoon. —Daddy? He's the least temperamental person I know, artistic or otherwise.

—That's because you didn't know him when he was young. You never saw him with his violin.

—I didn't even know he played one.

—Oh, yes. Started when he was six. He loved that violin, practiced for hours and hours. Poured his heart out across those strings. He had the soul of a great *maestro*. And the technique of a hod carrier. He couldn't make his fingers and bow convey the passion of his inner spirit, his understanding of the joy and pain of the human condition, the fierceness and grandeur of the universe. Abby's crystal-blue eyes cloud. —But he didn't know it. His ear heard only what was in his heart. So he kept on playing.

Reggie lowers her spoon, spellbound.

Abby takes a breath, briskly straightens the napkin in her lap. —One day his teacher prepared a surprise. He had all his pupils cut records.

—Oh no.

—To give their parents at Christmas. Arthur was so proud, so sure it was going to be a great success, he hadn't bothered to listen to it— Abby smooths the table cloth, stares at her hand. —I can still see him sitting in the chair beside the Christmas tree while his father put the record on— Reggie waits as Abby absently fusses with the silverware. —It was the first time he heard himself. The way the rest of us heard him.

Abby looks up, her eyes pained as Reggie has never seen them.

—That night he smashed the record. Then he smashed his violin.

Reggie stares, incredulous. —He went a little crazy.

—Yes. All artists are a little crazy, I think. Especially if their artistic flow is dammed.

Reggie shakes her head slowly. —Poor Daddy. And he never played again?

Abby smiles wryly. —He had nothing to play. We offered to buy him another violin, of course. He wouldn't even discuss it. He closed off and made clear the subject was never to be opened again.

—He was that hurt.

Abby shrugs. —Hitting the wall of one's limitations can be very hurtful. He was sixteen— She stands, goes to the sideboard —But it's an ill wind blows no good, they say— sets the salad bowl and platter of sandwiches between them. —Strangely enough, that's how he got into anthropology— She watches as Reggie checks over the triangles—cucumber, tuna, egg salad, creamed cheese with chopped olives— takes one of each. —He turned to religion, in an effort to find some explanation for the vagaries of life, and an answer as to how man was meant to deal with them.

Reggie looks startled. —But Daddy's an agnostic, Abby.

—Yes. The final result of his studies. But then he was a seeker.

Abby helps herself to salad, talks around bites. —He attended churches of all denominations, spent long hours reading and thinking. In college, he took courses in philosophy and theology. He became particularly interested in comparative religion and the religions of the ancients. From there it was a short step to the religions of primitives. Hence, into anthropology. She picks out a sandwich. —Specializing in ritualistic music.

Reggie's eyes widen. —He came full circle, Abby.

Abby nods, pleased with her granddaughter's perceptiveness.

—He had his music, restored central to his heart. In a context where it had primal meaning in man's structuring of life.

Reggie's amazed. She's never heard any of this. She works back over the story, chewing absently, wondering what application it has for her. —But he was only crazy for a short while, Abby, when he destroyed the record and violin. He didn't carry it on for months and months.

—Would you call his over-night flight into religion, that lasted for years, sane behavior? Or was he haunted, driven by a need to make sense of his loss and disillusionment, so he could forgive and accept God's betrayal?

Reggie takes a small serving of salad. —If that's craziness, then half of mankind's off kilter.

—Very probably.

Reggie shakes her head. —No. He was constructive in his actions, he found a purposeful way to work out his problem.

—Well— Abby studiously studies her sandwich —maybe there's a message in that.

Reggie's distress returns. —Yes, but, Abby, Daddy *knew* why he was unhappy. And he knew exactly what he had to do about it.

—Did he now? He learned he could not play as he wanted, he smashed the instrument and evidence of his failure, then promptly said to himself, Obviously, the solution to all this is to read the Bible.

Reggie laughs in spite of herself. —But it worked, didn't it?

—So might going to a psychiatrist.

Reggie immediately sobers. —So is that what you think I ought to do then?

—I think there are many routes to a destination, Reggie, psychiatry, in this case, being one. It's the route Maggie would think of because it's the one most frequently resorted to these days, and therefore the one that comes most readily to her practical mind. But you're a person of imagination. I think that's part of your problem.

—What? That my imagination's gone wild on me? Or that I've lost it.

Abby considers. —Let me tell you another story. You know I went to Paris to study art.

—When you were nineteen. Your mother was against it, but your father finally agreed.

—It wasn't considered proper in that era, especially for an upper-class Bostonian debutante. They were afraid it would taint me as a bohemian and damage my prospects for marriage. But I was a peer of O'Keeffe and Nevelson, only a little younger, and infected by the times. I was determined to follow my dream— Abby's eyes turn roguish. —So I boycotted all the eligible young men who came around until Daddy finally reasoned that if I didn't get this out of my system I'd never settle down— She's primly pleased. —He also wisely reasoned that by giving his approval he was glossing it for our social set with a coat of acceptability. He was a man of some prominence. His glossing carried some weight.

Reggie grins. —He also gave his approval because you threatened to run off to Paris anyway, with or without it.

Abby looks mischievous. —Well yes— She reaches for a pear, her face suddenly softens. —But what you don't know, Reggie, is that while I was in Paris, I fell madly in love— Reggie's face registers astonishment. —Oh, yes— Abby deftly slices and cores the fruit. —A tall, slender young man, full of passion and vitality. And terribly talented. He was one of my painting instructors— Abby carefully arranges the slices on her plate. —Paul Pierre . . . An inner sigh, a whispering of soft wind. Reggie sits quietly. Abby looks up, once again no-nonsense —The love of my life— briskly, as if brushing her hands of it.

Reggie lets out her breath. —What happened?

Abby shrugs. —What could happen? My parents and I had agreed upon one year. I refused to come home. My father came to get me. And in the end, I had to go.

Reggie nods, her look sympathetically understanding. —You had to honor your contract.

Abby snorts at such idealistic folderol. —Honor had nothing to do with it. I ran out of money.

—But what about your trust fund?

Abby looks as if Reggie's lost her senses. —Why do you think it's called a *trust* fund? It's held out of your control until you're deemed of an age to be trusted. You ought to know about that.

And indeed Reggie does. Her own trust still requires her father's signature if she wishes to draw upon it. She's thirty-five . . .

—And you were only twenty.

—And as I had proved to my parents, not ready to be trusted.

Reggie slips into thought. —So you returned to Boston— She's remembering her own wretched wrenching from Harden and Casey. —It must have been terrible for you.

—Yes. I cried a lot— Reggie nods, again knowingly sympathetic. —But not so terrible as you might think— Reggie looks up, startled. —There had occurred a kind of resolution. My parents' worst fears had been realized, while I had realized my dream. And none of us had died from it. I came home clear on the difference between the luxury of dreams and the requirements of reality, and with an acceptance of what I would have to give up for what I would gain. I recognized I was part of a tradition that was ultimately Bostonian and not Parisian. I guess you might say I grew up.

Reggie struggles to grasp this. —You never went back to Paris?

—Oh years later. But not because of Paul Pierre.

—You didn't try to find him?

—I was tempted. He'd become a well-known painter, of the post-Impressionist *avant-garde*. But I was with Calvin.

Reggie fiddles with a bunch of grapes, her face wistfully pensive. —So you never saw him again.

—I didn't say that at all— Reggie jolts from her doldrums. —Paul Pierre came to find *me*.

—Where? You mean *here*? In Boston?— Reggie's instantly alert. —When? Before or after you were married?

—Before.

Reggie's finding the analogies of this story uncanny. She plucks at the grapes. —Just like Casey came to see me— Abby waits, guarding a small secretive smile. —But how? I would have thought your parents would refuse to let you see him.

—Oh they would have. Had they been given the opportunity. Paul Pierre arrived unannounced.

—He didn't even warn *you*?

—He'd written. Many letters. My parents intercepted them.

Reggie's aghast. —They didn't *read* them?

—Of course not— Curt, frowning; such an invasion of privacy would be unthinkable. —They put them away for safekeeping.

—But how— Reggie's eyes search her grandmother's face in distress. —How did you feel? I mean, what was it like seeing him again?

Abby's mouth purses. —Uncomfortable. Awkward— Reggie's clearly not expecting this. —I might even say embarrassing.

—You didn't love him anymore?

—I loved him very much. He was still the same beautiful, wild young man. With the same materially indifferent presence he affected in Paris. He would have been fine in Soho or Greenwich Village. In our living room, he looked impecunious and slightly unkempt.

—He didn't fit— Reggie's reliving her own disillusionment. —Like Casey. When he showed up in his sailor suit.

—Another beautiful, exciting young man.

—He brought rolls of adhesive tape, Abby. He kept making me cut strips to lift the lint off the blue serge.

—He wanted to make his best appearance. All he had were his pride and uniform.

Reggie's sunk again in dejection. She always considered Casey's visit a miserable failure, leading directly to what happened. —He and Maggie never did get along.

—They were in each other's way.

—She did admit though that she liked the way he looked out for me.

—He adored you, Reggie. That was clear to all of us. He was a big fish from a small pond, who'd come to make his leap into your larger pond. But he misgauged the distance and fell a little short, one gill in water, the other out.

—He floundered . . .

—And blamed your family for it— Reggie glances over. —But everyone of us, including Maggie, tried to be as hospitable to him as we knew how.

Reggie nods resignedly. —I know.

—With Paul Pierre, there was one major difference. Unlike Casey, he hadn't the slightest desire to be part of the family. To the contrary: he'd come to take me back to Paris and save me from corruption. As a vehement socialist, he hated everything we represented. He resented our house, our clothes, our silverware. We argued furiously. I refused to apologize for being born wealthy, I didn't feel I should have to defend my family's right to enjoy a life of privilege. Our ancestors had worked hard for it. And I didn't see how giving away all our money was going to solve the problems of the world's poor. We'd contributed a great deal in time *and* money toward helping the underprivileged. He even resented us for this, referring derisively to our *noblesse oblige*. Our differences were irreconcilable. We had a clean ending.

Reggie's eyes stay fixed on her grandmother as she gravely absorbs this. —And you've been happy?

Abby considers. —I've been . . . she searches —*satisfied*. Yes— She nods decisively, definitely. —My life has been quite satisfactory.

Reggie sits unmoving for a long moment, her eyes troubled and distant, head tight and snarled, mind working to untangle so much new information. Trying to sort ideas and meanings into a pattern that might provide answers for her.

She lowers her gaze, fumbles for grapes. —What happened to the letters?

—Paul Pierre's? Oh, my parents gave them to me eventually. Years later, when they were long past doing damage.

Reggie plucks at the grapes, drops them one by one onto her plate. —I destroyed Casey's— Plucks, drops. —I wish I hadn't— Plucks. —I'd like to hear his voice— Abjectly drops. —It's the one thing I can't remember.

Abby studies her granddaughter as stems grow bare and grapes pile. She sighs. —Go back, Reggie— Reggie looks up, uncertain she's heard correctly. —Yes. To Harden. Go back. Retrace your steps, revisit your memories. And perhaps you'll find a new route home. To resolution and satisfaction.

Reggie stares, her face round and flat in astonishment. Of all the advices she'd anticipated, she'd never once conceived of this. But something deep in her gut slips into place. Pieces pull toward a center. Shards find a fit.

She closes her eyes. Her body feels connected again, part of her. Hers. For the first time in months, she feels she can breathe.

She does so, deeply, opens her eyes, sees her grandmother quietly watching her.

—Why is it, Grabby, you always understand?

Abby looks into the green-and-gold-flecked hazel eyes, so lost and unnaturally shiny. She smiles, face creasing softly.

—What'll you have, tea or coffee?

Reggie descends by the driveway, stops halfway down, turns to look back. Abby waves from the steps, silver hair a halo in the sunlight. She looks so much a part of the house.

A grand house, stately and gracious, warm and comfortable, sprawled on its secluded, broad-lawned knoll, protected by trees and gardens. Blue-gray, pre-Victorian, with wide overhung veranda, large windows generously giving light, gabled servants quarters on the third floor, oversized fireplaces throughout. And a deep bay in the sitting room where Reggie spent hours curled on the cushioned window seat reading *Jane Eyre, Anne of Green Gables, Green Mansions, Anna Karenina, Wuthering Heights.*

Was it possible some day she might be worthy of this house?

SCENE 31

Reggie pulls her hand through her hair, trying to rub sense into it, trying to force out a decision. She has to make up her mind.

For days now, since her talk with Abby and encounter with Maggie, she's been torn in two. She feels as if she weren't crazy before, she's going crazy now.

Should she return to Harden? Or should she go to a psychiatrist? Should she open Pandora's Box and fly with her dementing specters? Or should she stay in her coffin, lid closed, and fight her demons in confined darkness? Is hers a ferment that needs to be exposed to sunlight and air, or will she have a better chance of grappling in close quarters? Either way there will be problems, that will undoubtedly unleash more problems. But she sees no middle ground. And she has to reach resolution.

She still resists a psychiatrist. She honestly does not believe she is maladjusted or neurotic. She has no history of mental disturbance, she has never been difficult. Perhaps a little willful and high-strung, as Maggie used to accuse, but that was when she was young. For years, as Maggie should be the first to acknowledge, she's been a model citizen.

She does not see herself sitting across a desk from some detached hired stranger, spilling her innards out. The thought alone bores and offends her. She does not feel this inner turmoil of hers is something that can be cured by sifting through her entrails with the sanitized tools of scientific inquiry. No. This is a particular, personal ailment, requiring a particular personal remedy, which she alone can prescribe. Which leaves her tearing her hair.

She slumps over her desk, making no pretense at writing, which is the excuse she's been giving her family these last few days for locking away in her study. She's a wreck. She can't eat; her stomach's a churn of acid. She can't sleep; her eyes are red and darkly circled. She can't think; her head's a constricted miasma. She's cranky and short-tempered. She hasn't even bothered to dress decently, has simply thrown on baggy pants and a blousy smock.

She feels like she knows she must look, like a futile straw-stuffed scarecrow, a floppy farcical boogeyman stuck in the middle of a ravaged field to ward off derisive blackbirds. And what with her current hair-tearing, she's messed her short curls into shocks of ragged peaks, like bunches of tied cornstalks.

She's enwrapped dark and deep, lost in desolate quandary—when her insulated incubusy is suddenly shattered by blaring music *She looks in the mirror and stares at the wrinkles that weren't there yesterday.* Glen Campbell barreling down the hall and through the door like a battering ram.

She jerks upright, stupefied and trembling from the abrupt invasion. She feels rudely shucked, nakedly tender.

She thinks of the young man that she almost married. What would he think if he saw her this way?

She bolts from her chair, crosses the room in three strides, and slams the door wide, cornstalks vibrating against the increased blast of volume.

She slowly starts dancing, remembering her girlhood . . .

Katelyn and Lindsay stand behind the portable record player set at the end of the hall floor.

—WHAT'S GOING ON HERE?— Red black outrage above country western insult.

Katelyn and Lindsay, startled by this unexpected response, shrink back, smiles arrested.

Such are the dreams of the everyday housewife . . .

—WHO PUT THAT ON?

—We did, Mummy— Bravely, uncertainly.

. . . you see everywhere . . .

—WHY?

. . . any time of the day . . .

Shifting anxiously. —We wanted you to know—

—*WHAT?*— Barging up the hall, bearing down.

The photograph album she takes from the closet . . .

—We understand— Tremulously, losing courage.

. . . and slowly turns the page . . .

—WHAT? WHAT DO YOU UNDERSTAND?

Katelyn ducks behind Lindsay.

An everyday housewife who gave up the good life for me.

Legs spread, hands on hips, cornstalks turned to Medusa snakes writhing, Reggie glowers —I AM NOT YOUR EVERYDAY HOUSEWIFE.

The hall door to the family room flings open, Howie steps into the breach. —What's all the racket?— Takes in Reggie towering, Glen yowling, the girls cowering, backed against the wall, eyes wide, faces white.

In one swift movement, he shoves past Reggie, kicks the phonograph, raking the needle across the record in a nerve-grating screech, and is at the girls' side, pulling arms, cradling shoulders —Come on— gently steering them, heads averted, eyes fluttering frightened sidewise glances, out and around their mother, as she stoops over the phonograph.

—What's *wrong* with her?

—Shhhhhh. I'll explain later. Right now, why don't you go outdoors, maybe take a bike ride. It wasn't your fault. Don't worry. It'll be all right.

Reggie's vaguely aware of their hesitant scuffles down the hall and dismayed whispers, but she's momentarily stunned past caring, examining the scratched record and broken needle-arm.

The hall door firmly closes on silence.

Reggie spins around, on her feet again, to confront Howie, fists clenched.

—You broke—

—Shut up, Reggie!— He charges toward her, grabs her arm. —You and I are going to talk— Drags her down the hall.

She twists sideways, tries to wrench free, trips. He yanks her up, shoves her into the bedroom, slams the door, pulls her to a stop with a sharp jerk. —I've had enough. Do you hear me, Reggie? Enough!— He shakes her, like a terrier with a rat. —I will not let you do this. You can do what you want to me— He whips her out, fingers biting bruisingly into her arm —But you will not take it out on the girls!

Reggie stares, as much fascinated as frightened. She's never seen Howie like this: face white, skin tight, ears flat, eyes narrow, lips thin, cheekbones and chin razor sharp. Crazily, she feels like giggling.

—And get that stupid grin off your face!— Reggie raises her hand to cover her mouth. —There's not a thing funny about this.

—No— shaking her head, eyes wide, immediately, obediently deadly sober.

—And you're not going to con me again. So forget your playacting.

—By why?— a plaintive whine. —What did I do, Howie? . . .

His face goes black. He pulls her near, meanly tempted, then shoves her away, as if to rid himself of her. —Don't give me that shit!

She stumbles backwards, the backs of her knees hit the bed edge. She topples —I was writing— struggles to sit —The music. It startled me, I—

—You think the girls and I believe that? You think we don't know what's going on here? That we don't track your every mood and movement? For five months now you've had this household standing on its head, tiptoeing around you, trying to understand. But we don't, Reggie. *I* don't understand. And I'm tired of trying.

—The girls are worried sick. They're afraid. Anything they say or do might upset you. They follow you around, watching and listening, whispering after lights out, trying to think up ways to help you. What can we do, Daddy? they ask me. How can we make Mummy happy? And I don't know what to answer.

—I know— Wretched, head hanging, hands twisting.

—You showed them those photographs, told them about Arizona and Harden. Head lifting. —Only a few things.

—They found your records, listened, trying to understand, looking for a way to reach you— His lip curls sarcastically. —I guess they thought they were being loving.

—It was just the shock, Howie, I couldn't think—

—Save the excuses, nothing justifies . . .

—I'm sorry.

—You can save your sorries, too. We're all sorry. It doesn't change a goddamn thing. And things do have to change, Reggie. Because I'm telling you, I can't go on like this. I've had enough, I'm through with your nonsense. Either you get yourself together or you get out!

Reggie stops breathing, swallows hard, heart crashing around in her chest, pulse racing in her throat, ears pinging.

—Howie?— wailing disbelief. Can this be Howie?

—No. Don't try that on me. I mean it. I love you, I love our girls. I love our life together. But I will not live like this. If you want another life, fine. You're free. Take it. But the girls and I have some right to *our* happiness.

—Please— Reggie's face lifts, supplicates. —Please. Just give me six weeks. I know I've been a mess, I know I've made a mess of things, oh such a mess. But I think I know what to do. My talks with Abby, Maggie. I know what I have to do— She breathes. —I have to go to Harden.

—I don't care what you do, Reggie, or where you go. Harden, a psychiatrist—

—You've talked with Maggie.

—You don't honestly believe you're the only one involved in this? The only one frightened and lonely?

—Six weeks, Howie. Please. That's all I ask. Six weeks. I'll go to Harden. If that doesn't work, I'll go to a psychiatrist.

So the route is determined.

ACT II

SCENE 1

CHAPTER (?)

Smokey was on trial. Her past had finally caught up with her. She was taking the witness stand to purge herself, so she could be granted a new life.

The evidence was in. Casey, Fred, and the Bureau had pursued every line and angle, followed up every name, date, transaction, and dollar she'd given them in her little black book. Their cases were built, and they felt they were solid. All that awaited was Smokey's testimony.

The time had come to revisit the scene of the crime.

Smokey mounted the stand.

"Raise your right hand, please. Do you, Smokey Lorraine, swear to tell the truth, the whole truth, and nothing but the truth, so help you God?"

"As well as I understand it."

The judge leaned over. "Please, Miss Lorraine, a simple yes or no will suffice."

"Oh. Sorry, your Honor." A bedazzling smile. "Yes."

"The prosecution may proceed."

Each day, Smokey appeared at court disguised as Ann Carter: flowing black hair, trim tailored dresses in subdued colors, two-inch heels. Nothing seductive, nothing spectacular. She also had her dark glasses, presented as a good-luck joke by Glory, the same style Glory wore.

And each day, she surreptitiously scanned the courtroom crowd, the press and other authorized persons jamming the halls, the evil- and well-wishers pressing against the cordons running down the courthouse steps. She knew she'd see it, the face she knew would eventually be there, *had* to be there, to put into action the final phase of her long deliberated and carefully orchestrated plan.

On the third day of the eighth week, after she'd disposed of three major and four minor figures, Smokey spotted him, quietly watching from the bottom of the steps, behind the barricades. Vincent Bogatta. Tall, dark, handsome, mid-thirties. Smart. Tough. Sexy. They'd slept together.

Vinnie—whose life rested in her hands.

"Vincent Bogatta," Casey had said. "What do you know about him?"

"Everything."

"His name isn't on the list."

"He didn't do anything."

"What do you mean, he didn't do anything? He ran Artie's club, he knew everyone Artie knew, he must—"

"The worst you can accuse Vinnie of is a little backroom gambling, and a little high-class prostitution. I'm not going to finger Vinnie for that."

"Why? Were you sweet on him, did you two have a thing going?"

"I sang and danced for him. And once in a while we shared drinks and talk. Vinnie looked out for me, Casey, in some pretty rough times, when I needed a protective friend. Artie and the boys trusted and respected him, but he wasn't part of the rackets. He was an honest business man, or as honest as you get running a club and hanging around that crowd."

"But he must have known something, he must have—"

"He knew how to keep his eyes, ears, and mouth shut, and his mind a blank. He grew up on the South Side of Chicago, a street kid, with a drunken father and no mother. We had a lot in common. He learned to survive. What Vinnie wants out of life are exactly two things—to make a lot of money and to stay alive. How's that make him any worse than the rest of us?"

Casey had eyed her skeptically, speculatively.

"Forget Vincent Bogatta, Casey. My shirt tails are dirtier than his."

So Casey had dismissed Vincent Bogatta. And Smokey had heaved a relieved sigh. But not so relieved as the sigh she heaved when she saw Vinnie watching her from behind his dark glasses and barricade as she descended the courthouse steps between Casey and her bodyguard.

She quickly but subtly changed her movements: twitched her shoulders and hips; shortened her steps, slightly pigeon-toed; tilted her head to the right—in a perfect imitation of Glory's walk. Or, as far as Vinnie knew, that of her assumed Ann Carter. As she drew abreast of Vinnie, she quickly lowered her own dark glasses, smiled directly, challengingly into his eyes, then turned her head, replaced the glasses, and closed her face as if the moment hadn't happened.

The next morning, she was ready. As Casey bent to help her out of the guarded car, she looked over his shoulder and saw Vinnie front line behind the barricade. As she passed, she raised her hand, as if to straighten her glasses, revealing to him the white slip of paper clutched in the palm of her hand. He gave an imperceptible nod.

That afternoon, Vinnie was in place. As she approached him, Smokey lurched in front of her guard, stumbled sideways, and fell into the barricade. Vinnie grabbed her from the front, the bodyguard hurried to upright her from behind. Casey was immediately beside her.

"What happened?"

"These damn sling pumps. My heel twisted out and I lost my balance."

Casey glared at the offending shoe. "Don't wear them again."

Smokey contritely nodded and let Casey whisk her into the car.

But the note had been passed.

It's a funny feeling I have, sitting in this plane all by myself, no Howie beside me, no girls in the seat ahead. I've never flown by myself. And the last time I flew was three years ago, when Howie took me to London. I love to fly. I love to travel. Doing something new, seeing something different. Going somewhere.

I should be feeling sad, upset and concerned, that's what my mind tells me. Reggie, this is a serious business you're embarking on, with unknown, possibly serious consequences. And I did. Yesterday, while I was packing. Last night, when I tried to talk to Howie. This morning, when we kissed and said good-bye. I cried. The girls did, too. But I took a taxi to the airport. Howie and I agreed: I couldn't quite expect my family to wave me a fond farewell. It would be too hard. And under our circumstances, not exactly appropriate.

But what I'm feeling now, from the moment I entered the plane, is release. And anticipation, like a child on an adventure. I'm wondering what the movie is, and what they'll serve for breakfast. I'm going to order a Bloody Mary as soon as the stewardess comes around.

I wish the conversation with Howie had gone better. I hate leaving him like this, so cold and angry, with so much distrust and distance between us. I wish I hadn't tried to explain, made one last attempt to smooth things. Everything I said only made it worse. All Howie can understand is that I'm unhappy with my life, and that he's a major part of it. But I guess that's the reality, and there's nothing can be done about it. At least not for the time being. No sense brooding, I have to look ahead.

In less than seven hours I'll be in Albuquerque. The very thought makes my heart jump. The Southwest. I've reserved a car at the airport, and a room at the Radisson. I tried to find the place where I stayed with Maggie and Daddy, but that was years ago. I couldn't remember the name, and I wasn't about to ask Maggie.

I'm a little worried about the changeover in Houston, only forty-five minutes, and I don't know how far I'll have to walk or run. Coming into Chicago the winter Howie took me skiing in Aspen, our plane was so late we missed our connection. Howie always took care of everything, I never had to pay attention. So I'll just have to ask a lot of questions, that's all. I'm sure it won't be the first time they've had to deal with a fledgling grown woman let loose in the world on her own.

I don't know what to do about Maggie. I feel terrible about the way things ended. I wanted to call her but I just couldn't. There was so much to say and no words adequate. Abby said she'd see what she could do. And I guess that's the way I'll have to leave it.

I'll hang my dresses, freshen up, then take a taxi into Old Town. There are two wonderful trading posts where I'll pick up gifts for the family. I'm not going to add insult to injury by bringing home things labeled from Harden. And I want to buy a few clothes suitable for the West. Most of my things at home smacked of the East: beaches and sailing. And the fabric was wrong. You can't wear synthetics in heat, unless they're blended with a lot of cotton. Then I'll have dinner at that fantastic Spanish-colonial restaurant in the middle of the block, providing it's still there.

I've been craving Mexican food. I could eat it three times a day, and intend to. Howie hates Mexican food. That's because he's never had the real thing. You can't get decent Mexican food in the East, only pseudo. And the girls haven't even tasted it.

The two seats next to me aren't occupied, thank god. I'm not in the mood to make small talk with strangers, and I'm exhausted with thinking. I just want to snuggle into the dull hum of the engines, look out the window, and empty myself.

I'm so tired. . . .

We're flying above a solid bank of fluffy white cloud, sheer blue sky surrounding . . . limitless, no horizon . . .

. . . I'm suspended . . .

In the beginning, there was only *Tokpella*, Endless Space. No winds blew, no shadows fell, no life stirred. All was empty black stillness. Only Tawa, the Sun Spirit and Creator, existed, along with a few lesser gods. Tawa regretted the barrenness. He took the Endless Space and, putting into it some of his own substance and breathing into it his breath, created the First World and first life. But these were not people, merely insect-like creatures who lived in a dark cave deep in the earth.

Tawa was disappointed. "What I have created is imperfect. These creatures do not understand the meaning of life. They see but they do not comprehend."

So he called his messenger *Gogyeng Sowhuti*, Spider Grandmother, to lead them on a long journey. And while they were traveling, Tawa created the Second World and changed the creatures into animals that resembled dogs, coyotes, and bears. They had fur, webbed fingers, and tails. But still, Tawa could see, they did not grasp the meaning of life.

So again he called Spider Grandmother to lead them on a journey. This time, while they traveled, Tawa created the Third World. He made the atmosphere lighter and gave water to moisten the earth. When the animals finally emerged, they no longer had fur, webbed fingers, and tails. "Now," Spider Grandmother said, "you are no longer merely creatures. You are People."

The People were grateful. They built villages and planted corn. Spider Grandmother taught them to weave blankets and cloth, and to make pots of clay. Maasaw, Ruler of the Upper World and Owner of Fire, showed them the secret of fire. So now they could cover their bodies, cook their food, bake their pots, and have warmth. And for a time they lived in harmony.

But gradually the *powakas*, or sorcerers, began to spread evil. They made medicine to injure those they envied or disliked. They caused the People to fight among themselves, and turned their minds from virtuous things. The People became lazy, greedy, and licentious. And worst of all, instead of seeking to understand the meaning of life, many began to believe they had created themselves.

Finally, the old chiefs and medicine men, who had not forgotten that Tawa was their Father, sought to find a way to save the people who were still good and leave behind those who were evil. They created a catbird out of clay and sent it to explore the place above the sky and to seek refuge with Maasaw, whose heavy steps they could hear over their heads. Maasaw consented to let the good of heart come to the Upper World.

Spider Grandmother and her two grandsons, the young warrior gods *Pokanghoya* and *Polongahoya*, came to help the good people. They planted a bamboo and gave them a song to sing to make it grow straight and tall. Each time the people stopped to catch breath, the bamboo stopped growing and a joint formed on the stalk, and when they started singing again, the bamboo resumed growing. And so the good people climbed the bamboo through the *sipaapuni*, the doorway in the sky, the joints providing footholds.

When they reached the Fourth World, Maasaw greeted them and divided them into tribes, naming each. But before he turned his face away and became invisible, he gave special instructions to those he named the Hopi. The Hopi clans, he explained, were to travel separately, and all the clans were to make four directional migrations before they could arrive at their common permanent home. Only after each had gone to the farthest *paso* where the sea meets the land in each direction—west, south, east, and north—could they come together again, forming the pattern of the Creator's universal plan.

Spider Grandmother had further instruction: "This is the land of Maasaw, Caretaker of the Place of the Dead. So people will always be in the presence of death. You will learn about the forces of nature in your travels. The stars and moon, the sun and clouds, and fires in the night will show you which way to go. And in time, you will find the land meant for you. But never forget that you came from the Lower World for a purpose. Those who forget will lose their way. They will disappear in the wilderness and be forgotten."

So The People started on their migrations, the path of one crossing the trail of another, until finally they were led to the plateau between the Colorado and Rio Grande Rivers. It was a high, vast land of dramatic beauty, but with scant rainfall and few rivers or streams for irrigating corn, squash, and beans. But The People knew this was as it should be. They had to depend on the power of their ceremonies and prayers to bring rain and snow, control the wind, regulate the flow of underground water, prevent flash floods, and insure germination and the reproduction of all life.

There would be no easy life to make the people soft and lazy. They would remember and preserve their knowledge of and faith in the supremacy of their Creator, who had brought them to this Fourth World after they had failed in the previous three to understand the meaning of life.

SCENE 2

Well, all I can say is, Eisenhower's hot love affair with the German autobahn leaves me cold. Interstate 40 may be bigger, faster, and safer than Route 66 but it has no heart or soul. The Main Street of America they used to call 66, because it connected so many small towns. Now as I whiz along 65 miles an hour in my air-conditioned rental car, bypassing every town, I haven't the slightest urge to stop and look, to investigate and get acquainted. No enticement—unless you're enamored of flimflam tourist traps, sleazy fast food, cheap plastic motels, and chain gas stations.

I'm thoroughly disgusted. All those colorful four-corners and backwoods burgs Ike turned into blanched ghost towns, cut off from their life blood, the traveling American. All those personalized small businesses he forced into dehumanized bankruptcy. All those dispossessed, repossessed people. Where did they go? Did he compensate them for their loss? Give them relocation funds? Not that I heard of.

To both sides of me, somewhere in the distance, are Indian reservations: Laguna, Acoma, Zuni. I've been to all of them, as well as the Rio Grande and Jemez pueblos: Santa Ana, San Felipe, Santo Domingo, San Juan. To the north is a town called Regina, named after me, Daddy joked. I've been there, too. And to Taos, and Santa Fe, and Los Alamos. And Chaco Canyon and Bandelier National Forest. I look at my road atlas and say, Yeah, I've been there. Daddy didn't pass up a place that had anything to do with Indians.

Some of the most beautiful country in the world, at least some of the most beautiful *I've* seen. Georgia O'Keeffe country. I think of Abby. I miss her, and for a moment I wish she were here. But only for a moment. I need her back where she is, with Maggie. And I need to be alone.

O'Keeffe's folded hills and striped cliffs really do exist, I've seen them. Chalky layers of gray, green, yellow, blue, red, pink, purple. And I promise myself on the way back I'll take time to see them again, along with a lot of other scenic places I remember. But for now, I'm in too much of a hurry.

I'm already one day behind schedule. I planned to stay only one night in Albuquerque. But when my wake-up call came yesterday, I literally couldn't get out of bed. I completely collapsed. I slept until ten, had huevos rancheros, slept for another few hours by the pool—I was as pale as a banana slug—had margaritas and an early dinner—enchiladas and chile relleno—and was in bed again by seven thirty. I was so exhausted, I couldn't even read.

But this morning, I feel great!

I'm up at four-thirty, to be on the road in time for sunrise. And my effort isn't wasted. I keep watch out my rear-view mirror, and when the light begins to lift behind the mountains, I pull over to the shoulder and take my perch on the trunk of the car.

First light comes as a soft gray, suffusing into the night like a gentle tide, pushing back moon and stars. The gray gradually diffuses into a wash of translucent sea green, which flows into a wash of shimmering lemon yellow. The silhouetted mountains blend from deep indigo to pale cerulean to vibrant lavender. A flush of peach announces the imminence of the sun, which suddenly cuts above the now-mauve mountains in a fiery slice of orange. The violet and blue streaks of the desert flee before the wave of fire, to hide beneath scrub and rocks as cobalt shadows.

I wait until the sun has become an intense white ball, burning out moon and stars, bleaching desert, and making its warning felt of the heat to come. I think of Abby again, how I wish I'd taken her painting lessons more seriously. I'd like to have done justice to this. But I doubt if even Abby could. Abby's bold, at times even daring, in the rendering of her provocative flowers, but she always retains a line of delicacy. It takes a rawly exposed inner eye, unflinching against the desert's flattening glare, to see through to and capture the magnitude of mass and space and the vividness of color.

I wish I could write like that.

I stop for breakfast in Gallup. Following my road map and the signs, I turn off 40 east of town onto one of the few remaining stretches of Old 66—they call it U. S. 66 *Avenue* here—and take my time, savoring the approach, the low spare houses, the out-of-era businesses, the dusty dry buffness covering all.

I want to throw my arms around the heart of town, it's exactly as I remember. I park on Aztec—the streets are practically deserted—and go in search of the cafe on the corner. It's right where I left it.

I take a booth toward the back. The same baby-blue Formica and leatherette trimmed with chrome, spiked chrome coat racks dividing. Only a little more scratched and scuffed, dirty cotton stuffing poking out of gaping slashes.

The waitress smiles, Hi, Honey, slaps down my flatware, water, and menu, and bustles away. No paper placemat featuring the town map edged with advertisements of local businesses, like in the old days. Napkins are in a holder next to the salt, pepper, ashtray, and ketchup.

The waitress returns with coffee, sloshed in the saucer, and stands ready with pencil and pad.

I smile up. —I'm sorry, I don't know what I want yet.

—Take your time, Honey— and she hurries back to her friends in the front booth I dislodged her from.

The menu offers nothing Mexican, but I'm not disappointed. It takes me several minutes to decide among corned beef hash with two eggs, creamed chipped beef on toast, or biscuits with sausage gravy. Fare you'll never find on a Boston menu, at prices equally undreamed of.

I close my menu and give my attention over to my companions. Besides the one with my waitress's boisterous buddies, three other booths are occupied: a man with his wife and two children, an elderly couple, and two girls in their late teens or early twenties. The man and wife are trying to coax their young daughter into eating instead of fussing and whining. While the older brother takes advantage of their distraction to leap around in the aisle, spin on the stools, and swing on the coat racks. The older couple is exchanging bites and sharing assessments. The girls are bent head-to-head talking intently, about boys I'm willing to bet. And from the salty language, rude guffaws, and CB references, the waitress's friends up front have to be rig drivers. Several lone cowboys sit at the counter, hunched over their plates, thoughtfully sipping coffee and puffing cigarettes. They discourage conversation.

With one exception, the waitresses are in Levis, tight over butts and thighs, western shirts, and cowboy boots. My waitress is distinguished by a red bandana around her neck. Most appear to be in their thirties or forties, but in this unkind clime, who can tell.

The one exception is a woman who has to be close to sixty, at least thirty pounds overweight, with hennaed hair in an every-hair-sprayed-in-place beehive and to-the-shoulder earrings. Her uniform is bulging green western slacks and yellow satiny western shirt, emblazoned over hefty bosom with sequins and embroidered flowers. She commands the cash register.

My stomach is growling. I've been sitting expectantly for several minutes now, back erect, hands folded, closed menu pushed conspicuously to the table's edge. But I can't compete with the CBers. I signal a passing waitress.

—Excuse me, but would you mind telling my waitress I think I'm ready.

She turns, hands on hips, and hollers to the front. —Hey, Elaine, your customer's tired of waiting.

Elaine grudgingly pulls from her booth, snubs out her cigarette, still talking, takes a final swig of coffee, and heads toward me, full of smiles, hips swinging, not a care in the world.

—So what'll it be, Honey?

I order the biscuits with sausage gravy.

—Orange juice?

I nod.

—It's frozen. We ain't got fresh.

—Then tomato juice.

—It's canned.

—All right.

She ambles off.

An Indian woman comes in the door, a Navajo I think from her dress. Denim western shirt over long green broom-stick skirt, dirty white sneakers, and heavy bunched pink socks. But from her features, I can't be sure. Her hair hangs lank and stringy, not tied back in a bun or cut short in a neat bob. The customers look over curiously at her entrance, then uncuriously look away. She's carrying a rectangular board covered with black velvet on which she's tacked a heavy turquoise and silver necklace. She makes the rounds of the tables, starting in front, holding the board out, receiving averted eyes, negative shakes, frowns, curt No's. She moves down the line at the counter. One cowboy refuses to acknowledge her, she bumps the board against his arm, he turns on her. I can hear the sharpness of his words. She backs away and doggedly proceeds to the next man.

I wait for her to reach me, fascinated, not thinking about how I'm going to respond. I've always wanted a squash blossom necklace.

She shoves the board at me. I can't take my eyes off it. Eighteen inches of graduated, hollow die-stamped silver beads, spacing ten large turquoise nuggets sprouting fluted silver blossoms at least an inch long, the turquoise pure and hard, traced with a faint matrix, untreated by silicone. Old style. The good stuff Indians made for themselves. The questions flash through my mind. Where did she get it? Why is she selling it? Why doesn't she take it to a trading post?

I reach out a hand, heft. Heavy. In Albuquerque I saw necklaces like this going for over a thousand dollars.

—How much?

For the first time I look in her face, and am surprised at how young she is, not over thirty.

Her eyeballs skitter and roll back in her head, for a moment half moons beneath her lids. Her face shines with soft moisture, which I suddenly realize from the pallor beneath her walnut skin, must be cold sweat. My heart goes out to her. I think I have the answers to my questions. She's sick, she needs medicine. She's hungry, perhaps starving. And it's Sunday, the posts are closed.

Her eyeballs roll back down and try to focus. She teeters, I resist an impulse to steady her.

—Five hundred dollars— The words are thick, guttural, and come at me on a sour wave of alcohol. And it's not even nine in the morning.

I pull back my hand, shake my head.

She pushes the board at me. —How much?— Demanding. —Three hundred?

—No. I'm sorry.

She leans toward me, desperate, aggressive. —One hundred.

I can smell her body. I want to draw away as far as possible, into the booth corner. At five hundred it would have been a bargain.

Elaine shows up with my plate, no juice. —Come on, Naomi, the lady wants to eat.

—She buy— Belligerently.

—You interested in the necklace?

—Fifty! Fifty dollars.

—It's worth thirty times that.

—I know.

—You want it, you might as well take it.

I look longingly at the necklace, shake my head.

Elaine shrugs. —Somebody else will.

—Thirty!

—It's a real steal.

I try not to show my misery. —I can't.

—Okay, Naomi. That's it, we're closing shop— Elaine starts shoving the woman toward the door.

I jab at my biscuits, drag my fork around in my gravy, trying, like the parents in the front booth with their daughter, to talk myself out of fussing and whining and into eating.

I knew alcoholism had become a real problem among the Indians. I'd seen signs of it even when I lived in Harden. But with the men, not with the women. I understand how low this woman's life has sunk, the despair, the poverty of soul as well as of mind and body. But there's nothing my fifty or five hundred dollars can do, except supply more bottles to push her lower. The problem's too large, too complex. It's not about drinking, it's about being. I wonder if she—Naomi—is one of the girls they yanked out of reservation homes and ported off to boarding schools in Phoenix. Uprooting, with no provision for replanting.

Naomi. So many of the Indian girls in Harden had biblical names: Judith, Ruth, Rachel, Mary. . . .

I've looked forward to biscuits and sausage gravy for years. It sticks in my craw.

I continue on Route 66 out of town. I'm going to stay with what little they've left me for as long as I can. It's a relief to be off Ike's super assfault. Instead of skimming over the surface barely in touch with the land, on 66 I feel intimately rooted in it. I can relax and take my time. No watching out for erratic tourists harassed by scrapping kids and exhausted by too many miles. No artful dodging of game-playing trucksters out to bully a lone female to break the monotony.

I *have* to take my time. Dynamite didn't blast a straightaway here. The narrow two-lane road with its skimpy scrabbly shoulder follows an old Indian trail down and up arroyos and around natural land forms. My light economy compact bucks and shimmies over the ruts and wash-board patches. Too fast over a drip and I'm in the air, one uncontrolled curve and I'm in the desert.

I want to lose myself in the beauty of the land and my satisfaction at navigating it, but I can't shake the experience back at the cafe. I'm agitated by an undefined sense of responsibility, and angered by my continued coveting of the necklace. One part of my brain approves me for holding onto my scruples, another part derides me for being a fool. A third part shakes its head over me for having the argument at all. I turn on the radio, to take me out of myself and brighten the atmosphere.

I'm jarred by a twang of country western music. Of course, I laugh, what did I expect? Grinning, I hook into the brash rhythm, bobbing my body. But after a minute, I'm dissatisfied, it isn't what I'm wanting. I press the search button and skip from station to station, looking for Willie Nelson or Waylon Jennings, Merle Haggard or Johnny Cash, Tammy Wynette or Loretta Lynn. Or someone who sounds like them. But I don't recognize a name, voice, or song. Even the styles are different. I hear the influence of rock, and rhythm and blues, and soul and gospel, and jazz, and cajun. I'm dated, out of tune and out of time.

It's been years since I've listened to country western music. I stopped. After that night. . . .

I jab the button off, aggrieved and prickly. Like I'd like to fight someone.

Up ahead, coming at me, I see a sign. WELCOME TO ARIZONA. I wait for the anticipated leap of excitement, but it doesn't come. Instead I get a twinge of anxiety. I drive in a funk, wondering what's happened to my joyous reentry into the high point of my youth.

But gradually the land pulls me in, soothes, lulls . . .

I roll down the window, turn the air conditioner full blast, take the wind in my face, hair flying.

Hot, dry, pungent . . .

It tranquilizes . . .

Mesmerizes . . .

Cliffs Solid red sandstone blocks mineral-streaked flat-topped rising abruptly above white sandbeds wet-stained by underground waters Like the Colorado River at the bottom of the Grand Canyon trickles of prehistoric overland torrents that once cut sheer sides

Rugged buttes defiant survivors jutting atop eroded red mounds rough rubble tumbled boulders crushed rocks dotted with green shrub and spiky white grass

Toppled red sandstone slabs pitched sideways piled aloft forming uprights platforms arches windows of sky shadowed pockets Pock-faced rock creature crevices edifices for small life desert habitation dangerous dark

Sunburned windwhipped sandblasted icecracked waterlashed the core endures withstands stripping triumphs into the trueness of its nature into its essence the beauty of its heart . . .

I lift my head, stare around. For a moment, I'm completely disoriented. I don't know how I got here, for that matter, where I am. But I've stopped, pulled over to the side of the road, and I'm writing. I've dug out my notebook and I'm writing.

I read the words. Foreign. I don't remember a thing. I find this alarming, that some part of my brain could take over without consulting me, without my knowledge or consent. This could be highly dangerous. My conscious mind would never have let me park on this treacherous shoulder.

I put the notebook and pen on the seat beside me and carefully pull onto the road, with every intention of keeping frontally focused.

I pass the Petrified Forest, the Painted Desert, and enter Holbrook. The town looks better than I remember, larger, newer, more prosperous. I wonder what could possibly explain this. I was never a fan of Holbrook, except for one thing. I lean forward, watching to my left. And there it is: large Mama teepee in a semicircle of Baby teepees. I laugh out loud, the same disbelieving reaction I had the first time I saw it. The Teepee Motel. My first sign that this migration my father had brought us on was not beyond all hope.

And I realize, in surprise, that this is true: the land had not spoken to me. My father had driven us through the same high-colored cliffs, the same indomitable buttes, but I had not understood their language.

JOSEPH CITY   10 MI
WINSLOW   33 MI
HARDEN   61 MI
FLAGSTAFF   91 MI

My surroundings have become vividly familiar. We must have covered this stretch dozens of times. I concentrate, trying to see it the way I did the first time, with young Reggie's eyes. The eyes of a protected, presumptuous teenager who'd never been farther south than Washington D.C. or farther west than Philadelphia. She'd known green all her life, and cities and suburbs. She'd never been exposed to poverty, of land or otherwise.

She'd been mildly interested when they'd started out; New Jersey and Pennsylvania were green. But Ohio and Indiana had bored her, Missouri had depressed her, Oklahoma had appalled her, and the Texas Panhandle had finished her off. She'd probably been in shock by the time they reached New Mexico, and hadn't even seen the cliffs.

She'd received her WELCOME TO ARIZONA and watched the land go flatter and flatter, drier and drier. Become a baked crust of yellow dirt relieved by only an occasional scrawny shrub or skeletal tumble weed, or low jumble of rocks she was sure was a decimated hill. She saw that same sign—HARDEN 61 MI—and knew it was the end.

SCENE 3

—My god! I don't believe this place. It's the end of the world!

Maggie swings around in her seat, Reggie's prepared.

—Don't use the Lord's name in vain.

—I knew you were going to say that.

—Then why do you make me say it so often? If you don't want a nag for a mother, don't make me one.

Reggie grins, thinking she's working with natural material. —I was praying.

She looks out the window, spots in the barren distance a lone black mound. Her eyes fly wide. —What's that, Daddy?

—What?

—That giant ant hill— She sees in her mind's eye monsters with mandibles the size of icemen's tongs.

Daddy laughs. —That's not an ant hill, it's a burnt-out cinder cone. You're going to see a lot of them around here. They're all through the high desert.

Now she's visualizing great belches of black smoke, flying chunks of fiery rock, hissing rivers of molten lava gushing down on her. The earth rumbles.

—I'll die here, Mummy, I mean it. My life's passing before my eyes.

—And, please, Reggie. Don't dramatize. It's too hot.

—No. I'm serious! Look out there. That's what happens to anything tries to live here.

—Oh, it isn't going to be all that bad— Daddy humoring, the perennial optimist.

Maggie gives him a hard tight look, then stares out the window.

They drive in silence. Daddy pulls erect, leans right. —See those signs? Get ready for some diversion— Maggie and Reggie look skeptical. He slows as they approach: a line of five plaques set on poles, spaced every hundred feet. Reggie reads:

> IS HE LONESOME
> OR JUST BLIND—
> THIS GUY WHO DRIVES
> SO CLOSE BEHIND?
> BURMA-SHAVE

Reggie giggles, delighted.

Maggie smiles. —The old Burma-Shave signs.

—There ought to be more. I'm surprised we haven't seen any earlier— Daddy's pleased to see his family boosted back to life and the living. —So keep your eyes peeled.

—I can't— Reggie squints, her hand over her eyes. —The sun's too bright.

Maggie sighs heavily. —Where are the sun glasses I bought you?— Reggie rummages in her purse, holds up the glasses. —Put them on— Reggie perches the glasses on her nose, obediently strikes a pose. —I don't know why you weren't wearing them all along.

—They're too big. And there wasn't anything to see.

Maggie sighs again.

Reggie returns to the edge of her seat, watching right, head tilted up to keep the glasses from slipping down. After a moment, she gives a jump, points. —Here come some more!

> DON'T TRY PASSING
> ON A SLOPE
> UNLESS YOU USE
> A PERISCOPE.
> BURMA-SHAVE

—And look, Daddy. We're coming to a hill.

As they approach a curve, she reads:

> AROUND THE CURVE
> LICKETY-SPLIT
> A BEAUTIFUL CAR
> WASN'T IT?
> BURMA-SHAVE

Reggie's impressed. —They're performing a safety service.

Maggie's sardonic. —Something you won't see much anymore. A corporation with a social conscience.

Daddy hrumphs cynically. —A social conscience that sold the American male into putting away his brush and mug, and made Burma-Shave the leading shave cream in the country.

Maggie frowns disgust. —It figures.

The signs are gone now. I've been watching and haven't seen a one. Probably all pulled up and carted off by collectors.

Casey made his own set, his idea of contribution to social conscience. He and Les put them up one night, just outside Harden:

> HERE I SIT
> BROKEN-HEARTED
> CAME TO SHIT
> AND ONLY FARTED.
> BURNING-SHAME

They were up two days. I was surprised they lasted that long. But in retrospect, I suspect time was allowed for word to spread so the town could enjoy a good laugh. They expected such creative high jinks from their up-and-coming youths. It was the spirited stuff from which successful men came.

But I'm wrong: five signs in a row. It's ridiculous I should feel so happy. I check my mirror, slow:

DRINKING DRIVERS
—NOTHING WORSE
THEY PUT THE QUART
BEFORE THE HEARSE.
BURMA-SHAVE

A few yards beyond, a clump of markers. I don't know why I call them markers, they're crosses. Simple wooden crosses. White. To catch the glare of headlights, leap up at you out of the night, fly at windshields, arms spread. Skeletal warners, ghostly reminders.

I count four, a fifth off to the side where a body'd been thrown from the impact.

I squeeze my eyes tight, shake my head, forcing away images, refusing, denying . . .

I feel betrayed. Please, no more Burma-Shave signs. I was happy. I'd gotten over the Indian girl. I was beginning to look forward. I'm wondering now what, if anything, on this trip I can trust.

A hump on the right slowly pulls into view as a black-and-white police car. I don't need to see the sign

HARDEN
Elevation   5,167
Population   4,573

to know I've entered the city limits. If this squad car is still here, I can bet money there's another on the western edge of town, along with a twin to the billboard 500 feet ahead.

Irritable tourists, hell-bent to get past the desert and into California, spot the black-and-white, pump brakes, cruise past, recognize the decoy for what it is. Then smirking, press foot to gas pedal, gaining just enough speed to break the limit before they hit the signboard, the only to-the-ground signboard between here and Albuquerque. But frazzled tourists don't note such subtleties. They whiz past and, lickety-split, out from behind the billboard pulls the lurking sheriff's car, red lights flashing. The deputy—now the one smirking—times them between police car and billboard with a stopwatch.

The city coffers have been greatly enhanced by cocky out-of-staters who underestimated the crafty local yokels.

I slow to a decorous 25 and, as I pass, check the driver's side. But it's empty. When I was last here, the town fathers were more serious about their game playing. They had a decoy deputy manning the decoy squad car. I laugh, spirits again lifted, remembering that deputy.

We were out at the Antlers, the roadhouse on the way to Flagstaff. They'd serve anyone, especially on a slow night. This had to be Saturday, the *big* drinking night. The whole gang was there. Except for Herren, who wasn't part of the gang except in his own mind, was never invited, and showed up only if he caught word. And for Janie, who didn't like to party and took a stiff-necked pose when we tried to entice her.

We'd taken over the bar, a rowdy row of twelve, leaving just enough room at one end for a few cowboys. Three couples huddled in the dim booths. Cowboys, real cowboys—and real cowgirls, for that matter—don't sit in booths unless they're with a date. Even old marrieds prefer the bar.

The Antlers has a nice mellowed-gold atmosphere, true West. A big lodge-type room with shellacked knotty-pine walls, high rough exposed beams, wide-planked dance floor, and big color-lighted jukebox that plays nonstop. The long bar's rimmed with heavy oak, curves at the ends, and has separate pine-backed stools. Its poured resin surface is inlaid with coins, bullets, belt buckles, bottle labels, and other memorabilia of the Old West. But I don't like it. The walls are hung with the heads of dead animals. Deer, antelope, elk, big-horn sheep, even a dusty bison. I express myself clearly when we first come in on the subject of killing for sport. But no one else seems to think there's a thing wrong with hunting. Even Casey. He and his dad, he tells me, supply rabbit for their table two or three times a year, and venison when it's in season. His big ambition now is to bring in a javelina.

It's the first I've heard that Casey knows how to handle a gun. I like the image but not the reality. I wonder why I haven't heard about it before.

Faye, Billie, and Betts are drinking boiler-makers—bourbon shots with beer chaser. Casey still won't let me drink, so I order a 7-Up.

Betts leans across me to the bartender —Make it a ginger ale. And another shot— then turns and smiles at me slyly. I don't understand but I don't argue.

I get my ginger ale. She nods. —Drink up— I drink. —That's enough— I stop. She dumps in the shot, looks at me encouragingly. —Bourbon and ginger. Easy-down for a beginner— Billie's grinning. Faye looks like a cat ready to swallow a canary. —Just sip— Betts instructs.

I sip and try not to wince. Rawness coated with sweetness. But I'll get it down no matter what.

Faye, watching me critically, seems satisfied, turns back to hunch over the bar. —That goddamn Janie— We know what she's talking about. —She doesn't belong with this group.

Betts downs her shot. —So maybe that's why she isn't with us.

—Fine. Then let her find some other crowd to hang around with.

—Why?— Billie pauses in the nursing of her beer. —Just because she won't drink?— Billie likes Janie.

I'm glad I've passed the test. I too could be up for blackballing.

Faye scowls. —She acts like she's got a corncob up her ass.

Billie laughs.

Betts takes a swig of beer. —I don't think she's forgotten the slumber party.

Faye glares, belligerently. —What's that got to do with the price of hogs?

—You ever apologize?

—Hell no. Why should I? She was drunk, she needed sobering.

—Maybe she's not crazy about the possibility of another slap.

—Screw you.

Billie's anxious about the turn of conversation. She doesn't like anything that even hints of disharmony. She wants everyone to be happy. She lifts her chin. —Yeah, Faye. You ruined poor Janie for life— Faye looks over, pugnacious. Billie grins. —You made a confirmed teetotaler out of her.

—Shit— But Faye has to laugh.

Having restored good humor, Billie looks around for fresh entertainment. Her energetic body can't stand sitting still, and she's been perched on her stool now for over an hour. She looks up the bar at the boys, milling among themselves, laughing and joking.

—Hey you guys. Anybody wanna dance?— They look over, then go back about their business.

She shoots her slug, gulps beer, and slides off the stool. Her short legs hit the floor, she totters, the stool teeters, and I can see the alcohol hit her. She's been drinking steadily and not moving.

She heads up the bar, hips swinging.

—Okay, suckers. Who's the lucky guy gonna be?

They shift uneasily, grin.

—Come on— She gives a sexy little twist. —I wanna dance.

—So go dance.

She fixes on the most vulnerable. —How about it, Glenn?

The guys laugh. —Yeah, go on, Glenn, give the lady a break— Shove Glenn toward Billie.

He shrinks back, face red. —You know I can't dance.

Billie pushes past Glenn into their midst, hands on hips. —Okay, Les. Let's go— She dances for him.

Les holds up his bottle. —I'm drinking.

—Up yours.

—Why don't you ask Trixie?

—Shit— a toss of the head. —I gave up girls when I was twelve.

—Then maybe it's time you tried 'em again.

—All right, you sonsabitches, to hell with you. I'm goin' out and find me a *real* man— They laugh. —Oh yeah? You think I can't?— They snicker. —Watch this.

Billie flounces across the dance floor, calls over her shoulder —Come on, Faye.

Faye looks over at the boys, eyes twinkling, shrugs, and follows Billie. The boys watch with grins.

At the door, Billie stops, turns, flips them the finger. They laugh, scuff the floor, swig beers. All except Casey, who doesn't like me to be exposed to such things.

He detaches himself from the group, saunters toward me.

—Hi, Hon. How ya doin'?— Big smile.

—Fine.

—Miss me?— He sidles up, face sweaty. He's left me for the boys all evening, he expects me to say yes? He puts his arm around my waist —Ahh, I'll bet she's been lonesome down here all by herself. But you know you're still my best girl— and tries to kiss me. I shove him away. He always gets smoochy when he's been drinking and I don't like it. I find it insulting.

He spots my empty glass. —Hey, Marty, the little lady needs a drink. Whaty'ya want, Honey? Another 7-Up?

I turn directly to Marty. —Ginger ale, please— Betts grins.

Marty sets down the glass, Betts catches his eye, holds up two fingers.

Casey slaps down money. —You need anything else, Honey? You sure? All ya have to do is holler— He chucks me under the chin —I don't wanna neglect my girl— and swaggers back up the bar.

I reach for the shot glass, pour it in myself. I'm drinking this one without a straw.

Betts toasts. —Bottoms up.

I toast back. —Here's to your rusty dusty.

Betts chokes. —*Shit*— But the look she gives me is worth the whole damn evening.

Billie's back in twenty minutes, Faye grinning behind her. I don't know how she thought it up, whether she had it in the back of her mind all the time or was just struck with sudden genius. But Billie has her date.

She's dragging the sheriff's decoy deputy.

Billie's five-feet-four, the deputy is life-size, the right size in life for a man evidently being six feet. She has him around the waist, his painted face on a level with hers, his twisted legs trailing behind him. He's in full uniform, except for no gun in his holster and no boots on his toeless feet. I wonder if he's wearing underwear, and giggle.

In Wexler first-aid class they gave us stuffed cotton dummies just like this one, made decent by T-shirt, socks, and boxer shorts. Their floppy flesh-colored bodies and shiny plastic faces had been worse than any cadaver we could imagine. We'd had to cover their staring sightless eyes before we could practice on them.

The Antlers has come to life. The boys are hooting and calling.

—Hey, Billie. Who's your date?

Billie holds out the dummy. —Meet Deputy No-Dick.

The crowd goes wild. The lone cowboys at the bar turn around on their stools. Even the lovers in booths lift their heads grinning.

Billie takes the deputy into dance position. —All right, you spineless bastards. Eat your hearts out— Faye hands her a shot, Billie downs it and starts dancing. Someone yells —Hey, Marty. Turn the jukebox up.

Billie does a lively two-step, bouncing No-Dick from side to side, her feet at about his knees, his calves flipping around behind him. The crowd claps, yells, cheers, whistles.

No-Dick's limp thighs slip between Billie's.

—Oh, no. No-Dick's gettin' dirty.

—Hey, No-Dick. Get outta there!

Billie kicks No-Dick's thighs away, not missing a step or beat of music.

—That's it, Billie. Kick 'im.

—Get 'im in the balls.

She twirls with him, No-Dick's legs flying.

Grabs him up, tosses him in the air, his arms and legs flapping.

Catches him by the waist, his head flopped over backwards. Double-time stomps, her face in his crotch.

Slings him between her legs, jitterbug style. Catches him by the hand, spins him flat to the floor in a circle.

It's quite a show. I'm fascinated by her inventiveness.

She pulls No-Dick up, arms flung around her neck. Dirty dances. Bends in a sexy dip.

Their legs tangle, she stumbles, falls flat on him. The crowd laughs.

She humps him. They roar.

Casey's at my side. —Come on.

Billie wraps her arms around No-Dick, rolls over and over across the floor, ending at the boys' feet, spread-eagle, laughing and gasping, No-Dick on top of her.

—Come on.

—What's the matter?— I'm laughing so hard I can hardly speak.

—We're leaving.

Betts looks over. —What's your problem, Colter?

—Stay outta this.

—Don't be a horse's ass.

He grabs my arm. —I said we're leaving.

I'm still laughing. I try to step off the stool. But his hand has me off-balance, I'm a little lightheaded, and weak from laughing. I slip, and land on the floor, sitting and laughing.

—What the hell's wrong with you?— Casey glowers over me. I can't stop laughing. —Are you drunk? Have you been drinking?— He sniffs my glass. —Who gave you liquor?— I laugh. He glares around the room, the boys smiling nonchalantly, fingers latched in front pockets, the girls staring back, eyes wide, cheeks sucked in, pictures of innocence. Things have quieted considerably.

—Goddamnit!— He hauls me up and half-shoves, half-drags me toward the door. I'm still giggling and gasping.

The last thing I see, before he pushes me out the door, is Deputy No-Dick in my stool at the bar, finishing my bourbon and ginger.

SCENE 4

The squad car and billboard are on the west side of town, just as I predicted. A blown-up Marlboro Man watches my return approach. But I know the enticing promise of his smile is empty. No white sheriff's car hides behind to spring out at me. Deceptions aren't what they used to be.

I've traversed the length of town, just to get a feel of it. My first impression, to my happy surprise, is that it hasn't changed that much. Untrue to the conventional wisdom, things do not seem smaller; if anything, they seem bigger, except for the Rialto, which looks badly run-down. The Mexican theater, on the other hand, has a recent coat of red-and-white paint. Walgreen's has a tacky new black-and-green plastic tile face. Babbitt's has added large plate-glass show windows and looks even more prosperous. No Indian women sit in the shade of its awning nursing babies the way they used to do. I wonder why.

Herren's trading post looks less prosperous. I wonder what's become of Freddy. La Descansada looks untended and barren, no geranium window boxes, no climbing riots of bougainvillea. But behind the high garden walls, who can tell, perhaps the roses still thrive.

The secret garden. I think of Dorothy.

I stop for gas at the Texaco where Dean worked. He smelled of grease and oil when he kissed me.

Then I try to decide on a motel. There are several now to choose from; I remember only a few rundown mom-and-pop types when last here. I've already ruled out the Marco Polo and Motel 6, big with truck drivers and rumpled families. The walls will be thin; I'll be privy to night-time phlegmy smoker's hack, squalling babies, and the rhythmic rocking of beds.

I vacillate between the Best Western and Travelodge, and decide on the former. It's across from a 76 truck stop. If I want good down-home cooking—and I do—this is where I'll find it.

I check in, unload the car, hang my clothes, and go in search of Harden. I have a rough agenda, but there never has been any question about my first destination. I find the street without a false turn, but I can't find the house. I have the right block, I'm sure of it. But I have to go back and forth three times before I realize this is it. My god! This is *it*?

I park across the street and sit in numbed shock. It couldn't have been this tiny and bleak when Casey lived in it. And yet it had to be. The scruffy Bermuda grass has dried to a coarse stiff yellow, but even green it wouldn't do much to help. This is what Maggie saw, and Daddy. This is what frightened them so. In Boston, this is one step up from poverty.

I stare at the unrelieved squat brick box and try to imagine what it must have been like for Casey. Young, spunky, bright, proud and impressionable, shipped off to military academy on scholarship, a form of earned charity. Where he mixed with boys his equal and better, came in contact with lives more affluent and more respectable than his, and in general received an education beyond Harden's offerings. Then he came home to this. What must it have done to him? His feelings about himself, about his family? Were the ideals and dreams there before private school or fostered by it?

I don't want to look at this sad little place any longer. It raises too many unsettling questions I'll never be able to answer. But if I'd seen clearly enough to ask them then, it might have explained some things.

Mr. Colter doesn't live here anymore. I learned that from the telephone directory, along with his new address. And with the help of the town map I got at the motel office, I find my way to his new residence: a small plain bungalow in a low-cost tract just a few blocks north of the Ferguson house. Yellow wood siding, with narrow concrete drive, detached one-car garage, neglected postage-stamp yard, and a few thirsty shrubs. In this dry land, it takes money to water.

Mr. Colter finally bought Catherine her house. No picket fence with climbing pink roses but a definite improvement. I wonder if Casey helped out. He had to have been out of the Navy by the time they got it. Did he send home his service pay?

I wonder how long Catherine had it to enjoy before she died. And what the inside looks like. Did she manage some new furniture?

I wonder what happened to Denny. She'd be in her late twenties now, probably married and with a family. Did she make it out of Harden or is she still here, to cheer the declining years of her father?

I never understood what made Casey join the Navy. It couldn't have been just to get out of Harden. He was determined to go to college, as soon as he saved the money. We'd planned our future on it. He even got a letter from TWA offering to send him for flight engineer's training, plus pay him $350 a month. Which, by any count, was better than becoming a sailor. Yet one day he called: Hi, Honey, guess what? I've signed up to sail the seven seas.

This is where our troubles began, I think. When Casey joined the Navy.

I wonder what Casey's wealthy Southern Belle thought when she saw this meager little house. His Georgia Peach, his Louisiana Mardi-Gras Queen. She knew him as a Navy veteran, a college football star, a soon-to-be FBI agent. A man of color and daring. A hero. What did she think when she came home with him the first time and saw this dismal hick town? Did she recognize its inhabitants' heroism for what it was or was she disdainful, dismissive? Did she have second thoughts about Casey and her marriage?

Maybe Casey was racing around town in her little red sports car alone because they'd had a fight and she was locked away in the bedroom. Maybe he didn't introduce her to his friends because she refused to meet them. Maybe she was embarrassed to be here, and ashamed of Casey.

I won't disturb Mr. Colter's peace. I won't knock on his door and say, Hi, remember me? What's the point?

The Ferguson house hands me a good laugh. Someone has converted the entire front yard into a sand-bedded cactus garden. Cholla, ocotillo, pincushion, barrel, prickly-pear. Three yucca, now in full waxy-white bloom. Not a bad idea if the house were an adobe Spanish or pueblo-type. But in front of a white frame with concrete porch, metal chairs, and asphalt roof?

I spend the rest of the afternoon going up and down streets, passing slowly before old haunts: the Bailey house, the Franks house, Janie's, Faye's, Trixie's. I never saw Ruthie's.

The McElvrey house looks the same. I wonder if they're still there. The old library has undergone considerable repair and is once again a residence. I wonder what happened to the children's books, and Maggie's pillows, rug, and chair. And to Story Time.

I wonder about Dean. Maybe I'll look up the McElvreys.

The town has flourished and, as with Holbrook, I wonder why. What could be the economic base? The high school has a lawn, and parking lot, and tennis courts, and new bleachers and playing field. There's a municipal park, and on the east edge of town, a low-income housing project. In the days of Betts and Dean and Janie, the promising youth got out as fast as they could. Leading the town fathers to worry that Harden would gradually dry up into an old-folks ghost community. But clearly, a solution has been found, new blood has been infused.

North, the town has expanded into the desert several blocks with large, well-kept, well-landscaped California ranch and split-level houses, and a modern elementary school. I don't have to ponder why long; to their side is an extensive new hospital.

In my day there were two hospitals: the Santa Fe for railroad employees; and the General, an over-crowded, rundown, ill-equipped, inadequately staffed string of rooms made over from an old motel right on Route 66. Now they have HARDEN HEALTHCARE CENTER.

Twenty years too late. A recognition I don't want to ponder. I'm suddenly tired and dejected. Maybe because I'm hungry. I haven't eaten since breakfast. In the course of my explorations, I've scouted restaurants. Daddy has a friend, a professor of paleontology, who before every trip—business, vacation, or holiday—carefully plans out every meal, where he's going to eat, what, and when. He has nothing on me.

I freshen up, get the motel manager's recommendation, and head into Mexican Town. It's been cleaned up and, to my relief, looks relatively safe. The houses are tiny and crude but for the most part they're houses. Only a few that could be classified shacks or shanties, with scattered lean-to's on the fringes.

Jose's Cocina is a low adobe with heavy wood doors and strings of dried red chiles hung from the low outside rafters. The small interior is lit by slanting westerly sun and dimly flickering candles. I bury myself in the menu and excruciate over a decision.

Finally settling on the complete dinner, I set the closed menu down, and almost immediately the waitress is at the table. I look up. And lose my order somewhere in my constricted throat.

She studies me coolly, arrogantly, indifferently. She hasn't changed a bit, at least not in demeanor. Her face is thinner and harder. There's a ragged scar to the side of her left eye curving into her high cheek bone. But other than that, she's the same.

She doesn't recognize me. Perhaps doesn't even remember me.

I force myself to smile. —*La combinacion completa, por favor. Y una Margarita*— I can hardly get the words out.

She doesn't blink an eye, scratches two sharp marks on her pad, and flings away.

But I'd recognize her anywhere.

Juanita Gutierrez.

The leanest and meanest in the whole gang.

The Mighty Midgets, they called themselves, averaging no more than five-three, beauty queen Dolores Torres being at five-five the tallest, Juanita a close second. The Spunky Spicks, Betts called them, in fonder moments. Pachuca Putas was Faye's epithet. They were tough, haughty, and defiant. They walked legs stiff, shoulders high, heads back, arms out at their sides, three abreast down the halls to force you around them. Don't mess with us, their dark eyes flashed, and for the most part we didn't.

But in gym class and after-school athletics, it wasn't so easy. We were thrown together in intimate competition, and we competed, our side against theirs, even though we were often on the same side. There were twelve of them, enough to form their own team for any sport. But Stafford and Loomis always split them up. No doubt to keep trouble down, and possibly in the idealistic hope that through the exercise of team work and good sportsmanship, we'd learn to play together. Which we did, with divided loyalties.

We girls had no tennis courts, limited badminton facilities, and only once-a-year springtime use of the swimming pool. Soccer and field hockey were unheard of. So we played a lot of softball, basketball, and volleyball. The Midgets were good at these; they could be practiced on home lots with minimum equipment. But you never found them on the school swimming team anymore than you found them at the city swimming pool. And though they had the spirit of swift runners, their legs weren't long enough to make them successful track competitors.

Basketball I was lousy at, not being aggressive enough. In softball I shied from the ball, having been hit once, a stunning blow to the chest. Track I hadn't really explored, since it conflicted with swimming. But volleyball I knew. I had a strong sure serve and a swift hard spike. I did best in the front and back line, in the middle I was adequate.

On this particular day, I had just finished my serve, during which we'd taken the lead in a close, heated, see-sawing game. I was in the front line, the ball came flying over the net, dropped.

I lunged to the right, bumping into Dolores, scooped it high and spiked, hard, over the net, to bring the winning point.

My teammates jump up and down, clap, cheer. Except for Dolores, who pushes toward me, hands on hips.

—What the hell you think you doing? That was my ball.

I stare at her. —It was between us.

—Like hell it was. You reach across, you push me. You take my ball, you score my point.

I shrug. —What difference does it make? We won.

She pushes her face into mine. —It make a big difference. It was my ball. You steal my ball, you steal my point.

I take a step back. —It's a team sport.

She smiles meanly, eyes narrow, and forces me back another step. —Oh yeah? You're not on my team— She pushes me. —What you know about team sport?— By now, the girls have stopped jumping around and are silently watching. —You wanna know about sport? We teach you.

Juanita, on the other side, ducks under the net and steps between us. —Yeah— Now it's Juanita's turn to push me. —We teach you. We teach you good, you— I get a rapid barrage of Mexican invective of which I recognize only isolated words but get the general meaning.

—Chocha— she spits. —Puta— Then slaps me.

I don't have time to think before Faye's there beside me. She shoves Juanita back. Juanita rebounds and slaps, sharp to the cheek. Faye slugs, hard to the chin. Dolores leaps forward. Faye grabs her by the shoulder, spins and knocks her to the floor. Juanita recovers, yells and springs. The next thing I know, it's a gang fight, the Mighty Midgets against the Gutsy Gringas. Betts, Billie, Faye, Trixie, Ruthie. Slapping and slugging, punching and pushing, hair-pulling and shirt-tearing, cussing and swearing. And believe it or not, right there in the middle is me.

It doesn't last long, maybe a minute or five, before Stafford and Loomis get word in the office and come running; we usually referee ourselves. But by the time they arrive, the Gringas have clearly cleaned up. Ruthie is flinging Bernice around by the hair. Trixie has stomach-punched Gloria against the wall. Faye has Dolores with her arms pinned behind her. Betts is sitting on Juanita. And I'm on the floor, holding onto Angie's leg for dear life, yanking her down every time she tries to stand up.

Looking back on it now, I suppose it's funny. But at the time it was deadly serious. I had become a scrapper, a street fighter, a town tough, with the scratches, bruises, and welts to prove it. I wore them proudly.

In the shower, under the hot spigot, fingering my bruises, steam billowing around us, I turned.

—Thank you, Faye.

She scowled. —What the hell for?— disgusted that I should be so stupid as to even mention it. —You're part of the gang.

Catherine was right. Faye made it up to me.

SCENE 5

I'm so tired by the time I get back to my motel room, I can hardly stand up. The day has been long and draining, and the *combinacion completa* and three Margaritas too much. I'd like nothing more than to just fall into bed. But I can't, I have one last thing to set in motion. I splash water on my face and go to the phone.

I hadn't told Betts I was coming. I wanted to feel my way in, find my own timing. The time has come. I sit on the edge of the bed and stare at the phone, puzzled as to why this should suddenly seem so difficult. I'd been looking forward with such excitement. But many of my reactions today haven't been what I expected. *I* haven't been what I expected.

I'm just tired . . .

I dial. One of the kids answers.

—Hi. May I speak to your mother?— Rude, not to identify myself.

—*M-o-o-o-m*. Telephone!

—Hello?

—Hi, Betts, it's Reggie.

—*Reggie.*

—You'll never believe where I am. Right here in town.

Beat. —You're in Harden?

—Can you believe it? It was spur of the moment or I would have called sooner— I take a breath, launch too fast into my rehearsed lie. —My folks are in San Francisco. I was flying out to meet them. I stopped in Albuquerque to change planes. And I suddenly thought, My god, I'm so close. I may never be this close again. So I called my parents, told them I'd meet them a few days later, changed my ticket, rented a car, and here I am.

—My god. Where are you?

—At the Best Western. Across from the 76.

—I'll be right down.

—No, don't, Betts. I'm absolutely pooped. I'm going to put myself to bed.

—I told you you could stay here.

—I know. But to tell you the truth, I need some time alone. I'll explain later.

—Okay. How about tomorrow then? Come for lunch.

This is harder than I imagined. —Well, I thought maybe I'd take the day to drive around. Look the place over, you know, visit some old haunts.

—Okay.

Breath. —But I'll tell you what I would like. Do you think you could get some of the girls together? Faye, Trixie, Ruthie?

—Sure. They'd love it. When?

—I know it's awfully short notice. But how about tomorrow night?

—What's tomorrow night? Monday. I don't see why not, they won't be doing anything. I'll call them right now.

—I don't want you to go to any trouble. I'll bring food and drink. What do they like to drink? Beer, wine?

—Wine's fine. And maybe a large bottle of coke. But don't worry about stuff to eat, I'll take care of that.

—I don't want you to fuss.

—It won't be fancy. And why don't you come early, for dinner.

—Great. That way we'll have some time alone together. I'm dying to meet your family.

—They've heard all about you.

—What time?

—I'll have the girls come at eight. We'll eat around six.

—Perfect. I'll see you tomorrow night then.

—I better tell you where we live.

—I have a map. Just give me the address.

I tug my clothes off into a heap on the floor, turn out the light, flop into bed. I don't even brush my teeth. I can't understand what's wrong with me. I should be full of anticipation. Instead I feel two-faced, conniving. For some funny reason, I get weepy. I turn my face into the pillow, fall asleep almost immediately. But I'm troubled all night with fitful dreams I don't remember.

CHAPTER ?

The car stopped at the curb, Casey reached for the door handle. Smokey put her hand on his thigh and held him back. He turned quizzically. She bowed her head.

"I can't, Casey." Her voice quavered. "I just can't go back into that apartment." He waited quietly. He understood the strain she'd been under, he'd seen other witnesses crack. "The phones are tapped, the walls are bugged, there are guards under every bush, cars on every corner." Her fingers dug into his thigh as she fought tears. "It makes me feel like a hunted animal."

"I know it's hard, but it's for your protection."

She shook her head. "I can't take it any longer."

"Just a few more days. We're almost over."

She lifted her face to his, cheeks streaked with tears. "Please, Casey—take me home with you." He stared. "Let me stay with you and Glory and the kids. Let me feel like a human."

"I can't do that, Smokey." His face showed how much it hurt him to deny her.

"Yes, you can. It's just for a few more days. You said so yourself."

"The worst is over. We have just a few minor—"

"Then it shouldn't matter so much. I've done my damage, it's too late—"

"It's never too late with them. You know that."

"If I were with you, I'd be protected."

"They could have a contract out on you right now."

"So let them hit me. I don't care anymore. At least I'd die a human." She could see him wavering. "I could go pack a bag and late tonight slip out through the back. You could pick me up on the other block. They'd think I'm still in the apartment."

"It's against my better judgment."

"Your single most important charge is to take care of your witness. So take care of me, Casey. Let me walk around and talk unmonitored. Let me fuss in the kitchen with Glory, and laugh and play with the kids."

Casey sat for a long moment, his face set hard in conflicted decision.

"All right," he turned to her. "But if for any reason in the next days I change my mind, there'll be no questions, no argument."

Her eyes looked full into his. "No questions. No argument." Her hand squeezed his thigh. "Thank you, Casey." It was an effort for him to look away.

Smokey packed her bags and waited. Casey had given his instructions: No one was to know except for the agents in the house, who would escort her, and the guards in the back, who would have to let them through. He wanted the stakeouts to remain on their toes and the routines to continue unchanged. Everything had to appear as normal as possible. The fewer people who knew, the fewer chances of leaks. He would get a policewoman to assume her place in the apartment.

At eleven thirty, clothed in black turtleneck and black slacks, Smokey made her furtive escape. By twelve thirty, she was sipping cocoa with Glory.

In spite of my disquieting dreams, I feel better in the morning, refreshed, renewed in spirit. I shower and dress quickly, no makeup but plenty of body lotion and face moisturizer. My skin doesn't like the hard water and dry heat, anymore than does my hair. I give it a double dose of conditioner, rub with the towel, then fluff with my fingers. And it dries in a cap of natural curls and waves almost as perky as I get in Boston. Nothing like a good cut.

I dart across to the truck stop and, after one reassuring glance at the menu, order the creamed chipped beef. After my huge dinner, I decided I should go easy. But tomorrow, corned beef hash. The next day, pancakes with maple syrup. After that, country-fried steak and eggs with hash browns. Then maybe I'll be ready again for biscuits and sausage gravy.

I have my agenda clear in mind, I don't have to write it down, even though I brought my notebook. I'm just worried about time, there's so much to cover. And I'll have to change clothes before going to Betts's. I've worried about that, too; what I'm going to wear. I don't want to appear East-Coast preppy, but I can't really present myself as Southwest shitkicker. So I've prepared myself with my shopping in Albuquerque: wash-and-wear sea-foam-green Levis-styled pants with matching sea-foam-green T shirt. Leather sandals on my feet, leather belt at my waist. No jewelry.

It seems this trip, to my consternation, is presenting me with a lot of worrying.

I'm worried now that the high school will be closed; it's only eight thirty and school's not in session. But a lone secretary sits behind a desk in the front office, talking a mile a minute over the telephone. She looks up as I enter.

—Just a minute, Marge, there's someone here— She holds the receiver aside and smiles at me. —Can I help you?

—Yes. I used to go to school here. I'm back in town visiting. And I was wondering if I could just look around a little, to kind of relive old memories.

—Why, of course, dear. What's your name?

—Reggie Patterson— She draws a blank. —I only went here one year. But my best friend is Betts Bailey.

—Oh, *Betts*. Of course— The secretary beams. —Everyone knows Betts. Go right ahead, dear— And she returns to her telephone. —Anyway, Marge . . .

I wander down the hall; it looks the same, even smells the same; of oiled floor-mops and heated teenage bodies. I peek in rooms; the same fixed bulletin-boards, the same straight rows. As Maggie pointed out later, these unvaried straight rows should have given me my clue right off. The desks weren't bolted down but they might as well have been. Along with the students' minds.

I turn into one of the rooms, freshman or sophomore whatever; the second floor was for junior and senior endeavors, a kind of physical hierarchy. I slide into one of the desks, rub my hand across the worn initialed blond oak. I think of my adjustment here. It was true culture shock. My first week I spoke up in class, just like I did at Wexler. I wasn't aware yet that spontaneous student participation wasn't exactly smiled upon. I was an ignorant immigrant.

At Wexler, we arranged our seats in groups, circles, or around a table seminar-style, dragging portable bulletin- and black-boards with us. Our decision depended on the assignment, learning mode, and what we felt like. We never chose rows. If someone wanted to be alone or study on her own, she was free to remove to a corner. Information was presented as fuel to fire our thinking, not as an end within itself. We were encouraged to discuss, question, comment, even challenge. We often engaged in heated, passionate arguments.

Information, understanding, analysis, evaluation, and insight, said a banner on the wall: *This is the route to knowledge.*

When I was finally made to understand that at Harden teachers were authorities not facilitators, and that my role as student was to read, listen, take notes, and regurgitate facts, I was furious. I threatened insurrection. I refused to cooperate. I demanded to go back to Wexler. I would not accept such restrictions on my intellectual freedom. I would not be relegated to a puppet. I gave Maggie and Daddy a really bad time.

They sat in their living-room chairs, watching me pace up and down, listening to my ravings and rantings.

—What's the matter with you?— I accused. —Don't just sit there. *Do* something!

Maggie regards me coolly. —What is it exactly you think we can do? Overthrow the system? Upend their whole world? This is more or less what we expected.

—Great!— I glare. —Why didn't you tell *me*?

Maggie shrugs, purses her mouth primly. —We didn't want you to set up any premature biases— Looks at me pointedly. —We wanted you to *adjust.*

I'm silenced with disbelieving outrage.

When in Rome, Daddy cautioned.

Moderation in all things, Maggie warned.

They were afraid I was going to create a scene in class, a situation that would alienate me from my teachers and set me apart from the other students. I took their instruction under wily advisement. I wasn't anymore crazy about my becoming a pariah in purgatory than they were. I became a model of virtuous control and obsequience, better even than old Clydene Orton, who couldn't, was constitutionally *unable* to, hide her lamp under a bushel.

I no longer volunteered. I answered and questioned only when called upon. And with such humble timorousness neither teachers nor fellow students could be threatened. But I did so with calculated vengeance. I had a point to prove, a case to make: I would not be held down. I would not be muffled. My hand was still the one most frequently up in class, and when it went up, I made sure my observations were still the most incisive.

I was a worthy adversary.

I think of Casey.

What if I'd left here? What if I'd gone back to Wexler after that first month? I was willing to leave him without a second thought.

I slowly slip from the desk, walk back into the hall.

I'm thinking of Betts and Billie. Trixie and Ruthie.

What if I'd *never* left here? What if this was all I'd ever known, all I'd been allowed? I think of Katelyn and Lindsay, try to see them walking these halls. They would have been different persons. Might not have been at all.

Oh, Casey. Oh, Katelyn and Lindsay. Where would we be now?

The padded door closes behind me with a soft *whuff*. I stand, letting my eyes adjust. The auditorium is larger than I remember, yet more intimate, its heavy dark silence portentous, like a church.

I scuff down the sloped aisle, the balls of my Keds gripping the rubber runner, and take a seat in the center. I sit for a long while, staring at the empty stage, trying to visualize myself singing and dancing and posturing across its bare, lusterless boards. But I can't. It all seems so long ago. So unreal.

Another person.

All that keeps coming before my eyes are the stiff black-and-white photos I gave the girls, those unfortunate photos. I was reaching out, intending something else, another message. But what? What was I trying to say? What was I asking? How could I have communicated so wrongly?

I have become muffled after all. Or perhaps I should say muddled.

Whatever I came to recapture is no longer here. I rise resignedly from the worn plush, push up the seat, trudge up the aisle, vaguely acknowledge the door's soft *whuff* behind me.

The athletic complex is connected to the back of the main building by the girls' gym and a long enclosed outside corridor. I push the bar on the gym door and quickly step in. The high light spacious emptiness has a strange effect on me. I feel a pull toward the center, to fulfill it. But the glossy surface of the floor looks fresh, vulnerable to shoe imprints. I stay to the edge and listen. And suddenly realize that this is exactly what I'm doing: I'm listening. That this is what this room holds for me: sounds. The scrapes, squeaks, and pounds of sneakered feet; the thuds, slaps, and thunks of balls; the whoosh of nets, the thwang of backboards, the screech of whistles; the shrieks, yells, screams, and laughter of teenage girls.

I hear only their echoes.

I move to the inside hall, past the gym office, toward the locker room. The moment I enter, I'm overwhelmed and lifted by a transport of smell: scented soap, drugstore cologne, disinfectant, mildew, and sweat. The present becomes past, the past present. For a disorienting moment, I'm fifteen.

Of all the retainers of memory, the strongest and most reliable is the nose.

I step into the gang shower, half-expecting to see Faye, Billie, Ruthie, Trixie, Betts. I stand in the middle, looking at the white tile walls, the pitted concrete floor. And have a sudden urge to tear off my clothes and turn on all the spigots, full blast.

But I don't. And as I leave, I feel sorriness about this, sorriness for the part of me that's gone that would have done it.

I try the swimming-pool door and, to my surprise, find it open. My luck holds out: no one's in it. They used to commandeer the pool in summer for swimming and life-saving classes, to add to the school's revenue. If I'd stayed, I could have been an instructor.

I climb the concrete steps to a block of shade and sit contemplating the motionless aqua. An outdoor pool, used only in warm-to-hot weather, and still no overhang. People in the bleachers swelter, but it's great for the swimmers. I still remember how good it felt to crawl out of its unheated water and get hit by the sun. We dried in minutes. And by the time our next event came, we were so hot we practically jumped the gun to get back in. It made for eager swimmers.

We took the regional championship that year. I won first in the crawl and backstroke, second in diving, and third in the sidestroke. I guess I showed Freddy Herren.

Betts was our manager, keeping track of our gear, leading the singing on the bus, and helping me, as team captain, out with the locker-room pep talks. I can still see her sitting pool-side, in her oversized blue-latex swimsuit, her massive arms and thighs radish red. Her fair skin didn't take kindly to the sun. It took her several burns to tan, and her nose peeled all summer. We'd throw wet towels over her but, in her excitement of encouragement, she kept leaping up off the bench, dumping them to the concrete.

She couldn't swim, at least not well or easily. She kept sinking. But she loved the water, and she floated beautifully. She'd lie there on her back, arms spread, eyes closed, white-capped head bobbing gently. What did it matter if her legs dragged downward? The mounded rise of her breasts and stomach kept her buoyant. She floated before and after every meet, it was our good-luck charm. She was more than our manager, she was our mascot.

With Betts, who needed a rabbit's foot?

I smile at the blistered pool-side bench. Yes. She was my mascot. What did it matter if I showed Freddy Herren, if we won or lost, if I placed first or last?

What did it matter if Betts's legs dragged? She kept afloat.

The sun has come over the wall, glinting off the water in blinding shards. My patch of shade has abandoned. I feel the heat pounding my head and shoulders. My face is sweaty, I taste salt on my lips. I place my hands on my thighs and reluctantly rise. At the door, I shield my eyes and take one last look. A shimmering rectangle of molten gold.

I head for the girls' gym with no hesitation. I tear off my clothes, step into the gang shower, and turn on all the spigots, full blast.

I thank the secretary on my way out. If she notices my wet hair, she doesn't comment.

—How was it, dear?

—The same. Exactly the same.

She smiles, so glad.

The trophy and yearbook cases are in the foyer just inside the main entrance, along with the announcement board. I start to look for our trophy, then stop myself. What does it matter?

At the announcement board, I take out my pen and notebook, print neat and large, and tack my message in the middle of the dated notices:

Information, understanding, analysis, evaluation, and insight: This is the route to knowledge.

Outside, I step back into the road and take a long look at the brick walls and steel-sashed windows. Without this—the experience, the expansion—where would I be now?

The Hopi do not approve of awards and prizes, of trophies and names on plaques and scrolls. This is as true for adults in their crafts and work as it is for children in their sports and grades. The traditional Hopi does not believe in individual importance, position, or gain; rather he refuses to seek high office, avoids exhibiting exceptional talent or ability, and strives for humility at all times. There is no personal accumulation of wealth, so there is no inherited material status. Everyone lives in the same type of house, wears the same sort of clothes, and eats the same kind of food. Everyone works and the value of everyone's work is equal. The only person exempted from labor is the religious leader, whose time and energy are given to prayer and meditation for the benefit of all.

The Hopis do not engage in competitiveness because they believe it is harmful. Those who fail to win will feel inferior, and possibly envious of the winners. Those who win will feel superior, and possibly disdainful of the losers. This is injurious to all. If a woman makes a strong and beautiful pot she may rightly take pride in it, as may the man who raises a good field of corn. But they will do wrong if they compare with others, even in their minds; for the thought alone has power to damage.

The only allowable reward is the achievement itself. The only accordable honor is that merited by piety and dignity of character.

SCENE 6

I need food. It isn't noon yet but revisiting memories is hungry work.

I drive to Dairy Queen, a must on my agenda, and enjoy its sameness, down to the last fluorescent light bulb, while I wait for my brazier burger, french fries, and two large cokes. I drink one coke as I drive, but save the rest; I have plans.

It takes me a while, but I finally find it: the road out to the flat where Casey took me for Fourth of July fireworks. Only this time I'm not looking for fireworks, I'm looking for a turnoff.

I slow, trying to see through the swirl of red dust. It's somewhere along here. I'm trusting I'll feel it. And I do. I swerve left onto the narrow barely visible track and bump along over rocks and ruts, straining toward the distance. I begin to worry. I don't remember its being this far out. And then I see it: a small lone formation of red sandstone suddenly projecting up out of miles of scorched flat.

Castle Rock.

If you use your imagination, you can see the ramparts, the central donjon, the turrets. I park by the scattered remains of hundreds of campfires, grab my lunch sack, and climb. I've worn my new Levis and old sneakers just for this excursion.

Natural footholds, helped along by generations of boots, provide access up one side the impressionable rock to a pretend parapet, which widens at one end into a platform where a king might stand regarding his fief, or watching his advancing enemies.

I find my throne, carved high in the tallest turret, unload my sack, and settle down to my picnic. The burger is cold, the fries soggy, the coke watery. But up here, in the shade of the rock, the hint of a breeze underscoring the silence, it seems food fit for a queen. Even one twenty years vanquished.

How many times did we come here? Two, maybe three? They all blend into the last.

Casey had told me to wear shorts, just the way he did that night he took me out to the airport and set me up with Max. He liked to show me off. But Maggie didn't. So I'd put a skirt over, which I discarded the moment I got in the car. I hadn't thought to bring sneakers. So I was stuck with my Bernardo thong sandals, which were right for the skirt but wrong for the shorts and desert. But it didn't really matter, I knew we wouldn't be doing much climbing. Mostly at Castle Rock, we stand around and drink. At least everyone else does. After the Antlers, Casey watches me like a hawk, still expecting me to stay a Boston Proper lady. Once in a while, Betts'll slip me a sip of her beer, but never enough to get a buzz on.

We have a slow fire going, by now well-bedded with embers; the guys bring wood in their pickups and car trunks. We stand at the fire's edge, lean against the rock, sit on dislodged boulders, the light flickering across our faces, pulling figures and features out of the dark: a crossed leg here, a hand holding a can there, a bent profile. Cigarettes glow off and on, like flitting fireflies.

Tex is playing his guitar. Now and then he'll get into something lively that'll stir us into scuffing around in the dust. Or an old favorite that'll draw us into a sing-along. But most of the time he just sits up on his rock, one leg bent up, the other dangling, hunched over his guitar, lost in his chords and runs.

—Hey, Billie. Whyn't you and Reggie sing?

—Yeah.

The crowd is getting restless, they want to be entertained.

Billie and I have discovered we harmonize well together, she taking the alto, me the soprano. We have several songs, a few where Betts joins us in close three-part harmony.

—Okay. What'll it be?— Billie flips her cigarette into the fire.

—How about "Waiting Just for You"?— Casey looks at me from across the fire.

Billie and I take position side-by-side, Tex strums the opening, we pick up.

You have to leave me, all by myself, dear, and I been cryin' the whole night through.

But I keep tellin' everybody, I'm waitin' just for you.

Casey moves forward, his eyes locked on mine, his look significant. It won't be long now before I have to leave Harden.

You know this waitin', can drive me crazy. Don't mind this waitin', it's nothin' new. And I'll be tellin' everybody, I'm waitin' just for you.

I sing directly to him, his eyes, as he sips his beer, never leaving mine.

May be a long time, before I see you, so we can do what, we used to do. But I'll be tellin' everybody, I'm waitin' just for you.

A spatter of applause, each pair of clapping hands sounding separate, alone in the night.

Casey comes for me, pulls me into the dark, against the rock. He leans over me, one hand braced above my head. We kiss. He smells of cigarettes, tastes of cold wet beer. His body sinks warmly into mine.

—Hey, Case. Where the hell's the beer?

He jerks from the kiss. —Goddamnit— Calls back over his shoulder. —In the trunk.

—No it ain't, I looked.

He reluctantly pulls his body from mine, lifts his hand from the rock.

—Then try Walt's car.

—I did. There ain't none there either.

—Shit— He spins on his heel and stalks off.

I stay leaned against the rock, watching him mingle with the phantom others as they move in and out of the light, waiting for him to return. When he doesn't, I feel lonely, forsaken.

I feel . . . something crawl onto my foot. I freeze. It's slow. And big.

—Casey— I try to make my voice shrill enough to reach across to him but not loud enough to disturb whatever it is.

It moves.

—*Casey.*

He hears, looks up in my direction. —What's the matter, Honey?

—There's something on my foot.

He comes hurrying, slows, stops. —Shit. Don't move— He takes my arm. —And don't look down.

I'm rigid. The thing keeps coming, laboriously, across my sandaled instep.

—Just stand still.

Tex has stopped strumming, the crowd has gone quiet, a few have moved forward.

—What is it, Case?

—A sonofabitch centipede.

—Shit!

—Don't move, Reggie— Billie seems to be calling across miles.

—One of the poisonous kind?

—They're all poisonous, stupid.

I'm tracking every filamented movement, leg by leg, my eyes riveted on Casey.

—Just stand still, Honey, let 'im go his way.

I feel the outside half of my foot go free. I finally have the courage to look down.

It's huge. A least three inches long and almost an inch wide. And dark. It must have a thousand legs. I watch as it finally crawls off.

Casey's hand tightens, I can feel the imprint of every finger.

—Lift your foot, Baby.

—Which one?

He looks at me angrily. —What the hell's the difference, just lift!

I lift. He slams his boot down, grinds viciously. —The dirty sonofabitch.

I fall back against the rock, the gang flocks in.

—Jesus christ.

—Holy shit!

—What a *ugly* bastard.

I pull my feet up, arms around my legs, chin on my knees, smiling. . . .

—My hero— The voice cuts sarcastically across my reveries. I practically fall off the rock. —Our brave cavalier— it simpers. —Again to the rescue.

I stand, look around. But she's nowhere to be seen. She said she wouldn't be caught dead back in Harden. I thought I'd be safe here.

But there's no mistaking, it's Smokey's voice all right.

I sit back down. If I'm very quiet, maybe she'll go away.

—So then what happened?— She's somewhere rudely behind me. I stare at the horizon. I refuse to acknowledge her. —What happened then, Reggie? You trying to tell me you don't remember? Or you don't want to remember.

I reach in my bag, take out a cigarette. This is where Billie taught me to smoke. I inhale, deeply. Frown. Exhale, slowly. —It wasn't a centipede.

—*What?* Speak up, Reggie— She's leaning into my ear, almost shouting. —I can hardly hear you.

I study the scattered char below.

—It wasn't a centipede, Casey.

He looks up glaring. I know immediately my mistake.

—What the hell was it then?

I shrug, make my voice small and contrite. —A millipede.

—Who gives a shit— Casey grabs the can Les holds out to him, guzzles. —It's dead now.

Billie steps to my side. —You okay, Reggie?

Casey takes a defiant stance. —Of course she's okay. I killed the sonofabitch— He kills his beer, bends the can, throws it into the desert—he knows how I feel about littering—and swaggers off toward the fire, scouting up a new beer.

Betts silently hands me a can, I take it.

The gang hangs around, still anxious about me.

Casey turns and regards us, legs wide, head back, silhouetted against the fire.

—Hey. What's wrong with everyone around here? Let's have some fun, some noise, some music. Come on, Tex— Tex starts to pluck half-heartedly. Casey raises his beer. —Here's to conquering the Wild West— He chugalugs. Some of the guys lift cans with him.

—Come on over here, Reggie. Sing for me— I stay where I am. —Did you hear me? Come over here.

—I don't want to.

—Whaty'ya mean? I said come over here. I wanna hear my girl sing.

Billie steps in front of me. —And *she* said she doesn't want to.

—Who asked you?

—You did, asshole. We sing together.

They stare each other down.

—To hell with you then— A sudden big grin. —*I'll* sing— Casey toasts with his can, in a gesture that looks very much like Up yours. —Hey, Tex. Do "Honky Tonkin'"— Tex fingers an introduction. —Come over here, Les, help me out. You know this one.

Casey sings, imitating Hank Williams. Les's drunken falsetto isn't much help. Casey keeps it up a few bars, then laughs, throws his head back, and chugalugs, spilling beer down his front. Billie turns away in disgust.

As the evening wears on, Casey gets drunker and drunker, and louder and louder. I stay away from him, trying not to watch or listen.

But then I see him stumbling around by the cars, bent forward at the waist, Les beside him. I hear this sound, then Casey's curses. And I realize with horror that he's vomiting. I don't think, I just run.

By now I've had a few beers myself.

—*Casey.*

He turns, furious. —Get out of here!

—I want to help.

He sees my face. —I don't need your pity.

He's overcome with a new paroxysm. He stoops over the splattered pool of yellow, hands braced on his thighs. His body jerks violently, the retches tear from the root of his guts. He's into the dry heaves. It's terrible. The sound, the smell, the dribble on his chin, his helplessness. I don't know what to do.

I reach out a hand to hold his forehead, the way Mummy would do. He spins on me, face contorted beyond recognition. —Get away from me, you shithead!

I stumble back, stunned, appalled by his face, the epithet. I'm afraid to face the crowd. But as I return to the fire, no one looks up, as if they haven't heard.

We prepare to leave. The guys kick out the fire, the girls collect beer cans. Casey shows up with my skirt.

—Come on.

I shake my head.

—It's time to go home.

—I'm not going with you.

—And why the hell not?

—You've been drinking.

He stands stiff and steady, arms out. —I don't have a drop of beer in me— Grinning, trying to make a joke of his vomiting.

—I'm going with Betts.

He scoffs. —And you think she hasn't been drinking?

I take my skirt, face him squarely. —Well, at least she's not an ugly, foul-mouthed, sloppy drunk.

Betts, Billie, and I drive in silence, enjoying the cooling breeze blowing across the open windows. I have my sandaled feet braced up against the pickup's dashboard. They're filthy.

Billie lights a cigarette, drags, passes it to me. —Don't be too hard on him, Reggie.

I remove my Sen-Sen, puff, without inhaling. —He made a complete ass of himself.

Billie shrugs. —Yeah, well. It did kind of go to his head.

I pass the cigarette to Betts. —Too much beer did.

Betts looks at me. —I guess the way he sees it, he saved your life.

I return the Sen-Sen to my mouth, suck, look straight ahead.

—Millipedes aren't poisonous.

Billie laughs, short, sharp, ironic.

—Shit— Betts's grin is wide. —Don't tell Colter that.

SCENE 7

I don't see or hear from him all the next day, and that suits me fine. But that evening, at seven thirty sharp, his car pulls up at our curb. I peek through my blinds, then scurry to listen at my cracked door.

Maggie greets him at the screen.

—Hi, Mrs. Patterson. Reggie isn't expecting me but if it's all right, I'd like to talk to her.

Maggie and Daddy have been aware, from my sullen reticence about the evening, that things have gone wrong between Casey and me. But they've been tactful enough not to pry. I'm sure Maggie's hoping it's something major that'll split us up.

Maggie hedges. —Well, I don't know. She's resting. I'll see if she wants to be disturbed.

Then I hear Daddy. —Come on in, Casey— My mouth pinches in irritation. Just like Daddy.

—No thanks, Mr. Patterson. If you don't mind I'll just wait here.

Maggie hush-foots down the hall, softly knocks, then finding the door ajar, pokes her head in.

—Casey's here— A whisper.

—Well tell him I'm out— Loud.

—He says he wants to talk to you— Hissed, conspiratorial.

—About what?

—He didn't say— Her eyes glint, eager, hopeful. And that's what makes me change my mind. She's been out to get him all year.

I slide off the bed, flounce past Maggie, barge across the living room, and confront Casey through the screen.

—What do you want?

—I'd like to talk to you.

—What about?

He looks uneasily at my parents. Maggie's resettled in her chair across from Daddy, both innocently absorbed in their reading.

—About our little disagreement.

—All right. Talk.

I see his anger flare then get doused. This is costing him a lot of cold water.

—I was hoping we could talk privately.

I consider him haughtily, then open the screen and settle decorously on the wicker settee. He sits beside me.

—First of all, I'd like to say I'm sorry— I nod, hands prim in my lap, not looking at him. —Does that mean apology accepted?

I consider. —I guess.

—No hard feelings?

—I didn't say that. There's a lot we need to talk about.

—All right, then let's talk. Where would you like to begin?— His voice gets louder. —At the party?— I glance over, suddenly aware how close we are to the screen, and how well our voices carry.

I stand. —Why don't we move onto the lawn. It's cooler there.

Casey grins smugly.

I drag a cushion from the settee with me. Maggie's nursed the grass into greenness but it still itches.

Casey sprawls on the lawn, plucks a blade, chews on it. —So why are you so mad at me?

—Because you made a complete fool of yourself.

He pulls at the grass. —I guess I had too much to drink too fast.

—You were chugalugging.

—I was so scared, Honey.

—Don't call me Honey.

—All I kept thinking was, My god. What if she gets bit?

—So that's why you walked off and left me standing there? Because you were so worried about me?

—I was just so relieved.

—Bull shit!

—Don't swear.

—Why not? You do.

—I'm a man.

—I don't believe in a double standard.

—Well if there's no double standard, why didn't *you* kill that centipede?

I don't correct him. And I have no answer. —All I know is a man doesn't call the woman he *says* he loves a shithead.

Casey hangs his head, digs at the lawn. —I shouldn't have said that. And I *do* love you. I guess I was just . . . I didn't like you seeing me like that.

—Then you shouldn't have drank so much. A man doesn't have to buoy himself up with beer and go swaggering around like a big macho honcho to prove—

—Are you telling me I'm not a man?

I look at him. —You are in some ways. In other ways, I think you need to grow up.

He studies me, trying to decide whether to get angry or acquiesce.

I press my advantage. —All I can say is that a man doesn't treat a woman like a piece of baggage he can drop off or pick up whenever he feels like it. God made woman out of man's rib, not out of his foot. She was meant to serve as an equal at his side, not get kicked around by him.

His face gets obstinate.

—God took woman out of man's side so he could keep his arm around her and protect her. She's *of* him, not the same as him.

I look at him, hard, intent. —She's his other half. When man and woman give themselves to each other in love, they become one.

He returns the look. —And what God hath joined together, let no man put asunder.

I get his message, lift my chin. —Well, if you're such a man, why are you putting us so much asunder?

It amazes me now that we could have said such things. He was seventeen. I was fifteen.

It isn't on my agenda, but I know where I have to go. I grab my bag and picnic remains and climb slide down the rock.

I'm not dressed properly. I'm wearing a braless tank top. In Italy I was refused admittance to a church because of my uncovered shoulders. Howie had to lend me his jacket. I decide to risk it. I figure if God can accept me the way I am, so can a small-town church.

It's one of the oldest buildings in town, an elongated rectangle of sandstone block set bluntly on Route 66, the wide steps leading directly up from the blank concrete sidewalk to the heavy double wood doors. The entry is so dark after the outside glare, I have to stand a moment to let my eyes adjust. But even blinded I'd know where I am by the close smokey cling of candle wax and incense.

I cross myself with holy water, soft-foot up the aisle, genuflect. When in Rome . . .

I'm the only petitioner. But others have been here recently. Votive candles splutter on the tiered table to my left, signaling feebly their wafted prayers.

I think of the Hopi. Does God receive a candle's breath in enclosed darkness, I wonder, better than an eagle's feather afloat on the air?

I sit down on the hard rump-polished pew, concentrate on the painted carved-wood figure above the altar, the twisted Crucifix of a fair-skinned, fair-haired young man who'd given himself in hope of saving me. And the dark-skinned, black-haired supplicants who make up at least a third of this parish, filling the back rows, and don't at all resemble their savior.

Religion was important to Casey; he knew exactly what he believed, how, and why. The Church gave him his faith, and ritual gave him a way of avowing and reaffirming that faith.

I believed that God was within and that we avowed and affirmed our godliness by our actions. I didn't believe in blind faith, and had an aversion to ritual. The one time I attended mass with Casey, Catherine, and Denny, I was embarrassed, it seemed pagan and unintelligent.

—You can't reject our faith out of ignorance— Casey and I'd been arguing and Casey was getting angry. —At least we believe in something. Your father's a damn atheist.

—He is not— Now I was getting angry. —My father believes devoutly.

—Oh yeah? In what?

—In keeping an open mind. That all things are possible and impossible.

—And that's not being an atheist?

—He says it's his definition of an agnostic.

Casey snorts. But he can't argue. Now we're into *his* area of ignorance.

He glowers. —Well, I don't care. If you're going to become my wife, you have to become a Catholic.

—I don't see why. I'm not forcing you to become a Unitarian.

—I'm not forcing. I'm just saying if we're going to get married, we have to be married in the Church.

—And we can't if I'm not Catholic?

—We can't go up to the altar. We'd have to stay outside the railing.

—So what difference does that make?

—I want our marriage fully recognized by the Church.

—It's recognized by God. Isn't that enough? You said so yourself: What God hath joined together—

—The Church is God's emissary here on earth. Our union has to be sanctified by the Church. I don't want our kids raised in a divided family. We have to think and *believe* alike.

He became like a martinet on the subject. Rigid, dogmatic, repeating the same tired ideas over and over in the same tired words. There was no getting around it: if I wanted to marry Casey . . .

So I began Catholic instruction. Covertly. Maggie would have died, and

Daddy probably would have followed soon after. Once a week after school, Casey drove me to catechism. I was beyond the usual age for confirmation. But when Casey explained our circumstances, the priest allowed me to attend; by special dispensation of the Pope, I suppose. I sat in the back row, tall behind the elementary-school heads, intending to keep a low profile. Just listen and learn, Casey had directed.

And I was doing all right. Until we came to confession. Which got into the hierarchy of the Church. Which for me was synonymous with hierarchy of religion. I hadn't known it before, but I was a confirmed egalitarian.

—But why?— I pressed the priest. —Why can't I confess and ask forgiveness directly from God? Why do I have to go through an intermediary?

Unitarians are like that; they look everything in the face point blank and question.

The priest took me aside to answer me in private; he said I was confusing the younger students.

—Ahhhh— he smiled wisely, benevolently. —It is the psychology— He appealed to my arrogance. —I'm sure you understand psychology— He explained patiently.

—Man is like a child. He will not be sorry for what he can get away with. He will steal the cookie from the jar, eat in secret, and feel not only pleasure in the forbidden sweet but pride at his cleverness. Theft is a sin. Gluttony is a sin. Pride is a sin. He will be guilty but because he has not been made to feel his guilt, he will not learn from it. He will steal a car. He will deal in drugs. He will make profit from prostitutes. He will become a fat and drunken lecher. He will see himself as superior, outside the laws that govern other men. He will become a power unto himself. He will use and misuse others to his selfish advantage. This is directly against the teachings of the Church, which are Christ's teachings, which is God's law.

I'm fascinated. I haven't taken my eyes off his eyes and mouth. Or moved a muscle.

He smiles. —Are you with me?

I nod. I'm seeing a gigantically obese crime lord, stuffed in a Jaguar, fondling a wanton woman, and munching a hashish-laced chocolate chip cookie.

—Good— He takes breath, leans back in his chair. —Now. What if on the other hand, the father comes home that evening, takes his son on his knee, says, How did your day go, my son? and the boy happily and eagerly tells his father all the wonderful things he did. The father pats his son, smiles, says, I'm proud of you, my son, and I love you. Then he says, And did you do anything you shouldn't have done?

—The child is immediately aware of his guilt. He can lie but he knows his father is bigger and smarter than he is. He can ferret out and see things in ways the boy does not understand. The boy cannot risk being caught in a lie as well as his cookie theft. He cannot risk going against the father's authority and disappointing his love. He confesses. And in so doing, the full weight of his guilt comes to bear. He recognizes his wrong and is sorry.

—The father instructs his son in the evils of gluttony, stealing, and pride. The child learns, and in the child is the man. The child feels relief at having his burden lifted, and gratitude toward his father for lifting it. Confession is good for the soul. It humbles us and restores us to the path of righteousness. The father blesses the child with a hug then says, Now, pray to God for forgiveness.

I pluck at my skirt, trying to think of further objections, but I can't.

Catherine gives me my rosary, rounded garnet and cut-crystal beads, with a tiny silver crucifix.

Hail, Mary, full of grace, blessed art Thou among women and blessed is the fruit of Thy womb, Jesus . . .

I sit outside the curtained box and confess. I can hear the closed-in priest shift in his seat, once in a while breathe. At the end, he chastises and instructs me, then prescribes my penance.

I count my beads. *Holy Mary, mother of God . . .*

But I don't feel relieved or grateful. I'm troubled, something keeps jabbing at me.

. . . pray for us sinners now and at the hour of our death.

—But how can I be such a sinner? I'm only fifteen. I haven't had that much of a chance— I'm leaning so close to the curtain, it flutters with my words. I resist an urge to yank it aside.

The priest sighs. —You were born in sin.

I'm aghast.

He describes Original Sin. The transition of souls. Heaven, Hell, and Limbo. I hadn't yet read Dante.

SCENE 8

I feel loss. A hollow, empty sadness. My mind is dark and fuzzy. I haven't prayed in years. Maybe that's what's wrong with me, what's missing. I close my eyes, grasp the pew-back in front of me, and slip to my knees. I feel them hit the prayer bench. And a sudden image flashes: women on their knees—in thin, worn-shiny black dresses, black veils over their heads—crawling up steps. It was in Mexico, when I went with Maggie and Daddy. I don't remember what town or city, what church or cathedral. I remember the crawling women, work-rough knees dragging over punishing stone.

I look down, expecting reddened scrapes, blood-oozing scratches, and see dust. Dust on a crinkled skirt.

My head lowers onto my hands, my eyes squeeze tight, lids stinging. A dusty crinkled skirt, the tag of a cotton flannel blanket . . .

It was Friday night, no game, the boys were off somewhere. Faye, in her car with Trixie, Ruthie, and Janie, was following Betts, in the pickup with me and Billie, as we cruised up and down, looking for a little excitement. We'd just been out to check the Antlers. And on the way back we pass a big tent surrounded by cars and pickups.

Betts slows. —Hey, this might be interesting— She swings in, Faye follows and pulls alongside her.

—What the hell you doin'?— Head out the window, over bent arm.

—You ever been to one of these?

—Hell no.

—You wanna go?

Faye ducks back in, checks, pokes her head out. —Sure. Something different . . .

We park, pile out.

I hang back uncertainly. —What is it?

—A tent revival. You up for it?

I shrug. —Why not?

I was fifteen. What did I know about good and evil?

The tent is large, dingy gold, with dirt floor, and three sections of folding wooden chairs. At the front is a wooden dais with podium, flanked by two baskets of gladiolas, and a piano. Light glares mercilessly from huge round globes on tall rods spaced around the sides. As we enter, the pianist is pounding out "Come, come, come to the church in the wildwood."

We take seats toward the back, behind a young woman cradling a blanketed baby.

The piano pounds. We look around, smile at one another. Friday night. Fun.

The preacher enters from a back slit in the tent and steps up to podium. He's a medium-built man with thick wavy black hair, dressed in a brown suit, yellow shirt, and club tie. There's a microphone. He starts in, sweet, persuasive, seductive. He welcomes the crowd. He's so glad we've come, to see our shining smiling faces, so eager to enter into a communion of souls, to share the spirit of God.

He talks about the spirit of God, becoming fervent. His face lifts, glints with light. His voice catches us up, carries us with its passion. God is Good. God is Grace. God is Love. God is Mercy. God, Who so loved the world that He gave His only begotten son, Jesus Christ, that whosoever believeth might not perish but have everlasting life.

Jesus Christ our savior, the sacrificial lamb.

God our Father, the salvation of our souls.

If we shall only enter into the Kingdom of God, we will inherit the Kingdom of Heaven.

He waxes poetic on the Kingdom of Heaven, the glories, the beauties, the rewards. The angels singing, St. Peter at the pearly gates holding out his hand, Welcome. Welcome, my children. Welcome to the promise of God, the Kingdom of Heaven.

Praise the Glory of God. The minister throws his hands heavenward. Let us pray, lowers his head, hands clasped in front of him. *Our Father, Who art in Heaven . . .*

We bow our heads . . .

Thy Kingdom come, Thy will be done, on earth as it is in Heaven . . .

. . . sneak looks, catch each others' eyes . . .

Amen.

. . . look up.

Let us praise God, let us build His Kingdom here on earth.

Men in poorly cut dark suits leap up, start passing deep-sided baskets through the crowd, row by row. They come to us, we look at each other. Betts raises her closed empty hand, lowers and opens it, quickly passes the basket. We get the idea, follow suit. Janie puts in fifty cents. Billie digs in her Levis, drops in a quarter. Faye glares at her.

The men carry the baskets forward, pile them on the dais. The minister again raises his arms, calls upon God, to bless this contribution to the establishment of His Kingdom, to the continuance of His Work here on earth, to the efforts of His humble servant.

Oh, bless me, my Father, that I may be worthy to help lead Your poor straggling flock in the Paths of Righteousness. He lowers his head, regards the crowd earnestly. For who among us, my sisters and brothers, can do without the teachings of Christ, the Way of the Truth and the Light?

Without God's Word . . . he looks at us sorrowfully, compassionately . . . we are lost sheep, ignorant, wayward. Weak, fallible mortals, stumbling in sin and sloth.

We . . .

He shifts gears, starts to list all our failings. He doesn't miss a one. We cheat, lie, steal, covet, and envy. We give into avarice and gluttony. We curse and blaspheme. He grows lurid in his descriptions of our baseness.

I'm spellbound, we all are, sitting mouths agape, eyes wide. This is a much better show than we'd anticipated. We're sucked in, slink down in our seats, feeling shoddy, flawed, vulnerable, and guilty.

We fornicate and commit adultery. . . .

Now he really gets down to it. *Sex.* The filthiness of sex. He dwells on it, face dark, eyes gleaming, tongue wrapped around his voice, relishing our twisted hungers and depravity.

We're fascinated, stuck to our seats.

Communion. He shouts out at us a new term, *physical communion* is an act of God for procreation only. A sacrament to be engaged in only by those whose union has been recorded by the state and recognized by God. Without God's blessing, without lawful husband or wife, such an act between man and woman is *un*lawful. A crime against society and church. Without rightful father for your child, you are a whore, a viper at the breast of your family, a rotten spot in the shiny apple of your community, a pox upon the healthy flesh of your country. *An abomination in the sight of God.*

We shift uneasily. This is getting a little more than we'd bargained for. And then we notice the woman in front of us. She's rocking, rocking back and forth, and moaning. Faye looks at Billie, Billie kicks Betts, Betts nods. We watch as the woman rocks harder and harder, cradling her baby, moaning and sobbing.

The minister is shouting, exhorting. *Repent,* oh you sinners, repent. You adulterers, you fornicators, you liars and cheaters and stealers. Those of you who covet and envy, who curse and blaspheme, *repent.* Ask God's forgiveness!

The dark-suited men leap up again and start passing their deep-sided baskets.

The piano plays, the preacher sings. "What shall I give Thee, Master? Thou hast given all for me. Shall I give less, of what I possess? Or shall I give all to Thee?"

The baskets pass.

Yes, God! I will pay. I will pay for my sins.

I will support Your Church, Your Kingdom here on earth. I will pave my road to Heaven.

Yes, Lord! I will support Your minister, who is here to show me The Way.

The woman fumbles in her purse, drops in a handful of dollars. We pass the basket without pretense, we're too engrossed in her.

The baskets reach front, the preacher accepts them, looks heavenward. Thank You. Thank You, God. Thank You.

The piano starts up again, softly. "I come to the garden alone . . ."

Bless you. Bless you my people, *God's* people. God's lost lambs returned to the fold.

Let God see how sorry you are, how repentant. Come forward, those of you who believe in God, who ask His forgiveness. Come forward, those of you who would inherit the Kingdom of Heaven. Humble yourselves. Let God hear your prayers. Bow down. Bow down.

The people come forward, kneel in the dirt in front of the dais. The preacher passes his hand over their heads, in the air, looking heavenward. Oh, God, we call upon You. Please forgive these poor sinners. They know not what they do. We ask You, heads bowed, on bended knee, to show us Thy Mercy. We beseech Thee, bless them, restore their souls.

The woman has gone down on her knees, in the dust, clutching and rocking over her baby. She's crying, sobbing . . .

—Oh, God. Forgive me. I didn't know, I didn't mean to. He said it was all right. He said it was because he loves me.

—He loves me, God, please make him love the baby. Tell Mama it's all right, make Mama forgive me.

—Make Mama understand. I'm not bad, God. I did it because of Roy. Because of You, God, because Roy said God gave me to him to love.

—Oh, God. Forgive me.

—Please. Forgive me.

She wails into the baby's blanket. —I wanna go home.

Billie's crying.

Faye stands. —Let's get out of here, I've had enough.

Trixie looks around at us. —Do something. *Help* her.

Betts shoves aside the chair in front of her, bends, gently lifts the woman. —Get up. You're getting dirty.

I reach for the baby.

The people around are trying to ignore our small commotion.

The woman stands, gives up the baby, past resistance.

She stares, cheeks streaked with dust-edged tears. —I'm already dirty.

—Shit— Faye starts pushing out through the chairs.

From behind, her straight hair pulled back severely from her plain face, the woman looked older. But now that we see her, we realize she's no more than our age, possibly younger.

—Do you have a car?— The girl nods. —Then let's go to it.

The minister is winding down, assuring us of God's Love, His Blessing, His Forgiveness, His Tender Mercy. But we're not in much of a mind for it. We guide the girl between chairs, surround her, and escort her out the tent.

She hovers at the side of her old Packard as if unsure what to do next.

—Where do you live?

The girl looks startled. —With my grandmother.

—Can you drive?

She scans Betts's face, eyes still wide and glazed. Nods.

Billie opens the car door.

The girl stands there a moment, then slides in, studies the dashboard without recognition. I wait, holding the baby. She connects, fumbles in her purse, inserts the key in the ignition. I step up, hand out the baby. She starts, as if in sudden remembrance. Reaches, lays the yellow cotton-flannel bundle on the seat beside her.

Billie hangs onto the door edge. —Look. You aren't dirty. Just because you had a baby doesn't make you bad.

Faye steps up. —You wanna blame somebody, you oughta blame this Roy guy.

Color comes to the girl's cheeks, her eyes show a spark of life.

Trixie puts in her two-bits worth. —Yeah. Where is he anyway? Why isn't he here with you, down on *his* knees in the sand?

—He lives in another town.

Janie finally gets up her courage. —Well, if he loves you, he should marry you.

—He can't— The girl blinks, stares. —He's already married. To my mother.

—Shit!

—Jesus christ.

Betts pulls Billie back, closes the door. —Get in the pickup.

We watch as the girl backs up, gives us one last look out her window, face a round white blank, then drives away.

We straggle to the car and pickup. Faye pauses at her door, hands in her back pockets.

—Where now?

Betts turns on her. —Where the hell you think? You feel like partying?

Faye shrugs.

We load up and head for home.

Betts roars up 66, screeches to a stop. Kicks the gas, yanks a hard left, burning rubber. Floors it, throws the steering wheel right, down gearing. Takes the corner on two tires, pitching me onto Billie. Grabs the wheel as it spins back, righting us with swerving jerking bounces.

I straighten back up.

Billie looks over. —It's all right, Betts.

Betts glares through the windshield. —No it isn't— Guns the engine, double shifts viciously. —I'd like to believe in God.

—I can't— I pull the garnet-and-crystal rope through my hands, shake my head. —I can't become a Catholic.

Casey takes my hand, plays with the rosary in it. We'd driven to the north edge of town, where we always seemed to go to work out our problems, looking toward the sloping sky and rising horizon.

—You have to.

Again I shake my head. I can't meet his eyes. —I don't believe that, that babies are born with sin. They're born pure, straight from Heaven. We commit our sins in life. Our *own* sins. Why should we have to pay for the sins of our fathers?

Casey strokes my hand. —We're all products of who and what we come from.

—That's so fatalistic. So defeatist. If we're born damned, why try?

—That's why we're baptized. To cleanse us of our fathers. Purge us of the past. Purify us for a new life dedicated to God.

I hate it when he talks like this. He sounds so fanatical, like a Pentecostal or Holy Roller. I pull away my hand.

—How? By splashing water on the heads of dead babies who never had a chance to decide on a good or evil life?

I'm nonplused by my sudden rush of feeling, by how much this matters to, and incites, me. I'd heard stories about how babies, stillborn, their heads barely out of the birth canal, had been hurriedly sprinkled with unsterilized water, infecting and thereby endangering the life of the mother.

Casey responds accordingly. He stiffens and pulls back. We're going to fight, it's going to be a bad one, but I can't stop myself. I'm seeing those babies, drifting in space, their little arms reaching legs kicking bodies twisting, suspended in grayness, through no fault of their own.

I turn on him as if it's his fault.

—Priests are no better than any other man, just because they've been to seminary, taken an oath of celibacy. They have no right to judge me or anyone. How can that priest tell me I'm wrong for the things I've done with you, that I've sinned and need forgiveness? I'm not sorry, for any of it, and I refuse to let him make me ashamed and dirty me.

I've worked myself into a fury.

I glare at Casey. —How can it be a sin to love? That priest doesn't know how I feel, what we have between us. He's never been with a woman, he's never loved, not like normal people. Priests don't have normal feelings, they have to close them off, deny, repress. And look what happens, look at all those babies found in the basements of nunneries. The stories you read about young girls and boys who have been molested by their priest, the—

Casey viciously twists the ignition, guns the motor, grinds into gear, and peels us out of the desert, in a flurry of spinning wheels and spewing sand. He drives in a rage, too fast, running stop signs. I grip the door handle. He swerves into the curb, slams the brake, knocking me into the dashboard.

I kick open my door.

He turns on me. —You're a narrow-minded, self-righteous, protestant bigot!

I throw my rosary at him.

It was the end of catechism.

It was almost the end of us.

We avoided each other like we were sidewinders for days. Our eyes were miserable as we passed in the hall and averted our faces. Then one afternoon, I found him outside gym, waiting for me.

It was hard, he looked at the floor before he could look at me.

—I talked to Father Martinez. You don't have to convert. You just have to agree to raise our children as Catholics.

It was hope. We picked up the torn threads and retied them. We could marry, live together, have children. They'd go to catechism, genuflect, cross themselves with holy water. And in the meantime, at home, I could teach them other values, different ways of thinking and believing. As adults, they could make up their own minds. Better a base against which they could later rebel than no base at all, I reasoned. From information, understanding, analysis, and evaluation come knowledge.

It was a compromise.

I look around the church, inhale the smokey sweetness. Maybe I was wrong after all; maybe it wasn't the Navy: It was right here our troubles started.

I stare at the carved wooden crucifix. This frail, painted son of God, body and head wounded and bleeding, does not give me affirmation, does not give me hope. Does not make me believe in love, charity, justice, and mercy. I feel rotten, miserably fallible. Weak, wayward, lost. And resentful at being reminded of it. But I can't blame God, even though He's handiest. No. I lift wearily from my knees.

The source of my problems, like their answer, lies much closer.

SCENE 9

CHAPTER ?

Smokey had prepared carefully, like an actress studying her script. She had planned far ahead, considered every possibility, and counted on luck, her shrewdness in human behavior, and her powers of persuasion. And she had planned, considered, and counted right.

Vinnie showed up Wednesday, she passed the note Thursday, by Friday she was secretly ensconced with Glory and Casey.

And now it was Sunday, the day she'd prayed for, the day most perfectly suited to her plan.

Sunday. The day Casey and Glory, with little Denny and Les, went to mass.

Glory hovered at the door, clutching her purse, looking for all the world like a parody of Ann Carter. "Are you sure you don't want to go?" Casey and the children hovered behind her.

Smokey smiled. "I'm sure. But thank you anyway."

Glory gave a little shrug and ushered the children out.

Casey hung back. "You gonna be all right?"

"I'll enjoy the peace and quiet."

"A little church might do you good."

She grinned. "I'm past saving. You know that."

He grinned back. "Yeah. I know."

"And that's exactly the way you like me."

His eyes held hers a long moment, then he followed after Glory.

Smokey watched as Glory minced down the walk: shoulders and hips twitching from the waist, steps small and slightly pigeon-toed, head tilted to the right. Smokey waited until the car was out of sight then quietly closed the door and turned into the room with a heavy relieved sigh.

The anxiety had been intense. But they'd gone. And finally Smokey had the house to herself.

She glanced at her watch. Nine forty. They always went to ten o'clock mass.

Ten o'clock sharp, the note had said. Newgate Shopping Center. The phone booth outside the A&P.

Glory's A&P.

Smokey moved quickly, surely. The phone in the combination kitchen/family room had an extra long extension cord. Glory was a phone person, she spent hours talking to friends and making little business calls. She liked to walk around and potter while she gossiped.

Smokey unclipped the cord from the phone and jack, carried it into the master bedroom, and, removing the short cord there, reclipped it into the master phone and jack. She then carefully dragged the phone into the bathroom and closed the door. If Casey's house was bugged, they might or might not skip his bedroom, but they most certainly would leave him bathroom privacy.

Smokey looked again at her watch, took the paper from her slacks pocket, and slowly dialed.

She wasn't worried about Casey finding and tracing the number. With all Glory's miscellaneous calls, one more or less on his bill would pass unnoticed.

Vinnie answered on the first ring.

"Hello."

"Long time no see, Vinnie."

"I thought it was going to be a lot longer."

"Sorry to disappoint you. But you know me. Full of my little surprises."

"Yeah. That's what Chuck and Louie found out. Only I don't think they're seeing twenty-five-to-fifty years as so little."

"Them's the breaks. So how're things at the casino?"

"Okay."

"You enjoying being big boss?"

"I think of you now and then."

"I'll bet you do."

"Fondly, of course."

"Of course."

'What's on your mind, Smokey?"

"A little exchange."

"Why do I get nervous when you say little?"

"How would you like to keep enjoying your freedom?"

"That's what I always liked about you. No beating around the bush."

"Five million, Vinnie." She'd anticipated the pause.

"You know I don't have that kind of money."

"No. But you can get it. I know the workings behind the casino. Remember, Vinnie? *My* casino."

"Our casino. We were partners. Remember?"

"My seventy, your thirty. Now it's all yours, since I so conveniently got blown to the list of the nonliving. That must be nice for you, Vinnie. But I don't hear any thank you's."

"How much time?"

"Five days. Today's Sunday. I expect my payoff Friday."

She gave him time to consider.

"What if I can't make it?"

"I think the Feds would be more than happy to have you fingered as Artie's top hitman."

"You got it all in that little black book?" Vinnie's voice was ugly. She smiled. He'd throttle her on the spot if he could.

"I've got it all in this *little* black head. I'm an actress. Remember, Vinnie? I can memorize my lines. Shall I recite them for you? Miami, 1982. Thursday, September 4, 11:20 P.M. . . ."

"Where do I make the drop?"

"Friday I'm taking the day off, to get my hair and nails done. Yvonne's Beauty Salon, 1427 South Sam Houston. My appointment's at ten, I'll be done around twelve. There won't be a guard. Make it casual. Just walk in and leave the case for me at the desk."

"You know, Smokey, I liked you better as a blonde."

"Like I said—them's the breaks. We do what we have to do. Five days, Vinnie. Five million."

"You're a bitch, Smokey."

"And don't you forget it."

She hung up, and smiled. She'd planned, she'd prepared. She'd calculated the sum carefully. He'd never meet it.

Betts's house is two blocks west and one block south of Mr. Colter's, in a cul-de-sac of small would-be ranch types that look almost like mobile homes. White aluminum siding with black shutters. Narrow overhung concrete porch with metal outdoor furniture. A strip of lawn with a clump birch, and shrubs around the house. Marigolds line the walk and encircle the posted mailbox. Neat, and modest.

I no sooner stop the car than Betts comes out the front door. She meets me on the sidewalk, face shining. The joy I'd been missing on this trip finally floods over me. She grabs me in her big arms, I want to bury myself in her substantialness. My eyes water.

She steps back, we take each other in, grinning absurdly.

—My god. You look just the same.

—So do you.

And she does. Face maturer, laugh lines deeper, hair in a side part and bob, but otherwise the same. She's wearing a tailored cotton dress, in a small floral print. I throw my arms around her wide midriff. —Oh, Betts, I'm so glad to see you.

The kids are hanging around just inside the door, shyly eager, all with Betts's grin. Betts counts them off, pointing a finger to the top of each head.

—Jennifer. Ten.

Tall and slender, long hair, on her way to being a beauty.

—William, we call him Will. Eight.

Stocky, shocked crewcut, the cocked chin and assessing look of a show-off or mischief-maker.

—Amy. Six.

Her mother, I know from pictures, at that age. Tomboyish, direct, hair in an androgynous cap.

—Jonathan, Jonny. Four. The baby.

Sweet, gentle, a cowlick at his crown and wisps across his forehead.

Each child is different, a distinct personality, as Betts would encourage. The girls honey-blonde like their mother, the boys dark, I assume, like their father.

Betts scowls at her crew. —All right, you've met her. Now get out of here.

The kids give me last grins then scatter, giggling, up the hall.

—You have them well trained.

—I have to. Else I couldn't live with them— She grins.

—They're darling, Betts.

—Yeah. They're good kids, I have to admit. But like all kids, they have their problems. Jenny likes to put on airs, I have to keep her on the ground, among us common folk. Will pushes, to see how far he can go and how much trouble he can cause. Amy has a temper, she'll fly into a fight before there is one. And Jonny's always getting his feelings hurt, he can't look out for himself. I can't stand princesses, bullies, hotheads, or crybabies. So they keep me hopping.

And it's clear to tell how happy she is about it.

The small area immediately to the left of the front door—there is no entry— has been made into a family room, the knotty-pine walls covered with the children's art work, no concern given to tack holes. The board-and-brick shelving exhibits cardboard and cloth dioramas, a lopsided clay bowl, a glue-glopped popsicle cottage, a cocoon on a leaf in a Mason jar, sparrows' eggs in a nest, rocks, shells, a dried-weed arrangement.

The bookcase is stuffed with children's books, many showing torn spines and disarrayed pages. The 13-inch TV on top of the case is surrounded by water-filled food jars holding toothpick-stuck potatoes and avocado seeds sprouting exuberant leafy tendrils that reach for the TV and hang down over the books.

Betts's old black upright piano stands at the end of the tiny area, a worn saddle blanket over its bench. Piano books, sheet music, and hymnals are stacked on the floor beside it against the wall. A steer's skull decorates the right corner of the piano's high top. The left corner, nearest the window, is occupied by a cage with two love birds. An imitation Indian blanket of heavy cotton flannel has been neatly tucked over the crushed cushions and thin back of the couch under the window. Doilies disguise its threadbare arms.

Betts has led me into the kitchen, talking away about her children. She could stretch out both arms and touch the cupboards above the stove with one hand, the cupboards above the sink with the other. I stand at the end of the serving bar that divides cooking from eating section, listening while Betts checks pots, lifts dishes from the cupboards, pokes around in the refrigerator. I'm completely relaxed, happy just to be in her presence.

She turns and regards me.

—So. What'll you have? Iced tea or coffee?

—Coffee, of course.

We settle at the heavy pine table, on large wooden chairs made comfortable by tied-on cushions. Betts pushes my mug toward me and reaches for an ashtray, box matches, and cigarettes.

We light up, exhale, smile at one another.

—I wanna hear all about you but so do the other girls. So I'll wait. That way, you won't have to repeat yourself.

—I'd rather hear about you anyway.

—You just about heard it all.

—What about your teaching? You said you were substituting.

—Yeah. As often as I can. Which isn't all that often, maybe six or eight times a month. I'd like to take more, we need the money, but the kids always have something. The flu, the measles, the chicken pox. And Jonny's in preschool only three days, I can't leave him.

—What do you teach? Elementary?

Betts nods, smiles wryly. —The whole shibbang. Kindergarten through eighth. It's tough, keeping on top of that many grades. But in two years, when Jonny starts first grade, maybe I can go back full time. I did it for five years, before Jenny was born.

—What happened to nursing? Last I knew, you were at Northwestern.

Betts reaches to the ashtray, taps ash. —My dad got sick. Cancer. He was really bad off. They decided there wasn't anything more they could do for him in the hospital, so they sent him home— She shrugs. —My mom couldn't handle him alone.

—Why didn't you go back?

—I lost my whole third year. It would have taken too long, Mom needed me, and we didn't have the money— She leans back in her chair. —So I decided to go to Flag, get a teaching credential. I could be home weekends.

—I did it in two years, took overloads, went straight through summer school— She stubs out her cigarette. —And it hasn't been all that bad, I'm good at teaching.

—I'll bet you are.

—And it's helped me with the kids.

—So where'd you meet Josh? At Flag?

Betts laughs. —Would you believe? At the Grand Cafe— Her face creases with humor. —He's a Chinese-food freak— She looks over at me. —He's from Brooklyn.

Her smile softens. —It was summer, between school sessions. I was waitressing, to add to my paltry teaching salary. Josh had just moved to town, as an accountant with Santa Fe. He came into the Grand almost every evening. We got to be friends, talking and joking; he's a great joker.

—One night he said, You know, you're the biggest Chinese I ever met. I said, What makes you so sure I'm Chinese? He said, From the way your eyes squint when you laugh. I said, So maybe I'm Japanese. He said, Too bad you aren't, you'd make a great sumo wrestler. I said, Sumo or not, I can outwrestle any man any day. He said, I don't think I believe that. I said, Would you like a demonstration? He said, My backseat or yours? I said, I drive a pickup. He said, Great. I drive a Volkswagen. The bed of a pickup seems just about the right size— She's chuckling.

—So that's how I got asked out on my first date— She strikes a match, watches it flame at the end of her cigarette.

—My god. Your first date? In the back of your pickup?

She laughs, blows out the match. —I took Monday night off, a slow night at the Grand. He drove me all the way to Flagstaff. To another Chinese restaurant. In his Volkswagen. You can imagine how I fit in that. He had a lot of problems with his gear shift, we had a lot of laughs— She looks at me, seriously, but with her eyes still crinkled. —He outwrestled me in every match. And we have Chinese every Monday.

I feel my chest squeeze around my heart. I'm staring at a woman in love.

Josh comes home at 6:15. I don't know what I expected; I had no expectations. But he meets them all. A warm, gentle, intelligent man, shorter than Betts, slighter in stature. But who wouldn't be except a Japanese sumo wrestler? Dark curly hair, receding at the hairline and thinning on top, dark-rimmed glasses. He smiles all the time.

He's happy to be home, happy to see Betts, happy to be with his children, who grab his legs and arms, hang on and around him. They hug and kiss, tussle, chatter, tease and joke.

I watch.

The dog, a black mongrel with white nose, paws, and tail-tip, bounds off the living-room couch at Josh's entrance and skitters among the legs, barking for his share of attention.

The cat, a tiger-striped alley, wanders in, interested in the commotion, but finding it too hectic, leaps up onto the table, for a more philosophic view. Eventually bored, he languidly springs to a chair to the floor, and superiorly strolls out.

It's Jenny's night to set the table; she instructs Jonathan in laying out the flatware. The kids clatter and scrape into their chairs, bow heads. It's Amy's night to say grace.

Dinner is a huge pot of spaghetti with marinara meat sauce, light on the meat. A huge wooden bowl of salad—lettuce, cucumber, and tomato—with bottles of Italian and French dressing. A loaf of Italian bread sliced and heated in foil with bottled garlic spread. And, of course, presweetened iced tea with lemon. Dessert is ice cream bars from the freezer.

The children dominate, laughing and talking simultaneously. But amazingly enough, listening too, frequently interrupting one conversation to interject across the table into another. Betts and Josh smile and laugh, comment and question, praise and console, giving each child equal attention.

The dog makes the rounds begging, but it's a favorite meal, no one spares him bites. Except Jonathan, who drops him unwanted tomatoes which the dog mouths and also drops.

The cat prisses across the kitchen, disdaining to look right or left, pushes open the laundry-room door; I hear the scratching, catch the smell. The family is no more concerned with him than he with them.

It's Will's night to clear; Jonathan collects and carries in the flatware. Betts washes, I dry. There is no dishwasher.

There aren't enough leftovers for lunch; the remains of spaghetti and salad are mixed in a bowl for the dog, who gobbles them up, still somehow managing to eat around the tomatoes.

Josh opens up a cardtable. I go to the car for the wine and coke. Betts brings out potato chips and onion-soup/sour-cream dip. I was hoping for tortilla chips and salsa, maybe a little guacamole, or even jalapeno cheese or bean dip.

Betts bends over her arrangement of plastic cups and paper napkins. —Oh. I forgot to tell you in all the excitement— She looks up. —Janie's coming— My heart thuds to my feet. She grins. —Isn't that great? She's home visiting.

I manage to smile back. —Great!

Does Betts know? Do all the girls know? My joy is gone, my sense of command and composure forsaken.

SCENE 10

The girls arrive promptly at eight, one on top of the other. Faye first with Ruthie, followed by Trixie, their glances avid, shy, curious. Just like when I first met them, only older, more hooded, though not disguised. Betts lets the children get in on the greetings, then Josh shooshes them up the hall.

We stand around, awkwardly, uncertainly, trying to get the feel of how to go about this. I'm a stranger in their midst, someone they used to know.

Betts is telling the kids good night. So it's up to me.

I grab a plastic glass. —Who wants wine?

Faye laughs. —Who doesn't?

I busy myself pouring and passing out glasses, furtively making my assessments.

Faye has changed the most. She's exchanged her horn-rims for jeweled opalescent harlequins, and is wearing large dangle earrings with her flowered shirt and tan slacks. But her efforts at femininity only serve to emphasize her lack of it. She seems no longer just tough but hard, a surface defense penetrated to the core. Her freckles have faded, as has all her color, inside as well as out. Her auburn hair, which she's permed, has dulled to an undistinguished brown. I see hints of gray. And in her eyes I catch shadows of distrust and swift judgment. Her mouth looks set for ridicule.

Trixie's flitting around, sipping her wine too quickly, talking too much, laughing too loudly, too shrilly. She's thin, too thin, dressed in Levis, embroidered western shirt, moccasins, and, from the looks of it, all her Indian jewelry.

—Shut up, Trixie— Trixie gives Faye a hurt look, clamps her mouth shut in midsentence. —And sit down. You're making me nervous.

Trixie looks around. She has five choices: the couch against the long wall, the straight-backed dining chair to its left, the upholstered twin chairs to its right, or the backless bench under the window. At the moment, she's by the stuffed chair nearest the bench. She sits.

Betts comes charging in from the hall. —Did everyone get something to drink?— We raise our glasses. —Good. Then—

The doorbell rings. I know it can be only one person. I back into Faye, laugh, apologize, step behind her.

Janie enters, quickly takes stock. She smiles around, says Hi. To everyone except me. I tell myself not to get paranoid; maybe she didn't see me.

Janie's gone through a transformation; she's actually pretty. Her light-brown hair curves soft and wavy around her face. She's lost weight. She's still chunky, but her casual cotton suit is carefully styled to disguise it. Her fingernails are painted a bright red.

Betts gets a glass. —What'll it be, Janie?

Janie looks at the table. —Coke will be fine. With ice.

Faye laughs. —Still teetotalling, huh, Janie?

Janie gives her a tight superior smile, takes the glass, and passes into the room. She always was reserved and sure of her own mind; but now she seems more than confident, beyond reserved. I think of Clydene.

I decide what the hell, and come out of hiding.

The women find their places, Faye and Ruthie on the couch, Janie in the other twin chair, between Trixie and Ruthie. I've been hanging around the armed dining chair, hoping to commandeer it, in case I need to beat a fast retreat: it's nearest the kitchen. Betts sets the chips and dip on the coffee table, then settles on the bench.

—Well whaty'ya think, gang, doesn't Reggie look great?

They look at me. I blush. Trixie and Ruthie smile, even Faye. Janie studies me.

—Come on, Betts, you're embarrassing me. We all look great— Faye snorts. —It's really good to see you guys. I can't tell you how glad I am you could come— I feel inane.

—How long has it been?

I have the exact figure —Twenty years.

—Jeez.

—That long?

—Don't tell me it seems like yesterday.

—It seems like another century.

—Yeah.

—God.

—So what've you been up to?

They focus on me. I see their interest. I'd thought, in my envisionings of this get-together, of how comforting it would be to finally unburden myself to these women I was so comfortable with as a teenager. Like sitting around Catherine's table. But I look in their time-touched faces and find I can't.

I consider, shrug. —Not much really. Driving taxi. Fixing dinners.

They laugh and nod.

—Yeah.

I've left a void they help me fill.

—So you've got kids?

—Two girls. Eleven and thirteen.

Trixie perks up. —I've got two boys. Eighteen and fifteen. Maybe we should fix them up.

Ruthie looks at me wisely. —Take my word, there'll come a day you'll *wish* you could still taxi them.

Ruthie has lost her demure, vacuous prettiness. She still wears her straight black hair cut square below her ears and pulled to the side with a tortoise barrette, perhaps to retain her youthful image. But her body has thickened, especially around the middle, her thighs are heavy, and in spite of her girlish pink-polyester pant suit, she looks matronly. But she's no longer vacant. Behind her dark eyes I see a mind working, and in her still-sweet face I see strength.

The girls look at her with concern.

—Any word yet?

Ruthie shakes her head.

—How long has she been gone this time?

—Two, going on three weeks.

—Don't worry, she'll be back.

Ruthie considers her knees. —Maybe that's what worries me. I don't know which is worse.

There's a silence. Betts looks at me. —We're talking about Ruthie's daughter Mary.

Trixie leans forward. —She has problems— Faye glares, Trixie pinches her lips tight.

Ruthie shakes her head. —No, it's all right, it's no secret— She looks at me. —She's into drugs. She met this older guy from the projects, the low-cost housing east of town.

I nod. —I saw it.

—She changed overnight, became another person. We did everything we could to break them up, even had him arrested. One night Mary stole our car and took off with him. We didn't see or hear from her for five months, the police couldn't find her.

—Ruthie and Glenn were frantic.

—For all we knew, she was dead. Then one day she showed up.

—Without the car.

—Told me they were married.

—She was only fifteen.

—She was pregnant. He'd sent her home, for me to take care of.

—While he stayed in Phoenix, supposedly working.

—But more likely dealing drugs.

Ruthie smooths her polyester.

—I thought we could start over again. We didn't hear from him. Mary got more and more like her old self. Then one day, when the baby was three months, she went to the store. And never came home.

—And that's the way it's been for three years now. Mary'll take off, months at a time, then suddenly show up.

—When she's out of drugs and money.

—And good old Ruthie here always takes her in.

Ruthie looks at Faye. —What do you expect me to do?

—She made her bed. Let her lie in it.

—I should just kick her out? She's sick, she needs help. You've seen how she looks.

—She's a druggy. You're just making it easier for her. And for Tyrone. They oughta raise their own kid, learn some responsibility.

Betts jumps in. —And just what kind of life do you think the kid'd have? What chance?

Faye turns on Betts. —What chance do you think she has here? You've seen the other mothers.

I pick up on the information. —Ruthie, you have the child?

Ruthie turns to me, her face a conflict of anger and sorrow. She smiles, her eyes light softly. —She's beautiful. The sweetest thing. The best disposition.

Trixie adds support. —And really smart.

Faye spits it at me. —And she's black.

I'm stunned. I don't know how to respond. I think of Katelyn and Lindsay. I think of all my liberal ideals.

Janie clears her throat, smooths her skirt. —Have you tried to get Mary into a hospital or some kind of program?

—She has to volunteer herself. And if I force her to, she doesn't stay.

Janie nods, crosses her leg. —Well, actually, the drugs are only symptomatic. If you're going to cure the drug problem, you have to deal with the whole construct. The familial and societal as well as the physical and mental.

The girls stare.

Betts looks at me, with a little smile. —Janie's married to a doctor.

For the first time, Janie looks at me directly. —An internist. We have a private practice. I manage the office. We believe in the holistic approach.

I return her look. I want to say, Yes, I understand, I know what you're talking about. But she knows I do; that's why she's telling me. I'm interested in holistic medicine, I believe in it too, I'd like to talk about it. But I also sense in Janie's look another motivation, one deprecating to the other women, that I don't want to play into. I simply nod.

Betts heaves to her feet, smiling. —So where would you begin, Janie? Family counseling?

Betts ambles to the card table, smiling, and returns with a jug of wine, smiling, as Janie launches into her recommended course of therapy. The women hold out their glasses, and as they catch Betts's face, they too assume pleasantly attentive smiles.

Janie's pontificating on about the current use of drugs in our society. —And it's not just drugs, it's the whole spectrum of substance abuse, including alcohol. You'd be surprised how widespread it is, across all classes and age groups. We're constantly on the alert for it among our patients. The problem is to identify them, they certainly won't tell on themselves, and get them into treatment before they ruin their bodies and lives.

Faye looks over at Trixie. —You hear that, Trixie?

Trixie gives a little start, frowns. —I'm not into drugs.

—What's that in your hand?

—The same that's in yours.

Betts and Ruthie are watching, Janie comes right to the point.

—You're too thin.

—You think I don't know it? I can't eat.

—Cigarettes kill the appetite and make you jumpy.

Trixie's been chain-smoking. The ashtray beside her is already half-filled with butts. —It's that damn ranch, it's making a wreck of me— She grins around at the girls. —I keep seeing snakes.

Ruthie and Faye laugh, Betts fills me in. —Last year when Trixie and Curt were opening the house up, they found this huge diamondback.

—In the bedroom closet, of all places.

—He'd come in out of the cold to hibernate.

—He was over six feet.

—God knows what I would have done if Curt hadn't been there.

—Probably the same thing you did then.

They laugh.

—She went screaming out the back door.

—Curt couldn't get her back in.

—He had to carry her.

—Kicking and screaming.

Even Trixie's laughing. But I can't. I have a mortal fear of snakes. —My god. How'd you get him out?

—Curt blew his head off.

Trixie grimaces. —Then hung him outside and made me watch him twist until sundown. Then he cooked him over an open fire. He and the boys had great fun out of it, kept licking their fingers and smacking their lips, saying it was better than chicken. But I couldn't taste a bite— She turns to Janie. —So you see? Is it any wonder I smoke too much and can't eat?

Janie's looking slighted. —I didn't know you and Curt bought a ranch— She casts around accusing glances. —When did all this take place?

Trixie looks toward us for help. —Oh, I don't know. Not that long ago really. Just a couple of years.

Faye's eyes are tight, her smile thin. —You're not here that much, Janie. And when you are, we usually learn about it afterwards.

Janie stiffens. Trixie fidgets in her chair. —And it's not all that much, not a ranch really. Just a four-room shack.

Faye's sardonic. —With no phone, no gas.

Trixie perks. —But we have a good well. And when Curt fixes the windmill, we'll have electricity.

Betts's grin is wry. —But no television.

Janie's frowning. —What do you do for heat?

Trixie tries for nonchalance. —We have a potbelly in the living area and a wood burner in the kitchen.

Janie digests this. —What about plumbing— Trixie looks puckish. —You mean you have an outdoor privy?

Betts laughs. —And a big chamber pot.

—You can bet I'm not going out there at night.

Janie's appalled. —And you live like that all year?

Trixie's chin goes up. —We come in for the cold months— For some reason, she turns to me. —And the barn and stockades are new. And the rangeland is the best— Her eyes dart toward Janie. —That's really what we bought it for.

I smile encouragingly. —Sure. You can always fix up the house.

Trixie's face brightens, she reaches for her cigarettes. —We have thirty head.

Janie sits upright. —That's not enough to make a living on.

Faye's voice is a threat. —No, but it's a damn good start.

Even Ruthie's bristling. —And Curt's only thirty-eight.

Janie looks at us, shakes her head. —I'm not being critical. I'm just worried, about the way she's living, about—

Trixie pulls erect, reaches for her wine. —We do all right. Curt has his job.

—You mean he's still at the feed and fuel? But— I can see where Janie's mind's going, mine's following the same track. —Where is this ranch, anyway?

—North. Out by Walker's place.

—But that's over twelve miles.

—So what?

—You don't expect to find range in the middle of town.

—No. But how— Janie shakes her head. —Does Curt commute?

Faye's laugh is derisive. —You can tell you've become a suburbanite.

—I'm just trying to get the picture.

Betts slaps her hands on her thighs. —Look, Janie, why don't you just come out and ask? The answer is yes. Trixie's out there most of the time by herself. Curt stays in town at his mom's. With the boys. They have school and their social lives.

Trixie prisses smartly. —But they *commute* out on the weekends— We laugh, she flicks a look at us, pleased and proud. —And he gets time off during the calving and selling seasons.

Janie's studying Trixie intently. —But you have all those lonely evenings.

Trixie twitches a shrug, gives her an uneasy grin. —That's why I smoke so much.

—Shit— Faye lurches forward on the couch —Let's drink— downs her wine.

Betts stands, downs hers, goes for another bottle.

Trixie hesitates, aware of Janie.

I raise my glass. —Here's to Trixie and Curt, the next cattle barons.

Trixie drinks with me, her eyes smiling over the rim of her glass.

Betts passes with the bottle, we hold out our glasses for refills, except for Janie, who's staring at her barely touched coke. I should have brought diet.

We light cigarettes, except for Janie, who never smoked, and Ruthie, who's quit.

—Shit— Faye sprawls back on the couch, exhales a thick cloud. —So what else's new?— She laughs.

The wine's getting to us. I've brought three gallon-jugs of Gallo, and we're doing justice by them.

I decide it's time to close in.

—So what's Walt been up to?

Faye laughs. —Shit. Poor sonofabitch. We never should've been born twins, we keep having the same lousy luck. Sometimes I think we're living each other's lives— She looks over at me. —You heard about me, I suppose?— I shake my head. She leans forward, considers the glass in her hands. —I guess I might as well begin with the beginning.

She sighs.

—I was working out at the Antlers, waitressing, sometimes filling in as bartender. I met this guy, a rig driver. He started coming in regular, one or two times a week, whenever he passed through. One thing led to another, and we got married.

—Walt wasn't doing much, picking up jobs here and there in construction. Jerry, the truck driver, set him up rig driving. One night on the road, in a bar, he ran into Tex.

I give a short laugh. —I don't believe it.

—Yeah. That's what we all said. Seems Tex served only eighteen months out of his five years.

—They gave him time off for good behavior— Scoffing laughter.

—Shit. The jails were just full.

—And he hadn't learned one goddamn thing. He was still living off the money of lonely old women. He had this big roll. He talked Walt into going down to Texas. They started hanging around rodeos. Tex was a real con artist. He could set up anything, as long as it was illegal. Craps, poker, cock-fights. Anyway, Walt met this gal, a blonde, blue-eyed, died-in-the-wool rodeo queen. He went crazy over her. And after he'd followed her around for about a year, they got married.

Faye looks up while Betts refills her glass, then hunches over, arms on her knees.

—I'd had my fill of Jerry. His favorite form of relaxation after a long haul was to come home, get mean drunk, and try to beat up on me. So I divorced him. I was kinda at loose ends. It was a bad time. I still had my job at the Antlers, but I felt my life was going nowhere. So I said, What the hell, took what money I had, and went off to join Walt and Arlene.

Faye looks up, grins crookedly. —And like I said. The same damn lives. I met this rodeo king, an honest-to-god, rough-and-tumble bronc and Brahma rider— She looks down. —His name was Kenny.

Trixie chimes in. —I wish you could've seen him.

Faye nods. —He wasn't all that good-looking. But he had something— She swirls her wine. —I fell madly in love. And after I'd followed him around a while, he married me. But the rodeo circuit's a tough life. You're always on the road, facing injury or death. It's hard on a marriage— She stares into her glass. —He took to staying out nights. And when he did come in there wouldn't be anything left of him for me. He'd either be all boozed up or all loved out, and usually both. We had some terrible fights. I tried to punch him out. One night I packed his bags, kicked him out, and told him never to come back— She laughs, it hurts. —And the sonofabitch never did.

She drains her glass. —Last I heard, he was running around with some blonde rodeo groupie.

—Probably Walt's wife.

—Yeah— Faye grins, humorlessly. —They'd be just about right for each other.

Betts gets up for a potato chip. —And Arlene, Walt's wife, did the same damn thing. Started running around. Finally just took off.

Faye reaches for a chip —Like I said— scoops dip, munches, licks fingers. —The same lousy luck.

I consider. —Where's Walt now?

—Right here. We live with our parents— I stare. Faye stares back. —I know. I feel the same damn way. But we come and go as we want, have our own lives. And one of these days, we'll own the house.

I have no adequate response. I get up for chips and dip.

I offhandedly concentrate on loading a chip. —What about Les? Betts said he's a deputy with the sheriff's department.

—Not anymore— I catch something in Ruthie's tone, look up. —He's dead.

I'm so startled I jab the chip in my chin. —Jesus christ.

Trixie giggles. —This is getting to be some party.

Faye hands me a napkin. —He was fooling around with another deputy's wife in a trailer camp over in Holbrook. The guy caught him, they got in a fight, and Les shot him.

—He tried to plead self-defense.

—But the other guy wasn't wearing his holster.

—I guess he couldn't stand the thought of life in prison.

—So he hung himself.

—With his belt. In his jail cell.

—My god— I look at Betts. —This must have just happened.

She nods. —About two months ago.

—My god.

I sit back down in my chair.

Trixie looks around primly. —That's what happens when you give a little man a big badge and big gun.

I take a deep breath, try to look and sound nonchalant. —I hear Casey went into law enforcement, too— My heart's pounding.

Faye looks surprised. —Who? Colter? I didn't know that.

Betts frowns. —Sure you did. The FBI. Down in Galveston.

Ruthie laughs. —Him and Les. They saw too many movies.

Faye scowls. —Colter was an asshole.

My head jerks. I'd heard him called that before, I didn't remember. I try to grin. —I guess we all acted like assholes from time to time.

—Not like Colter— Faye's tone is vicious. —He was particularly shitty.

I freeze a smile.

Betts's eyes are pinched. —Faye still blames him for Billie.

I flinch, no longer making any pretense at smiling. —I thought you liked him, he was part of the gang.

—We put up with him.

—Because of Les.

—The guys liked him okay.

—He was always trying to act big.

—He thought he was better than us.

—Yeah. Remember that time he came home? In his wife's little red sports car?— Trixie looks over at me. —He went roaring all over town, making sure everyone saw him. But he couldn't be bothered looking any of us up.

—Or introducing his wife.

I'm having a hard time breathing; my chest seems to have caved in, collapsed on my stomach. I'm thinking of Casey, the Casey *I* remember. I feel a need to explain, defend.

—Maybe she was jealous. She didn't want to meet his old friends.

Trixie shakes her head. —Les said it was him.

—She was too good for us.

—We were an embarrassment.

—He didn't want to damage his image.

I'm staring at Betts's sculpted carpet, trying to deal with this. —So none of you ever really liked Casey?

—Even Les finally got fed up.

—Casey and his Rich Bitch had this big expensive wedding.

—Les was sure Casey was going to ask him to be best man.

—He didn't even get invited.

—Casey had some guy from college.

—A football player.

Betts is studying me.

—Oh, he wasn't all that bad. Just a little cocky maybe. You probably saw a lot more in him, Reggie, you knew him better.

Trixie looks up, covers her mouth —Oh. That's right— giggles. —I forgot. You went with him.

I flush. —Only a year.

I don't look at Betts; she knows my lie. I don't look at Janie for fear she does too.

Faye snorts. —That's all the time you lived here.

—Yeah— I grin. —But what a year it was— I'm recovering. I look at them, trying to be light while letting them see I'm serious. —The best year of my life.

They smile.

—We had some pretty good times.

—Yeah.

—Boy were we wild.

—Not that bad.

—Well we seem wild to me now.

—We did some crazy things.

—Remember that time we . . . ?

They lapse into the good old days. This is what I came for, what I'd anticipated, the reliving of memories. I let myself relax, lean back in the chair, sip my wine and listen, gradually recollecting myself.

—Remember how we . . . ?

—And . . .

—Remember when we . . . ?

—And what about that time the guys rounded up all the dogs they could find and let them loose downtown?

—God. There must've been over two dozen.

—All barking and running around, growling and fighting.

We've warmed into our old camaraderie. We don't think we're young again but we remember that we were. And that's good to have.

Janie looks at her watch, stands. —I hate to break this up, but I really have to be going.

She makes her good-byes quick. —It was really great seeing you all— Her glance does not include me. —Next time I'm in town, I'll call.

Faye smiles cynically.

Betts closes the door behind her, turns back into the room. Everyone's grinning.

—Janie's come up in the world.

—Shit.

Ruthie lifts reluctantly from the couch. —I guess I better be getting, too. Latonya wakes up at six.

Faye pushes up. —And I guess that means me, too. I'm driving.

Trixie starts to gather herself, puts her glass on the table, reaches to snub out her cigarette, bumps the glass, grabs for it, and knocks the ashtray to the carpet.

—Oh shit— She stares helplessly at the litter of ash and butts.

Betts stays right where she is. —Don't worry about it.

Trixie gives the mess one last befuddled look, clutches her purse, and totters toward us.

—You gonna be all right?

—I'm just going to Ma Wheelocks's— Trixie grimaces. —And you know how I love that— She tries to smile, her eyes wince. —That's what Janie doesn't understand. I'd rather be out at the ranch.

She trips out the door.

—Take it easy.

—Drive slowly.

Faye and Ruthie turn to smile.

—It was really good to see you again, Reggie.

—Next time, don't stay away so long.

Betts nods toward Trixie, heading down the walk. —Follow her.

I linger at the door, look up at Betts. —Thank you.

She smiles. —What the hell for? We're the ones oughta thank you. We haven't gotten together like this in years. We had a ball.

—You don't sit around over coffee and have cow sessions?

—Hell no. Who has time?

—So you talk on the telephone?

—Mostly we just run into each other in town— She sees my face, understands. —Things aren't what they used to be.

I nod, look down.

—So why don't you come over tomorrow? We'll have a long lunch. I never did have a chance to catch up on you.

It's hard to meet her eyes. —I'd love to. But I have to get on to San Francisco. My mother called.

Betts's look is disappointed but she doesn't question, doesn't push. —Okay. Next time.

We hug.

—I'll write.

—Good luck— She squeezes my arm. —Come back soon.

I'm too choked to answer.

I drive to the north edge of town, where the sharp-starred sky closes over and holds me fixed on the horizon. I need the focus, the grounding. I'm swirling in a nebula of thought and feeling. Betts and her round-cheeked family. Faye and her abusive husbands. Trixie and her solitary drinking. Janie and her red-nailed righteousness. Ruthie and her stricken daughter and mulatto granddaughter.

I think of my liberal New England upbringing and the respect I was taught for diversity. No. More than that. The appreciation and valuing of races, religions, and cultures different from my own. Daddy, after all, is an anthropologist. Maggie's a student of literature.

Then I think of Katelyn and Lindsay. It's not color, I tell myself. It's class. A socioeconomic problem. This son-in-law of Ruthie is poor, the product of poverty, a drug addict and pusher. From a government tenement on the outskirts of an unaccepting western town where the inhabitants believe in yanking yourself up by your boot straps.

But I bounce around in the hollowness of my hypocrisy.

Of all the European conquerors and colonizers of America, only the Anglo-Protestants couldn't accept intermarriage with the Indians. All the others— the Spanish and Portuguese, the German and French—mixed blood freely and lawfully, creating a new race, the *mestizo*. But this was white man with brown woman. How did it work the other way round? Brown man with white woman?

The Hopi rarely intermarry. It's discouraged. This man is black, probably the son of a Santa Fe porter. Where are his boots?

If he were a graduate of Harvard could I accept him? If I were Ruthie, if he were on my doorstep, in my daughter's bed, father of my grandchild, I would have to.

If I were Faye, hungry for the love of an exciting, virile man, I too might reduce myself and accept humiliation.

If I were Trixie, alone in an isolated shack with no plumbing or electricity, I too might drink.

I squirm uneasily. I feel shredded, stripped bone-bare. Well at least we didn't talk about Leonard Bernstein and the Boston Pops. We didn't hash over the merits and demerits of book banning. We didn't weigh shopping trips versus catalogue ordering. We didn't fuss over someone's upcoming party and whether we would or would not be invited.

And we didn't discuss Katelyn, Lindsay, and Howie. I didn't allow it. Like me, Trixie, Faye, and Ruthie had come to the party eager to swap stories, share histories. But when they'd given me my opening, I'd put them off, just as I'd put off Betts. And like Betts, they didn't press. Didn't get offended. Instead they'd offered their friendship by being more open with me than I could be with them. It wasn't a fair trade. Not fair at all. Or honest.

But what was I to say? How was I to begin? Was I to tell them about the shallowness of country-club socializing? The banality of alumnae meetings? The inanity of Junior League? The phoniness of fancy dinner- and cocktail-parties?

Was I to tell them about the emptiness of my marriage to a handsome, highly respected lawyer, a caring husband and devoted father, who provided me with a nine-room house and six-figure income? How could I explain loneliness and meaninglessness of direction in a life so apparently plentiful? So beyond their possibilities. So outside their expectations.

I could have tried, I could have trusted; as I could have trusted with Cissy. But it would have taken too long, all night, and in the end, they would have done the same as Cissy. They'd have made the right commiserating sounds, given the right soulful looks and supportive nods. But they wouldn't have understood. They'd have judged. And as with Cissy, I couldn't withstand their judgment. My own is far more damning.

And equally confused.

How do you explain starvation while holding a cornucopia?

I start the car and drive slowly back to the motel.

How does a woman like me, weak and flabby from a soft life, dare ask sympathy from women who live so close to the bone? Whose flesh has hardened to muscle to carry heavy burdens I'll never even have to consider.

The next day, I move to the Travelodge. It isn't that I don't want to see Betts again; I just don't want to be caught in a lie.

It's time to move on.

SCENE 11

CHAPTER ?

Thursday night, Smokey became violently ill. It started at dinner. In the middle of unwary family banter, she suddenly dropped her fork. It clattered onto her plate.

"I'm sorry," she said, looking around apologetically. "But I don't feel so good."

She tried to rise, her knees buckled, she sank back into her chair, grabbing at the table. Glory shoved to her feet, Casey was immediately beside her.

"I'm sorry," she said again, looking up at Casey. "But I think I need to go to bed."

Casey helped her down the hall, while Glory scooted ahead to turn on the light and pull down the bedcovers.

Smokey hunched on the edge of the bed, watching vacantly as Glory hunted up her robe and nightgown. She'd started trembling.

"Do you want me to help you get undressed?"

Smokey shook her head. "No. No, I'll be all right." Her teeth were chattering. "All I need is a little rest."

Glory laid the robe and gown beside her, looked uncertain. "Okay. I'll just go clean up the dishes then, and get the kids in bed. But I'll be back soon, to check in."

Casey studied Smokey worriedly from the door. "I'll be right out here in the hall. Just call."

She nodded, staring at the floor.

But by the time Glory got back, Smokey's condition had worsened. She was rocking back and forth in the bed, arms gripped around her body, moaning softly.

"Why didn't you hear her?" Glory accused Casey, as she hurried to the bathroom for cold compresses.

"What's happening?" Smokey pleaded. "What's wrong with me?"

But they couldn't quiet her, and by midnight Smokey'd sunk into a kind of panicked delirium. She shook uncontrollably. She cried hysterically. She clutched her throat and gasped.

"I can't breathe. I can't breathe!"

"God—what is it?" Glory dithered in the middle of the floor, wringing her hands. "Is it seizures?"

Casey bent over Smokey, trying to free her grip on her throat, trying to pin her arms, trying to control her convulsing body. "Just let me handle this."

Smokey jerked up and grabbed Casey, eyes wild. "Help me. Help me!"

Glory took a short stumbling step forward. "Do you think we should call the doctor?"

Casey cast a quick, angry look over his shoulder. "I said let me handle this! Leave us."

Glory shifted from foot to foot in concerned confusion, then withdrew, closing the door behind her.

Smokey pushed away from Casey, tore back the sheets, and leapt from the bed into the bathroom, slamming and locking the door.

Casey could hear her gut-tearing retches, her sobs and groans, the flushing toilet, the running water.

Smokey reemerged, white-faced and spent, the sides of her hair draggling in wet tendrils across her cheeks and forehead, the front of her gown clinging in sopped streaks to her body.

"I can't, Casey . . ." she lurched forward. "I can't." He reached to catch her. "They're going to kill me. Don't you understand? They're going to kill me!" She jerked away from him and collapsed to the floor, tearing at his shirt, grabbing his belt, clawing his pants legs as she went down.

She lay on the floor, sobbing and gasping. Casey bent and gently lifted her, lowered her onto the bed, arranged the pillow under her head, smoothed her dripping hair from her face, straightened her damp nightgown, and covered her with the dry sheet and warm blanket.

Smokey stared at him, without recognition, seeing something beyond. "I'm going to die," she whispered.

"No, you're not. I promise you. Just take it easy, try to go to sleep. I'll be back in a minute."

Casey left her panting and trembling, staring wide-eyed at the ceiling.

He used the phone in his den. "Fred. We've got a problem. A witness on the verge of crack-up. . . . Yeah. It's been too much. She's had it. . . . We've been through this before, you know the calls to make. Just get me tomorrow off. I'll have her back on her feet by Monday."

Casey sat by Smokey deep into the night, until her body had quieted, her breathing was even, and she'd slipped into an exhausted sleep. He studied her face a moment, then bent to kiss her forehead.

"It's all right, Honey," he whispered against her now-dry temple. "Nobody's going to get you. Not while I'm here."

He touched her cheek, rose from the bed, turned out the lamp, and stumbled toward the den, leaving the door slightly ajar.

A few hours later, Glory pushed the door open and tiptoed in, carrying a tray. The dishes rattled. Smokey's eyes flew open, she bolted upright with a scream.

Glory stopped dead in her tracks. The dishess rattled. "Oh—I'm sorry. I didn't mean to frighten you, Ann. I thought you'd be awake."

Smokey stared at her. "Where's Casey?"

Glory smiled brightly, her best bedside manner. "Sleeping on the den couch, poor dear. He was so worried about you, he stayed with you almost all night."

Abruptly Casey came charging in, clothes disheveled, gun ready in his hand, eyes frantically searching the room. "What happened?"

Glory nervously smiled. "It's just me, dear. I guess I frightened Ann."

Casey glared. "What the hell are you doing in here?"

Glory's smile faltered. "I brought her breakfast." She held out the tray, the dishes rattled.

"Did I ask you to?"

"No."

"Did she say she was hungry?"

"No, but . . ."

"Did I tell you to leave her alone, that she needs complete quiet?"

"Yes, but . . ."

"Then do as I say. There are things here you don't understand."

Glory's head went high, shoulders straight. "But I want to understand." Her hands gripped the tray. "After all, she's my friend, too."

Smokey hadn't counted on this. She'd wooed Glory to make her a friend as an expedient: to get into her good graces so she could get into her household. Now here Glory was being that friend, concerned, caring, even, unbelievably, standing up to her husband. Smokey would have laughed if the situation hadn't been so desperate.

She glanced furtively at the clock on the bedside table, and was filled with panic. Real panic. This had been her best job of acting, and most demanding. In her need for a quick nap, she'd let too much time get away.

She clenched her fists and began pounding the bed. "Stop! Stop—I can't stand this!" She started rocking and panting.

Casey hurried toward her, glowering at Glory as he passed. "See what you've done?"

Smokey looked up, her face twisted with torment. "Please. Please, Glory. Don't feel bad. I know you mean to help. I just need to be alone." She gave her a quavering smile. "I'll be all right. Just go on with your daily schedule." She squeezed her eyes tight, "Please—just act normal," gasped and cried out, "Oh, god—*please*. I want everything to be normal!" She started shaking and sobbing.

Glory stood irresolutely holding her tray.

Casey turned to face her. "Are the kids gone to school?" Glory nodded stubbornly. "Don't you have errands to do?"

"Of course I do."

"Then do them." His jaw and eyes broached no argument.

Glory turned to Casey, to Smokey, back to Casey.

Casey touched her arm. "I can't explain, but this is serious, Glory." His look held hers, his fingers tightened. "Trust me."

Glory's eyelids fluttered, she smiled tremulously, nodded loving obedience.

"I'll just hurry and dress."

Smokey watched from the corner of her eye as Glory tripped out with the tray, small steps slightly pigeon-toed, shoulders and hips twitching from the waist, head tilted to the right. The dishes rattled.

Smokey flung herself over, face to the wall, buried in the bedclothes. Casey touched her shoulder.

She jerked away. "No, please—just leave me alone."

Casey hesitated. "Do you want anything to eat or drink?"

"No."

"All right. I'll be outside. I'll leave the door ajar."

"I know," Smokey's voice came muffled from the pillow. "All I have to do is holler."

Smokey listened intently as Glory clattered about from bathroom to bedroom to kitchen. Heard Glory's quick, low exchanges with Casey. Heard the close of the kitchen door, heard the car back down the drive. Heard silence.

Heard Casey's muffled movements in the kitchen, living room, study.

Heard the phone ring.

Smokey jumped, looked quickly at the clock. Ten forty. She went stiff with the intensity of her listening. Heard Casey answer, his voice low and even, then pause, blurred. Pause. Brusque. Pause. Sharp. Pause.

Anguished?

She pressed against the wall, pillow over her head.

Moments later, hours, years, cars pulled up, in the drive and at the curb. Doors opened and slammed. The front door opened. Heavy scuffling feet. Deep hushed voices.

Smokey waited, face to the wall, buried under the bedclothes and pillow.

Someone came into the room.

"Smokey?" Casey. His voice flat and hollow. She didn't answer. "I have to leave." She didn't stir. "Fred's here. He'll look out for you. There are stakeouts..."

She flung the pillow off her head, spun over and up, her eyes wild and desperate.

"They're here, aren't they? They're out there! Oh god. I knew it, I knew they'd find me."

Casey's face was ashen, his eyes bottomless black. She'd never seen such pain, such despair.

"They're going to kill me!"

He stared at her, then turned on his heel and left.

Give him time, Smokey smiled. He'd get over it.

She sank back on the bed and rested.

The news item of Glory's death was not allowed to reach front page.

> An as-yet unidentified woman was shot to death this morning on the sidewalk outside Yvonne's Beauty Salon, 1427 S. Sam Houston. The assailant, also as-yet unidentified, was described as a Caucasian male in his middle-to-late thirties, of medium height and build, wearing a gray sweat shirt, Levis, white running shoes, dark glasses, and a light-blue golfer's hat pulled low over his forehead. Witnesses state the suspect was looking into the windows of Martin's Pharmaceuticals next door to the salon when the victim approached from the north. The suspect turned abruptly from the window, bumped into the woman, then continued up the street at a rapid pace, as the woman fell to the sidewalk. Two witnesses, also as-yet unidentified, tried to lift her. It was then they discovered blood on her blouse. The suspect had disappeared.
>
> The victim was shot point-blank through the heart. Death was instantaneous. Motive is presumed to be theft as the woman's purse was missing, and one witness stated she saw the assailant tuck something that looked like a purse under his sweat shirt.
>
> A deputy at the scene of the crime, who wished to remain anonymous, stated, however, that it was an odd mugging, since purse snatchers don't usually shoot to kill, and from witnesses' accounts, it appears the man was using a silencer.
>
> Anyone with information regarding this crime is asked to call the following number:

The number given was Casey's private Bureau line.

No follow-up stories appeared, and the victim's name was never released. Vinnie, of course, also remained unidentified. But Smokey knew he wouldn't be breathing easily. The contents of Glory's snatched purse would reveal the true identity of his victim. As murderer of an FBI agent's wife, he'd be placed on the list of Most Endangered Species.

Smokey had to laugh. He should have known better than to try to match wits with her.

It had taken arduous planning, daring risk, and a lot of cool-headed fast-on-her-feet thinking. But she'd gotten what she wanted—as she always did. Her single-minded objective these past twenty-two months: Casey's freedom.

SCENE 12

The new library is on the west side of Harden, near the cemetery, the poor section, and Indian Town. I'd like to think this is intentional, for the sake of token balance. The east side has the high school, the new hospital, the new elementary, and the new municipal park. For kids from Potter's and Indian Town, without a bike or available parent with a car, it's a long hard walk. One few would make even to school if they weren't bused. Maybe with books more readily at hand, they'll have a chance to discover the possibilities of life they aren't otherwise going to learn about in Harden.

The building is a basic one-story adobe rectangle, but bordered with sandstone planters bedded with evergreen cypress. Three sides are faced with high wide windows that let in airy light and give an enticing view of the shelves of books. To the side is a parking lot with bike racks. And in front—on an actual lawn with sidewalk and flags of the state and nation—there's a mounted burnt-wood sign HARDEN CITY LIBRARY. Maggie would be encouraged; it looks like an honest-to-goodness library.

And inside, it smells like one: cool, clean, lofty yet intimate, redolent with inked treasures buried on paper between hard covers. People whisper and walk softly in libraries not only out of consideration but out of reverence. If anyone were to ask me the smell of enlightened reflection, I'd have to say a library.

It's the right place for me today. I'm not feeling like much. Tired. Slow. Moody. I didn't sleep well last night. A combination of wine, cigarettes, and bad dreams. It's not hard to decipher their source and meaning. I'd think my subconscious could come up with better disguising. But Janie's surprise appearance is having its repercussions.

Let it go, Daddy had said. Some things are better forgotten.

Sound advice. And I'd taken it. But now it seems my dream censor is pulling out on me.

It's left me vulnerable, with a need to protect myself.

I'm not sure exactly what I'm doing here, except I guess I hoped I'd run into Dorothy. But when I don't see her, I'm relieved. I'm not much up to interacting. Finding the old library returned to a house was a loss. It had been important to Maggie, and therefore to me. Maybe that's why I've come: in search of continuity.

I wander up and down, probing shelves, noting categories, number of books, variety of titles. It's a solid, well-rounded collection. Maggie would be pleased.

I drift toward the corner, a snug alcove—and come up short. Maggie's rocking chair. Maggie's braided rug. Maggie's blue and red and yellow floor pillows. Shelves of children's literature. Colorful pictures, puppets, dioramas. A flannel storyboard. And to the side, on the wall, a plaque: THE MARGARET HARRINGTON PATTERSON CHILDREN'S NOOK.

My heart zigzags, leaps. I feel it behind my eyes, inside my head, throbbing at my throat and temples. I fumble into the chair, to catch my breath, and find myself rocking.

A hand touches my shoulder.

—Are you all right?

I look up. And start crying.

—Oh god, Dorothy. She'd be so proud.

The woman stares at me. —Reggie?

I suck back my tears and nod.

—Reggie Patterson?

The tears start flowing again.

She goes down on her haunches in front of me, like a parent with a kindergartner, looks in my face, takes my hand. —Would you like a glass of water?

I shake my head, smile, try to resume some size, some stature. Some adulthood.

—I'm sorry, Dorothy, I was just so overcome. This will make Maggie so happy.

Dorothy stands, looks around the alcove. —Yes— She smiles. —I think we fixed it pretty much the way she wanted. We sent her photographs. But of course that's not the same as seeing it in person.

I stare at Dorothy's knees, trying to sort the meaning of this. —Maggie knows about the Nook?

—Why of course— She's startled. —That was the whole idea. To honor her— Her face goes soft. —She did so much for Harden. If it hadn't been for all the advice she gave me on fund raising, we might never have gotten the library. I sent her a complete packet on the dedication: the newspaper writeup, the mayor's speech, the brochure with her picture on it. She suddenly realizes. —Didn't you see it?

I'm too hurt to lie. I shake my head. —She never said a word.

But why? Why didn't she? A whole children's section. Dedicated to her, my mother.

Or didn't I listen?

Dorothy smiles affectionately. —That's so like Maggie. She never was one to wave her own flag.

I lift from the chair —Well you've done a terrific job— trying not to sound as punctured as I feel.

—Thank you.

She turns to me eagerly, face alight with questions. Opens her mouth . . .

I get there first. —How's Dean?

—Oh— thrown off course —He's fine— but recouping rapidly. —Doing quite well, as a matter of fact— She smiles. —He was just made president of the state dental association.

I'm startled. —I thought he was in medicine.

Dorothy looks confused, embarrassed. —I guess you didn't hear— Her eyes cloud. —He left medical school, right after his wife died.

—Oh. No. I didn't hear.

—He said filling teeth was as close as he ever cared again to get to suffering.

—I'm sorry. I didn't know she died.

I didn't even know Dean had a wife.

Dorothy nods. —Leukemia. It was tragic. She was so young. They tried everything; but they didn't know then what they know now. Dean gave up all his other studies. Became a kind of expert, poring over medical books, researching case histories, writing letters, phoning specialists all over the country. And when they couldn't save her, he blamed himself— Dorothy looks at me. —It's been years now. But it scarred him for life.

My eyes answer her sorrow. —He never remarried?

Dorothy shakes her head. —He still mourns Leanne. His only salvation is work. He puts in long hours, never takes vacations, belongs to more philanthropic and professional organizations than you'd care to shake a stick at. Makes all kinds of money he's not the least interested in spending. He puts it into the clinic he's set up for the indigent— She smiles, shrugs. —So. That's how Dean is.

—I'm sorry, Dorothy.

And I mean it.

—I know— She looks into my eyes. —But I guess we shouldn't be. He's a caring, socially committed person.

—A humanitarian.

She looks surprised, as if the word hadn't before occurred to her. —*Yes.* That's how Dean's made up for his loss.

My mind clicks, my vision blurs. I'm suddenly rushed with images: Daddy and his violin. Abby and her painter. Ruthie and her daughter. Faye and her cowboy. Trixie and her bottle. Scotty. Catherine. Howie. *Howie?*

I blink, force myself back to Dorothy. —Please be sure to say Hi to Dean for me.

—I will.

I'm backing away.

—It's been wonderful seeing you. I can hardly wait to tell Maggie about the Nook— I'm sidling toward the door. —She'll be so glad I saw it.

—You're not going, are you?

I look at my watch. —I have to.

—But we just started talking, there's so much I want to know. About you, your family, Maggie. You didn't even tell me what you're doing in Harden.

I'm almost to the door. —I wish I had time.

—How long are you going to be here?

—Actually, I'm leaving right now.

—Oh no.

—I just have to pick up my suitcases.

—I was so hoping you'd read for Story Time.

I stop. —You still have Story Time?

—Why of course— Her smile is brilliant. —What would the Maggie Patterson Nook be without Story Time— Her look is conniving. —But no one can read for us the way you did.

—Well— I vacillate, calculate. —I *could* arrange to come back through Saturday.

—Oh, Reggie, could you? It would be so wonderful. That'd give me just enough time to get a notice in the paper and an announcement over the radio— She wags her head. —Yes. We even have our own radio station now. All your old fans will come, I'm sure of it. Most of them are still in town— She laughs. —With *their* children— Claps her hands. —Oh what fun we'll have!

—Okay— I grin. —Story Time. On Saturday— She clasps her hands in front of her with a joyful squeeze, smiling widely. I remember now why Maggie was so fond of Dorothy. —What time?

—How about morning? Would morning be all right? Around ten thirty or eleven?

—Ten thirty.

—Then we can go for lunch. What shall I do to help you?

I consider. —Nothing. I'll take care of everything.

I haven't the slightest idea what this means. But I know I will.

I hug my feeling of warmth as I head back into town. Story Time. Can you imagine? Just like old times. An impulse, an unplanned visit. And look how it ended. Perhaps I should trust my impulses more often. I smile as I run through books in my head, trying to decide on a selection.

I approach the liquor store, reminding me I'm out of wine. I make a quick swerve to the curb. Next door is a small magazine and tobacco shop, with a newspaper rack in front. I want to be sure to pick up a paper.

The *Harden Times*, a thin 11 x 14 publication devoted to business advertisement and every scrap of local interest possible, used to come out once a week on Monday. To take advantage of the socially and sensationally newsy weekend. And to allow for last-minute writing by the volunteer staff and off-hours printing by the part-time editor. Now there's a full-time editor, the manager of the Best Western's informed me, and the paper comes out twice a week, Monday and Friday.

I'd left my unopened complimentary copy in the motel room when I'd fled to Travelodge. I want to look for names I might know, get a fix on the town's activities and prosperity.

I buy two bottles of chardonnay, a pack of Virginia Slims, and head for the newsrack. I reach, and stop, stunned. Top center, just below the banner and date line, is a face I know. Too well. Halo of back-lighted hair, icy smile, impenetrable frosty eyes.

Hello Clydene Orton.

Her senior yearbook picture. Who the hell knows what she looks like now, but we sure know what she's doing.

I skim quickly. Clydene Orton, graduate of Harden High, valedictorian, recipient of the DAR and American Legion awards, has been named Dean of Women of some college, some town in Utah. It's a long article, two columns, listing her education—BA, MA, PhD—her achievements, her affiliations, her missionary and church work, her parents and siblings. All it neglects is her salary. And her marital status. Her children. Her domestic obligations. The time spent taxiing, planning meals, running errands, attending functions in support of her husband.

Clydene *Orton*, I assume, has no husband or children.

She's Dean of Women.

So, Clydene, not only did you have the last laugh, you've had the *last* last laugh.

Good old Clydene. Do you know, I wonder, about Les? Les, who hanged himself in his jail cell by his own belt, for shooting his lover's husband. Les, who was, unbelievably, your sweetheart.

We'd see Les with Clydene, more and more often, at her locker, walking her to class, driving her home. But he refused to talk about her, not even to Casey, an unknown for Les, who liked nothing better than to brag about his conquests.

We all watched and wondered. Were they or weren't they? Did they or didn't they? With Les, it was fascinating conjecture. He never went out with women he couldn't screw. And Clydene was the Ice Maiden. We couldn't even imagine her kissing. We never saw them touch.

But the night of the Prom, we knew for sure.

The prom *I* decorated, the night that was to be Casey's and my final triumph.

He'd fussed over what I was going to wear, my jewelry, my makeup, how I was going to fix my hair. Which was long by then, below my shoulders. He made me describe over and over my dress, because I wouldn't show it to him. Maggie had paid for it, but Abby had designed it. Three tiers of yellow organza edged with seed pearls, yellow satin cumberbund, dyed-to-match satin pumps. Strapless. Ankle-length. It was a beauty.

Clydene floated in, on Les's arm, frosty shoulders luminescent above a froth of icy-blue tulle, the color of her glittering eyes. And they'd been voted king and queen of the prom.

Clydene's last laugh.

Casey had been furious. He'd been so sure it was going to be us. He'd laughed and talked heartily, making the rounds of couples, slapping shoulders, passing compliments, winning voters over with that infectious charm. He'd been the showiest dancer on the floor; I thought he'd finally made it as Dean McElvrey.

Les stood quietly aside with Clydene, danced only the slow numbers, holding her decorously, like she was a fragile treasure. Casey looked wonderful in his white dinner jacket and maroon tie and cummerbund, his tanned, blond good-looks vibrant and vital. But Les, with his dark, lean, brooding handsomeness, looked even better. One was effervescent, the other seductive. Casey sparkled, caught you up and made *you* sparkle, like a magnetic nebula of whirling energy. Les mesmerized, sucked you in, like a fiery moth to a dark flame.

Casey wouldn't dance with me after the crowning. —What's holding that thing up— he glared at me. I looked down. —You're sure no sweater girl— I had to admit I wasn't; Clydene's pristine bosoms were ampler. And I had to admit his judgment hurt, as if my breasts were to blame for our not winning.

It separated us.

Afterwards we went to La Descansada with the gang, Betts in her blue taffeta, Billie in plaid, Trixie in white, Ruthie in pink, Faye in turquoise. Walt, Curt, Glenn in white dinner jackets. Everyone with their date, except for Betts. Casey and I sat next to each other, but we didn't talk. We didn't look at each other.

Did I eat? I don't remember. Did I place my napkin on my lap, smile politely? Did I pick up fork and knife? I don't remember.

Clydene and Les weren't with us. Where were they? Out secret.

Secrets.

Secret haunts, secret hauntings.

Secret pleasures . . .

Hungry searchings . . .

SCENE 13

My room is dark and stuffy. I'd left early, hadn't turned up the air conditioner, hadn't opened the drapes. The dark closeness seems right. I'm tired, trembly tired. My exhilaration from Dorothy has evaporated. I know it's lunch time, but I don't want to eat. I lie down on the bed, but I can't sleep. Too much commotion. In and out. Here and there.

I light a cigarette, taste its harshness, feel it aggravate my already unsettled stomach. I open a bottle of wine, fill my water glass. The wine cuts through the acridness, soothes the abused inner tissues. I lie back on the bed, braced against my pillows, and stare through the smokey staleness at the draped window edged by the closed-out light.

Midday. In a cheap motel room. In a nondescript desert town. Drinking and smoking. I feel like a derelict. Stranded, between a past I can't let go of and a future I can't reach out to. Regretting, feeling dark, thinking dark thoughts, facing darkness I can no longer hold off.

Seeing dark men.

Les. Howie. Tommy. Men who by the simple possession of black hair and shadowed jaw seem also possessed of heightened mystery, intense sensuality. Whose bottomless black eyes seem deeper, more penetrating, profounder, capable of uncanny insights and uncommon knowledges, of exciting promises. Secrets . . .

Like Les's eyes that night at the prom, when he looked at Clydene.

Like Tommy's eyes. . . .

I'd catch him, looking at me, lost in my face, scanning my skin, peeling it back layer by layer to get at the essence. Probing at the bone, the slope of my nose, the rise of my cheek, the arch of my brow, the curve of my jaw. His eyes would meet mine and he'd look away, without a flicker, without embarrassment. Without acknowledgment. He made me feel exquisite, like a meissen figurine. And uncomfortable.

But he never looked below my neck, not that I was aware of. And his talk was always harmless, always. No come-on's, no sexual innuendos, no verbal advances.

Harmless.

I knew Janie had a brother, the girls had talked about him, Tommy and his exploits were something of a legend. Even the guys stood somewhat in awe of him.

He's a genius, Betts said. He's a crazy bastard, Billie said. He's a sexy sonofabitch, Faye pronounced. I think she'd had her eye on him.

But Tommy was uncatchable, by anyone. His parents, the school, and, as it turned out, even the Navy. No one could keep up with him, or hang on to him once they found him. He could—and evidently would—do anything. Name it— art, music, the humanities; football, baseball, basketball, track—he did it, and did it better than anyone. Including wild, body-denying carousing. He was the survivor of several car crashes. And particularly gifted in the sciences. But nothing held his attention. The penalty of his brilliance. He'd take something up, find how easy it was, and drop it.

He became a frequent truant, and when he was sixteen he hopped in his car and lit out across country in search of new challenges. He worked on a ranch, in the oil fields, for the railroad, on the docks. I think in my mind, I began to see him as a kind of latter-day Jack Kerouac.

Janie wrote. It was the summer before my sophomore year at Vassar. Tommy had joined the Navy and was stationed at New London. He'd settled down, straightened out. The rigid discipline of the Navy seemed to be what he'd needed. But lately he'd been sounding restless again. The family was worried. They wondered: Maybe if he knew someone who knew his family. Maybe if he had some place he could go off-base. Could she give him my name and number? Could he maybe come visit?

I wrote back, Sure. I didn't even discuss it with Maggie and Daddy. We were always hospitable. It was part and parcel of our New England upbringing. It came with the territory. How could I go back on that?

So one afternoon Tommy showed up, in tight long-legged navy-blue bellbottoms, twisting his white cap in his hands. Even with the stories, I wasn't prepared. He was over six-foot-three, long-waisted, broad-shouldered, muscularly thighed. Dark—and immensely attractive. But he didn't seem to know it. Which made him all the more attractive. He was courteous. He almost bowed to Maggie. He shook hands deferentially with Daddy. He ducked, shrugged, looked up through lowered eyes, no mean feat when you're almost six-four. My heart went out to him. Poor guy. No wonder he was at loose ends. He's lonely. A landlocked cowboy from the West remolded as a seafaring sailor in the East. A rattlesnake in salty water.

I never gave a thought to Casey. This was no transgression; it was a simple human kindness.

Tommy stayed for dinner. He was shy, hesitant, modest. I couldn't connect him with those harum-scarum escapades.

We said at the door as he left, It was nice meeting you, Tommy. You're always welcome.

He took us at our word. He came again for dinner. We sat out on the patio. Daddy was experimenting with barbeque. Maggie was tormenting herself with homemade ice cream, in an old-fashioned machine that required rock salt and manual cranking. Tommy cranked for her.

He called to invite me to a movie, "The Magician," by Ingmar Bergman. I was impressed by his choice, and even more impressed when we discussed it. His observations, haltingly, almost apologetically offered, were astute and imaginative. He understood Bergman and his symbolism. Better than I did.

Let's face it, Tommy fascinated me. Dark, intelligent, sensitive and perceptive, rumored ungovernable, like a fierce westerly blowing destructive sand before it. But I'd never seen that side of him, not the slightest hint, except in those skinning, flesh-layering looks.

Late one afternoon, he called. He wanted to see me. There was an urgency in his voice I hadn't heard before. It made me uneasy. I said I wasn't sure, what did he have in mind? He said there was a fair in town, a kind of carnival: rides, amusement booths, tent shows. Would I like to go?

I'd never been to a carnival. It sounded like fun. The kind of fun Maggie and Daddy didn't allow me. I said I'd love to. I told Maggie and Daddy we were going to dinner and another movie.

I met Tommy at the door. He seemed different, more relaxed, more assured. He quietly but definitely took me in tow, maneuvered me to his dark-blue Ford, situated me in my seat, lifted my skirt out of the door and tucked it around me. In his new attentiveness I felt an undercurrent of possessiveness, which I had qualms about but which was nonetheless flattering.

He chatted conversationally while he drove, taking the lead, looking over at me and smiling more than usual. No fumbling uncertainty, no self-doubting humility.

I'd been aware of a sharp aroma in the car that was vaguely familiar, but I hadn't bothered to place it. I was too intrigued by the transformation in Tommy. He was drawing me in, making me feel I'd known him much longer, and much better.

He mounted a hill, pulled off onto a rough viewpoint, and stopped the car. Below us, in a small flatland, was the carnival, a fallen galaxy of glittering, whirling, dipping bright lights, in the center of which the circling green-and-red constellation of the ferris wheel seemed to be lifting it back into the sky.

I sighed. —How beautiful.

—I thought you'd like it.

He opened his window, then leaned across to roll down mine. The rise and fall of mingled musics punctuated by barkers' calls floated to us.

The sound of the hemispheres.

I turned to him, dreamy and breathless. —It's like a handful of scattered gems. Diamonds, sapphires, topazes. The ferris wheel is an emerald and ruby necklace.

Tommy's eyes scanned my face, darker than ever. —A fairy treasure. For a fairy princess— His voice was darker also. I turned away.

After a moment, he reached over, I thought for me. My heart stopped, I prepared myself to handle his amorous advances. Instead, he opened the glove compartment, took out a bottle. I recognized it immediately, and the unidentified smell. Vodka.

He offered it to me, I shook my head. I was struggling with conflicting emotions. I'd been afraid he was making a move on me. The vodka was even more unsettling. I was wishing now I'd been right in my first assumption. The lesser of two evils. At least I'd know what to do.

And complicating my consternation was an awareness of disappointment; I'd wanted him to make a move. So I could at least have the opportunity to reject it.

Tommy raised the bottle, tilted his head back, and drank deeply. I could hear the gulps and gurgles as the vodka level rapidly lowered. He recapped the bottle and set it beside him.

Staring out the window, he started to talk, about my mother and father, how nice they were, how nice they'd been to him. How good it was to have some place to come, away from the base, instead of just wandering. Some place that made him feel like home.

He talked about home, his home, his life in Harden, his family. How he'd upset and worried them, how crazy he'd been, how he'd messed up his life. How he'd turned over a new leaf in the Navy and was making a fresh start. He'd finished his GED, signed up for radar training, and if things went well, he hoped to get into officers' school. He'd already started studying for the test.

I felt compassion for him, and warmth. The entrusting of another's mistakes, disappointments, and aspirations has the tendency to do that. I wanted to be worthy of that trust. I told him everyone deserves a second chance, that I was sure he could pass any test he took.

He looked over at me. He said that was one of the things he liked about me, I was so sensitive. He started talking about how sweet I was. How lonely he'd been. How he needed my support and understanding. And how he wanted to be a friend.

He put his arm around my shoulders. It had been a long time since I'd felt like a cherished, protected female. I guess I gave in to it. I let him. And when he leaned over to kiss me, I let him do that, too.

It was a long kiss, slow, deep, quiet. I hadn't realized how hungry I was to be kissed. I sank into it. I didn't even mind the bitter tinge of vodka. Tommy'd been drinking on and off while he talked, but after my initial disconcertion, I hadn't thought about it. I was more involved in sharing his confidences.

His left hand found my waist. Gradually it moved up, until it was resting on the side of my breast. He started rubbing, slowly, methodically. There seemed no reason to object; it wasn't actually on my nipple.

I waited for something to happen. Nothing did. We sat like that for a long while, a very long while, kissing, the same kiss, his hand massaging, around and around. He never moved it forward, toward my nipple. His body never became impassioned, demanding. He never pulled me close. His lips never worked over mine greedily, his tongue never flicked or thrust. We were simply locked in a contact, caught in a frozen moment, that was pleasing and comforting, but strangely asexual.

His breathing quickened, held a rhythm, then gradually subsided. Satisfied, or exhausted, he pulled away and reached for his bottle. It was empty. He got out of the car and went to the trunk. When he returned with another bottle, I knew it was time to leave.

I looked at my watch, and was alarmed. There would be no time for the carnival. I asked him to take me home. He was quiet and withdrawn as he drove, almost sullen. I blamed it on his anger over missing out on the carnival. I too would have liked bright lights, crowds, and excitement.

The next morning, I felt terrible. I had betrayed Casey. He knew I was dating, it was part of our agreement; so I could participate fully in college life. But it was understood, for social purposes only. No other man was to touch me, not even a good-night peck on the cheek. If a man couldn't be satisfied with just my company, Casey decreed, then he wasn't worthy of it.

I had crossed the line. I had broken our agreement. I was guilty. And ashamed.

The side of my right breast was sore. I waited for the tell-tale bruise. I kneaded it for weeks, fearing the retributive cancerous tumors. I refused to answer the phone, jumped whenever it rang. Maggie and Daddy screened for me. I told them Tommy had made a pass and I never wanted to see or hear from him again. I left it for them to figure just exactly what constituted a pass.

Tommy called several times. They told him I wasn't home. They were polite but definite. He got the message. He stopped calling. I began to breathe easier.

Then one Saturday evening about three weeks later, Tommy pulled into the drive. I saw his car and something inside me snapped. I was furious, that he should have such effrontery, that he should feel free to just show up, in our driveway, on our doorstep, without invitation or advance notice. Such an infringement on our hospitality, such a breach of courtesy, such an invasion of our privacy. Surely he knew he was no longer welcome.

I confronted him at the door, ready to fight.

—What are you doing here?

He stood hunched, twisting his white cap, his eyes dark and sorrowful, confused and hurt.

—Why won't you see me?

—Because I don't want to see you.

—Why won't you at least talk to me?

—Because I don't want to talk to you.

—Why? What did I do?— He twisted his cap.

—I made a mistake. I never should have gone out with you, not even to a movie. I'm sorry and I apologize.

—Why?

—Because I'm going with somebody else.

—Who?

—That has nothing to do with you.

His dark sorrowful eyes narrowed. —I think it does. Who?

—That's none of your business.

—Some college guy? Some smartass with a frat pin?

—I told you, that's—

—Or some guy from Harden? Some simple jerk named Casey Colter?

I stared at him.

—You leave Casey out of this.

Tommy's hurt confusion had become hard meanness.

—Then you shouldn't have led me on.

—I didn't.

—You shouldn't have given me those coy smiles and come-hither looks.

—I didn't.

—Then why did you let me feel you up?

—I didn't!— I was almost screaming. —And don't you dare say I did.

—Oh yeah? Well, what do you call what we did that night?

My fists were clenched at my sides. I glared at him, letting him see my cold superiority.

—We kissed. You put your arm around me. That was all. I made a mistake.

I'm sorry. Now I just want to forget.

I turned my back and started into the house.

He grabbed my arm.

—Yeah, well I can't. You led me on. You made a fool out of me. You made me a bigger jerk than poor sucker Colter. And I'm not going to let you get away with that— He looked over my shoulder. —Where're your parents? I want to talk to them.

—You can't— I faced him defiantly, blocking the door.

—Oh yeah? Who says I can't?— He shoved me aside, leaned into the doorway. —Hey, Mr. and Mrs. Patterson. It's Tommy Smithson. I'd like to talk to you.

His yell could be heard all over the block. Fortunately, it was a large block, with wide lawns between houses, and separating trees and hedges.

Tommy waited. —I guess they're not here— He smiled. And I suddenly realized he'd known that all along. He'd been patrolling the place, prowling around and spying. He'd probably seen Maggie and Daddy drive off. Saturday night; they always had a social engagement.

—Get out of here!— I was screaming. —And don't come back. I never want to see you again. And neither do Maggie and Daddy. You've taken advantage of our hospitality, you've abused our friendship. You're a low-class clod who doesn't know how to behave in polite company!

His dark face went black. He spun on his heel, slammed into his Ford, and peeled out down the drive.

I slammed our door, to second the slamming of his, feeling courageous and triumphant. And that, I congratulated myself, mentally brushing my hands, is the end of that!

I was nineteen. What did I know about good and evil?

Tommy returned just before twilight. It was July; the sun set late. I heard him first, roaring up and down the street, gunning the engine, grinding gears. That was how he announced himself. Like a threatening gorilla, gnashing his teeth and pounding his chest.

And when he'd finally growled enough, he swerved up the drive and came to a skidding stop. I watched from behind the front curtain as he charged toward the door, staggering and swaggering, a vodka bottle in his hand, another bulging his back pocket. He dispensed with the doorbell. He raised his fist and pounded.

I held my breath and waited for him to go away. He didn't. He pounded.

—Come out of there, bitch!

I slipped away from the curtain, tiptoed toward the door. I could hear him pacing, his heavy steps rough and uneven across the brick landing. He paused, drinking, I imagined.

He pounded.

—Come out! I know you're in there!

I stared in panic at the unlocked door. I hadn't been prepared, hadn't taken precautions.

—You better come out. If you know what's good for you.

Heart pounding, I leapt to the door, turned the dead bolt, slipped the guard chain. I knew he heard me.

I froze, listening. He who hesitates . . .

By the time the true meaning of the silence registered, it was too late. Tommy was at the plate-glass patio door, where he could see fully into the room and up the four stairs to the hall landing.

—Come outta there, you bitch. You hear me? I wanna have a talk with you.

I crouched in the hall behind the stairs bannister, where I could see him across the sunken family room but he couldn't see me.

—Yeah, I wanna talk— He chuckled. I didn't like the sound of it. —I wanna explain the facts of life. I wanna teach you a few things.

He stumbled around, swigging at his bottle, muttering and laughing to himself. Suddenly he spun, shouted at the door.

—You need a lesson. You hear? You're not gonna get away with it!— He lunged, stopped inches from the glass, legs braced, shoulders hunched, arms stiff, face twisted. —This is your last chance. Either you come outta there, or I'm gonna come in and get you!

I looked around in desperation. I had to do something, before Tommy tried the unlocked door. I peeked around the bannister. He had his face and hands pressed to the glass. I crawled out on my hands and knees, slid to the first step, extended a leg toward the second, until I was sure he saw me. Then I scrambled up and ran up the hall to the front door. I unbolted the bolt, unchained the chain, opened the door, waited a few seconds, slammed the door, rebolted, rechained, and raced as fast as I could back to the family room. My ruse had worked. The patio was empty.

I had just enough time to slide the patio-door bolt and shove the guard bar into place before Tommy came lurching around the side of the house. He was too drunk to run fast; he took as many steps sideways as forward. I ducked behind the bunched-up drawn drape and hugged the wall, heart pounding, chest heaving with short dry gasps.

Now he was really angry.

—You dirty bitch, you scheming two-timer. I warned you. Now you're really gonna get it!

I heard a tinkling smash.

—Come out, my sweet beauty. I have something for you. A little present— His voice was crooning, it was ludicrous; he sounded like a trashy gothic novel. —Let me see that pretty face. Let me fix it for you. So you can't bait some other hungry fish. So no other man will look at you, long for you, want you the way you made me want you. You cheating bitch, with your simpering smiles, and cutesy ways.

He was winding down, mumbling now more than crooning. I lifted the back edge of the drape, peeked out. Tommy was glaring at the door, brandishing the jagged neck of his broken bottle.

I needed help. There was no getting around it. I was in over my head.

Tommy's knees suddenly seemed to give out, he pitched forward, caught his balance, and stood there looking around, disoriented. Then he set the jagged bottle on the patio and reached for his back pocket. He was momentarily distracted, turned away, as he struggled to free his second vodka bottle. It was now or never.

I tore across the room, up the stairs, into the kitchen. I couldn't take time for a backward look, couldn't worry whether he'd spotted me. I grabbed the telephone, dialed O.

—Operator, *please*. This is an emergency! My name is Reggie Patterson. I live at 41 Greencrest Road. My parents aren't home. And there's a madman out there trying to carve me up with a broken bottle.

There was a shattering crash and heavy thud. I screamed and threw down the receiver.

—Call the police!

I could only hope the operator had heard me as I sped for the front door.

As I passed the family-room stairs, I glimpsed Tommy making his way in over a shower of splintered glass. He'd thrown Maggie's redwood coffee table through the door. He saw me, roared, and fell over the table.

I needed those precious seconds. My hands were shaking so hard, it seemed to take hours to unbolt and unchain the front door. I prayed Tommy would stumble on the stairs, giving me more critical seconds.

I was at the bottom of the drive when I heard the slam of Tommy's car door and the furious revving of the engine. I had counted on his chasing me on foot. In his condition, I could easily outrun him to the nearest neighbor. But he wasn't that drunk; he still knew his best weapon.

I ran like I'd never run, and it still wasn't fast enough. Tommy had the accelerator floored, I could hear him gaining on me rapidly. I glanced over my shoulder, and stopped, paralyzed. He was heading straight for me. He flashed on his head lights, blinding me. But not before I caught his face, hunched over the steering wheel, grinning into the windshield. Consumed, monstrous. What he couldn't have, no one would have. What he couldn't master would have to be destroyed.

At the last second, I jumped. Tommy went whizzing by, inches from me, the wind from his car flattening the tall grass. I went rolling down the embankment as Tommy's car crashed into the telephone pole, sheering it off at the point of impact and causing a second thunderous crash. I was still lying on the damp ground, clutching grass and crying softly, when the police found me.

Daddy filed charges. Tommy stood captain's mast and spent weeks in the brig. There was talk of dishonorable discharge on the grounds of psychiatric instability. But Tommy passed the tests, as he could pass any test. Except, now, those for officers' training.

Tommy's car was totaled. But except for glass cuts in his knees and hands, Tommy emerged unscathed. He'd survived another crash.

I wasn't so lucky. But the injuries I sustained didn't show up until later.

SCENE 14

I awake at 4:30, feeling lousy, my mouth like the bottom of a bird cage, thinking of Howie. He'd been in my dream, just how I can't remember, but I keep seeing his eyes, dark and sorrowful, hurt and confused.

Howie, whose eyes were what first attracted me. Who looked at me quietly, deeply, tenderly, and made me trust and love him. Who made me believe he would provide for me and protect me, and cherish and honor me above all others.

Howie knew me as I was, the whole sordid story. I told him, about Casey, about Tommy. He said it didn't matter, it was in the past, it had nothing to do with us, who we were now, where we were going.

Howie, a dark man but not a man of darkness, not like Les, not like Tommy. A man of gravity. A man who took responsibility, dependability, loyalty, and trust earnestly. A man who tried, who cared, who stood by me. Who stands by.

I didn't fall in love with Howie, but I was grateful. I was a beached craft, mired in sand, mast aslant, sails slackened. He lifted and carried me to safe water, set me afloat again. And he loved me.

He could love me.

When Casey couldn't, not like that.

Yet I stayed in love with Casey.

I feel myself sinking again, the room closing in. The smell of the cigarette butts and wine dregs is making me sick to my stomach. I force myself to get up, before the pit becomes so deep I can't dig out.

I open the drapes, turn up the air conditioner, flush down the cigarette butts, rinse the ashtray and glass.

I brush my teeth, shower, fluff my hair, put on fresh slacks and T shirt, and drive to the 76 truck stop. I need sustenance.

I order meatloaf with mashed potatoes and gravy. My stomach is a small, tight wad, eating itself. It takes me a long time, chewing and swallowing slowly, waiting between bites, clearing my gullet with water, but I get it all down. And after a while, I feel better.

I know what I have to do.

I go to the phone the minute I'm back in the room. I clear my throat, practice Hello, Hello a few times, trying to make my voice sound strong and natural. I listen while the line rings, fighting cowardice. It's the first time we've talked since that terrible omelette morning.

—Hello.

—Hi, Maggie. It's me. Reggie.

She takes it in stride, only the slightest pause.

—Hi, Honey— I close my eyes. An endearment I haven't heard in years.

—I thought I'd just check in. How are things going there? Is everybody all right?

—Yes, we're fine. Everything's fine, Reggie— The words are weighted. Is she trying to tell me it's all right between us? —How are *you*?

—Okay. I'm still here. Still sorting things out. But I'm thinking— I feel a childlike need for her. —I'm not sure about what. But I'm thinking, Maggie.

—That's good, dear.

—Would you do me a favor?

—Of course.

—I can't call Howie. He's at the beach with the girls. We agreed: I'm not to call them. They need time alone, too. But would you call him, Maggie? Tell him I'm okay. I'm okay and I'm thinking. I'm thinking about him, Maggie.

—I'd be glad to. Any other messages?

—Yes— I take a breath. —I'm sorry, Maggie.

Do I hear a sigh? —So am I.

I pluck at the telephone cord.

—Just stay with me, Maggie.

—Yes, don't worry. We miss you, Reggie. Come home soon.

I pack my bags, except for what I'll need in the morning, and load the car. I'd planned to spend today revisiting the Painted Desert and Petrified Forest. Instead I'd dissipated. I'd lost a whole afternoon. But perhaps not. Perhaps this was something I had to go through. Rocks and sand will be there tomorrow. I have a mountain to climb.

I set the alarm and start out early, pick up a picnic basket and thermos at Babbitt's, bread, cheese, fruit, and iced tea at Safeway, and head east, back through Winslow, Joseph City. On the other side of Holbrook, I come up on 77, and without second thought, veer onto it. So much for the Petrified Forest.

Trust your impulses, I'd told myself yesterday.

I'm trusting.

The Colorado Plateau is a region of remarkably varied faces. I'm heading due north, elevation 5,000 and getting higher. Bold buttes, sandy washes, shallow basins, bubbling springs, winding rivers, layered canyons, sunken deserts. Undulating flatlands covered with green-gold grasses dotted by scattered herds of grazing sheep and cattle. Distant mountains.

The sky is light blue and high, wispy with clouds. The rocks are red, the dirt is gray, the sand is white, the sun is yellow.

How many times did I take this road with Daddy? Three or four? Not many. He preferred 87, which goes through the Little Painted Desert and comes out at Second Mesa.

Drifts of pink sand veil the dark-gray asphalt, innocent remnants of vicious side-long slashes of wind storms that can pit car paint, push a Buick off the road, and topple Volkswagens. Hot, vengeful winds that sweep across the land, reclaiming everything—foliage, people, sheep—with a coating of stinging dust. I think of Maggie and her furious summer-long battle against the blasted-in silt that filmed venetian blinds, window sills, and table tops. And that turned to red mud on the white paint when she tried to wipe it with a wet cloth.

I think of Casey grinning smugly as he watched. And I have to grin.

Daddy had two more sabbaticals after Hopiland but he never went out in the field again. His year with the Hopis was a kind of high point, a peak experience, and it changed him. He gradually moved away from ritualistic music, more and more toward religion. Or back to religion, Abby would say. He became a museum and library scholar, reading, teaching, writing, thinking. And sometimes he shared his thoughts.

But even now, when he talks, no matter what the topic, he almost always comes around to the Hopis.

I pass a circular, earth-covered hogan next to a small lone tree, in the scant shade of which a gray-haired woman kneels weaving at her vertical loom. Three black-haired children play with some goats. Chickens scratch in the clay. A dog on his haunches watches. Two young men tinker under the hood of a battered pickup, in the bed of which sits a 50-gallon barrel.

I've officially entered Indian Country, the huge, wealthy, encompassing Navajo Reservation, nearly sixteen million acres, in the heart of which lies the tiny, poor, constricted Hopi Reservation, about five-hundred square miles. I hear Daddy's voice: An island of peaceable village-oriented dry-land farmers surrounded by a sea of aggressive nomadic herders bounded by the continental shores of the White Nation.

Once, all this belonged to the Hopis, as part of the Sacred Circle granted them by Maasaw, God of Life, Death, and Fire, and Guardian of this Fourth World of the Hopi.

This, Maasaw promised, would be theirs to build their homes on and take their subsistence from, until the beginning of the Fifth World, so long as they followed the *Potskwani*, the commandments for living and livelihood he also gave them. Their boundaries extended from the Colorado River west to the Rio Grande River east, and from the northern mountain forests to the southern deserts.

Century by century, decade by decade, it was taken from them. By the Spaniards, who came for their riches, and finding none, settled for their souls and slave labor. By the White Man's government, who wanted a transcontinental railroad to the California gold fields, and land for exploitation and expansion. By the Navajos, who, defying their agreement, kept encroaching in large numbers. And, again, by the federal government, who ignored its treaty and let them. Until finally the Hopis were left with but a postage stamp of their original envelope.

A low-moving cloud of dust ahead gradually resolves itself into a jumble of sheep. I slow, knowing what to expect. A stately Navajo on horseback calmly steps onto the road and comes to a stop in front of me, without so much as a flicker in my direction. I put the car in Park and settle back to watch his prized flock stupidly amble across. It'll take a while. The flock is large, and sheep get confused when you try to move them with purpose. They keep stumbling and bumping into each other. The man—tall-waisted, weathered into his sixties or seventies, in Levis, boots and bandana sweatband—sits erect, reins held high, on his sorrel— also highly prized—and stares into space. His space. While his sheep dogs—the most highly prized of all—nip and nudge the sheep into obedient procession. When the last ewe has safely cleared, he pushes the horse forward with a barely perceptible press, and I'm allowed to pass. Not that I was there to begin with.

A thin line separates from the horizon and the southern end of Black Mesa lifts into sight, like a slab cut from the surrounding static buff and gradually elevated into the electric blue.

The Center of the Universe.

I ease my foot on the accelerator so I can come up on it slowly, the way Daddy used to do, to absorb the pinks, peaches, and purples as they focus into the cliffs, crevices, and shadows of First Mesa.

I take a deep breath. Daddy's breath.

Polacca, at the base of the sheared-off mountain, is a shock. I remember it as a small combination grocery store/trading post and a few scattered houses. It's become a regular town, complete with telephone poles, power lines, and TV antennas. Daddy'd told me about this, the new communities being funded by HUD. But I'd forgotten. Or chosen to.

I guess the residents—reasoning that they no longer had need to fear the invasion of unfriendly neighbors, and thus fortify themselves on top of an inaccessible mesa and subject themselves to its privations—had decided there could be no harm in enjoying the modern conveniences of the lowlands.

But I wonder about their reasoning.

So, Daddy has told me, do some of those still up on the mesas. The definition of progress has to be carefully considered.

I park facing the southeastern slope and climb out. The sudden blast of heat after the air-conditioned car almost bowls me over. The sun is intenser here, beating down through the high thin air with little to filter and soften it. It strikes the hard-baked clay and bounces back, meeting itself coming down with such accumulated energy that it becomes actually palpable. You feel it, as a hot thickness enveloping you and sapping your will and strength. You smell and taste it, as a golden sweetness drying your nose and mouth and swelling your tongue. And you sometimes see it, as a wavering wall rising above rock and asphalt, like a vertical sheet of shimmering water.

I lean against the fender and stare six-hundred feet up. When Daddy first brought me, you couldn't see a sign of the villages, not even at this close range, nothing to betray human habitation. The way up was a scary bumpy switchback that coiled tighter near the top. A ledge scraped by hand out of dirt and around rock for ponies, burros, and wagons, barely wide enough for one car, with a sheer drop down. Now it looks paved, and as I watch, two cars meet and pass without one getting pushed over the cliff's edge or the other crushed against its wall. Antennas and power poles, like in Polacca, mar the skyline. But they stop short of Walpi.

Walpi, stronghold of Traditionalists who continue to struggle, even well into the twentieth century, to honor their contract with Maasaw.

From here, it looks like a rubble of rock cluttering the southwestern tip of the mesa. From up there, it's a huddle of low two- and three-story houses hugging the edges of the narrow ledge around a central plaza, pine-bole ladders reaching out of underground kivas and leaning shadows against bleached adobe walls.

Up there, you can look across a thousand square miles. South, toward the Petrified Forest, an eroded badlands strewn with fallen totems of agate and jasper logs; and the Hopi Buttes, a jagged line of volcano throats, cinder cones, and basalt thumbs. North, toward Monument Valley, a sculptured expanse of thousand-feet high free-standing redrock formations; and Canyon de Chelly, steep-sided sandstone shelter of prehistoric cliff dwellings and *Hisatsinom* pictographs. West, toward the Grand Canyon and Little Colorado, site of the *Sipaapuni,* the reed in the sky dome through which the Hopi emerged; and the San Francisco Peaks, home of the Kachinas.

And east, toward the rising sun and Tawa, the Great Being.

The first time Daddy brought us here, it was March. Bundled in knit caps, lined gloves, and padded parkas, we stood at the edge of Walpi's lofty parapet while Daddy pointed out our surroundings. An icy wind wailed in from the west and whipped around us, bringing the smell of snow from the San Francisco Peaks to our red noses, and the sting of chilled sand from the desert to our numbed cheeks. The yellow-gray screen of a sandstorm shifted across the tablelands south, and the sun through the dirty haze slanted an eerie ochre cast. There wasn't a dot of green in sight.

We had come for a baby-naming ceremony. Daddy had made friends with a man named Frank who carved kachina dolls at the Northern Arizona Museum. It was Frank whose grandson was being named, and it was he who had invited us.

We tumbled out of bed at three to be on the mesa before dawn. The night was black, without moon or stars to define any silhouette or shadow of life. We drove in silence, leaning forward, caught in a sense of helpless, almost frightening unrealness, as we sped through the unbounded dark, our headlights swallowed before they could confidently find the white line.

It was predawn when we reached the foot of the mesa. Before he started up, Daddy warned —I don't want to hear a word— and he didn't. Maggie, after one incredulous look, gripped her door handle, squeezed her eyes tight, and clamped her mouth shut. I pressed to the window, clouding it with my shallow breath, as I stared in dumbstruck fascination at the prospect of my imminent crushed death.

—Okay— Daddy sighed, reaching the top and grinning over at Maggie.

—You can look now.

Maggie looked, but she didn't let go of her door handle. What she was seeing against the graying sky was what I saw: a connection of rude, flat-roofed hovels, barely distinguishable from the dirt and rock, laid out around a series of small courts, with narrow side streets running helter skelter.

I don't know what I expected. I'd certainly seen enough photographs. But I guess I'd imbued them with a kind of mystical otherworldliness. This was the real thing, and there was no room for romance. It wasn't that I was disappointed, just dismayed. And from the look on Maggie's face, I suspect she was having the same reaction.

But as Daddy threaded the woody between the dark houses, around the deeper ruts, and into Walpi toward a splash of light, my excitement returned. He parked in a small clearing surrounded by the crumbled walls of a collapsed house, and led us toward two softly glowing windows. At the sound of his hushed knock, the door cracked to allow a slit of light to reveal us, then swung wide. I saw the outline of a short stocky man backlit by pulsating warmth. Daddy smiled, shook hands, exchanged greetings, and the man ushered us in.

We stood in a small, low-ceilinged room with a hard-packed earth floor swept spotlessly clean. The pulsating light, I saw, came from two kerosene lanterns and a curved fireplace, the only source of heat that cold morning. Coiled plaques and kachina dolls decorated the walls, and bunches of herbs and roasted-and-dried ears of sweet corn hung from the smoky rafters. Here and there a downy eagle feather dangled from a short cotton string fastened to a small painted stick stuck into the closely packed brush and earth that covered the cross poles. *Paavaho*, prayer sticks, gifts from the winter solstice ceremony signifying a blessing on the house and its occupants. The front windows looked out onto the village street, the back windows onto the desert and distant fields below.

This was an old-fashioned house. The newer ones, I knew from Daddy's descriptions, were larger, had more rooms, with plastered ceilings and stone-slab or linoleum floors. There would be a coal-fed stove or hooded fireplace with chimney, cabinet with cooking utensils, table with chairs, even a couch. But here there weren't even screens on the windows or a screen door.

The family looked up with interest as we entered, but only Nancy, Frank's wife, came forward. The rest acknowledged us as introductions were made with quick, flashing smiles, then went on about their work.

This was my first close contact with Hopis. Certainly I had seen them in Harden, passed them on the street, sat with them in class. But that had been in my land, now I was in theirs. I was the outsider invited in, if not accepted, at least good-manneredly tolerated. The honor being extended was to my father; I had ridden in on his coattails. I felt awkward, alien. I wanted to change my skin. I tucked my chin, smiled through humbled eyes, croaked my hellos. I was regarded with friendly silence. The Hopis are not a garrulous lot. It made it easier to hide my discomfort.

We stood to the side while the family finished its preparations. Nancy returned to the pots simmering in the fireplace. As maternal grandmother, she was hostess of the event and responsible for preparing the food and gifts. Alice, the paternal grandmother, was busy setting out on the floor a mat, towel, basin, and small bowl of creamy liquid. Nancy's younger daughter Frances knelt behind a hollowed stone metate set in the dirt floor, grinding blue cornmeal into a fine flour with the stone mano held in her two hands. And in a special corner of the fireplace, Nancy's mother, a broad-hipped, full-bosomed woman, dipped the meal mixed with water from a bowl and spread it with her hand in a thin layer over a rectangular polished stone, heated beneath by a small fire. I wondered how she managed that without blistering her palm. Finished rolls of the *piki* bread were stacked at her side. Raymond, Nancy's father, sat on a stool in a corner, winding yarn onto a spindle.

A vigorous, elderly man entered, and without concern for our presence, poured water into a basin from a pitcher, rolled up his sleeves, and began washing his face, neck, arms, and hands. Then smoothing his blunt-cut steel-gray hair with his wet hands and tying a bright bandeau—the traditional Hopi hat—around his forehead, he turned his attention to the family.

This, I decided, had to be Frank's father, Johnny. A staunch Traditionalist who did not approve of his son's friendliness with the *Pahana*. He was a *Kikmongwi* from a long line of *Kikmongwit* who had cared for their villages without writings, laws, courts, or money systems. The *Navoti*, the Prophecies, had warned of a time when the white men would come with materialistic philosophies, technologies, and pollutants that would disturb Mother Earth. And that would distract the Hopis from their spiritual responsibilities, end the ceremonies, pit Hopi against Hopi, and destroy their way of life. He saw us as their representatives. I wanted to apologize, explain myself. It mattered that he, more than anyone in the room, should like me.

Suddenly the room came to life with the arrival of the mother and baby, accompanied by four women, the aunts. Nancy took a kettle off the hearth and poured water into the basin. One of the aunts took the baby from the mother and positioned herself on her knees before the basin, the baby held above it. Alice knelt beside her, and taking an ear of corn handed her by Nancy, began rubbing the creamy liquid from the bowl over the baby's head. I was witnessing, I realized with quickening heart, the ceremonial hair-washing. The cream was yucca soap, the corn was a perfect ear, a "Corn Mother," symbolizing the mother of life.

Although the light outside was now beginning to compete with that inside, the women didn't hurry. I glanced around the room. The faces were shining, a soft blend of humor and dignity, intent on the baby. No sign of tension, no wince of anxiety or frown of frustration. No sense of pressure. Only a calm, accepting poise. An attitude of peace with the world.

Until a few decades ago the white man's calendar was unknown among the Hopi. The Hopi believe in living each day as it is and not counting their length of time on earth. For them, time is a flow of past and future cupped in the present.

The mother accepted the dried and blanketed baby, then passing the Corn Mother over him four times from navel to head, she named him, wished him a long life, a healthy life, and on the fourth pass, a productive life in his work. The aunts, each wishing to be godmother and each with her own Corn Mother, did the same, giving him a name from the clan of her mother or father.

The mother takes the baby in her left arm, the Corn Mother in her right hand and, with Nancy, leaves the house. The rest of the family remain behind, except for Frank, who, after a discreet moment, steps to the door and, to our surprise and his father's frown, motions us to follow. He leads us past Sichomovi and the Tewan village of Hano, just beginning to stir, to where the mother, grandmother, and baby stand on the eastern edge of the mesa.

The Hopis define three phases of dawn: the purple flush, when the shape of man is first outlined; the yellow glow, which reveals man's breath; and the red splash of sunrise, in which man stands proudly revealed in the fullness of his creation. These three phases mark the dawn of life and man's evolutionary journey, as they now mark those of the baby.

As the disc of the sun clears the horizon, Alice steps forward and holds the baby up to the sky, while the mother passes the Corn Mother over him and repeats words Frank tells us mean, "Father Sun, this is your child. Now is he seeing the sun for the first time. May he grow so old that he has to lean on a crook, proving he has obeyed the Creator's laws."

The lifting sun reminds the Hopis to always face life with a full, radiant countenance. The women reach their hands toward the sun, gather the white light, and rub it over their bodies. Then we turn and hurry back to the house, looking over our shoulders as Alice and the mother draw cornmeal paths toward the sun for this new life.

During our short absence, the house has been transformed. A large mat has been spread on the floor and laid with an abundance of food. A tiny, wrinkled woman with clear, alert eyes, erect bearing, and thick white hair twisted in a bun at the nape of her neck has joined the party. She takes the baby and laces him into a cradleboard, which is viewed by the Hopis as an early conditioning to the restrictions of their difficult way of life.

With the return of Nancy and the mother and baby, the family is ready to begin the breakfast feast. We settle on small mats around the floor table. Gradually the family becomes comfortable with our presence. Their glances and talk shift to include us. They name and give descriptions of the food, their ingredients and how they're cooked. Nancy speaks of the baby's lineage, how he is related to each person in the room, and how he inherits his clan membership from his mother and must marry outside that clan.

And it is the clan, Johnny interjects gravely, that is the most important, for it determines a person's standing in both religious and secular matters. It is the heart of the Hopi society.

The Hopi, I learn, are matrilineal. The land and homes belong to the women, distributed through the authority of the Clan Mother, the matriarch head-of-household and caretaker of the clan's most sacred religious objects. This is the tiny white-haired woman.

Frank tells of how he met Daddy, and encourages Daddy to talk a little about his work. Daddy's humble, modest, and careful. He describes his interests as mainly in the area of music. He admits to being a professor, but defines himself more as a scholar, a student of life. He doesn't mention religion, and he doesn't refer to his study of "other" cultures, for fear the term might be misinterpreted to reflect on the Hopis as primitive, alien, barbaric.

His audience is no less cautious. They listen attentively but silently, no comments and, above all, no questions.

Do not ask questions, Daddy advised us before we left home, no matter how innocent they may seem. They will be considered intrusions and will be met with courteous but unmistakable distancing.

Daddy had instructed me, by way of analogy: At a dinner party in Boston, would you pry into the inner workings and relationships of your hosting family?

I had been indignant: Of course not.

Well, the Hopi smiles now grouped around us seemed to say, we are no less civilized.

The aunts clear up. The mats are rolled up against the wall. Maggie, now feeling accepted enough, comments on a bowl she admires. Nancy beams and admits it's hers. Encouraged by our surprised appreciation, she brings out more of her ware: tall jars, squat bowls, curved plates. The walls are thin, the color even, with no burn spots, the designs lyrical. She's obviously a master potter, and Daddy says as much. Nancy beams again, and explains how the pieces are made. But the true success of a piece, she says, is in the firing. Then she asks if we'd like to see her kiln.

We eagerly pull on our outer clothing and follow to the windy tip of the mesa. Nancy's is the largest in a cluster of rounded hogan-like kilns, and has a fresh coat of white plaster. It's in a special place, she tells us, a position of honor, because of the standing of her family, which is one of the oldest in the village. She states this simply, as a matter of fact, but I feel her pride. She then takes us through the exacting task of firing.

We stand huddled into ourselves for a long, brave moment, surveying the blustering, swirling expanse below, while Frank draws in the dust with a stick the map of the Hopi migrations. It isn't an exact map, he explains, for it describes the journey of the soul. Then we head back toward shelter and warmth.

It's time to go. Maggie has brought the baby a gift, a plushy powder-blue blanket with satin binding. As we make our good-byes, Nancy hands Maggie the admired bowl. Maggie's so touched, her eyes actually mist.

But the greatest gift is the one I receive as I hold out my hand and say thank you: the crinkled smile in Johnny's eyes.

SCENE 15

The mesa swims, tilts, lifts. I steady myself against the hot fender. Not even ten and the sun is getting to me. I make a tactical retreat.

I feel like a sissy, sitting in the air-conditioned car. But I don't want to end up like Maggie. She never did acclimate. She refused to stay home from the few dances Daddy invited us to and, even with her broad-brimmed hat, she always came home with a pounding headache that lasted into the next day and made her sick to her stomach. I've brought no hat. It never occurred to me I'd need one. Time was, I could stand out on the mesas all day bareheaded. The cool of New England has weakened me.

I lean forward and crane upward, trying to see through the tinted glass. I wonder if Frank and Nancy are still up there. Twenty years. Given the longevity of the Hopis, they could all still be living, except for the great-grandmother. Even Johnny could be alive. And Johnny would never leave Walpi.

I'd like to go up, see if I can find them, but I'm not sure I'd be welcome. Especially as I am: a lone White female in pants and T shirt. The Anglo tourists' misuse of Native American hospitality finally became such an issue as to get widely publicized and make them, on many reservations, *personae non gratae*. Daddy wrote one of the first scathing articles. We didn't have to go abroad, he said, to be the Ugly American.

I remember those tourists, in shorts with cameras around their necks, how ashamed I was, how embarrassed. I didn't want to be seen as one of them. Why did they come, I wondered? driving long, hard miles to stand under the torturous sun so they could gawk at what was for them little more than a sideshow. They had no understanding of what they were watching, and no respect for what they didn't understand. No awareness that this was a religious ceremony and that their behavior was not only rude and offensive but sacrilegious. They scuffed across the center of the plaza, disrupting the sacred cornmeal lines, unmindful that the Hopis stayed to the sides. They talked and laughed loudly, looked around boldly, insensitive to the Hopis' quietness and averted eyes.

They took the seats of the Hopis on the adobe benches attached to their homes, scattered candy and gum wrappers. The village priest had to make the rounds, admonishing them not to take pictures, and when one man did anyway, the camera was yanked from his neck. A threesome of beer-drinking men was asked to leave the mesa.

The Hopi are distinguished by sobriety. They are one of the few Indian groups that has never developed a native intoxicant, believing that no man can rightly indulge in anything that will cause him to lose command of himself.

But overriding all this, I remember the beauty. Nothing can detract from that. Even the crass *pahana* got caught up once the kachinas arrived.

I squint up at Walpi and see them almost as vividly as I did then. Dramatically commanding personages in white kirtles and long woman's sashes embroidered with red, green, and black, the colors of sun, growth, and rain. Fox pelts hanging from the back, symbols of courage. Their bodies smeared with black corn smut. Their torsos painted with the white crescent moons of friendship. A circle of blue yarn over one shoulder across their chests. Black yarn around their wrists. A strip of sleigh bells below their left knees, a turtle shell filled with rocks or deer hooves below their right. In their right hands, a gourd rattle. In their left, a twig of spruce and downy eagle feather. Sprigs of spruce stuck in their blue arm bands. Ruffs of spruce around their necks. Skirts of spruce flaring over their kilts.

Spruce, the branching throne upon which the clouds rest, with the magnetic power to pull the rain in.

On their heads they wore great three-tiered *tablita* painted sky blue with white clouds spilling black rain, the tier corners tufted with heads of wild wheat and eagle and parrot feathers. In the center, above the half-yellow half-blue face-mask, arched a red rainbow over a field of white, on which was painted a frog or butterfly. Each mask was distinctive, like the body decoration, expressing the originality of its designer.

I memorized every detail, and once safely back in the car, drew a sketch which Daddy later had me redo in color. I used poster paints, the way the Hopi do, to give it the right feeling. Daddy made it the cover of his book.

The Hemis Kachina.

The Niman Dance: the Home Coming.

I realize that this is what I'm visualizing. Of the four or five dances I saw, this is the one I most remember. Here on First Mesa. The first weekend of July, the same time of year as now. My last dance, and my last trip to the mesas. In a few weeks, we'd be leaving for Boston. Maggie had already started packing.

The Home Coming. The end of the Summer Solstice and the beginning of the Winter Solstice. The return of the kachinas to their home in the San Francisco Peaks and the repeat of their dances in the Underworld, where the seasons of the sun and phases of the moon mirror-reflect and alternate rhythmically with those of the Upperworld. Day and night, summer and winter, birth and death. Two sides of one coin. The Pattern of Creation, the Road of Life.

Home Coming. The departure of the gods, leaving behind cold and darkness.

We arrived at dawn, to set up our folding chairs in a place that would provide good vantage and shade in the afternoon. Women were sweeping out. Children splashed in rain puddles reflecting cloud-streaked blue. Dogs scratched fleas. Chickens ruffled in sand baths. Gradually the villagers gathered, men and children standing along the walls, women and babies sitting on chairs and cushions. The sky lightened, low-hanging cumulus parted, the plaza hushed, eyes focused on the eastern edge of the mesa.

The image came first, the vision. Suddenly the tip of a headdress appeared above the ledge, tufts of wheat, fluttering feathers. The tableau rose, then the face mask. The body climbed, arms and chest, hips and legs. Slowly they ascended, one by one, set foot on earth. The Emergence. They came toward us, steadily, a long line of supernatural beings, mortals imbued with the eternal, moving in stately reverence. I count them: thirty Hemis Kachina followed by nine *Katsin manas*.

The Katsin manas are female impersonators, wearing black woman's dresses and red-bordered white mantles, their legs thickly wrapped in white buckskin boots. The flat half-masks are yellow under a long fringe of red-yarn bangs, with feather beards. The black wigs parted in the center form maiden's butterfly whorls over their ears. Each carries a hollow pumpkin shell, notched stick, and deer or sheep scapula.

The dancers pause at a rock-slab altar to drop cornmeal and ask a blessing. An old man in ordinary dress carrying a *paaho* meets them and leads them into the plaza, marking the path with sacred cornmeal from the burlap sack around his neck. They stand along the south side, facing east, while the priest, the Kachina Father, goes down the line, sprinkling each with cornmeal. Nothing breaks the silence, except the single cry of an eagle tethered atop a roof. Then the Kachina Father goes to the head of the line, the leader shakes his rattle, and the mystery play begins.

The sound comes second, a deep insistent drone, strangely muffled by the leather masks *Hummm, Hummm, Hummm* rising and falling, up and down, in a low limited register *Hummm, Hummm, Hummm* rivetting, mesmerizing.

The leader starts in the center. The dancers join in on cue, taking up the song one at a time, down both sides of the line to the ends, where the weaker and neophyte dancers are positioned. *Hummm, Hummm, Hummm* encompassing the vision until sound and vision are one. *Hummm, Hummm* encompassing the plaza until we're all one.

And as they sing, they dance.

Strong legs lift right feet to the same height and bring them down at the same moment with a solid stomp, while left heels raise slightly. Raise, lift, stamp, raise, lift, stamp, in interwoven rhythm with the chant, each raise and stamp punctuated by the chunk of turtle shells and jingle of bells, in close succession that blends in one three-part pulsation, with curious skip beats and pauses interspersed. The gourd rattles provide a steady background, a dull rolling-surf sound. *Whoosh whoosh whoosh.*

Chingle, thump, chunk, chingle, thump, chunk, whoosh whoosh whoosh, fringed deerskin moccasins pound upon the earth-drum, taking from it strength and power. *Hummm, hummm, hummm, Hummm, hummm, hummm* throats open to the sky, taking from it breath and light. Feet and voices vibrate the air above and ground below, stirring up the gods. *We are here. Hear us.*

The dancers move in perfect unison, knees slightly bent, arms bent up at the elbows, bodies contained, slowly swinging. Left, pause, right, pause, left again, backward and forward. The manas have come up alongside the Hemis, to form a double line, rotating as a single unit in opposite directions.

I watch, and as the dance progresses begin to understand the Father's function: to guide and encourage the Kachinas. He signals the dancing to start, calls out instructions, directs the line to shift, repeats the words of the song. And in between, walks up and down the line, "feeding" the dancers with cornmeal, and delivering, interchangeably, what sound like prayers and pep talks.

The music stops abruptly, leaving a stunned stillness. We look around, disoriented, self-consciously brought back to ourselves. The dancers stand at ease, arms at their sides, watching the leaders prepare for the second movement. The Kachina Father leads them to the east side, facing north.

Women hurry up with folded quilts, blankets, towels, lay them in a row. The manas kneel, facing the men. A second priest with a Corn Mother scatters cornmeal on the dancers. A priestess follows, sprinkling especially the kneeling manas, whose wigs are now becoming white with powder.

For the third figure, the dancers move to the north side, facing west. The manas place their green-and-yellow pumpkin shells mouths down on the ground, their left hands hold the sticks over the upended bottoms, and with their right hands they begin scraping the scapulas over the notches. The sound is eery, uncanny. A coarse grunting tone, a deep hollow rasp, a dull resonant squawk, but not unpleasant. It fills the plaza.

The dancing begins again. The steps seem more vigorous, the singing stronger. And I'm certain now: the song is gradually changing. I hear subtle variations, more highs above the lows, trickier, quicker shifts in tempo. I whisper my observations to Daddy and he says, Good for you. Maggie frowns and goes, *Shhhh*.

Then the dancers file out of the plaza and disappear over the ledge to their dressing shelter beneath the rock, where they unmask, eat, and rest in preparation for the next round.

There is no fourth position, for life is still in progress in this Fourth World, the perfect pattern waiting to be fulfilled or broken.

The dance continues throughout the day, at regular intervals, dawn to sunset, and we stay for it all. At the longer noon break, we retire to the back of the woody for our basket lunch. Maggie's an experienced picnicker, sandwiches are what she does best. Mayonnaise and mustard wait cool and fresh in the ice chest, along with lettuce, tomatoes, and fruit. But the thing we hit first is the jug of iced tea, lemon, no sugar.

By the time we return, the plaza is packed. Visitors from other villages have been arriving steadily all morning, on foot, by pony or burro, by wagon or pickup, along the way picking up passengers. But now they crowd the walls and rooftops. Men and boys in Levis and shirts faded to the hues of sky and desert. Women in simple ready-made dresses of gingham or calico. Older matrons in black with bright Spanish shawls. Girls in flowered skirts and white blouses, white socks, and shiny patent leather or pastel slippers. The younger carry babies hanging in shawl hammocks across their backs. A few of the older, more flirtatious attempt nylons, high heels, and clinging rayon-jersey dresses. Attire not socially smiled on or practically sensible.

The sun burns down from its zenith. Great cottonball clouds hover in the quivering blue, a few drift leisurely across the dun, dropping purple shadows. There isn't a breath of moving air.

The dancers enter more frequently now, and each time they return they bring gifts. At sunrise, they come with armloads of whole, green corn stalks, the first harvest of the year. In late morning, they bring gourd rattles and bows and arrows for the boys, kachina dolls for the girls. They also bring bowls, baskets, or washpans of food: small ears of colored corn, little red-cheeked peaches, various kinds of green and yellow melons. Some offer piki bread. But there are also hard-boiled eggs, store cakes with gooey frosting, Twinkies, and popcorn balls.

The children come forward shyly, but only after they're sure their names have been called. There's no pushing or shoving, no snatching or grabbing, no greedy vying for more. And the kachinas, peering through the eye slits of their masks, make sure each child and family gets a fair share.

By five o'clock, the light has changed. The sun hangs orange in the west. Blue shadows dapple the golden desert, drop from roofbeams, spread in cooling blocks across the plaza. To the far northwest, a storm blackens the horizon. Closer, a towering thunderhead trails a curtain of rain and shoots up tiny streaks of lightning. A breeze raises puffs of dust and brings the soft aroma of wet sand, creosote, and cedar. The air caresses.

The leaders are beginning to look tired and drawn. The dancers must be nearing exhaustion. But their dancing and chanting are as quick and lively as ever. I sink, drift, my head woolen with the steady hum, chinkle, stomp, chunk, my eyes glazed with the rhythmic sway of color. A strange lightness comes over me, I lift, and suddenly I hear them, I think I understand the words.

Oh Great Being, Creator of us all, rocks, rivers, plants, and animals, all that make up this beautiful and beneficent world. Bring us rain, give us abundant crops, bless us with the continuation of life, so we may complete our evolutionary journey.

I want to cry. I clench my jaw and fists to stop myself. And I believe. I believe that the kachinas are among us, that their spirits are in these boys and men who have prepared themselves through sixteen days of meditation, abstinence, and purification to become worthy receptacles of the kachinas, communicators between the living and the dead, and messengers for their people. To dance on the womb of the world and send out prayers for harmony between nature and all living creatures.

At six, the dancers make their final appearance. Then the priests and priestess remove the turtle shells and sprinkle the dancers with meal. The Kachina Father delivers his farewell:

Now it is time that you go home. Take with you our humble prayer, not only for our people and people everywhere, but for all the animal kingdom, the birds and insects, and the growing things that make our world a green carpet. Take our message to the four corners of the world, that all life may receive renewal by having moisture. I am happy that I have done my small part in caring for you this day. May you go on your way with happy hearts and grateful thoughts.

The kachina leader shakes his rattle to show the Father's message has been accepted and will be delivered, and it's over. Life is in full flower, the first fruits are in, the kachinas' work is done.

In silent procession they file through the narrow streets to the mesa's western edge. For a brief moment, their unearthly shapes are outlined against the sunset's fire, then they disappear over the edge.

No man follows.

SCENE 16

I close my eyes, wanting to call them back, hold the spell. But gradually the sound recedes, the air stills. I open my eyes, and am startled by the mesa's solid reality, its vivid nearness. I sit quietly, waiting, hoping for the vacuum to fill. I roll down the car window, let in the sun-hot air to swirl around with the air-conditioned cool. Nature mediating with man.

The best possible solution in this impossible world.

I look at my watch, and am again startled. I put the car in gear, take one last look. It's all right, it doesn't matter that I can't return: I remember.

I head up Second Mesa and pass Shipaulovi, almost a ghost village now, the houses used only during ceremonies. The result of the modern Polacca-type project below, where Route 87 comes in. Shungopavi has a new library, Maggie's told me. But I don't stop, even though I know she'd like to hear about it. I'm hungry. And the thought of the bread, cheese, and fruit in my basket palls. My mouth balks, my stomach blanches. I want something hot, spicy, and exotic. And I think I know where I can get it.

I lean forward, watching out the window, and suddenly I see it. A complex of chic, ultra-contemporary, pueblo-style buildings. The new Indian Cultural Center: motel, museum, gift shop, and restaurant. I turn in, my mouth watering. Traditional as well as Anglo food, the brochure said.

I park near the gift shop, and as I pass can't resist a quick step in. The room is filled with beauty begging to be possessed. Cases of jewelry and carved fetishes. Shelves of baskets and pottery. Walls of paintings and kachina dolls. Piles of rugs and saddle blankets. Racks of blouses and sashes. Boxes of moccasins and boots. I'm overwhelmed with a baser hunger.

I step up to a case. Trays and trays of rings, bracelets, pins, earrings, necklaces. Silver, gold, turquoise, coral, ebony, mother-of-pearl, lapis, ivory. Hopi overlay, Zuni channel, Navajo cluster. Old and new style, primitive craft and high art. I start picking. This, this, this.

Next to me, a plump, gray couple smacking of the Midwest hums and haws over a selection. To their other side is a teenage Hopi girl in a cheap Anglo dress with ruffles and lace, and long Navajo earrings, her hair wrapped in a straggling French twist. Her mascaraed eyes are narrow and crafty, her scarlet mouth set in the lines of inured resentment.

The woman paws through the trays in front of her, lifting a ring, trying it, putting it back. —Oh, I don't know— She bends, peers through the glass side. —How about that one?— The Hopi woman behind the counter stoops, points. —No. The one to the left— The Hopi woman points. —No. In front of it.

Couple and clerk are lost in the rows inside the case. The girl takes advantage of their distraction. Quick as a hawk she reaches and snatches a large turquoise ring. As she pockets it, her eyes meet mine. I see the challenge.

I quickly calculate my alternatives. I can turn her in. Then what? I can reach over, retrieve the ring from her pocket, and quietly return it. Will she fight me? I doubt it.

Or I can do nothing. I can tell myself this is none of my business and turn my back.

But it *is* my business. Behind the challenge in her eyes, I see something else: confusion, fear, vulnerability. Something that reminds me of Katelyn and Lindsay. Katelyn and Lindsay, who go to a private school paid for by their mother and father, live in a nine-room house with their own bedrooms, and enjoy closets and drawers full of tasteful clothing. Who have every opportunity and the confidence that they always will have.

This girl goes to government schools, where she also has been taught the values and skills of succeeding in the White society around her. While she comes back to a communal room of adobe and stone on an isolated mesa, with no money to buy the vestments of acceptance and little promise of getting it.

I walk out. There were many things in that shop I wanted. Things for me, and the girls, and Howie; for Maggie, Daddy, and Abby. I could have helped support Indian artisans, Indian livelihood, Indian culture.

By buying?

I've lost heart for lunching at the Cultural Center. As I drive away, I have one haunting regret. I wish I'd asked the girl, Do you realize you're stealing from your own people?

But no; young as she is, this girl is past caring. This is not her first shoplifting; she's too hardened and experienced. She's already placed herself outside her community. A community that believes that the essence of life is to have a "good heart." Which includes lack of materialism, freedom from greed, and honesty.

Let her keep the ring. In her pocket she carries the sorrow and shame of this nation.

I try to put her out of my mind, focus on my immediate surroundings. I don't want anything to ruin my memory of the mesas.

All around me I see signs of change, new buildings, new ruins. Elementary day schools located near the villages. An on-reservation hospital. An on-reservation high school. When we lived in Harden, teenagers were bused 120 or more miles a day to and from Winslow, Holbrook, or Harden. Others had to leave the reservation the whole nine months to attend government boarding schools, like the Phoenix Indian High School.

At the New Oraibi Community Center on Third Mesa, a banner across the front advertises the coming appearance of the Keams Canyon Rock Band. The picture shows teenage Hopi boys in brilliant blue satin shirts with red sashes. In the parking lot I pass a boy in a green team jacket with white lettering SECOND MESA HORNETS. A coal miner, probably from the controversial giant strip mine on Black Mesa, has decorated his hard hat with traditional Hopi and clan symbols. Prayer feathers, instead of a St. Christopher medal, hang from the rearview mirror of his pickup.

The bulletin board inside the Center announces a jackpot rodeo to be held on Third Mesa, aerobic dance sessions for women, a teen club. There are notices from the Hopi Housing Authority, and the Tribal Council. The Council is another source of dissension with Traditional village and religious leaders. They regard it generally as the puppet government of the U.S. Indian Bureau and not representative of the people, therefore not legitimate. I've come here in search of food, but there isn't even a lunch counter. My basket lunch is getting more and more attractive.

I drive on. Old Oraibi, the oldest continuously inhabited settlement in the country, looms up more desolate and forbidding than ever. I don't see a sign of life. In a hidden crevice at the base of the mesa are the bells, vestments, and chalices, the swords and armor, of the *padres* and *soldados*. The only evidence remaining of their oppression are the ruts carved in the mesa's sandstone top by the heavy church beams. The huge logs, dragged by Hopis from hills forty to a hundred miles away, were taken to rebuild their destroyed kivas. Then the walls, quarried and laid by Hopis, were razed to the foundation and carried away stone by stone, and the rubble scattered to the six directions.

And in an unknown gulch somewhere outside the village, covered by a layer of rock and three centuries of obliterating sand, lie the bones of the priests and soldiers.

It is not a time the Hopi like to speak of, a time of shame and sadness. The Spaniards had desecrated their sanctuaries, disrupted their ceremonies, taken their wives and daughters, and tried to destroy their way of life. Finally forced by the need to protect their homes and religion, the People of Peace were driven into killing.

No matter how hard I try, it seems I'm not going to be allowed to hold onto my feelings of joy and affirmation at First Mesa. I keep getting confronted with upsetting memories of the past and troubling questions about the future.

Even Hotevilla presents a confusion of conflicting contrasts. Small terraced gardens, irrigated by a spring just below the mesa's rim, stretch down the gentle slope. A gray-haired, red-bandeaued farmer digs moisture-robbing weeds with his broad-bladed Hopi hoe. A pickup loaded with laughing male youths tears past him and out onto the road ahead of me, leaving behind a wake of turbulent dust. In the village, TV antennas and power poles end abruptly, demarcating the new section from the old. Two boys play hoops at a homemade backboard just feet in front of an old kiva, its spindly ladder pointing toward the blazing noonday sun.

Hotevilla was established as the result of a quarrel among the Hopis over their relationship with the White man and his Christianity, resulting in distressing divisions of brothers, families, and clans.

It seems Johnny was right, Maasaw knew whereof he foretold.

The Navoti also prophesied roads in the sky, and vehicles that could move over the ground faster than deer. And of being able to talk to one another over great distances, through closed windows and doors. And of walking through darkness with light.

But, Maasaw said, you can survive these disturbances. If you stay together, you will gain not just life but good life. You will live forever, together with other people.

Oh, yeah, Maasaw? And just how do you propose they accomplish that?

The mesas are behind me. I've come down onto the low stretch of State Highway 264 between Hotevilla and Moenkopi. I approach the eroded white-, black-, and red-striped walls of Coal Canyon, my eye out for a picnic spot. I'm starving. According to legend, a Hopi girl leapt to her death off the cliffs here, and now she dances in the canyon on nights of the full moon. I imagine her. Black hair twisted in butterfly whorls, white maiden's blanket wrapped over her left shoulder, white deerskin moccasins spiralled thickly up her legs. Making her feet small and dainty as they silently lift and stamp, lift and stamp, turning her slowly in the luster of white light from the sky-filling orb above her.

But that's just the end of the story. Why did she jump? What would make a Hopi girl take her life? Suicide is not a Hopi thing. It had to be more than a rejecting lover. More than an unwanted pregnancy. The Hopi are accepting of illegitimate offspring, demanding only that the parents assume their responsibility. No, it had to be something uncommonly grievous.

I hear a whirring, a click click click, like the spinning of a bingo basket. I concentrate, waiting for the aligning numbers. They fall into place.

Perhaps she wasn't a despairing maiden at all. Perhaps the woman who haunts the canyon is the Jimson Weed Maiden, a trouble-maker with the power to make people insane.

Or the Outcast Woman, the ghost of a young woman in a white wedding robe who preys upon men, a creature of dreams and darkness.

I'm so surprised by these strange associations and why they should suddenly leap to mind, I keep right on driving, completely forgetting my picnic. Next thing I know, I'm approaching Moenkopi Wash.

I feel a sense of relief, a release from disquieting connections, as I slowly cross over the shifting bands of red-and-white sand, streaked with the ribbony paths of underground waters, and grooved with the channeled rush of recent downpours. There's a tightness in my throat, a greediness in my chest. I think of Maggie on our first trip to Flagstaff, leaning out the window, hair flapping like spaniel ears, gulping in the clean, cool air. I'm gulping with my eyes.

I know exactly where I'm going to lunch.

I check my rearview mirror, then swerve across the road onto a small outcrop of packed dirt. I grab my basket and thermos, and climb down to a slab of rock overhung by a shading ledge. The village is directly below me. I can see the villagers moving about, hear an occasional dog bark. The air carries the moist pungence of irrigation and wood smoke.

It's not on a mesa top and it's forty miles from the other villages, still Moenkopi is my favorite setting. The houses are mostly one-story, regularly grouped along the plateau ridge overlooking the wash and facing the crumbling cliffs opposite. There's more green here, clumps of mesquite, low cypress, and bunchgrasses. The fields stretch close behind the village, neatly plotted, divided here and there by post-and-barbed-wire fences. And boundaried by a curving line of willows, cottonwoods, and scrub bushes following the spring bed. Moenkopi, "the place where the water flows." And site of the most outrageous show I've ever witnessed. I grin just thinking about it.

SCENE 17

The day had gotten off to a bad start. We had left behind schedule and arrived late. Daddy was upset because the dance had already started, and Maggie was upset because he was upset and I was the cause. I was upset because I didn't want to be there; I'd wanted to stay with Casey and the gang, who were spending the day at Jack's Canyon. My last-ditch resistance had cost us precious time.

Daddy wouldn't drive into the village during the ceremonial, so he parked on an outcrop overlooking the village to wait for intermission. Maggie, who couldn't stand doing one thing while you could be doing two, pulled out the picnic hamper and we silently ate our breakfast of hard-boiled eggs, ham and cheese on rye, and bananas. A thermos of milk for me, coffee for Maggie and Daddy.

The undulating hum floating up to us on the soft morning air had an ethereal quality, a calming effect. We watched as the dancers filed out of the plaza into a small courtyard behind the houses and removed their masks, plopping down onto benches, wiping brows, sipping cups of water. The women followed, passing around baskets of fruit. The men nibbled apples and peaches, hunched over between their knees with slices of melon.

We shouldn't be watching this, Daddy said, and we hurried into the car. By the time we entered the village, our quills had been smoothed and we were talking.

But still I couldn't get involved in the dance. I was thinking about Casey, missing him, wondering if he was missing me. It was the Tasap Kachina, that much I remember, because he and the Navajo Maiden who dances alongside him are the Hopis' interpretation of their troublesome neighbors. But the dance was slow and monotonous, enlivened only here and there by a quickened sequence of intricate calls and turns. In between I drifted, visualizing Casey laughing and horsing around with the kids, fantasizing our future together, nursing my loneliness and longing. And my grievance with my unsympathetic parents.

So I don't remember exactly what interlude it was, except that it was afternoon, when I was suddenly jolted out of my dreamy doldrums by a burst of noise and activity. A group of outlandish characters had boisterously charged into the plaza, shoving and shouting, trying to trip or knock over one another, taking fighting stances, brandishing fists, threatening punches.

The crowd was delighted. So was Daddy, who'd been hoping we'd be treated to some clowns. He'd seen the *Koyemsi* or Mudheads on one of his trips without us. But these were the *Koshari*, the Hano clowns, also known as the striped clowns for the black-and-white stripes encircling their arms, legs, and bodies. They wore nothing else but a short-flapped, black breechclout with a bunched white cloth tied loosely around their middles, and a striped cap sprouting two tall horns tufted with dried corn husks.

The clowns had taken their argument to the audience, pushing and pulling, talking a mile a minute at the top of their lungs, each vying to be first to get out his side of the story; pointing fingers and name calling; looking hurt, aghast, outraged; turning supplicating hands and faces to the crowd, asking sympathy, and judgment in their favor. The crowd laughed and jeered at them.

Tiring of their quarrel, the clowns fall into a game of tag, chasing around the plaza, hooting and hollering, challenging one another with rude, coarse noises. Tag becomes leap frog, a straddled jumping over crouched backs, which ends in a rollicking jumble of arms and legs rolling and wrestling in the dust.

One clown attempts a headstand, another catches up a leg and makes a wobbling display of hopping and balancing on one foot, a third juggles two oranges. The crowd rewards them with prizes of food, which the clowns grab and gobble, stuffing mouths with whole rolls, dribbling chins and chests with watermelon, burping and belching. They then scamper around the plaza rubbing their bellies, begging for more, which they're mischievously given in great quantity, since according to the rules, they have to eat everything offered.

They're tossing beanbags among themselves and their audience, when a piercing Tarzan-like yell shatters the air. The clowns stumble back in astonishment, some literally bowled over onto their fannies, eyes wide, mouths agape in fear and wonder.

A short, stocky, round-bellied man stands on the rooftop of the house opposite the plaza from us. He's coated from brow to bare toes in a thin layer of sacred pink clay, his head wrapped in a clay-coated scarf stuck with spikes and curls from the corn plant, his groin cupped in a clay-coated loincloth. Other than that, he's dispensed with even the breechflap. I try not to stare at the enormous bulge of his crotch.

—Who is it?— Maggie whispers.

Daddy's clearly excited. —A Hopi Clown. A real treat. They don't often appear.

The clown steps to the edge of the roof with great dignity, and takes a commanding stance. Eyes rivet on him, breaths hold in abeyance. He raises his arms, lowers them, raises them again, as if to fly. And steps off the roof. The crowd releases its breath in one stunned gasp. With incredible agility and timing, the clown twists his body and at the last second grabs the roof edge. The crowd twitters nervously, feeling foolish in its relief. He dangles there, kicking and jerking, staring at the ground in terror. It's two stories down.

A second clown, similarly clay-caked and unclothed, saunters onto the plaza, takes one look at the roof, grabs his head in alarm, and rushes to his partner's rescue, jumping up and down beneath him. But his arms won't reach.

Clown Two dashes back to the alley, pantomimes a whistle, and waves on a third clown, who climbs over Clown Two's back onto his shoulders, and pushes Clown One—scrabbling and heaving, muscles straining—up the wall to safety. The crowd laughs and claps.

But now the problem remains as to how to get Clown One down. Clown Three is struck with inspiration. He ducks into the alleyway and returns dragging a large coil of rope, which, between them, the three clowns manage to secure and tautly string across the plaza to a rooftop with a ladder. It never occurs to any of them to carry over the ladder, which, of course, is part of the nonsense.

Clown One then prepares to tightrope walk. The crowd tenses again as he takes his first teetering steps, cries out as he slips and topples, laughs as he grasps the rope, slides down it, and ends bottomside-down, dangling by his hands and ankles, over the center of the plaza. Clowns Two and Three have great fun tickling and teasing him, swinging him back and forth, pushing him harder and higher, until he swings over and over the rope in wide, jerking arcs. He releases at just the right moment to tumble into their outstretched arms. The crowd laughs and claps vigorously as Clown One finally sets foot to ground.

He stands surveying his audience, legs spread, hands on hips, belly pushed out over his protruding pelvis. He spots a White woman in trim dress and white sunhat, perched stiffly on a camp stool, face averted, lips tight with distaste, eyes pinched with disapproval. He switches out a hip, lifts a limp wrist, and minces toward her, eyelids demurely lowered, mouth primly pursed. He stops directly in front of her, flipping his wide hips, fluttering a condescending hand, mimicking her with such bald but good-humored accuracy that even she has to finally give in and join the crowd in laughter.

The clown abruptly spins around and scowls at the sniggering Hopis, who immediately sober. He stalks up and down their ranks, singling out individuals, caricaturing their idiosyncrasies, making fun of unHopi ways, puncturing pretenses and vanities. He calls in the other clowns to act out little skits, which are clearly, even to an outsider, parodies of village life, spoofs of local gossip, satires lampooning group foibles and follies. When the clowns score a direct hit, the Hopis laugh raucously.

The clowns rest back, rocking on their heels, bouncing at the knees, nodding and looking immensely self-congratulatory. The central clown scratches his belly, grins, ventures lower, scratches his crotch, grins wider. The crowd quiets, grinning expectantly. He tucks a hand into his loincloth, explores, eyes rolling.

Maggie turns in alarm to Daddy, eyes signaling in my direction.

Daddy's tone holds a hint of humoring. —Oh I don't think it'll hurt her. It's all in good fun— But his smile doesn't reassure Maggie. She frowns.

I lean forward to confront her directly. Does she think I can't hear? —After all, Maggie, I'm almost sixteen— Her frown deepens. —What do you expect me to do? Cover my head?— Her mouth opens. —And if you're not careful, they're going to spot you as their next target— That does it. She snaps her mouth shut and abruptly turns back to the show, the picture of unperturbed, smiling interest. Which gets harder and harder for her to maintain.

The clown has finished with his fumbling and, flashing a sly leer, pokes out from the side of his pouch a long skinny green chili, wrinkled and hooked on the end. The crowd titters. The clown appraises his produce, shakes his head and, with a shrug, yanks it out and offers it to his partner. The second clown studies it, considers his sagging cloth, tries the pepper for size, then looking disgusted, throws it over his shoulder.

Clown One commences searching again and comes up with a second chili, long, thick, curved, and fiery red. This is much more to his liking. He holds it erectly in place and struts around, showing off his prize. The men chuckle openly, the women snicker behind hands. The clown prowls the crowd, picks out women, married matrons, and flicking his tongue or rolling it around his lips, thrusts at them obscenely. The women turn their heads, hide their eyes behind fans, pull scarves across their faces. But they're all giggling, even the young and unmarried.

I'm amazed, and overcome with embarrassment. I don't know which way to look; certainly not at Maggie. But as I watch, the Hopis' merriment seems strangely innocent, no dirty smirks, no knowing looks, no furtive glints or veiled darknesses. Just good healthy fun at a harmless joke. The clown's blatant lasciviousness provoking their laughter has demystified sex and defused it of its power and potential danger.

The clown swaggers to the center of the plaza, gesturing grandiosely to his waiting comrades about his prodigious endowment and prowess. The other two clowns slap their thighs, shake their heads, ooh and aah in wonderment. But as they admire, their bodies gradually slump, knees sag, faces droop, heads hang. Clown Two crosses his thighs to hide his inadequacy. Clown Three covers his with his hands.

Clown One falters in his braggadocio, regards his deflated friends, pats them sympathetically. Then with a reluctant last look, gallantly offers up his red chili.

Clown Two snatches and happily stuffs it into his loincloth. Clown One rummages again and comes out with two bell peppers, which he magnanimously presents to his other friend. Clown Three hefts their satisfying roundness, squeezing and nodding approval, then pops them into his pouch. Groins plumped and chests puffed, Clowns Two and Three pose proudly for the audience's appreciation of their new manhood.

But now Clown One's sac is empty. He considers it dejectedly, plucks at its limp folds. Then throwing out his arms, shrugging and grinning broadly—*c'est la vie*, what the hell—he turns and walks off the plaza. His buddies fall in beside him, arms around his shoulders. They're both a head taller but as they exit, it's his strong back our eyes follow.

Afterwards, on the way home, Daddy instructs us.

By acting the uncouth buffoon and burlesquing unadmirable qualities, the clown has provided not only comic relief but sugar-coated object lesson, and catharsis. To take on himself the taboos of his society and serve as judge and censor, this clown must be a member of one of the two most potent priest groups, a man of great stature among his people, revered for his service, wisdom, and piety. How else, Daddy laughs, could he get away with such profaneness?

But he doesn't escape uncastigated. During the clowns' performances, special kachina whippers often appear with switches of willow or yucca to flog them for their unseemly antics, as part of the symbolic purging of the whole community. Before returning to their homes and families, clowns, like the dancers, must undergo the ceremonial washing of hair and body. And to insure internal purification as well, both must take emetics every morning of the retreat and after the final dance. Their phenomenal strength and endurance, then, becomes spiritual.

SCENE 18

I fold up my lunch and leave my ledge with reluctance. But the air is cooling, a breeze has come up. And there are no Hopi Clowns to purge me. As Daddy said, they don't often appear.

I gas up at Tuba City. Two boys are buying an automobile battery to power their video entertainment. This strikes me as somehow symbolic, I'm not sure of exactly what, but since lunching at Moenkopi, everything's suddenly cumulating with the color and size of significance.

Something is stirring. Glimmerings. Intimations of connections. Not the disturbing connections of Coal Canyon; these are uplifting.

I drive west, toward the sun, now past zenith, body alert over the wheel.

My mind's working. I'm listening with a stiffened ear. A message is about to be delivered.

I turn south on State Highway 89, onto the section they call the Painted Desert Scenic Drive. A moonscape of crusty black-and-buff mounds and depressions, reminding me of the tailings and slag heaps around the copper mines in Southern Arizona. Completely barren. A wasteland of nature burnt to cinders and ashes. A graveyard of mountains crumbled to the dirt through which they once erupted. Ashes to ashes. Dust to dust.

The land of the unliving. The end of the world. A good place for a beginning.

I feel an igniting excitement.

I ease my foot on the accelerator as I approach Cameron, an excellent trading post and restaurant where I can get the Mexican food I've been craving, and pick up Indian gifts for the family. Then I put my foot down and buzz by.

An idea is sparking.

At the turnoff to the Grand Canyon, I vacillate a minute. I'd reserved a room at the Fred Harvey Lodge, planned to watch sunrise wake the slumbering walls into striations of purple, blue, and gold. Maybe take the mule train down and spend a night at the Phantom Ghost Ranch at the bottom. Watch sunset flame the towering sculptures into masses of orange and red, then extinguish them in blankets of blue and purple. But now I have a more pressing purpose. I drive on.

An idea is firing.

I pass Wupatki, a prehistoric community of over eight-hundred rooms, with ball courts, chambers, and towers of a sophisticated architecture denoting a highly advanced civilization. Abandoned now. In ruins. A national monument of fallen walls and broken artifacts, of only passing fancy to tourists. But a proving ground of continuing interest to archaeologists. A mounded stockpile of human debris and buried pits of garbage, to be dug up, sifted through, and speculated on. Like dried bones, to be picked over in gnawing search of telling flesh.

I push on, foot heavy on the pedal, hands gripping the steering wheel, body arrowed toward the glaring road, as if that'll get me there faster. I barely glance at the red top and black sides of Sunset Crater as I whizz past, regretting for only a moment the roping lava flows, slashing squeeze-ups, dripping ice caves, and steaming fumaroles I'll be missing and that used to fascinate me.

Like the cinder cone's compressed core, molten ore is roiling to the surface.

An idea has taken hold. I'm burning.

The Museum of Northern Arizona presents me my hardest decision. Daddy's old hangout. I'd like to walk its cool, beamed galleries again, linger over its exhibits, browse in its gift shop. Sit on a pine bench in the sunny innercourt, admiring the Indian rugs and blankets stretched across the white walls under the shaded overhang. Visualizing Frank with his cutting tools hunched over a cottonwood root. Thinking of Daddy and all I learned from him.

It was here Daddy guided me through my first lesson in the cycle of creation. In the museum's small front rooms, dioramas and bas-relief maps display the geological history of the Colorado Plateau: How the earth cooled and contracted, crinkling the crust into mountains, that eroded to a great plain. How the hot pent-up interior pushed for release, erupting volcanoes and tilting up great blocks of strata, that wore down to low hilly country. How the seas washed in and receded, forming floodplains and sand dunes. How glaciers covered the San Francisco Peaks then retreated, carving lake basins and valleys. How the Colorado River raged, cutting a mile-deep canyon, and subsided. And how the whole plateau was finally lifted 7,000 feet above sea level.

Trilobites evolved, then fish, then amphibians, then primitive reptiles, casts of their disintegrated bodies trapped between eras of sedimentary rock. Dinosaurs came, and left, leaving behind their skeletons and footprints. Great mammals— mammoth, ground sloth, prehistoric deer—roamed, then wandered off to extinction. Other animals arrived: bison, antelopes, mountain lions. And finally, humankind.

All the beauties of this land—the starknesses and majesties, the variegations of its plant and animal life—were accomplished by a persistent weathering and resurgence through the ups and downs of time. Old forms deteriorate, but in their remains, new ones arise.

It was a big learning for a fifteen-year-old, one I soon forgot. I'm glad to be reminded of it now as I slowly pass the museum, its field-stone walls and Spanish-tile roof tucked on a small sun-and-shade-splashed clearing amid a forest of tawny-barked ponderosa. In my mind's ear I hear the nearby creek as it tumbles over black basalt rocks through the wide brush-covered ravine. In my mind's nose I smell the sun-warmed pine sap and spicy needles.

But as much as I may want, I can't stop. I'm consumed.

My idea has arisen full-formed on the horizon.

I head toward it, hell-bent. Flagstaff is only two short miles down the hill. I turn in at the first motel advertising a vacancy, quickly register, drag in and dump my luggage, and dig out my notebook. Propped against the pillowed headboard, notebook braced on my bent thighs, I flip hurriedly through the pages of writing: Smokey's adventure, waiting for the next episode. But I'm impatient with it now.

I have bigger things in mind.

I stop at the first clean page, glance at my watch—two forty—and frantically start writing. I can't get the words down fast enough. I try to slow myself, so that when I go back I can decipher my writing.

The thoughts are all there, they found their form in the car. I just have to put them in order.

I write all afternoon. By six, I'm hungry. I finish off my bread and cheese with one hand while with the other I keep on writing. The going is slower now, harder. I puff thoughtfully on cigarettes, nibble grapes, go through the coffee, tea, and Sanka provided by the motel, with a little electric heating pot. Somewhere along the way, I turn on lights.

I finally put down the last word, stare blankly at it for a moment, then resolutely close the notebook and lay it on the bed beside me. I'm exhausted, aching all over. I close my eyes and slump into the pillows. But there's no hope of sleep. I'm all jazzed up, nerves jangling, brain still buzzing, from cigarettes, caffeine, and hours of intense thinking. I need to relax. I check my watch: ten twenty. The liquor stores will still be open. I grab my purse and, at the last minute, remember a sweater. Even in late June, the nights this high get chilly.

The sky surprises me. It's almost white with moonglow and glittering stars. Last time I saw it, it was sun-dazed blue. The cool twinkly brightness unknots my muscles, the fresh piney air clears my head. By the time I return, I'm ready to celebrate. I settle back on the bed with wine, cigarettes, and notebook, prepared to enjoy myself in a halo of self-congratulation.

I'm distraught. I can't believe what I'm reading. A preconscious dashing of notes, sketchy clues to an as-yet unexplored mystery. Little more than the wordy outline of a story.

After my first dismayed shock, I move wearily to the desk, shove aside the TV, lay out wine, cigarettes, and notebook, and resignedly plunk down in the stiff-backed chair. It's clear what I have to do. I dig in my heels for the real work.

Children are a tough audience. It can't be long, I'm dealing with short attention spans. But it can't be too short or they'll feel cheated. It can't be complex; I don't want to lose their interest by talking over their heads. On the other hand, it can't be simple; I don't want to insult their intelligence by talking down to them. The idea is to stretch their thinking, make them reach, without overchallenging. And I have adults to contend with, too: parents who will hopefully continue my story.

It's a tricky line to walk. I rewrite, teetering, living on crackers and peanut butter stocked up on at the liquor store. And despair and frenzy. I barely touch my wine, but I go through a pack of cigarettes.

I finish at four fifteen a.m. I pour a glass of wine and read it over, slowly, out loud. It's not good enough. Not nearly. But I can't do any better, at least not now. I've had it. I'm sick and tired of it. I toss it on the desk. I still have Thursday and Friday, I tell myself.

It's out of ill-humored determination to defeat defeat that I set my alarm for eight.

When it goes off, I burrow under my pillow, wanting to cry out, Please don't make me. But I don't know who I'm whining to. I doggedly shower and dress, fix my last packet of coffee, and take it out onto the cottage stoop. The moment the light hits me, I feel better. It's one of those rarefied high-mountain mornings where there seems to be no sky, only trembling space waiting to be filled.

For the first time, I take note of my lodgings. A string of rustic timber-and-shake cabins backed against a forest of pines and aspens. Decidedly run down. Seedy, would be Maggie's word. I wander into the patchy dark, crunching pine cones, listening to birds, and come out into a bright meadow vibrant with wildflowers: blues, pinks, purples, whites, yellows, a spike here and there of red. I stoop to identify, and am amazed how quickly the names come to me: larkspur, lobelia, fleabane, penstemon, columbine. Names Maggie taught me.

This was her special project, her contribution to our Hopi sabbatical: the collecting and cataloging of high-desert wildflowers. She guiltily plucked one flower and one leaf of each variety, fretting and fuming about people who picked indiscriminately and jeopardized the plants' propagation thus survival. She never took from the first plant, but rather, in the Hopi way, prayed to it, explaining her purpose, asking permission, and expressing thanks. Then went on to the second plant.

She pressed and preserved her specimens on ivory paper between plastic, labeling in her small precise handwriting the name, date, locality, and Indian use of each plant. She couldn't draw or paint, there was no artist in her, she ruefully confessed. But her leather-bound pages were as beautiful as any illustrated book.

By the time I finish my coffee and leave the meadow, I'm eager for the second half of my project.

List in hand, I'm on the streets of Flagstaff and outside the art store before it opens. And in less than an hour I'm back at the cabin with sketching pads, pencils, sable brushes, tubes of acrylic, three 14 x 20 blocks of 140 pound cold-pressed watercolor paper, and enough food, cigarettes, and wine to last me through the day and night. I lift the shades, pull back the curtains, open the door wide, and turn on all the lights, simulating as much as possible the lighting of the library. Then dragging desk and chair to the northern window and arranging my supplies, I commence to pretend I'm an illustrator.

In contrast to writing, the sketching starts hard then gets easier. I swirl outlines, spiral masses, trying to be rhythmically free and spontaneous, the way Abby taught me. I've planned twenty pictures, a daunting number, but simple single-subject compositions that won't be too demanding. I take a late lunch break, absently chew tostadas while I assess my lined-up products, mark changes, and start again. At last satisfied, I lightly transfer my first three sketches to the pebbled paper and, heart pounding, prepare to realize my ideas in color.

I work back and forth among the three blocks, wetting the first with broad horizontal strokes of clear water, then washing on loose areas of color; moving to the second, wetting and washing; on to the third. Then back to the first, with a smaller flat brush, to layer on patches of deeper, brighter color; to the second; then to the third. When the sheets are dry, I define my subject in black with a small pointed brush, cut off the pages, and repeat the process.

I miss the free-spirited flow and luminous transparency of watercolor. But I wasn't brave enough to take on its own-mindedness on this my first venture in years as an artist. The acrylic is less fluid, more opaque, less vibrant. But I have better control over it. I watch for the mistakes, the unanticipated blotches and wanderings, that will challenge me to creatively adjust my original idea to "use" these "accidents." The hallmark, Abby once told me, of the true watercolorist.

Besides, I haven't time to redo.

I get caught up, wetting, washing, layering, adjusting, defining. I forget my trepidation, my heart quiets, and at midnight, when I quit, I'm not the least tired. I may not be "true," and I'm certainly no Abby, but, surveying my accomplishments, I'm satisfied. They're clear and bright, cleanly defined so as to be recognizable at a distance, and fresh with unrefined energy. I sleep soundly and by eight I'm up and at it again.

I munch soggy burritos and cold tacos, sip cloudy instant coffee, smoke an occasional cigarette when there's reason for contemplative pause. The wine sits in its brown bag unopened.

At seven p.m., I fold my tents, load the car, and check out. By eight I'll be in Harden, by nine thirty I'll have had dinner, by ten I'll be in bed.

SCENE 19

I take my time, driving with one hand, elbow out the window, savoring the breeze in my hair. No need to rush now; I'm happily cooled and flattened. Not a bubbling bump or steaming vent on the surface, not a rumbling protest of the interior. The altitude declines steadily, the trees thin and fall back with the mountains, the road straightens. My mind merges with the twilight. And I find I'm thinking of Casey.

Yesterday was to have been my day in Oak Creek Canyon: Casey's and my place.

Our first trip, we brought Denny. To Slide Rock, a slippery trough carved into a steep incline of redrock where the creek becomes a channeled waterfall. Bathing suits and butts protected against the abrasive sandstone by cut-off Levis, our feet in old tennis shoes, we plummeted down—laughing and shrieking, the water rushing around us in sprays of sparkling light and blossoms of bursting white. To plunge into the swirling pool at the bottom, where the less adventurous or water-logged languorously posed on ledges and toppled slabs for suntans.

We stayed until our box of Levis gave out, then Casey fed us on hamburgers and root beer at a roadside A&W. But Denny still hadn't had enough. So Casey drove us to the white barnlike roller rink, where Denny and I, hand-in-hand, decorously circled, while Casey showed off for us in the center. He skated backwards, and on one foot, making figure eights, twirling. He was a natural athlete, had almost perfect control over his body.

Skiing at Humphreys Peak, he shooshed daredevil down the mountain, in Levis and wood skis with bearclaw bindings. While I, in fashionable stretch pants, with the latest in fibreglass skis and safety bindings, conservatively stem-christied. He watched my traversing descent grinning widely, sun glinting off his dark glasses, teeth white against his winter tan. Then he gave me lessons. He liked to instruct me, with much the same proprietary playfulness he did Denny. He was self-taught, I'd learned from professionals. But I obediently followed his every direction, listening to the husky brush of his voice, watching the expressive movements of his eyes and mouth, savoring the protective guidance of his hands, adoring the agile shifts of his body.

Our next trip to Oak Creek was for just the two of us. The night before, I'd packed a picnic lunch: tuna sandwiches, stuffed eggs, potato salad, chocolate cupcakes, and presweetened iced tea. I wanted to impress Casey with my culinary talents. I hadn't so much as boiled a potato before, and the preparing took me over four hours.

Casey located a secluded cove by the creek with a small sandy beach and deep pool banked by low-hanging trees and rounded boulders. The peace of the suspended air and soughing stream made us quiet. We played gently in the icy water, kissing and clinging, twisting and turning, entwined against the current. He pulled me close, wrapped his legs around mine, cupped my buttocks and pressed my pelvis into his. Ran his hands up and down my body, feeling the slick flesh of my exposed midriff, the goose-pimpled rise of my breasts. Then he pushed away and floated, eyes closed, mouth smiling softly, the stiff ridge of his groin outlined by the sun.

I languidly stroked downstream, to a large boulder that looked the perfect spot to sun. I reached to pull myself up—and suddenly felt Casey's hands grab mine, pinning my arms and dragging me slowly but forcefully back. Shhhhh. His breath was lulling in my ear, but I heard the warning. I looked up and saw the sinuous black line of a sunning water moccasin stretched across the white rock, right where I had been about to place my hands.

Casey had to carry me to the beach, I couldn't walk. He lowered my feet and held me for a long minute, lips pressed against my water-splattered crown, grip around me so fierce I was afraid I was going to pass out. When I finally had strength to support my own weight and look up, his eyes were pinched tight and his face was ashen.

We ate lunch, me drained and wistful, Casey subdued and thoughtful. We tried to joke about my "cooking." I refused to go back in the water. Sitting side-by-side, we quietly talked. Casey reviewed his plans for college, the money he'd saved, the scholarship he hoped to get. It was the first I'd heard about the sporting goods store he wanted to open, in a small up-and-coming town like Prescott.

He skipped pebbles across the water. We watched the rings widen.

Then he asked me to marry him.

We'd talked about it before, many times, but always in a light fantasizing sort of way, like teasingly testing the waters. Like kids playing house.

This was for real. A formal proposal from a serious young man willing to make a commitment now.

I said yes.

Then we made love on our beach towels and Maggie's checkered picnic cloth.

I'm watching the earth suck the last sip of light from the sky, thinking, Yes, that's right: We made love. Our few excursions before then, we'd had sex. The unlovely overheated strugglings of novices in the cramped quarters of a car searching for essential meaning in a basic drive.

But that day, for the first time, we made love.

He laid me back. I stared at the patches of light-diluted blue above the trees. He gently worked off my bathingsuit. I arched my back and lifted my hips to help him, watching the leaves shift in the breeze.

He explored and stroked my body, kissed my neck, my breasts and stomach, while I explored and stroked the sky.

He crouched over me, spread my thighs, but he didn't enter. He pressed against me then held, unmoving, insinuating his presence. I pressed back, reaching to grasp and encompass him.I could feel myself opening.

He slipped in slowly, by inches. I was no longer seeing the sky and trees; every sense was focused on that tantalizing gradual entry. There was a spot, deep, an aching hunger. I strained, my walls tightening, to pull him to it. My legs were shaking. He slid out, and started slowly in again. I pushed down hard, forcing his full penetration. The relief was so intense and the pain so sharp, my throat closed on it. He covered my cry with his mouth. I threw my arms and legs around him. He gripped my hips and stopped their movement. He held me still, then slowly began rocking. I raised to meet him, in small countering circles. The sky was in my head, the leaves were in my body, rippling faster and faster in the wind that was lifting and carrying me.

It was my first orgasm. I buried my face in Casey's shoulder and wept from the sweetness and surprise of it. Casey finished off with a flurry of thrusts, and came across my stomach. I gathered the milky fluid and rubbed it over my breasts and stomach. We lay in each other's arms, Casey's lips on my neck, my eyes on the sky, until the sun was low and we were goose-bumped.

The road narrows into darkness.

Do Howie and I make love? Yes, I guess we do. Of a quiet, restrained sort. No unseemly acts, unorthodox positions, or disturbing noises. Howie's not comfortably demonstrative. He can be grandly expressive across a legal desk or on a court floor, passionately eloquent. But outside professional confines, he's uneasy with strong emotion, unsure of his ability to handle it. Control is the operative word. Abandon is the frightening one.

We certainly don't enjoy unabashed sensuality, that joyous, free seeking after pleasure that gives pleasure, no orifice or fold unexplored. He's never known such intimacy. Neither have I. But I intuit it. And that intuition makes me want to cry.

I'm driving too fast, outrunning my headlights. I realize too late. The road swerves left, a low stone abutment looms up right, directly in front of me. I slam on my brakes, tires skidding on sand, squealing on asphalt, and come to a violent stop inches from disaster. Knuckles clenched white, heart pounding, I stare as my headlights slice through the swirling dust. The deep arroyo slips silently under the bridge. The spikes of the barbed-wire fence glint sharply. I know where I am.

I slump over the wheel and start to cry.

This shouldn't be happening.

Images fly at me, searings from the past, like firings from an alien spaceship.

This shouldn't happen.

Casey hunched over, hands in his back pockets, staring at the ground . . .

Reggie sitting on the embankment, arms locked around her knees, rocking and sobbing . . .

This shouldn't have happened.

She'd been so excited. They'd planned weeks ahead, Casey and the gang. A big blowout at Pine Lake. Reggie's last weekend. Her Going-Away Party.

They'd met at Betts's house and loaded into three cars, Casey, Les, and Freddy driving. Herren hadn't been invited but he showed up anyway, acting like he had been. So Betts said, What the hell, let him drive. That way she could get as drunk as she wanted. The trunks of the cars rode low with beer.

There'd been a feeling of high festivity: voices high, laughs loud, heads back, eyes bright, cheeks colored. Everyone had dressed especially. The girls in colorful dirndl skirts and low-cut peasant blouses, the guys in Levis, tooled boots, and fancy shirts. They stopped just outside town to break their first case, and by the time they got to the lake, everyone was happily half-smashed. Except Reggie; Casey still wouldn't let her drink.

Reggie'd been to Pine Lake before, with Casey, Denny, Scotty, and Catherine. Casey'd rowed their rented boat to the middle of the lake, where Scotty'd outfitted them with poles, and they'd spent the day laughing, swimming, and pulling in perch. Scotty taught her to bait her hook and play her line. Casey taught her to row. Catherine made a funny story out of meeting and marrying Scotty. Scotty talked about his job on the railroad, and made that funny, too. All three—Scotty, Casey, and Catherine—told jokes, most of them off-color.

Late in the afternoon, they rowed back to shore, where Scotty built a fire while Casey taught Reggie to clean fish. Then Catherine fried their catch in a heavy cast-iron skillet. Reggie didn't care much for fish, but as she sat in the evening air eating the thin crispy bodies dipped in egg and cornmeal, and served with coleslaw and sliced tomatoes, she thought nothing had ever tasted better.

Her first fishing trip. And last. Now she was returning for her first—and possibly last—down-and-out cowboy stomp.

The forest around the lake was dotted with cabins, private and rental, but the "town" itself was exactly four buildings: the boat-and-bait shop; the general store and post office; the hotel, bar and restaurant; and the dance hall. Saturday night was the *big* night, and it took some doing to find parking slots close enough for beer runs. The band was in full-swing, its brass and strings twining enticingly through the trees half a mile down the road. The dance floor was packed, a jam of twirling, strutting, stomping bodies.

Reggie wasn't sure she wanted to join the crush. It wasn't that she was worried any longer about dancing with Casey; they'd become smoothly practiced partners. She just didn't relish getting poked and bumped. She bruised easily. But Casey gave her no choice. Grabbing her up—elbows out, butt switching—he swayed her backwards into the fray, clearing with the best of them a spot to swing his "little lady."

That's what he'd been calling her ever since they'd tromped up the shaky plank steps onto the scuffed shellacked floor. It made her laugh. That and his sudden thick drawl. She knew this adaptive-ham side of him, the theatrical chameleon who changed colors according to his surroundings, then had to go one better. It was integral to his personality. And most of the time it delighted her. She'd watch him expand into role playing and get caught up in it, acting out her part to encourage his. It added intensity, an exhilaration that heightened. Most of the time. When he didn't go too far.

And tonight Casey was in rare form, dancing like a dust devil, whirling Reggie around in a flurry of spins, dips, and little half-turns and quick-steps he'd never tried before. He seemed driven by the music and a need to do justice to the occasion. Reckless in his laughter. Lavish in his attention. Extravagant in his mood. She'd never seen him higher. Or more handsome.

He glowed with a kind of wild magic. And it rubbed off on her. She didn't miss a step but rather lifted with him on a keened edge that anticipated his every move. She'd never felt more alive, or more beautiful. And for that vitalness of being, she would have followed him anywhere.

But for all Casey's efforts to shine on her and show her off as Starlett of the Stomp, she was not. The walls were lined with cowboys avidly eyeing cowgirls, ready to ride in, drop their lasso, and place their brand. Everyone danced, even Betts, whose light-footed, big-bodied heartiness seemed particularly popular with the older men. Even Janie, whose staid indifference seemed to reassure the younger and less seasoned or adventurous.

But it was Billie—hands on hips, chin cocked, eyes flashing—who was clearly Queen of the Crop. Her devil-may-care vivacity had them standing in line, cutting in, stumbling over themselves to get their hands on her and meet her challenge. She left them dazed and panting, crotches turgid. She twirled on, from one man to the next, laughing and daring. Billie, who knew better than anyone how to play this hilarious hungry game.

The sign said No Drinking or Smoking on Premises, so there was a steady flow in and out as dancers fueled up and fagged out, a few hitting the bar next door but most swigging out of stashed bottles. Casey made frequent trips to the car, dragging Reggie with him. She was beginning to worry about his drinking. But she didn't want to say or do anything that might ruin this special evening. So she waited quietly to the side while Casey finished kidding around and cussing with whoever else happened to be out.

Something was brewing, she heard sharp clips of anger, saw pointed toe-jabs at the ground. But when she asked, Casey refused to answer.

—Please, Casey— She tugged at his sleeve, sought his eyes. —Don't start trouble tonight.

He touched her nose softly. —Are you my little lady?

—You know I am.

He grinned. His finger slipped to her lips. —Then leave some things to the man.

And he picked her up and swung her around and around, leaving her giddy and laughing.

Casey's spirits stayed on the high track, but his body began to slow down. He was sweating, and once in a while he missed a step. They started dancing less and milling around more.

He stopped to wipe his brow. —Come on, let's take a break.

—We just had one.

He laughed. —That was an hour ago.

Reggie didn't want to argue. But she also didn't want Casey to make another beer run. She looked at the crowd between them and the door. It had gotten thicker, louder, and drunker.

—Let's just rest here— She pulled him toward two chairs. —I'm too tired to fight that crowd.

—Awww— he tried to tease her into compliance. —That's what you have me for. I'm a football player, remember? I'll run interference.

She shook her head. —I'm staying here. You can go without me.

—What? And leave my little lady alone with all these rowdies? I'd come back and find you'd been snatched up and carried away. No sir. I'm not letting you out of my sight.

Reggie sat down obstinately.

—All right— Casey looked around. —Come on then— He grabbed her hands and yanked her out of the chair.

—What?

—Come on— He tugged her toward one of the windows, a large glassless opening shuttered from above by a plywood flap now propped up by side supports. —Just follow me.

He dropped her hands and without a backward look, braced himself on the window edge, swung over, and dropped out of sight.

Reggie screamed and ran to look down. Casey was just springing up, arms out —Ta *tah*— grinning widely. —Okay. Now it's your turn.

Reggie stared. —Are you crazy?— The dance hall was elevated on stilts to allow for when the lake flooded. —It's got to be over ten feet down.

—*I* did it.

—I'm a girl.

—Oh? I thought you didn't believe in a double standard.

She grinned. —I'll get dirty.

—No you won't— He smiled, his most beguiling, and held out his arms. —I'll catch you.

—You *are* crazy— She was gauging the drop.

—Crazy about my girl. Crazy in love. Crazy with the strength love gives me.

Reggie grimaced a grin at him, shaking her head, climbed onto the sill, and jumped.

Casey caught her, staggered backwards, and went down on his back, holding Reggie on top of him, out of the dust.

—See? Didn't I tell you I'd catch you?

She was laughing, arms around his neck. —You're a crazy son-of-a-bitch.

He kissed her —Don't swear— and stumbled up, lowering her feet to the ground, hands around her waist.

—That's why you never have to be afraid— She looked up, his eyes held hers. —I'll always be there to catch you.

The gang had agreed to meet at eleven. The band didn't quit until twelve but Reggie knew it would take time to get everyone rounded up. The drive back was an hour and a half, in the dark maybe longer. And she absolutely had to be home by two.

Her parents had granted her a special late night in honor of her party. But she'd known they'd never consent to Pine Lake; they weren't ignorant of Saturday-night dance-hall stomps. So she'd told them the party was at Betts's house.

Maggie'd sensed something. Reggie'd overheard her in the kitchen with Daddy. —Do you think we ought to call? Just to be sure there are going to be adults?

Reggie's heart had flip-flopped, her mind raced to spin out covering webs. But Daddy had saved her.

—We have to trust, Meg.

And Reggie's conscience had writhed with shame.

She couldn't be late, no matter what.

Now she anxiously checked her watch as the gang casually straggled in, rummaged in the trunks for beer, looked ready to wander off again. Eleven twenty, and they still weren't all in. She saw Curt and Walt staggering around in front of the bar and, with a quick word, sent Betts to fetch them. Then she spotted Faye outside the dance hall, pinned against the wall by an amorous cowboy. She couldn't send Billie, she was too bombed; she'd never come back. And she didn't want to send Casey; he'd been officiously ordering everyone around but at least he was keeping them corralled. So she went herself.

By the time she got the pelvis-grinding cowboy peeled off and Faye peevishly back at the cars, whatever was brewing had reached a head. Casey, backed up by Walt and Curt and loosely circled by the gang, was squared-off against Freddy.

—You're a goddamn poacher, Herren. A stinking squatter, staking out on other guys' territory. Pushing in where you're not wanted. You may think you're hot shit 'cause your daddy has money and you drive a big car. But you're not. No one likes you.

Freddy was belligerently holding his ground. —Oh yeah? Sez you and who else?

Walt's chin jerked up. —Sez me— He'd been pugnaciously waiting his turn. —I say you're a big-headed small-pricked sonofabitch, Herren, who wouldn't know where to stick it if he could find it.

—And I say fuck you.

Casey went rigid, took a stalking stride past Walt toward Freddy, arms stiff, fists clenched.

—What'd you say to my buddy?

For the slightest second, Freddy wavered, pupils dominated by the whites. He knew what was coming but there was no way out, he was in too far. He tossed back his head, eyes narrowed, smile defiant.

—I said Fuck You, Colter.

Casey drew back his arm and threw his punch with the full weight and momentum of his body, landing it squarely under Freddy's lifted jaw and sprawling him flat to the ground.

Walt and Curt stepped up, stood over him, shoulders hunched, fists bunching, throats growling satisfaction. The crew crowded in, waiting for Freddy to rise. When he didn't, Betts went down on her knees beside him.

—Jesus christ. He's out cold. His head hit a rock.

—Shit.

—What'da we do now?

—Get water.

—Where?

—At the lake, you stupid sonofabitch— Billie had abruptly sobered.

—Get him a beer.

—Get Les's bottle.

Casey hovered at Freddy's feet, hands still loosely clenched.

Betts looked up. —Nice work, Colter— Her face was pinched with disgust.

Casey shifted uneasily, looked around.

The group had drifted off, arguing in low heated voices, damning or defending Casey, casting worried looks toward Freddy.

Casey shouted after them. —Where's Les's bottle?— Demanding, as if he was tired of waiting.

—With Les— A flat voice.

Casey scanned the dark. —Les!

His call bounced across the lake and sank into the pines, sharp and alone in the sudden quiet. The band had stopped playing.

—Forget Les— Another flat voice. —He left over an hour ago.

—With that hot tamale he was pawing all night.

—They're probably shacked up at the nearest motel.

—If her husband hasn't caught up with 'em.

A rude laugh.

Casey stood stock-still.

—You mean there are only two cars?

—Good for you.

—Now you get it, Cowboy.

—*Shit*— Casey kicked dust for a minute, then resolutely spun on his heels and swaggered back to Freddy.

—Hey, fella, how ya doing?— All ebullient smiles and buddily concern.

Freddy was on his feet, looking dazed, one arm over Betts's broad shoulders, the other braced by Reggie.

—How the hell you think he's doing?— Betts's eyes snapped. —He's got a lump the size of an egg on the back of his head.

But Casey wasn't hearing, he'd lost his smile. He was tugging at Reggie.

—Come on over here, Honey. He doesn't need you anymore. He can stand on his own two feet.

Reggie slapped at him. —Get away from me, Casey. Haven't you done enough for one night?

—Awww now, Honey— He tried to reach for her again. She shoved.

—Just get me out of here! That's all I ask. Just get me home, Casey!

—Okay, Honey. Right this very minute. That's exactly what I'm doing— He turned to Freddy. —How about it, buddy? You think you're ready to drive?

Freddy attempted a smile. —Sure. What the hell. Just a little bump— He laughed shakily, took his arms from around Betts and Reggie.

Casey held out a hand, Freddy ignored it and started toward his car. His knees buckled. Betts rushed up and caught him.

—Shit— Freddy shook his head groggily. —Just a little disoriented, I guess— He stood straight, looked around —Just gotta get my bearings— and did his best to walk a steady path around his car, leaning a hand against it once or twice.

He fumbled in his pockets, lost his balance. Betts grabbed and righted him.

—Okay, Herren, give me the keys— She held out her hand.

—No, no. I'm fine— He laughed —See?— raised his arms straight out at his sides. Bent them and touched his nose with his index fingers.

—Please! Please!— Reggie was frantically tugging at Betts, pulling on Casey. —Can't we just get into the cars?

She turned to the waiting others. —Please, you guys. Just get in the cars. It's almost twelve thirty!

Freddy opened his door and slid under the wheel. Casey slammed the door behind him, then surveyed the hovering cluster.

—Okay, everyone, you heard the little lady. Let's load up— He beamed. —Who's going with Herren?— His beam broadened. —And who's going with me?

It was a loaded moment, strained with silence. Feet shuffled, faces furtively checked one another. Billie stepped up, chin cocked.

—I wouldn't drive with you, Colter, if you were the last chariot to Heaven. You'd flog the goddamn horses to death before we ever got there— She started around Freddy's car, stopped and turned. —You're an asshole, you know that, Colter? A flaming asshole.

Faye wouldn't leave Billie. She climbed in next to Freddy, then Billie flounced in beside her. Freddy started his engine.

Walt wouldn't leave Casey; he headed for Casey's car. Curt wouldn't leave Walt. Trixie went with Curt.

Betts saw Reggie's misery. —I'm going with Reggie.

That left the backseat of Freddy's car for Glenn, Ruthie, and Janie.

They made Freddy lead out.

—Remember, Herren, we're right behind you.

—Just keep our headlights in your mirror.

Betts shook her head. —I don't like this.

But after the first thirty, toughest, most dangerous miles, they were convinced Freddy was all right. He was negotiating curves smoothly, accelerating evenly, staying on his side of the line. They all relaxed. Except Reggie.

—What'll I tell my parents? Why will I say I'm late?

Curt, Walt, and Casey helped her make up excuses, getting fanciful, waxing farcical, trying to hold onto fun. The good, possibly believable ones, Betts and Trixie tested out, plying questions, pushing limits, pursuing fine points, the way parents would. Until they finally got tired of it and let Reggie fret on her own.

It didn't matter, she knew. The best they could come up with would be a flimsy, shabby lie.

She checked her watch for the twentieth time, calculating it against the speedometer.

—My god. We'll never make it!— Her hand clutched Betts's wrist.

Casey smiled confidently —Sure we will— fingers tapping the dashboard in time with the country-western music. He started singing, winsomely, mock-mournfully, with cracking falsetto, glancing over at Reggie. *I've never seen a night so long, When time goes crawlin' by. The moon just went behind a cloud, To hide its face and cry.*

When Reggie refused to acknowledge him, he checked the rearview mirror. —Hey, Walt. You still alive back there? How about helping me and Hank out? *The silence of a fallin' star, Lights up the purple sky. And as I wonder where you are, I'm so lonesome I could cry.*

But Walt was asleep.

Curt was necking with Trixie.

Betts was sullenly smoking.

Casey finally gave up and they drove in silence.

Reggie stared at the road, head dull from the hum of the engine, eyes dry from counting down miles as they were sucked into their headbeams and swallowed under the car . . .

. . . *long lonely highway black asphalt two lanes white line dividing stretching on forever telephone poles lone felled pines merging into horizon into nothing . . .*

Betts suddenly jerked alert. —Shit.

Reggie started. —What?

—Where're Herren's tail lights?

Casey craned forward. —He's pulled ahead of us.

—Sonofabitch— Walt lurched upright.

Curt and Trixie stopped necking.

—I'm doing sixty, he must be doing at least sixty-five.

—He's outrunning his headlights.

Casey put his foot to the gas. Leaning forward, they searched the dark.

Suddenly, two spotlights probed the night ahead.

—What's that?

—Slow down!

A low stone wall blazed up in their headlights. Casey slammed on his brakes, threw the wheel, and came to a sliding stop sideways across the road.

—Jesus christ.

They climbed out.

—Oh god.

—*Shit!*

—Oh god oh god oh god . . .

Freddy's shiny black sedan had hit the abutment head on, reared up, and plunged over, landing with its left side wedged against the arroyo bank, nose up, lights sheering off cockeyed, right front door sprung, country-western music blaring out across the night.

They scrabbled down the embankment into the swirling dust. Freddy was pinned by the steering wheel against the trapped left door, blood oozing from his nose and forehead. The windshield on his side was smashed. Faye was sprawled a few yards up the arroyo, arm beneath her, leg bent at an unnatural angle, the side of her face slammed against a rock.

Billie was caught in the barbed-wire fence, like a sparrow impaled by a shrike, wings outspread, downy head thrown back, flesh torn and bleeding, feathers softly ruffling in the wind.

Ruthie, Janie, and Glenn were toppled on top of one another in the backseat, too stunned and frightened to yet react, but otherwise unharmed. Casey and Curt wrenched the door open and pulled them out. Glenn stared unseeing into the distance, arms heavy at his sides, while Ruthie clung to him, face buried in his shirt. Janie wandered off in search of solitary solace, which she found in the black arch under the bridge.

Walt kept talking to Faye. Betts held Billie's hand and stroked her hair. Curt and Trixie went for help. Casey stood helplessly watching, hands stuffed in his back pockets, shoulders hunched, jaw muscles silently working. Reggie rocked and sobbed.

—For christ's sake. Turn off that goddamn radio!— Walt's anger was jagged with despair.

Casey walked to the car, looked in, shook his head, and backed off. —Leave it on for Freddy.

Freddy suffered a brain concussion, cracked ribs, and fractured sternum. Faye's leg and shoulder were broken, and she almost lost an eye. Billie had multiple contusions, internal injuries, and a broken neck. The volunteer ambulance took too long. The hospital was inadequate. Before they could airlift her to Phoenix, Billie died.

SCENE 20

I climb out of the car, slide down the embankment, and stagger toward the fence, tears streaking my face and neck. I glare at the single white cross. I hate it. With all the viciousness in me. I yank it up, crack it across my knee, snap it with my hands, and strew the pieces in six directions. Billie deserved better than this.

As I stumble back toward the car, my toe stubs against a hard object, sends it clinking in front of me. I stare, then stoop. A fractured triangle of pinkish sandstone. I pick it up, scrape my fingernail across its soft surface, leaving a chalky white line. The desert is littered with them. Flat impressionable fragments, like pottery shards waiting to be matched and fitted into a restored pattern.

I start collecting, choosing those the size of a child's hand. When my arms are full, I load them in the trunk and return for more.

At the Travelodge, I layer them carefully in my picnic basket, and put the basket by my clothes for tomorrow. Everything else stays packed. Then I take out my story. I leaf through quickly, marking pages with the decisive changes I determined out there on the desert. Then I reread slowly, to make final revisions and polish. I feel no joy, no accomplishment. Only a sense of deep commitment, a weighted wanting to fulfill debts too-long outstanding.

I lie in the dark finally allowing myself to remember the rest of that violent night, forcing myself to face it for what it was: a break in two threads of my life.

Maggie and Daddy were waiting; the sheriff's department had called the parents. They stood in the middle of the living room, blinds up, door wide, every light on. The sky was graying with dawn. The glare bouncing off the white walls and their shadowed, anxious faces made them and the room seem otherworldly. Like encapsulated space travellers momentarily hovering above earth, staring out of their bright cube at a strangeling. I wouldn't let Casey come in with me; I had to face this alone.

I could see from their hollow eyes and drawn faces how distressed they were.

I could also see, from their sharp jaws and tight mouths, that they were angry. Daddy, in the grip of strong emotion, goes quiet. Maggie gets voluble. She gave me one quick checkover to reassure herself I was all right, then let loose, furious in her relief that it hadn't been me.

But from the way she raged she made me feel that she wished it had been, that it would have been better for all of us.

She and Daddy were thoroughly disgusted with me, sick with shame and disappointment. I had betrayed them. Looked them in the eye and bald-facedly lied. I had deliberately gone against their judgment, flouted their authority, disregarded their feelings and the wisdom of their experience. They could never trust me again. I was willful, arrogant, self-centered, and duplicitous, determined to have my own way no matter what.

And look what it had cost: If I had refused to go to Pine Lake, insisted on having the party at Betts's house, Billie would be alive.

She had more to say, all along the same line, but I stopped listening. I waited, stonily respectful, eyes never leaving her face, until she wore out and ordered me to my room.

I walked down the hall, limbs stiff and unreal, like a wooden soldier, quietly closed the door, and lay down on my bed, fully clothed, in the garments of the living. While I pulled over my head the bedcover shroud of the dead.

Maggie tried to undo it the next day, explaining her state of emotion, apologizing for not saying things quite the way she meant, for perhaps being too strong. But my unblinking silence unnerved her, she floundered, and turned to Daddy. He was distressed, I could see that, as he judiciously hunted for soothing words to heal over Maggie's previous cutting ones. But his discomfort, like Maggie's, meant nothing. I sat patiently, studying their eyes and mouths, until they were finished.

They waited for my response. Daddy searched my face, trying to get into my eyes. I closed them off. —All right— he finally sighed. —I guess you can go back to your room— I dutifully obeyed.

—Please, Reggie— Maggie called after me. —Just think about what we've said.

I couldn't think about anything else.

The funeral was closed-casket. The ten of us—Betts, Janie, Ruthie, Glenn, Walt, Curt, Trixie, Casey and I, and Les—were seated together specially, in the second row behind Billie's family. That Les should be included with us seemed an affront and filled me with dark resentment; I was harboring the suspicion he was the one really to blame. The other mourners fixed on us a kind of fascinated attention. We were the survivors, lighted with the grace of life, still dusted with the closeness of death. Like a row of votive candles flaming in a cave, staving off inevitable dark.

I hadn't talked to anyone, not even Betts or Casey, since that night; Maggie and Daddy were keeping close guard. I came together again with my friends in that funeral parlor. We were strangers. We couldn't talk. We couldn't make eye contact. We sat side-by-side lost to each other in our isolated thoughts.

When the time came, I watched them rise one by one and pass before the coffin, each placing a single white flower. I saw Trixie criss-cross herself and go down on her knees, saw Curt gently lift and drag her away. Saw Betts spread her broad hands on the coffin top, heard her silent prayer.

But when Casey stood and reached for me, I knew I couldn't. That cold, hard, hermetically sealed, traitorously gleaming box had nothing to do with Billie. I pushed his hand away and looked in the other direction. He went up without me.

I stared at the white rose waiting in my lap, heard the slow shuffle of feet, the occasional muffled word, the scuff of my friends as they returned. But I couldn't go up there. I wished someone would take my hand, tell me it was all right. But I knew it wasn't. There was something wrong with me. Something terrible.

I stumbled out with the other mourners, vaguely aware that Casey was beside me. The sudden dazzle of light blinded me. I stopped on the stoop, dazed and disoriented. I saw Maggie and Daddy on the sidewalk below, waiting for me. Catherine and Scotty stood a few feet behind and to the side. I started down the steps, gaining momentum, at a run by the time I reached the bottom. I clutched out a hand, Catherine opened her arms, I crashed into them, face crushed into her shoulder. And cried, uncontrollably, for the first time since that night.

Catherine held me, patted. Soothed and crooned. —It's not your fault, Reggie. She knew!

She looked up at Casey, hunched beside me, head low, eyes squinched, mouth twisting. —It's no one's fault— She stretched out a hand, pulled Casey to her. —It just happened.

We huddled against her. —Death can't be explained— Her eyes caressed us. —Neither can life— She stroked Casey's hair, my cheek. —We just have to make the most of it.

I wanted to believe. I searched her face, trying to find my conviction. But it was no use. I knew: I was responsible for Billie's death.

I felt Catherine stiffen, saw her lips and eyes tighten, her look directed over my shoulder. I didn't have to turn around to know who was there.

I reluctantly pulled away, fingers clutching, clinging to her arm, dragging along her sleeve. Then let myself be led away by Maggie and Daddy.

I didn't see Casey again. We left the next morning; we'd already delayed our departure to attend Billie's service. Casey called to ask if he could come over, but Maggie wouldn't let him. Then Catherine called. I heard Maggie explain how worried she and Daddy were about me, my zombi-like state, my rigid control, my refusal to eat or talk. Delayed shock, they thought. She was sure Catherine understood; they couldn't risk anymore upset, anything emotional.

Catherine understood. Maggie covered the receiver and repeated to Daddy: Catherine suggested that perhaps leaving the boy I loved without so much as a good-bye would be quite upsetting. More emotional perhaps than a few parting words.

Maggie and Daddy finally agreed to let Casey talk to me.

There wasn't much to say.

I love you.

I love you.

You'll always be my girl.

There'll never be anyone but you.

Don't forget that.

You're all I'll ever want.

Don't forget that either.

I'm a one-man woman.

I'll write.

I'll write, too. Every day.

Think of me.

Always.

We'll be together.

Soon. . . .

It took three days on the road, half the way to Boston, before I could speak again to my parents. But it wasn't the same as before. I wasn't the same.

I lost Billie that night.

I also lost my mother.

I could forget. But I couldn't forgive.

SCENE 21

I wake before the alarm goes off. I'm a frazzled stringmop; dingy, wiped-up and wrung-out. I seem to have aged overnight. There are circles under my eyes, lines around my mouth, creases in my forehead and a dent between my brows.

Story Time is to begin at ten thirty. I'd checked with Dorothy from Flagstaff, told her I'd be there by ten. I arrive at nine, the time the library opens. Dorothy's surprised, but immediately drops everything to help me. She's excited; they're expecting a large crowd. They've advertised over the radio, in the newspaper, sent flyers home from school.

I rub my forehead. —How many do you think? Fifty?

—Oh, at least!

It suddenly hits me with a shock that Betts might show up with her children. Maybe Trixie with her boys, Ruthie with Latonya. I don't know why this never occurred to me. Too caught up in the glow of starring again in Story Time? Perhaps. But, I now realize, once I headed for Hopi Land, I left Harden behind me, cut myself free from treacherous false memories and those attached to them.

I think fast. If any of the girls should show up, I'll simply tell them I stopped over on my way back to Boston. Just for Story Time. Dorothy had originally invited my mother, to honor her. But she'd had to stay in San Francisco with my father. I'm her stand-in. Flimsy. But I can pad it, fancy it up.

I nod, dully assess my space, pull the rocker into the nook, turn it around to face the outer room, set my basket and folder beside it.

Dorothy's fluttering, anticipating my every move, clapping her hands, talking a mile a minute. I can't take it. I force myself to smile, try to relate, but it's sapping my energy. And I have precious little.

I put my hand on her arm. —I'm sorry, Dorothy. I don't mean to seem unappreciative. But I really do need time alone.

—Oh. Oh, of course you do— She laughs. —Like an actress going over her lines, getting ready to go on stage— She motions toward her desk —I'll just finish up what I was doing— hesitates —You're sure there's nothing?

—No, no, I'm fine.

—If you need anything— she backs away —I'll be right over here.

I'm aware of her now and then, peeking at me. But I'm too busy, going through my story, memorizing, rehearsing.

The Hopi had no written language until recently. They preserved and carried their history in memory. The oral passing-on of these legends and myths, mothers to daughters, uncles to nephews, is an important part of a youth's initiation into tribe and clan, and integral to the kiva ceremonies. I'm not going to read my story. I'm going to tell it. In the Hopi way.

At one point, Dorothy ducks back in. —I'm sorry, Reggie. I hate to disturb you. But I forgot just one thing. When I introduce you, is there anything special you'd like me to say?

I pull myself from the pages. —Yes— I look at her. —Tell them I'm the daughter of the librarian Margaret Harrington Patterson and the anthropologist Arthur Claredon Patterson, and the granddaughter of the artist Abigail Claredon Patterson. Who are responsible for today's story.

Her eyes widen, her mouth rounds.

—And tell them it's dedicated to Billie Franks. Who lived right here in Harden. She smiles moistly. —That's lovely, Reggie. I wish they could be here.

I smile back, finally a true smile. —They are.

I sit quietly in my rocker and watch my audience slowly gather. Children, ranging in age, I'm guessing, from four to twelve. Mothers, in their twenties and thirties. Grandmothers, the mothers back then. I scan these older faces, looking for familiar features. A few return my smile. Do they know me? They have a better chance at me than I have at them; I'm the only one in this chair. Would they recognize me on the street?

Dorothy guides the children into places on the floor. For the adults, it's standing room only; they form a long back row. We wait for late-comers. I hold my breath. But no Betts, Trixie, or Ruthie. Then Dorothy steps up. Mothers *shoosh*, children quiet.

—Today, ladies and gentlemen, young and older, we are privileged to have with us Story Time's *first* storyteller. She is none other than the daughter of Margaret Harrington Patterson, well-known to all of you as the librarian and generous benefactress responsible for our wonderful children's nook, and the originator of Story Time.

—She is also the daughter of the social anthropologist Arthur Claredon Patterson, author of, among other books and articles, the highly acclaimed *Hear Us, Tawa: Hopi Music and Dance,* which is right over there on our shelf.

—And she is the granddaughter of the colorful Boston painter Abigail Claredon Patterson.

—She would like to credit these three people, who have been so influential in her life, for today's story. And she would like to dedicate it to Billie Franks, who was born, lived, and died right here in Harden.

—And now ladies and gentlemen— she turns toward me with a flourish —the original storyteller of Story Time— I hear the fanfare. —*Regina Patterson Kendall.*

Dorothy has her own flare for drama.

My audience claps enthusiastically, faces eager and smiling, full of ready acceptance.

Just like old times.

I take a deep breath. —Good morning, boys and girls, mothers and grandmothers. It's good to be back— and I find I mean it.

Suddenly, I'm bursting with smiles.

—Today I have a special story. One no one has heard before. It's about a little boy named Billie. A Hopi boy.

I scan the young faces. —How many of you know who the Hopi are?— I raise my arm encouragingly. Most look blank, a few lift hands timidly. I reward them with radiance. —Good for you!— I make eye contact with one of the older, braver-looking boys. —Why don't you tell us. Who are the Hopi?

The boy grins proudly. —Indians!

—Yes! That's right— I beam on him. —The Hopis are a tribe of Native Americans who live right up there— I gesture north —just sixty miles away, one short hour from you. In Hopiland.

—So you can say Billie is almost your next-door neighbor. And like your neighbor, Billie is very much like you. He goes to school, plays ball, likes video games. But in some ways, Billie is very different from you. That is because the Hopis live in a special way, which I would like to tell you about. And that is why my story today is called— I flourish high my title page —*Billie of the Hopi Way.*

The children, and adults, study Billie's three-quarter profile, chin cocked, eyes crinkled, as he smiles into the sun. Looking for all the world like a young black-haired, brown-skinned Billie Franks.

A strip has been taped across the top of the sheet to correct the title, which before last night read *Donny of the Hopi Way.* The manuscript has been marked with the same correction.

I slip the title page to the bottom of the pile on my lap and arm myself with the next two pictures.

—Billie lives on a flat-topped mountain called a mesa— I pass the picture slowly. Their heads turn with it. They make me smile.

—In a flat-topped village called a pueblo. The houses are called pueblos, too— I give them time to absorb pueblo and mesa.

—There are houses and stores right here in Harden that look like pueblos. How many of you have seen them?— Many hands go up. I smile, nod.

—But there is one thing in Billie's pueblo you won't find here in Harden. And that is a kiva— I brandish high my kiva. —A kiva is a large, round, underground room where the men and older boys, like you— I smile at one of the older boys, he pulls tall —go to learn how to follow the teachings of their gods. Just as you do when you go to Sunday School and church to learn about *your* God— I see a mother frown. —So a kiva is a little like an underground church.

She's still frowning.

—If you think of the pueblo and its fields as the body of the Hopi Way of Life, then the kiva is its heart.

I try not to look at the frowning mother.

—Billie isn't old enough yet to go into the kiva. He's only ten. How many of you are ten?— Several hands go up. —But when he is old enough, Billie will have special lessons, and he'll learn special songs and dances. Then he'll put on a special costume. Like you do if you're an altar boy or member of the choir— In spite of myself, I glance at the frowning mother. Her disapproval has deepened to a scowl. —Only Billie's costume will look something like this— I hold up my Hemis Kachina. The mother bristles. What is the problem here? Is she offended by the analogies? —Then he'll sing and dance in a long line with his uncles and cousins, to send the Hopis' thanks to the gods and ask them for their blessings. Just as you and your family do when you sing hymns and say prayers.

The mother pushes into the sitting group, grabs up an arm, and marches away with her prospective altar- or choirboy.

I'm totally nonplussed. I sit stone-still, holding up my Hemis Kachina.

In all my careful planning, it never occurred to me that what I was doing might be objectionable.

A youngster in the front twists to stare after the departing couple. —Where's Andrew going?

—Shhhh

—Mommy, where's Andrew—

—To the bathroom.

—No he isn't, his mom just took him out the door— We hear the thunk of the door.

—Be quiet!— A girl in jeans and red T shirt has risen on her knees and is glowering at him. —I want to hear the story.

Her voice carries angry authority. The crowd settles down. I pull myself together and wait for their attention, looking coolly confident, as if nothing at all has happened. But as I lower the Hemis I was so proud of, I find my hand shaking. I try to keep the tremor from climbing my arm to my voice.

I tense my body and smile.

—Now, the Hopis have lived in this part of the world for many, many years. Over a thousand, and that's a lot of years. Longer than any other people have been here.

—And before that they lived in three other worlds. Yes! Believe it or not, this is not the Hopis' first but their *fourth* world— I tick off three and hold up four fingers.

—And they came to this Fourth World for a very special purpose: To learn to be true humans.

I catch a face watching me intently; a woman with mannishly cut gray hair. My insides shrink. Another dissenter?

—Because, you see, in the Third World before this, The People didn't do as Tawa, the Sun Spirit and Great Creator of All, told them— I hold up Tawa, watching the grandmother. —"Forget all evil," Tawa said. "Be People of Peace, and live in harmony with Mother Earth and all her plants and creatures."

—For that is the *soul* of the Hopi Way.

The grandmother smiles and nods grimly. I feel smally encouraged.

—But instead, the people became greedy, lazy, and quarrelsome. So they had to start over in a new world.

I take a breath.

—Now, in the Third World, the people were just The People. Some were light-skinned, like you and me, and some were the color of Mother Earth, like Billie. But they all lived together as brothers.

I sense tension.

—But as The People climbed through the doorway in the sky, they were met by Maasaw, Ruler of the Fourth World.

As I hold up my Hopi climbing the bamboo reed, then Maasaw, I assess my audience. The children are studying the pictures, the mothers are studying the children, the grandmother is studying the mothers.

I forge ahead.

—Maasaw divided The People into tribes. A tribe is something like a very big family. Then he gave each tribe a name to call itself, a different language to speak, and a different direction to follow. But before the tribes started out, Maasaw said to the Hopi: "A time will come when strangers will take over your land and try to rule you. They will want you to give up your way of life and live as they do."

Yes. There is definitely tension. And it's increasing.

—"But," Maasaw warned, "you must not fight the strangers. You must remain People of Peace and wait for The One who is to deliver you."

I concentrate on the young faces. —Deliver means to rescue or free— They look back, wide-eyed but still with me. Thank you, Maasaw.

—Now when they heard this, the Hopis were greatly frightened. They looked at one another in wonder— I look around in wonder.

—"And who," the leader asked, "is this One to be?"

—Then Maasaw answered. "On a certain day, in some distant time, a person whose name is not yet known will come from the direction of the rising sun. To bring friendship, harmony, and good fortune to the Hopi."

I brave a look at the mothers and grandmothers.

—"And this person shall be Pahana, your long-lost White Brother."

I feel the tension ease.

I smile back at the children. —Can you say that? Pa-ha-na. Good! Pahana. The Hopis' long-lost white brother.

I take another breath. I'm making it. I'm going to make it.

But I'm short on pictures for this section. I try to make my voice the captivating force. I go for drama.

—But now the Hopis were worried. "When the White Brother comes," they wanted to know, "how will we know he is the True Pahana and not a wicked person who will destroy our way of life and scatter our people?"

I ignore the back row.

—And Maasaw said, "Yes, that is true. You must be sure of the True Pahana."

—So Maasaw picked up a small flat stone and carved on it the picture of a man. Then he broke the tablet in two and gave the half with the head of the man to the White People, and the half with the body to the Hopi. Then he said: "When the special Pahana arrives, let him bring with him this piece of stone. If it fits together with the Hopis' piece and the broken tablet again becomes whole, the Hopi will know he is the True Pahana. The brown and white brothers will be together and their lives will become one. As they were once long ago."

The children stare, some blank, some quizzical, many grinning, amused by my play with face and voice.

I grin back. Then reach into my basket and hold up a triangle of sandstone.

—What do you think this is?

They pull straight, squint at it.

—Does it look like anything in the story?

A girl with a ponytail, one of my brighter listeners, pipes up. —It's like that rock. The one the man in the spotted mask drew the picture on.

I dazzle her with a smile. —Yes. That's it exactly!— She darts prissy sidewise glances, smiling smugly. —This is just like the stone Maasaw gave the Hopi and White People.— The others eye her enviously.

—Now, I want you all to stand— They struggle to their feet, twisting and stretching. —Because I have something for you— They rivet attention on me.

I throw open the basket.

—Maasaw has sent these to you— They crane to see.

I load my arms with rocks. Dorothy steps up, questioning with her eyebrows.

I nod. She loads her arms, too. We pass out the flat reddish sandstone.

—Maasaw wants each of you to have a stone. For a very special reason. Which I'm going to tell you about in just a minute.

They accept their stones, assessing the others'.

—Does everyone have a stone?— They nod. —All right, are you ready?— They nod. —I want you to listen very carefully.

I look at them intently, they stand motionless. I lower my voice, they lean toward me.

—When you get home, Maasaw wants you to draw a picture. He wants you to get something strong and sharp, like a nail or a stick— I hold up my stick. —Then he wants you to carve on your stone a picture of your face and head. Like this.

I demonstrate, scratching my sandstone with the outlines of a spikey-haired, kewpie-faced head, then pass it before the children.

—See? Do you think you can do that?— They nod.

—All right. Tell me again. When I get home, what am I going to do?— I speak slowly, mouthing deliberately, leading them with me in stumbling chorus. —I'm going to draw a picture on my stone of my face and head.

—Good! Now let's all sit down again. While I finish Billie's story.

They sit, clutching their fist-sized slabs. I love their avid attention, their fascination with my eyes and mouth, their young impressionableness. The adults seem relaxed now too. Thank you, Tawa.

I exhale a sigh of relief and pick up my sandstone rock.

—So. The tribes went their separate ways. And it came to happen just as Maasaw said it would: The Hopis found their home up on the mesas. They built their pueblos and planted their fields. The strangers came to overrun and rule them. And the troubles for the Hopis began.

—The Hopis waited for the White Brother to deliver them. But he didn't come. And so their troubles went on. And on and on. Until now they are Billie's troubles.

I show them Billie again. He's no longer smiling.

—Billie loves his family. Just as you love yours. But he's worried for them.

—Billie's father Frank is a very important man, a village chief. It is Frank's job to lead his people according to the laws Maasaw gave the Hopis. Frank believes his people should live simply, farm their land, and do their dances. Just as they've been doing for years and years and years.

—Frank believes in the old ways.

—Roy, Frank's brother and Billie's uncle, is also important. He's a member of the group set up by the United States government to make decisions for the Hopi.

Roy thinks the old ways are too hard. He thinks electricity, and running water, and television sets, and houses off the mesas will make life easier for the Hopi.

—Roy believes in the new ways.

—But Frank says the White Man's new ways will disturb the Hopis' old ways, and the people will become lazy, greedy, and quarrelsome. Just as they did in the Third World.

I'm refusing to look at the back row.

—So the two brothers argue. Sometimes they don't even speak. Which, Billie knows, is not right for People of Peace. And this makes Billie unhappy.

I lower my pictures of Frank and Roy, and raise Robert. My young listeners perk at the sight of the boy in bright blue shirt and red sash, holding a guitar.

—Billie's brother Robert agrees with Uncle Roy. Robert plays in a rock band. When he finishes high school, Robert wants to get a job off the reservation, just like Uncle Roy, and make a lot of money and drive a shiny car. He doesn't want to spend time in the kiva.

—This upsets Billie's and Robert's grandfather Johnny. Johnny is a high priest, a man of great wisdom and good heart. Like the minister or priest of your church— I don't give a damn who reacts how now, I have to do this. —Johnny knows how important it is for his people to keep their promise to Tawa the Great Creator and live with Hopi honor. But if the young men don't come home to learn their lessons in the kiva, there can be no songs and dances. The Hopis' prayers won't be heard, the gods won't send rain, the crops won't grow, and the Hopi Way of Life, like the corn stalks and melon vines, will wither away and die.

It's too much. My pictures of withered stalks and wilted vines mean nothing to the children. I've lost the little ones. They're looking around, fidgeting with their clothes and fingers. The older ones are drifting.

I speak louder, with more animation.

—Johnny tries to talk to Robert about this, but Robert won't listen. He just laughs at his grandfather and calls him old-fashioned.

—This makes Billie unhappy. For it is not right to laugh at and talk back to your parents and grandparents.

I grab up my picture of Frances and hold it in front of my face, to block out the mother checking her watch.

—Frances, Billie's sister, agrees with Roy and Robert. But instead of arguing like Roy or laughing like Robert, Frances is silently angry.

The surly face of Frances, thankfully, recaptures interest.

—Frances worked very hard in school. She thought because she did well, she would sit at a desk in an air-conditioned office, where she could use her skill with words and numbers. Just like you like to feel good when you spell a word correctly or get the right answer in math. Frances wanted to earn a pay check, buy pretty clothes, and live in a nice apartment. But when she tried, she couldn't get a job. So she had to come back to the mesa. Where now she has little to do but help her mother grind corn and make piki bread.

My picture of Frances on her knees over a metate, mano in hand, pike rolls beside her, is too foreign and too detailed. I should have known better.

I drop Frances to the floor.

—Billie has seen Frances take things from the trading post, rings and pins she didn't pay for. He is afraid Frances is going to get into trouble. And this makes him unhappy.

I flourish high Nancy. Whose stoicism doesn't call for a flourish.

—Billie would like to talk to his mother about this. But Nancy already has too much to worry about. She works hard to take care of her family, help the men in the kiva, and still have time to make her pottery. And now her sister Zelda, who is a school teacher, is telling Nancy she must join a woman's group to learn to be her own free person.

I find myself working on the women, probing their eyes, exploring their faces. I pull myself back to the children, but my vision stays split, one eye still on the women.

—This also makes Billie unhappy because he loves his mother just the way she is, and doesn't want to lose her.

—The only person Billie can really talk to is his great-grandfather.

It's my second-to-last picture. I try not to panic.

—Jimmy is over eighty and going blind. But every day of good weather, Jimmy walks down the mesa-side to tend the family crops. And when he can, Billie goes with him, to help hoe and weed. And while he works, Billie tells his great-grandfather about his worries. And this makes Billie feel better because he knows Jimmy understands.

—But although Billie's great-grandfather understands his great-grandson's feelings, he doesn't understand his words. Because Billie speaks only English, and Jimmy knows only Hopi.

—And this makes Billie sad.

I'm no longer worried about my audience, I have only my feelings.

—So more and more, Billie stays alone, sitting and thinking. He understands now he is no longer Billie of the Hopi Way. He has become Billie of the Divided Way.

—And this makes him very unhappy.

I hold up my picture of Billie, facing the rising sun.

—That is why, each morning, Billie goes to the edge of the mesa, watching toward the rising sun. He is waiting for the return of the lost White Brother. He is hoping he will come before it's too late.

I hold up my etched rock.

—And that is why you must always carry Maasaw's stone with you. For one of these days you may meet Billie. And when you do, you will match your stone to his. If they fit together and the tablet again becomes whole, Billie will know you are The One: The True Pahana he has been waiting for.

I lower rock and picture and sit quietly, looking at the children. They look back, uncertain: Is she finished? Is she really finished? Dorothy decides I am. She steps up and vigorously starts clapping. My audience joins in, not so vigorously.

The children look around for mothers, struggle to their feet. I watch faces. A few of the mothers smile as they collect their children and turn to leave. Two mouth "Thank you," the others drift out without a word or look.

The mannish grandmother curtly nods with what I take as approval. Then shoving her daughter ahead of her, and yanking her grandson by his arm, she pushes out through the crowd. A broad mind and strong will of few words, I gather.

As for the children, I'm forgotten as soon as my story's ended. Except for the bright little girl with the saucy ponytail, who stands to the side regarding me curiously. I smile, she flounces her body, flashes a grin, and races after her mother.

No one comes up. No one says, How wonderful, Reggie.

I lay my story on the basket and slowly rise, leaving the empty chair rocking woodenly behind me. I hear Dorothy at the door, chattering brightly, thanking her brood for coming, reminding them of upcoming events. Then I hear the door close, then silence.

—Reggie? . . . Reggie? Where are you?

She finds me behind the shelves, crying.

—*Reggie.* Whatever's the matter?

I shake my head, a sob catches my throat.

She reaches in her pocket, hands me a handkerchief, lace-edged and smelling of perfume. It makes me smile.

I wipe my eyes.

—Oh god, Dorothy.

—It was *wonderful.*

—No it wasn't. It was awful, a total failure— I gulp back a fresh gush of tears.

She pats me. —You're just having after-show letdown.

I snuffle. —Did you see their faces? They couldn't come near me.

—They were overwhelmed, that's all. They didn't know what to say.

—They were angry. And embarrassed. For *me*.

—Don't be silly. I know my children and parents. They were sincerely impressed— She grins. —It just wasn't what they were expecting— I look at her. —They thought they were going to get *The Biggest Bear*.

I snort. But I'm touched. Twenty years and Dorothy still remembers. —Yeah. And instead they got *The Biggest Bore*.

Dorothy faces me sternly. —It was *brave*— I shrug. But I like the word. —You made them think— I pull away from the shelves.

Dorothy gives my arm a last bracing squeeze and bounces off for her purse, full of airy cheer. —Let's face it; it's time somebody retired that old bear. He's nothing but an escapee from an outmoded zoo.

I giggle, blow my nose. —More likely, a refugee from some ecological study.

Dorothy's waiting at the door. —Now. How about some lunch? As we say in these parts, I'm so hungry I could eat a horse and chase the rider.

I give my nose a last swipe, wad Dorothy's handkerchief, and stuff it in my purse. I know it can never be as we expected. I understand: Expectations court disappointment.

I give up and give in. I'm laughing as, arm-in-arm, Dorothy and I trip out to the car.

She takes me for a special treat to La Descansada. Thankfully, the interior is as lovely as I remember. The gardens are at their height, bursting with gladiolus, delphinium, and roses. The hollyhock are ten feet tall.

We linger longer than I'd wanted while I fill her in on Maggie and Daddy, Lindsay, Katelyn and Howie, answering all her questions, giving the bright side. It's after two by the time we get back to the library. I quickly grab up my basket and manuscript. We make emotional good-byes. I give Dorothy the title page to my story, with Billie's cocked-chin smile.

As I leave the city limits, I pass the empty squad car. I wonder where Deputy No-Dick is now.

Still dancing with Billie I'm hoping.

I head east on U.S. 40, foot heavy on the gas. I have no time now for the scenic, no kicks on Route 66. I'm staying strictly with the fastest and most direct, Ike's interstates all the way. I've studied the map, carefully calculated time and mileage. If I average sixty-five miles an hour, I can be there by Monday afternoon.

I should be excited. But my depression these last eighteen hours has been too heavy and deep-delving to shake easily, even given my brief respite with Dorothy.

As with my last leave-taking of Harden, Billie is going with me.

SCENE 22

I cried almost nonstop that first day out of Harden. If it hadn't been for Catherine, I wouldn't have been able to do even that. I couldn't eat. I couldn't sleep. Maggie and Daddy kept trying to draw me out. But I was completely closed off.

The second day I cried only half the time, but I started retching up bitter bile. I finally let Maggie coax me into forcing down some ice cream, simply in an effort to soothe my seared inner lining.

The third day I was no longer crying. But the black box I was locked in was sealed tight. I managed to keep down a bowl of Cream of Wheat for breakfast, and cottage cheese with fruit at lunch. I guess Daddy saw this as an encouraging sign, because suddenly, out of nowhere, while Maggie was driving, he started talking.

He told me a story.

It seems a young man of Oraibi wanted to know about death. He wanted to know where the dead went and what happened to them. He went down to where the dead were buried and asked them his questions, but no one answered. He asked his father, and his father said: "What we have buried in the earth is only the stalk. The breath has gone elsewhere and lives on."

But the young man was not satisfied. "How can you know this for sure?" he said. "No one has ever returned from the land of the dead. This is only what you have been told." And the father had to admit this was true.

So the young man continued to brood.

One day, out of his thoughts, an Ancient One came to him. This ancient one gave the boy medicine to stop his breath and make him sleep, so his spirit could depart his body. The father thought his son dead. So he had his sister wash the boy's hair in yucca suds to purify and prepare him for his journey. Then he dressed him in the clothing of the dead and buried him.

The young man traveled to Maski, the Land of the Dead. There he was met by a priest, who led him along the Trail of Death. The boy saw dead spirits, naked or in clothing of cactus, pulling heavy loads with only a bowstring across their brows, the string cutting into their bleeding flesh. They were going slowly, slowly, allowed only one step a year, and only one kernel of corn and one drop of water to sustain them, because in life they had done things that were not good.

The boy came to a fiery canyon and saw spirits thrown into the flames, where they writhed but were not consumed. The priest said, "These are persons whose evil deeds were so great they couldn't be forgiven."

As they went along, they passed a group of children playing in a field. When they saw the young man, the children ran away in horror, crying, "Oh, no, a living one is here. The smell of his body is too much."

"Why am I so horrible to them?" the young man asked.

"We here have discarded our bodies," the priest said, "and left them back where we were living. To us, the bodies of the undead are not clean. We look upon you here just as you, back in the land of the living, look upon the dead."

Then the children were sorry for their rudeness and brought the young man a melon. They gathered around him and laughed as he ate because he was hungry for the substance, while in the Land of Maski they eat only the spirit of the food.

At last they came to the end of the trail, where the young man saw a beautiful village gleaming white in the pure sun, against a brilliant blue sky. As far as the eye could see stretched fields of flowers, where people strolled, gathering bouquets. Others rested on benches along the houses, faces smiling, turned toward the sun. A young woman sat at a worktable singing while she smoothed clay coils into a pot. The only sound was her high clear voice.

"This is the pueblo of those who have lived good lives," the priest said.

It had now come time for the young man to return to the living.

"Do not forget Maski," the priest told him, "the land where the spirits live. When you get back, make prayer sticks to remind the living of us. In return, we will send Cloud People to water your fields."

Then the priest blessed and bid the boy good-bye.

"Do not forget the past."

So at last the young man knew for certain: When the dry stalk of the body goes into the earth, it stays there and the flesh falls away. But the breath of life takes the trail to the west, toward the shores of the setting sun.

And now he also knew it was true, what the old people say, that the clouds that come from the west are a gift from the dead ones in Maski. They are Hopi ancestors who themselves once prayed for rain.

But when the young man got back to the land of the living, he was met by Spider Grandmother, who said, "You cannot go back to your home the way you are. You are contaminated with death. You must be purified."

Then she prepared a large earthen tub of secret herbs and scalding water, and made the young man get into it. There his skin was boiled. Then she inserted the thorn of a cactus through his scalp and twisted it until the young man's skin split at the bottom of his feet and she could pull it off over his head. Then she threw the skin into the fire and burned it.

"There," she said. "Now the contamination of the Land of the Dead has been removed. You may return to the living."

And so the young man went home. But he returned with new understanding: When man dies, he wakes. When the body ceases, the soul begins. There is no dividing line between life and death. They are one and the same.

I didn't say anything for a while after Daddy finished; I was thinking about the story and what it had to do with Billie. But that's when I started speaking again. I wanted to talk about death. But Billie's death was too painful. Daddy's telling of Hopi death gave me a safe way in.

I asked him a question, I don't remember what. But I saw him and Maggie take deep breaths, exchange looks, then sag flat, as if punctured by relief.

But I remember Daddy's answer.

When a Hopi dies, he explained, he is buried facing east, for that is where the sun rises, and the direction of new life. It is also the direction from which the True Pahana will come, which is also a rebirth. And the body is placed in a sitting position, so that when the right time comes, the spirit will be able to rise quickly.

Then, like the sun, the spirit will travel west to return to the Underworld, where it will be reborn and emerge again, up the bamboo reed, the umbilical cord, through the sipaapuni, the navel of the earth, into the Upperworld.

This Hopi explanation gave me hope, and a way to live with my grief. I saw Billie amid a field of flowers, bathed by the western sun, waiting to be born again and return to us.

Now as I travel east, I try to imagine her that way again. But all I can see are sun-gold clouds and fields of orange flowers. Is it possible Billie has already made her return journey?

Harden is behind me and I know, like Billie, I won't be going back again. But as I watch the sun slip behind the horizon I feel, at last, peaceful acceptance.

I spend the night outside Albuquerque. A truck-stop dinner: liver with onions and bacon, mashed potatoes on the side, tapioca pudding for dessert. No wine before or after; I have to be fresh for the long drive ahead. I don't want to arrive with shadowed, blood-shot eyes.

But I have a hard time getting to sleep. My mind's working overtime, busy fulfilling its own requirements. Next thing I know, I'm writing.

CHAPTER ?

Smokey read the news clipping for the hundred-and-tenth time—once for each lousy day she'd been in this lousy town—and laughed out loud, bitterly, sardonically.

What a joke. What a sublime double switch. For all her careful planning and calculations, she'd never foreseen this outcome. In all her dangerous maneuverings and clever machinations, she'd never once anticipated this risk.

What a mockery.

The Bureau and law authorities had assumed, as she'd intended, that the assassin's bullet had been meant for Smokey Lorraine, disguised as Ann Carter, a look-alike for Glory Colter. It had been the end of Smokey's testifying. It had also been the end of her life among the living. She'd been placed in the Witness Protection Program and whisked out of sight and sound to a safety so remote and barren even God had forsaken it.

She laughed again. So here she was back in Harden. Where she swore she'd never be caught again. Not even dead.

Casey had been so proud of himself. He'd thought it sheer inspiration—returning Smokey to her childhood home—where she could recapture her youth and promise, before she went so sadly, badly wrong. She could start over, he said, have the second chance she'd begged him for, the new life she wanted free of the mob. He thought he was looking out for her best interests. Doing her a favor.

"No one," he said, "would think of finding Smokey Lorraine in Harden."

Not even Smokey Lorraine.

She paced the cheap sculpted carpet, her long legs trim in white slacks, her painted toenails vivid in white thongs, her mascaraed eyes and frosted lips finely outlined. At least here she could be a platinum blonde again; small consolation. Her embroidered Mexican overblouse she'd purchased on a sneak trip to Albuquerque. Her turquoise earrings, bracelets, and rings she'd picked up on a sneak trip to Cameron.

She was waiting for Casey. His first visit since her relocation.

Her dislocation.

She hated her new house, a small white aluminum-siding ranch with black trim and window awnings that looked just like a mobile home, stuck on a cul-de-sac, with no entry, no decent dining room, and marigolds around the mailbox.

Marigolds, for christ's sake.

"What's wrong with marigolds," Casey had asked.

"They stink."

"So what?" he'd laughed. "They keep away the bugs."

She hadn't thought his pun funny.

And she didn't think he was doing her any favor.

She kicked the blue-and-green tweed couch. She hated her new life. Little Denny and Les were two blocks away, with their grandmother and grandfather, where she could be with them every day. Take them shopping, on little outings: roller skating, bowling, swimming, picnics out at Jack's Canyon. Where, Casey instructed, she could practice being their mother, an eventuality Smokey was finding increasingly repulsive.

Janice, Casey's sister, and her husband and four kids lived on the north side of town, in a modern split-level near the new elementary school and hospital. Smokey was expected to join them for dinner every Sunday, along with Denny and Les and Casey's parents, after they'd all gone to mass. So she could get used to being part of a family, Casey had further instructed. Something she knew nothing, and cared even less, about.

She'd kicked around—abandoned by her mother, left to take care of an often-absent but adoring alcoholic father—and she'd done just fine. She still had her cache of money. For all the good that was doing her.

She didn't get her five million. She grinned. Not that she'd expected she would. But she got from Vinnie what she really wanted.

And they didn't get Vinnie. She grinned again. Not that she'd wanted them to. No sir, old Vinnie was still out there somewhere, probably at the casino, having the time of his life. Business as usual for Vinnie.

And if she knew her man, Vinnie knew she was still out there somewhere, too, *not* having the time of her life. Out of business for Smokey.

Was he looking for her, waiting for her to pop up again like a bad penny, ready to cash in on her as he had before; as she'd let him; as she'd cashed in on him? Bad penny though he knew her to be, she'd been lucky for Vinnie, and he'd done her more than a few return favors. They were good partners, a good team, using each other to get what they wanted, which was the same thing. And they'd had fun playing the game together, winning, sharing their gains. They understood each other.

Was Vinnie ready, she wondered, to consider a new partnership? A different kind of challenge? He was thirty-eight, past prime for a hit man, pushing his luck. With his looks and education, and the casino money behind him, he could do whatever he wanted. It was time to go legitimate. Or at least on the face of it. And Vinnie was smart enough to know that.

As a high-rolling, power-brokering professional, he'd need a high-class, inner-salon hostess who was wise in the manipulation of men, money, and influence. Someone who had no compunctions about using her feminine wiles to help him get what he was after. And Vinnie knew that, too.

She'd set him up to get rid of Glory, and he'd gone for it, hook, line, and sinker. But Vinnie wouldn't be holding that against her. Of that she was sure. No, he'd be laughing, enjoying her little joke, applauding her cleverness, her unscrupulousness. She'd beat him at his own game, at his tables. He'd be waiting to win back his bet and even the score. He'd be waiting for the next throw.

He'd kill her for five million; he'd keep her alive for ten. Smokey had no doubt about her capabilities. She'd be worth at least that to him. Which Vinnie also knew.

A shiny new red sports car pulled up at the curb. Casey's effort to overcome grief and meet his widower's life with a bright face.

Smokey stuffed the news article into the drawer of the side table and rushed to the door, yanking it open before Casey had a chance to ring the tinny bell.

"Oh, god, Casey—" she flung herself at him. "I'm so glad to see you!"

Casey was not all hugs and kisses. He stood stiff, arms limp at his sides, while Smokey clung to him. She slid a quick look at his face. He was not smiling. She didn't understand this cold distance, but she did understand she had to break through it quickly.

She grabbed his hand. "Come in—where I can greet you properly." She dazzled him with a smile, laughed with quivering emotion. "I don't want to shock the neighbors." He let her pull him into the room.

She threw her arms around him, pressed her body against his. "Oh you feel so good." Lavished his face with kisses. "I've missed you so." Buried her face in his neck. "I've been so lonely." And started to cry, tears wetting his skin, breasts heaving against his chest.

She could feel him begin to respond. His body relented. His arms reluctantly went around her.

"I love you, Casey," she sobbed, hands gripping his shirt, eyes imploring. "Don't ever leave me."

"No." He was looking over her head. "I won't."

She pulled back from his woodenness. "Are you all right?" Her eyes searched his face. "No. Of course you're not. How insensitive of me." She gripped his arm. "Forgive me." She touched his cheek. "I was just so happy."

He removed her hand from his face.

"I've resigned from the Bureau." His tone was as flat as his expression.

She dropped her hand from his arm. "You've what?"

"I'm to be relieved as soon as I finish my current cases."

Smokey took a step back. "But why? You love the Bureau, Casey. It's your whole life."

Casey's eyes were hard on hers, his lips a thin bitter line. "I'm not fit anymore to serve as a special agent. I've lost the right to carry the badge."

Smokey's senses warned her not to pursue this. She faltered, backed away toward the couch. "But what . . . what are you going to do?"

"Open a sporting goods store."

She stopped in her tracks. "A sporting goods store?" Her voice failed to a whisper. "Where?"

"Here."

"Oh no."

"And why not?" Casey was watching her closely. "It's a perfect location, close to all kinds of recreation. We can supply the schools. Sell roller blades and bikes."

Smokey's pulse was rapid in her throat, her breathing shallow.

Casey's eyes met and held hers with challenge. "This is our home town. My parents are here, and my sister. The kids can grow up with their cousins. We'll have kids of our own, maybe two or three more." He smiled, without warmth or humor. "I think five's a nice round number. Harden's a good place to raise a family."

Smokey stepped back, shaking her head. "I can't, Casey."

His eyes narrowed. "You can't what?"

"I can't live in Harden."

"Oh but I think you can."

Smokey's hands fluttered. "I'll die here."

Casey laughed, short and harsh. "You're already dead. Remember? Conveniently in pieces at the bottom of the Atlantic Ocean."

Alarm bells went off all over Smokey. She turned away. Her shoulders hunched pathetically. Her voice choked miserably. "And maybe that's where you wish I'd stayed. I've been nothing but trouble for you."

Casey softened slightly. "No. But I think it's time we had a little talk."

Smokey's head lifted. "About what?"

"About you, Smokey. And the truth." Her body stiffened. "If we're going to be husband and wife, there can be no lies between us."

Her shoulders straightened. "There aren't."

"I'm not so sure of that."

"You know everything."

"Yes. So I thought. And then I started going back over the trials. I kept coming across little things, things that didn't quite add up, or added up differently. I decided I'd better do some checking. I wanted to know exactly who this woman is I'm getting ready to take as my second wife."

Smokey whirled and flared at him. "I was your first lover."

Casey regarded her placidly.

"Your father was in the Navy."

"I know that," she snapped.

He smiled complacently. "And in the Navy, he specialized." Smokey folded her arms across her chest. "What was his specialty, Smokey?"

"How the hell should I know?"

"I think you know very well. What was his special division?"

"Why don't you tell me? You're the one with all the answers."

"He was in demolition. Your father was an explosives expert."

She met him eye-to-eye, shrugged. "So what?"

Casey studied her coolly. "So how did you get off that boat, Smokey?"

Smokey glowered, her lip in a pout like a petulant child's.

"I told you. Over and over."

"I want to hear it again."

She threw her arms out, turned away toward the window.

"My god—when will this ever end?"

"That's up to you. Tell me."

Smokey took a deep breath, recited in a dutiful singsong. "I started my period unexpectedly. I had no provisions." She looked over her shoulder insolently. "I'm a heavy bleeder."

Casey nodded, without batting a lash. "So you said. And so?"

She glared. "And so I took the motor launch to the mainland to get the supplies I needed."

"Why didn't you return?"

"It was sunset when I left. I told Artie I'd come back when it was light."

"Meanwhile, at four a.m., the boat blew up."

"That's what they tell me."

Casey sighed heavily. "The Bureau has scraps of the bomb that blew Artie and his boat to smithereens. I've read the lab report, compared it carefully with your father's Navy record. The materials in Artie's bomb are the same as your father used to make similar-type bombs."

"My daddy died when I was nineteen. I swear to you—he didn't do it."

Casey smiled, gently amused. "No," he said softly, "but I think it highly probable that before he died, he passed along his knowledge. To his very bright daughter." Smokey went rigid. "And I think I can prove this, Smokey."

"Then do it!" she spat. "Get it over with. Arrest me!"

Casey moved toward her, she jerked back. "That isn't the point of all this." He reached for her, she flinched. "I just want to get things straight."

He got her by the arm and guided her to the couch. "Sit down."

She sat, eyes starkly riveted on his. She was trembling.

"It's all right, Smokey," he said gently. "I understand. You had a hard life, a lot of bad things to go through, with no one there to help you. Artie was your first big break. You had to make the most of it. And you did. I don't blame you."

Smokey was listening so carefully, she had stopped breathing. She had also stopped trembling.

"And you were right; Artie would never have let you go and stay alive. Not with all you had in that little steel-trap black-book mind of yours. You did what you had to do. I understand that, too. And in the process, you did the State a great service. Because of you, the Bureau was able to make a major dent in the mob, which we can further use to break down the rackets. You undid your wrongs, you paid your debt to society. And you showed real courage. You earned your right to a new life."

Smokey was intent on Casey, reading every sign.

He regarded her reassuringly. "It's over now, behind us. It's time for a clean start." He took her hands. "You have nothing to fear." His eyes held hers. "A husband can't be forced to testify against his wife."

Smokey returned his look. He was driving a hard bargain. She sucked in a shakey breath, and nodded.

"Good," he smiled benignly.

She lowered her chin, looked up through misty eyes, faking a grateful smile. The love was back in Casey's face. He had complete control over her. She was dead. For the rest of her life.

He tenderly wiped his thumb across the mascara smudges beneath her eyes. "Now," he leaned forward and kissed her lifeless mouth, "go fix your makeup. My folks are waiting for us."

Smokey numbly rose, somehow made it to the bathroom.

Braced against the basin, she stared into the mirror at a face she barely recognized. The face of a woman who in ten years she wouldn't know at all. A woman prematurely aged, used up—like Casey's mother, like all the women in Harden—wearing cheap ill-fitting dresses and polyester pants from Babbitt's, pushing a baby carriage.

Well, Smokey, old girl, she leered at the face, you dug your own grave. I guess it's time to lie down in it.

The reflected image was ugly.

SCENE 23

I'm up at the crack of dawn and on the road in half an hour. I decided to dispense with breakfast and lunch; I'm noticing a little plumpness. What can I expect, eating like a Mexican peasant truck driver? I want to appear stylishly svelte, seductively starved.

I take Interstate 25 south, eventually to pick up Interstate 10 at Las Cruces and gradually curve east. I plan not to stop until I reach Comfort, a town selected out of several an hour or so this side of San Antonio strictly for the humor. A total of 780 tedious miles, 12 monotonous hours, to be filled with planning and preparation. I can't pay attention to my surroundings; hitting 80 miles an hour on open, unpatrolled sections, I have to keep focused on the road. My time schedule is exact, and it's tight.

But I know the dangers of this kind of driving. I force myself to take a break every two hours, get out of the car, stretch, do deep-breathing exercises. By ten, my stomach's gnawing on my backbone. By twelve, I'm light-headed. I pull into a dilapidated Texaco to fill up the tank and empty my bladder. Luckily they have natural spring water; I buy six bottles. I stuff my purse with packets of cheese and crackers. The lock on the bathroom door is busted, the floor strewn with soggy tissues, the toilet streaked and rimmed with rust. I have no choice. I gingerly squish across, brace myself in a noncontact squat, and hope no one barges in.

I arrive in Comfort at six thirty. I have no trouble finding a liquor store; in these towns, there's little other comfort. No wine outside of Gallo, so I buy a bottle of scotch. I get directions to a fast-food Mexican drive-in, take out two tostadas and three tacos. To hell with starving. I'm going to need my strength.

I scout out lodgings. The Flamingo Motel is just right. A low concrete-block on the dusty fringe of town and time, its pink paint blistered and peeling, its asphalt tile bleached and curling. No swimming pool, not so much as a cactus in landscaping; a vista of flat, parched desert. Besides the owner's, mine is the only car. But the signboard advertises my foremost requirement: a telephone in every room.

I open my suitcases to air out their sweating contents. No sense hanging anything; after ten minutes of wear, they'll be in the same condition. I sit on the edge of the bed and open my bottle of scotch. I drink to the plucked chenille bedspread. I drink to the chipped blond furniture. I drink to the faded plastic flamingo standing on one leg on the thin roof. When I have enough courage, I lift the phone and dial.

—Information?— A bored Texas accent. They always end sentences with a question mark.

—Yes. Galveston, please.

—Yes?

—The Federal Bureau of Investigation.

—The FBI?— Quickened interest.

—Yes.

—One moment, please? That number is . . . ?

I write it down quickly, replace the receiver, and stare at the scrawled numbers. I drink to the FBI. I drink to telephone operators. I drink to information. Then, taking several slow, deep breaths, I calmly and carefully dial.

—Federal Bureau of Investigation— No questioning Texas accent.

—I'd like to speak to Casey Colter.

—Casey Colter?

—Yes. Special Agent Casey Colter.

A pause. —I'm sorry. Agent Colter isn't here right now. It's after hours. The office is closed.

—I know that. But this is very important. I have to get in touch with him.

Pause. —Is this an emergency?

—Yes.

—Would you care to leave your name?

—No! I have to talk to him as soon as possible.

—I see. . . . Is there a number where you can be reached?

—Yes!— I squint at the phone face, give the number.

—All right. I'll see what I can do.

I gush breathy gratitude. —Thank you.

—Stay by your phone.

—Yes! Yes, I will.

I stay, tranquilly sipping scotch, toasting special agents, toasting drama school.

The phone rings in exactly fifteen minutes. I start so violently, I practically fall off the bed. I collect myself and slowly lift the receiver.

—Hello?— Hushed, hesitant, frightened.

—This is Casey Colter. Are you the party who called me?

The soft huskiness of his voice is so painfully familiar, for a moment I forget what I'm about.

—Oh . . . Oh yes. Agent Colter. I'm so glad you called. I have to talk with you.

I surprise myself. I didn't know what was going to come out of my mouth until I opened it. But it's pure Georgia Peach, southern-fried Mardi Gras Queen, sugar-pied Glory Colter.

—Who am I speaking to?

I hesitate. —I, I'm sorry. I'd just as soon not give that over the telephone.

—Where are you?

I whisper. —In a little motel outside San Antonio. I don't know the name. I just tried to find some place that might be safe.

It didn't matter; I knew he'd checked the number before he called.

—Why are you calling me?

—I need your help.

—I take it you don't feel free to talk.

—No. No, please. Could I meet you somewhere?

—Are you in danger?

—I, I don't know. I might be. *Please.* Could we meet?

—How did you get my name?

I take a deep breath. I hadn't counted on this. I grab the first straw that floats past my hand.

—A mutual friend. Someone you knew in college.

—At Texas A & M?

Cute, Colter. A little test.

—No. At Rice. From the football team. He said you were someone I could trust.

—Where would you like to meet?

—At your office?

—When?

—Tomorrow? I could be there by three.

He considers, makes his decision. —All right. Tomorrow. My office. Three. Do you know how to get here?

I scribble down his directions.

He hesitates.

—What should I do if you don't show up?

—I'll be there— And I slam down the phone, laughing hysterically.

That crazy damn Smokey. Who knows when she's going to crop up? Not me, not Vinnie, not even Casey Colter. With all his special agent training, she's still a match for him. A worthy adversary.

Look out, Casey. Smokey's on your trail.

I'm giggling so hard, this time I do fall off the bed. I sprawl on the thread-bare carpet, hiccoughing between giggles, trying to hold my breath.

Giggles and hiccoughs finally subsided, I settle on the floor, back against the bed, and happily consume two tostadas and three tacos.

I take Interstate 10 Bypass around San Antonio early, before the going-to-work traffic; cut around Houston mid-morning; drop south on Interstate 45, and reach Galveston shortly before noon. I congratulate myself. For a woman who's never traveled before on her own, my routing and timing have been perfect.

As in Comfort, I drive up and down until I find just the right place. But this time I'm going for luxury, nothing but the best. I choose the tallest, poshest motor-hotel on the strip, take a suite with full-wall window and private balcony overlooking the gulf.

I dig to the bottom of my suitcase, pull out a dress carefully wrapped with tissue, shoes, purse, pantyhose, black lace bra, and jewelry. I hang the dress in the bathroom, turn on the shower—hot, fullblast—close the door, and munch cheese and crackers while the dress steams and I review the local map. Then I shower, shave, lotion, coif, make up, and dress with the meticulous attention of a Miss America contestant. There isn't a wrinkle in my dress, a miracle fabric, bought at Boston Saks and saved expressly for this meeting.

My last touch is a liberal spray of cologne and dab of perfume at my throat and behind each ear. Very expensive. I'm as cool as a breeze in November.

I have little difficulty following Casey's directions, and arrive two minutes before three in the outer entry he told me about. I shove my dark glasses into place and push the intercom button, facing away from the security monitors.

A voice blares. —Your business, please.

—I'm here to see Casey Colter.

—Your name.

—He's expecting me.

The intercom buzzes off. I strike a pose in the middle of the floor, back to the elevator, and wait, listening for the elevator's descending hum.

The doors slide open. I give it a long, long second, then slowly turn. He's outlined by the elevator's softly lit interior, framed by its hard-edged door.

A surge of heat rushes through me. I feel it scorch my lungs, burn my cheeks.

He's wearing a tight navy-blue T shirt. The muscles of his chest and arms are harder, more developed, his shoulders broader. The lines of his thighs in gray slacks are strong. His crotch is a subtle bulge. He's let his crewcut grow out; he has waves. One's separated into loose curls above his forehead. I didn't know he had waves and curls. They soften the chiseled bones of his classic Greek features. He's golden tan. He looks taller.

I've never experienced such unmitigated animal longing. It shakes me and leaves me powerless, which for the moment, I hope, passes as composure.

He doesn't recognize me; he's busy trying to take my measure. Then his eyes shade and resolve into recognition. His face goes flat, his jaw hardens, his mouth becomes a tight line.

He nods.

—So. You finally found me.

Like I said: He's been expecting me.

I push down my nerves, waver a smile. —It wasn't easy.

His expression and tone are not friendly. —I didn't mean it to be. Are you the one who called?

I nod.

—Nice job. I always did suspect you had a streak of the southern bitch in you.

My tongue stings with a dozen bitchy things I could spit out about southern bitches and the men who marry them. Instead, I keep smiling. —It's what heats my cold New England blood.

He smiles. Grimly. But at least it's a smile, a chink.

I'm suddenly aware of how natural we are with each other. As if we'd talked, or quarreled, just yesterday.

He's considering me, with that same irritated impatience he always got when I displeased him.

—All right. As long as you're here, you might as well come up.

He turns and strides into the elevator.

I sedately follow. —Thank you. I'd love to see your office.

He gives me a quick look, chucks a laugh.

Another chink.

All the way up, he blatantly checks me over, going slowly from head to foot, not missing a detail. I pose nonchalantly, studying the elevator doors.

I know what he's seeing: a tall blonde with stylish Italian haircut; slim black dress with cap sleeves and deep V neck, large black buttons stopping above the knees, making a split to reveal trim legs in sheer black nylons. Wide patent-leather belt at narrow waist, patent heels on small feet, patent purse in dainty hands, clustered jet-bead earrings at delicate ears. I'm confident he can smell me.

I worked hard to put this together, and I've never looked better; I know it. And if I didn't, I'd know it now by Casey's face.

—Take off your glasses.

I take them off and look toward him.

He studies my face for a long moment. And I see in *his* face all the years. He's remembering.

He smiles, sincerely. —You look good.

—Thank you— I smile back, dazzlingly —So do you— wanting to touch him.

By the time we reach the sixth floor, we've relaxed into a kind of edged camaraderie. I feel the pull between us, that old magnetism that used to draw and hold us.

We step out of the elevator into a long corridor lined on the right with name-plated doors, on the left with a glass-topped partition, behind which are grouped the usual furnishings of an office: desks, telephones, computers, file cabinets. The place is surprisingly empty; I expected a bustle of important activity. Only four men mill around behind the glass. They look up at Casey's and my approach.

Casey suddenly halts in the middle of the hall and grabs me by the arm.

—Hey, fellows. Look what I've got here.

The men stop their work and move forward. Casey holds me out by the wrist, twisting me this way and that, as if we were dancing. I'm too startled to demur or blush. I'm pleased and flattered. Also embarrassed and a little angry.

—Isn't she pretty?— He beams at me.

—Very pretty.

Smiles. Murmurs of appreciation.

Congratulations to Casey.

—Boys, I'd like you to meet Reggie Patterson. An old friend from high school.

—Hi, Reggie.

—Nice to meet you.

—Reggie.

Casey takes my hand and, walking backwards, still smiling, pulls me down the hall. I wriggle my fingers at the boys good-bye.

He ushers me into one of the private offices at the end of the hall, pointing out the brass plate on the door: Special Agent Casey Colter.

I look impressed. —Very nice.

He gestures around the room.

I take in the large teak desk, the black leather chairs and sofa, the shelves of books and football trophies. Framed degrees and citations decorate the grasscloth walls.

—Very, *very* nice.

His smile tightens with vindication. —I guess you didn't think I'd come this far.

I look at him quietly. —I always knew you could do anything you wanted, Casey.

He returns my look, curtly nods. Then strides behind his desk and plunks down in his high-backed contour chair. And as an afterthought motions me into my low-backed armchair.

I sit across from him, knees together, back erect, hands folded on my shiny patent purse.

He leans forward, clasps his hands on the black blotter. —Now. What was so urgent? Why did you have to see me?

I'm taken aback; I hadn't planned on such directness. In my scriptings of this scene, I'd imagined we'd begin conversationally, take time to fill in the years, feel each other out. Skirt around and ease into it.

I take a breath, grabbing for fragments of my carefully prepared speeches. The words come haltingly. I can't meet his eyes.

—Well, things haven't been going too well for me lately. I haven't been happy. I'm feeling a lot of loneliness, a lot of dissatisfaction. A lot of emptiness in my life— I pause, hunting for the way to say it. —I keep thinking of the past. What was. What might have been— I look down —I guess I had to come back— fumble at my purse —to where I left myself— look up. —Try to work things through differently. Find a better ending.

There's a long silence. Casey's studying me thoughtfully.

—And you think I can help you with that?

—I'm hoping so. I've just come from Harden.

—I figured as much. Did that help?

—Yes.

—How?

—It helped me put pieces in place. Get a different perspective.

He leans back in his chair, hands behind his head.

—So. You think you still love me.

My head jerks. I feel the sting on my cheek.

I force myself to meet his eyes directly. —Yes.

His face is impassive.

—What do you expect me to do?

—I don't know.

What did I expect?

—Marry you?

I stare.

—I can't marry you, Reggie. That was fifteen years ago. I have a whole new life, a wife and family. Whom I love very much, and who make me very happy. I have no intention of leaving them.

I obediently register the pain.

—You have children?— I hear my deprivation. This is ridiculous. Of course I knew he had children. It's just the reality.

—Two— He smiles proudly, turns a double photo frame toward me. —Michael and Melissa.

Not little Denny and Les?

I study the blonde brown-eyed girl and brunette blue-eyed boy. They could have been mine.

—They're beautiful, Casey. Melissa looks just like you.

He's making no effort to disguise his pleasure. —And Michael is the spitting image of his mother.

I have to get away from this.

—Your wife. She must have dark hair.

This is killing me. Why must I pursue it?

Casey regards me with a small smug smile. —Long and black, the color of a raven's wing. And large thick-lashed eyes the color of lilacs— He's laying it on, tormenting me deliberately. —I met her at the beach. On spring break my second year of college. I fell in love with her on first sight. She was the most beautiful woman I'd ever seen.

I get the stab: Prettier than you, Reggie.

I lift my chin.

—Well that's what really counts.

He looks at me sharply.

I close the frame with a snap and hand it back to him.

—I'm happy for you, Casey. Happy that you're happy.

He pushes back in his chair, crosses a leg.

—So what's wrong with your second husband?

—My what?

—I see you're wearing a wedding ring.

I glance involuntarily at my ring. —I have the same husband I've always had.

—You were divorced.

—Where'd you get that?

—From the report I had run on you.

—The what?

—When you started harassing my dad. I thought I better have you checked out.

—I wasn't "harassing" your father. I telephoned him. Exactly once.

—That was harassing. He was afraid you were going to track me down, cause trouble. Try to disrupt my life.

—I'm flattered he should consider me such a threat.

—You're not.

—So why did he get so excited?

He doesn't answer.

I smile, enjoying my little advantage. —So what else did your report tell you?

—That you're a dorm mother at some private girls' school.

I burst out laughing. —I'm what? That's the funniest thing I ever heard.

His jaw juts. —Are you telling me you're not?

—Of course I'm not.

He's obstinate. —It's in the report.

—I don't care what's in your silly report.

He glares. —Then what are you?

—A mother. A simple wife and mother. With a house— I suppress a giggle. —No dorm.

He grabs. —You have children?

—I suppose your report told you I was barren.

He lurches forward. —How many?

—Is this an interrogation?— I'm finding this hysterical. —Two. Two girls. Katelyn and Lindsay. Would you like to see their pictures?

—That wouldn't prove a thing.

—My husband's name is Howie. I have his picture, too.

—They could be fakes. Pictures of anyone.

—So could those pictures— I nod toward his propped-up frame. He glowers. —This is ridiculous, Casey. Don't you see how crazy? Is this what the FBI's done to you?

He pulls upright. —I'm no different than I ever was.

I'm stopped.

—This is a violent, crime-ridden society, Reggie.

—What's that got to do with anything?

He expands back into his chair, full of self-righteous justification and importance. —It's my responsibility as a citizen, and my sworn duty as an agent, to do everything in my power to make it a safe place for my children— He fixes me with a pointed look. —And *your* children.

I stare at him. I know what I'm seeing: the chameleon ham, playing out for me his interpretation of the role of FBI agent. Or has this become his permanent coloration?

I ease back in my chair and cross a leg.

—So you run checks on all your friends? Anyone who happens to cross your path with undeclared intention?

—You can't judge people by their past or appearance. It doesn't matter whether you've known them before or not.

—That means I have an FBI file now, doesn't it?

—People change. I've seen pillars of the community become serial killers overnight. Kidnappers that look like college professors. Little gray-haired ladies turned arsonists. You never know anyone.

—So the message is, distrust everyone?

—It's a dangerous world out there. I guess I can't expect you to understand that, coming as you do from a life of insulated privilege— He's rocking in his chair, regarding me superiorly.

I'm resenting his smugness and condescension. The way I always did when he climbed up on his soapbox.

And I do as *I* always did: I square my jaw and climb up on mine.

I uncross my leg and lean forward.

—I don't believe in what you're doing, Casey. Using federal employees to run expensive checks and create potentially incriminating files on innocent persons. Who haven't even been given the right to explain or defend themselves, much less warning they're being investigated. I consider it a misuse of power and the tax payers' money.

He sprawls in his chair, eyeing me belligerently.

—I see you're still Miss Priss.

I react; he knows how I hate that epithet. —And I don't like what's happened to you. You're sounding like a flag-waving stiff-necked right-winged—

He lunges forward, lips tight, eyes narrow.

—Let me see your purse.

—What?

—Your purse.

I hold up my purse.

He stretches out a hand. —Give it to me.

—What?

—Hand it over.

I hand it to him.

He scowls at me while he turns the bag upside down and empties its contents on his blotter.

It's a mess: torn cellophane packets, crumbled crackers, cheese stuck to my wallet. I didn't have time to change purses selectively, I just dumped one into the other.

He picks through the pile. —I always did remember you as a messy person.

I'm incensed. —Then your memory's faulty— He looks at me. —I pride myself on my organization. My house is *always* clean and orderly.

He smiles tightly. —I'm glad to hear you've changed.

He's poking around inside my bag, squeezing the sides.

—I don't have a gun, Casey.

He arches his eyebrows, gives me a small, tight-lipped smile. —In this business, you can't be too safe.

—Oh honestly.

He sets the purse down, settles back in his chair.

—Now that you're satisfied I'm not dangerous, may I please have my belongings back?

He leans over the blotter, sorts out the cellophane, cheese, and crackers, tosses them in the waste basket, scoops the rest into the purse.

I grab it from him. —What brought that nonsense on? A new way to win an argument?

He cocks his chin. —It just occurred to me you might be some kind of subversive. From the way you were talking.

I start laughing —Oh, Casey— shaking my head.

He has the wits to look sheepish and grin.

He hunches over the desk, stares at his clasped hands, suddenly dark and thoughtful. When he finally looks up, he's shed his FBI skin. He looks stripped.

He sighs heavily. —What we had wasn't love, Reggie.

I steel myself.

—What was it then?

—I don't know. Puppy love. Infatuation— He shrugs.

Puppy love at age thirty-five? Infatuation for twenty years?

—I don't believe that.

—All I know is that what I feel for my wife, I never felt for you.

I grip my pain. I have to get through this. Whatever it is I'm doing here, I have to get to the end of it. —How is it different?

He spreads his hands, studies his palms. —It's quieter. More mature. Easier to live with. And easier to build on— He flexes his fingers. —My wife and I don't have the same high emotion as you and I had. The same intensity. I can't talk and laugh with her the way I did with you— He reweaves his fingers —But my feelings for her are deeper and stronger— and sets his reclasped hands on the blotter.

It's taking everything I have to hold on.

He finally looks up, shakes his head. —You and I weren't right for each other, Reggie. We were too different.

I sit very still, my look steady.

—You can say that for yourself, Casey, but you can't say it for me. I loved you. More than I've ever loved anyone. And what I felt for you was not puppy love. Not infatuation. It was real, as real as anything I've ever felt. Or hope to feel again.

He darts me a quick glance. I lift my chin.

—Maybe we aren't right for each other now; too many things have happened.

But we were right for each other then. And I don't ever want to deny that. Or forget it.

He stares at the space between us. Then pushing his hands against the desk, slowly shoves back in his chair.

—I'm sorry, Reggie. Sorry you haven't found in your marriage what I've found in mine. Sorry you're unhappy— He rises. He seems tired. —And sorry I can't help you.

I rise, too. With dignity.

—Oh, but you have. I realize now why I came here— He looks at me. —To exorcise ghosts.

He nods.

—Our problem wasn't that we were too different, Casey. We were too much alike. Almost the same person. And when you left me you took away a vital part.

—You left me.

—I'm taking that part back now.

We stand, memorizing each other's faces. I know mine must be looking like his. Behind his eyes I'm seeing the same hurt I'm feeling behind mine.

He starts around his desk. —I'll see you down.

—No. Please don't.

He hangs by the side of his desk.

At the door, I stop and turn.

—I love you, Casey. I always will. But that's the second time you've had to tell me you don't love me. I won't make you do it again.

The boys behind the glass look up as I pass. I wriggle my fingers, leaving them to wonder why Casey isn't with me.

I could tell them if they asked:

He's down at the end of the hall, in his private office with his name plate on his door, in his deep chair, behind his big desk, staring at the photos of his children. Where I left him.

I make it down the elevator in exemplary fashion, spine erect, shoulders back, head high. The way Maggie coached me. I'm aware my heart is jumping around, beating with sharp, erratic jabs, but I ignore it. I have to get out to the car.

I slide in, close the door. And that's the end of that. It hits me. I grab the wheel from the jolt. I'm a whirl of sickening, conflicting emotions: exhilaration, devastation; triumph, humiliation; rage and relief.

I can't cry. I can't laugh. I can't even turn the key in the ignition. So I sit there, in a closed car, in the dead heat of midsummer, in Galveston, Texas. Trying to untangle myself and grab onto a loose end that might help me get ahold of myself and out of this parking lot.

Suddenly I start trembling. How strange, I think, from a detached distance. What an interesting delayed reaction, as I watch myself practically shake myself apart. When the paroxysm finally spends itself, I'm depleted but calm.

You did it, Reggie, I tell myself. It's over. And you survived.

I sag in the seat, clinging to the steering wheel.

Now it's time to take care of yourself.

Yes. The nurse in me understands this.

I start the car and slowly leave the lot, without a backward glance at the imposing granite building.

SCENE 24

I drive up and down streets, until I find Ye Olde Wine and Spirits Shoppe. I buy two expensive bottles of pouilly fuisse and, getting directed to Nuevo Caterers and Cafeteria, pick up caviar, liver pâté, striped vegetable mousse, Bel Paese cheese, and assorted toast and crackers.

In my elegant bedroom on the top floor of my top-drawer transient residence, I strip myself of earrings, belt, dress, shoes, hose, and bra. I put on a caftan and, on the round balcony table, carefully lay out my provisions: my gourmet Band-Aids and gauzy connoisseur bindings. Then I move to the balcony edge.

Gripping the iron rail, I stare at the lowering sun—falsely enlarged, deceptively emblazened—and stretch toward its heat, willing it to absorb and consume me. Eyes burning, I turn away, toward the undulating sea—calm-surfaced, deep-fathomed—and lay myself across it, wishing its coolness could wash over and drown me.

Why did all this have to happen? Why did I have to hold onto a westering sun, seeing only the fiery brilliance, feeling only the heat and light, when all around me was encroaching darkness? Why did I have to turn away from the blue-shadowed troughs and white-frothed crests of rolling waves, denying the comfort of their repetitive rhythm, their reliable ebb and flow, capable of turbulence only when whipped by the elements?

I buried myself in desert sand when I could have been floating on the tide.

I think of sailing with Howie, how the sea is like the desert, everything a vast sweep: sweep of sky, sweep of cloud, sweep of sun and thin air. Sweep of horizon.

What am I going to do with the rest of this day? This unreal day so real I can't imagine getting past it.

I slump into the deep plastic-cushioned chair, pour a glass of wine, and toast. Well, this is it, Reggie, old girl. The end of the road. You've been chasing yourself until you've finally come full circle. Like a snake biting its own tail.

I feel the sting of my fangs. It's time to crisscross the flesh, suck out the poison, and swallow its bitterness. Like an antidotal serum.

I'm hearing our words.

We were almost the same person, I'd said.

It's time to think about that.

I'm no different than I ever was, he'd said.

Was that true?

I'd been stopped. I was seeing him. Perhaps for the first time. Was I also seeing myself?

It's time to think about that, too.

Was this man the same as the boy I'd fallen in love with? The burden I'd been dragging behind me all these years, allowing me only one step a year, a kernel of corn and drop of water to sustain me, the bowstring cutting my brow and restricting my thinking?

Was my vision that faulty? Or my memory? Had I clung to some falsely protected image of Casey in order to save my own?

I sit in my chair and watch the reflections on the water as the sun slowly goes down.

Casey and I did everything we could to stay together after I left Harden. We lived on letters.

Casey wrote once or twice a week, two or three pages, on both sides of cream-colored stationery, in a large distinctive hand—round vowels, generous loops, definitely dotted i's—with only a slight irregularity to the slant.

Reggie wrote every day. She and Casey had had a habit, for almost a year, of spending time each day—aimlessly driving around, getting a root beer, or simply sitting at a curb or along the side of some road—talking together. They'd tell about their day, what they'd said and done, their successes and disappointments, their sillinesses and concerns; anything that was on their mind or came into their head. And habits die hard. Reggie needed that sharing. She wrote Casey everything that mattered to her: about her school and classes, her friends and social life, her parents and family, her extracurricular activities. Giving him her thoughts and feelings, which she gave to no one else.

Casey's letters were full of similar news, but liberally spiced with humor, sprinkled with jokes and anecdotes. He never failed to respond to Reggie's confidences, making comment, asking questions, offering advice. Making her feel they were still in dialogue. Reggie couldn't wait to continue these conversations, rushing to the mail pile the minute she got home. She read and reread each letter, laughing at Casey's funniness, taking seriously his seriousness, admiring his well-constructed sentences and correctness of punctuation, his large vocabulary and colorful command of language. Loving this tangible evidence of his intelligence, personality, and character.

Casey wrote in his natural voice; in his letters Reggie could hear him. So long as she had his letters, Casey wasn't far away. She hid them in the cubbyhole atop her antique maple highboy next to her four-poster bed, in easy reach on nights of loneliness.

Once in a while Casey called, usually on a Sunday. But these phone conversations were unsatisfying. Their intermittency made them awkward, fragmented and stilted, as if with each one, they were getting reacquainted. In their letters, where there was continuity and time to consider their thoughts and wording, they had developed a kind of heightened sensitivity. They listened and answered with a deliberateness that brought them closer. The abrupt immediacy of the phone calls—and the jarring reality of the external voice in contrast to the internally heard voice of the letters—seemed only to emphasize the time and distance between them.

Gradually Casey called less and less, until they were relying solely on their letters. By the end of a year, Reggie's beribboned bundles had grown so bulky they had to be moved into a large grocery sack at the back of her closet.

It was in the spring of her freshman year at Vassar that Reggie received Casey's letter telling her he'd enlisted in the Navy. She was stunned. She wrote back immediately, without sensitive consideration, without careful deliberation, expressing her dismay honestly and succinctly. Where was the plan they'd made? What about college? What about business school and the sporting goods store? What about the offer from TWA? Hadn't he been talking lately about becoming a commercial pilot? What about *that*? Even flight engineer's training was better than being an ensign in the Navy. At least with TWA, he'd have some chance of getting into pilot's school.

Casey replied promptly, full of jaunty reassurance. He was still planning on college; he was still thinking about pilot's training. But Reggie was wrong: the Navy was a much better deal than TWA; it was a short cut. As a veteran he'd have the GI Bill, which would help him pay for college. And once he learned the ropes, he'd apply for pilot's school. As a naval pilot, he'd be an officer with officer's pay and officer's privileges, and married officer's housing. Maybe he'd even get into Annapolis. He'd figure out the details once he got there. Don't worry, Honey, he wrote. Trust me. I'm looking out for our best interests. My first concern is always our future.

Reggie let his jauntiness woo and win her. If her love for Casey meant anything, she told herself, he was right; she had to believe in and trust him. Anyway, she observed wryly, it was done. She swallowed hard and accepted his reassurances

But the swallow caught in her throat. Slowly she began to understand she was angry. Where was she in all this? *Our* future, he'd said. *Our* best interests. But he hadn't even bothered to consult her.

Once he settled into boot camp, Casey's letters picked up frequency. Sometimes he wrote daily. He was on a high of new adventure. Out of the sandy-beige of his boyhood into a world of watery-blue manhood. After the restrictiveness of military school, boot camp seemed like a wild out-on-his-own frolic. He fed Reggie funny stories about his barracks buddies, his daily regimen, the rigors of his training. He bought a new camera and sent snapshots. He looked wonderful in his uniform, his white cap cocked over one eye. Reggie let him woo and win her again.

Then one night several weeks into boot camp, Casey called, his first call in over six months. His last had been shortly after she'd entered college, when Reggie'd had to reassure him she still loved him, that nothing had changed between them, that she was still a one-man woman. Although she was now, as Casey called her, a high falutin' college girl.

Her roommate held out the phone. —It's for you— Then added in a whisper —It's a boy.

Reggie was, by now, used to phone calls from boys; but there was no one in particular. She accepted the receiver with indifferent curiosity. When she heard Casey's voice, she was taken completely off guard.

—Casey? Is that you? Is it really you?— Her excitement flooded the room. Her roommate discreetly left.

Everyone knew about Casey; his photographs covered Reggie's bulletin board.

—I can't believe it! It's so wonderful to hear from you.

—Why? Haven't you been getting my letters?— She heard the edge of irritation but was too elated to acknowledge it.

—Yes. Of course. I mean your voice. How *are* you?

—Okay. Yeah, I'm okay— His voice was strangely flat. —How are you?

—I'm fine, too. How's boot camp?

—Good. Really good. I like it. I'm learning a lot, things I never knew. Things you don't get in Harden.

She laughed. —I can believe that— She was feeling bright, giddy.

—They're preparing us for real life.

—You call the Navy "real life"?

—Sure. Sail the seven seas. See the world.

By now, Reggie was beginning to register Casey's distance.

—But not a woman in every port, I hope.

—No. They warned us about that— He tried to be light but Reggie sensed its falseness. —Like tonight. They showed us this movie.

—What? "Anchors Aweigh"?

—No— Impatient. —About venereal disease— He worked to bring the lightness back. —Now you're not going to get that in Harden.

—No— Reggie had pulled back. Her antennae were quivering uneasily. —Or in Boston.

—Yeah. It was really something. They showed us all these guys in close-up. No faces, nothing above the waist or below the knees. Actual cases. One guy had a swollen dick, thick pus coming out of the mouth of its glans; they call the head the glans. Another guy had these tight oversized balls. They looked painful as hell.

Reggie was hunting for appropriate response.

—Then they showed us these guys with deep, round, hard-rimmed sores all over their pricks, with pus under the crusty centers.

—Was this in color?

—Strictly black and white. But the narrator described it pretty vividly.

—I can imagine.

—One guy had chancres all over his balls. They call them chancres or lesions or fissures, sometimes ulcers. Another guy, where the disease was more progressed, had them on his butt and around his anus.

Reggie was surprised he didn't say bung hole.

—The worst was this guy with gangrene. The skin was literally rotting and falling off his dick.

Reggie was wondering where all this was leading. That there was a specific point of destination, she was absolutely certain. She knew Casey when he had an agenda, especially a hidden one. She could feel a line slowly being unwound, wrapping around her, dragging her with it. The trick was to stay unentwined and get there ahead of him.

She listened warily. —That was some training film.

—It wasn't *training*— Sharp. —It was *instructional*.

—I stand corrected.

Casey's voice grew dark and weighted. —Then they showed us the cause of it all. These women, their labia red and swollen, round indented sores inside the slimy lips, thick yellow pus dripping out of their vaginas.

—*Now* we're in color.

Casey had no time for humor. Good thing; because Reggie herself was no longer feeling so humorous.

—One woman had an abscess the size and color of an orange. Another had pusy bleeding chancres on her nipples.

—No faces, I'm assuming. Nothing above the breasts.

—And these wart things can spread. On this one woman, they were the size of dimes, in clusters all over her vulva, down her thighs, around her buttocks. She had this congested vestibule, bathed in pus, and inflammation of the urethra.

—You sound like a medical textbook. Your vocabulary has grown by leaps and bounds.

—Yeah. Well, like I said, I'm learning a lot. For instance, I never knew about the hymen.

It was the little pause, the off-handedness, that alerted Reggie.

Casey's voice was soft, insinuating. —You know about the hymen.

—Of course. I'm a woman. I went to private girls' school where they believe we should know about our bodies.

The sharp shift in his tone came as a shock. —Then why didn't you have one?

—What?

—Why didn't you have a hymen?

Reggie stared at the corner of the floor; she felt she was staring at the receiver. Not only had she not gotten there ahead of him, she hadn't even been going in the right direction.

—When?

—The first time we had sex.

Reggie saw the backseat of a car.

—I did.

—No you didn't.

Somewhere in the back of her mind, she realized she was treating this as if it were rational.

—How are you so sure?

Why was she being rational?

—You didn't cry out or bleed.

Now she was seeing a frail damsel in gossamer, wild eyed, legs spread, dropping the tell-tale stain on the white sheet for the gratification of the red-bladed, tale-telling puncturing knight looming above her.

She wanted to laugh, but couldn't.

—Casey, that went out with the dark ages.

—That's not what they told us in the movie.

She saw "us": Rows of young uninformed uniformed men hunched in their folding chairs, gawking avidly, like a private men's club watching a lewd smoker. Like a ball team hunkered on locker-room benches, luridly describing their groupie conquests.

—So what are you telling me, Casey? That you think I wasn't a virgin?

—I'm not telling anything. I'm simply asking.

—What?

—Were you a virgin?

—Why?

—You said I was the first. That we gave our virginities to each other.

—That's what I said.

—That we were bound forever in the eyes of God.

—That's what *you* said.

—So why didn't you have a hymen?

—Why should I bother to answer? You've already made up your mind.

—No. I'll accept whatever you tell me. I swear. It won't make any difference. I'll still love you.

—Then why ask?

—I just want to know.

—Why?

—I don't want there to be any lies between us.

Reggie understood the company she was keeping: Women with abscessed labia and suppurating sores, vaginas and nipples dripping pus. Diseased, contaminating, hymenless women. The cause of it all.

She also understood that her rationality had finally given way and she was coldly, cruelly enraged. She wanted to claw out, dig into Casey's unquestionable blameless, stainless flesh the stinging inflamed slashes she now felt all over hers.

—Yes. There was someone before you.

She felt the impact of her retaliation by the cold silence that followed. He'd asked for it. And she'd given it to him.

—Who?

—How does that matter?

—You're protecting him.

—I'm protecting myself.

—Do you still love him?

—I don't even remember his name.

Casey's silence this time gave off the raw electricity of shock.

—That's all I wanted to know— and he hung up on her.

Reggie was amazed at how well she handled herself in the days that followed, proud of her ability to rise above it. She didn't cry. Didn't fall apart. Didn't rave and rage. She calmly and quietly went about her college business. The ice she had bound herself in to get through the last minutes of her conversation with Casey had numbed her to the core. She ate heartily, slept heavily, making sure to be exhausted by the time she hit bed from late hours of studying and partying.

Reggie'd started drinking her senior year back in Boston. That's what everyone did, the purpose of a party. And she didn't have Casey to stop her. But she'd always been careful not to drink too much, not to get sloppy and make a fool of herself, do something she'd be sorry for.

The weekend after Casey's call, she watched herself with particular caution. She didn't want to do anything that might substantiate his assessment of her.

Because deep inside was a hot coal of despair that was slowly thawing her frozen resolve into a runoff of guilt.

She'd lied to Casey. She'd lashed out and hurt him as badly as he'd hurt her. Perhaps worse, because his wound had been out of propagandized confusion and ignorance. The one she'd inflicted had been out of consciously mean vindictiveness. She hadn't been understanding of his circumstances, she reproached herself. Hadn't tried to reason with and reassure him. Hadn't avowed her innocence. She'd let herself sink to the Navy's level. She'd destroyed trust and betrayed their relationship.

She began to put on the garments of her false confession as if they belonged to her.

She felt dirty, soiled, sullied—all the clichés—by the unwholesome company Casey had associated her with.

Why hadn't she cried out and bled? Instead, she'd thrown herself into her relations with Casey exuberantly, exultantly, ecstatically. As if, she acerbically thought now, she were a natural, born for this kind of work.

She remembered one night, late in spring, early in their experimentations. She'd been sitting on Casey's lap facing him. Don't pump so hard, he'd admonished, grabbing her writhing hips and thumping bottom. She'd been embarrassed, made to feel somehow unseemly and wanton. She'd climbed off his lap and sullenly refused to continue.

Where was her hymen when she needed it? Why hadn't she had one? Was she a whore from a previous life? A high-class geisha?

It took Casey two weeks to come around. By the time she got his letter,

Reggie was reduced to a mash of guilt, confusion, sorrow, and loneliness. The process had been slow and insidious, like the gradual reduction of a glacier, and equally impossible to stop.

Casey was apologetic. Remorseful and contrite. He didn't know what had gotten into him. He'd promised he'd understand. That he'd accept whatever she'd done, and still love her. He'd gone back on his word. He'd been stupid and selfish.

It was just hurt pride, he realized that now. Injured male ego. He wanted to be a better man than that. Would she still be his girl? They had their whole lives ahead of them. What did it matter what she'd done before she met him? She'd been young, didn't know what she was doing. He understood and forgave her. He loved her. He'd never love anyone else. Would she understand, forgive, and love him?

Reggie let him woo and win her. Again.

SCENE 25

Casey was to be out of boot camp in early summer. He wanted to come visit. We have to see each other, he wrote. We have to talk, we have to be together. Our lives have become so different and separate, I'm afraid we'll drift apart.

Reggie met him at the airport. He was glorious in his bell-bottoms, so perfectly suited for his narrow-waisted, broad-shouldered, long-legged body.

They didn't kiss; their smiles did. Their hands fluttered toward each other; but they didn't touch. In the car, they were tentative, eager to know each other again, anxious at what they might find. Intimate strangers. Casey kept watching her. Reggie kept smiling, hair blowing back from her face, as she tried to impress him with her maneuvering of the white Skylark convertible in and around traffic. Casey had taught her to drive.

—Whose car is this?

—Mine.

—When did you get it?

—At graduation.

—Why didn't you tell me about it?

Reggie looked over surprised. —I didn't?

—I would have remembered.

She turned back to the road, frowning. Why hadn't she told him?

For graduation, Casey had sent her a heart-shaped gold locket with a diamond in the center, his smiling face framed by the inside heart. She'd pressed her own smiling face in the heart opposite. She wore it all the time. She fingered it now and smiled at him.

For her birthday, he'd sent her a gold ankle-chain, her name on one side, Love always, Casey, on the other. She was wearing it now, for the first time. In Harden, all the girls wore gold ankle bracelets given them by their boyfriends; it was the sexy, proprietary thing to do. Just as the boys wore heavy silver wrist-chains from their girlfriends. Like the one she'd given Casey, which, she glanced over to see, he had on now. In Boston, both were considered cheap.

As she turned off the main road into the residential districts toward the low wooded hills, Casey's attention shifted from Reggie to his surroundings. She watched from the corner of her eye. He seemed entranced by the swells of green lawn, the carefully cultivated gardens, the substantial well-established houses. She took a deep breath and swerved up their drive.

—Well, this is it.

Casey eyed the large decorous colonial with what Reggie perceived as misgiving. Then he gamely folded out of the car, hoisted his heavy bag as if it were nothing to a man as big and strong as he, and swaggered to the front door ahead of her.

Maggie and Daddy were waiting; Reggie could imagine them lurking behind the bay curtains. Maggie opened the door before Reggie could reach the stoop. Daddy hovered in the dark hall behind her. They were all gracious welcome. Maggie was smiling effusively, disguising her rapid appraisals, first of Casey's sailor suit, then of Reggie's face. Daddy stepped up and shook hands vigorously.

As Reggie led Casey down the hall and up the stairs, Casey darted quick assessments. She could see him relax. The glimpses of chintz and crewel, of dark-patterned rugs and old-fashioned furniture, didn't seem so imposing. Maggie's precious antiques, so assiduously hunted out and painstakingly refinished, went unappreciated.

On further inspection—after he'd deposited his bag in his room, been shown his bath and towels, and followed Reggie down to the family room—Casey grew disdainful. Catherine would never leave magazines scattered across the table, newspapers all over the floor. She'd never allow those cluttered piles in the corner or this closed-off pungent odor. She'd have to air, tidy, and dust. And that shabby, shredded chair? That would have to go; Catherine could never live with that.

Reggie saw all this and grinningly understood.

These were Maggie's cat years. She had a handsome tom with impeccable papers, whom she sired out for a considerable fee. He was too precious to risk to the great outdoors. So in frustrated natural instinct, he'd staked out his territory in Maggie's deep-piled wool carpets. He hadn't missed a corner. Maggie sprayed and foamed constantly, with special expensive neutralizers, equally frustrated. But the cat's proprietary spray prevailed. The shabby, shredded chair was his scratching post.

Reggie read Casey's face, and for once was glad for Maggie's pets and casual housekeeping. Casey could contemptuously dismiss his initial intimidation and confidently stake out his *own* territory.

Maggie served lunch—sandwiches, of course—in the kitchen, to set a tone of low-key hominess. Daddy asked about boot camp. Maggie inquired after Catherine, Scotty, and Denny. Casey shouldered the burden of conversation manfully and mannerfully. He was polite and respectful without being deferential or defensive. Reggie was proud of him.

When Casey asked Maggie and Arthur would they mind if Reggie drove him around a little, to let him get a feel for the area, they readily wished them out the door. Relieved, Reggie could guess, to be free of the strain of entertaining him. Reggie hadn't told them about the phone call. If she had, Casey would never have made it past the front steps. As it was, Maggie still held no love for him. Daddy's feelings remained a mystery to everyone, possibly even to Daddy.

As Reggie started the car toward town, Casey grabbed the wheel.

—No. Into the hills. Where there aren't any houses. I want to be alone.

Reggie found a secluded turnoff beneath sheltering trees. She shut off the engine and turned toward Casey.

He looked at her. —Trade places.

She climbed over into the passenger seat while he slid behind the steering wheel. When she looked up from untangling her skirt, Casey was moodily staring out the window, the muscle in his jaw working. He did that only in strong emotion.

—I want to talk.

Reggie adjusted to face him and quietly waited.

—I'm sorry, Reggie. I told you that in the letter. I'm telling you now in person. I've thought about nothing these past weeks but that phone call. And I have to explain it to you.

He studied his thoughts, eyes troubled.

—I don't know what's happening to me, who I am, what I'm becoming. I feel caught in different worlds. One here— He risked a look at her. —One in Harden. And one out there— His eyes shifted back to the window.

He took a heavy breath, frowning slightly.

—I don't know. Sometimes I think it would have been better if Catherine hadn't sent me to private school. I'd be a simple shit-kicking hick from Harden.

No questions, no doubts, no aspirations. I'd be happy at TWA, I wouldn't care about the outside world. I'd settle down with some girl like Ruthie or Trixie and raise a bunch of kids, who'd marry right out of high school and start on *their* families. The boys would get jobs out at the airport or on the railroad, the girls would be kitchen beauticians or waitresses. Just like their mom and dad. Just like their *parents'* parents.

His eyes scanned her face. —I wouldn't want someone like you— He turned away again.

—But it's too late. I know about you. I know about that larger world. I know the possibilities. And I'm afraid of it. Afraid I won't measure up. That I'll do my best but no matter how hard I reach, it'll be beyond my grasp.

His shoulders slumped, his head bowed, his hands reached for the steering wheel.

—So I took it out on you. I guess I thought by reducing you to my level, I'd make myself bigger.

Reggie's eyes traced the lines of Casey's bent profile: the broad brow, the straight nose, the full lips and strong chin. Of all the things she loved about Casey, this was the one she loved best: No matter how wrong-headed or foolish he'd been, he was always willing to face himself and try to make amends.

She reached for his leg. Now was the time to tell him: I lied, Casey. I'm as guilty as you.

By now she'd been to the female doctor at the student health center. She could tell him about girls who rode bikes and horses, who swam and played tennis and took vigorous dancing lessons. By now, she could tell him why she didn't have a hymen. But something deep prevented her.

Casey turned to look at her, and as their eyes met she understood she could not make this easy for him. She could not give back so freely what he had taken so wrenchingly. He would love her with no doubts or she would not accept his love at all.

She lifted her hand from his thigh. —Thank you, Casey. I really appreciate that. It means a lot. And I understand.

Casey ducked a look at her, the look of a chastened boy trying to be a man. —What does it matter if you weren't a virgin?

—It doesn't matter at all.

—We were virgins in our hearts.

Reggie nodded, disliking herself for this penance she was exacting. And applauding herself for its success.

Casey turned and reached for her. Reggie twisted sideways and stretched across him. He put his arms around her and slowly bent his head. Reggie reached for his neck and lifted her face to meet his. They kissed, for the first time in two years.

The kiss was different from previous kisses. Not heedlessly hot and demanding but soft, tenuous, enquiring; asking to be fuller and deeper. And it made a difference. They clung, kissing and kissing, growing fuller and fuller with each other, going deeper and deeper, getting sweaty in the late-afternoon Boston cool. But they went no farther.

Casey pulled back with a jagged breath, eyes squinched. Whether from pain or pleasure, Reggie couldn't tell; she'd heard at college about "blue balls." She sat upright, straightened her clothes, then traded places. They drove back to the commodious unkempt colonial in close, comfortable silence.

But late that night in bed, after dinner out with Maggie and Daddy at a nice but unpretentious restaurant, Reggie realized she was ready for more. She appreciated Casey's consideration, his show of respect in not grabbing at her right off, his sensitiveness in not adding insult to injury. But now that they'd settled that, she wanted more. She sorted through words looking for the one that most precisely described her yearning, remembering Oak Creek. And that word was sweetness.

She lay there, feeling the need for it behind her ear, down her neck, in the cleft of her shoulder. She cupped her breasts; the nipples were erect just from the thought of it. She smoothed her hands down her abdomen, sucking in her stomach. Her fingers caught in the silky mons. She spread her palm and pressed. The ache for sweetness was urgent here. She extended two fingers and gently separated the lips, stroking into the hot, moist flesh. She caught her breath and arched. She'd never touched herself like this.

She allowed herself a moment of delicious pleasure. Then suddenly ashamed, removed her hand and rolled over. It took her a long time to go to sleep. Just before dawn she woke herself grinding against the mattress, on the edge of exquisite sweetness.

The next morning, shortly after Maggie's brunch of overcooked ham steak and undercooked waffles, Reggie announced she was taking Casey to see more of Boston. At the bottom of the hill, Casey stopped her.

—I'll drive.

Reggie didn't argue; she just hoped Maggie and Daddy weren't watching. The car had come with the explicit instruction that no one else was to drive it. But that caveat hadn't been clarified, And for this visit that includes Casey.

He drove them into the woods to the same spot as the day before, without a misturn. Reggie was impressed with his powers of observation and sense of direction.

He switched off the ignition and reached for her. Reggie was eagerly ready. They kissed for a long while, slowly and deeply, as if they'd learned from yesterday. But this time, they ventured further. Their kisses picked up pace, grew harder and greedier. They experimented with tongues. Casey sucked Reggie's lip, she licked and nipped his. He discovered her right ear and its sensitivity. She tilted her head, inviting him onto her neck, and moaned when he gently bit. They dragged and crushed against each other. He pulled up her blouse and put his hand on her warm midriff. She undid her bra and moved his hand to her breast. He groaned and enclosed it in his fingers. He squeezed, hard then lightly, learning the heft and give of the soft weighted flesh. He tugged and tweaked the taut nipples; rubbed in a circular motion, palms teasingly brushing. They were breathing heavily.

Casey pushed Reggie back across the passenger seat, shoulders against the door, where he could get his mouth on her. He kissed and nibbled, licked the salty streams in her shallow cleavage. While his hands slowly squeezed and stroked up her thighs, tickling the inner sides, spreading them wider and wider.

Reggie waited, eyes slitted, breath suspended, and gasped when he touched her mons, arching to meet his hand. He tucked his fingers into the edge of her pants, and she softly cried out. She wanted more, and more and more.

She grabbed for him and pulled him onto her. She wanted to feel his flesh, the way he was feeling hers. She wanted to explore his body, the way his was exploring hers. She wanted him inside her.

She yanked frantically at the flannel encasing his body; it was too tight, she couldn't get a grip. She reached for the lower edge of his tunic and tried to tug it up; it wouldn't budge over his ribs. She pushed him back and roughly began fumbling at the small buttons sealing off his groin.

—What're you doing?

—Trying to get this damn thing off.

—You can't.

Reggie stopped fumbling. —Why not?

—It's too hard— He crossed his hands over his head and started pulling and lifting. —See? It takes me ten minutes to get it on, what with the buttons and all.

Reggie stared, suddenly seeing them. Casey bound from shoulder to foot in uniformed correctness. She sprawled across the seat, legs wide, skirt up around her waist, naked breasts dangling, wetted crotch gaping. God knows what her hair and face looked like. She felt unseemly and wanton.

She struggled up and pulled down her skirt.

—What's wrong?

She retrieved her blouse and bra. —I just don't feel right about this.

—What? What'd I do?

She fastened her bra —Look at us— and primly plumped her breasts into the cups. —Would you call this equal involvement?

Casey looked around, at a loss. —I thought it was.

Reggie finished buttoning her blouse —In that?— and glared over at his uniform.

Casey looked down. —I'm in the Navy now.

Reggie shoved open the door —Well I'm not— and flounced out of the car.

Casey watched helplessly as she strode around the hood and stood impatiently waiting while he slid over to the passenger's seat. She bounced in behind the wheel, slammed the door, and started the engine.

—Where are we going?

—To see Boston— She looked over, smiled archly. —Don't you think it's about time? In case Maggie and Daddy ask questions?

They returned home just in time for supper. Maggie had planned early barbeque on the patio, something she did well since there was little damage could be done to corn-on-the-cob, mixed green salad, and Italian garlic bread. Daddy was in charge of the chicken.

Daddy served cocktails. Casey asked for beer but settled for bourbon. And it became immediately evident that Reggie's tour with Casey had come none too soon: the topic of conversation was to be Casey's impressions of Boston.

Reggie had crammed two days of her carefully planned itinerary for Casey's visit into one, to make up for yesterday's debit due to unforeseen circumstances. She'd whirled Casey through downtown Boston, up through Cambridge, across Arlington and Waltham, down as far as Wellesley. Then back over through Newton and Brookline.

She'd shown him Beacon Hill, Trinity Church, the John Hancock Tower, the Old South Meeting House, the site of the Boston Tea Party, the Custom House, Quincy Market, Paul Revere's House, and the Old North Church. She'd whizzed him through Harvard, Radcliffe, Tufts, Brandeis, Wellesley, Boston College, and her own beloved Wexler. But Casey hadn't set foot in one of them.

To compensate, Reggie'd kept up a constant line of guided-tour patter, filling Casey in on details as well as general information, and adding pieces of special or personal interest. Casey looked and listened attentively. If he minded this tied-in-the-car-for-hours, captive-audience exercise, Casey wasn't about to say so. And Reggie wasn't about to ask.

She was relying now, as Maggie and Daddy plied their questions, on

Casey's demonstrated powers of observation and memory. He got them through admirably. And by the time the evening was ended, they were both in a relaxed friendly frame of mind. They were able to kiss out on the patio. The events of the morning were behind them.

But not quite resolved. At least not for Reggie. She sat in her darkened room after the house was quiet, staring out the window, running back through the morning, trying to understand what had happened to her. And suddenly, she had an image.

She was remembering a bitch Maggie once had, a black miniature poodle, who'd produced a fine litter of show pups. Maggie had paid a handsome sum the second time around for an even better sire to produce an even better batch of prize winners. The bitch and young male were introduced, allowed to play together, until the breeders were assured the prospective mates liked one another and, when the critical time came, would perform successfully.

The bitch came into heat, the young sire was brought. The bitch was happy to see him. More than happy; she was needy. She immediately backed up and presented her swollen, dripping vulva. The inexperienced male couldn't believe his good luck. In an agitation of excitement, he mounted. The bitch braced her legs and, watching over her shoulder, waited for the relieving penetration. But at the last second, just as he was about to enter, the sire hesitated. Who knows for what reason. Uncertainty, over-excitation, unstable balance? But in that second he— and the two breeders—lost all. The bitch whirled on him, teeth bared, viciously growling, and thereafter refused to have a thing to do with him.

Reggie rose from her chair and closed the bedroom drapes, chuckling softly. She understood that bitch perfectly.

SCENE 26

Evidently Casey held his own late-night counsel. He appeared the next morning in slacks and polo shirt. When Maggie asked conversationally —What're your plans today?— Reggie looked uncertain but Casey had a quick answer.

—Well, being as I'm in the Navy now, I thought I'd like to see something of the ocean.

He grinned over at Reggie. She hurriedly picked up on his cue and nodded.

—I thought I'd take him to Marblehead. And Salem.

Maggie smiled. —That'll be nice— She started clearing the table. —And he might like Walden Pond. It's one of my favorites— She looked up from her dishes at Casey. —Are you interested in Thoreau's old stomping ground?

Casey looked at Reggie. —I am if there's enough time— The message in his smile made Reggie flush.

Oblivious, Maggie dumped her load in the sink and turned on the water. —Well, just be sure you're back in time to bathe and dress. We'll leave the house at five.

Casey strode ahead to the car and, standing by the passenger door, held out his hand. Reggie had no choice but to place the key in it. He settled her into her seat, tucking her skirt around her with intimate strokes, brushing her breasts as he leaned across to fasten her seat belt. Surprising her with a quick kiss as he pulled back to close the door. Surprising her with another as he slid into the driver's seat and turned the ignition. She risked a look back at the bay window as they started down the drive. But there was no flutter of curtain, no shadowy watching presence.

Casey drove with mock old-fashioned sedateness: back erect, arms stiff, hands tight on each side of the wheel, overplaying the steering. He didn't look at her, but Reggie could see his mischievousness. She found him irresistible when he was like this.

He took the road into the hills, as Reggie hoped he would. But instead of pulling off onto their previous spot, he turned into a narrow track he must have made note of earlier. Reggie gripped the hand rest and cast anxious glances as they bumped and bounced over the rapidly diminishing ruts. But Casey negotiated the encroaching branches and brambles without a scratch to the convertible's pristine enamel.

They ended in a tiny clearing, deep in the woods. On their other two outings, they'd kept the top up; but today Casey released the latches and slowly folded it down. They were surrounded by brown and green filtering blue and gold, emanating warm woodsy fragrance. Reggie inhaled with a deep inner sigh.

They sat for a moment in silence. Then Casey turned, his face no longer lightly playful but darkly intense.

—Get in the backseat— His voice came from deep in his throat, roughly edged.

Reggie hurried to comply. But after the delicate peace, she found the abrupt scrabbling around thumping seat backs and sharp slamming of doors unsettling, a rude disruption. As she and Casey faced each other across the interruption of tan imitation leather, she felt the need for a bridging connection—a soft kiss, a tender touch, a slow movement—to reestablish the sweet spell. Instead, Casey grabbed and pulled her to him, pushing her back and down, his mouth hard on hers, his body heavy, his fingers feverishly working at her buttons. She responded to his urgency and helped him. He immediately sat back and started tearing off his own clothes, letting her finish with hers.

She suddenly saw their disrobing as a kind of speeded-up struggle of body parts and bindings, as if in a fast-forward film: arms tugging up shirts; hands yanking open belts and zippers; feet kicking off shoes; fingers ripping down socks; legs shucking slacks, hips shrugging off skirt. The car was strewn with pieces of cloth and leather.

Casey unsnapped her bra; she shook it off. He twisted at her underpants; she lifted and slithered out of them. They finally sat side-by-side naked.

In the sudden stillness, Reggie felt foolish.

Casey looked at her, softly. His hands started roving over her body, slowly. He took her in his arms, gently. At last, Reggie was going to have her sweetness. She lost her self-consciousness and allowed herself to look down. The thick stiffness of Casey's erection was the most beautiful thing she'd ever wanted.

She sank back and reached for his neck, pulling his mouth to hers. She opened her body to him, forgetting the discomfort of the seat, the awkwardness of their position. She gripped his hips and insistently drew him to her.

He broke their kiss and sat up, reaching for his slacks, fumbling in the pockets. He came up with a small paper packet, from which he extracted a cream-colored disk; Reggie's first sight of a condom.

She watched in dismayed fascination as Casey rolled the dull rubbery sheath over his slick silky penis. She thought of the line, Like taking a shower with your raincoat on. But she understood the wisdom of his caution. She lay back and willed herself to be receptive.

But the condom was dry and tight, and so was she. Casey spit on his hand and rubbed the spittle over her and the condom. Reggie closed her eyes, not wanting to see his frowning efforts as he poked and probed at her. He finally accomplished entry. But his movements did not bring sweet pleasure, the joyous connection Reggie'd been waiting for. Did not recapture Oak Creek. Instead she felt assaulted, invaded by a foreign object.

The rubber dragged against her flesh. She cried out.

Casey stopped.

—What's wrong?

—It hurts. It's tearing me.

He pulled out, leaving, Reggie felt, the deflated condom stuck to her vagina. She was getting images, unwillingly remembering Casey's phone call.

She started to cry.

—Oh god, don't cry, Reggie.

—I can't help it.

—I didn't mean to hurt you.

—I know.

—I wouldn't hurt you for the world.

She was trying to stop sobbing.

—I'm sorry, Casey.

—It's all right.

—But I can't. I just can't.

—You don't have to

She struggled up.

—It's *that*— Her eyes stabbed at the rubber clinging in wrinkles to his now-limp penis. She expected to see blood on it. Or pus.

He plucked off the offending object. —I just didn't want us to take any chances— He bent toward her, his voice caressing. —We aren't ready for a baby yet, are we?

Reggie averted her face. —It's just so unnatural— She was feeling loss, of something taken from her, she sensed forever.

—I won't use one again.

He reached for her. But she shook her head.

—I can't. Not right now, Casey. I can't explain. I just need a little time— She tried to smile. —I'll be all right later.

They redressed in lonely, confused silence.

Reggie raised the convertible top. Casey surveyed their situation. Reggie wryly watched. —Well, do you think you can get us out of here?

Casey grinned. —I got us in, didn't I?

He backed them out without mishap.

On the road, he pointed the car toward town then stopped.

—Where to now?

—I guess we'd better do Marblehead and Salem. Walden Pond if there's time.

The smiles they gave each other were disheartened.

They never found time for "later."

It was Sunday, Casey's last evening. Abby had planned a dinner for Casey to meet the rest of the family; and for them to meet him. Maggie was not pleased about this; she'd tartly expressed her opinion: It's inappropriate. Like welcoming him as a prospective member when no intentions have been declared. She was still hoping Reggie would come out of her adolescent romance with Harden and grow up to a nice boy from Boston.

Reggie knew these things because Abby had told her, had wanted her to be forewarned. Abby had her own opinion about what it takes to grow up, her own definition of what it means to be adult. She believed uncompromisingly in the loyalty and support of family. If Casey was what Reggie wanted, then it was her family's duty to be there behind her. How can the melon be robust when the vine is pale and spindly? she'd been known to ask.

For Reggie, this dinner where Casey could finally meet Abby was the perfect culmination of his visit. But as they headed home from Walden Pond, Casey started asking questions: Who's going to be there? What're they like? How should I act with them? And Reggie realized he was nervous. Just be yourself, she told him; they're not people to worry about. Uncle Jack's well-meaning but a stuffy bore. Aunt Miriam's sweet but an airhead. Lawrence is at summer camp. Caroline's in Europe. A stroke of luck. She felt disloyal but it was the truth and the only way she knew to reassure him.

Abby, she told him, was the most special person in the world, her dearest and closest friend, the one who knew her best. And she realized with an unexpected pang that this also was the truth.

Casey worried over what to wear; he had only his flannels and the slacks he had on. They decided on the uniform. He posed for her in the living room, shinily scrubbed and shyly proud, anxious for Reggie's approval. She told him how nice he looked, how well the bell-bottoms suited him. His grin became boyish, his spirits buoyant. He handed her a roll of adhesive tape and, under his direction, she applied the wide strips over the breadth and length of the dark flannel, to remove every vestige of Maggie's lint and cat hair.

Casey's confidence continued high as Daddy drove them through the increasingly affluent suburbs, while Maggie supplied a listing of major street names and description of neighborhoods. But the sprawling gray Victorian, secluded on its high hill, backed by seemingly limitless forest, and surrounded by luxuriant gardens, daunted him. Reggie saw him pull back and assume protective indifference.

He was in punctilious command of himself as Abby greeted them at the door, almost courtly in his manner. But as Abby led them into the living room, his poise momentarily failed and he imperceptibly faltered. His smiles were eager, his handshakes enthusiastic through introductions with Jack and Miriam, but Reggie sensed his distraction, as, from the periphery of his attention, he took in gilded frames, Persian rugs, lustrous fabrics, and carved dark furniture.

Settled on the velvet loveseat next to Reggie, he maintained his smile and entered into the initiatory conversation, articulately answering questions about the Navy, Arizona, and Harden. But the edges of his smile frayed, his demeanor lost its sparkle, and his responses increasingly lacked vitality. The bravado tha had carried him through introductions had given out and left him subdued and flattened.

Reggie stepped in and started telling about their tour of Boston. Abby quickly served drinks.

The bourbon seemed to revive him. He relaxed back, crossed a leg. His winsome charm returned. He started telling stories, entertaining, wooing and winning, making the family laugh. Jack joined in by pontificating. Miriam became flirtatious. Daddy contributed a story or two of his own. Even Maggie seemed captivated. Abby served another round, her eyes knowing, her smile sly. And Reggie thought they were going to make it.

Then they went to table. The dazzle of the dining room after the soft glow of the living room set Casey back again. The light flooding from the large chandelier glinted off sterling and crystal, gleamed from china and polished wood, reflected in facets from the long mirror above the sideboard, and glanced off the glass restraining Abby's ornately framed flowers. Creating a pulsating brightness Abby hoped would—indeed intended should—also infect her guests. Instead, it intimidated Casey. As they entered, he stepped to the side of the door and let the others proceed ahead of him. Reggie stopped in front of him, providing a shield while he regained his bearings.

Abby had arranged her group of seven at one end of the mahogany table, which on larger occasions closely accommodated twenty. She curtly directed seating:

—Reggie, you and Casey, as my honored guests, sit to each side of me— She pointed.

—Jack and Miriam next to Reggie.

—Maggie and Arthur next to Casey.

As they took their places, Reggie saw the calculated dynamics behind this sociogram: Reggie opposite Casey, where she could maintain reassuring eye contact. Maggie and Arthur buttressing him on the left, Abby buttressing on his right. Jack and Miriam at a diagonal, cordoned off by the table and blocked, if necessary, by Reggie. Abby, of course, at the head, in charge.

Which she was, magnificently. In her sharp-eyed, soft-smiled strong voice, she controlled the conversation: raising topics, directing questions, focusing on her family, making them carry the weight. Drawing Casey in only when he could ᵔfortably contribute from his experience and knowledge.

ᵗt for all Abby's astute maneuvering and tactful orchestration, the dinner did ᵢly. Casey was unnerved by the presence of a butler, pulling back stiffly ᵕ black-sleeved arm placed or removed a dish. He approached warily ᶜods fancily presented: Coquilles St. Jacques on scallop shells, duck confit on arugula, celery and pear bisque in tureen, Beef Wellington on covered silver platter, little molds of green custard Maggie told him was asparagus. He didn't understand all the silverware; why two forks, two knives, and three spoons. He watched Reggie carefully to see which utensil she picked up when. He didn't understand all the wines, why a different one with each course, each a different color. He didn't understand the commotion over the Baked Alaska; to him, it was just cake a la mode with a crust of meringue. Reggie saw his expression and wanted to laugh.

He cut and ate with slow over-politeness, his eyes lowered while he chewed self-consciously, as if he were doing something primitively private in civilized public. Though servings were small and slowly presented, he couldn't handle the six courses. His plates were taken away half empty, his wine went barely touched.

In an unguarded moment, when the family was involved with itself, she caught him looking around. And she saw him as he must be seeing himself: a dark slash of wool in a pastel flow of tweed and silk: an intrusion. A misfit. And he knew it.

To her immense relief—and Casey's, she imagined—they finally retired to the family room for liqueurs and coffee. The lowlit informality of the simple fruitwood furniture and overplump paisley cushions loosened the family into mellow congeniality. The rich food and liberal wine didn't hurt. The family slumped back, knees spread, elbows on arm rests, arms across couch backs, jackets undone and belts released a notch over distended bellies. This was the room where they did their most hair-down talking. The room with the window seat where Reggie had spent hours crying over *Anna Karenina*, *Jane Eyre*, *Green Mansions*, and *Wuthering Heights*.

Casey, admitting it was his first, consented to try a brandy. Daddy, with his own snifter, showed him how to swirl and inhale before sipping. Casey's eyes flew wide.

—Wow!— he grinned. —It sure clears the sinuses.

The family laughed, and were reminded of their own first experiences with particular drinks. This led to recollections of wild college parties and youthful escapades, all of which were new to Reggie. There were jokes and kidding, and much laughter. And Reggie thought things were going to end well after all.

College days lapsed into an updating on college buddies, their whereabouts, fortunes, and family.

Daddy asked Jack what he thought about the stock market. Maggie asked Miriam about Caroline. They discussed the world situation, reviewed the news, argued issues. Among themselves. The family as usual; a close, closed circle.

Reggie glanced anxiously at Casey, to see how he was taking this. But he seemed happy enough just to be listening. Good, a small voice in her brightened; maybe he'll learn something.

On the way home, Casey chatted comfortably with Maggie and Daddy about the evening. What a nice time he'd had, how nice Jack and Miriam were, how much he liked Abby. He confessed he hadn't been in a house like that before, or had that kind of dinner. He admitted it overwhelmed him. But he really enjoyed it all. Reggie reached for his hand and squeezed, he smiled and squeezed back. He seemed to have regained his confidence.

In the hall, Maggie made her good nights. Casey asked, if she didn't mind, he'd like to sit up a little with Reggie; it was their last evening. Maggie looked uncertain. Daddy took her arm and guided her up the stairs.

Casey led Reggie to the patio and plumped her down on the plastic-cushioned ivy-patterned glider.

—Now stay there. Don't move. I'll be right back— And he bounded into the house. He returned in less than a minute.

He settled briskly beside her, on the edge of his seat, looking like a cat ready to burp a canary. He leaned to kiss her, tucked her hair behind her ear.

It was one of those humid New England summer nights, the sky close and heavy, the stars fuzzy, the moon pale and small. The air had the clean, sweet scent of mowed grass.

He looked at her softly, intently. Then held out his hand and opened it.

Reggie knew instantly what was in the tiny blue-velvet box. She stared into Casey's eager, expectant eyes and tried to smile.

—Open it— Casey prompted.

Reggie's fingers lifted, she looked down. Her heart skipped, her stomach lurched, her smile became frozen.

—It's beautiful, Casey.

—Put it on.

She stayed bent, trying to absorb the small diamond solitaire bolstered by an unimaginative gold mounting. She felt she was drowning.

She needed air. She lifted her head and gulped.

—I can't, Casey.

His face fragmented.

—Why not?

She looked at him, letting him see her pain, trying to show him her recognition of his.

—It's not the right time, Casey. Not the right timing.

—What's wrong with it?

She groped for words, her eyes imploring him to understand.

—We're not ready. We're nothing yet. You have to finish the Navy, I have to finish college.

—We could do that together.

—I'm only eighteen.

—That's the age all the girls marry in Harden.

She explored his face, helplessly.

—This isn't Harden, Casey.

He closed the box and clutched it back.

—Right now I wish it were.

She appreciated his correct use of the subjunctive.

He stood. —Well, I guess that's it— Reggie remained on the glider. —Are you coming in?

—No. I think I'll stay here for a while. I'd like you to stay with me.

—I think I better get to bed. I'm pretty tired. And I have to get up early— He paused at the door, without looking at her —Thanks for the nice day— then quietly slid the glass closed behind him.

Reggie sat up late again that night, staring out her window, miserable in her feelings but clear in her mind. In the morning on the way to the airport, she tried to explain more fully, with the words she'd carefully prepared, why she wasn't ready yet to get engaged. But Casey cut her short, dismissing it with airy indifference.

—Forget it. Don't make such a big deal. It doesn't matter, I don't really care. One way or the other. In fact, it wasn't even my idea. Catherine put me up to it— He grinned over at her. —Shit or get off the pot, she said.

Reggie laughed. That sounded like Catherine.

—So I shit— He looked back out the window. —And now I'm off the pot.

His good-byes were effected with the same breeziness.

—You still my girl?

—Of course I am.

—Stay that way— He gave her a brisk kiss. —I'll write. As soon as I get settled.

He saluted from the top of the ramp, cap cocked over his eye. Then giving her the thumbs-up sign, he disappeared into the dark hole of the plane's hatch.

SCENE 27

Casey had managed to get stationed at a naval air base. Though he'd learned that to be a pilot he had to be a college graduate, he was still working toward something in aviation. His letters came less frequently but with regularity. He wrote every Sunday, his letters arriving in Boston Wednesday or Thursday. Reggie replied the same evening, her letters reaching Casey Monday or Tuesday, after he'd written his next letter. So they were always out of sync, a week behind each other, their responses often like talking at cross purposes. Reggie registered a mild complaint, nothing more really than frustration. Without comment, Casey changed the pacing of his letters, answering only after he'd heard from her. They fell into a pattern of writing every other week. Once in a while, Casey skipped; Reggie didn't mind, she herself was busy.

Then in March of her sophomore year, Casey's letters stopped altogether. Reggie waited two weeks, unconcerned. Then three. The fourth week she wrote, saying she missed his letters. The fifth week, she wrote again, asking why he hadn't written. By the sixth week, she was seriously worried, she knew something had to be wrong. She decided to call.

With nothing more than his address, she tried to get his number. She made it through to the air base. She begged the operator into staying with her as they were shuttled from department to department, each connection a different call. But none could come up with Casey's barracks. Apologizing that there was nothing more she could do, the operator finally left her.

Reggie knew she was going to have to call Catherine. It was the last thing she wanted to do. But she had no other choice, she was desperate.

She dispensed with conversational openers.

—Catherine, it's Reggie. Can you give me Casey's number?

—Why? What's wrong?

—He hasn't written. For six weeks.

—*Six weeks.*

—I'm afraid something's happened to him.

—I'm sure I would have heard.

—I think something's the matter.

—Did you fight?

—No.

—Then what's going on here?

—That's what I have to find out.

Catherine gave her the number. —Call me. After you've talked with him. I want to hear his excuse.

Reggie called the barracks every hour on the hour, but Casey was never there. Finally the phone jangled. Reggie jumped from the bed, her heart pounding.

It was Catherine. —Why didn't you call? I got worried.

—I haven't talked to him. I made several calls, but he was always out. I left a message, Call Reggie. But he hasn't answered.

—It's almost ten his time. He has to be there for lights out. Give it a few more minutes. I'm sure he'll call.

And he did. At twelve minutes to eleven, Reggie's time.

Casey, too, dispensed with conversational openers.

—Why did you have to drag my mother into this?

—Did you get my messages?

—I got them.

—Then why didn't you call?

—I would have gotten around to it.

—I was worried.

—About what?

—Why haven't you written?

—I didn't have anything to write about.

—Are you all right?

—Why shouldn't I be?

—You sound so funny.

—So I sound funny. Why should you care?

—Because I love you.

—Yeah? Me and how many others?

Reggie stopped. How was she to answer this? She was up against a barricade of anger she had no idea how to breach.

—What's the matter, Casey?

—Guess who's on base with me?

—Who?

—Tommy Smithson.

Reggie's heart plummeted, then lodged in her throat. She knew now the face of her trouble, but not its nature. Her breathing became quick and shallow.

—Yeah. He got here eight weeks ago. He wants to fly high, too. We didn't know each other much in Harden, but since he's been here we've gotten to be great buddies. We have a lot in common— His voice twisted from angry to ugly.

—It seems we share the same woman.

—What?— Reggie couldn't believe what she was hearing, couldn't believe what was happening. —What are you talking about?

—I'm talking about his kissing you, feeling you up.

—Tommy told you that?

—He says you're a great fuck. Better, I gather, than I got.

—And you believed?

—So what was wrong with me? What's he got I haven't? Wasn't I big enough? Wasn't I good enough? Or maybe it's the other way around. You like 'em down and dirty, drunken bums like Tommy.

Reggie rallied what few wits she had left.

—You're calling me a whore.

—If the shoe fits.

She hung up.

She sat on the edge of the bed, waiting for it to hit her. When it did, it ripped her apart. No numbing cold to hold her together this time. She went out of control, screaming behind clenched teeth, convulsed with wracking sobs. She pounded the bed, charged around the room, throwing objects, kicking furniture. A housemate timidly knocked. Reggie rammed herself against the door and clicked the lock.

—Go away!

When Catherine called an hour later, Reggie was still crying but coherent.

—Did you talk to him?

—I wish I hadn't.

—You're crying.

—It was horrible.

—What did he say?

Reggie choked with a fresh flood of tears. —He called me a whore, Catherine.

—He *what*?

Reggie poured out the whole story, her words coming in breathy fragments broken by hiccoughing spasms as her exhausted lungs tried to grab air. But as she talked, she began to quiet and gradually gain control.

It took Reggie a long time in the telling. She had to go back to the beginning: Tommy's visit. She could hear the lighting and sucking of cigarettes on the other end, but Catherine didn't say a word. Reggie's relief at getting it all out was cathartic. Even if she didn't tell quite all, didn't give a quite truthful account of the episode overlooking the carnival.

She was working for protection. Something crafty had happened to her.

—And I didn't do a *thing*, Catherine. He showed up on our doorstep. He was lonely, a lost soul away from home. We took him in, fed him. I went with him to a movie or two. He was the brother of my girl friend. What else was I to do? We were being decent.

—And then he tried to kill me. Tried to cut up my face, tried to run me down with a car. Because I wouldn't accept his advances. Because— she sobbed —I was being true to Casey.

She snuffed back her tears.

—Daddy pressed charges. Tommy had to stand Captain's Mast. He spent time in the brig. And lost his chance at officers' school. And now he's wreaking his revenge, Catherine. And Casey believed him!

Catherine drew a hard breath. And released it with a disgusted growl.

—Tommy Smithson's a sick bastard. And though he's my son and it hurts me to say it, Casey Colter's a stupid son-of-a-bitch.

—I'm not a whore, Catherine.

—I know that, for christ's sake.

—I didn't deserve this.

—No. And Casey doesn't deserve you. Not if he's going to act like this.

—I love him, Catherine.

—And he loves you.

—But I can't take anymore of this.

—You shouldn't have to.

—I can't let him hurt me again.

—And he won't. I promise you. Just give him a little time, Reggie. He has some growing up to do. Some lessons to learn. But he'll make it. So will you. You've both been hurt. But you'll get past your pain and work things out together. I know you will. If you just give it some time.

But Reggie didn't get past her pain; didn't rationalize it away with some acceptable explanation; didn't change it to guilt as she had before so she could excuse and forgive Casey. This time, she fed on it, going back over their relationship, getting stronger with each recalled insult, growing fat on each resurrected injury. Her pain informed and honed her awareness, gave a keened edge to her life, a sharp bright poignancy. She felt most alive, most in touch with herself, when she was alone—studying in her room, walking on campus, sitting under the stars or trees—thinking about Casey. Remembering the times they'd had together, the things they'd said, the laughter they'd shared. And all they'd lost. She began to see it as a kind of tragicomedy, a betrayal of themselves, their past, and their future. A waste of so much potential. And so unnecessary. She began to withdraw, preferring her times alone with her sorrow. She began to see life through the eyes of disillusionment and estrangement.

Casey wrote, pages of intricate self-analysis and excruciating apology. Reggie read, and tore them up, page by page, into tiny pieces.

Casey telephoned. Reggie hung up on him, and felt sweet revenge, joyous disconnection.

Catherine phoned. Reggie explained—gently, sadly, patiently—that it was too late. She never wanted to see Casey again.

Then late one night, Reggie took her sackful of Casey's letters and fed them slowly into the family fireplace. The leap of the destructive flames in the dark room made her feel exultantly like Hedda Gabler.

Maggie and Daddy knew the romance was ended but didn't know why. They saw Reggie's distressed distance and tried to reach out to her. But Reggie refused to trust them.

—It's over. That's enough, isn't it?— Then she turned on Maggie. —You should be happy. After all, this is what you wanted.

She saw the hurt in Maggie's eyes. But hurt was something Reggie was becoming inured to.

She didn't even tell Abby. She wanted no one saying, even so much as insinuating, I told you so. She had to spare herself—and Casey—further humiliation.

Then one afternoon in early July, Reggie's telephone rang. The caller didn't need to identify himself.

—If you hang up, I'll come to your house.

—What? Where are you?

—Right here in town.

—How?

—I took a weekend pass. Hopped a cargo plane.

—What do you want?

—We have to talk.

—I have nothing to say to you.

—Then *I* want to talk.

—I don't want to listen.

—You've got to hear me out. I have so much to say.

—I don't have to do anything. And I've heard more than enough of what you have to say.

—Even the condemned man gets his last rites, doesn't he?

Reggie's mouth twitched wryly; she applauded this.

—All right, start talking.

—No. Not over the phone. I have to tell you in person.

—Then forget it.

—If you won't meet me, I'll come to the house and say everything in front of your parents.

—That's unscrupulously like black mail, isn't it?

—I have to see you.

Reggie considered.

—When did you have in mind?

—Right now.

—Where?

—Anywhere.

Reggie was intrigued. Her pain had taught her about power, the rewards of controlling, the satisfactions of manipulating.

—All right. We can meet at Abby's. She's at the lake. Do you remember how to get there?

—I'll find it.

—Park in the drive. Then take the path back to the left. There's a gazebo.

—How soon?

—One hour.

Reggie went as she was, in shorts and T shirt. She didn't give a damn how she looked. She told Maggie she was restless, had to get out of the house, go for a drive. It wasn't exactly a lie; but if it had been, it wouldn't have mattered. Lies were another thing Reggie'd become inured to. She contemplated how interesting it was that the only time she lied seemed to be when it involved Casey.

Casey's car was in Abby's drive when Reggie got there. He stood as she approached the gazebo. She took wide, swinging strides, flipping her hair and smiling. He was holding a bunch of flowers. She burst out laughing. —I don't believe this.

She took the flowers and tossed them onto the bench.

Casey maintained his smile.

—It's good to see you, Reggie.

—I wish I could say the same— She flounced down beside the flowers. —So what's all this you have to say?

Casey sat down beside her.

—You're not going to make this easy, are you?

—Why should I?

—I don't know where to begin.

—Try the beginning.

Casey took a deep breath, picked up the flowers. —I guess that's my childhood. What it was like growing up in a place like Harden, trying to belong. When all the time my folks kept telling me I *didn't* belong, that I had more to offer.

Reggie twisted impatiently —You told me all that. In your letter.

—You read it?

—Of course I did. Then threw it in the rubbish.

—That's all it was to you? Rubbish?

—No. I thought it was interesting. And made a lot of sense. Just like what happened to you when you went away to school. That made sense, too.

—But it didn't make any difference?

—In what? Your behavior?

—In the way you saw my behavior.

—It helped me understand it, yes. Better than I already did. But it didn't excuse it.

—I didn't mean it to.

—Then what were you going for, Casey? What are you going for now?

Casey plucked at the flowers. —You.

Reggie laughed. Rudely, sardonically.

—How? By telling me about your childhood? I'm interested in your adulthood. Or excuse me, perhaps I should say *manhood*.

Her smile was bitter.

Casey studied her. —You've changed, Reggie.

—And I'd say about time— She studied him back. —But you haven't. Not one bit.

Though he had. She saw it in the tiny lines around his eyes, the new crease pulling at the corner of his mouth.

Casey pinched a petal. —So you're not interested in the other things I have to say? About what the Navy did to me? What it was like coming out of boot camp into your life? How it felt to be rejected?

—I know all those things, Casey. You told me in your letter. And I told myself. Long before you wrote. They still don't excuse your arrogance, your jealous possessiveness, your suspiciousness and ugly temper.

She took a breath, gathered steam, relieved to be finally venting.

—You're completely self-centered, Casey, the whole world revolves around you. In all this, all I've heard about is you, *your* pain, *your* confusion, *your* conflicted childhood. I haven't heard a word about me, about what *I* felt like, growing up in a tight little world of money and influence, while right outside my door I knew children were starving— She's losing control. —About what my year in Harden did to me. About what happened when you went in the Navy. About what happened to *me*, Casey— She slumps —To me— and starts to cry.

Casey takes her hand. For a moment she lets him stroke it, then realizes and yanks it away.

—That's what I want to hear now, Reggie. About you. About what you thought and felt.

She looks up, her face streaked and tormented.

—God, Casey, where were you all the time we were talking and writing? Was it all about you? Didn't any of it have to do with learning about Reggie?

—I was always thinking about you. Trying to understand and know you. And I thought I did.

—Really? Then how could you have done what you did, said all those things? How could you have hurt me that way?

His face is stricken. —That's what I've been trying to explain.

—No. Nothing will ever explain that! Because that's the one thing I can never forgive. Your distrust. Your cruel disbelief in me.

—Please, Reggie. Can't we start over?

—How? Out of rubble?

—We could wipe the slate clean. Make today our new beginning.

Reggie's bowed over, shaking her head, sobbing softly.

—All I ask is one more chance. To prove myself. In ten days I get on an aircraft carrier— Reggie looks up. —I'll be gone overseas for two years— The dismay in her face heartens him.

—I'm not asking you to write, I'll write. I'm not asking you to love me. As long as you'll let me love you. I'm not asking anything. Except that you'll wait for me. And that you'll meet me. On July thirty-first, the last day of the month. The day after your birthday. To let me show you I've become a man.

Reggie stares, her eyes large and dark. Casey's implore.

—July thirty-first. Two years. I'll have only eight more months in the Navy. You'll be out of college. We'll meet. And we'll talk. That's all. Then we can see where we go from there.

Reggie's eyes are filling her mind with the memory of him.

—Will you wait?

Her lip trembles. She nods.

—Promise me.

And she promises.

SCENE 28

Reggie sucks a deep draught of wine, hunches over her knees, listening to the black soughing sluff of the waves.

And I promised.

Night has come in. Darkly, no moon. Boat lights dot the water, surprising in number, demarcating ocean from horizon.

God forgive me, I promised.

My food is gone. I'm on my second bottle. But I'm not through with this. There's more thrashing to be done, more excoriating of the flesh. More grain to be separated from the chaff.

I didn't think I'd see him again. I thought he'd forget me, that I'd forget about him. We'd be sailing different waters. I thought what we were doing was a last desperate effort to deny the damage we'd done, to belie our inadequacies, as individuals and together.

Casey wrote, every two or three months. I never answered. He sent gifts, for Christmas and my birthday: a Chinese lacquer jewel box, a Japanese kimono, a fan from the Philippines, a shell necklace from Samoa. I sent them to Catherine and Denny. Postcards came from New Guinea, New Zealand, and Australia; from Shanghai, Hong Kong, Singapore, and the Panama Canal. Casey was seeing the world, more of it certainly than I was. His experience was now larger than mine. I studied and partied, dated a little, drank a lot.

After Casey's and my good-bye tryst in the gazebo, I gradually crawled out of my dark shelter. I became a dedicated partier. I went anywhere I was invited, it didn't matter, so long as it involved people, booze, and laughter. And I was invited every weekend. I had gained a reputation as a bright spark to enliven any gathering. Like hard flint off of which to strike fire. I didn't care about this reputation; it carried with it a kind of quizzical respect. And I knew it didn't matter.

But wildly gay as I might drunkenly get, no one was allowed to touch me. And this gained me a reputation, also: Reggie, the glittering fun-loving Ice Maiden, the new Clydene Orton. It made me unapproachably desirable. I felt myself at last an accomplished woman, a success.

I met Howie the summer before my senior year, at a lawn party. He was in seersucker suit and white bucks. I was in flowered chiffon and floppy beribboned hat. He was attentive and gallant. I was bored and drunk. He himself was a little tiddly. We danced vividly. We talked avidly. We laughed excitedly, discovering complements and balance.

He thought I was beautiful and made me feel it. I thought he was a true gentleman, a sincerely nice guy. I saw myself bring out in him sparks and lustre he hadn't known before were in his reserved composition. He provided for me a rock I could bounce around on, leap off of, while he held me with a loose tether that kept me safely, securely grounded.

He gave me a stability I could rely on.

I married Howie in May, one week after I finished my bachelor's degree, two weeks after he finished law school.

THE SUNDAY NEW YORK TIMES

Regina Irene Patterson Weds Howard Vincent Kendall

Regina Irene Patterson, daughter of Mr. and Mrs. Arthur C. Patterson of Boston, was married yesterday to Howard Vincent Kendall, associate at Barringer, Livingston, Havighurst, Morrisey & Garrison law firm of Boston and New York. Rev. Malcolm Reid performed the ceremony at the Unitarian Universalist Society of Greater Boston.

The bride is a graduate of Wexler School for Girls and received a bachelor's degree cum laude in drama and theatre arts from Vassar College. She made her debut at the Cotillion. Her father is professor of anthropology at Harvard College. Her mother, Margaret Harrington Patterson, is Librarian in Charge of Children's Literature at Newton Public Library. Her paternal grandfather was Calvin MacLeod Patterson, senior partner in Patterson Baird & Saunders law firm of Boston. Her maternal grandfather was William Bradlee Harrington, chief executive of the Plymouth Rock Group, a securities brokerage in Boston. Her paternal grandmother is Abigail Claredon Patterson, a painter and philanthropist of Boston.

The bridegroom is an alumnus of Phillips Exeter Academy and graduated summa cum laude from Harvard College, where he was elected to Phi Beta Kappa and a member of the Fly Club. He received a master's degree in international affairs from Tufts University and a law degree from Yale University. His father, the late Martin Wiley Kendall, was president of Sterner, Leopold & Company, the Boston investment bank. His grandfather was Andrew Fitzgerald Kendall, pioneering founder and chairman of Kendall Ship Designers and Builders.

Christine Decker was maid of honor. Other attendants were Kathleen Bennett, Susan Stewart, Patricia Keenan and the groom's sister Elizabeth Kendall Fisher.

Kenneth Germaine Jr was best man. Ushers were Bruce Dempsey, Joseph Grayer, Peter Weatherill 3rd and J. Roger Hughes.

THE SUNDAY BOSTON GLOBE

Regina Irene Patterson Bride of Howard V. Kendall

Miss Regina Irene Patterson, daughter of Mr. and Mrs. Arthur Claredon Patterson, Boston, and Howard Vincent Kendall, son of the late Mr. and Mrs. Martin Wiley Kendall, Boston, were married by Rev. Malcolm Reid at the Unitarian Universalist Society of Greater Boston. A reception was held at the home of the bride's grandmother, Abigail Claredon Patterson, widow of Calvin MacLeod Patterson, both of Boston.

The bride was given in marriage by her father. She wore a fitted drop-waist dress of silk peau de soie. The sweetheart bodice, bell-shaped sleeves, and chapel train were accented with alencon lace and seed pearls. Her heirloom lace veil was bordered with alencon lace and seed pearls and had been worn by her grandmother. She carried white orchids and stephanotis from her grandmother's hot house and gardens.

Miss Christine "Cissie" Decker, Brookline, was maid of honor. Bridesmaids were Miss Kathleen Bennett, Worcester, Miss Susan Stewart, San Francisco, Miss Patricia Keenan, New York, and the groom's sister Mrs. Elizabeth Kendall Fisher, Manchester. They wore silk organza dresses each in a different pastel of lilac, yellow, pink, blue and mint with matching velvet ribbons around the waist. The circlet necklines, bouffant sleeves, and full skirts were edged with alencon lace. Their picture hats were also trimmed with velvet streamers. They carried baskets of pink carnations, yellow marguerites, purple lilacs, blue cornflowers and lily of the valley to match the flowers on their hats. The bridesmaids' outfits and the bride's gown were designed by Mrs. Calvin Patterson.

Best man was Kenneth Germaine Jr, Cambridge. Ushers were Bruce Dempsey, Chicago, Stephen Grayer, Princeton, NJ, Peter Weatherill 3rd, Milton, and J. Roger Hughes, Hartford, Ct.

The bride is a graduate of Wexler School for Girls and Vassar College, where she received a bachelor of fine arts degree cum laude in drama and theatre arts. She made her debut at the Cotillion.

The groom is an alumnus of Phillips Exeter Academy and summa cum laude graduate of Harvard College, where he was elected to Phi Beta Kappa and was a member of Fly. He received a master's degree in international affairs from Tufts University and a law degree from Yale University. He is an associate at Barringer, Livingston, Havighurst, Morrisey & Garrison of Boston and New York.

The couple will honeymoon in Hawaii, where they plan a three-week tour of the islands. They will reside in Boston.

Howie and I settled into a shiny two-bedroom apartment in a new complex not too far from town and Howie's office. It was my first flight into decorating. It wasn't good but not too bad; an unresolved conflict between Maggie's Queen Ann / American Colonial and Abby's Louis Seize/Regency. A conflict somewhat forced on me since most of our furnishings came from their basements and attics. I was enjoying my initiation into housewifery. As low man on the totem pole, Howie was having to put in long late hours. I spent my time alone learning to cook. I was determined to be at least better than Maggie.

I still don't know how Casey got my number. I'd broken communication with everyone in Harden, including Betts and Catherine. Casey knew no one in Boston except my family, and Maggie would have died before she'd let Casey back in my life. She adored Howie. The biggest gift I ever gave her was the day I married him. The biggest scare I gave her was the month before, when I tried to back out.

So it had to come down to Abby. But why? It has never been mentioned, it never happened. We know when to keep our own counsel.

—I hear you're married— Casey was trying to sound casual, but his voice was tight.

—Who told you?

—You thought I couldn't find you.

—I wasn't hiding.

—You didn't wait.

—I couldn't, Casey.

—You could if you'd wanted.

—It wasn't that simple.

—So that's another new thing I now know. Reggie Patterson What-ever-your-new-name-is— a twist of bitterness —doesn't keep her promises. You see, after all these years I'm still learning about you.

I didn't answer.

—You know what today is?

—No— But I did.

—July thirty-first. One day after your birthday.

I held my breath.

—So where do we meet?

—We don't, Casey.

—You're not even going to keep that part of your promise?

—I can't.

—You keep saying that. I can't, I couldn't. Have you become helpless?

I wanted to say yes.

—Well, unfortunately for me I *do* keep my promises. So I guess I'll have to come there.

—No!

—What's stopping me?

—You don't know where I live.

—I wouldn't count on that— I could hear his grin. —When does your husband— another bitter twist —get back?

It could have been a bluff. But how did he know Howie wasn't home, that he'd just left after dinner?

I couldn't take the risk.

And I wanted to see him.

—Fifteen minutes, Casey. That's all.

—I'll bring a stopwatch. The gazebo?

—No— I gave him directions to a small neighborhood park just a few blocks from the apartment. —It'll take me at least forty-five minutes to get there.

I tore out of my shorts and into a dress, a yellow calico with low-scooped neck, nipped-in waist, and full-circle skirt; one of Howie's favorites. I touched up my toenails and slipped on thong sandals. I decided against perfume; too obvious. Then I brushed my hair into a shiny silky bounce.

It was an easy walk. I made it in ten minutes. I didn't realize Casey had already arrived; I didn't know what his car looked like. Then I became conscious of a car parked a little ways down from where I'd told him and of the driver staring.

I walked toward him, my heart fluttering, knowing he was watching every step. I opened the door and slipped in beside him, taking a quick sidewise look.

He looked older, his features sharper, the creases around his eyes and mouth harder. He was deeply tanned, probably from shipboard. He'd freshly showered; his skin had that tight glow, and his hair was slightly damp. He smelled of soap and male warmth. I remembered the Rialto.

We sat for a moment in silence. He still hadn't looked at me. Then he lifted my hand and looked at my rings. I was embarrassed by their largeness and brightness.

—So. You're married— He set my hand back down.

I couldn't look at him. I was suddenly, and unexpectedly, ashamed. Deeply ashamed.

—Do you always do your housework dressed like that?

He was grinning. I had to grin back; I might as well have doused on the perfume.

He too had fixed up. He was wearing slacks and polished loafers. His white shirt was rolled up at the sleeves and open at the collar. The small pulse in his throat was lightly throbbing.

He studied me, and his face sobered.

—Why, Reggie? All I asked was two years.

I shook my head, looked down. —I couldn't. I couldn't last that long. I was too unhappy.

I could feel him considering my contrite profile.

—Are you happy now?

It took me a moment but I got it out. —Yes.

He looked away, out his side window. His elbow was resting on the lower edge, his hand gripping the upper. I could see the cords in his neck tighten, the muscles in his jaw bunch.

—Just tell me one thing— His voice seemed to come from a long distance, over great obstacles. —Do you love him?

He forced himself to look at me.

His question was hurting me as much as I knew my answer was going to hurt him. —Yes.

He winced, and gripped the steering wheel.

I saw his body stiffen, pump up, getting ready for the big one.

—As much as you loved me?

His voice was choked. I heard in it the boy I first met, the wounded boy from Harden who used to tell me his dreams and aspirations.

I didn't want to do this. It was the hardest lie I ever told. The one that cost me the most, and that made me the sorriest. But I owed it to Howie.

—Yes.

There was a long, heavy silence. Then Casey slammed his hand down on the steering wheel and sat back.

—Well, that's it then. The end.

He glared over at me. He was doing what he always did: covering his pain with anger. —Well, go on. Get out. What're you waiting for?— There was a catch in his throat.

I got out and slammed the door.

I started to run, I don't know why. Several yards up the sidewalk, I stopped and looked back. Casey was still sitting there. As I watched, he reached out his window and dropped a flutter of paper. Then he revved up the car and started toward me.

I panicked. For a terrified second I saw Tommy Smithson. I dodged behind a tree.

Casey swerved and braked to a sharp stop at the curb, leaning out his window, his face white and ragged.

—Go on, chicken shit! I never loved you anyhow.

Then he roared down the street out of sight, leaving behind the jagged saw of his voice slicing at me.

He was crying. Dear god, he was crying.

I stumbled back to where the car had been, bent over the paper fragments, picked them up. It was my graduation picture, the one I'd sent him for his wallet, along with an eight-by-ten for his dresser.

I didn't need to patch the pieces together to know how the words on the back read:

All my love.

Always.

Reggie.

I've carried the shards of that broken promise with me for fifteen years.

SCENE 29

I sit back and let the tears quietly trickle. What the hell. The cool salty breeze on their hot salty wetness seems a fitting union. Refreshing.

Yes. I laugh a little. I feel refreshed.

I'm also very drunk.

The boat lights have moved in and strangely converged, forming a bright almost-unbroken semicircle. I'm fascinated, mystified. What could be the significance?

I need significance.

When the fireworks go off, I leap up and burst out laughing. Of course. How silly of me, how stupid. How could I have lost so much track of time?

The Fourth of July.

I start applauding.

So symbolic. So melodramatic.

I love it.

I applaud it all. The arc of boats, the shooting stars, the soughing waves, the salty breeze and black sky.

I wrap myself in the sparkling sprays and watch until their last glitters sprinkle to sea and sputter to their salty death. Then I stumble to bed.

I don't set the alarm, I'll sleep until I wake; let time have its own reckoning. It's been a hard, heavy three days. I need rest before making a new start.

But my sleep is fretful, full of hard heavy dreams. Casey and Howie. Daddy and Maggie. Catherine. Abby. Floating in and out, in strange collision. I'm struggling among them. I can't grasp the connections.

Then I slip deeper. I'm out on the beach, my posh hotel behind me. I take off my clothes and wade into the water. The waves are low, the moon high. I swim out, toward the distant boat lights dotting the horizon. I swim into the cold black, my body warm in numbness.

I stroke, one arm over the other, stroking and stroking . . . and wake. It takes me a moment to get oriented; I'm still locked on that dark light-dotted distance.

Thank god, I tell myself as I shuffle to the bathroom, I'm a good swimmer.

I swallow down two aspirin and try to return to sleep propped up, hoping to assuage my throbbing head and the hangover I'm sure to have in the morning.

CHAPTER ?

Smokey knew these woods well. Her father had brought her here often to hunt deer. If it hadn't been for hunting, they would have gone hungry much of the time. She hated the soft beige bodies with their soulful chocolate eyes draped over the fenders of her father's ancient Ford. But she loved the food they provided.

Her father knew exactly what to do to take the gaminess out of the wild meat and make it tender and palatable. He skinned and gutted the carcasses, hung them by the heels for days to bleed and season. Then he cut them into steaks, roasts, ribs, and strips for jerky, soaking in brine, curing in smoke, giving them meat to last the winter.

He did all the cooking—when he was around, or off his back and moving. When he wasn't, Smokey shifted for herself and waited for his return, from whatever place or condition.

Zach Lorraine was a charismatic man—high in intelligence, long on laughter, low on incentive, and short on character. He could do almost anything—if he set his mind to it. And Smokey loved him. He was a song-and-dance man, a stand-up comedian, a tragedian worthy of Shakespeare and O'Neill. He was a crack-shot rifleman. And an expert on explosives.

The Navy had been the high point of his life, where he could pit himself against death and prove his cleverness and courage. After the war, there had been no place for him to go, no place he wanted to go. Without the energizing proximity of danger, everyday life palled. He sank to the depths commensurate with those few short years of heights. When he was drunk, he told Smokey all about himself. When he was sober, he taught her everything he knew. And in those extremes, Smokey learned the lessons of life. Her father left her a legacy that was now, once and for all, going to free her of Harden.

She crept forward soundlessly and chuckled softly as she remembered his hunting paraphrase: Walk softly and carry a big gun.

That was exactly what she was doing.

She watched keenly through the trees for the movement she was expecting. When it came, she smiled, slowly raised her rifle, put the finder to her eye and, bracing herself, pulled the trigger. She let her body bounce with the kick of the butt and absorb the repercussion.

The shot came as a sharp shock in the wooded silence.

She waited a few minutes for further sound or movement. But she was sure of her marksmanship. She lowered the rifle and quietly withdrew, her moccasined feet not leaving a dent or scuff in the soft-leaved path she'd carefully memorized.

She buried the gun and unused ammunition under a fallen log, on a high bluff the waters from melting snows and summer cloudbursts never reached. It would be years, maybe centuries, before they were uncovered.

Then she went home to wait.

The call took longer than she expected. It didn't come until the following afternoon. By then she was more than ready to get on with things. She volunteered to take charge of all the arrangements. The distraught family was relieved and grateful. She moved quickly and efficiently. She had everything set up in a day, over in two and a half.

The mortician had helped; the body had started to decompose, and there was little he could do with it. He suggested a timely service and closed casket.

The coroner had helped; he hadn't wanted to prolong the investigation and further distress the family; they were friends. Anyway, it seemed open and shut enough. He declared it a hunting accident, by party or parties as yet unidentified, and filed the case.

Now the family sat huddled in the small living room of the small brick bungalow as townspeople dropped in to express sympathy and sit awhile, offering comfort and support in this time of sorrow and trial.

Smokey answered the door and accepted the casseroles and baked goods with misty eyes and crushed smile.

"Thank you so much."

"So good of you to come."

"I know the family appreciates this."

She'd had to set up card tables along the wall; the refrigerator and kitchen table and counters were overladen. What a waste, she observed sardonically, as she made room for yet another casserole; half this stuff will rot.

Casey's mother clutched the newcomer's hand and sobbed into her commiserating face. "I still can't believe it."

"The damn fool," Casey's father said hoarsely, looking around at the small gathering. "I told him never to go hunting alone."

Well, Smokey smiled softly to herself, he wasn't exactly alone.

"I think he was trying to prove something," Casey's mother wept.

Casey's sister nodded. "He hasn't been the same since Glory was killed."

"Maybe he was wishing himself to join her," someone offered by way of consolation.

Father Martinez crossed himself. "God's will be done."

"Amen," the mourners murmured, some likewise crossing themselves.

Amen, Smokey echoed with a smile.

She was remembering the dark deep grave, the lowering of the casket, the scattering of earth, the strewing of flowers.

They had just laid Casey to rest.

It's after ten when I awake, feeling fuzzy and frowsy. I'm not up to showering. I brush my teeth, gagging, and splash water on my face, avoiding the mirror. I don't want to meet Dorian Gray.

I order room service and queasily nibble croissants coaxed down with tea, while I lethargically gather my clothing and organize my bags. I put the patent shoes, purse, and belt on the bottom, under T shirts and jeans. But I leave the black sheath hanging in the closet. It isn't that I couldn't get away with it in Boston if I pushed it; I don't want to. I'm almost thirty-six. That's enough pushing.

I'm seeing myself, yesterday. Prissing and preening like a self-struck debutante out to bedazzle and devastate with regret an old rejecting boyfriend. How ridiculous.

I laugh. The harshness shoots across my brain and reantagonizes my headache. I take two more aspirin.

Vanity, like pride, cometh before a great fall, Maggie used to caution. It seems now she had cause.

As I fasten the clasps on my suitcase, my eye catches the gold-embossed initials. RIP. I think of Rip Van Winkle, who slept twenty years and woke to find himself an old man.

Then I think of the other meaning. I see a headstone, a newly mounded grave, strewn with flowers. I rub my finger across the faded letters.

Yes, I think, so may you, Reggie. So may *we*.

I resist a last look from the balcony. The glare would be too much. As it is, I'm gingerly carrying my head in my hands.

But once in the car, I start to feel better. On the road again. Going somewhere. Getting ready for new adventure. Like a female Jack Kerouac. I grin. Or Huckleberry Finn astream on his raft. What the hell.

It's a blazing day, the sun striking down, dazing earth and sky into a white haze. In spite of my tinted windshield, dark glasses, and air conditioning, it disorients me.

Suddenly I feel scalded. My skin prickles and tightens, my head puckers and pinches.

A thorn is being twisted in my scalp and pulling off my skin.

A large shadow cuts across the road. I look up, and see a wide-winged arc in a tilted glide above me. The sun flashes off the glass and momentarily blinds me. When I can see again, the shadow and arc are gone.

I laugh at myself. How could it possibly have been an eagle? this far from mountain aerie and flying so close to the ground.

Then I remember what day it is: Tuesday, the fifth of July. Three days after the Homecoming Dance and the kachinas' return to the Underworld.

Time for the eagles' return with them.

Early in spring, the Hopi men go out from the pueblos to gather the eagles. The hunters lower themselves on ropes over craggy cliffs, or climb up precarious ledges, to remove from their nests the birds too young to fly. They bundle the eaglets on their backs into cradleboards, tucking beside them a small cornmeal cake, the spirit of which will sustain and comfort them.

Then the eaglets are reverently carried back to the mesas. Here their heads are washed and each is given a name and small doll, as if it were a human child. They are then taken to the rooftops and tethered by one leg to platforms built of logs, where they are fed daily—squirrel, rabbit, mice and sometimes meat from the store—and treated respectfully.

The eagle grows to be a mature bird, strong and vigorous, its feathers black, its tail marked with the white that flashes when it's in flight. Only this bird does not fly. It lifts its cries skyward and flaps its great wings. But it is always jerked down by its tether.

Although its beak is sharp and strong, and its talons long and wicked, the grounded bird does not lash out at its captors, or tear at the leather thong. It suffers its fate with dignity, as befits the Lord of the Air.

On the Day of Homecoming, the eagles are brought gifts: a small bow with arrows if it is male, a kachina doll and small woven plaque if it is female. At sunrise the morning after, the great proud birds are sent home.

No blood is shed in the eagle's sacrifice. A blanket is wrapped over its head, a thumb placed firmly in the hollow of its neck, and its life is snuffed out as gently as possible. When the body becomes cold, the feathers are plucked. The first perfect round feather is offered as a prayer to the sun. The others, including the down, are saved for use in home and ceremony.

Then the body is carried to the eagle burial ground west of the village. It is buried in a crevice in the rocks, with cornmeal, piki, tobacco, and prayer feathers, its head toward the setting sun. Stones are piled over it, bracing a small stick ladder, by which the eagle's spirit may ascend to that high realm whose invisible powers aid man on his long Road of Life.

The kachinas have departed, the summer is ended, and soon the Winter Solstice will return. The snows will blanket in white the tiny sand fields, the sparse fruit trees, the rocky hillsides. And Soyal will begin, the midnight ceremony that establishes life anew for all the world.

For now, out of dawn-darkness, germinating life is about to appear. The sun, reaching the southern end of its sojourn, is ready to return and bring strength to budding life.

But life must be paid for with life. The seed must give up its identity to become flower and fruit. The caterpillar must leave its cocoon to emerge a butterfly. The body must die to free the spirit so the soul may be reborn.

So the eagle must die.

My path has been crossed by a sacrificed eagle; even ghosts cast shadows. But I don't see this as ominous. It gives me hope.

I remember a story Daddy once told me, when I was young and afraid of the dark. A Hopi boy was returning home after staying too late at a dance. He was frightened by the darkness. Suddenly he saw someone ahead of him, someone who might share with him the terrors of the night. But as fast as he ran—and he was a swift runner—he could not catch up to the dark form. When the boy finally entered his village, the figure melted into the streets and vanished.

The boy was amazed and troubled by this as he told his father the strange story.

The father smiled and said: That was your shadow, my child. With its shape before you, you no longer worried about your fears of the dark. It led you home quickly and safely. Your shadow always helps you, if you will trust yourself to walk with it.

So I learned about shadows, that they're not necessarily darknesses to hide in or run from. Shadows can also guide and protect you.

SCENE 30

I'm taking a different route back from the one I came in on: 145 north through Houston to Dallas, then 135 up to Oklahoma City, where I'll pick up 140 west, back to Albuquerque.

Why take the old road when there are new routes to explore, new vistas to see?

Someone sitting next to me might find this hilarious right now: there's not a thing out there, nothing, except empty flatness. But as always, I respond to the vastness, its freedom, its starkness. Its drama.

Its boundless horizon.

I find it compelling. A clean slate, to be written on, like staring at a blank wall. My mind rushes in to fill it.

I imagine a mesa rising on the horizon, relieving the bleakness. I see a village, shimmering out of the rock. The people gather, sitting on chairs and standing on rooftops, silently expectant. The humming begins. I know this isn't right, the vision comes first. But I want the humming.

I watch the headdresses rise, the costumed bodies. I see the feet lift and stomp, hear the rattles. I'm trying to get the rhythm, the right sound, working in my throat, shrugging my body.

A voice cuts in sharply. —What the hell do you think you're doing?

I jerk so hard I swerve the car.

She's sitting in the passenger seat, in her pleated tennis outfit, one foot on the dashboard, her visored cap twisted sideways. She thinks she's being cute. Funny.

I am not at all happy to see her. She hasn't plagued me for days, I thought I'd lost her. In fact, I'm downright angry. I was enjoying my peace, my solitude.

—I'm singing.

She sneers. —You sound like a goddamn Indian.

I smile. Sweetly. —Thank you, Smokey— Then spit at her all my pent up venom. —And shut up! I'm sick and tired of you!

She pulls back, face crushed. —What did I do to deserve that?

I glare. —You know what you are, Smokey? A false pahana. A two-hearted powaka— I'm giving full vent. —The Jimson Weed Maiden. The Outcast Woman.

She hasn't the slightest idea what I'm talking about. But she gets the gist and has a ready comeback.

—Oh yeah? And what does that make you?

I stare at her, hating her, wanting to pull over to the side of the road and shove her out.

We drive in sullen silence.

She's hurt, sincerely hurt, eyes puckered, chin quivering, like an innocent misjudged child.

—Oh, Smokey. Why don't you grow up?

She casts me a dark look, flounces around in her seat, and stares out the side window. Every once in a while, I hear a sniffle.

After several miles, I relent. —How'd you like to go into show business?

Her voice comes muffled over her shoulder. —I *am* in show business.

—No, I mean legit. I'm going to start a children's theatre.

—You know I don't know anything about children. In fact, I can't stand them— She's whining. I suppress my irritation.

—Yeah, but you love dancing, don't you? You could be headmistress of dance. Better yet, how'd you like to be choreographer?

She twists around. —Are you serious?

—Sure. You'd be good at it.

She stares out the window, smiling softly, seeing her name on the program in bold black on glossy white.

I turn back to the road, studying the idea, thinking specifics. The Homecoming Dance. That definitely. It's a natural to end the season. We could begin with The Emergence, the obvious opener. Then I'd like to do a naming ceremony. And the clowns. Oh, I'll have to do something with the clowns.

We'll start conservatively, three or four productions the first year. All ritualistic and highly stylized. And all in pantomime. No lines to learn, only sound and movement. It'll be a cinch. Even a six-year-old can handle it. I want to get them early. While they're still impressionable. Like sandstone.

Katelyn and Lindsay will go crazy. I guess I'll have to include Buffie's little BMs.

And when we've done our best with the Hopis, we can go onto other tribes. The Navajos would be interesting. A healing ceremony, complete with sandpainting. Centering around a Medicine Woman.

The possibilities are unlimited. After the United States, we can move on to Asia and Africa. Wouldn't that set Boston Proper on its ear, thinking and shrinking? Their prospective preppies as Balinese and Pygmies.

I smirk, feeling gleefully wicked.

But they can't very well purse their lips and pinch their noses at what they've given such liberal lip-service to. We'll have 'em in our pocket. Make them put their money behind their *noblesse oblige*.

That's what's made the Mormons so successful among other cultures: they've worked with, not against, the established beliefs and traditions. Like the Catholics coopted pagan myths and holidays. In Hawaii I saw a church with surfboard altar and fishnets across the walls decorated with native artifacts. A moxy merging. The secret of conversion.

Maybe I could convert Boston. What a challenge. Buffie of the Hopi Way. Junie the first Hopi missionary. Sally as a Kachina Mother. We could form an adult improvisational society of clowns, parody one another, have monthly purgings.

I'm giggling.

Smokey grins over, wanting to join my fun. —You know, I think you and I are going to make a great team.

She's getting cocky again.

—You think so, huh?

Her eyes go crafty. —I could handle the singing, too.

—Oh?— I see her padding her credits. Smokey Lorraine: Music Director, Choreographer, Mistress of Dance, Singing Coach. —And what else would you like to take over?

She tosses her head. —I could really be a help to you. Keep things from getting soggy. Add a little pizzazz.

—I'm sure.

She grins, pulls her visor over her eyes. —You know what they used to say: Where there's Smokey, there's fire.

—Yeah. Well from what I know, we should call you Little Miss Firecracker.

She stops grinning.

I look hard at her.

—No more explosions, Smokey.

She lowers her eyes, petulantly contrite. —Can't we just let bygones be bygones?— A sad little sorry voice.

I consider her. She's not all bad. Not all self-indulged, hungry, adolescent connivance. And everyone can change.

—Sure. Why not?

I put out my hand and we shake on it.

I don't notice when she leaves. I'm too busy thinking up names for the theatre.

Kachina Enterprises?

Powaka Power?

By the time I stop for the night, I have everything worked out. I make my phone calls immediately.

—Daddy, it's me, Reggie. I have a proposition for you. How'd you like to be Director of Music and Dance, and Director of Research for a budding children's theatre?

—Well, I don't know— Of course I've caught him completely off guard.

—Well think about it. Because I'm Founder and Artistic Director, and I'm going to need all the help I can get.

—I—

—Is Maggie there? Put Maggie on.

I hear the receiver clunk to the table, the distant staccato of voices.

—Hello?

She sounds breathy. I guess from Daddy's reaction, she thinks something's wrong.

—Hi, Mummy.

I hear the sharp intake, and realize what I've said. My first "Mummy" in twenty years. I push past it.

—You know that space you said you could get for me in the library?

—Yes?

—Well get it. I'm going to start that children's theatre I was blowing such hot air about at Abby's birthday.

—What—?

—Daddy's going to be Director of Music and Dance, and Director of Research.

—Did—?

—And guess what, Mummy?— I'm getting used to the feel of the word.

—You get to be Executive Producer.

—Let me catch my breath.

—I haven't time. I have to call Abby and Howie.

—Are they—?

—Oh, yes. They get to play a part, too. I'm roping everyone in.

—Why that's wonderful, Reggie. I'm so excited.

—Stay that way. Just get the space. I'll see you in a few days.

I'm literally bouncing in my seat as I hang up. I'm doing it. I'm really going to do this.

My call to Howie takes more pulled-back consideration. I steady myself, review my wording.

—Hello.

Howie. The strong assurance of his voice.

Suddenly I see him. Howie getting the girls' breakfast. Howie romping with Maggie's dogs. Howie hanging Abby's pictures. Howie, laughing and smiling. The way he used to laugh with me.

I start to cry.

—Howie—

—Reggie? What's wrong?

—It's just so good to hear your voice.

—It's good to hear you, too, Reggie.

A sob catches in my throat.

—I'm coming home, Howie— and I know he understands all I mean to convey.

Home. I picture it. The crewel drapes, the chintz covers, the highbacked chairs. I pull myself together.

—And, Howie, I've found what I want to do. I'm going to start a children's theatre. In ethnic understanding.

—Hey that's great, Reggie.

—Will you help me?

—Of course. But I don't see much what I can do. You know I'm a lousy actor.

I laugh. It's true. It's one of the things I like about him. He's nobody but himself. What you see is what you get.

—But you're a bang-up corporate lawyer. How'd you like to become a Volunteer Lawyer for the Arts? I need you to set us up as a not-for-profit corporation. And maybe sit on the Board. I need you to monitor us legally. And— I start to blubber again —I need you, Howie.

—You have me.

I sniffle, feeling calmer. —And, and I was thinking, Howie. I'd like to do some redecorating. Get rid of the crewel and chintz. Paint the walls off-white, get some more contemporary furniture. Maybe bring in a little of the southwestern flavor. Like I did in the study. What would you think of that?

—I like the study.

—You do? You never told me that.

—You never gave me a chance.

—I know— I hear myself, snapping at him; see myself, pushing him away. —And I'm sorry— I take a hopeful breath. —So it's all right if I redecorate?

—As long as you leave the family room alone.

I laugh. —I won't touch your ship models and sailboat wallpaper.

How is it I can hear him smile?

—And don't tell the girls about the theatre. I want to surprise them. Are they all right?

—Just fine.

—And how about you?

—I'm good, too.

—Anything new to report?

—Yes. As a matter of fact there is— I hear his voice expand. —I got the partnership.

—Oh, Howie. That's wonderful! Congratulations! When?

—Five days ago. On Friday. They called me into Henry's office, gave me a big scotch and a little cigar, and shook my hand.

—I'm so happy! We'll have to celebrate. As soon as I get home. We'll have a party.

—Before or after you decorate?

I laugh. —Before, of course. The redecorating will take me years. And you know what else I'm thinking, Howie?

—*More?*

—Now that you have the partnership. That boat you've been wanting? Why don't we buy it?

—Now that's what I call *thinking.*

—We'll make it a sailing party. So start hunting for your boat.

—I know exactly where it is.

—I'll spend a few days in Albuquerque and Santa Fe shopping for the house and theatre. Then I'll fly home. And we'll have our party, Howie. A great big beautiful party.

—Sounds good.

—I'll call tomorrow.

—I'll be waiting.

I'm smiling ear to ear as I hang up.

Oh, Howie. Where would I be now?

I'm not kidding myself. I know what I'm going back to. The same thing I left behind ten days, and twenty-one years, ago. Nothing's changed. But maybe I'm a little different.

The Hopis believe that a man's thoughts have the power to affect his well-being. If his thoughts are happy and good, so will be he and his life. If they are unhappy or evil, he and his life will be thereby harmed. What a man concentrates on, he gives potency and calls forth. What he desires to keep at a distance and too weak to inflict itself, he refuses to give attention. Thus, if a man wishes to hold off illness and the infirmities of old age, he keeps his thoughts young and healthy. It is all a matter of cause and effect.

The Hopis also believe that a man's thoughts can affect others. But what he brings about for another, he himself reaps. The man whose thoughts are beneficial benefits. The man whose thoughts are destructive is destroyed along with his victim. Our thoughts come back to us.

Thus, thoughts become deeds. The thinking becomes the man.

The medium through which all this transpires is the spirit.

I'm seeing things differently, in a different spirit. So maybe my thinking is different. Maybe I can make my life different.

There are so many roles yet to perform. So many voices yet to speak. So many narratives to explore.

The Hopis believe that what is true for an individual is true for a group. Maybe my little theatre can make a difference.

I make my last call, to the lake.

—Abby? You're coming out of retirement.

—Who's retired?

—You. Sitting up there on that hill with your cultivated beds, hot houses, and canvasses of flowers. I'm inviting you into the real world.

—Oh? And where is that?

—The theatre, Abby. The stage. "All the world's—"

—Please. Spare me.

—I'm starting a children's theatre, Abby. Just like I said I would. Only this time it isn't a Let's-Top-Buffy bluff. I have it all figured out. I've even planned my first script. And you're going to be in charge of sets and costumes.

—Thank you so much for saving me.

—You're going to be *involved*.

—How much is this going to cost me?

—Ask Maggie. She's Executive Producer in charge of finances.

A short bark.

—That's what this whole thing's about, Abby. Involvement. We're going to have the children working on sets and costumes. They're going to learn to saw and hammer and paint and sew. We'll even bring in looms and teach them to weave.

—Sounds like a worthy undertaking, Reggie. And I wish you the greatest luck.

—Aren't you the one told me we make our own luck?

—Did I? How presumptuous of me.

—You can't yank yourself up by your bootstraps if you don't have boots.

—I can't argue with that.

—We have the boots, Abby.

—I'll bring my check book.

—Bring your drawing pencils and pad. And, Abby? You're gonna look great in a squaw's outfit.

She's laughing, one of the rare times I've heard her freely, unreservedly laughing. It's youthful, and comes from her gut.

I think I'm joking, but as I hang up I see her dressed in long green velvet broom skirt and burgundy velvet overblouse. She's loaded with turquoise. And her thick fine white hair is wrapped in a bun at her nape. My Spider Grandmother . . .

It was Spider Grandmother who led the Hopis out of the First World, and helped them climb through the doorway in the dome of the sky into the Fourth World. It was Spider Grandmother who told them, as they ascended, of the future they were facing:

Things will be different here. You will discover new ways of thinking and doing. You will be on a long journey, during which you must try to discover the meaning of life and learn to be true humans. For Tawa, the Sun God, did not intend for you to live in ignorance, chaos, and dissension.

It was Spider Grandmother who created the sun and moon so The People would have warmth and light, and could see all the beauties and wonders the gods had made for them on this earth. She is called Spider Grandmother because she can turn herself into a spider and crawl up into your ear, to whisper warning, advice, and guidance. She directs and protects you through your difficult trials, helps you make decisions on which your fate may depend, counteracts malevolent forces, and makes impossible tasks seem possible.

She is wise in her knowledge of good and evil, and tolerant in her understanding

of human temptations and weaknesses. Her realm is that of penetrating shrewdness.
And she is pliable in the hands of her grandchildren.

I order room service—three enchiladas swisse, with refried beans and rice, and a guacamole tostada on the side; no margaritas—and start scripting. I've thought up a new format to fit my new form.

PAHANA PRODUCTIONS, INC.

Proudly Presents

The Emergence

A Pantomime

by Regina Patterson Kendall

Sound & Movement	Stage Directions
	BLACK OUT. Audience sits in darkness.
	Gray light slowly suffuses back scrim.
	Adobe walls of a Hopi pueblo become discernible.
A low humming starts from orchestra pit. Grows louder. A Niman Kachina headdress appears above stage. First costumed body climbs ladder from orchestra pit to stage, followed by line of headdressed/costumed Hemis Kachinas and Mana Kachinas.	
Humming becomes more insistent. Dancers stand in line across stage.	Light suffusing scrim becomes brighter, more golden. Sky becomes bluer.
Humming stops. Total silence.	Sun bursts behind scrim.
Kachina Father, off stage, gives sharp command. Dancers turn sideways and, in perfect unison, start dancing.	

I get up in the dark and hit the road before dawn, trying to get a run on the sun. It's going to be another scorcher. Already I feel it pounding down on the car, trying to reduce us to sand. But not even the heat can beat me down. I'm flying so high my head's grazing the car ceiling. I have my window down, the air conditioner going full blast, the country-western blaring.

I'm getting to know the names and voices of the new kids in town. Then a familiar old-timer comes on. *Hel-lo*, Hank Snow.

I don't hurt anymore. All my teardrops have dried. No more walkin' the floor, with that burnin' inside.

I join in at the top of my lungs.

Just to think it could be. Time has opened the door. And at last I am free. I don't hurt anymore.

Hank's beaming me home.

In the Hopi's travels to the ends of the land in search of their true home, only those who kept open the doors on the top of their heads finally realized the purpose and meaning of their migrations.

For these migrations were themselves purification ceremonies. And the telling of the journey is as much religious as the ceremonies themselves.

SCENE 31

Chapter ?

The tall brunette pushed through the brass bank of heavy glass doors. Nice, very nice, she nodded as she took in the expanse of marble floor, high clerestoried ceiling, and dark lustrous wood-paneling.

She smiled sweetly at the security guard and walked sedately to the large directory.

Livingston, Havighurst, Morrisey, Garrison, Wallingford & Kendall.

She laughed. No wonder Vincent Bogatta changed his name. No room up there for a Southside Chicago dago. If he hadn't had other reasons, this would have been reason enough.

And already he was a partner. Junior, and maybe he'd had to leverage in with money and mob influence. But nonetheless not yet forty and he was a partner. She was proud of him.

She took the spacious burl-walled, soft-spoken elevator to the twenty-fourth floor, and stepped out into a wide foyer of buff and pale blue. She nodded again, at the plush carpet, the deep-seated chairs, the original paintings. She'd discovered from the directory that besides this floor, the firm also occupied the twenty-third and twenty-fifth.

A receptionist behind a curve of buff desk big enough for ten receptionists looked up at her brightly.

"May I help you?"

"Yes. I have an appointment. Ten thirty."

"Your name?"

"Ann Carter."

The receptionist ran a long red fingernail down her large appointment book.

"Oh. Yes." She looked up, still smiling her fixed red-lipped brightness. "Take this corridor here, go all the way to the end, turn left, and go to the end again. His name is on the door."

The brunette marveled at the muffled quiet. Even the click of computer keyboards, murmur of secretaries' voices, and ring of muted phones seemed absorbed into the walls and carpet. What went on behind all these closed doors was meant to stay private. It was amazing what money could buy. Including silence.

Including a revised past.

Including new identity.

She stood for a moment in front of the door, enjoying the name. Yes. Good. Very WASPish. Very upperclass. No one would suspect that under the reserved Anglo-Saxon exterior of the man bearing this name lurked a passionate Italian.

She smiled, and knocked on the door.

"Enter."

She smiled again. She loved theatre.

He rose as she stepped into the room and softly closed the door behind her. But his face remained expressionless. He'd been working intently at something on his desk and seemed preoccupied.

"Let's see," he looked down at his appointment book, "Miss Carter, isn't it?"

She was delighted. He was going to play the game.

She smiled and arranged herself neatly in the chair, knees crossed, hands folded on the patent purse in her black-linen lap, and waited for him to make the first move.

He outwaited her, his face interested but noncommittal.

She raised her hand and slowly removed the long black wig, letting a mass of platinum waves cascade over her shoulders.

He started and his eyes became wary. But he still wasn't giving anything away.

Okay. Let him have it his way. It was his game—and her throw of the die.

Smiling mysteriously, her eyes on his, she plucked off the Smokey Lorraine platinum and dropped it to the floor on top of the Ann Carter/Glory Colter brunette.

He stared for a moment then slowly began to smile, wider and wider, as she fluffed the curls on her crown and tweaked the peaks at her cheeks.

"How are you, Howie?" Her smile dazzled back. "Long time no see."

THE END

About the Author

Roberta Parry has published several short stories, two play monologues, two excerpts from *Killing Time*, and *Femme Tales*, a satiric re-vision of seven of the more sexist eighteenth-century Grimm Brothers' tales from the experience and perspective of a twentieth-century woman. She has completed three additional novels. One of her short stories was nominated for a Pushcart Prize. Two of her four plays have won awards and received full production. She studied with J. R. (Dick) Humphreys of Columbia and Walter James Miller of NYU. She also created the illustrations and cover for *Femme Tales,* as well as the cover for *Killing Time.*

She has taught elementary students, college undergraduates, and in-service teachers; written curriculum materials; been a freelance editor; and managed the offices of a pedodontist and an orthodontist. She now lives and works in Santa Fe, NM, where her watercolor paintings are shown in galleries and public exhibit spaces.

CPSIA information can be obtained
at www.ICGtesting.com
Printed in the USA
FFHW011036190819
54372072-60072FF

9 781634 139236